JEAN ANDERSON, food and wine, is t
is a frequent contri... .. ..ravel & Leisure, Bon Appetit, and Gourmet magazines, among others, and has received awards from the Portuguese government for her writing. She is the editorial consultant for this guidebook.

MARTHA DE LA CAL, author of a travel book on Portugal, has lived in the country for 20 years. She is a correspondent for *The Times* of London and *Time* magazine, and is a frequent contributor to travel publications.

THOMAS DE LA CAL was born in Portugal and returns there regularly from his current home in New York. He has contributed articles to *Connoisseur, European Travel and Life,* and other magazines. He has also worked on documentaries about Portugal for the National Geographic Society, the BBC, and NBC.

JANE GARMEY has written two books about the food of England and her articles on food and travel have been published in *The New York Times* and in *Diversion* and *Signature* magazines. She lives in New York City and travels to Portugal frequently.

DWIGHT V. GAST has travelled extensively in Portugal and has written about the country for *Art & Auction, Travel-Holiday,* and a number of other publications. He is the correspondent for Portuguese-American affairs for the Lisbon newsweekly *Tempo*.

MARVINE HOWE, on the staff of *The New York Times* since 1972, has covered Portugal and the Iberian Peninsula extensively. She also contributes articles about Portugal to the *Times* travel section.

CARLA HUNT is a freelance writer and contributor of articles to North American and international newspapers and magazines such as *Travel Weekly*. Her family has lived in Portugal since 1970, and she travels regularly to the Iberian Peninsula.

THE PENGUIN TRAVEL GUIDES

AUSTRALIA

CANADA

THE CARIBBEAN

ENGLAND & WALES

FRANCE

GERMANY

GREECE

HAWAII

IRELAND

ITALY

MEXICO

NEW YORK CITY

PORTUGAL

SPAIN

THE PENGUIN GUIDE TO PORTUGAL 1990

ALAN TUCKER
General Editor

PENGUIN BOOKS

PENGUIN BOOKS

Published by the Penguin Group
Viking Penguin, a division of Penguin Books USA Inc.,
40 West 23rd Street,
New York, New York 10010, U.S.A.
Penguin Books Ltd, 27 Wrights Lane,
London W8 5TZ, England
Penguin Books Australia Ltd, Ringwood,
Victoria, Australia
Penguin Books Canada Ltd, 2801 John Street,
Markham, Ontario, Canada L3R 1B4
Penguin Books (N.Z.) Ltd, 182-190 Wairau Road,
Auckland 10, New Zealand

Penguin Books Ltd, Registered Offices:
Harmondsworth, Middlesex, England

First published in Penguin Books 1990

1 3 5 7 9 10 8 6 4 2

Copyright © Viking Penguin,
a division of Penguin Books USA Inc., 1990
All rights reserved

ISBN 0 14 019.920 9
ISSN 1043-4585

Printed in the United States of America

Set in ITC Garamond Light
Designed by Beth Tondreau Design
Maps by Voltigraphics
Illustrations by Bill Russell
Copyedited by Anne Lunt
Fact-checked by Anne Ellis
Editorial Services by John Berseth and Amy K. Hughes

Except in the United States of America, this
book is sold subject to the condition that it
shall not, by way of trade or otherwise, be lent,
re-sold, hired out, or otherwise circulated
without the publisher's prior consent in any form
of binding or cover other than that in which it is
published and without a similar condition
including this condition being imposed on the
subsequent purchaser.

THIS GUIDEBOOK

The Penguin Travel Guides are designed for people who are experienced travellers in search of exceptional information that will help them sharpen and deepen their enjoyment of the trips they take.

Where, for example, are the interesting, isolated, fun, charming, or romantic places within your budget to stay? The hotels and resorts described by our writers (each of whom is an experienced travel writer who either lives in or regularly tours the city or region of Portugal he or she covers) are some of the special places, in all price ranges except for the lowest—not the run-of-the-mill, heavily marketed places on every travel agent's CRT display and in advertised airline and travel-agency packages. We indicate the approximate price level of each accommodation in our description of it (no indication means it is moderate), and at the end of every chapter we supply contact information so that you can get precise, up-to-the-minute rates and make reservations.

The Penguin Guide to Portugal 1990 highlights the more rewarding parts of Portugal so that you can quickly and efficiently home in on a good itinerary.

Of course, the guides do far more than just help you choose a hotel and plan your trip. *The Penguin Guide to Portugal 1990* is designed for use *in* Portugal. Our Penguin Portugal writers tell you what you really need to know, as well as what you can't find out so easily on your own. They identify and describe the truly out-of-the-ordinary restaurants, shops and crafts, activities, sights, and beaches, and tell you the best way to "do" your destination.

Our writers are highly selective. They bring out the significance of the places they cover, capturing the personality and underlying cultural resonances of a town or region—making clear its special appeal. For exhaustive, detailed coverage of local attractions, we suggest that you also use a supplementary reference-type guidebook, such as the Michelin Green Guide, along with the Penguin Guide.

The Penguin Guide to Portugal 1990 is full of reliable and timely information, revised each year. We would like to know if you think we've left out some very special place.

ALAN TUCKER
General Editor
Penguin Travel Guides

40 West 23rd Street
New York, New York 10010
or
27 Wrights Lane
London W8 5TZ

CONTENTS

This Guidebook	v
Overview	3
Useful Facts	19
Bibliography	30
Lisbon	35
Getting Around	64
Accommodations	65
Dining	67
Bars and Nightlife	72
Shopping	73
Day Trips from Lisbon	76
Costa do Sol	80
Sintra and Area	90
Northern Estremadura	97
South of the Tagus	107
Ribatejo	117
The Alentejo	151
The Algarve	180
Beira Litoral	201
Beira Alta and Beira Baixa	226
Porto and the Douro Valley	250
The Minho	290
Trás-os-Montes	345
Madeira	370
The Azores	401
Chronology	421
Index	434

vii

MAPS

Portugal	2
Lisbon	40
The Alfama	48
Lisbon Environs	78
Northern Estremadura	98
Ribatejo	120
The Upper Alentejo	153
Algarve East	185
Algarve West	189
Beira Litoral	204
Northern Beira Alta	228
Beira Baixa and Southern Beira Alta	242
Porto	260
Douro Valley	275
The Minho	294
Trás-os-Montes	348
Madeira	375
The Azores	404

THE PENGUIN GUIDE TO PORTUGAL 1990

OVERVIEW

By Jean Anderson

Jean Anderson, a recognized authority on Portugal and Portuguese food, is the author of The Food of Portugal. *She is a frequent contributor of articles on Portugal to* Travel and Leisure, Connoisseur, Food & Wine, Bon Appetit, *and* Gourmet *magazines, among others, and has received awards from the Portuguese government for her writing. She is the editorial consultant for this guidebook.*

And if Spain is the head of Europe, Portugal, set at its western extremity, where land ends and sea begins, is as it were the crown on the head." (Camões, *The Lusiads,* 1572)

Thus wrote Portugal's great epic poet. And yet to see Portugal on the map of Europe today is to suspect that this pint-size country can't offer much of interest. It's a mere sliver on the face of Iberia, a piece of real estate about the size of Alabama or Ireland enveloped by Spain on the east and north and pummeled by the Atlantic on the west and south.

Compared to Spain, Portugal is minuscule, which no doubt explains why travellers so often give it short shrift. Usually it's the add-on to a tour of Spain, a two-day dip that includes a dash across the Algarve or Alentejo before or after a day in Lisbon.

A huge mistake. Portugal has more to show than most countries ten times its size: Some of the world's sugariest beaches... tumbles of Roman ruins... Medieval walled towns that, except for a moped or two, look very much as they did 700 years ago... castles galore... vineyards so steeply terraced they might be Tibetan tea plantations... exuberant country festivals... red-brown plains scribbled with a calligraphy of cork oaks and olives... women sashaying down the road balancing everything on their heads from baskets of laundry to crates of chickens... shepherds in black sheepskin cutaways tending clouds of sheep... old men bending over nets... fishing villages so quaint they might have been knocked together by the folks at Disney.

To be sure, the Portugal you see today has been shaped down the millennia by a parade of invaders, aggressors, and occupants from shores as distant as Phoenicia, Greece, Rome, northern Europe, and North Africa. And, not least, from England. English blood flows in the veins of many Portuguese, which explains why you often see tall, blue-eyed blonds among these mostly small, olive-skinned, brown-eyed people. Even Prince Henry, the great navigator who in the 15th century slew forever the Atlantic's "demons of the deep" and launched Portugal's great Age of Discovery, was half British.

Who were the original Portuguese? No one knows. But some manner of men and women *were* living in the vicinity of Lisbon before the dawn of history, and in the Alentejo province directly east as well. They were probably simple hunter-gatherers; crude hand axes have been unearthed here, together with tools and weapons shaped of flint and bone. Scarcely 30 years ago a small painted cave was discovered about a half-hour's drive southwest of Evora, a district capital in the Alentejo, and the scribblings on its walls are believed to date back as far as 18,000 B.C.

Portugal abounds with menhirs and dolmens; so many of them are clustered in the Alentejo that some archaeologists now suspect that it may be the birthplace of a megalithic society that gradually moved northward, leaving in its wake the great standing stones of Brittany and, quite possibly, Britain's Stonehenge.

Unfortunately, the Portuguese have been rather haphazard about archaeology, so hundreds and possibly millions of valuable shards have probably been lost. Only recently have they begun to probe in earnest for the riches that may lie underneath the farmer's plow. The story is told of how three archaeologists—amateurs at that—while poking about in the fields of Medobriga, near Portalegre in the northeastern Alentejo, found three Roman bridges joined by a Roman road, two streets of Roman houses, and an imposing villa—all of this less than 50 years ago. And even more astonishing, all in a single afternoon.

Although dates can only be sketchy at best, it is known that Portugal was overrun and/or influenced by such diverse peoples as the Phoenicians, Greeks, Celts, Romans, Vandals, Alani, Suevi (Swabians), Visigoths, Moors, and Spaniards, in more or less that order (see the Chronology at the end of the book).

It was the Roman presence that the controversial 19th-century English explorer Richard Burton sensed the most strongly. It's true that the Romans developed the system of large farms that persists today in the Alentejo, that they introduced the secrets of wine making and built towns, aqueducts, and an elaborate network of roads. But Burton felt other resonances, too.

"Portugal, the western terminus of Rome's conquests, remains to the present day the most Roman of Latin countries," he wrote in 1869. "Her language approaches nearest to the speech of the ancient mistress of the world. Her people still preserve the sturdiness and perseverance.... Even in the present day, the traveller in Portugal sees with astonishment the domestic life of Rome, her poetry and literature, her arts and sciences."

Today's visitor to Portugal, however, is more likely to feel the presence of the Moor—understandable given the fact that Moslems occupied much of the country for more than 400 years and weren't finally driven from it, in the Algarve, until 1249. You see the Arabic influence in the squat, square houses of the Algarve and Alentejo forever being whitewashed, in the Op and Pop tiles that face buildings all over Portugal, in the arcaded streets and lacy wrought-iron grills. You hear it in the plash of fountains and trickle of water gardens, smell it in the orange blossoms, and taste it in the golden egg-and-almond sweets of the Algarve.

The extraordinary thing about 20th-century Portugal is that it's so unspoiled, so much itself despite the fact that it lies scarcely five and a half jet hours east of New York, significantly nearer than London or Paris. Still, if you want to see the Portugal of picture postcards, the Portugal of old, you'll have to hurry. Now that it has joined the European Community things are changing fast. Tractors are replacing teams of long-horned oxen, olive trees are being axed to make room for wheat, and *veiculos longos* (16-wheelers) from Germany, France, and Italy are barreling down the blacktops, smudging some of Europe's cleanest air.

Lisbon

The logical place to begin any tour of Portugal is Lisbon, the country's capital and the point of entry for most travellers. We all have images of this seaport on the Tagus river, thanks to Hollywood spy movies. The Lisbon they showed us was decidedly *chiaroscuro,* a city full of sinister types skulking in dimly lighted alleys, of dethroned royalty being smuggled aboard freighters, of spies courting counterspies in grimy basement *tascas* (bistros).

The real Lisbon couldn't be more different. Although it's a proper metropolis pushing 1.5 million in population, it's just an overgrown country town, a sunstruck place of low-rise, pastel buildings sprawled across seven hills, a city of broad palmy boulevards and jungly gardens. In what other world capital can you be awakened by a cock's crow? Where else can you see goats nibbling bits of grass, as you do on the slopes of the **Alfama** (the old Moorish quarter)? Or watch fishwives padding through cobbled streets balancing their inventories atop their heads? Or round a corner to find women grilling a lunch of fresh-caught sardines on little sidewalk braziers?

That notwithstanding, Lisbon is a cultural town with enough museums and galleries to keep you busy for days. And its proximity to the museums, castles, convents, and cathedrals of Belém, Queluz, Sintra, and Mafra, not to mention the beaches of Estoril and Cascais and the scenic attractions of the Arrábida peninsula just across the Tagus, makes it a perfect base for day trips.

All of these places are in the province of Estremadura, which in one direction spills south across the Tagus from Lisbon to the port of Setúbal 47 km (30 miles) away. On its way north from Lisbon to Leiria, where the Beira Litoral (West Central Portugal) begins, the other part of Estremadura ripples along the cliffy west coast for 170 km (106 miles), embracing vineyards, orchards of espaliered fruit trees, and cloth-sailed windmills whistling in the wind. From Lisbon, it's possible to loop deep into Estremadura to the south one day, to the north the next, and make it home before dark (see the Day Trips from Lisbon chapter).

Touring Portugal

Most people allow too little time for Lisbon. Too little, too, for the rest of the country. How long should you stay in Portugal? A week is the absolute minimum, two weeks better. Even then, you'll only be hitting the high spots.

Rental car is the best—some say *only*—way to go, especially if you stick with the scenic back roads. They're narrower than the primary roads, and more tortuous as well, but you *do* miss much of the heavy traffic. You also miss most of the crazy drivers who love to floorboard it on wider, straighter highways, passing on hills and riding your rear bumper if you're not travelling fast enough to suit them (you never are).

Every aspiring Mario Andretti loves to bomb up A 1/ N 1, the main north–south road linking Lisbon and Porto, 317 km (198 miles) north. But in truth the zigzag coastal route—via Ericeira, Peniche, Obidos, Nazaré, Marinha Grande, Figueira da Foz, and Aveiro—is more rewarding in every way. A good rule of thumb, unless for some reason you're in a tearing hurry: Stick with the secondary roads (the yellow routes on Michelin map number 437, far and away the most detailed of Portugal).

Because distances look so small on the map, people assume they can just zoom around Portugal. Not true. First of all, you can't average more than 100 to 125 miles a day on Portugal's twisting, two-lane blacktops. Nor would you want to, unless you're a *kamikaze* driver willing to view everything on fast forward. You should focus instead on two or three areas, pick a headquarters for each, then, once ensconced, set forth each morning in a different direction, returning to your home base at night so you don't waste time checking in and out, packing and unpacking. You might choose Lisbon and the Algarve or Alentejo, for example. Or Lisbon plus Madeira. Or Lisbon plus Porto and the Douro (or Minho).

In Portugal, perhaps more than in any other country, where you go and what you should do depends on your particular interests. You may be a sports enthusiast, for example. Or a history buff. Or a connoisseur of food and wine. Or an architecture nut. Or a nature lover. Or a collector of folk art. Or someone who just needs to get away from it all, escape the pressure of too many problems and too many people. Portugal can accommodate all these interests—but each involves a slightly different "Portugal."

Fun in the Sun

If all you want to do is thwack tennis balls, play golf, or deliver yourself to the sun, the **Algarve** is the place for you. The southernmost province, this skinny band of rumpled shore turns its back on the rest of Portugal and faces southward into the Atlantic, toward Morocco, which it resembles. Wind and wave have battered its 184-km (115-mile) coastline—from the *fim do mundo* (land's end) at Cabo de São Vicente on the west to the Guadiana river and the Spanish border on the east—reducing its rugged orange cliffs, here and there, to crescents of sand. Inland, mountains fence off the Algarve, separating it, body and soul, from the Alentejo directly north, and blocking much of the weather that blows down across it. The result: a "Mediterranean" climate that attracts the winter-weary of northern Europe by the jumbo-jet load.

The Algarve is Portugal's Riviera, an alternately creamy and craggy shore where golf courses, marinas, and fancy resort hotels and condos, sleek white boxes lined up along the sea cliffs like outsize refrigerators, have gobbled up farms and villages. In other words, a strip. Fortunately, vestiges of the old Algarve remain, and to find them you have only to veer off the bumper-to-bumper N 125 (the main east–west highway). In the hillside almond groves above Almansil, for example, it's strictly business at the market town of Loulé, where natives outnumber tourists ten to one. And westward, above the gridlock of Portimão, the red sandstone citadel of Silves doesn't seem far removed from its glory days as a Moorish capital.

Then there's the land's-end promontory of Sagres, where Prince Henry the Navigator retreated 570 years ago to plan his voyages of discovery. You can't help wondering what he'd think of the campers and caravans that have come to roost on his wild, heathery peninsula, not to mention the souvenir vendors at the gates of Cabo de São Vicente lighthouse.

There are other Algarve must-sees: the pottery at Porches, where you can watch artisans paint bowls and plates with ancient Algarve designs; the old Moorish town of Olhão, which might be a chunk of Tangier; and the cliffs at Ponta da Piedade, where great sandstone monoliths, red as iron rust, lounge in offshore waters like prehistoric beasts.

Two other choices for sun worshippers: Estremadura's **Estoril-Cascais-Guincho Coast**, which begins 22 km (14 miles) west of Lisbon (no shortage of golf, tennis, sailing, riding, and beaches here, although these last can be crowded), or the **Madeira islands**. Madeira itself boasts everything *except* beaches (you'll have to settle for hotel pools or sorry stretches of gravel). Neighboring Porto Santo Island has a beach that will forever be the envy of Madeira: six miles of sand the color of country cream. It also has a small, comfortable beachfront hotel—but very little else, unless you count the house where Christopher Columbus is said to have lived.

Architecture and History

For these you should combine Lisbon and Estremadura with the Beira Litoral and Alentejo or Minho province. You'll find dolmens and menhirs here, Celtic *castros* (fortified towns), Roman ruins, and at least a dozen living walled towns stuck in a Medieval mindset.

Lisbon itself is an architectural confection, a mostly 18th-century city, rebuilt after the cataclysmic earthquake of 1755. Its roots, of course, go deeper. You can find the fallout of centuries past at Castelo de São Jorge atop the city's highest hill (Roman, Visigothic, Moorish), in the narrow winding streets and stairs of the Alfama that lead up to the castle, and in the alfresco archaeological museum housed in the skeleton of the 14th-century Carmo (Carmelite cathedral) toppled by the great quake. You can also stride back across the centuries at suburban **Belém**, whose cache of museums includes the sugary Tower of Belém, a masterpiece of Manueline ("wedding cake") architecture and the spot from which Vasco da Gama sailed; the Jerónimos monastery, where da Gama and Camões, the 16th-century poet who immortalized his triumphant voyage in *The Lusiads,* lie buried; and, adjoining it, the Museu Nacional de Arqueologia e Etnologia (National Museum of Archaeology and Ethnology) filled with dusty fragments of prehistory.

Near enough to Lisbon for an easy day's outing in **Estremadura** are the castles and palaces at Queluz, Sintra, and Mafra. On a more northerly day trip you can easily visit Obidos, a cubistic walled town so perfect that the kings of Portugal made a practice of presenting it to their queens, plus the imposing cathedrals at Alcobaça (12th century) and Batalha (14th century; Prince Henry the Navigator's marble tomb is here). On the return to Lisbon there should even be time to detour 50 km (31 miles) east from Leiria to Tomar in the **Ribatejo** (it adjoins Estremadura to the east) to see the 12th- to 16th-century convent and chapel of the Knights Templar. Its convoluted "rope window," now encrusted with lichen, is by most accounts Portugal's most elaborate example of Manueline architecture.

The most extensive Roman ruins are those at Conimbriga (in the coastal **Beira Litoral**), a red-brick town of fountains, reflecting pools, and mosaics of stunning detail just south of the university town of Coimbra—itself worth a look, especially the 12th-century Sé (cathedral) and 18th-century gilded, muraled, and inlaid old library on the upper campus. You'll find more Roman ruins in the sprawling **Alentejo** province, which begins only 82 km (51 miles) east of Lisbon, occupies more than a third of Portugal, and butts up against Spain all along its eastern boundary. There's a doll-size second-century Roman temple at the provincial capital of Evora, and, in the regional museum just a few steps away, a courtyard of Roman relics.

Portugal's greatest cluster of prehistoric and megalithic artifacts can be found in the Alentejo, too: the painted Escoural Cave, 60 km (38 miles) southwest of Evora (it may date as far back as 18,000 B.C.), and the scatter of dolmens, menhirs, and cromlechs all about the central Alentejo.

There are also dolmens in the **Minho**, Portugal's most northerly province, notably the splendidly preserved Dolmen de Barrosa near the mouth of the Lima river. But the Minho's most significant sites are Celtic: Citânia de Briteiros and Castro de Sabroso (Portugal's oldest settlements), located 12 km (7.5 miles) southeast of Braga. Celtic ornaments, implements, and pottery unearthed at these ancient towns are on display in Guimarães (see also below) at the Martins Sarmento Museum. Note: While you're at Braga or Guimarães you may want to circle east into Portugal's remotest province, the **Trás-os-Montes**, or "Land behind the Mountains," to see the mighty rock at Outeiro Machado, which is completely covered with early Neolithic carvings. It stands 3 km (1.8 miles) northwest of Chaves, an old Roman town 129 km (80 miles) east of Braga.

Medieval fortress towns perch atop buttes and mounts all across the **Alentejo**. The most imposing of them face the Spanish border, hardly surprising given the fact that Spain and Portugal have squabbled for centuries. Two walled towns almost untouched by time—Marvão and

Castelo de Vide—cling to rocky scarps within 8 km (5 miles) of each other and about a half hour north of the textile town of Portalegre. Farther south, but still on the Spanish border, there's Monsaraz, an old Moorish citadel gripping a pedestal of rock 10 km (6 miles) east of the busy agricultural center of Reguengos de Monsaraz. There are other Alentejo walled towns, too: Evora, Elvas, Estremoz, Arraiolos, Avis, Evoramonte. Two beauties exist in the **Minho** as well, both high above the Minho river, Portugal's northern frontier with Spain: Valença do Minho and Monção. Every one of these is worth a visit.

So, too, is the Minho town of **Guimarães**, 55 km (34 miles) northeast of Porto, which is known as "The Cradle of Portugal." It was here, in the 11th century, that tiny Portucale (named for *Portus* and *Cale,* two towns on opposite banks of the Douro river that are known today simply as Porto), the territorial dowry of a Castilian princess, began to splinter off from Spain and become a nation in its own right. The final break occurred some years later, in 1140. Portugal's first king, Afonso Henriques, was born in Guimarães's 10th-century castle, a brooding pile of stone with sawtooth crenellations and nine fortress towers. (He was christened in the little Romanesque chapel of São Miguel on the castle slopes.) The castle stands on a hill outside Guimarães, a town that remains largely Medieval at heart and is thus of more than passing historical interest.

Religious Sites

Like every Roman Catholic country, Portugal abounds with cathedrals; every town of consequence has its *Sé*. And as if to underscore the piety of this nation, convents and monasteries of architectural and historical significance as well as of religious interest loom everywhere about the countryside (see the preceding discussion of historic sites).

Portugal's most famous religious site, the one to which hundreds of thousands of pilgrims come each year, quite literally on bended knee, is **Fátima**, in the **Ribatejo** province some 145 km (90 miles) northeast of Lisbon. On this desolate plateau rimmed by dour crags of granite "The Virgin of the Rosary" appeared to three small shepherd children on May 13, 1917. She reappeared five times, on the 13th of every month thereafter. By October 13, the date of her last appearance, 70,000 people had gathered, among them cynics ready to refute the children's story of the visions. They did not see the Blessed Virgin, but they do admit to watching strange celestial pyrotechnics: Storm clouds parted, then the sun seemed to spin out of orbit and hurtle earthward.

Today, millions of faithful dream of visiting Fátima at least once before they die, and there's no denying that it has become the Lourdes of Portugal. To the less-than-faithful it exemplifies the tawdry commercial side of religion. Fátima's Neo-Classic basilica (circa 1928), great colonnades arching toward a 215-foot central tower of white stone, is oddly clinical-looking. A strict dress code prevails; no shorts, halters, or minis allowed inside the hallowed shrine. And yet the souvenir shops lining Fátima's sprawling esplanade (it's bigger than St. Peter's Square in Vatican City) sell gimcracks of the most appalling taste. On the 12th and 13th of each month, from May through October, pilgrims converge on Fátima. The two biggest pilgrimages are always the first and last.

Portugal claims a number of additional pilgrimage sites, the two most important of which are **Bom Jesus do Monte** at Braga in the Minho and **Nossa Senhora dos Remédios** at Lamego in the Beira Alta. Both are exuberant examples of the Portuguese Baroque, walls of almost blinding whiteness trimmed with flourishes of granite. These two 18th-century shrines consist of steep double flights of stairs that go switchbacking up the face of mountains in crisp black and white. Pilgrims climb up on their knees, pausing to pray at the little wayside chapels all along the way. Braga's big pilgrimage takes place during Pentecost, and Lamego's is September 1 to 15.

Folk Art and Country Fairs

No one should leave Lisbon without touring the **Museu de Arte Popular** in suburban **Belém**, which showcases Portugal's finest handicrafts. Indeed, to stroll through its exhibits, arranged province by province, is to make a mini arts tour of Portugal. There's no quicker way to decide what pottery you like best, what embroideries and baskets, which hand-hammered metal cookware, which tapestries. Certainly, there's no better preview of the provinces, and no surer way to plan your crafts-oriented tour outside Lisbon.

The more rural the province, the more likely you are to see potters bending over their wheels, women seated in doorways making lace or embroidering linens, men weaving straw into baskets or hammering copper into cauldrons. And the greater your chance of happening upon a country market or harvest festival. The Portuguese National Tourist Offices (see "Information" in the Useful Facts section following) can mail you a list of the major fairs and festivals, together with their dates.

Portugal's biggest and best country fair takes place every Thursday in downtown Barcelos in the **Minho** province, about an hour's drive north of Porto. Here you can buy cotton blouses, aprons, placemats, and tablecloths embroidered in hot colors, many from the nearby coastal town of Viana do Castelo, which specializes as well in such things as delicately filigreed gold jewelry. You can buy the nubby, hand-knitted fishermen's sweaters of Vila do Conde, the lace of Trofa and Guimarães, all three Minho towns known for their handicrafts. There are flocks of brightly painted clay Barcelos roosters, renowned as the emblem of Portugal, and acres of brown pottery fancifully trimmed with hearts and flowers—immense dough bowls, tureens, casseroles, platters, and plates, all hand decorated in shades of yellow and white. And all absurdly cheap. Among the farm implements you'll find *cangas,* the intricately carved wooden ox yokes for which the Minho is famous. They're collector's items now, and they're being snapped up by decorators as well, who have discovered that they make dandy headboards.

The Saturday fair at Estremoz in the heart of the **Alentejo** is no slouch either, especially if it's pottery you're after. Laid out on the ground you'll find mounds of *tachos barros,* the terra-cotta casseroles beloved by every Portuguese cook, as well as dozens of unglazed clay water jugs of classic Roman design, piles of crude hand-painted earthenware, and platoons of the little festival figures unique to Estremoz. You can see more of these—shepherds, soldiers, and assorted saints—at the little Municipal Museum directly opposite the palatial Pousada da Rainha Santa Isabel at the top of the town, and you can even watch sculptors shape them in the atelier behind the museum.

To see country potters at work you've only to peek in the open doors of any *olaria* (pottery) at Redondo or São Pedro de Corval in the Alentejo (you can identify them by the huge terra-cotta amphoras placed at their entries, or by the racks of gaily painted plates). Portugal's most famous earthenware comes from Caldas da Rainha, in the coastal **Beira Litoral**, 88 km (55 miles) north of Lisbon. (See Day Trips from Lisbon.) The 100-year-old Bordalo Pinheiro factory here is big-time, employing 150 workers to turn out the cabbage-leaf plates, duck tureens, and honeybee honeypots prized by hosts the world over. Visitors are welcome at the company's ceramics museum, its shop, even in the pottery itself, where you can watch "slip" being poured into molds, then the individual pieces being glazed and fired.

For rugs and tapestries make your way to the white walled town of Arraiolos, some 30 km (20 miles) north of Evora in the **Alentejo**. These gros-point tapestries with curiously Oriental motifs are Portugal's finest, and most famous. But they aren't cheap. Still, you can beat the prices of Lisbon at any of the *fábricas* lined up along the main street (look for the *tapête* signs).

The island of **Madeira** has cornered the market on wicker and intricately embroidered linens. Both are very much cottage industries, so it's not unusual to see men near the village of Camacha peeling osiers (willow twigs) by the side of the road or piling baskets onto bicycles, motor scooters, or pickup trucks. Or, deep in the island's interior, to come upon a circle of women, shy and giggly, embroidering and gossiping the afternoon away. Once they've finished a respectable stack, the linens will be picked up, trucked to Funchal, washed, pressed, and packaged for sale in the boutiques you see everywhere around town.

The **Alentejo** (and especially the provincial capital of Evora) is headquarters for copper cookware, cork ice buckets and coasters, and bright wooden furniture strewn with hand-painted flowers. All are astonishingly cheap.

As for the decorative tiles (*azulejos*) you see facing buildings all over Portugal, the best place to buy them is **Lisbon**. There are half a dozen shops selling faithful replicas of antique tiles—and, of course, antiques stores where you can buy the real thing. See our Shops and Shopping section for Lisbon, or ask the Portuguese National Tourist Office for a list of shops (see "Information" in Useful Facts, below).

Most tourists become so smitten with Portugal's folk art that they buy and buy, giving little thought to how they'll get all their finds home. Luckily, there's a Lisbon shipper geared to solving just such problems (see "Packing and Shipping" in the Useful Facts section).

Food and Wine

No doubt about it: Portugal's best restaurants are in **Lisbon** (which see), and some of them are nothing more than neighborhood *tascas* where Mama presides over the stove and Papa waits table. The best way to get a gastronomic fix on Portugal is to visit Lisbon's morning market, the rollicking Mercado da Ribeira near the waterfront. If it's seafood you seek, do as the Lisboetes do and drive out to **Cascais** or **Guincho** beside the Atlantic. Lisbon, they insist, is too far "inland"—all of 25 km (16 miles)—for saltwater fish to be fresh.

Porto ranks second for food, but first for wine (although Madeira may dispute that because its wines are equally noble and its lodges just as adept at showing visitors about). You can visit any of the Port wine lodges on Porto's (the Douro river's) left bank at Vila Nova de Gaia, pausing at tour's end to sample the four basic types of Port: white, ruby, tawny, and vintage.

If Port wine is of particular interest, you'll surely want to drive up the **Douro** as far as **Pinhão**, 132 km (83 miles) east of Porto. This little village deep in the heart of the vineyards is devoted altogether to the production of Port. The stately *quintas* (wine estates) are here, many of them perched high in vineyards that stairstep up nearperpendicular slopes of buff-colored schist. The best time to visit is late September or early October, when the *vindima* (grape harvest) is on and folk songs ring from hill to hill. But you'd better make sure you have overnight reservations somewhere nearby. The best place, hands down, is the stylishly rustic 11-room **Pousada do Barão de Forrester** at Alijó, a half-hour drive beyond Pinhão. Although you *can* drive from Porto to Pinhão and back in a day, it's dangerous to try. The roads are roller coasters, pitch-dark after sundown, and murderous to navigate.

The Portuguese table wines best known outside of Portugal are the rosés of Mateus and Lancer's and the Aveleda *vinhos verdes*. Each of these wineries can be visited. The Lancer's (José Maria da Fonseca) operation occupies a good chunk of the little town of Vila Nogueira de Azeitão on the **Arrábida peninsula** across the Tagus from Lisbon, and both its old and new wineries welcome tourists. The other two wine companies are way up north: Aveleda at Penafiel, in the **Douro Litoral** maybe an hour east of Porto (a marvelous, gingerbready estate engulfed by subtropical gardens), and Mateus at Vila Real, some 77 km (48 miles) farther east at the edge of the **Trás-os-Montes** province. Its Baroque white manor house edged in black basalt looks just the way it does on every wine label, and it can be toured (as can its formal gardens). But the manor house today is a museum only. Mateus wine is now made several miles away in a modern plant as full of ducts, pipes, and tanks as an oil refinery.

One of the curiosities of Portugal is the little town of **Mealhada** in the **Beira Litoral** 19 km (12 miles) north of Coimbra. It's nothing more than a wide place in the road, but gourmets converge here from all over Portugal to feast upon suckling pig, the town's specialty. There are no fewer than a dozen restaurants serving it, most of them lined up along N 1, the Lisbon–Porto highway.

For what may be the most Portuguese of Portuguese food, you must spend time in the **Alentejo** province, where the hog reigns supreme, where the olive oil is deeply fruity, where markets sell bunches of coriander as big as bridal bouquets, and where most dishes contain enough garlic to blow a safe. Evora is pig heaven (especially a little back-street restaurant called **Fialho**). And Estremoz isn't far behind.

Portugal's main epicurean event takes place each autumn at the little farmer's town of Santarém in the **Ribatejo**, 78 km (49 miles) up the Tagus from Lisbon. It's the annual Gastronomic Fair, during which Portugal's best provincial cooks show their stuff. It lasts for days, brings folk dancers out in regional costume, and attracts artisans from all over the country.

Great Gardens

The Portuguese have the greenest thumbs on earth, and if you doubt that you've only to visit one of the country's famous gardens. **Lisbon** can claim three of them, and the surrounding countryside three more. A good place to begin is the Estufa Fria in the Eduardo VII Park, an extraordinary collection of botanical exotics under canopies of lattice or glass. Next there's the Botanical Garden, with its stately avenue of royal palms and neatly labeled specimens from the Portuguese colonies. Then, in suburban **Benfica**, Casa do Marqueses de Fronteira, an opulent 17th-century mansion (private) and gardens (open) that are as famous for their panels of antique *azulejos* as for their geometric plantings. Hans Christian Andersen, who spent some time here in 1866, described Fronteira as "lively and quite unusual... Italian in style and comfortably old-fashioned." From the main building, he continued, "a high terrace leads through the garden" where gallery walls "are covered with quite remarkable mosaic pictures—all of female figures representing, for example, Geometry, Astronomy, Poetry, etc."

You could probably spend half a day wandering through the extensive formal and informal gardens at the 18th-century pink palace at **Queluz** (Portugal's Versailles), 15 km (9.5 miles) west of Lisbon, where showers of bougainvillaea spill over walls paved with blue-and-white tiles. And another half-day at Monserrate, a few miles west of Sintra on the mountainous road to Colares.

Sintra has been called "Byron's Eden," because the great English poet, while staying in this mossy hideaway, wrote, "I must observe that the Village of Cintra in Estremadura is the most beautiful, perhaps, in the world." Thirty years later, another Englishman, Francis Cook, vowed to make a private Eden of **Monserrate**, his estate just west of town. Today, its steep slopes strewn with jungly plants remind you more of a tropical rain forest. But they *are* impressive.

The formal boxwood gardens at the Quinta da Bacalhoa at Azeitão on the **Arrábida peninsula** south of the Tagus are famous for their pavilions of early Moorish tiles and botanical symmetry. Quinta da Bacalhoa, now owned by Americans, has another claim to fame: Its smooth, well-balanced red table wine is Portugal's only true cabernet sauvignon.

Portugal's most spectacular garden is actually a forest, the 250-acre **Buçaco National Park** located 28 km (18 miles) northeast of Coimbra in the Beira Litoral province. The old royal hunting "lodge" here has been turned into a hotel. A good thing, too, because you could spend days strolling Buçaco's secluded paths, marveling at the *Green Mansions* majesty of a place where 400 native and 300 exotic species flourish among the waterfalls and reflecting pools.

In the north of Portugal there are two more important gardens, both at well-known wine quintas: the free-form floral groupings at Quinta da Aveleda at Penafiel in the **Douro Litoral**, and at Mateus, near Vila Real in the **Trás-os-Montes**, a meticulously pruned topiary separating two broad parterres, one worked out in great arabesques of greenery, the second in rigid geometrics. These two gardens are altogether different, and if you're in the vicinity of Porto or, better yet, Guimarães in the Minho, you can do them both in a day.

When the 15th-century Venetian explorer Cadamosto visited **Madeira** he exclaimed, "The whole island is a garden!" And so it is, an outsize nosegay that seems to float upon the sea. Because of the island's rich volcanic soil and near-perpendicular terrain, there are dozens of microclimates, some hospitable to orchids, birds-of-paradise, and poinsettias, some to calla lilies and hydrangeas, some to heather and gorse. In addition, there are two dreamy gardens shelved in the hills above the capital city of Funchal: the Botanical Gardens, devoted mostly to indigenous flora, and the Quinta do Palheiro Ferreiro. Here, among some 12 hectares (30 acres) of woodlands, Madeira's own spiky dragon trees and stately mahoganies coexist with South African proteas, Japanese loquats, Mexican blood lilies, and New Zealand fern trees, plus dozens of other botanical exotica from around the world.

To Get Away from It All

The ultimate retreat has to be **The Azores**, which have barely entered the 20th century. Or so it seems, even though there are modern hotels on most of the islands with all the expected amenities. Out in the countryside, however, even on the big island of São Miguel, donkeys outnumber automobiles at least two to one and life snoozes along in an earlier, easier manner. São Miguel is terrific for just poking around, inhaling the clean Atlantic air, and eating your fill of fish so fresh it all but swims to your table. So are Terceira, São Jorge (its sharp ivory cheese is superb!), Faial, and Flores. All of the Azores, in fact, will please nature lovers—indeed, anyone who craves peace and quiet instead of a bouncy brand of nightlife.

The mountains of **Madeira** are almost as quiet, especially the two isolated *pousadas* (government inns) perched high in the interior—just the place to catch up on your reading or maybe simply watch the clouds sail by. Well-marked trails lead across this dramatic roof of the world, and you needn't be an Olympic medalist to negotiate them with ease.

Honeymooners love **Buçaco National Park** (see Great Gardens, above); the otherworldly Serra da Estrela in the **Beira Alta** in eastern Portugal's mountainous midriff; also the 174,000-acre **Peneda-Gerês National Park**, created in

1970 to preserve the natural beauty of this gentle green "Switzerland of northern Portugal" (see **Minho**); and the snug little **Pousada de Santa Maria** in the Medieval walled town of **Marvão** (see **Alentejo**).

The hulk and the height of Beira Alta's **Serra da Estrela** (6,532 feet) startles many travellers. Skiers whiz down its slopes in winter, but for pure, unadulterated bliss you must come to these hardscrabble heights in late spring, summer, or early autumn. You'll be above the tree line, indeed often on top of the clouds, surrounded by a brutal beauty of barren crags, snowmelt lakes, and shingly fields of granite. In certain light at certain times of day it's easy to imagine that you're strolling across the moon.

There are several places to stay up here, but the pleasantest, surely, is down the mountain, across the western valley, and halfway up the facing slope. It's the cozy, chaletlike **Pousada de Santa Bárbara**, deep in a pine woods a few kilometers north of the village of Oliveira do Hospital (covered in our Beira Litoral chapter). Every bedroom has a balcony, and every balcony frames a view of this mighty "Mountain of the Star."

This overview gives you some notion of the riches that await you in Portugal. But there's an additional treasure: the Portuguese people, who are quick to greet every friend, every stranger with a hearty *"Bom dia!"*—"Good day!" Portugal may be tiny, but its welcome is as big as all outdoors.

USEFUL FACTS

Climate and Seasons

If you were to draw a line straight across the Atlantic from Washington, D.C., you'd hit Lisbon. And that surprises many people, because Lisbon *feels* like Florida. Palms, oleander, and bougainvillaea grow as far north as Porto (on a parallel with New York City), and, thanks to the warm, moist breath of the Gulf Stream, oranges and olives thrive along the banks of the northerly Douro river together with Port wine grapes.

As millions of visitors have discovered, summer is glorious everywhere in Portugal, so you'll have to fight for room at the inn (not to mention the beach). Sunny midday highs range from the 30s Celsius (90s Fahrenheit) in the Algarve and Alentejo to a few degrees cooler around Lisbon and points north. Even February can be balmy in the Algarve and Alentejo, with noon temperatures in the 20s Celsius (70s to 80s Fahrenheit). But don't count on it. Rain may swoop down from the north and lock you in for days, especially in the Alentejo.

The best seasons to visit mainland Portugal are late spring (mid-April to mid-June), although there is some chance of rain, and autumn (mid-September through October), when every village seems to stage some sort of harvest fair or festival. Portugal's rainy season begins in November and lasts throughout the winter, dreary days (or weeks) alternating with sudden bursts of sunshine. Only the Algarve, Portugal's southernmost province, is blessed in winter by a more Mediterranean climate, but here, too, it can—and does—rain.

On Madeira weather changes less from June to January than from seashore to mountaintop. Not for nothing is it called the "Isle of Perpetual June." Days are always sunnier on the south shore than on the north because the island's mountainous spine blocks most of the storm clouds rolling off the ocean from the north. Funchal and its big resort hotels, sprawled along a sheltered south-shore bay, enjoy a singularly mild microclimate. Here midday temperatures hang in the 20s Celsius (mid-70s to mid-80s Fahrenheit). Funchal's high season (more for social than climatic reasons) runs from December 15 to April 30. The busiest times of all are the Christmas holidays and Easter, when reservations must be made months in advance. The smaller, semiarid island of Porto Santo, located just 37 km (23 miles) northeast of Madeira, is flatter and more at the mercy of the elements: Its summers tend to be hotter, winters cooler.

The Azores are another story altogether. These nine mid-Atlantic islands, scattered across 650 km (400 miles) of open ocean, are colder and rainier than the Madeiras. You can be pretty sure of sunshine and shirt-sleeve weather with midday temperatures in the 20s Celsius (75 to 85 Fahrenheit) between May and September. The rest of the year, however, the islands can be buffeted by wind and rain, and local waters often grow so turbulent that even Azoreans shun the interinsular boats.

Entry Requirements
Nothing more than a valid passport is required of U.S., Canadian, British, and Australian citizens. There are no vaccination requirements.

Flying to Portugal

TAP Air Portugal and TWA jet daily from New York (or Newark) to Lisbon during the high summer season, less often in winter. There are also twice-weekly TAP flights to Lisbon, year round, from Boston and Los Angeles, and two nonstops each week between Boston and the Azores—one flight to Ponta Delgada on São Miguel Island and one to Lajes on Terceira. Air Canada and TAP Air Portugal both jet nonstop to Lisbon from Montreal four times a week, and Air Canada flies nonstop from Toronto twice a week.

British Airways and TAP Air Portugal maintain daily nonstop service to Lisbon from London's Heathrow Airport; TAP also hops once a day from Heathrow to Porto. In addition, British Airways jets six days each week from Gatwick to Faro in the Algarve, five times a week to Lisbon, and three times to Porto—all nonstop.

At present there is no direct service from Australia to Portugal. Other major carriers serving Lisbon and/or Porto include Air France, Alitalia, Finnair, Iberia, KLM, Lufthansa, Sabena, SAS, South African Airways, and Swissair.

Flying around Portugal and to Madeira and the Azores

There are no direct flights to Madeira from the United States, Canada, or Britain, so you must change planes in Lisbon. From Lisbon there are daily nonstops (sometimes several a day) to Faro, Porto, and Madeira, also to Terceira and Ponta Delgada in the Azores; in addition, there are three nonstops each week to the Azorean island of Faial. There are frequent flights via small prop planes between Madeira and neighboring Porto Santo, as well as among all the major Azorean islands, via SATA, the Azorean airline.

Customs

There are two different manned exits from the baggage area of each international airport in Portugal: one for those who have nothing to declare and another for those who do. Visitors over 17 years of age may bring in, duty free, two bottles of table wine, one bottle of liquor, 200 cigarettes or 250 grams (about 8 ounces) of tobacco, ¼ liter (about 8 ounces) of toilet water, and 50 grams (about 1½ ounces) of perfume. You may also bring in small quantities of tea or coffee for personal use.

Getting Around by Train and Bus

From Lisbon there are six crack trains a day to Porto (the Alfa service) as well as a morning and afternooon *rápido* to Albufeira and Faro in the Algarve, with connections for points east and west. In Portugal the only way to travel by train is first class, but fares are unbelievably cheap. Note: If you can prove you're over 65 or can produce a Eurorail Senior Card, you can travel by train in Portugal for half fare.

Like London and Paris, Lisbon has several different train stations, and the one you use depends on your destination. The three of most concern to the traveller are Santa Apolónia, Sul e Sueste, and Cais do Sodré. Santa Apolónia (Tel: 01-87-60-25), down on the waterfront just below and to the east of the Alfama at the corner of avenida Dom Infante Henrique and largos das Caminhos de Ferro, is Lisbon's central station, where international trains arrive and depart; it's the one you'll want if you're northbound to Coimbra or Porto. Sul e Sueste (Tel: 01-87-71-79), your point of departure if you're headed for the Algarve or lower Alentejo, is actually a ferry slip on the left side of praça do Comércio (Black Horse Square) as you face the water. You must board a ferry here, baggage and all, and cross the Tagus to Barreiro on the south bank of the river, where your train awaits. Cais do Sodré (Tel: 01-37-01-81), located on Lisbon's riverfront praça Duque da Terceira (four blocks west of praça do Comércio), is the spot from which three- and four-car electric "interurbans" whiz along the river Tagus to and from Belém, Estoril, and Cascais with commuter frequency.

Luxury air-conditioned buses with multilingual hostesses and on-board toilets make daily runs between Lisbon and Porto and Lisbon and the Algarve. The Lisbon–Algarve *express* buses of Rodoviária Nacional, the national bus company, are surprisingly posh. RN's main terminal, from which all express buses leave Lisbon, is located at 18-B avenida Casal Ribeiro (Tel: 01-54-54-39). You can buy your ticket here, too. Then there's Mundial Turismo, a strictly top-of-the-line private company that maintains frequent express service between Lisbon and Porto (four and a half hours) and Lisbon and Faro in the Algarve (three and a half hours). Its state-of-the-art buses offer about every amenity you could want (cushy reclining seats, air-conditioning, picture windows, hostesses, toilet). The company's main Lisbon office is at 90-B avenida António Augusto Aguiar; Tel: (01) 52-77-13.

Renting a Car

At Lisbon, Porto, Faro, and Madeira, all major car-rental firms maintain offices both at the airport and in town. It's also possible to rent a car on Porto Santo Island (in the Madeira group) and throughout the Azores. For most travellers, driving is the *only* way to tour Portugal effectively: you can set your own pace and poke around the back roads, visiting the towns time forgot. Although gasoline is very expensive, especially by North American standards, there's no shortage of modern service stations (more and more of them manned by English-speaking attendants), no lack of places to eat or sleep, and no dearth, certainly, of panoramas where you'll want to stop to *ooh* and *aah*.

The major Lisbon–Porto highway, called A 1 when it's four lanes around Lisbon and much of the way between Coimbra and Porto, becomes N 1 when it's only two lanes. It's the fastest north–south route. The four-lane stretches of A 1 are toll roads, too expensive for many Portuguese, so they're rarely crowded and a joy to drive.

Not so the old two-lane N 1 segments, which are often maddeningly thronged with cars, trucks, motorbikes, vans, even donkey or ox carts rumbling along the rights of way. And even though A 1 zooms you right up to the outskirts of Lisbon and Porto, traffic invariably screeches to a halt around both cities. Getting in or out of Lisbon you must contend with airport traffic as well as the usual suburban overload. Porto is ten times worse, maybe because it's Portugal's big industrial city and most of its factories are right on A 1/N 1, disgorging hundreds of vehicles onto it morning, noon, and night. So far, alas, highway engineers haven't figured out how to break up the bottleneck.

They've done a far better job with the fast new *auto-estrada* linking Lisbon and Setúbal on the Arrábida peninsula across the Tagus river.

All Portuguese roads, you'll be pleased to know, whether superhighway, primary, or secondary, are well marked and maintained. Still, many road signs confuse foreign drivers. For example, the arrows indicating that you should drive straight ahead often aim off toward the right—not sharp right, mind you, but vaguely. The logical conclusion, of course, is to turn right. Wrong! You should continue dead ahead. *True* right turns also point to the right, but the signboard itself is at strict right angles to the road. After a few wrong turns you'll get used to the Portuguese system of signposting, but in the meantime you can waste a lot of time retracing your steps. Here's a trick that may help: Each day before you set out, study your route carefully, noting whether there are any major turns along the way. Then jot down in big bold letters the names of upcoming towns and keep the list handy so you don't have to keep stopping to consult your map.

Here's another problem you'll encounter on the back roads. Village houses and shops open directly onto highways (no sidewalks), and cats, dogs, chickens, and especially children burst into the street without looking. They seem to have no fear of automobiles, so you must keep your wits about you at all times. Worse still, few secondary roads are lighted at night, and too many donkey carts, bicycles, motorbikes, even cars, have no taillights or reflectors. Whole families, moreover, often dressed in black (half the country, it seems, is in mourning), stroll the highways after dark, walking *with,* instead of facing, the traffic. So it's risky to drive after sundown, at least for now. But things may soon improve. Many highways are being straightened and widened thanks to recent infusions of funds from the European Community, which Portugal joined in 1986. Meanwhile, don't be afraid to drive throughout Portugal. Just exercise plenty of caution.

Always book a rental car well in advance (your credit card guarantees your reservation). As for licenses, all that's needed for Americans, Canadians, Britons, and Australians is a valid national license.

Pousadas (Government Inns)

"Government inn" has a grim ring, but this is no cot-and-candle operation. Portugal's *pousada* (poo-ZAH-da) program, begun in the 1940s both to provide local employment and to create a model other innkeepers might emulate, has grown into an impressive network. Today there are 30 inns scattered around the mainland, some of them truly palatial, plus two additional pousadas on the island of Madeira. The largest (the Santa Marinha da Costa at Guimarães in the Minho province) has 54 rooms and suites, but most pousadas offer no more than a handful, so you must make reservations well in advance. You should also know that there are three basic pousada categories:

- B: Small, snug, basically rustic inns located, for the most part, in out-of-the-way places. Although they have no delusions of grandeur, these pousadas offer nearly every amenity you could want (the government is busily renovating the older ones so that every room will have a private bath). Most are appointed with simple country furniture and local handicrafts. They often boast eye-popping views, gutsy home-cooked regional recipes, and wine lists featuring the best of the local output.

- C: There's a hunting-lodge look to many of these somewhat more elegant pousadas: beamed ceilings, terra-cotta tile floors, blazing stone hearths, wall-to-wall windows framing something of historic or scenic significance. Rooms tend to be small (and sometimes sleekly modern), but they can all claim private baths and sometimes balconies as well. Here, too, the cooking is done by good local cooks who have a way with soups, stews, and the devastating egg sweets for which Portugal is famous.
- CH: You'll find these strictly top-of-the-line pousadas in historic castles (Obidos, Palmela, Setúbal, Estremoz), convents (Evora, Guimarães), even occupying entire Medieval walled towns (the Dom Dinis at Vila Nova de Cerveira on the Minho river overlooking Galicia in Spain). All have been painstakingly renovated and modernized without sacrificing any of their architectural integrity, and many are furnished with rare antiques and pride themselves on their baronial dining rooms and Continental cuisine. Stick with the Portuguese specialties—they're almost always better prepared.

For details about pousadas contact the Portuguese National Tourist Office (see "Information," below) or your local travel agent. In the United States or Canada, you can book pousada rooms directly through Marketing Ahead, 433 Fifth Avenue, New York, N.Y. 10016; Tel: (212) 686-9213. Note: *Estalagems* (eshta-LAH-zhems), which often resemble pousadas, are privately owned inns, and some of them are very good, too.

The Manor House Program
Within the past few years it has become possible to stay at the *solares* (town houses), *quintas* (estates), *paços* (pal-

aces), and *casas* (simple country houses) of Portugal's nobility, aristocracy, and plain rich. It all began with a need for hotel rooms in isolated areas, in combination with a move to save historic properties from neglect or ruin. The Portuguese government made low-interest loans available to the owners of important houses if they would modernize them and make rooms available to travellers. Today there are dozens of fine private homes where you can stay in antique-filled rooms (most with baths *en suite*) in areas that you might not otherwise see. Many families participating in the manor house program speak English, and a few have been so caught up with the idea that they will, if you request it, serve lunch and dinner as well as breakfast, arrange tours of their area, even provide introductions to families whose interests you might share.

At the moment, several different agencies in Portugal handle bookings for several different manor-house networks, the best organized of which has published a four-color brochure featuring each of its properties and pinpointing their locations on an outline map of Portugal. For a free copy, contact: P.I.T., Alto da Pampilheira, Torre D-2, 8° A., 2750 Cascais, Portugal (Tel: 01-286-7958 or 01-284-4464). You can also obtain details about the manor house program by contacting the Portuguese National Tourist Office (see "Information").

What To Wear

Casual dress is acceptable during the day throughout Portugal, but this doesn't mean shorts, except at the beach. Miniskirts, tights, and tank tops may raise a few eyebrows, too, although Portugal's dress code isn't as staid or stuffy as it once was. At elegant restaurants in Lisbon, Porto, and Funchal, Madeira, coat and tie are usually de rigueur for both lunch and dinner. In the old days women were expected to cover their arms and heads when entering church. While this is no longer the case, it is still improper to enter skimpily clad.

In spring, summer, and fall you'll need lightweight clothes plus a sweater and raincoat (more for cool nights than for rain). Layering is the trick when travelling in Portugal, because there are often abrupt drops of temperature at night. And don't forget your sunglasses and sunscreen. You'll need them everywhere, not just at the beach.

Local Time
Mainland Portugal and the Madeira islands are on Greenwich mean time, which puts them in the same time zone as Great Britain, five hours ahead of New York, Montreal, and Toronto and eight hours ahead of California and Vancouver. The Azores are two hours behind Lisbon and Britain, three hours ahead of New York, Montreal, and Toronto, and six hours ahead of California. When it's noon in Lisbon or Funchal, it's 9:00 P.M. in Sydney.

Language
Portuguese may look like Spanish but it *sounds* nothing like it because the Portuguese slur so many syllables with *shhs* and *zhhs*. The *nh* in Portuguese is somewhat similar to the *ñ* in Spanish; Minho province, for example, is pronounced "Mean-yo." Until recently, French was Portugal's second language, and it's still widely spoken in the north, but English is fast gaining ground. The waiters and receptionists at every inn and eatery of consequence all speak English, as do many bank tellers and shopkeepers. Whether or not they speak a word of English (or you of Portuguese), however, the Portuguese are unusually accommodating, and you can usually make do with sign language. Many Portuguese don't much like being addressed in Spanish (given their long and uneasy relationship with the Spaniards, it's easy to understand why). And one last word of advice: When touring the wine lodges of Porto or Madeira, remember that *Sherry* is a dirty word.

Telephoning
The country code for Portugal is 351. The city code for Lisbon is 01; for Porto, 02 (eliminate the zero when telephoning from outside Portugal). In case of emergency when travelling about Portugal, dial 115. It's the equivalent of the U.S. 911, which connects you with an emergency operator who will summon the police, fire department, or an ambulance straightaway.

Electrical Current
Throughout Portugal it's 220-volt, 50-cycle AC. Americans and Canadians will need adapters plus assorted plugs.

Currency
The *escudo* (pronounced something like *ish-KOO-doe* and divided into 100 *centavos*) is the official monetary

unit of Portugal. As if to bedevil North Americans, the decimal point is written as a dollar sign. Thus 1,000$00 means 1,000 escudos (which, by the way, is called a *conto*). Portugal sets no limit on the amount of cash or travellers' checks that you can bring into the country, but does on what you're allowed to carry out: it's 50,000$00 in Portuguese currency and the equivalent of 100,000$00 in foreign currency.

Credit Cards

Access, American Express, Diner's Club, Eurocard, MasterCard, and Visa are widely accepted throughout Portugal. Gasoline credit cards are not.

Business Hours

As a rule, banks are open from 8:30 to 11:45 A.M. and from 1:00 to 2:45 P.M., Monday through Friday; in Lisbon, certain branches are open again from 6:00 to 11:00 P.M. In the Algarve, the bank at the Vilamoura Marina is open daily from 9:00 A.M. to 9:00 P.M. The bank at the Lisbon airport is open round the clock.

Shops open at 9:00 A.M. and close for lunch at 1:00 P.M., then reopen at 3:00 and remain open until 6:00, Monday through Friday. On Saturday the shops are open only from 9:00 A.M. to 1:00 P.M. Most big shopping centers are open seven days a week from 10:00 A.M. to 11:00 P.M. Note: In every community, at least one drugstore (*farmácia*) is open 24 hours a day, seven days a week; check the hotel concierge or local newspaper for the listing.

As for restaurants, lunch is served from noon to 3:00 P.M. (although fancier Lisbon establishments may not open until 12:30 or 1:00 P.M.) and dinner from 7:30 to 10:00 P.M.

Most museums are closed on Mondays.

National Holidays

All of Portugal observes New Year's Day, National Day (April 25), Labor Day (May 1), Camões' Day (June 10), Assumption (August 15), Republic Day (October 5), All Saints' Day (November 1), Restoration Day (December 1), Immaculate Conception (December 8), and Christmas Day. Good Friday, Easter, and Corpus Christi, dates that change from year to year, are also celebrated, so check a current calendar.

Packing and Shipping

It's easy to get so carried away with Portuguese folk art that you buy more than you can possibly lug home. The rug, tile, and linen shops will probably pack and ship what you buy. But how do you transport all that heavy, *breakable* country-market pottery? You'll be happy to know that there's a first-class shipper in Lisbon who will pack things meticulously, then send everything to your door. It's the International Travel Service, at 61-B rua Castilho, near the Ritz Hotel. But expect to pay plenty for their services, possibly five times what you spent for the folk art.

Cautions

The Portuguese say it's safe to drink the water everywhere (unless signs indicate otherwise), but they themselves always drink one of the fine local bottled waters. The most popular is Luso, a nonsparkling, mineral-rich water from the spa of the same name just north of Coimbra.

The surf in the Algarve is rarely rough, but along the west coast of Portugal, particularly at Guincho near Cascais and Estoril, it pounds in with awesome force and the undertow can be lethal.

Information

Contact these government tourist offices: In the United States, the Portuguese National Tourist Office, 590 Fifth Avenue, New York, N.Y. 10036-4704 (Tel: 212-354-4403); in Canada, the Office National du Tourisme Portugais, 500 Sherbrooke West, Suite 930, Montreal, P.Q. H3A 3C6 (Tel: 514-843-4623) or the Portuguese National Tourist Office, 2180 Yonge Street, Toronto, Ontario M4S 2B9 (Tel: 416-487-3300); in Great Britain, the Portuguese National Tourist Office, New Bond Street House, 1 New Bond Street, London W1Y ONP (Tel: 1-493-3873). In Australia, contact your travel agent.

BIBLIOGRAPHY

H. WARNER ALLEN, *The Wines of Portugal* (1963). Discussions of the demarcated and undemarcated wines, many of them unknown outside Portugal.

HANS CHRISTIAN ANDERSEN, *A Visit to Portugal, 1866;* translation from the Danish by Grace Thornton (1972). Portugal through the eyes of the famous Danish story-teller. Not among his best works, but fascinating nonetheless.

JEAN ANDERSON, *Henry the Navigator, Prince of Portugal* (1969). A biography of Portugal's visionary 15th-century scholar-prince and the story of Portugal's conquest of the Atlantic.

———, *The Food of Portugal* (1986). Recipes from Western Europe's most original and least known cuisine (worked out using American measures, ingredients, and implements), with advice for travellers about Portuguese inns, menus, wines, and foods.

W. C. ATKINSON, *A History of Spain and Portugal* (1960). A highly readable account of the two Iberian nations often at odds with one another.

CARLOS DE AZEVEDO, *Churches of Portugal* (1985). The Visigothic, Romanesque, Gothic, Manueline, Renaissance, and Baroque churches of Portugal captured in all their splendor by photographer Chester E. V. Brummel. Azevedo provides the narrative.

SAM AND JANE BALLARD, *Pousadas of Portugal* (1986). Profiles of Portugal's famous pousadas (government inns), many of them housed in historic castles and convents.

MARCUS BINNEY, *Country Manors of Portugal* (1987). Binney's text plus the lush four-color photographs of Nicolas Sapieha and Francesco Venturi add up to a voyeur's tour of Portugal's great houses, built over the past seven centuries.

DANIEL J. BOORSTIN, *The Discoverers* (1983). This history of man's quest to know the earth and its peoples includes an important section on the Portuguese discoveries.

C. R. BOXER, *The Portuguese Seaborne Empire, 1415–1825* (1969). A straightforward political, economic, and cultural history of the Portuguese part in the great expansion of the European powers; written by a leading historian.

ERNLE BRADFORD, *Southward the Caravels* (1961). A sailor follows the routes of the great 14th- and 15th-century navigators.

ANN BRIDGE AND SUSAN LOWNDES, *The Selective Traveller in Portugal* (1949). Shunpiking in Portugal with two women who love it and know it well. Bridge's husband was the British ambassador to Portugal; and Lowndes, the niece of Hilaire Belloc, was married to Luiz Marques, a writer and correspondent in Portugal for major English and American newspapers.

L. A. BROWN, *The Story of Maps* (1949). How cartography evolved through the centuries; the Portuguese have of course been one of the major forces.

ROBIN BRYANS, *The Azores* (1963). A highly personal introduction to these mid-Atlantic Portuguese islands.

LUIZ VAZ DE CAMÕES, *The Lusiads,* translated by William C. Atkinson (1952). Camões, the "Virgil of Portugal," wrote this epic poem in the late 16th century to immortalize his country's voyages of discovery, particularly those of Vasco da Gama, to whom he was related and who died the year he was born. But *The Lusiads* is also the story of Portugal itself.

SUZANNE CHANTAL, *Portugal, The Land and Its People,* translated by F. R. Holiday (1943). Personal impressions of each of the Portuguese provinces.

RUPERT CROFT-COOKE, *Madeira* (1961). The definitive story of Madeira wine.

G. R. CRONE (editor), *The Explorers* (1963). Profiles of the world's great navigators and explorers, including Magellan, da Gama, and other Portuguese.

C. DERVENN, *The Azores* (1956). A detailed look at this mid-Atlantic archipelago discovered by the Portuguese early in the 15th century.

JOHN DOS PASSOS, *The Portugal Story: Three Centuries of Exploration and Discovery* (1969). This important American writer of Portuguese ancestry turns his attention to the tiny land of his forefathers and details its role in leading Europe out of the Middle Ages and in opening up the world to Europe. His carefully researched history traces the evolution of Portugal from its earliest days through its Golden Age in the 15th century.

JOHN AND SUSAN FARROW, *Madeira, The Complete Guide* (1987). This British couple, now living on the island of Madeira, have written the most complete guide yet available to the "Isle of Perpetual June."

FRANCISCO ESTEVES GONÇALVES, *Portugal, A Wine Country* (1983). The most detailed book available on the wines of Portugal. Lavishly illustrated.

JOHN L. HAMMOND, *Building Popular Power* (1988). The story of Portugal's 1974 "Flower Revolution," especially the role of the workers and neighborhood movements.

RICHARD J. HARRISON, *Spain at the Dawn of History* (1988). How the Iberians, Phoenicians, and Greeks helped to shape Spain and Portugal.

WILLY HEINZELMANN, *Azores* (1980). Swiss writer-photographer Heinzelmann not only trains his lenses on the nine islands of the Azores but also examines their history, geography, economy, legends, and lore.

———, *Madeira* (1971). A portrait in photographs and words of the two inhabited islands in the Madeira archipelago: Madeira and Porto Santo.

ANTHONY HOGG, *Travellers' Portugal* (1983). Off the beaten path in Portugal.

A. C. INCHBOLD, *Lisbon and Cintra* (1908). A romantic description of Portugal around the turn of the century, with watercolor illustrations and sound historical background on places of interest in Estremadura.

MARY JEAN KEMPNER, *Invitation to Portugal* (1969). A well-written and informative exploration of the country, with evocative sections on bullfighting and fado.

WILLIAM KINGSTON, *Lusitanian Sketches* (1845). A tour of the north of Portugal during the mid-19th century, with particular references to the Anglo community in Porto.

CYNTHIA AND RALPH KITE, *Karen Brown's Portuguese Country Inns & Pousadas* (1987). A close look at more than 50 Portuguese inns and small hotels.

BJÖRN LANDSTRÖM, *The Quest for India* (1964). A profusely illustrated history of exploration from an expedition to the Land of Punt in 1493 B.C. to the discovery by Portuguese navigators of the Cape of Good Hope in A.D. 1488.

ROSE MACAULAY, *They Went to Portugal* (1946). This classic chronicles the journeys of celebrated travellers—Lord Byron, Tennyson, Palgrave, English royalty, William Beckford, and others—who went to Portugal, and tells what they found there and how the country affected them.

FREDERIC P. MARJAY, *Portugal and the Sea* (1957). This picture book with blocks of text documents Portugal's long-standing love affair with the sea.

A. H. DE OLIVEIRA MARQUES, *History of Portugal* (1976). A solid historical account of the formation of the Portuguese nation and the rise and decline of the empire.

MARIA DE LOURDES MODESTO, *Cozinha Tradicional Portuguesa* (1982). Although printed in Portuguese, this masterwork by "Portugal's Julia Child" is so profusely illustrated that flipping through its pages amounts to a culinary tour of Portugal. Anyone who knows Spanish or French should have little difficulty making sense of the recipes.

GUIDO DE MONTEREY, *Madeira, Isle of Flowers* (1987). A field guide to the extraordinary flora of Madeira.

SAMUEL ELIOT MORISON, *The Great Explorers* (1978). This abridged edition of Morison's classic history of the European discovery of the Americas acknowledges the valuable contributions of such Portuguese scholars and explorers as Prince Henry the Navigator, Bartolomeu Dias, Magellan, and Pedro Alvarez Cabral.

R. R. PALMER, *Atlas of World History* (1957). World history told via maps.

J. H. PARRY, *The Age of Reconnaissance* (1963). The story of how Europe discovered the rest of the world, from Prince Henry the Navigator onward.

———, *The Discovery of the Sea* (1974). The principal events of the great Age of Discovery (in which the Portuguese played a major role), covered with clarity and elegance.

RICHARD PATTEE, *Portugal and the Portuguese World* (1957). A useful study of the Portuguese principle of "biracialism" as a means of managing the far-flung empire.

MAGDELAINE PARISOT, ED., *Portugal, Madeira, Azores (1956)*. A hamlet-by-hamlet, museum-by-museum, stone-by-stone journey through Portugal, Madeira, and the Azores that is heavy on the history.

EÇA DE QUEIROZ, *The Maias* (1986). An entertaining and perceptive novel of 19th-century Portuguese society and manners.

ELAINE SANCEAU, *Henry, the Navigator* (1947). A well-researched and well-written biography of Portugal's most famous prince.

DON GLEN SANDY, *Madeira Wine at Home* (1988). The story of the Madeira wine industry, plus tips for serving and cooking with these noble wines.

ROBERT C. SMITH, *The Art of Portugal, from 1500 to 1800* (1968). A comprehensive survey of Portuguese architecture, sculpture, paintings, ecclesiastical art, ceramics, silver, furniture, and textiles, illustrated in color and black and white and with many floor plans of monasteries, cathedrals, and churches.

MURAT GEOFFREY TAIT, *Port, from the Vine to the Glass* (1936). Still the definitive guide to these fine wines.

JOHN AND PAT UNDERWOOD, *Madeira* (1987). John Underwood's photographs capture the many moods of Madeira.

FRANK VILLIER, *Portugal* (1963). A frank, sometimes dour, profile of the country and the people.

CAROLYN WALKER AND KATHY HOLMAN, *The Embroidery of Madeira* (1987). Two American teachers of needlework synopsize the history of the Madeira embroidery industry, then teach the essential stitches and techniques through the use of detailed how-to photographs and diagrams.

HELMUT AND ALICE WOHL, *Portugal* (1983). Travels through Portugal recorded in photographs and text. The accent is both architectural and historical.

DAVID WRIGHT AND PATRICK SMITH, *Algarve* (1965). Two insiders share the sights, sounds, and scents of the southernmost Portuguese province.

LISBON

*By Jane Garmey
with Martha de la Cal in Lisbon*

Jane Garmey has written two books about the food of England, and her articles on food and travel have been published in The New York Times *and in* Diversion *and* Signature *magazines. She lives in New York and travels to Portugal frequently. Martha de la Cal, author of a travel book on Portugal, has lived in that country for 20 years. She is a correspondent for* The Times *of London and* Time *magazine, and is a frequent contributor to travel publications.*

Lisbon has a special charm, constantly surprising you with unexpected contrasts and odd juxtapositions. It is a capital city with the feel of a sprawling village. Geographically tied to the rest of Europe yet culturally tugged by its affinities with Africa and the Orient, the city is at once exotic and homely. The exotic strain is a reflection of its Moorish history and the Século de Ouro (Golden Age) of the 16th century when, almost overnight, the city was transformed into the richest capital of Europe and became, according to the Portuguese poet Camões, "Princess of the world . . . before whom even the ocean bows."

Although it possesses only a few buildings of major architectural distinction, taken as a whole Lisbon is a city of great beauty. Its architecture fits together harmoniously, and it has an extraordinary natural setting, its buildings seeming to tumble down the seven hills on which the city is built. The sheer steepness of Lisbon's streets would be daunting were it not for the dramatic views and constantly changing perspectives that the city provides as you trudge, sometimes wearily, up and down its narrow streets.

Every surface in Lisbon seems to be patterned. House fronts are richly tiled and pavements are curlicued with mosaics, and this decorative extravagance is complemented by the brilliant light thrown off by the river, the muted colors, the scent of flowers, and the faint sea breeze, ever present.

MAJOR INTEREST

Neighborhoods
The Rossio area and the Baixa
The Alfama: old Moorish hillside quarter
The Chiado shopping district
Bairro Alto taverns
The suburb of Belém's museums and architecture

Sights
Castelo de São Jorge
Santa Justa Elevador
Quinta dos Marqueses de Fronteira
Mosteiro dos Jerónimos

Parks and Gardens
Jardim Botânico
Parque Eduardo VII: Estufa Fria

Museums
Museu Nacional de Arte Antiga
Museu Nacional do Azulejo (tile museum)
Fundação Calouste Gulbenkian (Gulbenkian Foundation)

Among travel writers of the past century, no European city aroused feelings more mixed than Lisbon. The Romantics, in particular, didn't know what to make of it. "Views like these exist only in climates like these," Robert Southey wrote in 1800. While delighting in the "voluptuous luxuriance" of Lisbon's riverside panorama, the English poet laureate was at the same time appalled by "the filth, the slops emptied from windows, the fierce and scavenging dogs, the deformed and diseased beggars." Later, he confided to a friend that things in Lisbon "look best at a distance."

Today's visitor will encounter a cleaner and more convenient city, about which modern Lisboetes tend to have mixed emotions. They are passionately attached to it but at the same time frustrated and exasperated by it. Despite its almost provincial charm, Lisbon has many of the usual problems of larger European cities—too much traffic, a growing population, not enough housing. It also has some problems that are less common—among them a recent revolution and, in 1975, an influx almost overnight of nearly a million dispossessed settlers from Africa, who came to Lisbon after Portugal's colonies won their independence.

Even though Lisbon's charms sometimes seem elusive to its residents, the city has been captivating visitors steadily since as long ago as the 12th century, when the first Crusaders arrived. They were not Lisbon's first foreign visitors. In the first century B.C. the Romans established a stronghold on the north bank of the river Tagus and named it Olispo, and then in the fifth century A.D., after the decline of the Roman Empire, the Visigoths invaded Olispo. They in turn were conquered by the Moors at the battle of Jerez in 711, and these new invaders fortified the city, improved the old Roman roads, and developed trade and agriculture.

In 1139 Afonso Henriques, the son of Henry of Burgundy, declared himself king of Portucale and persuaded some Crusaders to help him conquer Lisbon, which by then had a population approaching 15,000. On October 25, after heavy fighting, the Moors were driven out of the city, and by 1256 Afonso's son had moved the capital of his consolidated kingdom from Coimbra to Lisbon.

As the importance of trade and shipping increased, Lisbon's population, wealth, and importance also grew. But it was another century before developments in shipbuilding, the inventions of the compass and portolan chart, the competence of Portugal's navigators, and the ambitions of her rulers combined to make Lisbon a city of real significance. Endowed with a superb natural harbor on the edge of the known world, Lisbon was ideally situated to become the point of departure for many of the voyages of exploration that were to transform Portugal into a major economic force in Renaissance Europe.

But looking for the architectural underpinnings of this prosperous age—and indeed for any of Lisbon's early history—is a little like a paper chase after a windstorm. The sad fact is, the event that contributed most to Lisbon's architectural scene as we know it today was the earthquake of 1755, one of the worst cataclysms in modern European history. It destroyed most of the city; few buildings in the central part of Lisbon survived. Most of those that withstood the two main shocks on that fateful morning of November 1 succumbed to the fire and tidal wave that followed in their wake. More than 30,000 people died—about one quarter of the city's population. Lisbon was, literally, devastated.

The city that arose out of the rubble was very different in character from its predecessor. Portugal's despotic prime minister, the Marquês de Pombal, wanted to rebuild the city along rational 18th-century lines. The "Pombaline" approach called for strictly stylized houses and straight, wide avenues, geometrically balanced and rational. This attempt at coherent city planning lost momentum after a while, however, and never achieved the scope envisioned by Pombal. As a result, Lisbon has the feel and look of an unfinished city.

The politics of the present century have left their stamp on Lisbon as well. In 1908 King Carlos I and his son, Crown Prince Luis Filipe, were assassinated by anarchists in Lisbon's main square, the praça do Comércio. Two years later the monarchy was overthrown and a republic declared. Between 1911 and 1926, no fewer than 44 governments tried, with little success, to solve Portugal's economic and social problems. Finally, in 1928, Dr. António de Oliveira Salazar, an economics professor from Coimbra, was appointed finance minister and, with a series of austerity measures, proceeded to overcome many of the country's financial woes. He was made prime minister four years later and began using his political power to become the virtual dictator of a fascist regime.

Time stood still under Salazar's regime. It was authoritarian, conservative, and dependent on extreme censorship and a much-feared secret police, and it waged a long, unpopular colonial war to retain control of Portugal's African empire. Only in 1968, when Salazar suffered brain damage in a freak accident and was succeeded by his protégé, Marcelo Caetano, were some of the excesses of the old regime moderated and problems addressed.

Discontent continued to grow, however, until on April 25, 1974, a group of junior army officers with carnations stuck into their rifles staged a bloodless coup, "The Flower Revolution," in Lisbon. This event was such a relief to Lisboetes that they renamed the great Salazar suspension bridge over the river Tagus the Ponte 25 de Abril. A year later Portugal's colonies were granted their independence. As a result, Lisbon was flooded with huge numbers of *retornados* (refugees) from Mozambique, the Cape Verde islands, and Angola. Though most of the refugees have now been absorbed, housing continues to be scarce and shanty towns have grown up on the city's outskirts.

Since 1974, Portugal has made real economic progress, and Lisbon is at last catching up with other European capitals. Modern Lisbon, while much in evidence around the outer rim of the city, still keeps its distance from the older center and intrudes little except for neon lights, heavy exhaust fumes, and an excruciating rush hour. Visitors to Lisbon can still concentrate on the twisting streets (often too steep for cars), the tree-lined avenues, elegant squares, flowers and cafés, the well-groomed cats sitting in windows, and everywhere the pungent smell of sardines cooking on outdoor grills.

CENTRAL LISBON

The gateway to downtown Lisbon and the logical place to begin a tour of the city is the **praça do Comércio**, a large square that faces the river Tagus and is lined on its three other sides with Neo-Classical arcades. (It was here in 1908 that Carlos I and Luis Filipe were assassinated.)

The square is a magnificent architectural space on a scale with the piazza San Marco in Venice or the plaza Mayor in Salamanca. It is often referred to as "Black Horse Square," because at its center is a huge bronze equestrian statue of José I, the king of Portugal at the time of the 1755 earthquake. It is now no longer black but covered in a rich green patina. Sacheverell Sitwell, the authority on southern Baroque, thought it to be the most beautiful equestrian statue of its century.

A short walk west of the praça do Comércio is the **Mercado da Ribeira**, situated in a commercial neighborhood close to the waterfront. Here dozens of ships from all nations once docked offshore to deliver their cargo, but now there are only a few ferryboats to carry hurrying commuters across to the south shore of the Tagus.

If you like to rise early and are partial to chaos and color, the market (open every day except Sunday) is well worth a visit. It takes place in a huge two-story stadiumlike building shaped like a square doughnut. The wholesale operation downstairs is not particularly interesting, but upstairs you will find farmers selling their cheeses, a marvelous variety of olives, silvery braids of

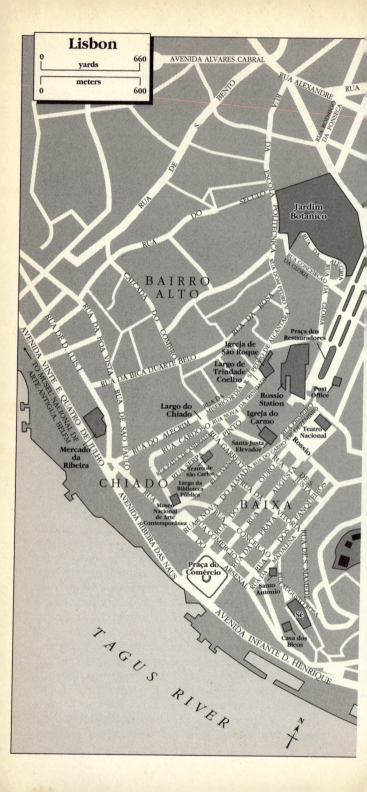

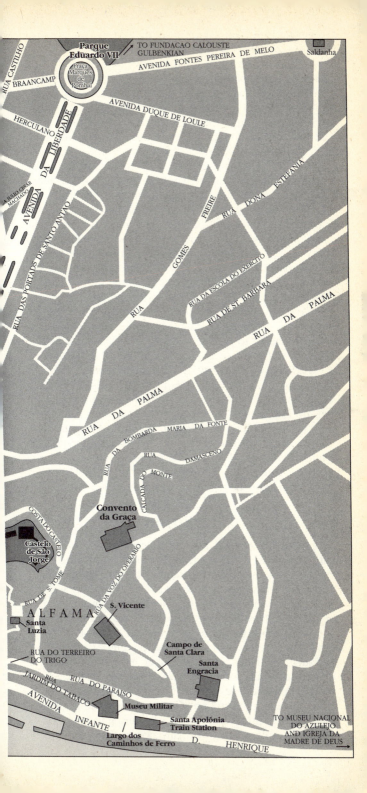

garlic, mounds of oranges, plums, grapes, and pomegranates, and everywhere women shredding kale that will wind up all over town in kettles of steaming *caldo verde*.

A triumphal arch on the north side of the praça do Comércio leads to rua Augusta, which, like many of the streets in the **Baixa**, or lower town, is open only to pedestrians. During the day street vendors, artists, and strolling musicians congregate here, but as soon as the shops and offices close, the neighborhood is deserted.

Both the praça do Comércio and the Baixa were planned and built in the 18th century under the supervision of the autocratic Marquês de Pombal. To rebuild the city, Pombal was given powers that Christopher Wren would have envied: What the earthquake did not knock down, his engineers did. The ruins of the Oriental and Medieval quarters of the city were leveled and replaced by the neatly laid out grid of the present-day Baixa. Sidewalks and sewers were installed, and the new buildings were ordained to be three- to five-story structures with virtually uniform façades and similar interior layouts.

The Baixa was designated a commercial area, and Pombal even went so far as to assign certain trades to certain streets: goldsmiths on the rua do Ouro and silversmiths on the rua da Prata. When Hans Christian Andersen visited Lisbon in 1866 he wrote in his diary: "On rua do Ouro, where all the goldsmiths live, shop after shop glitters with necklets, decorative orders, and suchlike glories." Today there are still many jewelers, but shoes now seem to be the dominant merchandise.

The Rossio

From the rua Augusta it's a quick walk to the Rossio, officially called the **praça Dom Pedro IV**, considered by most Portuguese to be the center of their capital. You come into a large, rectangular square filled with sidewalk cafés, neon signs, and flower stalls, and everywhere and at all hours there is an agreeable bustle and commotion. In earlier times the Rossio was the site of most of the city's public events, and Medieval morality plays, royal banquets, bullfights, carnivals, public executions, *autos-da-fé,* and popular uprisings have all taken place here. At the beginning of the 19th century its coffeehouses and cafés, including the still-present **Nicola**, became gathering places for artists and writers, and during the years of the Salazar dictatorship so many doctors, lawyers, and other professionals used to congregate here to criticize the regime that the square became known as the "wailing wall."

Today the Rossio is a hub of activity, with citizens and weary backpacking young tourists lounging around the fountains and statue of King Pedro IV. The open-air cafés and restaurants, **Pastelaria Suissa** and **Picnic** in addition to Nicola, are always crowded with tourists and local tourist watchers. (Unfortunately, the square is also popular with pickpockets and drug pushers.)

The restored **Teatro Nacional** stands at the north end of the square on the site of a former palace that served as the headquarters of the Inquisition in the 16th century. Here suspected heretics were condemned, tortured, and sent to the stake, as were Marranos, or "New Christians"—Jews who had been forced to convert to Christianity in 1496 by King Manuel I when he wished to marry the daughter of the Catholic monarchs of Spain, Ferdinand and Isabella. His future in-laws would agree to the match only if he expelled the Jews from Portugal, as they had done in Spain. But at least 60,000 Jews, mostly from Spain, had taken refuge in Portugal during the reign of Manuel's father, and many had become court advisors, financiers, and physicians or held other important positions. Manuel's compromise was to baptize them all and promise to ask no questions about their religion for at least 20 years.

This uneasy rapprochement came to an end after only ten years, with the murder of a "New Christian" who openly scoffed at the thought that a light suddenly reflected from a crucifix during a public mass was a miracle. His death triggered three days of terror and rioting, during which the mob hunted down and slaughtered several hundred Jews. Manuel executed 50 leaders of the mob, but his son, João III, hated the Jews and in 1536 established the Inquisition in Lisbon, with its headquarters in the Rossio.

To the northwest of the square is the **Rossio station**, one of Lisbon's main railway stations, a late-19th-century Victorian Gothic extravaganza. It boasts a huge, much decorated Moorish entrance that has recently been cleaned and restored. Some people find it grotesque, but those with a taste for the bizarre will like it.

Hidden away in the rua das Portas de Santo Antão, a block east of the Rossio, there is a small church, **São Luis da Francesca**. Seldom mentioned in guidebooks, it is worth a quick visit to see its 16th-century pre-earthquake painting of Lisbon, *Nossa Senhora do Porto Seguro* (Our Lady of the Safe Port), attributed to the Portuguese painter Amaro do Vale. Today the street is also rich in seafood restaurants. Here you can "menu-shop" and be courted by headwaiters until you find the best place for your favorite dishes. **Gambrinus**, at number 23, is noted for its excellent shellfish and is one of the best on the street.

North of the Rossio is the **praça dos Restauradores**, named for those who took part in the revolt of 1640 and restored a Portuguese king to the throne after 60 years of Spanish rule. Their deed is commemorated by a huge obelisk in the center of this square. Lisbon's central post office (conveniently open on weeknights to 10:30 P.M.) is on the east side, and the main tourist office, housed in the restored Palácio Foz, is on the west side. The Elevador da Gloria cable car off the plaza runs up to the Bairro Alto to the west (see below).

The praça dos Restauradores opens into Lisbon's main boulevard, the mile-long **avenida da Liberdade**. Both the square and the initial section of the avenue were built as a promenade in the 18th century, when the Rossio had grown full of beggars and Gypsies. To keep out all undesirables this promenade was enclosed by walls and a gate, within which fine ladies, perfumed, coiffed, and dressed in silks, strolled the tree-lined paths among rosebushes, statues, and fountains. After the Liberals came to power in 1821 the walls were torn down and the promenade became a public space, gaslit for dances and other festivities. In 1879 it was lengthened into a double avenue, lined with palms, and planted with a continuous stretch of water gardens. Because of its inherent elegance the street is often compared to the Champs-Elysées. Although it is still an avenue on a grand scale and is lined with open-air cafés, the Liberdade, like its Parisian counterpart, has lost some of its luster, as many of its better shops have been replaced by dull commercial offices. Nevertheless, walk up the avenue a little way to see the street mosaics of loops, dolphins, arabesques, and other motifs, among the best in Lisbon. British writer Brigid Brophy describes their "abstract curlicues of high fantasy, as though some very dotty but very grand duchess had dipped her train in ink and gone swishing down the hill."

West of the praça do Comércio but too far to walk (it's only a short taxi ride) is the **Museu Nacional de Arte Antiga**, rua das Janelas Verdes, 95. The museum, housed in a 17th-century palace close to the waterfront, has an excellent collection of 15th- and 16th-century Portuguese primitive paintings, as well as Italian, French, Spanish, German, Flemish, and Dutch art. Most of it was confiscated from Portuguese convents and monasteries when all religious orders were expelled from Portugal in 1834. Be sure not to miss Nuno Gonçalves's masterpiece *Retable of the Infante,* a mid-15th-century altarpiece worthy of comparison to the greatest Flemish paintings. Its six wooden panels show Saint Vincent, the patron saint of Lisbon, surrounded by kings, queens, bankers, doctors, knights, monks, and beggars, and on the left panel is a magnificent portrait of a mustachioed Prince Henry the Navigator. Three other world-famous paintings are also found here: Piero della Francesca's *Saint Augustine,* Hieronymus Bosch's extraordinary oversized triptych *The Temptation of Saint Anthony,* and Lucas Cranach's *Salome.*

There is also a large collection of gold and silver, reflecting Portugal's long relationship with Africa and the Orient, and carved ivory objects from Africa, Indo-European ivory-inlaid furniture, and Namban Japanese screens, among the finest of their kind. Painted during the 16th and 17th centuries, the screens show the arrival of the Portuguese in Japan. (The word *Namban,* in fact, means "barbarians coming from the south.") All the Portuguese visitors on the screens have very big noses, which must be how they were perceived by the Japanese.

The museum has a cafeteria that opens onto a garden, giving a pleasant view of the river, and in the summer tea as well as lunch is served here. Also close by—a hundred yards to your right when you come out of the museum—is the entrance to **York House**, a 16th-century monastery that has been converted into a particularly charming hotel. It is entirely hidden from the street, and a steep flight of steps leads to a courtyard filled with trees and flowers where, weather permitting, you can have a drink or a meal.

THE ALFAMA

The Alfama, on the hillside overlooking the Baixa and the river to the east of the town center, is the poorest but also the most picturesque district of Lisbon. This old Moorish quarter was built on solid rock, so it is one of the few parts of Lisbon that was not leveled by the 1755 earthquake. Hardly touched since Medieval times, it remains a maze of narrow alleys, cobbled and perpendicular, with overhanging eaves and stairs carved into the rock. Making sense of any map of this labyrinth is not easy; it is best simply to wander at random, soaking up the Moorish atmosphere as you head downhill from the Castelo de São Jorge, which sits atop the Alfama like a weighty crown.

Because the Alfama is extremely steep, the best way to see it is to take a taxi to the castle. Then, after exploring the ramparts and ruins, wander downhill to modern Lisbon. Sad to say, even the Alfama has caught up with the 20th century in one respect: There are purse and camera snatchers, especially during the high summer season, so be on your guard and carry only a small amount of cash.

Castelo de São Jorge

When the Moors conquered Lisbon in the eighth century they built a castle on the city's highest hill on top of earlier Roman fortifications. Portugal's first king, Afonso Henriques, captured this castle in 1147 and rebuilt it. The fortification served as headquarters for the kings of Portugal until the end of the 16th century, when a new royal palace was built on the river front in the praça do Comércio.

You enter the castle grounds through the Porta da Traição (Treason Gate), on the northeast side. Its two towers probably existed at the time of the Moors, as did the old walls, which measure between 15 and 30 feet thick. Though nothing remains of the original battlements, the castle walls, with their sheer drop of sometimes a hundred feet or more, offer unobstructed views of Lisbon across the red tiled roofs of the Alfama (now sprigged with TV antennas) and beyond to the Tagus, the Ponte 25 de Abril, and the distant hills of Sintra and the Arrábida peninsula.

Lisboetes come up to the castelo to relax, lunch on grilled prawns with *piri-piri* (hot red-pepper sauce) at the **Casa do Leão** (a state-run restaurant within the ramparts), and to stroll in the cool green gardens, where white peacocks preen beneath the olive trees. A Lisboete once remarked, pointing to a flurry of feathers, "The children of Lisbon have never seen snow. These peacock feathers are their snow."

Largo das Portas do Sol

As you leave the castle grounds, zigzag a few blocks downhill to the largo das Portas do Sol, a large square at the end of the rua de Santa Luzia. The square stands on the site of the old city gates, aptly called Portas do Sol (Gates of the Sun) because, facing east, they catch the first rays of the early-morning sun. From the square you will have yet another aerial view down over the Alfama as well as over the **Cêrca Moura**, an outdoor restaurant just off the square with a terrace that is a pleasant place to pause for lunch or a drink. It is known for its fresh orange juice (something of a rarity in Lisbon).

On the square is the **Museu Escola de Artes Decorativas**, part of the Ricardo do Espirito Santo Silva Foundation, housed in a 17th-century palace. Its elegant rooms, all facing an inner courtyard, hold a priceless collection of Portuguese furniture (including an exquisite rosewood game table), silver, and Arraiolos gros-point tapestries with strangely Oriental motifs. The foundation was established in 1953 in order to preserve traditional Portuguese craftsmanship in the decorative arts. It operates 21 workshops in another part of the palace, open each morning to the public, where students learn such skills as gold leafing, wood carving, furniture making, textile restoration, bookbinding, and iron working. Examples of their work are displayed in the museum.

Before heading down into the Alfama stop in at **Santa Luzia**, a little neighborhood church around the corner from the museum. It is built on top of the remains of the old Visigoth city walls and has on its wall a Baroque-framed panel of blue-and-white tiles showing the praça do Comércio as it was before the earthquake: carriages passing through, soldiers drilling with muskets, riders on prancing horses. Above is a large tiled image of Saint Lucia, surrounded by an elaborate border, in front of which hangs a lamp to illuminate her at night. In the summer neighborhood children splash in a big, shallow pool outside the church, while tourists and others sit around under the bright umbrellas of the outdoor cafés, enjoying the spectacular view across the Alfama to the opposite hill, with the church towers of São Vicente and Santa Engracia rising above it.

Map

Streets and locations:

- RUA DOS FANQUEIROS
- RUA DA MADALENA
- RUA DO REGEDOR
- RUA DAS FARINHAS
- COSTA DO CASTELO
- LARGO DO CHAO DO LOUR
- RUA DO MILAGRE DE ST. ANTONIO
- RUA DAS PEDRAS NEGRAS
- Igreja de St. Antonio
- RUA DE S. MAMEDE
- CHAO DA
- RUA DA PADARIA
- RUA DE S. MARTINHO
- AUGUSTO ROSA
- Largo da Sé
- CRUZES DA SE
- Sé
- RUA DO BARAO
- RUA DOS BACALHOEIROS
- RUA DE S. JOAO DA PRACA
- RUA DA ALFANDEGA
- Casa dos Bicos
- RUA DO CAIS DE SANTAREM
- ← TO PRAÇA DO COMERCIO
- AVENIDA INFANTE

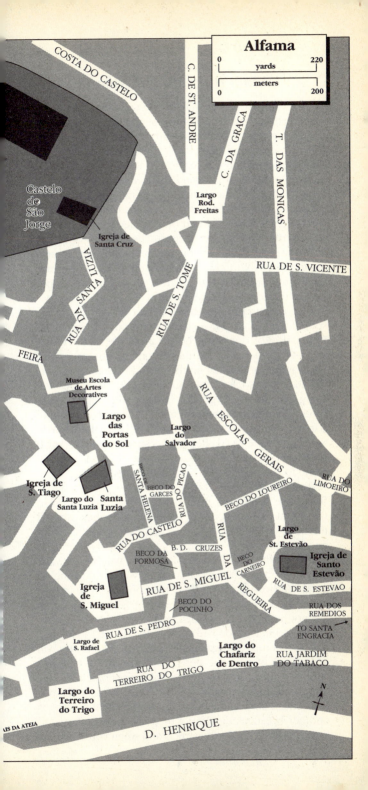

A Walk through the Alfama

As you walk through the Alfama you will pass along twisting streets and steep staircases opening into unexpected courtyards, past braziers of sardines grilling on almost every doorstep and women doing their daily wash at outdoor fountains. You will see houses whose front walls are entirely covered in blue-and-white *azulejos,* some with designs of such delicacy that the overall effect is like an outdoor wallpaper. Often the limestone trim of the doorways and windows is further ornamented with borders of narrow tiles decorated with stars. The craftsmanship that has gone into these marvelous façades is endlessly rewarding to the eye. Windows, which are often at eye level, are sometimes provided with shutters painted in subtle contrast to the color of the wall tiles.

If you are in the mood to seek out one or two of the special houses in the Alfama, walk from the largo das Portas do Sol down the beco (alley) de Santa Helena steps (right across from the decorative arts museum). Halfway down, turn left on the beco do Garces and then, in 150 feet or so, left again on the rua do Picão. This will bring you to the largo do Salvador; the superb 16th-century mansion of the counts of Arcos, with a beautiful Baroque balcony, stands at number 22. Leave the largo do Salvador by the rua da Regueira, a street lined with small shops and restaurants, and in about 300 feet you will come to the steps of the beco das Cruzes, on your right. At the corner is an 18th-century house whose upper floors are supported by carved ravens, those birds so important in the legends of Lisbon because they ushered the body of Saint Vincent, the city's patron, to the city in an unmanned boat.

If you follow the beco das Cruzes you will pass on your left, after about 100 feet, a doorway with a fine panel of *azulejos* showing the Virgin of the Conception. At the top of the beco das Cruzes, where you pass under an arch surmounted by a cross, turn left down the beco da Formosa. In 150 feet you will come to the rua de São Miguel, and, if you turn left again, after another 150 feet you will see ahead of you the steps of the **beco do Carneiro** (Sheep's Alley), so narrow that the houses on either side almost meet above you and in order to pass someone you must duck into a doorway. At the top of the steps is another breathtaking vista of tiled rooftops. Continue to wander down any of the streets and when you reach the foot of the hill you will be able to hail a cab to get to your next destination.

Every June, during the **Festas dos Santos Populares** (Festivals of Popular Saints), the Alfama explodes with revelry. The celebrations begin, as they have for centuries, on the eve of Saint Anthony's feast on June 13 in honor of Lisbon's—indeed, the Alfama's—own saint, for he was born here in 1195. First there's a huge costumed parade, sweeping exuberantly down the avenida da Liberdade from the praça Marquês de Pombal to the praça dos Restauradores. Then, around midnight, everyone heads for the Alfama to dance, drink, and enjoy *fado* singing until dawn. The festivities continue uninterrupted until the feast of Saint Peter on June 29. During this time the streets of the Alfama are brightly festooned with streamers and paper lanterns, and every corner, patio, and little square is turned into a makeshift café with music and dancing. The air is filled with the smell of sardines roasting over open fires, and everywhere women sell little pots of bush basil, believed to bring luck in love.

Lisbon's Great Churches

A short walk up the rua da Padaria, off the rua dos Bacahoeiros, brings you to Lisbon's **Sé** (cathedral), the oldest church in the city, built in the 12th century by King Afonso Henriques after he drove the Moors out of Portugal. It, too, was devastated by the earthquake and has been extensively rebuilt. Its two low towers and rather plain exterior are softened by a large rose window over a Romanesque doorway. The chancel is 18th century, but in the transept you can still see where the Gothic arches were imposed over the Romanesque. The ambulatory dates back to the 14th century, and in the chapels opening off it there are some interesting tombs. Lopo Fernandes Pacheco, a famous Portuguese warrior, lies with his bright-eyed little dog alert at his feet, and nearby his wife reads forever from her small prayerbook. In the ruined cloister lives an ancient raven, well tended by the sacristan. The bird is thought to be descended from the ravens of the Saint Vincent legend.

Tucked behind the cathedral is the little **Capela de Santo António**, built on top of the actual room where the saint, usually associated with Padua in Italy, is believed to have been born. He is the city's most popular saint, venerated in Portugal not for his knack of finding lost articles, as in most Roman Catholic societies, but for his successful matchmaking abilities.

On the hill directly northeast of the Alfama (about a five-minute cab ride from the cathedral) stand two important Lisbon churches. **São Vicente de Fora** (Saint Vincent outside the Walls) derives its name from the fact that it was built outside the old Visigoth city walls. It is a white limestone church with short twin towers erected between 1582 and 1627 on the site of a 12th-century monastery, at the command of Philip II of Spain a year after he had been crowned king of Portugal. The architect, Felipe Terzio, an Italian, used Il Gesù in Rome as his model but gave the church the same severity as the Escorial monastery near Madrid. The central dome collapsed in the 1755 earthquake, but the grandiose barrel vault and the enormous 18th-century gilt organ survived.

In the campo de Santa Clara, just behind the church, the **Feira da Ladra** (Thieves' Market) takes place every Tuesday and Saturday. This is the place to pick up anything from antique brass coach lamps to a copper coffeepot to video cassettes.

Across the campo is **Santa Engracia**, Portugal's great Baroque church, which is also the national pantheon. It is actually the third church on the site, and took so long to complete—almost 300 years—that a popular saying grew up around it: Anything that takes a long time to do is called *uma obra de Santa Engracia* ("a work of Santa Engracia").

The limestone used to build Santa Engracia is so white it looks like marble, and the church's four façades trace the architectural development of the Baroque style. The interior, both uncluttered and enormous, is shaped like a Greek cross and topped by a giant dome with semicircular vaults above deep alcoves. All around the walls are cenotaphs of Portugal's great historical figures. You can take an elevator to the upper gallery of the church and to the roof to see all of Lisbon spread out below.

Heading down to the river, you will come to the **Santa Apolónia train station** in the largo dos Caminhos de Ferro (about a five-minute walk). Right beside it is the **Museu Militar**, housed in the old national arsenal. This hodgepodge of Portuguese military memorabilia includes arms, sculpture, and paintings, as well as granite missiles used in the assault on Ormuz in 1552, 14th-century cannon, and relics from the Napoleonic invasions. In the Sala de Dom José is a reproduction of the enormous wagon used to transport King José's equestrian statue to the praça do Comércio, where it stands today. The Sala Vasco da Gama traces, object by object, Portugal's great Age of Discovery.

The Casa dos Bicos Area

On the rua dos Bacalhoeiros (Street of Codfish Sellers), close to the waterfront and to the west of the Alfama (on your left as you face the river), is the Casa dos Bicos (House of Pointed Stones), so named because it is covered with sharp, diamond-shaped stones. (That it was once actually covered with diamonds is only a legend.) Afonso de Albuquerque, a powerful Portuguese explorer and viceroy to India, built the house at a time when Portugal's overseas trade was expanding so rapidly that most of the city's life centered on the port area. Like so many other buildings in Lisbon, this strange structure was almost totally destroyed by the great earthquake, and only in 1983 was its restoration finally completed. You can't go inside, but its exterior design is so unusual that you should see it.

The docks and customs area around the Casa dos Bicos are now rather seedy. The hole-in-the-wall shops and rundown taverns make a very different impression from the quarter's character in the days of Lisbon's great "Spice Age," when the city rivaled London and Venice as a prosperous center of world trade and these streets were lined with the homes of wealthy merchants and shops selling silks, spices, and jewels, frequented by traders from every country in Europe.

A short taxi ride east along the river from the Santa Apolonia station or the Casa dos Bicos (watch as you go for a glimpse of the *Sagres,* Portugal's "tall ship," with red crosses emblazoned on her white sails; she is often in port) is the **Igreja da Madre de Deus**, one of Lisbon's real treasures, and the adjoining **Museu Nacional do Azulejo** (National Tile Museum). The church was built in 1509 by Queen Léonor to house the relics of Santa Auta, a Portuguese saint and one of the 11,000 virgins of Cologne who were slaughtered by the Huns as they were returning from a pilgrimage to Rome. A Manueline doorway, its twisted columns topped by trilobate arches in which carved pelicans and fishnets are entwined, leads into the church and suggests the opulence that awaits inside. The lower walls are lined with blue-and-white polychrome tiles, the upper walls and ceiling with ornately framed primitive paintings. At the center of the choir is a splendid lectern surmounted by a lamb, head held erect, holding a waving pennant.

The adjoining cloisters house the tile museum. When the Portuguese captured Ceuta in Morocco from the Moors in 1415, they allegedly saw and appreciated the beauty of Moorish tiles. When they returned to Portugal they brought back with them the art of making such tiles. While the earliest dated Portuguese tiles, those at the Quinta de Bacalhoa on the Arrábida peninsula across the Tagus (see Day Trips from Lisbon), go back only to 1565, by the 17th century tiles were all the rage, in such demand that they were even being imported from Holland. (Blue-and-white Delft tiles were in fact considered more desirable than the earthier local ones.)

In the museum you can see a dazzling display of four centuries of Portuguese tile making, including excellent examples of huge floor or "carpet" tiles. Among the museum's special treasures are two tiny tiles depicting King Charles II of England and his Portuguese queen, Catherine of Bragança, but its greatest prize is an enormous wall of blue-and-white tiles that runs the entire length of the gallery on one side of the large cloister. Here is a panoramic view of pre-earthquake Lisbon, and in it you can see the royal palace, the pointed towers of the cathedral, and many other landmarks of early Lisbon.

The museum also has a fine selection of Art Deco tiles and those by modern Portuguese painters, and a small shop where you can buy books about tiles and modern *azulejos*.

WEST OF THE BAIXA
The Chiado

The Chiado, to the west and uphill from the Baixa, is the most fashionable shopping area in Lisbon (see Shopping, below). Chiado is an improbable name for a city's main shopping district, as the word means "shrill or squeaking sound." It derives from the statue in the largo do Chiado of António Ribeiro, a 16th-century satiric poet known as "O Chiado."

The main shopping street of the district is **rua Garrett**, lined with outdoor cafés—such as **Brazileira**, long a gathering place of artists and writers—and shops. **Bertrand's** is a long-established book shop much frequented by English-speaking readers.

A disastrous fire, believed to have been set by a disgruntled former employee of one of the larger department stores, broke out in the early morning of August 25, 1988, and gutted four blocks of the Chiado. Rebuilding is now under way, but several stores have been forced to relocate, and it will be some time before the district fully recovers.

Just south of rua Garrett is the **Museu Nacional de Arte Contemporânea**, on the largo da Biblioteca Pública. The name is misleading, as it is not a museum of contemporary art but a large collection of 19th- and early-20th-century paintings and sculpture. (It is now, however, temporarily closed for renovation following the fire.) The city's opera house, **Teatro de São Carlos**, is a block away on the rua Serpa Pinto. This fine old building, built in 1793, is modeled on the Teatro San Carlo in Naples; its large porte cochère and imposing façade are also reminiscent of Milan's La Scala. It was supposedly outside this building, in 1809, that Lord Byron, visiting Lisbon for the first time, was struck by an angry husband for making advances to his wife.

The Bairro Alto

The rua do Carmo in the Baixa leads to the outdoor **Santa Justa Elevador**, one of the world's great cast-iron extravaganzas. Often mistakenly assumed to be the work of Gustave Eiffel, it was in fact built by the French engineer Raoul Mesnier de Ponsard in 1898. The city is built here on a virtual precipice; the rear entrances of some buildings are a full seven stories above their front doors.

The elevator lifts you a hundred feet and delivers you on a little bridge. You walk through a succession of open galleries, their slender iron shafts and arches displaying a heady mixture of Gothic and Moorish styles, to an observation plaza cantilevered out on all four sides. Intricate spiral staircases rise still farther to the uppermost deck, from which you get a thrilling bird's-eye view of Chiado and Baixa rooftops. A narrow iron bridge leads from the top almost to the front door of the ruins of the 14th-century **Igreja do Carmo**, once a vast church with three richly decorated naves. The vaulting fell in the 1755 earthquake, and now only the façades and roofless Gothic arches remain, open to the sky. The ruins are floodlit at night and serve as a dramatic reminder of Lisbon's past; there is a small, not very interesting archaeological museum in the ruins of the adjoining convent.

You are now in the Bairro Alto (High Quarter), which was not greatly damaged by the earthquake of 1755 and is one of the oldest parts of Lisbon. Many of its houses open onto broad steps with stone risers and smooth terrazzo treads, shaded by fruit trees carefully placed down the center, one at each landing, and by overarching grapevines, at which small boys often tug to reach the fruit. The 17th-century houses are now decayed, but here and there doorway and window decorations remind you of their more elegant past. Everywhere there are cats, just as in Princess Maria Leticia Rattazzi's day, when this great-niece of Napoleon remarked "The cat is an indispensable adjunct in Portuguese homes."

During the day the Bairro Alto is primarily a commercial neighborhood, teeming with small businesses and some of Lisbon's best-known restaurants, including **Tavares**, **Avis**, and **Bacchus**. But Lisboetes know the Bairro Alto for its *tascas*—mom-and-pop restaurants, usually no larger than one room, with the kitchen tucked somewhere behind a counter in the back and a smoking brazier set on the sidewalk outside the front door. While a grandmother tends the grill, the men and children of the family wait on tables and the younger women work in the kitchen. Around lunchtime it is always easy to tell which are the best of these *tascas:* Inside they are jammed with noisy eaters, and there is an eager line waiting outside.

Lunch in a *tasca* is simple, usually delicious, and inexpensive. Typically, it will begin with a plate of bread, cheese, and olives, then grilled fish—either *espadarte* (swordfish), *linguado* (sole), or *sardinhas.* (Portuguese sardines are fat, meaty, and succulent, nothing like the skinny creatures packed tightly together in tins.) Then comes a fresh green salad and a flan or piece of luscious ripe melon. The meal is almost invariably washed down with a bottle of the house *vinho verde,* that young, light Minho wine for which Portugal is famous. It all makes for a perfect light meal, one that is enjoyed every day by the vast majority of Lisboetes. At night the Bairro Alto becomes the center of Lisbon's nightlife (see Bars and Nightlife, below).

The rua nova da Trindade runs north from the Bairro Alto toward the largo de Trindade Coelho. If you walk along it you will come to the **Cervejaria Trindade**, an enormous beerhall/restaurant that is always crowded. Some of the walls are covered with 17th-century tiles, and supposedly this vast hall was once the dining room of the 13th-century Convento da Trindade, the first headquarters of the Inquisitor General.

At the far end of the largo de Trindade Coelho is the **Igreja de São Roque**. Its flat, undecorated façade is not particularly imposing, but in the interior is a famous chapel dedicated to Saint John the Baptist. It was commissioned in Rome in the 18th century by King João V and built there by the architects Luigi Vanvitelli and Niccolò Salvi. After Pope Benedict XIV dedicated the chapel, it was dismantled and brought to Lisbon in three ships.

The chapel is one of the most costly structures of its size ever built, carved entirely from semiprecious stones. What appear to be paintings of scenes from the life of John the Baptist are actually mosaic panels by Mattia Moretti. The sacristy is also sumptuous, with painted vaulting, chests of jacaranda wood, and three tiers of paintings depicting the lives of the saints. The **treasury museum** adjoining the church contains the most valuable art from the chapel, including two silver candlesticks, each weighing almost a thousand pounds.

From here it is only a short distance along São Pedro de Alcântara to the **Solar de Vinho do Porto**, the perfect place to take a break and your chance to pick and choose from a menu that lists a staggering number of white, tawny, ruby, and rare vintage Ports. Simply go into the bar and relax in one of the comfortable oversized leather chairs. This is a room with a massive fireplace, vaulted ceilings, and polished terra-cotta tiled floors that looks for all the world like a foreigner's attempt to re-create an English men's club. Your only obligation will be to sample a glass or two of Port and begin to appreciate its complexities and delights.

From here, the easiest way to get back down to the center of town is to take the **Elevador da Gloria cable car**. It stops right outside the door and then rolls down the alarmingly steep hill with the greatest of ease, depositing you in the praça dos Restauradores. If you still have some time, though, take a short taxi or bus ride up the rua Dom Pedro V, which becomes the rua da Escola Politécnica, to the **Jardim Botânico** (Botanical Garden), first opened to the public in 1873 and considered to have one of the best collections of botanical specimens in southern Europe. You will enter through a rather dusty alley lined with enormous palms before descending a stone staircase to a cool, green, hilly garden with large banana trees, cedars, jacarandas, conifers, and many other species of tropical and subtropical plants and trees.

NORTH LISBON

The north end of the avenida da Liberdade descends into the **praça Marquês de Pombal**, a manic traffic circle into which cars funnel from every direction. A marble Pombal, seemingly oblivious to the carbon monoxide and honking cars, surveys all beneath him from his perch high on a column in the middle of the circle. The despot is surrounded by lions—appropriate companions, as he had a reputation for devouring his enemies.

In addition to masterminding the rebuilding of Lisbon after the great earthquake and putting into action what was in effect the first large-scale urban construction program in preindustrial Europe, Pombal reformed the university, reorganized the army, and set up the Royal Bank. These extraordinary achievements were accomplished with such cruelty and vindictiveness that he was feared and hated throughout Portugal. He persecuted, imprisoned, and executed whoever opposed him, and even installed his brother as Grand Inquisitor so that he could use the Inquisition as a weapon against his enemies. When Pombal's protector, King José I, died in 1777, his successor, Maria I, stripped the marquês of all his powers and banished him to his estates in the Beira. It was a time of national rejoicing—hundreds of political prisoners were released and Pombal's effigy was burned in the streets of Lisbon.

The **Parque Eduardo VII**, named to commemorate that English king's visit to Lisbon in 1903, stretches nearly a mile uphill from the north of the praça Marquês de Pombal. Lisbon was the destination of Edward VII's first state visit abroad after his coronation, and he arrived in great pomp aboard the royal yacht, *Victoria and Albert,* which anchored in the Tagus. Seven thousand Portuguese troops lined the shore as King Carlos I was rowed out in the royal barge to welcome the English monarch. An endless round of celebrations marked the royal visit, culminating in the official opening of the new park.

The park provides a welcome expanse of green and an opportunity for charming walks among formally clipped boxwoods. Stop in afterward for a drink at the **Ritz Hotel**, which overlooks them. At the far end of the park are two of the best-kept horticultural secrets in Europe, the **Estufa Fria** (Cool House) and the **Estufa Quente** (Hot House), both opened to the public in 1926. The former covers an acre of land and is an enchanting oasis entirely enclosed by bamboo slats designed to keep out the sun but let in the air. In this protected Eden flourishes a sumptuous array of plants, bushes, and ferns, both tropical and Mediterranean. The flower beds are connected by winding paths; miniature bridges and stairways lead to an upper level. Everywhere there is flowing water—waterfalls, fountains, ponds, and streams. The air smells damp and rich, and the stillness is broken only by the sound of goldfish and carp breaking the surface of the water. The Estufa Fria leads to the Estufa Quente, its desert equivalent, which is similarly laid out. Being a hothouse with a glass roof, it is positively torrid, enjoyable only on cool days.

The Gulbenkian Foundation

From the park, it is about a five-minute cab ride to the **Fundação Calouste Gulbenkian**, situated at the juncture of the avenida Berne and the praça de Espanha. Created by an immensely wealthy (oil royalties) Armenian collector who spent many years in Lisbon and died there in 1955, the foundation is the foremost cultural center in Portugal. It has its own orchestra, choir, and ballet company, concert halls, cinemas, library, and two permanent art collections.

The Gulbenkian collection consists of works amassed by the founder over a lifetime. Gulbenkian was that rare combination, a billionaire with taste, and his art collection is impeccable as well as idiosyncratic. The first room you see on entering the museum contains a small but stellar collection of Egyptian sculpture. Be sure to look for the small, exquisitely detailed bronze cats in this room. The Islamic ceramics and carpets are unsurpassed, and lovers of Art Nouveau should be delighted by the fine Lalique jewelry. There are superb collections of coins, ivories, furniture, Chinese porcelain, and Japanese prints and lacquers, and a highly concentrated collection of European art, including canvases by Rubens, Gainsborough, and Monet. In particular, look for Renoir's delightful portrait of Madame Monet and the fine Degas self-portrait.

On the south side of the landscaped gardens behind the Gulbenkian Foundation is its **Centro de Arte Moderno**, with a large permanent collection documenting the development of modern art in Portugal, from such turn-of-the-century artists as Almada Negreiros and Amadeu de Sousa Cardoso to contemporary artists working in Portugal today. The Gulbenkian's garden, with a collection of modern sculpture, is one of Lisbon's most popular parks.

The **Jardim Zoológico**, Lisbon's zoo, is half a mile north of the Gulbenkian on the estrada de Benfica at avenida das Forças Armadas. Not far west of the zoo, off the rua de São Domingos (take bus number 46 or a taxi), is the **Quinta dos Marqueses de Fronteira**, a beautiful late-17th-century house set in terraces and formal Italian Renaissance gardens. The box hedges of the main garden are laid out in such a dense pattern that they appear to be a green carpet punctuated only by statuary and privet topiary. Beyond rise the red-and-white walls of the palace, its garden front a crazy quilt of panes, arches, and pilasters. At one side of the garden is a long water tank set against a backdrop of blue-and-white *azulejos* and a balustraded walk lined with marble busts in alcoves, large pyramids at each end.

The lower walls of the palace are covered with 17th-century tile panels depicting banquets, boats, houses, and most particularly cats—cats of all kinds, some staring quizzically at you as you pass, others offering you a fish. Perhaps the most memorable is a large panel showing a cat musicale—cat conductor, cat musicians—and, just next to this, a wonderful scene of a cat at the barber's, having a shave. And don't miss the grotto covered entirely in bits of Gaudí-esque broken china. (These are reminders of a visit by a king, long ago, who ordered that the china on which he had been served be broken so that no one else could ever eat from it.) Inside the palace is a huge library and more tile panels, these showing famous battles of Portuguese history in great detail. Fronteira is open only at the most unusual hours, so be sure to call before going; Tel: (01) 78-20-23.

If you have driven to Fronteira or are returning to town by cab, leave by the avenida 24 de Janeiro and then go left on the caminho das Pedreiras until you see, rising up in front of you, the other great sight in northern Lisbon, the **Aqueduto das Aguas Livres**. This huge water project, its 109 pointed arches spanning a distance of 11 miles, was built between 1729 and 1748. It survived the earthquake of 1755 and is still in use, as impressive as ever.

BELEM

Belém is situated along the mouth of the Tagus, 8 km (5 miles) west of downtown Lisbon. If possible, allow a full day for a visit, since there is so much to see. The best way to get to Belém is by taxi (approximately a 20-minute ride from the center of town). A tram (numbers 13, 27, and 49 all go to Belém) from the praço do Comércio will take about 45 minutes, depending on the time of day.

Almost every building, garden, cul-de-sac, and fountain in Belém has a history closely linked with the Portuguese Age of Discovery. With its fine natural harbor perched seemingly on the edge of the world, Lisbon was ideally situated to become the launching point for the exploratory voyages that were to turn Portugal into a major economic force. It was from Belém that Henry the Navigator, King João II, and King Manuel I sent ships into the uncharted Atlantic and down the coast of Africa on journeys that changed the world. Prince Henry's sailors, who departed from the Algarve, found the uninhabited islands of Madeira (1419) and the Azores (1427). In 1487 Bartolomeu Dias sailed south from Belém, but heavy winds forced him off his course, and when he finally sighted land he realized that he had unknowingly rounded the tip of Africa and discovered a new sea route to India. In 1497 King Manuel sent Vasco da Gama with three ships to sail around the Cape of Good Hope to India, and on May 18, 1498, the expedition reached Calcutta.

These voyages were made possible by Portuguese development of the skills of ocean navigation and by the invention of the caravel, a three-masted vessel with a roundish hull, a high bow and stern, and lateen rigging. The heavier, square-rigged ships used at that time could sail only with the wind, but the sails of a caravel could be manipulated to catch the wind more flexibly. Because the prevailing winds along the coast of Africa were from north to south, square-rigged ships could sail down the coast but couldn't return to Portugal, lending credence to the myth that the world was flat and stories of ships dropping off its edge. Only when Prince Henry's designers came up with the idea of the flexible, lateen-rigged ship were the explorers' ships able to beat successfully against the wind on their return trips—enabling Portugal to take the lead among Western nations in exploring the African coast.

During this period Lisbon became Europe's richest capital and Manuel its richest ruler. At the same time a distinctive form of architecture named for the king developed in Portugal. The Manueline style reflected the exuberance and excitement of the times, expressed by dramatic twisted columns, a Moorish feel, and a profusion of decorative maritime ornamentation including nets, waves, tropical leaves, anchors, sea beasts, shells, and sextants.

Since Belém somehow escaped most of the destruction of the 1755 earthquake, it boasts two extraordinarily fine examples of Manueline architecture. The **Torre de Belém**, built between 1515 and 1520, is its most distinctive landmark and has been a beacon for sailors for centuries. The top of this square tower, with its Moorish openwork balconies and turrets topped with melon-shaped domes, also affords one of the best views up and down the Tagus river. The peaceful beauty of its graceful stone exterior, however, conceals the underground dungeons of an armed fortress that guarded the mouth of the river.

Close to the Belém tower in the praça do Império park is the **Museu de Arte Popular** (Museum of Folk Art), interesting because it displays the folk art of the provinces and gives a clear picture of the diversity of Portugal. The museum is arranged so that when strolling through the rooms you feel as if you are actually moving from province to province. Beyond the museum stands the **Padrão dos Descobrimentos** (Monument to the Discoveries), a modern (but not too inspiring) memorial depicting Prince Henry the Navigator poised at the prow of a caravel, with explorers, painters, and poets behind him.

The other major piece of architecture in Belém is to be found at the **Mosteiro dos Jerónimos**, a white limestone structure covered with Manueline decorations. The monastery was built in the early 16th century on the site of the little chapel where Vasco da Gama prayed before setting out into the Atlantic. Since the money to build it came from the profits of the spice trade, it was said to be "built of pepper." The first of its architects was Diogo Boytac, who worked in the Manueline style. After 1516 the work was carried on by the Biscayan stonemason João de Castilho, who completed the vaults and columns, the cloister, and the sacristy. He was succeeded in 1540 by Portugal's greatest Renaissance architect, Diogo de Torralva, who worked on the chancel, the choir stalls, and the upper galleries. The final architect of the monastery was the classicist Jerónimo de Rouen, who completed the chancel and the interior of the transept, finishing in 1604.

The south wing of the monastery houses the **Museu Nacional de Arqueologia e Etnologia** and the **Museu de Marinha**. The former has an outstanding collection of ancient jewelry and some interesting prehistoric carvings, but it is a tired and uninviting place. The maritime museum contains a wealth of nautical history—maps, paintings, charts, artifacts, and models tell the story of a great seafaring nation with a rich maritime history. Next door is Lisbon's planetarium.

The rua de Belém, leading from the monastery to the Palácio de Belém, is lined with little restaurants, many with outside terraces. Behind one of these places, the Dionysus restaurant, and up some steps, there is a small cul-de-sac called **beco do Chão Salgado** (Alley of Salted Earth). A pillar dated 1759 marks the spot of one of the cruelest executions in Portugal's history: The Duke of Aveiro and other nobles, accused of attempting to assassinate King José I, were publicly hung and drawn and quartered, as were their families and servants. The Marquês de Pombal had their Belém palaces razed and the ground covered with salt to kill all vegetation.

The Palácio de Belém, now the official offices for the president of Portugal, was built in the 17th century and used as a summer palace by the kings of Portugal. The **Museu de Coches** (Coach Museum) in the old riding school of the palace is one of the famous sights in Lisbon. Constructed in French Empire style, it has a painted ceiling that is handsomely decorated with allegorical paintings and a gallery from which the court would watch skilled riders put Lusitanian horses (see the Ribatejo chapter) through their paces. Founded by Queen Amelia in 1905 (her pink riding cloak, presented to the museum long after she had been exiled, is displayed near the entrance), the museum has what is probably the finest collection of coaches in Europe. The most magnificent, such as one made in Rome in 1716 for the Portuguese ambassador to the Vatican, are extremely ornate and carved with writhing Baroque figures. The most charming is a miniature carriage used by King Carlos I as a child.

At the left of the praça de Afonso de Albuquerque,

which lies in front of the palace and museums, you can take a boat across the river to Porto Brandão, a small village where the **Mare Viva** restaurant specializes in fish and shellfish fondue and has a splendid view of Lisbon and its monuments.

North of Belém, up the calçada da Ajuda—not far but a steep enough route to warrant a taxi—is the enormous **Palácio Nacional da Ajuda**. Begun in 1802 on the site of an earlier wooden palace that had burned, it was never completely finished. A significant part of it, though, is open to visitors. The throne room and several other halls house interesting collections of jewelry, tapestries, and Saxe porcelain.

GETTING AROUND

Lisbon is a walker's delight. Many of the streets are roughly cobbled, though, so beware—this is not a city that takes kindly to spindly heels.

The airport is, fortunately, very close to the city, only about 20 minutes by bus. A taxi into town is, of course, considerably quicker and not expensive, about 450$00.

Taxis. On a map the layout of Lisbon looks quite simple, but this is deceptive; the city is built on several hills, and its many levels make it difficult for newcomers to find their way about. However, taxis are plentiful and cheap, and easier than renting a car, as parking is tight, traffic swift, and streets confusing to navigate. Within the city taxis charge a metered rate. Outside the city limits a driver is allowed to charge a flat rate. You should tip taxi drivers about 10 percent.

Buses and Trams. There is an extensive system of buses, trams, and even cable cars. Bus stops are clearly marked, and all display small route maps. You can buy tickets and get information from the orange-and-white Carris information booths scattered throughout the city. Three- or seven-day tourist passes are available, as are packs of 20 prepaid tickets (500$00). Otherwise you pay a flat fare when you board.

The brightly colored trams, covered with advertising, provide extremely efficient service. Many of them were made in England and predate World War I. Often the narrow streets they navigate are not much wider than they are, and from the open windows a passenger can almost touch the buildings. Bells ringing, people hugging the shops to get out of the way, shop goods almost within reach—a ride on a Lisbon tram is one of the city's chief charms, and a great way to window-shop. Don't worry about getting taken somewhere you can't get back from. Just get on the waiting tram at the end of the line and come back to wherever you started.

Aerial cable cars, *elevadors,* link some of the higher and lower parts of the city. (The Gloria line goes from the praça dos Restauradores to São Pedro de Alcântara, the Lavra line from the east side of avenida da Liberdade to campo dos Mártires da Pátria, and the Bica line from calçada do Combro to rua da Boavista.)

Subway. The Metro system has only two dozen stops and is easy to navigate. Stations are designated by large M signs. A tourist pass is valid on the Metro, or you can buy a book of tickets (400$00) from a ticket booth in one of the stations.

ACCOMMODATIONS

Hotel, residencia, and *pensão* (pension) are the three general categories used to describe accommodations in Portuguese cities. (*Estalagem* is a privately owned country inn, and *pousada* a government-run one, often in a converted monastery or castle.) The Portuguese Tourist Office gives hotels starred ratings. Rated hotels tend to be larger and offer such amenities as restaurants and room service. Residencias and pensions, also rated on a star system, are usually smaller and offer fewer amenities. Most are clean and charming and more personal than the larger hotels.

Since Lisbon is not very big, the area you choose to stay in will be a matter more of personal inclination than convenience. As a general rule, older neighborhoods have great charm but tend to be noisy, while the newer areas of the city, beyond the praça Marquês de Pombal and Parque Eduardo VII, are quieter and more elegant but lack the feel of the old city.

The telephone area code for Lisbon is 01.

Luxury Hotels

About half the rooms of the 310-room **Ritz Inter-Continental**, still considered the pinnacle of sophistication and comfort, overlook the Parque Eduardo VII. The rooms are large and elegant, all with baths reputed to be the most luxurious in Europe. The hotel has two restaurants, the lobby-floor **Varanda**, offering Portuguese specialties, and the downstairs Ritz Grill, by some accounts Lisbon's best restaurant.

Rua Rodrigo da Fonseca, 88; Tel: 69-20-20.

The **Tivoli**, with 344 smallish rooms, less expensive than the Ritz, is a popular choice for many visitors because of its swimming pool surrounded by a beautiful garden, its tennis court, its top-floor restaurant, and a terrace bar with wonderful views of Lisbon.

Avenida da Liberdade, 185; Tel: 53-01-81.

The **Tivoli Jardim** is under the same management as the Tivoli, and visitors have access to the Tivoli's pool and tennis court. Set behind its parent hotel, it is a newer building and slightly less grand.

Rua Julio César Machado, 7; Tel: 53-99-71.

The **Méridien** (318 rooms), next door to the Ritz, is Lisbon's newest luxury hotel. This member of the French chain overlooks the park and offers boutiques, a ground-floor brasserie looking out on the park, and a health club. The public rooms are very attractive, but the bedrooms—although attractively furnished and extremely light on account of their wraparound windows—are on the small side and anything *but* soundproof.

Rua Castilho, 149; Tel: 69-09-00.

The **Lisboa Sheraton** is a sleek, 30-story hotel with 400 bedrooms, every amenity (open-air heated swimming pool, health club, beauty parlor, and three restaurants), but zero charm—perhaps a logical choice for a business trip, but a poor one for a vacation, as it also tends to be filled with large tour groups.

Rua Latino Coelho, 1; Tel: 56-39-11.

The **Avenida Palace**, in the Rossio, is the most centrally located of the large hotels. It is noisy but will appeal to those who like the hustle and bustle of a busy, old-fashioned hotel. There are lots of gilt, silk brocade wall panelings, chandeliers, handwoven Portuguese carpets, and antiques. Most of the 95 bedrooms have recently been redecorated with traditional furnishings, and the bathrooms are spacious. The only meal served is breakfast.

Rua 1 de Dezembro, 123; Tel: 36-01-51 or 36-01-59.

Less Expensive Accommodations

For many people, **York House** is without doubt the most charming place to stay in Lisbon, despite its location quite a distance west of the city's center, toward Belém near the Museu Nacional de Arte Antiga. Called a *residencia* even though it has an excellent restaurant and offers full service, it is housed in a well-restored 16th-century monastery. You enter off an ordinary-looking street, go up a flight of stairs bordered on either side by trailing vines, fruit trees, and shrubs, and find yourself in one of the most delightful courtyards in all of Lisbon. In good weather, breakfast is served here. York House has long been a favorite of the British: Graham Greene always stays here, as did the hero of John Le Carré's *Russia House*.

There is a 12-room annex in an old town house down the street, known as **Residencia Inglêsa**. It is attractively furnished but extremely noisy, and unless you can get a room facing the garden it is not an acceptable alternative to the main building. At York House proper, too, you should ask for a room overlooking the courtyard, as the rooms overlooking the rua das Janelas Verdes are noisy.

Rua das Janelas Verdes, 32, Tel: 66-24-35.

The **Príncipe Real**, with 24 rooms, fits into the category of "fine small hotel" and has many aficionados who return year after year. It is in the neighborhood of the Jardim Botânico and has the intimacy and charm of a private home. The public rooms are cozy, the service is excellent, and there are fresh flowers in every room. The Ritz sends its overflow guests to this hotel.

Rua da Alegria, 53; Tel: 36-01-16.

The **Hotel Rex** has an excellent location near the Ritz and the Méridien and also overlooks Parque Eduardo VII. It is a good choice for those on a tight budget who would like a small, comfortable hotel with a friendly staff and a good restaurant.

Rua Castilho, 169; Tel: 54-81-81.

Albergaria Senhora do Monte is set on top of a hill near the Alfama. It used to be a small apartment house but has been converted very skillfully to offer 27 rooms, some with their own balconies. Views of the city are wonderful from the top-floor bar.

Calçada do Monte, 39; Tel: 86-28-46.

DINING

Not surprisingly, Lisbon offers the greatest variety of dining options in Portugal. What may be surprising is just how great that variety is. Lisbon's position as a port places seafood high among the city's specialties, as evidenced by the ornate displays of seashells in restaurant windows around the Rossio. Its role as capital also ensures that the bounty of Portugal's regional cuisines, such as *caldo verde* from the Minho and pork from the Alentejo, finds its way to the city's tables. And the glories of the former empire are reflected in a number of ethnic cuisines imported from Portugal's former colonies in Brazil, the Atlantic, Africa, India, and China.

Types of restaurants in Lisbon are as diverse as the foods they serve. The most popular and characteristic of Portugal are the *tascas,* the bistros concentrated in the Bairro Alto, which provide hearty meals in lively surroundings at low prices. Typical of Lisbon are the restaurants where you can hear *fado*—songs of life and love (haunting whether or not you understand Portuguese, such is their universality), usually sung by a sultry, black-clad woman backed up by a band of deadpan male guitarists. More recently, a growing number of sophisticated places whose chefs keep a close watch on international culinary trends have completed the dining scene.

A full-course meal in a Lisbon restaurant might begin with olives, sausages, shrimp, or a plate of the delectable goose barnacles called *percêbes,* perhaps accompanied by an aperitif of dry Port or Madeira. This might be followed by a regional soup, such as one of the local variations of *caldeirada* (a fish stew) or the specialty of coastal Estremadura, *açorda de mariscos* (made with shellfish, bread, and eggs and flavored with fresh coriander). A regional main course could be *pescada assada à Lisboeta* (hake baked with tomatoes, green pepper, and onion), accompanied by a dry table wine, *espadarte fumado* (smoked swordfish), or *lulas recheadas à Lisbonense* (squid with a stuffing that includes ham, of all things), washed down with a more full-bodied red wine. Although Lisboetes are nicknamed "lettuce eaters," most main courses are served with rice and/or potatoes, as elsewhere in Portugal, though greens are increasingly available. Typical desserts include *pasteis de Belém* (custard tarts), *torta de laranja* (orange torte), and *pudim Molotov* (a poached meringue topped with caramel or apricot sauce). A tangy alternative is *azeitão,* a creamy ewe's-milk cheese eaten with a spoon.

Dinner may be followed by a tawny or vintage Port, a Madeira dessert wine, coffee (*bica* is espresso, *carioca* approximates American coffee, *café* is somewhere in between), the eau-de-vie *aguardente,* or the cherry-flavored liqueur *Ginjinha.*

Of course, no Lisbon restaurateur will insist that you gorge on a full-course meal. And whatever you choose to order, be forewarned that Portuguese portions seem as boundless and Old World to the contemporary palate as the Portuguese Empire. Should you so desire, you can avoid any excess with impunity by sharing one portion (*uma dose*) with your dining companion or by asking for a half-portion (*uma meia dose*) for yourself.

Lisbon restaurants generally serve lunch between about 12:30 and 3:00 P.M. (1:30 is the most fashionable time for Lisboetes) and dinner from about 8:00 to 10:00 P.M. (the later the better for local atmosphere). If hunger strikes outside those hours, snack on a pastry at a *pastelaria* or buy a croquette, cold fish or meat, a roll, or a sandwich at a café.

Many restaurants are closed Sundays, and reservations are recommended at the fanciest establishments, where jacket and tie are appropriate attire for men. Prices are much lower than in other capitals and usually include a service charge, but it is good form to add a 10 percent tip to the bill. Most larger restaurants accept credit cards.

The telephone area code for Lisbon is 01.

Portuguese Restaurants

Aviz (rua Serpa Pinto, 12-B; Tel: 32-83-91) is the grande dame of Lisbon's restaurants, serving such rich dishes as *bacalhau conde de guarda* (salt cod and whipped potatoes au gratin), *migas à Minhota* (a ham-and-garlic stove-top stuffing), and *arroz a pato* (duck, sausage, and rice fricassee) in an ornate, Empire-style setting.

Another old-guard establishment (the oldest, in fact—it opened in 1784—and also arguably the smallest, so be sure to reserve) is **Tavares** (rua da Misericórdia, 37; Tel: 32-11-12). The specialty of *santola* (spiny crab) can be seen making grand entrances in two luxurious dining rooms.

Tágide (largo da Academia Nacional de Belas Artes, 18; Tel: 32-07-20), opened by former employees of Tavares, serves refined versions of such Portuguese classics as *sopa Alentejana* (garlic soup) in sumptuous salons overlooking the Alfama.

Casa do Leão (Tel: 87-59-62) is actually in the Alfama's main landmark, the Castelo de São Jorge. As at many stylish Lisbon restaurants, its menu is part French, part Portuguese. Stick with such Portuguese items as *presunto* (the Portuguese answer to prosciutto) from Chaves coupled with *ananas* (pineapple) from the Azores, perhaps followed by *gambas grilhadas* (grilled prawns).

The French-inspired menu at **Michel** (largo de Santa Cruz do Castelo, 5; Tel: 86-43-38) has a loyal and well-heeled following in Lisbon. Its menu, based mainly on seafood, could be described as "nouvelle Portuguese."

Casa da Comida (travessa das Amoreiras, 1; Tel: 68-53-76) is a lavishly decorated place serving trimmed-down Portuguese food to a like crowd of Lisbon sophisticates.

More classic are the historic Portuguese recipes reinterpreted at **Conventual** (praça das Flores, 45; Tel: 60-91-96), where dishes once literally fit for kings are served up in the setting of a former convent.

The ambience of **Clara** (campo dos Mártires da Pátria; Tel: 55-73-41) is a bit more open, with spreading magnolia trees providing the outdoor background for such specialties as garlicky baby octopus and lamb grilled with green peppers.

Gambrinus (rua das Portas de Santo Antão, 23; Tel: 32-14-66) is Lisbon's finest fish house, where you can sample sea bass prepared in the Minho way with bits of smoky ham, or baby clams gilded with olive oil, a recipe invented by 19th-century Portuguese poet Bulhão Pato.

Another seafood restaurant is **O Pagem** (largo da Trindade, 20; Tel: 37-31-51), where Portuguese fishermen's tradition provides stuffed squid, baby eels, and braised salt cod.

Sua Excelência (northwest of the city center at rua do Conde, 42; Tel: 60-36-14) has no set menu, but owner Francisco Queiroz will tell you what he's found at the market that day and how the chef can prepare it, to order. One recurring dream is chicken Moambo, braised Angolan style with dendê oil, eggplant, and okra.

Perhaps Lisbon's best regional restaurant, **Pap'Açorda** (rua da Atalaya, 57; Tel: 36-48-11) serves hearty, basically Alentejo, food (besides its signature dish, *açorda de marisco à Pap-Açorda,* a shellfish, bread, and egg soup, flavored with fresh coriander, from coastal Estremadura) to an enthusiastic crowd of young professionals.

If you'd like to venture from strictly Portuguese cuisine, the **Ritz Grill** (Hotel Ritz, rua Rodrigo da Fonseca, 88; Tel: 68-41-31) is the place to go. Its menu is mainly French, but the uncommon quality of such locally produced dishes as smoked swordfish and *queijo da serra* (ewe's-milk cheese) are as good an argument as any for Portugal's inclusion in the European Community.

Ethnic Restaurants

For a more exotic experience, **Monte Cara** (rua Sol ao Rato, 71-A; Tel: 68-87-38) serves the spicy, African-influenced cuisine of the formerly Portuguese Cape Verde islands, accompanied by equally spicy strains of live Cape Verde music.

Comida de Santo (calçada Eng Miguel Pais; Tel: 66-33-39) offers such Brazilian dishes as *feijoada* (black bean and pork stew) and *vatapá* (a fish stew) in an intimate, tropical setting.

The food of Mozambique is the specialty of **Laurentina** (avenida Conde Valbom, 69; Tel: 76-02-60), its robust seasonings hopped up by a sauce made from the *piri-piri* of neighboring Angola. (The fiery condiment has become a staple on Portuguese tables of every ethnic stripe.)

Velha Goa (rua Tomás da Anunciação, 41-B; Tel: 60-04-46) serves the Indian-influenced specialties of the former Portuguese colony of Goa. Try *xacuti,* fried chicken served in a sauce of coconut milk laced with numerous spices.

Of the numerous Chinese restaurants in what is still, after all, the home capital of colonial Macao, **Tun Fon** (avenida Fontes Pereira de Melo, 6; Tel: 57-76-85) is perhaps the best, with *gambas doces* (sweet-and-sour prawns) that manage to be familiar and fresh at the same time.

Fado

The Bairro Alto has been the spiritual home of *fado,* plaintive folksinging, for a number of decades now, and most of the well-known houses are found there. Dinner usually begins around 8:00 P.M., the fado between 10:30 and 11:00 P.M. You can go after dinner and just order drinks, but in the more popular places it may be difficult to find a table.

The most upscale of Lisbon's fado clubs is **Senhor Vinho** (rua do Meio-à-Lapa, 18; Tel: 67-26-81), where some of the country's best-known Lisbon and Coimbra *fadistas* perform and the regional Portuguese cuisine is perhaps the best of the lot.

Lisboa a Noite (rua das Gáveas, 69; Tel: 36-85-57) is another choice for fado, here sung Lisbon style by owner Fernanda da Maria, one of the leading exponents of the genre. The food here is also better than most.

A Severa (rua das Gáveas, 51; Tel: 36-40-06), named after the colorful and somewhat disreputable lady who was fado's greatest idol until the appearance of Amalia Rodrigues, is one of the oldest traditional fado houses in the quarter. It also includes folk-dancing shows, so it is a good place for non-cognoscenti. A Severa is closed on Thursdays.

Adega Machado (rua do Norte, 91; Tel: 36-00-95) is another Bairro Alto house where the classical fado is mixed with lighter folk dancing and other regional music in the interest of more general appeal. It is a big, cheerful place where the food is also quite good. Tends to get crowded; no closing day.

—*Dwight V. Gast*

BARS AND NIGHTLIFE

Bars of the Anglo-American type have established themselves as a feature of nightlife in Portuguese cities in recent years. They usually start to come alive around 11:00, as Lisboetes tend to frequent them after dinner. **Procopio**, in a little cul-de-sac near largo do Rato, is one of the oldest, catering to the thirsts of many of Portugal's leading politicians, artists, journalists, and their like. It is publike, with lots of bric-a-brac, and somewhat on the dark side (alto de São Francisco, 21; Tel: 67-28-51). **Pavilhão Chines**, in the street where many of Lisbon's antiques shops cluster on the edge of the Bairro Alto, is another comfortable, civilized place for a drink, and has a billiards table in the back room beyond the magnificent mahogany bar (rua Dom Pedro V, 89; Tel: 32-47-29).

The liveliest live-music bars in Lisbon are the ones that feature African music—quite often the Cape Verde variety, which blends Latin American rhythms with the African beat. In this sort of place, a minimum consumption charge, high but not crippling, gets you a part of the action. **Lontra**, not far from the Palácio São Bento, is a popular one (rua São Bento, 157), and so is **Clavi di Nos**, in the Bairro Alto (rua do Norte, 100). Also in the Bairro Alto, the samba club **Gafieira** is the liveliest Brazilian bar in town, usually packed with expatriates from Lisbon's sizable Brazilian community (calçada do Tijolo, 8). At **Copodetres** you get music of different sorts, from chamber to jazz, with an occasional poetry reading thrown in (rua Marcos Portugal, 1, cornering on praça das Flores). Undiluted jazz can be heard in the **Hot Clube de Portugal** (praça de Alegria, 39).

Discos

The chic circuit consists of half a dozen places. They tend to be pricey and are sometimes exclusive when it comes to letting in natives, but foreigners usually don't have any trouble getting in. **Banana Power** is a Lisbon jet-set haunt where the host is the postmodernist architect Tomas

Taveira. There is a separate bar and restaurant (rua Cascais, 52, in the Alcântara dock area). **Ad Lib** is very expensive, fashionable, and smooth, but a bit on the staid side (rua Barata Salgueiro, 18). **Stones** (rua Olival, 1) and **Stringfellows** (avenida Oscar Monteiro Torres, 8), equally chic, are younger in spirit. Superchic in Lisbon at the moment means **Alcântara Mar** (rua da Cozinha Economica, 11), a converted factory in the run-down Alcântara dock area. It can hold 2,000 people and usually does. You pay an entrance fee here that buys you the first drink. Closed Mondays and Tuesdays. **Bairro Alto** (travessa dos Inglesinhos, 50, in the Bairro Alto) is another huge place (a converted sawmill this time) and also very "in." The decor, created by architect Helder Oarita to reflect all of Lisbon's history, is imaginative, and so is the entertainment. In addition to disco, you get live music and can expect anything from clowns to fire-eaters.

SHOPPING

Lisbon is not the place to look for high fashion, but it is a wonderful source for traditional crafts and handmade goods, and you will find prices extremely reasonable in comparison to the rest of Europe.

Major Shopping Districts

The main shopping areas in Lisbon are the **Baixa**, the **Chiado**, and the streets around the **Rossio**. Stores are generally closed between 1:00 P.M. and 3:00 P.M. but stay open until 7:00 P.M.

Rua Augusta, a pedestrian street with a small arts-and-crafts market at its southern end, is the main shopping street in the Baixa. **Madeira House** at number 131–135 is a good stop for cotton sheets, linens, and embroidery at reasonable prices. Shoes are inexpensive in Lisbon, but the styles and materials are for the most part disappointing. One of the better shoe shops is **Helio**, in the Chiado at the beginning of the rua do Carmo. **Casa Canada** (rua Augusta, 232) and **Galeao** (rua Augusta, 196) both have a good selection of handbags and luggage. Lisbon is not noted for its designer fashions, but you will find elegant, simple, and beautifully tailored clothes at **Ana Salazar**, Portugal's best-known designer, who has two shops in Lisbon (rua do Carmo, 87, and avenida de Roma, 16-E).

The Chiado is considered Lisbon's most fashionable shopping area, despite the recent fire in 1988. Although the two main department stores in the Chiado were destroyed by the fire, **Ranniro Lea**, a small, rather old-fashioned department store on the rua Garrett, was not damaged and is worth a visit. Be sure to take a ride in its hand-painted elevator, made in Paris at the turn of the century.

Tiles and Pottery

Vista Alegre (largo do Chiado, 18) and **Casa Leonel** (rua do Carmo, 71) offer good selections of Vista Alegre porcelain from the town of the same name in Aveiro. **Fabrica da Sant'Anna** (rua do Alecrim, 95) is the place to go for Sant'Anna tiles, still made and painted by hand in the same way that they have been done since this tile-making company was founded in 1741. You will find a large selection of sample tiles to choose from, as well as hand-painted bowls, lamps, jars, jardinieres, and figurines. If you want to see how the tiles are made, the **Sant'Anna** factory in Belém (calçada Boa Hora, 96) is open to the public.

Berta Marinho is another good source for handmade and hand-painted reproductions of traditional tiles. Her showroom (calçada Conde de Penafiel, 9-A; Tel: 87-60-18) is near the Castelo de São Jorge. **Viuva Lamego**, a tile shop at largo do Intendente, 25, always has a wide selection of modern tiles and pottery—plates, dishes, and planters.

Crystal and Jewelry

Portuguese crystal is much valued for its high quality. **Casa Leonel** (rua do Carmo, 71) offers a good selection, as does **Atlantis**, a store with several branches, one of them in the same building as Vista Alegre (see above).

There are any number of jewelers and silversmiths in Lisbon. **Eloy de Jesus** (rua Garrett, 45) and **Sarmento** (rua do Ouro, 251) are both noted for their silver filigree work; **Barreto and Gonçalves** (rua das Portas de Santo Antão, 17) offers a good selection of antique jewelry.

Linens and Rugs

For fine linens and embroidered tablecloths, visit **Lavores** (rua Aurea, 175–179). **Casa Regional da Ilha Verde** (rua Paiva de Andrada, 4, just off the rua Garrett) has beautifully embroidered table linen and blouses and lace from the Azores.

Hand-embroidered rugs from the town of Arraiolos near Evora are treasured the world over. Known for their bold colors and Oriental motifs, they cost far less in Portugal than abroad. Several Lisbon shops specialize in Arraiolos rugs: **Casa Quintão** (rua Ivens, 30) offers the largest selection of patterns and also takes orders for custom-made rugs. They can reproduce any design you choose and are familiar with the intricacies of shipping, insurance, customs, etc.

Traditional copperware is another popular Portuguese handicraft. The **Centro de Turismo e Artesano** (rua Castilho, 61) and **Francisco Ramos** (rua das Portas de Santo Antão, 3) stock a good selection of excellent copper cookware, priced from one-half to two-thirds lower than overseas.

Two Chiado stores destroyed by the fire have now relocated: **Ferrari** sells the best chocolates in Lisbon and can be found on the escadinhas de São Francisco, and **Martins and Costa**, Lisbon's most exclusive gourmet food and wine shop, is now on the rua Alexandre Herculano, close to the praça Marquês de Pombal.

Antiques

Antiques lovers are in for a treat in Lisbon. There are antiques shops all along **rua da Escola Politécnica**, which becomes rua Dom Pedro V. The best ones—and there is a whole cluster of them—are at the top end of **rua Dom Pedro V**. Here you can find marvelous furniture, silver, and paintings. This is also the place to find reasonably priced, particularly beautiful 18th- and early-19th-century hand-painted plates and tiles. **Solar** (Dom Pedro V, 68–70) offers the best selection of antique tiles in all of Lisbon, many of them salvaged from monasteries and palaces. At the back of the shop and down a rickety flight of stairs is a real treasure trove: thousands of tiles sorted according to century. You can find everything from extremely rare 16th- and 17th-century examples to wonderfully colorful Art Nouveau and Art Deco.

Another good place to find antiques is the **Feira da Ladra**, a lively flea market held every Tuesday and Saturday at the campo de Santa Clara, near the Alfama.

DAY TRIPS FROM LISBON
ESTREMADURA

By Marvine Howe

Marvine Howe, on the staff of The New York Times *since 1972, has covered Portugal and the Portuguese-speaking world extensively. She also contributes articles about Portugal to the* Times *travel section.*

Lisbon is the center of its own private universe. Within a short radius, the rich diversity of landscapes provides many delightful excursions. Pampered gardens and parks cohabit with tropical forests and a profusion of wildflowers; Riviera-type playgrounds rub shoulders with untamed Atlantic shores. Roman walls, Moorish fortifications, and Medieval castles and churches bear witness to a long and multicultural past. Noble manors and luxurious villas mingle with modest fishing ports and farm villages.

Despite the variety of sights, the distances among them and from Lisbon are not large, and so it is possible to visit many of these points of interest by taking day trips out of Lisbon. You may wish to stay overnight, however, in one of the seaside hotels, country manors, or converted castles along the way. These accommodations are generally good and often better than those in Lisbon. And there is always a good restaurant at hand, with hearty fare and wine.

The main drawback of day trips is that the traffic on the

highways can be very heavy at rush hours and over weekends, and often extraordinarily reckless. The best way to avoid strained nerves is to take the train or an excursion bus—but that doesn't give you much opportunity to get off the beaten track or do any spontaneous exploration.

If you want to explore the Lisbon region, Estremadura, on your own by car, you can do it in several easy radial excursions, with Lisbon as the point of departure. Westward, there's the Costa do Sol, a 30-km (18-mile) string of beaches and bays along the northern shore of the Tagus river and out along the Atlantic coast. Here is the cosmopolitan resort of Estoril, with its grand casino, international auto-racing track, golf courses, and fashionable hotel pools and bars. Nearby, the ancient fishing village of Cascais has become a popular vacation site, with sailing in the bay, a nightly fish auction, pleasant seafood restaurants, discos, and a bullring. Just to the northwest lies the Sintra mountain area, including the Colares valley and the plain of Mafra. Sintra itself is a fairy-tale town, often shrouded in mist, with mysterious palaces, dense forests, moss-covered walls, narrow winding streets, antiques and handicraft shops. Mafra, to the north, is a modest town totally dominated by the massive 18th-century palace-monastery and basilica, which has splendid marble statuary, a museum of sacred art, and a magnificent library. Another track takes you farther north to Nazaré and other Atlantic fishing port–resorts and the monument towns of Alcobaça and Batalha. South of the Tagus a circuit includes Caparica beach, the scenic Arrábida coast, and the newly developing isthmus of Tróia.

MAJOR INTEREST NORTH OF THE TAGUS

Costa do Sol
Beaches and dramatic scenery
Estoril (casino, golf, restaurants)
Cascais (fish market, shops, fair, bullring)
Guincho (rugged cliffs and sandy beach)
Cabo da Roca, the country's westernmost cape

Sintra
Castles and manors, music festival, parks
Palácio Nacional
Castelo da Pena
Moorish castle fortifications
Capuchos monastery
Monserrate botanical garden

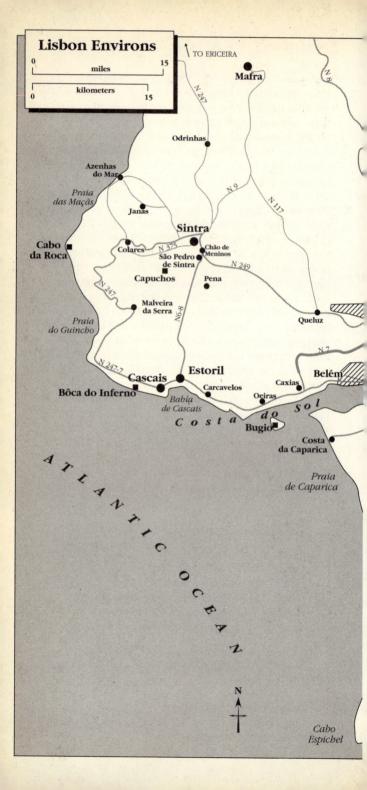

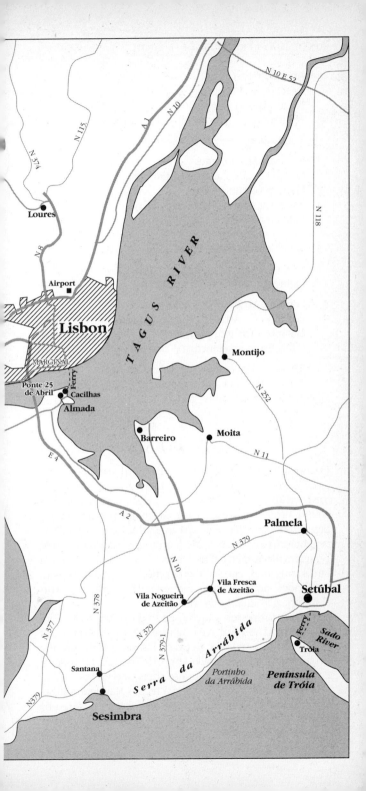

Atlantic Coast
Beaches and fishing ports
Nazaré beach
Peniche (port, prison museum, islands)

The walled city of Obidos

National Monuments
Queluz (palace and its restaurant)
Mafra monastery-palace
Alcobaça's Santa Maria monastery
Batalha monastery

MAJOR INTEREST SOUTH OF THE TAGUS

Costa da Caparica beach
Palmela (castle, church, pousada)

Serra da Arrábida corniche
Portinho da Arrábida (protected cove)
Sesimbra (fishing port, fort)
Cabo Espichel (sanctuary, chapel)

Setúbal's Igreja de Jesús, castle-pousada
Azeitão (market, winery, palace)
Tróia (Roman ruins, golf, beach)

COSTA DO SOL

Just outside Lisbon to the west on the northern shore of the river Tagus lies the Costa do Sol, a series of pastel riverside towns with small beaches and gardens that flower year round. Bright orange tile roofs adorn old manors and cottages, modern villas and apartment buildings alike. The vegetation is essentially Mediterranean: umbrella pines, bougainvillaea, date palms. On the mostly sunny days from late spring until late fall the beaches here are lined with sunshades and cabanas and crowded with sun worshippers, particularly on weekends.

Ancient fortresses, which used to guard the coast from brigands and hostile forces, stand along here as symbols of Portugal's imperial past. Between Lisbon and the sea, the broad Tagus is well travelled by NATO vessels, oil tankers, container ships, trawlers, cruise ships, and yachts.

A spectacular highway known as the Marginal follows along the river's edge and on stormy days is battered by waves. The river, being very wide here, is changeable, sometimes shimmering and serene, other times somber or blustering. Beyond the Lisbon city limits there are few notable monuments, yet the ensemble of weathered rose- and olive-colored mansions, chipped tile walls, neat whitewashed apartments and villas, and evergreen gardens has a special beauty.

Leaving Lisbon, the Marginal first passes the suburb of **Belém**, generally treated as part of the city. Here is the stately pink Presidential Palace, the sprawling Gothic **monastery of Jerónimos** (attached to which is a museum of Iberian antiquities and the Navy Museum), the lavish little fortress called the **Tower of Belém**, and the famous landmark Monument to the Discoveries, honoring Prince Henry the Navigator.

Beyond Belém, you might pause to see the exotic fish and marine plants and ship models at the **Vasco da Gama Aquarium**, located in the small town of Dáfundo. In the neighboring village of Cruz Quebrada to the west, a slight detour takes you to the National Soccer Stadium, a lovely amphitheater, built of stone, hidden in the wooded hills.

Worthy of a stop is **Oeiras**, 17 km (10 miles) west of Lisbon, with its broad, sheltered beach. In the old part of town there's a charming 18th-century Baroque church. Nearby, the Marquês de Pombal's fading pink quinta, once the site of the Gulbenkian Museum, now belongs to the Agricultural Institute. It is not open to the public, but visitors can obtain authorization to see the formal gardens and Waterfall of Poets, with statues of Homer, Virgil, and Camões by Machado de Castro. Write to the Director da Estação Agrónoma Nacional, Quinta do Marquês, 2780 Oeiras, Portugal.

On the western outskirts of town is an austere, sand-colored 16th-century fortress, **São Julião da Barra**, built by Dom João III, the founder of Portugal's colonial system. Opposite the fortress, in the middle of the river Tagus, stands the Bugio, a circular tower with a lighthouse marking the sandbar where the river waters meet the sea.

Between Oeiras and Carcavelos to the west, in a desolate field, is a low white building with a blue tile roof and flags usually in full sail: the headquarters for NATO's Iberian command. Special permission to visit the facilities, which are not open to the public, can be obtained by writing to Cinciberlant, Reduto Gomes Freire, 2780 Oeiras, Portugal.

Now a popular seaside resort with a broad beach, **Carcavelos** used to be a farm town, surrounded by vineyards. In recent years the farms have been pushed inland by modern villas, apartment buildings, and hotels. Carcavelos is known for its "aristocratic" topaz-colored dessert wine. A reminder of the town's bucolic past is the large weekly fair (on Thursdays), with displays of fruits and vegetables as well as household utensils, clothing, pottery, and basketware.

All along the coast here are pleasant seafood restaurants where Lisboetes enjoy long working lunches on weekdays or take their families on weekends. For example, **Saisa**, at Carcavelos on the cliff overlooking the sea, offers moderately priced fish that is fresher and tastier than that served at many luxury establishments in town.

Estoril

There are at least four Estorils west of Carcavelos: Santo António de Estoril, São Pedro de Estoril, São João de Estoril, and Monte Estoril. But these distinctions need not normally concern you, because the four are grouped together and generally referred to by the generic name.

Estoril first came into prominence at the turn of the century as a winter resort for the rich and aristocratic. It was during World War II, when Portugal remained a neutral haven in Europe, that Estoril gained its international fame. The casino, the grand Hotel Palácio, and its palatial villas made a perfect setting for espionage and other intrigues.

After the war this garden by the sea was discovered by exiled royalty seeking a refuge where they could live as they were accustomed. Estoril became known as the center of the Golden Triangle, home to such distinguished figures as Don Juan de Borbon, father of the present king of Spain; Umberto II, former king of Italy; the late King Carol II of Romania and his morganatic wife Magda Lupescu; Simeon II, former king of Bulgaria; the prince of Thurn and Taxis; Charles Hapsburg; and Henri, the count of Paris.

In recent times, however, royal or ex-royal residents have progressively been replaced by wealthy Portuguese and foreign visitors or retirees drawn by the relaxed, pleasant, affordable way of life here. Estoril today is not a playground where the rich and famous come to be seen, but rather a place to live well and *not* be seen. Monte Estoril, in particular, has managed to preserve a certain Victorian charm.

Lately, Estoril and southern Portugal have been discovered by a new sort of aristocracy, sportsmen attracted by the year-round good sports weather. There's an international championship golf course at the Estoril Golf Club north of town on the way to Sintra, another course at the Estoril Sol Golf Club (farther out toward Sintra), and a third designed by Robert Trent Jones, located in the Parque da Marinha, just west of Cascais.

Auto racing is a fairly new attraction at the Autódromo (auto racetrack) located on the road to Sintra from Estoril. The World Championship Formula One is held here every September. The Centro Hípico da Costa do Estoril in the Marinha area has horses for hire. Swimming pools and tennis courts are found in the main hotels.

Once famous for its white sand and calm waters, the Estoril beach—and in fact most of the beaches along the Costa do Sol—has been badly polluted in recent years. Now, however, work is under way to reconstruct the sewers all along the coast. The Estoril beach, called the Praia do Tamariz, has been cleaned up and is now considered safe for bathing. But it is so popular with local residents in summer that visitors usually prefer to stay by the hotel pool or drive to one of the wilder Atlantic beaches nearby to the west.

Nightlife revolves around the glittering casino complex and discreet hotel bars. Restaurants, and their clientele, are more formal than those in neighboring Cascais. One of the best-known landmarks here, the **Estoril Casino**, is open to anyone who has a passport or other identity card to prove he or she is over 18. This long, low, modern building is set in a flowering park with an illuminated fountain and mushroom lamps. The casino's roulette and baccarat tables are usually busy, as are the slot machines. For nongamblers there's a large nightclub and restaurant with international entertainment, a cinema (which frequently shows American films), shops, and several bars.

Yet to be discovered by international festival-goers, the Estoril Music Festival offers first-rate concerts at moderate prices from mid-July to mid-August. Concerts are held in the Estoril cathedral, the Cidadela (fort) beyond the fishing port of Cascais, and other dramatic settings.

Because Estoril's hotels are known for comfort, good service, and amenities, some visitors prefer to make this their base and commute to Lisbon. The old-world **Hotel Palácio**, where royalty did reside at one time, still has great style. Facing the casino gardens, the Palácio was built in 1930 and is said to have served as an important base of operations for Allied agents during World War II.

Today well-to-do Europeans and North Americans who want to impress Portuguese contacts tend to stay here. It is common knowledge that when in Estoril, the thing to do is to have a meal or drinks in the Palácio's gardens beside the heated pool.

The **Hotel Atlántico** has wonderful sweeping views of the coast. This large hotel hasn't got the charm or snob appeal of the Palácio and is a little too close to the railroad, but it is conveniently situated on the border between Estoril and Cascais. It has a saltwater pool and a popular terrace bar, and many of the rooms have balconies overlooking the sea.

Then there is the **Hotel Estoril-Sol**, a huge concrete-and-glass block, which is actually located within the town limits of Cascais. Old-timers say the late authoritarian ruler, António de Oliveira Salazar, drove past the Estoril-Sol while it was still under construction and lamented, "If I were the dictator they say I am, that monstrosity would not be going up here." While the hotel does mar the harmony of the coast, its guests enjoy a privileged position. From their private balconies *they* can't see the hotel, and they can view the river (as far as Lisbon), the bay of Cascais, and way out into the Atlantic. Conveniences include an Olympic-size pool, a health club, a sauna, a bowling alley, and a disco.

Restaurants in Estoril also attract many people from Lisbon. Somehow the sea air makes the fish seem fresher and the service better. Two fashionable retreats are frequented by people who want quality attention and are willing to pay prices comparable to those in London or New York: **A Choupana**, built into the cliff overlooking the sea at the entrance of São João do Estoril, serves splendid broiled lobster and *santola* (crab), and the **English Bar**, in a rock garden on the hill just off the Marginal at Monte Estoril, offers an admirable grilled sole.

Shopping is easy in Estoril because the main shops are located in the Arcadas do Parque, pleasant arcades on either side of the casino gardens. There are several good shops for women's clothing, and gifts for all the family can be found at either the **Bazar do Parque** or **Regionalia**.

If you are looking for something different in the way of gifts, you might try **Cerâmica de Bicesse**, a workshop where ancient tiles are restored and exact reproductions made. Take the road marked "Bicesse" from São João do Estoril and drive north about 5 km (3 miles).

Cascais

A couple of stone's throws west of Estoril along the coast, Cascais is altogether different in substance and spirit. Although it has become a popular holiday resort with fashionable boutiques, restaurants, and discos, it retains the flavor of a fishing village. In the old quarters, nonetheless, graceful mansions are a reminder of Cascais's former role as summer residence for Portuguese royalty. King Luís I actually resided in the Cidadela, a 17th-century fortress that dominates the bay and is now used by the president of the republic for official receptions. It is only open to the public for occasional concerts. Many well-to-do Portuguese keep summer places in Cascais, and there is a substantial year-round foreign colony, mostly British. Some critics warn, however, that development is getting out of hand, with new high-rise buildings going up on the outskirts toward the lovely village of Malveira da Serra.

The main attraction of Cascais is its little harbor, alive with bright-colored fishing boats and a bustling fish market, just off the main square. The best show in town is the nightly (except Sunday) auction at the market, where local fishermen and women present their wares.

At the end of the bay the Clube Naval de Cascais, a yacht club located at the base of the citadel, welcomes visitors, who may anchor their yachts in season (June to October) or rent a boat for the day. This is also the point of departure for half-day cruises of Cascais bay.

There are a few sights in Cascais. The **church of Nossa Senhora de Assunção** has a painted wood ceiling and walls lined with 18th-century tiles and paintings by Josefa de Obidos and José Malhoa. In a park across the way the **Conde de Castro Guimarães Museum**, formerly a private mansion, contains a good collection of Chinese porcelains, ancient maps, and tiles of the 16th and 17th centuries.

The town's main shopping area, near the railway station, is rua Frederico Arouca, now a pedestrian zone. It sports a number of fashionable dress shops, jewelry stores, and gift shops. One place to find an excellent gift is the **Atlantis** crystal boutique. The nearby grocery has the best country bread around.

Another place for concentrated shopping is the **Pão de Açucar**, located just off the Marginal at the entry to Cascais, coming from Estoril. This shopping center is open weekends and evenings, when most other shops are closed, and includes specialty boutiques for cosmetics, leather goods, and gifts.

One of the best shops for *azulejos* is **Isto e Aquilo**, on the largo de Misericórdia in old Cascais. Here you can find attractive hand-painted reproductions of 17th- and 18th-century tile panels or single tiles.

For modern tiles of traditional inspiration, there is **Ceramicarte** on the largo da Assunção, just opposite the church. The shop contains all kinds of ceramic tiles, jugs, plates, and vases decorated with fish and other sea motifs, as the local potters have done for some 4,000 years.

An open market is held on the fairground in the center of town every Wednesday. Itinerant vendors offer fruits, vegetables, flowers, clothing, and hardware. The market is not really geared to foreign visitors, but there is usually interesting pottery, woodcarving, and basketware on display.

Cascais's restaurants are usually noisier than those in Estoril, and less expensive. Tucked away behind the fire station on avenida Vasco da Gama, **Apeadeiro Restaurante** features succulent grilled lamb chops and pork chops, sardines, and sea bass at prices local people on holiday can afford. On the rua das Flores, just behind the fish market, there's a string of pleasant seafood places. The clientele is democratic: leaders of business and industry next to budget-conscious students and civil servants. **O Pescador**, for example, serves an outstanding sole meunière; **O Batel**, nearby, specializes in shellfish paella. On the main street, **João Padeira**, in an old bakery decorated with millstones, produces splendid roast goat.

The discos cater to Lisbon's golden youth. Currently in favor is **Coconut's**, a complex of disco, bars, and swimming pool cum ocean terrace, located on the road to the Bôca do Inferno. Also popular is **Palm Beach**, perched on the hillside at Praia da Conceição. There are also several *fado* (Portuguese folk song) houses, which seem somewhat out of context in modern villas, so far from Lisbon's old Bairro Alto—but the music isn't bad. The place to go for serious fado these days is **Forte Dom Rodrigo** on the road to Birre, a suburb of Cascais—most local taxis know the spot. The show doesn't get started until after 10:00 P.M.

Two hotels in Cascais should be visited, if only for lunch or tea, because of the view. **Hotel Baia**, a nondescript building on the main square, has a terrace whence you can survey the action on the beach below. On a nearby promontory stands the **Hotel Albatroz**, a small luxury inn that was once a private mansion. The hotel is beautifully furnished with antiques and has an elegant dining room and terrace, with a view of the entire coast as far as Lisbon. Try to get one of the rooms in the original villa; those in the new wing have less charm and character.

The Atlantic Coast

Around the corner from the protected bay of Cascais is the wilder Atlantic shore. Although civilization in the form of restaurants, hotels, and sports facilities has made inroads, the landscape along here has a desolate natural quality, and it is still possible to find an unpopulated beach.

Follow the coast road west out of Cascais to the **Bôca do Inferno** (Mouth of Hell), a strange formation of arches and caverns carved out of the cliffs by fierce waves. A great place for a leisurely lunch is the **Furnas Lagosteira** here, overlooking the Bôca, where you can select your own fresh lobster on the rocks and watch the waves battering the cliffs while you eat. (Lobster is expensive everywhere in Portugal, however; it might be wiser to settle for fish.)

Farther along the coast you will come to the Guia lighthouse on a rocky point and the lovely pine forest of the **Parque de Marinha**, with the spacious lodges and villas of the Quinta da Marinha, a large resort complex, mostly hidden by the trees.

At Quinta da Marinha itself there are a number of luxury villas with two or three bedrooms at what is called the **Aldeamento Turístico Marinha Village**. Rooms here should be booked well in advance. In the middle of the woods, the Clube da Marinha offers horseback riding, tennis, and golf, and is open to visitors.

A couple of miles beyond the lighthouse, in a clump of umbrella pines, is the **Estalagem Nossa Senhora da Guia**. (An *estalagem* is a privately operated inn, whereas a *pousada* is government-run.) This large villa of the 1920s, with typical red-tile roof, white stucco façade, and high ceilings, was completely renovated and opened as an inn in 1984. Every room has a spacious new bath decorated with attractive *azulejos*. A generous pool on the front lawn overlooks the sea. Many British and American guests come here to relax or enjoy the facilities of the Quinta da Marinha, a few hundred yards away.

Farther inland lies the Cascais bullring. Purists prefer Lisbon's Campo Pequeno, because, they say, the Atlantic coast is too windy for the bulls, but on hot summer days the spectators here at least enjoy the breeze.

The sea road, now heading north, continues on past large scattered boulders, sand dunes, and stretches of fine, uncluttered sand: This is **Guincho**, which means "scream" in Portuguese, referring to the almost continuous howling of wind and waves. Even on a calm day the breakers keep up a subdued roar. In summer the surf generally subsides enough for swimming or wave-jumping, but even the best swimmers must beware of the strong undertow.

An imposing fortress on a rocky promontory here has been converted into the **Hotel do Guincho**, an exclusive haven with 36 rooms and exceptional sea views.

Poised on the low-slung rocky cliff at Guincho, the **Porto de Santa Maria** restaurant is a favorite place for weekend family outings. The specialties of the house are *arroz de marisco* (shellfish rice), a noble form of paella, and *lulas al ajillo* (braised squid in garlic). On a nearby cliff the **Estalagem Muchaxo** overlooks a broad, sandy beach and a swimming pool. This inn, with two restaurants, is so popular that it seems to expand every year.

From Guincho to **Cabo da Roca**, the westernmost point in Portugal and in Continental Europe, the road winds north past bleak hills and along rocky cliffs overlooking the sea. It's a spectacular drive if you have time, but many people prefer to go to Cabo da Roca west from Sintra, across the gentle Colares valley. The remote and usually windy cape was best described by the Portuguese poet Luiz Vaz de Camões as the place "where the land ends and the sea commences." Cabo da Roca is a wildflower sanctuary and remains unspoiled. There's a working lighthouse and a small Turismo office, where certificates are available to testify that you have journeyed to the Continent's westernmost point. The local restaurant, **Refúgio da Roca**, serves excellent sea bass and a famous shellfish soup.

THE SINTRA AREA

Somehow Sintra, on a mountain northwest of Lisbon and north of Estoril, has not been spoiled by time or by its successive waves of visitors, from Roman and Moorish armies to English and German romantics—and Portuguese and North American vacationers. It is still a magic mountain with fairy-tale castles, thick forests, and abundant waterfalls, all generally veiled in mist.

Sintra's special charms have been celebrated by numerous well-known English writers who fell unabashedly in love with the place. Poet laureate Robert Southey lived here with his uncle from 1796 to 1801 and wrote passionately of the landscape, calling it "my paradise—heaven on earth of my hopes." That diligent traveller Lord Byron spent only a brief time in Sintra but consecrated it in *Childe Harold* as "glorious Eden." He called the village "the most delightful in Europe." William Beckford, who felt quite at home among Portuguese nobility, had several lengthy sojourns in Sintra between 1787 and 1799, living first in Ramalhão Palace, at the base of the mountain, and later in Monserrate. His letters describe the gardens, woods, cataracts, and sea as "a Royalty of Nature."

Some excursions combine Sintra with the lavish 18th-century palace of Queluz, and Mafra, the massive, austere palace and monastery (also 18th century). But it's best to devote at least one day to Sintra and another to its surroundings.

If you are driving from Lisbon, take the inland *auto-estrada* marked "Estoril" to get out of town. Just beyond Monsanto Park turn onto the N 117 and follow the signs to Sintra. The highway goes through rolling countryside, increasingly encroached upon by light industry and urban development.

Queluz

A slight detour on the way to Sintra from Lisbon will take you to the 18th-century Baroque **Palácio Nacional de Queluz**, 15 km (9.5 miles) northwest of central Lisbon. Unfortunately, this beautiful rose-washed monument is surrounded by uninspired apartment buildings. Sometimes called Portugal's Versailles, the palace of Queluz was built by Pedro III, consort of Maria I, known as the Mad Queen, who had come to know Versailles during her ill-fated engagement to Louis XV.

In modern times the palace has served as a guesthouse for state visitors, including Queen Elizabeth II and U.S. presidents Eisenhower and Reagan, as well as a venue for special musical events. Generally, however, it is open to visitors. Perhaps more than the palace itself, the royal gardens, laid out by French architect Jean-Baptiste Robillon, evoke Versailles, with their neatly clipped box hedges, ponds, flower gardens, cypress trees, and statuary. Special points of interest inside the palace include the Music Room, with splendid crystal chandeliers; the Throne Room, with magnificent gilt woodwork and mirrors; and the Ambassadors Hall, decorated with fine marble. If the palace proper is closed, at least visit the kitchen, which has a huge fireplace, giant spits, a 15-foot-long marble worktable, and a rich array of shining copper pans. Now known as **Cozinha Velha** (Old Kitchen), this is one of the most elegant restaurants in the area and serves the best of Portuguese cuisine. Among the many specialties is *linguado suado* (steamed sole) submerged in a velvety cream sauce with mushrooms, carrots, and onions. But the crowning glory is the pastry cart with its "royal sweets"— luxurious little cakes, made of egg yolk and sugar, whose secret recipe has been passed on from the royal chefs.

Sintra

Back on the main road, heading west from Lisbon, you come first to **São Pedro de Sintra** (30 km/18 miles) at the bottom of the mountain, where one of the best country fairs of Portugal is held on the second and fourth Sunday of every month. Good bargains are found in all kinds of pottery, woodwork, basketware, and other handicrafts, as well as clothing, leather goods, antiques, and imitation antiques. Popular with the fair crowd is **Adega Saloio**, a typical tavern nearby at Chão de Meninos square in São Pedro, serving sausages, grilled goat, and other local specialties. For more cosmopolitan dining there is the **Solar de São Pedro**, also located in São Pedro de Sintra, on praça Dom Fernando II. Specialties include *coxas de rã à Provençal* (frogs' legs), the currently fashionable *filetes de tamboril* (monkfish), and especially tasty tournedos.

The modern part of Sintra farther up the mountain, where the railroad station is located, is called Estefânia. Here, where the shops are less touristy, is the place to get the best *queijadas* (cheese-and-almond tarts). Then turn west at the crossroads and follow the signs marked "Vila," leading to the old part of town. You might wish to make a stop at the **Sapa** pastry shop, located at the beginning of the Volta da Duche, across the valley from Sintra Vila and the Palácio Nacional. Sapa's *queijadas* are reputed to be the best in the region, and its *nozes* (walnut sweets enveloped in caramel) are beyond belief. This is also an excellent site for taking photographs of old Sintra and the valley. Volta da Duche, a horseshoe drive with a magnificent view of the countryside, leads to the Palácio Nacional, easily distinguished by its two immense cone-shaped chimneys (see below).

A little beyond the palace is the government tourist office (Turismo), located in a distinguished old mansion with a permanent museum and other exhibits. Turismo, open daily including weekends, is the best place to begin a visit of Sintra and find out about local events, which include a regular Son et Lumière program, concerts sponsored by the municipal council, and Sintra's annual music festival. This last takes place in July, with concerts, recitals, and ballet presented in the Palácio Nacional, Seteais, Queluz, and some of the grand manors of the region.

The Turismo staff also provides information about restaurants, shopping, lodgings, and taxi and horse-carriage fares, and gives away maps for walking tours of the region. Walking about the cobblestone square and narrow alleys and stepped streets of the Vila is a delight, but, beyond that, Sintra's peaks are high and the roads steep and winding; most visitors would do well to take a carriage or car up to Castelo da Pena, Cruz Alta, the Moorish castle, and other lofty sights.

A few steps from the Turismo stands the Estalagem dos Cavaleiros, formerly called Lawrence Hotel (currently not open to the public). A small plaque notes that this is where Lord Byron stayed when he visited Sintra, and according to some people this is where he was inspired to write *Childe Harold*.

Also behind the palace stands one of Sintra's most controversial buildings, the bulky modern **Hotel Tivoli**, which seems out of character with the rest of the town. Sintra needed more hotel space, but there is a consensus that the hotel should have been designed to fit in with the old pastel palaces and manors, or should at least be enshrouded in greenery. The hotel's clients (who of course are spared having to look at the building when they're inside) have a superb view from private balconies and from the panoramic restaurant, and need only cross the street to visit the Palácio Nacional.

Also located next to the palace is the modest **Hotel Central**, built at the beginning of the century, with a lovely tile façade. The terrace of the Central is a strategic place to view the goings-on of Sintra or meet friends for a *galão* (café au lait) or a stronger drink.

The Sintra district is known for its handicrafts: pottery, basket-weaving, stone- and marble-cutting. In Sintra, the **Central Bazaar**, next to the Central Hotel on the main square opposite the palace in Sintra Vila, has a broad selection of local craftwork.

Palácio Nacional

The Palácio Nacional was built by King João I in the 14th century on the ruins of a Moorish fortress, and has subsequently undergone many alterations, making it a fascinating conglomeration of Gothic, Moorish, and Manueline styles.

With sharp eye and wit, Portugal's irreverent 19th-century novelist Eça de Queiroz, in *The Maias,* paints a gracious, if devastating, tableau of "this massive, silent palace without fleurons or towers, seated patriarchally among the houses of the town, with those lovely windows that give it a noble and royal look, with the valley at its feet, leafy, dense and fresh, and on high its colossal chimneys, disparate, summing up everything as though that residence was all kitchen built on a scale to suit the gluttony of a king who daily devours an entire kingdom." Unfortunately there are no guides available, and only irregular tours accompanied by Portuguese-speaking guards.

Of special interest are the 16th- and 17th-century *azulejos* in the Sala dos Arabes, the Sala das Sereias (Sirens' Room), and the chapel, said to be among the finest tiles of the Iberian Peninsula. Equally interesting is the Sala das Brasões (Coats of Arms Room), whose walls are lined with blue-and-white-tile hunting scenes and battles. On the octagonal ceiling are painted 72 coats of arms of all the noble families of the 16th century. One has been effaced, that of the Tavora family, which was caught in a conspiracy against the throne. Also impressive is the Sala das Pêgas (Magpie Room), the ceiling of which is painted with little birds carrying standards in their beaks with the royal motto Por Bem (all for the good). As the story goes, Queen Philippa caught King João in the act of kissing one of her ladies-in-waiting, and he responded with bravado, "Por bem." As this incident was the subject of relentless court gossip, the king had the ceiling painted with magpies, symbol of gossip, to remind everyone of his motto.

Pena

The **Castelo da Pena** is located on top of one of the highest peaks of Sintra mountain on what was the site of a 16th-century Hieronymite monastery. From a distance the building is quite imposing, but close at hand it resembles a Hollywood stage set, with its jumble of crenellated walls, forbidding dungeons, pointed turrets, and golden domes. It was rebuilt by the 19th-century German architect Baron von Eschwege as a summer residence for Queen Maria II's consort, Ferdinand of Saxe-Coburg-Gotha. The only authentic part of this ostentatious mock-Medieval palace is a small chapel near the entrance, with 17th-century tiles and an alabaster altar by the 16th-century sculptor Nicholas Chanterene.

Without doubt, however, the best part of Pena is the view, which is overwhelming. Just below the Jardim das Camélias lies a forest of every kind of tree brought back from all over Portugal's erstwhile empire. Beyond, the green valley of Colares spreads out to the sea.

At the highest point of the Sintra range is **Cruz Alta**, a stone cross. The site can be reached by car, to provide a great view of Pena and the Costa do Sol. On the crest of one of the lower mountains stands the **Castelo dos Mouros** (Moorish castle), built in the eighth century and now largely in ruins. From its tower and crenellated walls you can get a different view of Sintra's great moss-covered granite boulders and of the gentle countryside below.

Before going back down to the town, follow the Estrada da Pena (also known as the EN 247-3) westward along the mountain crest through thick forests to **Capuchos**, one of the most astonishing sights in the region. Deep in the woods, this 16th-century Franciscan monastery was built out of large boulders. The monks' cells were lined with cork against the extreme humidity, and their meager furnishings were also made of cork.

From Capuchos, you might want to make another slight detour a short distance to the southwest, but still in the mountains. Follow the sign for **Peninha**, another peak with a splendid panoramic view of the valley and the sea. There is a small chapel here whose walls are lined with handsome 18th-century tiles recounting the life of the Virgin.

You may wish to continue westward down and out of

the mountains from Peninha to join the road to Colares (EN 247) and circle back to Sintra from there. People generally prefer to backtrack to Capuchos and to the Pena road, which leads back down to Sintra Vila.

Seteais and Monserrate

From Castelo da Pena, take the Estrada da Pena, which twists its way down through the luxuriant park to largo Ferreira de Castro. Turn left onto the road to Seteais, past vine-covered stone walls, palatial mansions, and Moorish manors. This is the EN 375, which leads to **Seteais**, a stately 18th-century palace built by a Dutch consul, Daniel Gildemeester. The royal arch of triumph marks the fact that King João VI once stayed here. This was long considered the site of the signing of the Treaty of Sintra between the Duke of Wellington's forces and those of French marshall Junot during the Peninsular Campaign, but now there is some doubt.

Seteais means "the seven ayes" in Portuguese, which some people interpret as exclamations of sorrow, others of delight. In 1955 the palace was converted into the luxury **Hotel Palácio dos Seteais**, reputed to be one of the finest in Europe, with outstanding cuisine and service. Most of the rooms are decorated with murals, and the dining room and bar have landscapes said to be the work of Jean Pillement, an 18th-century French painter much appreciated in Portugal. All the furnishings are either antiques or replicas of antiques. The formal garden in front and the boxwoods in the back are meticulously kept. Prices match those of luxury hotels in other, more expensive, European countries, but some recent guests have noted a decline in service. Nevertheless, the decor and the views of the mountain and valley are exceptional and worth a stopover, at least for tea.

Continuing on the EN 375 (sometimes called the Estrada de Monserrate), you pass near two delightful 16th-century *quintas* that have been opened to paying guests. Just before you reach Monserrate Park, turn right down a steep dirt road to the **Quinta de São Thiago**, initially a convent belonging to the monks of Pena. Tastefully decorated and furnished with antiques, the quinta has nine rooms with private bath, a suite, a music room, a swimming pool, and a tennis court. Elegant meals are served in the family dining room, built in the 1960s with an 18th-century-style painted ceiling and candelabra. The owners live at the quinta and willingly share their family stories with visitors. (Some guests complain that the lady of the house can be somewhat overpowering.)

Some people wishing to explore the region prefer the **Quinta da Capela**, which is located off the same road and just beyond Monserrate. This ancient, sprawling country home has a lovely old chapel, 11 rooms with baths, a conference room, and a minipool, gymnasium, and sauna. The owners do not live on the premises.

Monserrate itself is undoubtedly one of the finest parks in the country, with exotic trees and flowers from all parts of the world: cedars of Lebanon, African palms, mahoganies of Brazil, and a profusion of local flora from camellias to rhododendrons. The original **Palace of Monserrate**, where the 17th-century English romantic writer William Beckford used to entertain his noble Portuguese friends, has been torn down. The present palace is an Arab fantasy with arches and bulbous cupolas built by Sir Francis Cook, Viscount Monserrate, in the 19th century. It is closed, but plans for renovation are said to be under way.

The Monserrate road winds west along the side of the mountain through lush vegetation and then zigzags down to the valley of Colares. Along the way are several handsome old quintas. The finest is the **Quinta do Vinagre**, built in the 16th century and located on the outskirts of Colares.

Colares

Compared to the lush, dramatic Sintra mountain, the valley of Colares is a peaceful landscape of vineyards, narrow winding roads, and whitewashed villages, with an occasional ancient manor and a scattering of new villas. English poet and art critic Sacheverell Sitwell writes that it could be some part of Tuscany.

The village of Colares is a small rural center 6 km (4 miles) west of Sintra, and its principal monument—the **Adega Regional de Colares** (local wine cellar)—is well worth visiting. The grapevines are grown in a sandy soil that protected them against the phylloxera blight in 1865 and gives the wine its distinctive aroma. Colares red wines are rich and full-bodied, ruby-colored and somewhat astringent when young, turning a velvety deep garnet with age. The white wines are straw-colored with a nutty flavor. A good place to test the local wine is **Casa da Ponte**, a popular restaurant near the Colares bridge. A specialty of the house is the rich *sopa à pescador* (seafood soup).

It is only a few miles to Cabo da Roca (see the Costa do Sol section, above) and several pleasant seaside resorts, frequented mainly by Portuguese families. **Praia das Maçãs** northwest of Colares, has a broad sandy beach with relatively calm surf, a restaurant, and a place to change. **Azenhas do Mar** to the north nearby is a lovely little village built into the cliffs, with a natural swimming pool carved out of the rocks.

A mile or so inland lies the village of Janas and the 16th-century **church of São Mamede**, an unusual circular building with classical columns, said to have been built on Roman ruins.

Little known and only partly excavated Roman ruins are found at **Odrinhas**, a village 10 km (6 miles) north of Sintra on the road to Ericeira. There are ruins of a fourth-century villa with a mosaic floor, a chapel, and strange monoliths. A small museum on the site contains Roman columns and tombstones found in the area.

An interesting expedition is to visit the pottery workshop and museum of **Eduardo Azenha** in the village of Santa Suzana, on the road to Ericeira (EN 247) just north of the archaeological site at Odrinhas. A farmer-artist, Mr. Azenha has re-created Portuguese village life of 100 years ago in ceramic. He sells small figures, windmills, Nativity scenes, and the like for reasonable prices.

Not so easy to transport are the marble statues and tables for sale at a number of marble factories in Montelavar and Pêro Pinheiro on the EN 9 road to Mafra from Sintra.

Mafra

To get from Sintra to Mafra another way, take the road to the fishing port of **Ericeira**, but turn inland just before entering the town of Ericeira itself—unless you want to get a closer look at the cliffside dwellings and lively harbor or stop for fish at one of the town's popular restaurants. Since Ericeira is the home of that unusual Portuguese specialty, *açorda de mariscos* (or "dry" shellfish soup), you might want to stop at one of the fish restaurants in town, such as **Toca do Caboz**, and give it a try. The basis for the soup is stale bread, marinated in shellfish stock and beaten well, then cooked with olive oil, garlic, and fresh coriander, to which eggs and shellfish are added. If the timing is right, it all tastes like some heavenly soufflé. Ericeira is best known as the port from which the last king of Portugal, Manuel II, set sail for exile on October 5, 1910, when the monarchy was overthrown.

A 9-km (5-mile) drive through rolling farmland then takes you to the **Palácio Nacional de Mafra**, which looms over the surrounding villages like a proud monument to the lost empire. Indeed, Mafra rivals the Escorial in Spain in grandeur, but is very different. It reputedly took 50,000 workmen 18 years and a fortune from Portugal's former colony of Brazil to build this vast structure, completed in 1735. It was King João V who commissioned the German architect Friedrich Ludwig to build this ambitious work.

The Baroque monastery-palace is built of ivory-colored marble, darkened by lichen, time, and the elements. The basilica, crowned by a large cupola, stands in the center of two long wings, with a domed tower on each end. Giant marble statues of the saints stand guard at the entrance. The interior is richly decorated with marble statues and bas-relief. These works are by artists of the School of Mafra, a group of foreign and Portuguese sculptors especially commissioned for the project, among them Joaquim Machado de Castro, one of Portugal's finest.

The royal apartments, hospital, pharmacy, and monks' cells are open to the public, as is Mafra's jewel, the library. This splendid long gallery with vaulted ceiling contains some 35,000 books, many rare editions among them. The palace also has a small museum with works of religious art.

Try to visit Mafra on a Sunday afternoon around 4:00 P.M., when the carillons are played. Dom João V ordered more than 100 carillon bells to be cast in Belgium for Mafra; they have recently been restored and have a beautiful sound.

NORTHERN ESTREMADURA

Estremadura province is an extremely varied swath of land, stretching from the great pine forests and green hills of the Leiria region in the north to the cork oak and olive groves of the Arrábida peninsula in the south, bounded by the Atlantic cliffs and beaches on the west and the Tagus river valley to the east.

A limited day tour of the northern reaches of Estremadura should include the Medieval walled town of

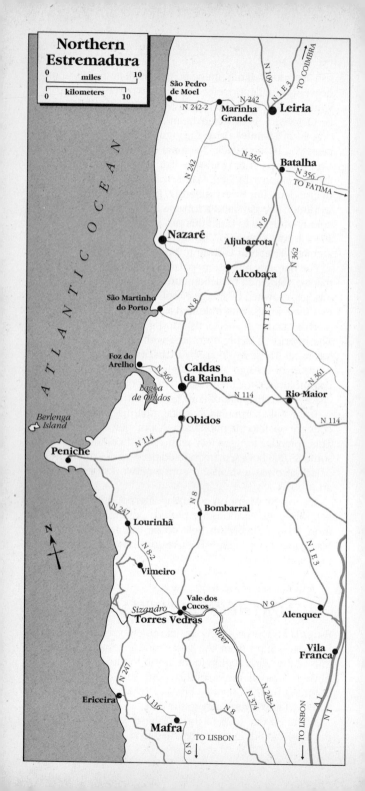

Obidos, the colorful fishing village of Nazaré, and the magnificent monasteries of Alcobaça and Batalha.

For those who travel by car and have more time, however, there is much more to see and enjoy in this area. Leaving Lisbon, take the N 8 route north to Loures (a road that used to wind through lovely old farms and vineyards but now goes through just another dormitory suburb). Stop at Loures to see the church with its fine 15th-century calvary.

Continuing north through rolling farmland, vineyards, and marble quarries, you will come to **Torres Vedras**, a busy industrial town and wine center. An old fort stands on the hill here overlooking the Sisandro river, which has served as a natural defense since Roman times. Torres Vedras played an important role during the Peninsular Campaign, when the Duke of Wellington ordered the construction of fortifications that stretched from the Tagus river to the Atlantic near Mafra and successfully blocked the advance of the French army. Remnants of these fortifications are still visible here and there in the fields.

In town, the **church of São Pedro** has a lovely Manueline doorway, 16th-century medallion-shaped tiles, and noteworthy primitive paintings in the chapel. The nearby Chafariz dos Conos, a Gothic fountain long since dry, dates back to the 14th century.

A short detour east along the river leads to **Cucos**, a spa with thermal waters and hot mud baths, good for rheumatism, arthritis, gout, and other ailments. There is an old-fashioned hotel on the site, but accommodations are better in Torres Vedras, which has several modest hotels and pensions. Or you may wish to stay at the **Quinta de São José**, 15 km (9 miles) east of Torres Vedras. This farm with vineyards is open to paying guests. Meals are served and there is a swimming pool. There are only seven rooms with baths, so reservations should be made in advance.

Another spa is located a few miles northwest of Torres Vedras at **Vimeiro**. The mineral water of Vimeiro is Portugal's Perrier, recommended for kidney diseases, digestive problems, and some skin ailments.

Take the direct road north from Torres Vedras to Peniche through **Lourinhã**, a farm center that goes back to Roman times. The parish church on the hill, built in the 4th century, is noted for its rose window and handsome tile balustrade. The 17th-century misericord contains some especially fine sculpture and religious paintings.

Peniche

An important fishing port today, Peniche stands at the end of a promontory 35 km (21 miles) north of Torres Vedras on route N 8-2/N 247. Its steep cliffs made it a natural site for the **Fortaleza**, built in the 16th century to protect the coast. Later this fort was used as a prison, and only after the overthrow of the dictatorship in 1974 were the last of the political prisoners set free. Today the old prison cells have been turned into an antifascism museum, a school for lace making, and a ceramics workshop.

Among the fine buildings in Peniche is the parish **church of São Pedro**, the fishermen's church, with such relics as a model of a sardine trawler, nets, and buoys. The 17th-century misericord has some outstanding paintings by Josefa de Obidos, a remarkable artist of the time, and a fine series of paintings by her father, Balthazar Gomez Figueira. The **chapel of Nossa Senhora dos Remédios** has 18th-century tiles attributed to António de Oliveira Bernardes and a magnificent view of the cliffs.

The liveliest part of town is the newly built fishing port, located at the eastern part of the isthmus, where giant seagulls await their prey. The best time to see the action is early in the morning, when the trawlers return with their catch of tuna, sardines, or whatever is in season. Sardine season runs from the end of May through October. You can find them almost anywhere in Portugal, but the sardine capital is Peniche. Stroll along the avenida do Mar, at the base of the fortress, and you'll see a dozen restaurants with charcoal grills outside, mainly for sardines. In Portugal, fresh grilled sardines are fat, juicy, and succulent, and except for the name have almost nothing in common with their small, pallid cousins in cans.

If you happen to be around on the first weekend in August, don't miss the festival of Nossa Senhora de Boa Viagem. On Saturday night a candlelight procession goes from São Pedro to the harbor, where a priest blesses the fishing fleet. The ceremony is followed by a fair.

Depending on the time and the weather, an excursion to **the Berlengas** can be delightful. This archipelago of extraordinary red rock formations, 12 km (7 miles) out to sea, is a national bird sanctuary, and all kinds of migratory birds can be seen around its crags and caverns. During the season, from June though September, a regular ferry makes the trip of about one hour from Peniche harbor to the main island. On Berlenga get a good fish lunch at the inn, located in the 17th-century **fortress of São João Baptista**. Then take a walk along the rocky plateau to see the lighthouse and the fishermen's cottages on the beach.

Obidos

Although Obidos now stands 10 km (6 miles) inland, this ancient walled town east of Peniche on N 114 once guarded the coast; but over the centuries the shore silted up, leaving only what is now called the Lagoa (lagoon) de Obidos between the town and the sea. The Romans—and possibly the Celts before them—built a fortress here. In the 8th century the Moors occupied Obidos, and held it for more than 400 years. It was such a beautiful town in the 13th century that King Dinis presented it as a gift to his wife, Queen Isabel, a pretty gesture that became a royal tradition.

Today Obidos retains the flavor of a Moorish casbah. Crenellated walls and towers surround the castle, the small whitewashed homes bedecked with geraniums and bougainvillaea, and the narrow cobblestone streets. The castle itself has been converted into the elegant **Pousada do Castelo**, but reservations are required far, far in advance; there are only six rooms and three suites. The pousada's chef specializes in such Portuguese classics as *frango na pucara* (chicken baked in a terra-cotta pot with tomatoes, onions, ham, and lots of garlic); and *bacalhau à bras* (dried cod scrambled with eggs, onions, and potatoes and garnished with black olives). At least stop for a meal or take a walk along the ramparts to admire the view. Turned into a royal palace in the 16th century, the pousada has a spectacular carved Manueline doorway and windows. Inside, the furnishings are antiques or exquisite reproductions. There is an immense calm about the place that makes it easy to relate to times past.

On the shady main square stands a 15th-century fountain and pillory with the coat of arms of Queen Leonor. Here is the misericord built by Queen Leonor, and beside it the **Municipal Museum**, with archaeological discoveries, ancient arms, and paintings from the school of the extraordinary 17th-century primitive artist Josefa de Ayala, better known as Josefa de Obidos. Several of her finest paintings can be seen here in the **church of Santa Maria**, built on the foundations of a Visigoth temple. The tomb of Josefa de Obidos is located in the church of São Pedro.

At the southern end of town is an impressive 15th-century **aqueduct**.

On the road north to Caldas da Rainha stands the vast 18th-century Baroque sanctuary Nossa Senhora de Pedra, which was never completed.

While the Obidos area has not been designated specifically as a wine-growing region, it does produce some high-quality wines. The red Obidos is bright ruby and smooth, and the white is lemon-colored, with a fruity essence.

Caldas da Rainha (the queen's hot springs), as the name implies, is the place where the queen used to take the cure. In the 15th century Queen Leonor found the sulfuric waters so therapeutic for rheumatism and respiratory diseases that she had a hospital built on the site. Today, people still flock to the Hospital Termal Rainha Dona Leonor to bathe in the curative waters.

Also dating from Queen Leonor's time, **Nossa Senhora do Pópulo**, founded as the hospital chapel, is a good example of Manueline architecture, its inside walls lined with 17th-century tiles and its altars decorated with 16th-century Moorish tiles.

The spa's other claim to prominence is its pottery, the delightful green cabbage-leaf ware that makes such appetizing soup bowls and salad plates. There is also a line of oyster-white ware, particularly effective as fish platters. The daily market now has only a couple of pottery stands, but there are half a dozen shops with a wide selection on the rua da Liberdade in the center of town. The National Ceramics Fair is held in Caldas da Rainha in mid-July.

The works of Rafael Bordalo Pinheiro, a local potter and caricaturist, can be found at the **Bordalo Pinheiro Factory Museum** and the **São Rafael Pequeno Museum**, located on the street named for the potter and devoted to pottery. The factory, **Faianças Artisticas Bordalo Pinheiro**, open to visitors, continues its founder's tradition, turning out cabbage leaves and other nature ware and folk figurines.

In the pleasant municipal park, the **Museu de José Malhōa** contains works by another outstanding native son, the turn-of-the-century naturalist painter Malhōa, whose murals and paintings of contemporary life and heroes of the past are found in many public buildings in Lisbon.

From Caldas da Rainha go west on N 360 to pick up the coastal road northeast to Nazaré at Foz do Arelho. The coastal road goes through the national park and several delightful resorts. Foz do Arelho is a village with a broad beach and the modern **Foz Palace Motel**, with tennis court and boats for hire. A little farther up the road is São Martinho do Porto, which has a protected beach and a fine bay for sailing and other water sports.

Nazaré

Nowadays, Nazaré should be visited *out of* season. This quintessential fishing village, with its fabulous long beach with an immense cliff blocking one end, its multicolored fishing boats, and its fishermen in plaid trousers and women in black, was discovered by summer vacationers, especially the French, in the 1960s, and seems to have been posing for photographs ever since. But in the spring, fall, and even winter the town relaxes and seems genuinely glad to receive visitors.

There are really two Nazarés: the Praia, or beach area, and the Sítio, a 360-foot-high promontory, the cliff of which forms the northern end of the beach. The main part of town, with numerous cafés, restaurants, bars, hotels, and *pensões* (pensions), is located at the Praia. A popular seaside boardinghouse is **Pensão Ribamar**, located near the Turismo office. There are no frills, and only 11 of the 19 rooms have a private bath, but the location and rates are difficult to beat. Nearby, on the main square, praça Sousa Oliveira, are several good seafood restaurants, such as **Restaurante Mar Bravo**, that specialize in shellfish. Expect prices to be almost as high as in the Lisbon region.

Souvenir shops at the Praia offer attractive fishermen's sweaters and capes. The fishermen's quarter, just back from the beach, is a maze of small whitewashed houses and alleys. In the not-so-old days, the fishermen used to pull their Viking-style boats up on the beach with oxen, or later tractors, but this tradition was eliminated when a harbor at the southern end of town was built, where trawlers and flat-bottomed fishing boats are now anchored.

To reach the Sítio from the Praia, you can either take the funicular (in season) or drive up to the lookout, which has a magnificent view of the coast. Here is the minute white chapel of **Nossa Senhora da Memória**, and nearby, a pillory with an inscription that says in Portuguese: "Before and after his first voyage to India, Vasco da Gama came to pray at Our Lady of Nazaré."

At the chapel near the edge of the cliff, somebody is bound to recount the story of the miracle of Dom Fuas: On one very misty day during the Middle Ages, Dom Fuas Roupinho, a local notable, was chasing a deer, which leaped off the cliff. Not aware of the danger, the horse and rider followed, but were saved by Our Lady of Nazaré. Believers even point out the horse's footprint on a rock overlooking the sea. At the far end of the promontory stands the São Miguel fort and lighthouse, built in the 16th century.

The **church of Nossa Senhora de Nazaré**, a large 17th-century building with a handsome Baroque door, twisted pink marble columns, vaulted ceiling, and tile scenes of war and peace, dominates the main square of the Sítio. During the annual pilgrimage of Nossa Senhora de Nazaré, in the second week of September, worshippers carry a statue of the Virgin from the church down to the sea, a statue that during the 4th century was reportedly brought back from Nazareth in the Holy Land by a pilgrim. For this reason the town is called Nazaré.

Alcobaça

A few miles inland of Nazaré, to the southeast, is Alcobaça, located on the Alcoa and Baça rivers on route N 8. This is the site of the grandiose **Santa Maria monastery**, built in the late 12th century by King Afonso I to commemorate the capture of Santarém from the Moors earlier in the century. The vast abbey, which became the headquarters of the Cistercian order, was badly damaged during the 17th to 19th centuries and restored on several occasions, but the beautiful Gothic door and rose window are part of the original structure. The church, with three long aisles, massive walls, and pure lines, is considered a masterpiece of Cistercian architecture. Especially moving is the **Cloister of Silence**, dating from the 14th century, with vaulted ceiling and graceful columns. The most astonishing part of the abbey is the monumental **kitchen**, with a huge fireplace in which the monks could roast half a dozen oxen at once. They could also procure fish from the stream running right through the room— and enjoy a constant supply of fresh water.

The cathedral of Alcobaça is best known for the tombs of Portugal's star-crossed lovers King Pedro I and his beloved, Inês de Castro. As a young prince, Dom Pedro was bonded by a marriage of state to Constanza, Infanta of

Castile, but deeply loved her lady-in-waiting, the beautiful Inês. Learning of his son's illicit romance, King Afonso IV had Inês banished. When the Infanta died in childbirth, Dom Pedro sent for Inês and resumed the liaison openly, having several children by her. King Afonso, however, never accepted the liaison, fearing the influence of Inês's family and possible claims of Castile to the Portuguese throne. Unbeknownst to Dom Pedro, the king had Inês murdered at Coimbra, in her home, which is today called the Quinta das Lágrimas (Manor of Tears).

When Dom Pedro succeeded his father as King Pedro I, in 1357, he found the assassins and had them executed. Announcing that he had been secretly married to Inês, he had her body exhumed and carried in a torchlight procession to Alcobaça. There her corpse was crowned queen and members of the court were compelled to bow and kiss her hand. Dom Pedro had two magnificently carved tombs built with panels portraying their love story. Lifelike statues of Inês and the king recline on the tombs, which are placed so that on the Day of Judgment the two lovers will gaze into each other's faces when they rise.

Alcobaça is another pottery center, producing its own distinctive blue-and-white ware with floral designs. A number of shops and stalls on the square near the monastery offer everything from candlesticks and vases to statuary.

You can also visit the showrooms of the many pottery factories in the area. **Vestal Faianças de Alcobaça**, for example, produces a variety of cachepots, candleholders, garden ornaments, and miniatures.

Batalha

There is not much to see in Aljubarrota, northeast of Alcobaça on N 8, except a small monument honoring the heroes of what the Portuguese call "The Battle." This was the decisive victory in 1385 of the poorly organized Portuguese forces against the much better equipped army of Castile, which saved the country from Spanish domination for 200 years. King João I had made a vow to construct the finest church in the realm to honor the Virgin if she helped him to defeat the forces of King Juan I of Castile. True to his word, King João had built what even today is the most magnificent monument in Portugal, the **monastery of Batalha** (originally called Santa Maria da Vitória), 12 km (8 miles) north of Alcobaça on N 8 and then N 1. Until a few years ago the road passed at a respectful distance, giving a breathtaking view of the majestic building. Then, despite a clamor of protest, the new highway up to Leiria was built so close to the monastery that the perspective is lost. Nevertheless, Batalha is a notable sight, especially at sunset, when its burnished limestone turns to gold.

The flamboyant ensemble of towers, buttresses, vaults, columns, and arches is a masterpiece of Portuguese Gothic. A splendid portal, decorated with a statue of Christ and 100 other biblical figures, leads into the sober, beautifully proportioned **cathedral**. Remarkable 16th-century stained-glass windows depict scenes from the lives of the Virgin and of Christ. In the **Capela do Fundador** the tombs of King João I and his English Queen, Philippa of Lancaster, are placed so close that their reclining statues are holding hands. Lining the walls are the tombs of their six sons and a grandson, each bearing a motto. Among the sons is Prince Henry the Navigator, whose motto was "The talent to do well."

On the opposite side of the church, the **Claustro Real** (Royal Cloister) is a marvelous combination of Gothic arches and richly carved Manueline decoration. In the chapter house lie the tombs of two unknown soldiers from World War I, one of whom died in France, the other during the African campaign. The stained-glass window, dating from the early 16th century, shows in vivid colors the Passion of Christ.

In the back of the church a Manueline door of the 16th century leads to the Capelas Imperfeitas (Unfinished Chapels). This large octagonal building with seven chapels, begun in 1435 by King Duarte, was to contain his tomb and that of Queen Leonor, but he died before the work was completed. The descendants seem to have lost interest in the chapels, and the columns and the passage to the church were never finished.

Just across the square from the Batalha monastery is the pleasant **Pousada do Mestre Afonso Domingues**. It has only 21 handsomely furnished rooms, so reservations are advised. There's also a first-rate dining room, which serves the best of traditional Portuguese fare like *caldo verde* (green soup), thin shreds of the local cabbage in a potato-onion broth with bits of sausage or pork.

From Batalha you can return to Lisbon directly south on the N1 highway, a drive of only about an hour and a half.

SOUTH OF THE TAGUS RIVER

Southern Estremadura, or the Arrábida peninsula, is a gentle land of olive groves, vineyards, wooded hills, and many unsullied beaches and coves. There are splendid castles at Setúbal, Palmela, and Sesimbra. Setúbal has several fine churches, particularly the Igreja de Jesús, with its extraordinary twisted columns. And across the bay, at Tróia, a sophisticated new resort is growing up beside the Roman ruins.

Before the opening of the bridge over the Tagus river in 1966, going south from Lisbon was quite an adventure, and not really a one-day excursion. Although the ferry ride to the Arrábida peninsula took only 20 minutes, psychologically it was much farther, and the roads and tourist facilities were very poor. Even today the southern environs of Lisbon are less developed than the north, although some places, such as Almada, are catching up quickly—perhaps too quickly. Now, with the bridge, the Arrábida peninsula is so convenient to Lisbon that its sights are sometimes overlooked in the rush for the beaches and the warmer waters of the Algarve. If your time is very limited, there are some fine sheltered beaches just south of Lisbon. The principal attraction to the peninsula, however, is not its beaches but the **Serra da Arrábida**, a gentle mountain range located on the southern coast. The region has several splendid castles, and the drive along the corniche is comparable in beauty to that of the Amalfi Coast in Italy.

At first the handsome suspension bridge was called the Ponte Salazar in honor of the dictator, who had ordered its construction. After the young captains launched the Flower Revolution on April 25, 1974, the name of the bridge was changed to the Ponte 25 de Abril.

Modeled after San Francisco's Golden Gate and built by U.S. Steel, the bridge has only four lanes—totally inadequate for weekend traffic. Originally planned to include a railroad bridge on the lower level, the bridge appears unfinished. Although vehicles cannot stop on the bridge, you can drive slowly and appreciate the spectacular view of Lisbon and its seven hills, particularly when approaching from the south.

Some people prefer the leisurely route by ferry. It is a pleasant minicruise and a good opportunity to take pictures of the Lisbon skyline and the assortment of boats plying the river. Ferries leave Lisbon from the river station at the southeastern corner of Terreiro do Paço and from the Cais do Sodré railroad station. They land at **Cacilhas**, a rather nondescript bedroom town with several popular restaurants overlooking the river. Many Lisboetes come here to eat fresh fish and gaze at Lisbon. You can also walk along the river to see the Cristo Rei in the neighboring town of Almada, or get a bus on the main square and go to Caparica beach, west on the Atlantic coast.

If you are driving, shortly after the toll gate on the southern end of the bridge you come to the turnoff for Almada and can drive right to the foot of the **Cristo Rei**. Inspired by the Christ of Rio de Janeiro, this statue is smaller and seems to be overwhelmed by its own pedestal. An elevator takes you up to the foot of the statue for an admirable view of the Tagus, Lisbon, and the entire Arrábida peninsula.

Caparica

Return to the main highway and continue a few miles to the exit marked "Costa da Caparica." Lisboetes flock to Caparica on weekends, because the long, crescent-shaped beach is more protected than the Atlantic beaches north of the Tagus and less polluted than the river beaches. On weekdays you can find long stretches of sparsely populated beach and a number of restaurants where you can get a good fish meal. Try **Varanda do Oceano**, on avenida General Humberto Delgado. The gorgeous sea view is usually matched by the quality of the fish. There are several hotels and pensões, and most of the restaurants have modest facilities for changing.

If you prefer, take the little train that runs (daily in summer, weekends spring and fall) along the 20-km (12-mile) beach, and get off at the southern end of the line, where you can bathe or picnic in the privacy of sand dunes.

To reach the Arrábida mountains, go back to the A 2 superhighway leading southeast to Setúbal, but first take a detour to **Palmela**. The Castelo do Palmela was already an important defensive post in the 12th century, when King Afonso Henriques captured it from the Moors. Later, in the 15th century, the Order of Saint James established its headquarters in the castle, adding a church and monastery to the complex. Today the monastery has been turned into the **Pousada do Castelo de Palmela**, which has 29 rooms, an attractive dining room in the old refectory, a comfortable lounge in the cloisters, and spectacular views of the mountains, Lisbon, and the broad Sado estuary. The church, restored, contains the tomb of Dom Jorge de Lencastre, son of João II and the last master of the Order of Saint James. At the foot of the castle wall, the **church of São Pedro** is interesting for its lovely 18th-century tiles telling the story of Saint Peter's life.

Setúbal

Back on the main highway, head south for Setúbal, an important industrial town dating back to Roman times. Always a busy fishing port, Setúbal is today a center for fish canning, shipbuilding, auto assembly, and cement production.

This industrial aspect should not deter you; there are a number of interesting sights in and around Setúbal. The **Igreja de Jesús**, located on the praça Miguel Bombarda, a little to the left as you drive into the city on the N 10 from Lisbon, was designed in 1491 by Diogo Boytac. It is an outstanding example of Manueline art, with columns like twisted ropes, ribs crisscrossing along the high vaulted ceiling, and walls decorated with fine 17th-century tile panels. The Gothic **cloister** adjoining the church has been converted into a museum, with archaeological remains from the region and a good collection of tiles dating from the 15th to the 18th centuries. It also contains paintings by 15th- and 16th-century Portuguese primitive artists, particularly one known simply as the Master of Setúbal.

Very different is the **Igreja dos Grilos**, so named because of the crickets that still sing there in the summer. This church is located on avenida Jaime Cortesão, just beyond the railway line. Its elaborate 18th-century Manueline altars are of rose-and-white marble. Tile panels depict the life of Saint Augustine.

The **Regional Archaeological and Ethnographic Museum**, on the main promenade, avenida Luisa Todi, features local folk arts and crafts, as well as exhibits about the fishing, textile, and cork industries in the area. A **Municipal Gallery of Visual Arts** is installed in the Casa do Bocage, birthplace of the 18th-century poet Manuel Bocage, located on rua Bartissol near the Grilos church.

It's not easy to find the **Pousada de São Filipe** (another castle-turned-inn), but the view from the top is worth the effort. Follow the signs scrupulously and you will reach the Estrada do Castelo de São Filipe on the western side of Setúbal. The road twists and turns upward to the castle, which is perched on a promontory high above the city. From the terrace you can watch the ferries scuttle back and forth across the Sado river to the Tróia peninsula, and on a clear day it seems you can see halfway to the Algarve. There are only 15 rooms, so reservations must be made well in advance. If you haven't got a room, make it a point to have lunch here anyway. The dining room is on the second floor, with a spectacular view of the sea and generally superb food and service. Try a local specialty like the grilled red mullet with oranges and olive oil—Setúbal style. This fortified castle was built in 1590 by the Italian architect Felipe Terzi on the orders of King Philip II of Spain, when the country was under Spanish rule. His aim was twofold: to defend the estuary against the English, and to keep the Portuguese population in order. The old chapel is adorned with tiles recounting the life of Saint Philip.

The Arrábida Area

Leave Setúbal by the avenida Luisa Todi, heading west to join the corniche road (the N 379-1). Shortly after leaving the city you will come upon an unsightly cement factory spewing fumes for miles around. But don't be deterred, because beyond this the road is breathtakingly beautiful.

After Setúbal, the road west climbs through the wooded foothills of the Arrábida range and proceeds along the mountain ridge. The thick pine and cypress forest, bright wildflowers, brick-colored ravines, and sapphire sea all have a Mediterranean luminosity. Down below, a cluster of whitewashed buildings surrounded by forest is the 16th-century Convento Novo. A sign indicates the footpath to Formosinho, the highest peak of the range.

Farther on, take the side road marked **Portinho da Arrábida**. This steep descent leads to one of the finest beaches in the area, with white sand and clear, clean water. There's a pleasant boardinghouse-restaurant overlooking the beach, **Pensão Residencia Santa Maria da Arrábida**, where you can get a snack or a fish dinner. The nearby **Santa Margarida beach**, accessible only by boat, enchanted the English poet laureate Robert Southey at the end of the 18th century, with its natural grottoes and transparent waters. In recent times, however, the grottoes have been badly defaced. From Portinho, go back the same way (there isn't any other) to the N 379-1, which now turns inland and makes a steep ascent, passing through pine and cypress woods. Then the landscape opens to vineyards and olive groves, and you come to the inland route, the N 379. Turn westward on this road past rolling hills, orchards, and farm hamlets. Just beyond the village of Santana you will see a sign for Sesimbra, on a road to the left. As the road winds its way down to the sea, you get a magnificent view of the coast and the mountain range.

Sesimbra has been an important fishing port since Roman times but is increasingly a holiday resort. The crenellated walls of **Sesimbra castle** dominate the town and provide a wonderful view of the coastline. Originally a Moorish fortress, the castle was badly destroyed by the 1755 earthquake, but has since been restored.

The main attraction of Sesimbra, however, is the fishermen's harbor at the foot of the cliff. Every morning, trawlers bring in their catch of swordfish, eels, sardines, or whatever is in season, and a lively auction is held in the afternoon. East of the port lies a protected bay with a swimming beach, water skiing, sailing, and other water sports.

The old part of town is built along the cliff, with steep alleys and steps leading to the port. It holds the **Igreja Matriz**, a parish church from the 17th century with a handsome marble pulpit and woodcarvings, halfway up the hill on rua João de Deus. The prison fort of Santiago, also from the 17th century, is in the center of town by the sea. From the fort take the shore road, called avenida dos Naufragos, westward, and you will encounter several good seafood restaurants. **Algamar**, for example, serves a copious *caldeirada* (fish stew) for two and tender squid stuffed with shrimp. The same road leads to the fishing port.

To leave Sesimbra you must go back up the hill. Take the road with the sign for the **Hotel do Mar**. Built into the hill on terraces, the hotel is tastefully decorated and has magnificent sea views; it is a favorite weekend abode for affluent Portuguese and foreign visitors.

From Sesimbra, the road climbs north to the village of Santana, then winds west through country villages to **Cabo Espichel**. The landscape changes dramatically as you reach the windswept cape, which is covered with low brush and heath. In ancient times people used to make pilgrimages to the **shrine of Nossa Senhora do Cabo**, in a setting that looks like the end of the world. The two long rows of arcaded buildings where pilgrims used to stay, long abandoned, are now used on weekends by people from Setúbal (and occasional squatters). The church, built in the 17th century, is decorated with gilt woodcarvings and a painted ceiling, now badly deteriorated. Beyond, standing on the edge of the cliff, is a small white seamen's chapel decorated with tiles depicting fishing scenes. A fishermen's festival is held here on the last Sunday in October to honor Our Lady of the Cape.

Azeitão

Back at Santana, take the inland route northeast through vineyards and olive groves to the important wine center of **Vila Nogueira de Azeitão**. In the center of town stands the 16th-century Tavora Palace, which belonged to the dukes of Aveiro. The palace is now rather dilapidated, but there are plans to restore it and turn it into a museum.

On the first Sunday of every month Azeitão is the site of one of the best regional fairs in the country, offering a wide range of products from cattle and poultry to pottery and leather boots. The fair drew such crowds that it had to move from the central square to a large field on the outskirts of town.

Azeitão is also the home of one of Portugal's leading table-wine producers, José Maria da Fonseca. Visitors are welcome to tour the original factory cum residence and small museum, located in the center of town. The factory, founded in 1834, still produces a delicate, honey-sweet muscatel, Moscatel de Setúbal.

Fonseca's modern winery, on the outskirts, is also open to visitors. Here some of Portugal's best-known wines are produced. The soft, mellow, red Periquita wines, a favorite with Portuguese wine connoisseurs, are reasonably priced and increasingly popular abroad. Another outstanding Fonseca wine is the very dry white Branco Seco. Better known internationally are the Lancer's red, white, and rosé wines, in their distinctive clay jugs, produced specifically for export.

Two other distinguished wines from the Setúbal region are João Pires, a dry white table wine from Pinhal Novo, and the Quinta da Bacalhoa, a rich red wine that is Portugal's only true cabernet sauvignon.

Nearby, on the outskirts of Vila Fresca de Azeitão, is the 16th-century **Quinta das Torres**, which has been turned into an inn and is an ideal spot for a romantic weekend (although some have found it dreary).

After Vila Fresca, take the N 10 heading back to Setúbal and within a few minutes you will come to the **Quinta da Bacalhoa**, which dates back to the end of the 15th century and was once inhabited by Afonso de Albuquerque, viceroy of India. The manor, which now belongs to an American family, has been beautifully restored. Sitwell describes it as "a lovely half-caste of the East and West." The formal gardens, with clipped boxwoods, fountains, and bamboo and fruit trees, are open to the public. Here too is a pavilion lined with 16th-century tiles. One panel, relating the story of Susannah and the Elders, 1565, is the oldest dated tile panel in the country.

It is possible to stay at the Quinta da Bacalhoa, but arrangements must be made well ahead of time because there are only three suites (six bedrooms). The owner, Thomas W. Scoville, lives in Washington, D.C., and rents the quinta, including its staff of seven, to families or groups for a fortnight or longer. Summer is usually heavily booked in this national landmark, but spring and fall can be even nicer.

Tróia

Portugal's newest holiday resort, the town of Tróia, can be a side trip or a day's excursion in itself. To get there, return to Setúbal port, where there are frequent ferries crossing the Rio Sado estuary to the narrow Tróia peninsula thrusting up from Lower Alentejo. Downtown Setúbal is a confusing maze, but if you follow avenida Luisa Todi eastward to the end, then turn right, you will come upon the Doca do Comércio, the commercial port. From here a car ferry (which also takes pedestrians, cyclists, and motorbikers) leaves every half hour for the 20-minute cruise to Tróia. Out of season the ferry goes every hour.

Tróia was known by the Romans as Cetobriga, and was an important fish-preserving town until it was swallowed up by the sea during the fifth century. Just a few years ago Tróia was the ultimate place for beachgoers seeking privacy. You had to have a private boat to get to the isthmus, where there was nothing but sand, pines, and intriguing glimpses of Roman ruins under the waters.

For those who loved the old Tróia, the high-rise apartments and hotels, the discos, cinemas, restaurants, and bars look like some kind of alien city that landed here by error. The new Tróia is for vacationers who enjoy a self-contained resort with modern comforts, entertainment, and sports facilities in a splendid, accessible site.

Generally called the Torralta Tourist Development, Tróia is really a family resort with two large aparthotels and several smaller ones. These are hotels that provide apartments—not rooms. Each apartment contains several beds, a private bath, a balcony, and a fully equipped kitchen. **Aparthotel Magnoliamar** and **Aparthotel de Tróia** have swimming pools and tennis courts, restaurants and nightclubs. The new Tróia golf course, designed by Robert Trent Jones, is one of the finest in the country. Also, every June, there's an international film festival here.

Nature buffs can still get away from it all at Tróia. The developers have kindly concentrated their constructions, at least for now, at the northern tip of the isthmus, leaving long stretches of sand dunes, pine forests, and secluded fishing villages to the south virtually untouched. Bird- and animal-watchers can sight dolphins, otters, wildcats, and all kinds of birds, including storks, herons, and eagles, in the **Sado Estuary Natural Reserve**, which covers a large part of the Sado marshes and Tróia woods.

The **Roman ruins**, dating back to the beginning of the first century A.D., lie along the Sado, about 9 km (5 miles) east of the tourist development. Archaeologists have uncovered the remains of a temple, a burial place, baths, numerous villas, and salting tanks, but much remains to be excavated.

GETTING AROUND

Because distances are short and many of Portugal's treasures are found off the beaten track, the best way to visit Lisbon's surroundings is by car. Cascais is normally only about 45 minutes from Lisbon along the scenic Marginal, or river Tagus, highway from Lisbon. Sintra takes about the same time, except during morning and evening rush hours (8:00 to 10:00 A.M. and 6:00 to 8:00 P.M.) and weekends. With the superhighway now reaching Setúbal, the trip there is about a half hour, except during the weekend rush, when it can take an hour just to get across the bridge. Even the drive to Nazaré and the northernmost reaches of the provinces takes under two hours, not counting stops.

This said, there are several caveats. Except for the few superhighways, most roads are narrow and not very good. The local drivers are often reckless and seem oblivious of the country's appallingly high accident rate. Fuel and car-rental prices are high compared to those in North America or Britain.

But do not despair. Commuter trains run all day and late into the evening along the Costa do Sol from Lisbon to the sea. It is a 45-minute ride from Lisbon's Cais do Sodré station, near the Ribeira central market, to the end of the line in Cascais. There are also frequent trains to Sintra from the Rossio station in downtown Lisbon, also about a 45-minute ride. The northern Leiria line goes from Santa Apolónia station near the Military Museum in downtown Lisbon to Obidos and Caldas da Rainha, a journey of about one hour.

In addition, the state bus company, Rodoviária Nacional (RN), goes almost everywhere, and its rates are inexpensive. The bus terminal is located at 18 avenida Casal de Ribeiro in central Lisbon. Several bus companies also organize day tours of the Lisbon environs; check with your hotel.

ACCOMMODATIONS REFERENCE

▶ **Hotel Albatroz.** Rua Frederico Arouca, 2750 **Cascais.** Tel: (01) 28-28-21.

▶ **Hotel Atlántico.** Estrada Marginal, 2765 **Estoril.** Tel: (01) 268-0270.

▶ **Quinta da Bacalhoa.** Vila Nova de Azeitão. For information/reservations contact Thomas W. Scoville, 3637 Veazey Street NW, Washington, D.C. 20008. Tel: (202) 638-2405 or (202) 686-7336.

▶ **Hotel Baia.** Avenida Marginal, 2750 **Cascais.** Tel: (01) 28-00-55.

▶ **Quinta da Capela.** Estrada de Monserrate, 2710 **Sintra.** Tel: (01) 929-0170.

▶ **Pousada do Castelo.** 2510 **Obidos.** Tel: (062) 95105.

▶ **Pousada do Castelo de Palmela.** 2950 **Palmela.** Tel: (01) 235-1226 or 235-1395.

▶ **Hotel Estoril-Sol.** Parque Palmela, 2750 **Cascais.** Tel: (01) 28-28-31.

▶ **Foz Palace Motel.** Estrada Marginal, 2500 **Foz do Arelho.** Tel: (062) 97413.

- Hotel do Guincho. Praia do Guincho, 2750 Cascais. Tel: (01) 285-0491.
- Aparthotel Magnoliamar. 2900 Tróia. Tel: (01) 44151 or 44154.
- Hotel do Mar. Rua dos Combatentes do Ultramar, 10, 2950 Sesimbra. Tel: (01) 223-3326 or 222-3422.
- Pousada do Mestre Afonso Domingues. 2440 Batalha. Tel: (044) 96260.
- Estalagem Muchaxo. Praia do Guincho, 2750 Cascais. Tel: (01) 285-0221.
- Estalagem Nossa Senhora da Guia. Estrada do Guincho, Quinta da Marinha, 2750 Cascais. Tel: (01) 28-92-39.
- Hotel Palácio. Parque do Estoril, 2765 Estoril. Tel: (01) 268-0400.
- Hotel Palácio dos Seteais. 8 rua do Bocage, 2710 Sintra. Tel: (01) 923-3200 or 923-3250.
- Pensão Ribamar. 9 rua Gomes Freire, 2450 Nazaré. Tel: (062) 46158.
- Pousada de São Filipe. Castelo de São Filipe, 2900 Setúbal. Tel: (01) 23844 or 24981.
- Quinta de São José. Freiria, 2590 Sobral de Monte Agraço (near Torres Vedras). Tel: (01) 284-4464.
- Quinta de São Thiago. Estrada de Monserrate, 2710 Sintra. Tel: (01) 923-2923.
- Hotel Tivoli. Praça da República, 2710 Sintra. Tel: (01) 923-3505 or 923-3855.
- Quinta das Torres. 2929 Vila Fresca de Azeitão. Tel: (01) 208-0001.
- Aparthotel de Tróia. 2900 Tróia. Tel: (01) 44221 or 44224.
- Aldeamento Turístico Marinha Village. Quinta da Marinha, 2750 Cascais. Tel: (01) 28-90-78 or 28-92-97.

Pousadas can be booked through Marketing Ahead, 433 Fifth Avenue, New York, N.Y. 10016; Tel: (212) 686-9213.

RIBATEJO

By Thomas de la Cal

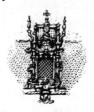

Thomas de la Cal was born in Portugal and returns there regularly from his current home in New York. He has contributed articles to Connoisseur, European Travel and Life, *and other magazines. He has also worked on documentaries about Portugal for the National Geographic Society, the BBC, and NBC.*

The Ribatejo is the geographical and agricultural heartland of Portugal. Sandwiched between the coastal province of Estremadura to the west and the rolling expanse of the Alentejo to the east, this triangular region roughly to the northeast of Lisbon is known for its bulls and bullfighters, horses and horsemen, wines and large estates, shrines and religious militants. It is also the guardian of genteel Portuguese values such as chivalry and honor.

The Ribatejo owes its name, economy, topography, and character to the river Tagus (*Tejo* in Portuguese), which originates in Spain and runs in a southwesterly direction through Portugal before spilling into the Atlantic Ocean 16 miles west of Lisbon. Legend has it that on his epic journey Ulysses ventured up the Tagus. In the millennia that followed, the fertile banks of the river drew northern and southern invaders alike, including Crusaders from Cornwall, France, and the Rhineland, who were given lands in the Ribatejo in return for their help in liberating Lisbon from the Moors. Before the construction of dams in the 20th century to divert part of the flow to irrigate the surrounding farmland, the river was navigable all the way to the border with Spain, and served as an important commercial route between the two countries. Today, despite the dams, the Tagus continues to bring devastating floods that transform the small towns on the plain into mini-Venices. The people of the region have learned to live with the unpredictable Tagus, making the best of the good years and facing the bad with stoicism and grace.

The Ribatejo is divided into three distinct areas: the *campo,* the *barrio,* and the *charneca.* The *campo,* which is also known as the *Leziria* or *bord-d'água* (by the water), is a rich alluvial plain where irrigated fields of rice and wheat, vineyards, and vegetable gardens thrive. It also boasts vast pastures that bloom with a rainbow of colors in the spring, produce most of the country's beef, and serve as grazing land for the horses and wild bulls so dear to the heart of the typical Portuguese male. The bulls are tended by colorful *campinos* (herdsmen) generally dressed in white shirt, red cummerbund, scarlet waistcoat with silver buttons, green stocking cap, thick white stockings, black breeches, and a black wool jacket usually draped ceremoniously over the shoulders. These Portuguese cowboys are usually armed with *varas* (wooden poles) to help in handling the bulls. Not surprisingly, it was here on the vast estates of the *campo* that Portuguese bullfighting had its origins. The wealth of the region has helped develop a basically happy people, reflected in their lively folk dances and music.

In contrast, the *barrio,* on the hilly west bank of the Tagus, is wilder. Large areas, particularly in the north, are covered with sagebrush and ferns. Nonetheless, olives, figs, and grapes are grown where nature permits. Some of Portugal's best wines are produced in the *barrio.* The people of this area are more serious, dress in darker colors, and have slower-paced dances than their neighbors in the *campo.* They are also more religious. This may be due in part to the fact that during the 12th century the *barrio* served as a critical line of defense for the Christians in the north against the Moors who controlled large tracts to the south. The remains of a string of castles and monasteries built by the Knights Templar, a military order that reached its peak of power and influence between the 12th and 14th centuries, still dot its hills and rivers. And the fervor has not died down: One of the largest centers of religious worship in the world today—Fátima—is situated in the *barrio.*

The *charneca,* the flat southern fringe of the Ribatejo, borders the east bank of the Tagus estuary. Its poor, sandy soil sustains pine and eucalyptus trees with an occasional vineyard or grainfield. The *charneca* is also called the *mar de palha* (straw sea) because of its extensive grasslands, and includes the Reserva Natural do Tejo (Tagus Nature Reserve), which stretches 20 miles from the mouth of the river to Vila Franca de Xira. The reserve serves as a resting station for migrating birds such as flamingos and wild ducks, on their way between North Africa and northern Europe. Pollution from neighboring cement factories and steel and paper mills, however, is taking its toll on the flora and fauna of the *charneca:* Once-plentiful dolphins have been driven away, a thriving oyster industry has been wiped out, and the few remaining fishing communities in the area are endangered.

The route mapped out below begins in Lisbon and heads northeast up the west bank of the Tagus past bull country and then through wine country and the city of Santarém to the former Templar capital of Tomar. After a detour to Fátima, we explore the region generally south of Tomar, cross the Tagus at Abrantes, and follow the river down the other side in a southwesterly direction over the Ribatejo plain back toward Lisbon. The route ends in the heart of bull country, at the border of the *charneca* and across the river from Vila Franca de Xira.

MAJOR INTEREST

Fine regional food and wine
Spectacular vistas of the Tagus river and plain
  (from Santarém and Abrantes)

Festivals
Bullfight festival at Vila Franca de Xira
Annual Feira do Ribatejo at Santarém
Golegã's national horse show
Tomar's biennial feast of the Tabuleiros

Rota do Vinho (wine route)
Santarém's churches and museums
Convento de Cristo of the Knights Templar in
  Tomar
Unspoiled beauty of the lower Zêzere river valley
Shrine of Our Lady of Fátima
Fairy-tale castle of Almourol

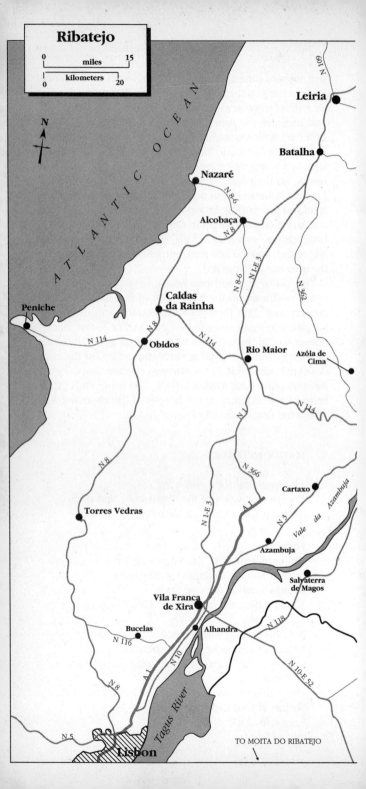

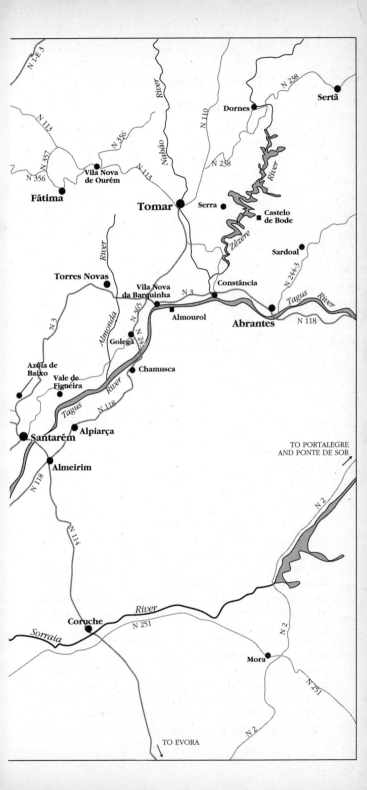

The Food and Wine of the Ribatejo

The Ribatejo, the second largest wine-growing region in Portugal, is known for its great selection of fine everyday wines. The British have known and drunk them since the 12th century. In fact, Shakespeare alludes to them in *King Henry VI, Part Two,* when Horner fortifies himself with a cup of *charneco* before fighting the tragic duel with his apprentice. The white Bucellas, whose grapes grow on the hillsides of the Trançāo river valley just north of Lisbon, became popular with Wellington's officers during the Peninsular Wars against the French. It is not known for certain whether it was the Teutonic Knights, who settled the area in the 12th century, or the powerful Marquês de Pombal, the country's prime minister from 1756 to 1777, who first introduced the Riesling-style grapes to the valley. What is certain, however, is that the soil and climate produce a wine that is quite different from that of its native Germany. The Arinto and Esgana Cāo grapes, grown in a lime-and-sulfur-rich soil, yield a straw-colored, slightly acidic wine that goes well with fish and fowl. The older reserve Bucellas are less tart and more popular among connoisseurs. At the Camilo Alves cellars (which also bottle the heavier Dāo and smoother Bairrada wines sold under the Caves Velhas banner) in the town of Bucelas, between Lisbon and Vila Franca de Xira, some of these finer wines are stored in large oak barrels.

Farther north, you will encounter full-bodied reds in the *barrio*'s Cartaxo district and smoother claret-styled Serradayres wines from the slopes of the Serra do Aire (Mountain of the Air), which borders the Estremadura. Fruitier wines can be found on the east bank of the Tagus around Alpiarça and Almeirim, while stronger spirits such as the wine-based *aguardentes* (brandies) and humbler *bagaços* are fashioned in the former Templar capital of Tomar, located in the Nabāo river valley north of Santarém.

The food of the Ribatejo is as varied and hearty as its wines. The river Tagus yields a bounty of fish, which is the principal ingredient of the delicious concoction known as *sopa de peixe* (fish soup). Regional delicacies include Cartaxo's *açorda de sável,* a shad soup laced with oil, garlic, and coriander and thickened with bread; and Golegā's *ensopado de enguias* (eel stew). Farther north, the Nabão and Zêzere rivers are known for their *lampreia* (lamprey), which is stewed in its own blood and red wine, with surprisingly delicious results.

Meat, of course, is popular in the southern ranch areas, where charcoal-grilled *entrecosto* (steak) and wood-fired *espetadas na vara de loureiro* (kebabs on a laurel stick) are the local favorites. The smoked *toucinho* (bacon) of the *charneca* graces all varieties of soups and bean dishes, as do the rice-filled *morcela de arroz* (blood sausages) of the northeast. *Borrego* (young male lamb) and *cabrito* (kid), however, are the favorite meats, particularly in the *barrio,* where they are grilled, fried, stewed, and roasted.

Like their countrymen in general, Ribatejanos are addicted to sweets, a taste they inherited from the Moors and developed in the convents of the region. *Fatias de Tomar* (egg-yolk sponge shaped into little ovals, then bathed in cinnamon syrup), *tigeladas* (firm yet foamy custards baked in earthenware dishes and decorated with dustings of cinnamon), and *palha de Abrantes,* nuggets of almond paste covered with golden "thread eggs," which resemble nothing so much as bits of straw (*palha*), are some of the diet-wrecking delectables of the region. The fruits of the *campo* are a less caloric alternative, particularly the *morangos* (strawberries) of Almeirim and the green-and-black *tendral* melon and white-and-yellow Ribatejano melons, sold fresh from roadside stands during the summer months. Cheese lovers should try the goat and sheep varieties made in the mountain areas. The best known are the small herb-scented sheep cheeses of Tomar, which taste of wood smoke and nuts.

VILA FRANCA DE XIRA

Situated on the west bank of the river Tagus, 32 km (20 miles) northeast of Lisbon, this city of modern apartment blocks and smokestacks is bypassed by travellers most of the year. However, during the first weekend of July visitors flock to the *colete encarnado*—the major event of the Ribatejo's bullfighting season. The festivities, which are named after the scarlet waistcoat of the *campino,* include bull running and herding competitions in the streets, bullfighting in the town's arena, displays of the region's lively folk dancing, which is similar to the Spanish fandango, and outdoor snacking on grilled sardines, pork steaks, and chicken.

The *corrida,* or bullfight, originated in both Portugal and Spain in the 16th century. Introduced by noble *cavaleiros,* or horsemen, bullfighting began as a way to train horses and men for battle. Over time, however, it became a popular spectator sport. In the early 18th century the Portuguese and Spanish styles of bullfighting began to diverge after King Philip V of Spain took a dislike to the sport and frowned upon the nobility taking part in it. The Spanish public went on to lavish their attention on the *matador* (literally, "killer"), who was generally of the peasant class and who fought on foot. The Portuguese, meanwhile, kept the *cavaleiro* as their main attraction. By the late 18th century the first official bullrings began to appear in Portugal, and horsemen such as the Marquês de Marialva became heroes of the national sport. (The word *marialva* later became a synonym for masculine pride and bravery.)

Portuguese bullfighting has not been without its controversies. In fact, ever since the late 18th century an always passionate and sometimes violent argument over whether or not to kill the bull in the ring has divided bullfighting aficionados. Since 1933 a ban on such killing has been in effect, and heavy fines are imposed on those who disobey the law. Critics argue that the ban deprives the bull of a noble death in the heat of battle, leaving him instead to be butchered in the slaughterhouse hours later. It should be mentioned, however, that bulls that have distinguished themselves in the ring are allowed to live; their superficial wounds inflicted by the *farpas* (darts) are treated, and then they are put to pasture in order to improve the breed.

The Portuguese bullfight is a lively and spectacular affair. In it, a *cavaleiro* dressed in 18th-century livery charges the bull and places the *farpas,* or long darts, of varying sizes in the back of its neck, all the while trying to avoid the horns of the enraged animal. Both horse and rider have to draw upon their tremendous skill and years of practice working together as a team. Once the *cavaleiro* has placed a minimum of four *farpas,* he turns the ring over to the *forcados,* a group of eight men dressed in rustic 19th-century garb—short jacket, breeches, white stockings, and green or red tasseled stocking caps—who confront the bull in single file to perform a *pega.* The *cara* (face) at the front of the line taunts the bull until it charges. When man and beast are about to collide, the *cara* leaps over the bull's horns, wraps his arms around its neck, and holds on for dear life. The other men then jump on the bull and try to bring the pair to a halt. More often than not, the bull manages to fling the *cara* in the air like a matchstick and pummel the rest of the crew. Developed in the 18th century by ranch hands and named after the pitchforks they used, *forcados* are unique to Portugal (those of Vila Franca, Santarém, and Lisbon are considered the best). The *forcados* are not paid for their bone-breaking efforts, but being a *forcado* is the ultimate test of bravery for a young Portuguese male, a sort of coming-of-age ritual.

Bulls are raised in the salty marshlands of the Ribatejo (ocean tides push as far as 30 miles upriver) as well as in the wooded areas of the *charneca* and the Alentejo. The young *toros bravos* (wild bulls) are separated from their mothers at an early age and, with a minimum of human contact so they don't become wise to the sport, are tested for their courage. At these *tentas* (tests), the bulls are prodded with long poles or challenged with a cape to see how they react. The most spirited bulls are selected and separated from the more docile ones, which are then slaughtered for their meat.

Also of special interest in this area is the short, stocky Lusitano horse, named after the pre-Roman tribes of Portugal, which has been esteemed for its quick reflexes and courage. (Its legendary maneuverability is due to the position of its hind legs, which are tucked well underneath the body axis. This gives the horse excellent balance and allows it to stop on a dime and accelerate quickly.) Reputed to have been the first saddle horse in Europe, the Lusitano was prized by the Romans, who established remount depots in Portugal to supply their cavalry with the breed. In the 14th century King Fernando established laws regulating the breeding and raising of all Portuguese horses. When nobles were not off fighting their rivals or the Moors, they and their horses trained by pitting themselves against wild bulls. Less lethal equestrian games were also performed at court and on large estates throughout the country. The Napoleonic invasion in the early 19th century practically destroyed the Lusitano breed, which was reduced further with the coming of mechanized warfare. After the First World War, horses were retired from the battlefield and the emphasis shifted to the bullring.

Today horse farms in the Ribatejo are spearheading a revival of the Lusitano. Enthusiasts can visit the **Centro Equestre da Leziria Grande** at Povos, between Vila Franca and Alhandra. Coming north from Lisbon on the E 80, get off at the first Vila Franca exit and swing back south on the N 10. The center is one kilometer (about half a mile) from the exit. Re-creating the elegance of the 18th-century Portuguese aristocracy, horsemen at the center dress in satin livery and perform beautiful equestrian ballets that combine both classical and popular dressage. The center, which also breeds and sells horses, offers typical Ribatejano lunches to groups and stages bullfighting spectacles in its outdoor bullring. Call ahead to find out the schedule of events and to make reservations; Tel: (63) 22781.

Portuguese horses can also be admired at the **Estação Zootécnica Nacional** (the national stud farm) at Quinta da Fonte Bela, outside Santarém, as well as at the annual national horse show in Golegã in November. At the latter you will also see patrician landowners dressed in traditional riding dress, which includes flat-rimmed hats and tight-fitting waistcoats and pants, competing in horse and carriage competitions.

Of historical interest in the Vila Franca de Xira area are the Torres Vedras defensive lines south of Vila Franca on the N 10 at **Alhandra**, which were built by Wellington to defend Lisbon against the French in 1810. At the end of the lines is a statue of Hercules, a tribute to the defenders who held against the French.

THE ROTA DO VINHO

This pleasant wine route from Vila Franca follows the N 1 north to the N 3, which traverses a wide vine-combed plain flanked by the rolling hills and olive groves of the *barrio* on one side and the Vale da Azambuja and the river Tagus on the other. The town of **Azambuja**, 19 km (12 miles) from Vila Franca, was given to Childe Rolim, son of the Count of Chester, in the 12th century by King Afonso I in return for his assistance in liberating Lisbon from the Moors. Today Azambuja is a prosperous farming town with a quaint main square.

About 13 km (8 miles) farther along the N 3, in the heart of the wine country, is the town of **Cartaxo**. Here you can park at the largo Vasco da Gama beside the bullring and walk to the other sights. Directly northwest, via rua Serpa Pinto, is the largo São João Baptista, a charming square where there is an ornate 16th-century

Manueline Cross and the **Capela do Senhor dos Passos**, which is all that remains of the former Solar dos Sousa Lobatos, where Wellington installed his headquarters during the winter of 1810–1811. Southwest of the chapel, behind rua de Batalhoz, is the **Museu Rural e do Vinho** (Rural and Wine Museum), on rua José Ribeiro da Costa, where you can savor (and buy) an assortment of regional wines, inspect traditional wine-making and agricultural implements, and shop for regional handicrafts, including earthenware pottery with hand-painted wine motifs.

On the eastern outskirts of Cartaxo is the 17th-century **Solar dos Chavões** manor house and restaurant, the ideal spot to partake of the region's full-bodied, fruity wines and sample the regional cuisine—pork, fried eel, *sopa de peixe,* and Cartaxo's very own *açorda de sável.* This former home of the counts of Unhão is surrounded by pines and vineyards. To get there, take the road to Santana for about 2 km (1.25 miles) before turning left toward Vila Chã de Ourique. The signposted property is on the right, or eastern, side of the road about 2 km north.

SANTAREM

Santarém is on the N 3, just 13 km (8 miles) north of Cartaxo. The unofficial capital of the Ribatejo, the town is also known as the *varanda* (verandah) of the region because it sits on seven hills overlooking the Tagus river and its fertile plain. It also has a number of interesting churches, has witnessed a host of miracles, and stages lively food and folk fairs.

The origins of Santarém are shrouded in legend. According to one account, Ulysses visited Lisbon in 1215 B.C., had an affair with Prince Gorgoris's daughter Calipso, and left before their son, Abidis, was born. The infuriated prince had the baby placed inside a basket and thrown into the waters of the Tagus. The high tide carried the basket upriver to the present site of Santarém, where it was discovered by a she-wolf who raised the child as her own. Years later, the boy was captured by royal hunters and taken to the court of the prince, where his true identity was revealed to his mother when she noticed the child's unique birthmark. Gorgoris, who had not been able to father a male heir, relented and welcomed Abidis back into the fold. Later still, after the youth had ascended to his grandfather's throne, he had a town built on the site where he had been found by the prince's hunters and named it Esca-Abidis, or food of Abidis. Later, invaders from the north called the town Escalabis.

Santarém's current name dates from the seventh century. According to another legend, there lived north of Santarém, in present-day Tomar, a beautiful nun by the name of Iria. Her beauty was such that it caught the eye of Britaldo, the son of the governor. Failing to gain her love, Britaldo took to his bed with a high fever. When Iria visited the young man and cured him by placing her hand on his forehead, her reputation as a healer was made. Father Remigio, her tutor, also could not control his passion for her. When his advances were rebuffed, he slipped the young nun a potion that swelled her stomach, making her appear pregnant. Hearing that the nun was pregnant, an enraged Britaldo had her murdered and her body thrown into the waters of the Nabão, where it eventually floated down into the Tagus and washed up at Escalabis. The priest eventually repented and confessed his sin. Hearing about the tragedy, the king changed the name of the town where she had washed up from Ecalabis to Santa Iria. The Moors altered the name to Xantarim, and the later Christians called it Santarém.

There is a statue of Santa Iria in the old riverside neighborhood of Ribeira, on the N 114 toward Almeirim. The statue, which stands on a pedestal, was commissioned by Dom Dinis in the 14th century. During floods it serves as a marker to gauge the water level. It was generally believed that if the waters reached the toes of the statue, everything downstream, including Lisbon, would be washed away. Flood waters reached the feet in 1979, but Lisbon was spared.

From the Phoenicians to the Romans, from northern to southern hordes, the strategic importance of Santarém has attracted traders and invaders. The Moors, who stayed the longest, were finally expelled in 1147 by King Afonso Henriques and a band of daring knights, who scaled the city walls under cover of night and surprised the sleeping garrison. From the 13th through the 16th centuries Santarém was popular with the Burgundian and Avis dynasties, who enjoyed the pleasures of the hunt in the surrounding area. Royalist and patriotic, it was the last city to lay down its arms in 1580, when Philip II of Spain invaded and captured Portugal. In 1810 it was taken by French forces under Massena, who then plundered its churches and palaces. During the Guerra dos Dois Irmãos, or War of the Two Brothers (1831 to 1834), the absolutist king Dom Miguel established his final headquarters in Santarém. (He was defeated outside Lisbon by forces loyal to his brother, Pedro.)

Most of the important sights in Santarém are within walking distance of one another. You can park in the northeastern corner of town beside the colorful tiled market across from the town hall and enter the old quarter through the remains of a Gothic tower to the south. The 17th-century **Igreja do Seminário**, a former Jesuit college that now serves as the city's cathedral, is the most prominent building on praça Sá da Bandeira. Vestiges of its palatial beginnings (it was built over a royal palace) can be detected in the elaborate cornices and windows above the Baroque façade. The interior, mostly marble, is cold and somber. The 19th-century Portuguese writer Almeida Garrett called it reactionary architecture: "There is no soul, no genius, no spirit in those heavy masses, devoid of elegance or simplicity; but there is a certain grandeur that imposes; a solid base, a calculated symmetry, cold proportions which reveal something of the century and the order which it characterized." Of a similarly cold nature was the 14th-century execution that took place outside the church: According to legend, King Pedro I oversaw the extraction of the hearts of two men who, following orders issued by Pedro's father, who was worried his son would be influenced by the Spanish, had murdered his beloved Galician mistress Inês de Castro.

A more pleasant experience can be had directly south at the **Casa d'Avo**, rua Serpa Pinto, 62, a beckoning tea and snack house lodged in what was formerly a palatial town house where the city's doyennes meet to trade the latest gossip and nibble on freshly baked Portuguese and English pastries. Farther down the street, on Visconde Serra do Pilar square, is the elegant **Igreja de Marvila** with its ornate 16th-century Manueline doorway and lavish interior, which boasts walls covered with colorful 17th-century neo-Mudejar tiles.

Veering east onto rua Conselheiro Figueiredo Leal, you'll come across the **Museu Arqueológico de São João de Alporão**, which is housed in a 13th-century Romanesque-Gothic church and contains treasures dating back to the days of the Roman occupation. The most impressive pieces, however, are the stone carvings taken from the churches, houses, and palaces of the area, particularly the beautifully carved balcony by Mateus Fernandes above the entrance and the Flamboyant Gothic tomb of Duarte de Meneses, Count of Viana. It must have been these and other works that led Almeida Garrett to comment that "Santarém is a book written in stone." The tomb was built to house a tooth (item number 615)—all that remained of the count after he and a small band of Portuguese knights were hacked to pieces by the Moors. The knights were in the process of covering the retreat of King Afonso V during his disastrous campaign in North Africa.

Across the street is the 16th-century **Torre das Cabaças**, in which King Manuel had eight arches built to represent the eight senators, or *cabaças* ("gourds"), of the city who had, according to him, misused his funds on this nondescript clocktower. Farther east, at the end of the avenida 5 de Outubro, you come to the **Portas do Sol** (Gates of the Sun), which were part of the former city walls. The gates open onto lovely gardens that overlook the river Tagus and the Ribatejo plain. Before entering the grounds, look for the stone crypt jutting out of the **Igreja de Santa Maria da Alcáçova**, which is the final resting place of the Jewish wife of a Christian knight who had asked to be buried beside her. The Catholic authorities granted the knight's wishes by placing her tomb beside his—but outside the church. On your left as you enter the gardens are the remains (two Gothic doors) of a former royal palace that was destroyed by the earthquake of 1755. Excavations in the southern corner of the gardens have uncovered what are believed to be the remains of Phoenician dye vats.

The snug **Portas do Sol** restaurant is lodged in the former wood-and-brick guardhouse overlooking the gardens. Its relaxed atmosphere and good food draw city officials and local intellectuals alike. Customers can enjoy grilled food on an outdoor patio during the summer.

The lovely 14th-century **Igreja da Graça**, southwest of the Portas do Sol, has an exquisite rose window, carved from a single piece of stone, that deftly makes use of the sunlight to give the appearance of glass. The church, which has been restored to its original Gothic appearance with the removal of all the extraneous elements added over the years, contains several important tombstones, including that of Pedro Alvares Cabral, the discoverer of Brazil. Cabral's discovery, made by accident in 1500 when his ship was blown off course on his way around Africa to India, was not deemed important at the time, partly because of a behind-the-scenes smear campaign by his archrival Vasco da Gama (which also explains why his simple, unassuming tombstone does not record his discovery).

On the other hand, the 15th-century tomb of Dom Pedro de Meneses is a sumptuous display of wealth and power, and contains the remains of Dom Pedro and his third wife surmounted by the carved reclining figures of the Dom and his first wife; their daughter paid for the sumptuous tomb. The word *aleo,* inscribed in the stone, is significant. One day, while Dom Pedro was playing the cricket-like game of *truque* with the king, news arrived of a revolt in Ceuta in Morocco. Dom Pedro lifted his *aleo,* the club used in the game, and told the king not to worry; he would go to Ceuta and restore order there with the *aleo.* And so he did. Dom Pedro's *aleo* became a symbol of power in Ceuta and to this day hangs on the statue of Our Lady of Africa there.

The sacristy of the 14th-century **Igreja do Santíssimo Milagre**, next door on rua Brancamp Freire, holds a crystal flask that is said to contain the blood of Christ. According to the 13th-century legend surrounding the flask, a young Catholic woman asked a Jewish *curandeira* (faith healer) how to stop her husband from beating her. Told to return with a holy wafer, the young woman feigned taking communion in church, wrapped the wafer in a cloth, and started back to the old *curandeira*'s home. Before she arrived, however, blood began to ooze out of the cloth. Terrified, the young woman rushed home and hid her bleeding bundle in a chest by her bed. But during the night, she and her husband were awakened by rays of light streaming from the chest. A priest was summoned and found, upon opening the bundle, that the wafer had been miraculously converted into a glass flask containing blood. During the French occupation of the early 19th century, the flask was taken to Lisbon for safekeeping. When the French departed, however, the people of Lisbon refused to return it, so a delegation from Santarém visited Lisbon and told its inhabitants that a man wearing boots with cork soles would walk across the Tagus at midnight. As all of Lisbon was at the dock waiting to witness this miracle, the delegation from Santarém took advantage of the opportunity to recover their flask.

The **Campo da Feira** is located near the bullring in the western corner of the town. It is here that the Feira Nacional de Agricultura, more commonly called the Feira do Ribatejo, is held. The one-week event, which begins on the first Friday in June, includes horse shows, riding competitions, bullfights, *campino* races, bullrunning, and folk-dancing competitions. This is a colorful, popular fair, and accommodations are virtually impossible to find while it is running. But Lisbon is less than an hour away via the N 114 and E 1 *auto-estrada,* so commuting is relatively easy. Another popular event is the 12-day Festival Internacional de Gastronomia (International Food Festival), held between the end of September and November 1, at which you can savor regional cuisines as well as admire folk arts and handicrafts from all over Portugal, including the Azores and Madeira. The exposition is housed in one of the big fair buildings, where each province sets up its own elaborate booth. Most are decorated to look like a local town or house or country estate, and each showcases the area's most famous foodstuffs, wines, pottery, cookware, and other crafts. (Items are also for sale.) In addition, each day a different province prepares a regional feast for everyone at the festival. The Alentejo, for example, might bring the chef in from Fialho in Evora to prepare *açorda à Alentejana* (bread-thickened, egg-drop, garlic soup greened with fresh coriander), *porco à Alentejana* (braised pork and clams), and *queijadas de Evora* (little cheese tarts). Local folk dancers (in costume) and musicians perform throughout the meal, recipes are given out, and the local wines are served.

Two of Santarém's most popular restaurants are located on the fairgrounds. Don't be put off by **O Mal Cozinhado**'s name (Badly Cooked). This bistro, situated on the north side of the fair grounds, is known for its regional menu (which includes fresh bull from the ring next door), rustic decor, thatched bar, and checkered table cloths, and reflects the rural ambience of the area. Impromptu *fado* sessions are held on Friday evenings, when reservations are recommended (Tel: 043-23584). The songs here are slightly more spirited than the mournful chants sung in the old quarter of Lisbon. The large air-conditioned **Restaurante Castizo** (the term for a local man) is next door to the equestrian ring. Decorated to look like the courtyard of a typical Ribatejo ranch, the restaurant has a mixed menu featuring such regional specialties as *caldeirada* (fish stew), *sopa de peixe,* and *feijão com entrecosto* (grilled steak and kidney beans).

Before leaving the city, take the time to see the 13th-century **Igreja de Santa Clara**, on avenida Gago Coutinho e Sacadura Cabral, in the northeastern part of the city. Apart from an elaborate Gothic tomb with Renaissance additions—the final resting place of Dona Leonor, the daughter of Fernando III—the former Franciscan convent contains interesting murals (said to depict part of the order's secret initiation rites) uncovered during restoration work in the 1940s. There was a tunnel from the convent to the former **Mosteiro de São Francisco**, but it has not been unearthed.

The 17th-century **Igreja de Santa Iria**, with its unusual Gothic Cross, stands on a promontory overlooking the riverside section of Ribeira. Legend has it that a noble of the area convinced a young shepherdess to surrender her virginity by promising to marry her. When the nobleman failed to comply with his end of the bargain, the distressed and by then pregnant shepherdess presented her case to a magistrate, who proceeded to summon both parties to the church. The shepherdess asked the image on the Cross for a sign to show she was telling the truth. Suddenly, the right arm of Jesus slipped from its position on the Cross and pointed accusingly at the nobleman, who then agreed to the marriage.

Staying in the Santarém Area

Accommodations in Santarém proper do not do justice to its monuments. The **Hotel Abides**, a 27-room establishment in the old quarter near the praça Sá da Bandeira and the Casa d'Avo tea house, is clean and boasts pure country charm and service. Its ground-floor restaurant is decorated with regional pottery, tiles, farm implements, and bullfighting artifacts. There are also four manor houses with guest rooms in the vicinity of Santarém. The 19th-century **Quinta da Sobreira**, owned by the Count of Penha Garcia, is located about 10 km (6 miles) northeast of Santarém off the N 365. The three rooms with private baths are decorated with antiques, and guests are also given access to the large living room, a well-equipped kitchen, a pool, and riding facilities. About 3 km (2 miles) northwest of town off the N 362 is the large agricultural estate of **Vale de Lobos**, in Azóia de Baixo. It was here that the Portuguese historian Alexandre Herculano spent the last years of his life (1867 to 1877), running a farm. Accommodations are spartan, but the home and large grounds retain their 19th-century charm. The **Casa dos Cedros**, farther up the valley, in Azóia de Cima, has nice grounds and three comfortable bedrooms, while the medium-sized **Casal da Torre** manor house is situated on the southern outskirts of Santarém and has three large bedrooms, several salons, a kitchen, and a garden.

If you like horses, the **Estação Zootécnica Nacional**, the national stud farm at Quinta da Fonte Bela, 7 km (4 miles) southwest of Santarém via the N 3, will appeal to your equestrian fancies. The government-run farm lends out its stallions to horse breeders with registered mares, and also schools horses in the art of dressage. In addition to Portuguese breeds (Lusitano and Alter), the Estação raises Arab, Andalusian, and English thoroughbreds.

The towns of Almeirim and Alpiarça on the east bank of the Tagus, about 7 km (4 miles) from Santarém via the N 114, are also possible excursions (see below for descriptions of both).

Golegã

This quaint town of whitewashed houses sits on a high plain above the river Almonda, 31 km (19 miles) north of Santarém via the N 365. It was named, so the story goes, after a *galega* (Galician) woman who ran an inn where King Afonso Henriques stayed between military campaigns in the area. Some historians disputed the story, but that did not stop the town fathers from making a woman the centerpiece of Golegã's coat of arms.

The handsome 16th-century Manueline façade of the **Igreja Matriz** was designed by Boytaca, the genius behind the fabulous Manueline monasteries of Jerónimos in Belém and Batalha, near Fátima. The church is on the rua do Campo; you'll see it as you enter town on the road from Santarém. Directly west, on rua José Farinha Relvas, is the **Atelier Fotográfico de Carlos Relvas**, in the elegant Victorian home of the former Portuguese statesman, farmer, and amateur photographer after whom the museum is named. In Relvas's former studio is a collection of early photographic equipment and some of his landscapes and portraits. Open daily (closed at lunchtime) except Mondays.

Golegã is also known as the equestrian mecca of Portugal. Its annual **Feira Nacional do Cavalo** (formerly called the Feira de São Martinho) is held during the first fortnight in November and draws horse enthusiasts, breeders, and bullfighters from every region of the country. The horses are paraded around the fairgrounds and compete in all kinds of events, including carriage races. The riders wear tight-fitting Ribatejano riding clothes and flat-rimmed hats. Cool nights are made more appealing with roasted chestnuts and *água-pé* (foot water), which is derived from the skins and pulp left after the grapes have been pressed up to three times. Mixed with water and left to ferment for two or three days, this is a powerful drink.

If you want to mingle with the equestrian crowd and the local landowners, head for the "**Central**" restaurant at largo da Imaculada Conceição. Housed in the former residence of one of Portugal's premier horsemen and bullfighters, Manuel dos Santos, the restaurant is known more for its bullfighting and equestrian decor and atmosphere than for its food. House specialties are large steaks and *açorda de sável,* porridgy, bread-thickened shad soup spiced with coriander and garlic.

The **Quinta da Cardiga**, owned by the wealthy Sommer family, is a magnificent sprawling estate on the banks of the Tagus, 4 km (2.5 miles) north of Golegã, just off the N 365. Famed for its beauty as well as its wine and cheeses, the estate is surrounded by forests and vineyards. The house has an elegant Italian façade and its own private chapel with a 16th-century door and several towers with glass-enclosed cupolas. The property was originally owned by the Knights Templar and came into private hands in the 19th century, when religious orders were banned. The public can visit the estate and, in season, buy its produce.

Leaving Golegã for Tomar, take the N 365 north for 4 km (2.5 miles) to the N 3 junction, where you connect with the N 10. The steeple of the **church of Nossa Senhora da Assunção** is to the west 2 km (1.25 miles) down the road at Atalaia. If you have time, stop and examine the arcaded doorway of this Renaissance church, along with its colorful tiled interior of figurative and geometric designs.

TOMAR

Tomar, with its cobbled Medieval streets, ancient waterwheels, and parks, lies on the bucolic banks of the river Nabão, 135 km (84 miles) north of Lisbon. The crenellated battlements of a castle erected in 1160 by

Gualdim Pais, grand master of the Order of the Knights Templar in Portugal, dominate a hill above the town. Behind the castle walls is the Convento de Cristo, the former headquarters of the Templar order, and its successor, the Portuguese Order of Christ.

The Knights Templar were established in Jerusalem during the Second Crusade (1119) by French knights who vowed to defend the Holy Sepulcher, protect pilgrims, and fight the Moors. At its peak the order had over 20,000 members and 9,000 castles, estates, and manor houses, and it controlled one of the largest banking concerns in Europe. In 1260 the Knights Templar broke up into three groups—knights, priests, and men-at-arms—and soon made enemies in the Church hierarchy; local prelates resented that the order was answerable only to the Pope. The Knights' wealth and power were also viewed as a threat by various sovereigns in Europe. In 1307 Philip V of France had the order's properties confiscated and its members arrested and accused of heresy, idolatry, and homosexuality. In 1312, when the order was disbanded by Pope Clement V under pressure from Philip, many of its members took refuge in Portugal. King Dinis, who was sympathetic to the banished order, found a way to circumvent the ban in 1320, by creating the *Ordem de Cristo* (Order of Christ). The new order assumed most of the trappings and properties of the disbanded Knights Templar, and Tomar became the organization's headquarters.

The new Order of Christ played a significant role in the great discoveries of the 15th century. Prince Henry the Navigator, its most famous member, funded many of his explorations from the order's coffers, and the caravels under his command were emblazoned with its Cross. In the 16th century King João III converted the Knights into monks and joined the three Portuguese orders (Cristo, Avis, and Santiago) under one banner. The 19th century saw the demise of the order. In 1810 the Convento de Cristo was sacked by Napoleon's armies. The final blow was delivered in 1834, with the disbanding of all religious orders in Portugal. Squatters moved into the abandoned monastery and remained there until this century, when it was turned into a national monument. There are stories and books written about a lost Templar treasure buried somewhere on the grounds. The fortress convent and the Templar are described in Umberto Eco's novel *Foucault's Pendulum*.

The Convento de Cristo

The monastery (built over a period of six centuries, from the 12th to the 17th) is an impressive structure. The remains of this sprawling complex, which is surrounded by a 12th-century wall containing stones taken from the ruins of the town on the site, include a huge bell tower, a rotunda, seven cloisters, and a church. Although the lavish gold furnishings of the monastery have long disappeared, the building still contains some of the most impressive stonework in the country, designed by such 16th-century Portuguese masters as Diogo de Arruda and Diogo de Torralva. The genius behind the ornate 16th-century Plateresque doorway, however, was the Spaniard known in Portugal as João do Castilho.

The religious nerve center of the monastery, the neo-Byzantine **charola** (rotunda), consists of eight pillars supporting a two-story octagonal structure crowned by a cupola and was designed after the Holy Sepulcher in Jerusalem. (Knights of the Order are said to have heard mass inside the rotunda mounted on horses.) After it was damaged by lightning, King Manuel had the *charola* restored with Manueline flair. The **main cloister**, the 16th-century Claustro dos Filipes, was built during the reign of King João III. Legend has it that João was so upset when his father, Manuel, married Leonor, the woman he, João, loved, that he disavowed his father's cherished Manueline style and looked elsewhere for inspiration. Historians point out, however, that Portugal's Golden Age was winding down and that the exuberant Manueline style that characterized it was in decline anyway.

Philip II of Spain is said to have been crowned king of Portugal in the main cloister in 1581, after he took advantage of Portugal's disastrous campaign in Morocco. The tiny holes in the pavement around the fountain, which was designed by Diogo de Torralva and used to be fed by an aqueduct, capture excess water and channel it into an underlying cistern. There are also several rooms under the cloister where initiation rites were carried out by the monks and where the luckless souls suspected of heresy were tortured during the Inquisition. The tomb of Balthazar de Faria, who introduced the Inquisition to Portugal during the reign of João III, is discreetly hidden in the upper terrace of the northeastern ablutions cloister.

From the terrace of the cloister of Santa Bárbara

(which is reached by a spiral staircase in the main cloister) you can admire the magnificent **Manueline chapter window** sculpted by Diogo de Arruda. The window, with its array of natural and maritime motifs, is considered not only the best example of Manueline art in Portugal, but also the most allegorical tribute to the Portuguese discoveries. Ropes, anchors, masts, shells, driftwood, nets, and even the Old Man of the Sea are carved in the stone of the window, and the artichokes lining it are a reminder that the Portuguese navy used them as a source of vitamin C to combat scurvy. The British Order of the Garter and the Golden Fleece, bestowed on Prince Henry the Navigator (his mother was a Lancaster), are represented by a chain and a ribbon encircling the two turrets flanking the window. Also carved in the window are the royal emblems of Manuel I (a blazon and armillary sphere) and the Cross of the Order of Christ, the two powers that made the Age of Discovery possible. The Convento de Cristo is open every day but is closed on holidays and at lunchtime.

Around in Tomar

Tomar proper was built over the Roman city of Nabancia (from which the river Nabão derived its name). Laid out in the form of a cross by Prince Henry the Navigator, its Medieval quarter, with **praça da República** at its center, is located on the west bank of the river and still retains much of its flavor and charm. Here you will find the former palace of King Manuel I (now converted into the town hall) and the 15th-century **Igreja de São João Baptista**, which has a Flamboyant door and pulpit carved by French artisans and a painting of the Last Supper by the 16th-century Portuguese master Gregorio Lopes.

The biennial **Tabuleiros festival** is held in the square during the first fortnight of July. With roots in an ancient fertility festival dedicated to the goddess Ceres, it was co-opted in the 14th century by the Brotherhood of the Holy Spirit—the latter founded by Rainha Santa Isabel as a means of gathering donations for the poor. Today, during the festival, young women dressed in white parade around the streets carrying on their heads a *tabuleiro* (platter) of bread that's often as tall as themselves. These *tabuleiros* consist of some 30 loaves of bread threaded onto rods that are attached to wicker baskets decorated with paper flowers, leaves, and stalks of wheat. Sometimes the platters are topped off by a dove. The bounty was symbolically offered to the Holy Spirit as represented by the dove, which in turn was the symbol of universal fraternity espoused by the cult. The festival, which had been all but forgotten, was revived in 1961 after it was re-created for a movie. It is also celebrated in Brazil, the Azores, and Portuguese communities in North America.

Just a block south of the praça da República, at rua Dr. Joaquim Jacinto, 104, is the synagogue, or **Museu Luso-Hebraico**, the only well-preserved vestige of Medieval Jewish worship in Portugal. Used briefly in the 15th century by the Jewish community in Tomar before the Royal Edict of 1496 ordered the Jews to convert to Christianity or leave Portugal, it subsequently served as a prison, a storehouse, and a cellar. It was finally acquired in 1923 by a Polish Jew, Samuel Schwarz, and was given to the state. The rectangular building, with its marble pillars and vaulted roof, now houses Hebrew tombstones and Jewish memorabilia from all over Portugal as well as gifts from Jewish organizations around the world. The water jugs lodged in the corners are an ancient method of sound-proofing a room. Excavations in the house next door have uncovered the remains of a room where Jewish women took ritual baths. The museum is closed at lunchtime.

Farther east, a five-minute walk across the Ponte Velho on rua Marquês de Pombal, is the former **Convento da Santa Iria**, named after the beautiful nun (see Santarém). The riverside property is now privately owned. To visit its Renaissance chapel, you need to apply for the key at the Turismo office on avenida Dr. Cândido Madureira; Tel: (043) 33095.

Parque Mouchão, a quiet corner of Tomar lined with aspen, poplar, and elm trees, is on a tiny island in the middle of the Nabão river that's connected to the west bank by a bridge. The entrance to the park is embellished by a huge wooden waterwheel of the Moorish style, the kind that was used for centuries to irrigate the area via a system of pottery buckets. The elegant **Estalagem Santa Iria** on its north side is being refurbished and expanded to 21 rooms, and is expected to reopen by the summer of 1990. Its spacious rooms and restaurant look out on well-landscaped grounds and the tree-lined river. Somerset Maugham stayed here when he visited Tomar, and though he intended to stay only for a weekend, he fell in love with the area and remained for two weeks.

Directly north of the island, on the west bank of the

river, is the **Hotel dos Templários**, an 84-room establishment with all the modern conveniences, including air conditioning, curio shops, a hairdresser, game room, tennis court, outdoor swimming pool, and discotheque. Its restaurant has an extensive menu, which includes both national and regional dishes, including such local specialties as *lampreia com arroz* (lamprey cooked in its own blood and wine and served on a bed of rice) and *fatias de Tomar* (poached egg yolks dipped in cinnamon syrup). For starters, you can nibble on *queijinhos de Tomar*, the snowy sheep cheeses that are a cottage industry of the region. These can be accompanied by a semi-dry Convento Tomar reserve white from the Adega Cooperativa de Tomar. The Adega sells wine to the public and is located on the outskirts of Tomar at Algarvias, on the road to Torres Novas. To burn off some of the calories after dinner, climb the 365 steps that start beside the hotel to the **Capela de Nossa Senhora da Piedade**. From here you can admire Tomar, the river, the Templar convent on the hill, and, to the east, an old silk factory.

For more adventurous fare, try **Chico Elias**, at Algarvias, a kilometer southwest of Tomar on the road to Torres Novas. This country bistro is housed in a converted farmhouse, which stands alone on a ledge to your right as you turn a corner of the winding N 358. There is no sign, but the outside is gray and its iron doors are painted green. The restaurant is owned by Dona Ceu, a dynamic and imaginative cook whose creations include *feijoada de caracóis* (snail stew with sliced sausage and smoked ham), *coelho na abóbora* (rabbit stewed inside a gourd, cooked in a wood-fired oven, and served with rice), and reportedly the best *leite creme* (custard) in the region. Part of the secret behind the popularity of the latter is the old-fashioned iron pan that is heated in the wood-fired oven and used to brand and brown the caramel topping. Customers, who include the area's businessmen and visiting foreign ambassadors, frequent Chico Elias for its food rather than its spartan decor, which consists of grapevine lamps, red-tiled floors, and benches. Reservations are a must; Tel: (049) 31-10-67. No credit cards.

THE LOWER ZEZERE VALLEY

The damming of the lower Zêzere river has created the largest and one of the most enchanting man-made reservoirs in Portugal, one known for its pristine waters, abundance of fish, and sweet-smelling pine forests. Fishing and water sports are popular, particularly at **Castelo de Bode**, the crest of the dam at the southern end of the reservoir, 13 km (9 miles) southeast of Tomar via the N 110 and N 358-2. The moderately priced **Pousada de São Pedro**, a state-run inn with eight modest rooms in the main house and seven in an annex, faces the dam. Its main features are a fine restaurant and a terrace bar that overlooks a valley lined with olive vines and mimosas below the dam. Pleasure cruises down the river are available on the *São Cristóvão,* a modern two-story ferry that leaves from the Castelo de Bode dock near the Pousada. The two- and four-hour trips can be booked from the Hotel dos Templários in Tomar (Tel: 049-32121) or at any travel agency.

The **Estalagem Ilha do Lombo** is a secluded island retreat in the middle of the river Zêzere, 16 km (10 miles) east of Tomar. To get to it, leave Tomar on the N 110 headed north toward Coimbra, then turn right at the second traffic light, and follow the signs to Serra and Ilha do Lombo. After Serra you'll arrive at a white house that serves as the post office, garage, and mainland dock for the inn, which is across from it. The modern inn itself, shaded by mimosas and blessed with the sweet perfume of orange blossoms, has 17 large double bedrooms with red-tiled floors, ornate bamboo furniture, and balconies facing the water. There are two indoor restaurants and a poolside grill, as well as a rustic bar with a fireplace. Guests can explore the river by pedal boat or on the inn's ten-person boat, which looks like a smaller version of the *African Queen.* Lodging reservations here and elsewhere in the area are a must in the summer season.

The **Estalagem Vale da Ursa** is a modern family-run inn on the wooded banks of the Zêzere, 30 km (19 miles) northeast of Tomar via the N 110 and N 238. Its 12 airy bedrooms, glass-enclosed restaurant, outdoor pool and tennis court, and pine-and-marble bar overlook the lake some 165 feet below. The inn has an excellent restaurant, too, featuring such specialties as *sopa de peixe à Vale da Ursa* (a rich soup containing both local river and sea fish), *bacalhau dourado* (creamed, baked dried salt cod), and *borrego na caçarola* (lamb stewed in an earthenware pot with onion and tomato sauce). On Saturday you can savor *maranhos,* the inn's weekly special, which consists of sheep's belly stuffed with sausage, onions, mint, and other herbs. The inn is near **Dornes**, a former Templar stronghold with a Medieval tower and church that crown a tiny peninsula overlooking the Zêzere to the north.

FATIMA

The religious sanctuary of Fátima, which lies 30 km (19 miles) west of Tomar via the N 113 and N 356, toward Leiria and Batalha, is the largest ecclesiastical complex dedicated to the worship of the Virgin in Portugal as well as one of the most famous Catholic shrines in the world. Situated in the Cova da Iria hollow, where the Virgin is said to have first appeared to three young shepherds—Francisco, Jacinta, and Lucia—on May 13, 1917, calling for peace in a world beset by a terrible war, the shrine attracts hundreds of thousands of faithful every year. (Subsequent monthly visits by the Virgin in the form of cosmic phenomena were witnessed by a growing number of pilgrims, until she made her final appearance on October 13, 1917.) Francisco and Jacinta died young, but Lucia, the only one with whom the Virgin had actually conversed, continues to live a cloistered life as a nun in a Carmelite convent in Coimbra.

In 1930 the Church acknowledged the importance of the site by establishing the Shrine of Our Lady of Fátima. Today, the faithful camp out in the concrete esplanade in front of the shrine and hold all-night vigils by candlelight. Many show their fervor by walking on their knees to the shrine, which consists of a huge esplanade dominated by a Neo-Classical basilica that contains the tombs of Jacinta and Francisco. The neighboring **Museu de Cera de Fátima** (Fátima Wax Museum), on rua Jacinto Marto, tells the religious story of Fátima in 28 scenes. Also within walking distance of the shrine is the clean and simply furnished **Hotel Dom José**, with a reputable restaurant to suit the austere needs of pilgrims.

The town of **Vila Nova de Ourém**, 8 km (5 miles) northeast of Fátima via the N 356, is tied to Fátima's name and history by legend. According to that legend, the Templar lord of the region in the early 12th century, Gonçalo Hermingues, known as the Traga Moros ("Moor Devourer"), captured a Moorish woman named Fátima on one of his military expeditions. Of course, he fell in love with her, married her after she converted to Christianity and changed her name to Oureana, and settled down with her on his large estate, which he named Fátima, and which included the land around the present-day shrine. When his bride died, the former Traga Moros became a monk.

High on a hill overlooking the town is an imposing Medieval **castle**, which is open to visitors. The castle belonged to the counts of Ourém until the 14th century, when King João I seized it and gave it to a court favorite.

SOUTH OF TOMAR

The **castle of Almourol** is one of the scenic wonders of the Ribatejo. Built in the 12th century by the grand master of the Templar order, Gualdim Pais, over the ruins of a Roman fortress, it sits in timeless splendor on a tiny island in the middle of the river Tagus between Constância to the east and Vila Nova da Barquinha to the west. The island and its fortifications, which were mentioned by Strabo in a chronicle of his travels over 2,000 years ago, have always been the stuff of books and legends. In Francisco Morai's epic romance *Palmeirim de Inglaterra,* the British Crusader Palmeirim fights the giant Almourol for the hand of the beautiful Polinarda. Just as Palmeirim is ready to give in, another giant by the name of Dramusiando comes to his aid and slays Almourol.

The castle itself is surrounded by ten circular towers, which command a wonderful view of the hilly and verdant countryside, and is said to be haunted by the daughter of the Christian mayor of Almourol and her Moorish lover, who eloped, leaving the girl's father to die of grief. Excavations on the island have unearthed Roman artifacts and coins as well as the remains of a tunnel that is believed to have linked the castle to the shore.

To get to Almourol from Tomar take the N 110 and N 358-1 to Constância, where you turn right at the bridge and onto the N 3 and head toward Vila Nova da Barquinha. After 3.4 km (2 miles), turn left at the sign for Castelo de Almourol and drive another kilometer or so to the river, where you'll have a fabulous view of the castle and a choice of visiting it and/or circling the tiny island by boat during daylight hours.

Constância

Were it not for a paper mill operating on the south bank of the river, Constância would be one of the most picturesque towns in the Ribatejo. Its whitewashed houses and narrow cobbled streets lined with purple bougainvillaea climb the slopes of a hilly embankment where the Zêzere river flows into the Tagus. Cedar and olive trees dot the landscape, and colorful painted boats line up at the town's steep dock. It was here that the great Portuguese poet laureate Luiz Vaz de Camões was exiled from the court between 1547 and 1550 for falling in love with a lady-in-waiting to the queen. Today his statue graces a square facing the two rivers at the western end of town. Nearby, a plaque indicates the now-ruined house by the water where the author of Portugal's epic poem *The Lusiads* is believed to have lived during his stay here. It was also from Constância that the Duke of Wellington launched his successful campaign against the French at Talavera during the Peninsular War.

The 19th-century **Palácio de Constância**, which once sheltered Queen Maria II on one of her tours of the region, is now a bed and breakfast 11 months of the year (it's closed in December). Guests are offered a choice of four rooms furnished with Portuguese antiques, and have access to a large Victorian-style drawing room with fireplace, self-service bar, and card tables. The second-floor landing is graced by a painting of a priest by the 16th-century Spanish master Zurbarán, and there's a private chapel lined with tiles and marble down the hall. Some 200 yards east of the town hall there is a sign to the palace pointing to the left. The road becomes narrower and takes you directly to the gate of this property.

The **Falcão restaurant** next door, rua Luiz de Camões, 33-A, is one of the area's best and is frequented by the town's businessmen and resident artists. The restaurant, like the palace, is owned by the aristocratic Falcão family, which may account for the smart decor. The cooking is mainly country, with Ribatejano delicacies such as snowy *queijinhos do céu* (sheep cheeses) and firm *tijeladas* (egg custards) complementing its extensive fish menu. Wild game dishes such as partridge and rabbit are served during the fall hunting season. The restaurant is closed on Tuesdays.

Constância has not had only unwilling artists like

Camões in residence; the 20th-century poet and actor Vasco de Lima Couto also lived there. His house, which adjoins an antiques shop at largo Azevedo Machado, 2, has been converted into a museum and contains his writings and theater memorabilia as well as a collection of modern Portuguese paintings; open afternoons. José Ramoa Ferreira, who runs the museum and its adjoining antiques shop, also owns the tiny town's art gallery at rua Luiz de Camões, 28, west of rua Falcão. Ferreira is a talented art scout who exhibits some of the best of Portugal's modern regional and national artists. Constância is also known for its colorful *minas* (cloth-and-cane dolls) and miniature wooden river boats. A good selection of dolls is for sale at the home of Maria José Filipa at rua dos Ferreiros, 13.

Abrantes

Recent development has marred the former beauty of Abrantes, 16 km (10 miles) east of Constância, but not the spectacular view of the area from its hillside **fortress** on the north bank of the Tagus. The Romans named the city Aurantes (Golden) because of the gold that washed onto the sandy banks of the river there. In the Middle Ages Portuguese kings made it the bulwark of their northern line of defense during the Christian Reconquest, and General Junot and the future Duke of Wellington both made it their headquarters (in 1807 and 1809 respectively) during the Peninsular War.

Today Abrantes is best known for its delectable *palha de Abrantes,* an egg-thickened almond paste that is sprinkled with "thread" eggs, called *palha* (straw). The pastry cook at the **Hotel de Turismo** is not only an accomplished *palha* cook, but also whips up other Ribatejo sweets. The hotel's air-conditioned restaurant, with its fine vistas of the town and countryside, provides the ideal atmosphere in which to sample these sweets. The 15th-century **Igreja de Santa Maria do Castelo**, next to the castle, serves as the temporary quarters of the city museum. Inside, the Gothic tombstones of Lopo de Almeida, the second count of Abrantes, and his wife, and a 15th-century statue of the Virgin and Child are among the more interesting pieces in the collection. The museum is closed Mondays and at lunchtime.

The town of **Sardoal**, 11 km (7 miles) north of Abrantes on the N 2/N 244-3, is known for its mineral waters, picturesque stone-carved squares, and elegant manor houses, and is one of the last unspoiled Ribatejano towns. The **Igreja de Santiago e São Mateus** contains a collection of seven religious paintings by an unknown 16th-century artist who signed his work only with the initials *M.N.,* and is thus called the monogram painter (M.N. also appears in other church work in the southern village of Montemor). He was a master of the brush who managed by skillful strokes to convey a lyrical mysticism in his subjects. The paintings have figured in major Portuguese and European exhibitions and will probably be moved to a regional museum sometime in the future.

THE EAST BANK OF THE TAGUS

Crossing to the opposite bank of the Tagus at Abrantes, you follow the N 118 southwest over the flat, fertile Ribatejo plain past farming towns and fields irrigated by the river. The **Casa Museu dos Patudos** at **Alpiarça** contains the fabulous art collection of Republican statesman José Relvas. Among the treasures decorating his 19th-century manorial home are a fine sampling of Portuguese masters going back to the 15th-century "Primitives," paintings by Spanish greats such as Zurbarán and Murillo, and many other fine works by accomplished European artists. The collection also includes rich Flemish tapestries and Portuguese and Oriental carpets from the 17th to the 19th centuries, as well as china and porcelain from Europe, China, and Japan. The 18th-century *azulejos* in a room adjoining the dining room were originally from the convent of Santo António in nearby Chamusca. The museum is on the southern outskirts of town and is generally open on Thursdays, Saturdays, Sundays, and holidays. Call before visiting; Tel: (043) 54206. Alpiarça is also known for its sweet muscatel wines and its reed chairs.

The neighboring town of **Almeirim** is considered the dining room of the Ribatejo. It is here, for example, that *sopa de pedra* (stone soup) is believed to have originated—or at least to have been perfected. According to legend, after a mendicant monk was refused a meal by the people of the village, he played to their curiosity and gradually tricked them into providing him with the ingredients for a delicious "stone soup" by starting to boil a pot of water with a stone in it. As they doggedly demanded to know what else went into the soup, the monk would oblige by revealing another ingredient, which the townspeople would then supply.

Today, there are several restaurants in the vicinity of the bullring that serve the soup in addition to a variety of other delectables. Success has not altered the rustic look of the oldest and most venerated of these, **O Toucinho**, but it has allowed the owners to open an annex next door. You enter the former through a busy kitchen where the smell of bread baking in a wood-burning oven provides a welcoming reception. In the restaurant itself, waitresses cater to your needs in small rooms furnished simply with wooden benches and tables. Apart from its mouth-watering *sopa de pedra,* O Toucinho specializes in grilled meats such as *rinzada de borrego* (lamb ribs) and large steaks. Customers can also choose between the simple house wine or the better-quality Quinta da Alorna whites, produced just up the road. The annex in the neighboring square is decorated with bullfight pictures. Both are closed on Tuesdays and during the month of August; Tel: (043) 52237.

The tiny **Museu Etnográfico** is housed in the Casa do Povo nearby on the southern side of the rua de Coruche between the bullring and the town center. In it you will find the full range of Ribatejo folk culture, from household items to traditional dress. There is a nicy, shady garden on the grounds.

During the 15th and 16th centuries Almeirim was a hunting retreat for the royal family, which built two now-defunct palaces here. Today, in addition to its *sopa de pedra* and wines, Almeirim is known for its leather goods, tin work, and iron stoves. Its sweet yellow melons, sold at roadside stalls, are also revered. There are several shops in the town center flanking the praça da República and the gardens. (The square is to your right as you enter town.) The "Chico Leonor" antiques shop is located at rua Manuel Andrade, 13, in front of the post office. A nice time to visit the town is market day, the first Sunday of every month; the annual wine festival (March 10 to 12) is also popular with visitors.

The 19th-century **Palácio da Alorna** estate is about a kilometer south of Almeirim on the road (the N 118) to Salvaterra de Magos. The wine cellars of this sprawling complex are open to the public, and its semi-dry Quinta de Alorna wine should not go untasted. The estate, which was built for the Countess of Junqueira, is one of the last of its size and splendor to be built in the region.

From Almeirim you have a choice of routes back to Lisbon. The fastest is via Santarém and the E 1 *auto-estrada*. Or you can continue south along the east bank of the Tagus through rich cattle country until you join the N 10/E 52 and cross the river to Vila Franca de Xira, where you meet the E 1 to Lisbon.

If you are in the region during September, however, you might want to stay on the east bank and visit the former fishing village of **Moita do Ribatejo**. The town, which is situated in the southwestern corner of the *charneca,* celebrates a lively annual pilgrimage called the *Romaria de Nossa Senhora da Boa Viagem* (Our Lady of the Good Journey). This colorful event, which takes place over the second weekend in September, includes bull-running in the streets, bullfights, a colorful fair, and the blessing of the fleet by local priests.

From Moita do Ribatejo you can make your approach to Lisbon from the south, crossing the Ponte 25 de Abril. This three-hour drive takes you first through the large bullfighting estates and cattle farms around Salvaterra de Magos and, on the west bank, Vila Franca de Xira. After Samora Correia, the alluvial flats of the Tagus Nature Reserve, covered with grassland and wild flowers, do justice to the area's nickname—the *mar de palha,* or straw sea. Egrets, flamingos, and storks are common in these parts, bordering the Tagus estuary. The N 118 finally gives way to the N 119 as you make your way toward Alcochete on the estuary past salt pans exploited since Roman times.

The N 5 and N 11 then take you past cork factories at Montijo and canals with the last remaining wooden Tagus sailing vessels. Up to the middle of the century, before bridges connected the north with the south of the Tagus, an armada of these lovely painted boats was the only link between the two banks of the river. Some of the last shipbuilding facilities can be sighted at the entrance of the dock at Moita do Ribatejo. From the quay you can peer at Lisbon looming majestically across the water to the northwest. Several watermills spot the horizon to the west. The watermills, which were built over the marshes to harness the energy from the tide waters, are mostly idle now.

GETTING AROUND

The major cities on this route are linked by train and buses from Lisbon. Trains to the major Ribatejo towns of Vila Franca de Xira, Santarém, Tomar, and Abrantes leave frequently from the Santa Apolónia train station located by the waterfront at the eastern end of the city below the Alfama quarter. The service is regular and inexpensive. For information, Tel: (01) 87-60-25. Buses to these destinations depart several times a day from avenida Casal de Ribeiro terminal, which is a short cab drive northwest of Lisbon's center; Tel: (01) 57-77-15. The buses are modern and comfortable. There are also daily bus tours of the Ribatejo, which can be booked at travel agents.

The best way to tour the region, and at your own pace, is by car. All the major international car-rental companies have offices at Lisbon's international airport and the major hotels. Give yourself three to five days to take in all the sights. Bridges cross the river Tagus at Vila Franca de Xira, Santarém, Chamusca, and Abrantes. The only *auto-estrada* is on the west bank and runs 45 km (28 miles) from Lisbon to Aveiras de Cima. The rest of the Ribatejo's roads are fairly well marked and paved, but be prepared for delays in farm areas, where tractors and trucks share the road with smaller vehicles. It takes on average three hours (without stops) to drive the 135 km (84 miles) from Lisbon to Tomar.

ACCOMMODATIONS REFERENCE

▶ **Hotel Abides.** Rua Guilherme de Azevedo, 4, 2000 **Santarém**. Tel: (043) 22017.

▶ **Casa dos Cedros. Azóia de Cima**, 2000 Santarém. Tel: (01) 80-09-86.

▶ **Casal da Torre.** Rua Nova da Torre, 29, Vale de Santarém, 2000 **Santarém**. Tel: (043) 76224 or (01) 88-64-93.

▶ **Hotel Dom José.** Avenida Dom José Alves Correia da Silva, **Fátima**. Tel: (049) 52215; Telex: 43279.

▶ **Estalagem Ilha do Lombo. Serra**, 2300 Tomar. Tel: (049) 37128.

▶ **Palácio de Constância.** 2250, **Constância**. Tel: (049) 93224.

▶ **Estalagem Santa Iria.** Parque Mouchão, 2300 **Tomar**. Tel: (049) 32427.

- **Pousada de São Pedro.** Castelo de Bode, 2300 Tomar. Tel: (049) 38159.
- **Quinta da Sobreira.** Vale de Figueira, 2035 Santarém. Tel: (043) 42444.
- **Hotel dos Templários.** Largo Cândido dos Reis, 1, 2300 Tomar. Tel: (049) 32121; Telex: 14434.
- **Quinta Vale de Lobos.** Azóia de Baixo, 2000 Santarém. Tel: (043) 42264.
- **Estalagem Vale da Ursa.** Cernache do Bonjardim, **Lago do Castelo de Bode,** 6100 Sertã. Tel: (074) 67511; Telex: 52673.

Pousadas can be booked through Marketing Ahead, 433 Fifth Avenue, New York, N.Y. 10016; Tel: (212) 686-9213.

THE ALENTEJO

By Jean Anderson

For travellers hurtling from Lisbon south to the Algarve or east to Madrid, the Alentejo is that endless stretch of cork oaks and olives that takes forever to cross. It seems as broad and flat as the Australian Outback or the Texas prairie—and every bit as boring, because the main roads slice across plowed ground, bypassing everything of interest.

How can tourists in a hurry know that cached about these red-brown plains are dolmens, menhirs, and cromlechs that predate those of Brittany? Or that there are tumbles of Roman ruins? Or Medieval walled towns so white they might be icebergs strayed off course? Or rambunctious country fairs and festivals?

How can they know that the provincial capital, Evora, was once a cultural center, with artists and writers in residence from as far afield as Paris? That the sugar-cube town of Arraiolos, piled up on its castle hill, is famous the world over for its gros-point tapestries and rugs?

How can fast-track travellers know that this is the land of the potter, the weaver, the wood-carver? That it's a place where shepherds, rather than stand idly by their flocks, whittle willow branches into cooking spoons or clip weeds into topiary? A land where women still kneel on riverbanks to do the family wash, where girls stroll home from the village well bearing clay amphoras atop their heads, where cooks don't stint on garlic, onions, and olive oil? Of course they can't. The Alentejo (meaning, literally, "across the Tagus" and pronounced allen-

TAY-zhoo) doesn't flaunt its charms the way the Algarve does. And its allure, nothing more than basic, unspoiled Portugal where life eases along at a slower tempo, is more subtle than seductive. About the only thing the tourist barreling across the Alentejo discovers is that it's BIG. It is in fact Portugal's biggest province, sprawling from the Algarve border 320 km (200 miles) north to the upper reaches of the Tagus river and Beira Baixa, bumping up against Spain all along the way—for centuries a source of friction.

The Alentejo, in short, occupies more than a third of the Portuguese mainland, and it isn't all cork oaks and olives.

MAJOR INTEREST

Museum town of Evora
Tapestry town of Arraiolos
Dolmens, menhirs, cromlechs, and the Escoural painted cave near Arraiolos
Market town of Estremoz
Pottery towns of Redondo and São Pedro de Corval
Ducal palace at Vila Viçosa
Fortified town of Elvas
Medieval walled towns of Monsaraz, Marvão, and Castelo de Vide

The Portuguese themselves rarely spend time in the Alentejo. Hunters come out in autumn to shoot rabbit and quail; but most Portuguese, being sun worshippers, prefer to vacation somewhere along their 500 miles of Atlantic shore or at Madeira. And you can scarcely blame the Portuguese hoteliers for assuming that most foreign visitors are beach buffs, too; doubtless they are. At any rate the Algarve, Cascais and Guincho west of Lisbon, and even the northerly Minho beaches, where the Atlantic runs cold, don't lack for modern resort hotels. In fact, you could consider them overbuilt. The Alentejo, though, has been forsaken, and that may very well be its salvation, although the shortage of good hotel rooms doesn't make it easy for visitors. The lesson here: Make sure that your hotel reservations are confirmed before you set foot in the Alentejo, because otherwise you may find yourself stranded with no place to lay your head. So we'll take care of that first.

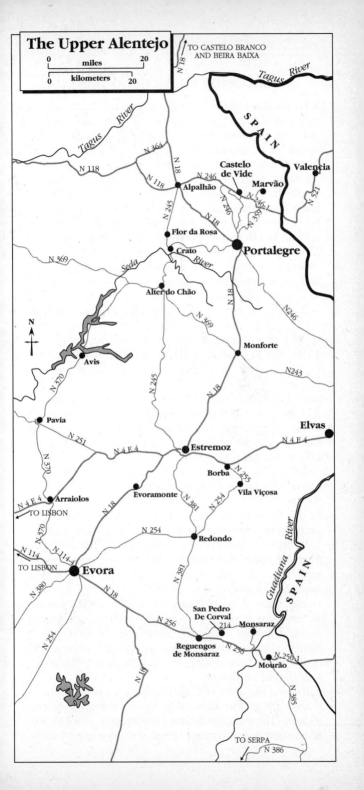

Choosing an Alentejo Base

With the Alentejo possessing so few first-class hotels, it isn't practical to move from place to place, staying in a different area every night, as you might do elsewhere. It makes far more sense here to pick a central home base from which you can make day trips, setting out in a new direction each morning. Distances are short enough within the visitor's Alentejo for easy circle tours that won't leave you exhausted at day's end or rushing to make it home before dark. In fact, the Alentejo's narrow, unlighted blacktops are *dangerous* to drive at night, because there are donkey carts creaking along in utter darkness—not to mention motorbikes, decrepit trucks, and cars with headlights missing and sometimes no reflectors or taillights at all.

Fortunately, two of Portugal's most palatial pousadas couldn't be more centrally located. In the provincial capital of Evora, about one and a half hours east of Lisbon, there's the 32-room **Pousada dos Lóios**, occupying a 15th-century convent (its rooms may be cell-size, but they're blessed with big marble baths). Scarcely a 40-minute drive to the northeast of Evora, the even more luxurious 23-room **Pousada da Rainha Santa Isabel** (a 13th-century castle crammed with honest-to-God antiques) crowns the old walled town of Estremoz, on the N 4/E 4, the main Lisbon–Madrid highway.

There's also the little country-rustic **Pousada de Santa Maria** in the mountaintop walled town of Marvão, but it's in the far north of the Upper Alentejo, almost on the border of the Beira Baixa, and is thus not well located to be practical for our solely Alentejo strategy (it's about a two-hour drive north of Estremoz, and 45 minutes farther from Evora). Besides, its 14 small rooms are invariably booked months in advance by honeymooners or those seeking a quiet retreat where they can catch up on their reading. Finally, there is the 17-room, split-level modern **Pousada de São Gens** at Serpa, in the upper reaches of the Lower Alentejo. But like the Marvão pousada, it's too far removed from the Upper Alentejo's major attractions to make a very handy home base. Evora, for example, lies 107 km (67 miles) to its northwest.

If you'd like to try bed and breakfast at a private manor house, there are two other good centrally located choices. The first, **Monte dos Pensamentos**, is a folk-art-filled country gentleman's retreat with four guest rooms (private but not *en suite* baths) located 1.5 km (1 mile) west of Estremoz within view of N 4. The second is the sumptuously renovated eight-room **Solar dos Peixinhos** (circa 1611) on the southern edge of Vila Viçosa, just 18 km (11 miles) southeast of Estremoz. Either the Evora or the Estremoz pousada, or a manor house, would make a handy headquarters for touring the Alentejo.

Whoever said "There's no shade in the Alentejo" must have had the southern half of it in mind, the Baixo, or Lower, Alentejo. You will cross it in about two hours if you are driving north on N 2 from the Algarve toward Evora or Estremoz. Except for rows of eucalyptus parading along highway shoulders, there's almost nothing to filter the sun that burns down without mercy on this old granary of Rome. There are gnarled cork oaks here and there, and the occasional spiky aloe or fiery burst of wild poppies, but there's little to shield the boulder-strewn fields or seas of grain billowing north to the town of Beja and beyond.

There isn't much in this monotonous brown stretch to keep you from hurrying on to the Alto (Upper) Alentejo, which *does* offer plenty of interest. You may wonder as you look at the map, however, about that long stretch of western Alentejo Atlantic coastline sweeping north from the Algarve border all the way to the Tróia peninsula (see Day Trips from Lisbon). There are occasional secluded crescents of sand tucked at the base of high ocher cliffs between Odeceixe on the Algarve/Alentejo border and the pin-neat white village of **Porto Covo** some 70 km (44 miles) north. With its weathered fishermen lounging on scarlet park benches, its plane trees pruned into umbrellas, and its flowery central plaza, Porto Covo is as picturesque as any movie set. The Lower Alentejo beaches are often difficult to reach, however, and the Atlantic pounding in upon them is apt to be both cold and ferocious. North of Porto Covo, the Alentejo shore flattens and is lined much of the way with spartan hotels and bungalows that are used by Portuguese families who can't afford anything better.

If you'd like to explore these windswept beaches for a day or so on your way to your Upper Alentejo headquarters from either the Algarve or Lisbon, there's a funky castle-inn at the old Phoenician stronghold of Vila Nova de Milfontes at the mouth of the Mira river just 20 km (12.5 miles) south of Porto Covo. The waterfront stone **Castelo de Milfontes** is privately owned, and its eight guest rooms are often filled with friends and relatives of the hosts. Still, if you make reservations well in advance, you will be able to stay here. The two choicest rooms are in the *torre* (tower) because they have *en suite* baths and huge rooftop terraces overlooking the sea.

As for the Upper Alentejo, you'll be pressed to see as much of it as you'd like in five days. The best possible place to begin your tour is Evora, the provincial capital, of which one native son wrote: "No other town in Portugal but Evora was able to tell me with purity and beauty that I am Latin, Arabian, Christian, Peninsular, and Portuguese." How better to summarize all the different peoples who have had a hand in shaping the Evora of today?

EVORA

Prehistoric man was the first to come Evora's way, how long ago no one knows, although he has left plenty of dolmens, menhirs, and other monuments scattered about for archaeologists to ponder. The first people of influence here were the Romans. From the second century B.C. to the fifth century A.D., Evora, Caesar's Liberalitas Julia, was a powerful seat of Roman Lusitania. The Visigoths followed, but they left little mark even though they occupied the area through the sixth and seventh centuries.

Next came the Moors, who captured Evora in 715 and held it until 1166. It's their presence that lingers everywhere. Later, the kings of Portugal made this little Alentejo hill town the royal seat of preference. João I, father of Prince Henry the Navigator, went so far as to proclaim Evora Portugal's second town (after Lisbon). During the Renaissance some of Europe's finest sculptors, artists, and writers settled in and made Evora, for a time at least, the Portuguese Montmartre. Evora fell to Spain toward the end of the 16th century and slid into a lengthy decline that continued even after it regained its independence in 1637. It was at the foot of the old Roman temple here, however, that 20th-century rebels met to plot the Flower Revolution of 1974 (see the Chronology).

Today Evora is a surprisingly sophisticated town of 35,000, an educational and cultural center, Portugal's fifth most important town (after Lisbon, Porto, Coimbra, and Guimarães). And now that UNESCO has named it a World Treasure it has spiffed itself up. All of the broken street lights along praça do Giraldo have been replaced, all of the gaps in the intricately mosaicked black-and-white sidewalks have been filled in, all the walls have been scrubbed clean of political graffiti. The townspeople have even repainted their houses, fringed their windows with geraniums, and hung out the welcome mat for all who would come this way.

As you approach Evora from the west or south—which you will if you're coming from Lisbon or the Algarve—you see it pyramiding up above the cork orchards like a giant pile of sugar cubes, blinding in its whiteness against the blue, blue Alentejo sky.

The best plan is to aim right off for the **Pousada dos Lóios**, letting the pousada directional signs (a little house with smoke coming out the chimney) guide you past the Medieval town walls, then up through a maze of narrow cobblestone streets to the top of the town and the second-century Roman temple standing there. The pousada faces the temple, and if you arrive early enough in the day (before late afternoon) you should easily find a parking place in this broad square, maybe even at the inn's door. (See Choosing an Alentejo Base, above, for more on this pousada.)

Your next stop should be the Turismo office on the west side of praça do Giraldo in the city center, a four-block stroll downhill from the temple along rua 5 de Outubro, to pick up leaflets pinpointing the locations of the dolmens and menhirs in the countryside around Evora, as well as city maps outlining fast, medium, and slow tours. It lists—awesome thought—18 major points of interest, and every local chauvinist can no doubt recommend twice as many. Not for nothing is Evora called the "Museum Town." More than half of its attractions, however, are churches, so unless ecclesiastical architecture is an obsession, you can skip all but three houses of worship, which we will discuss.

Evora deserves at least a full day. You'll find that the most sensible way to stroll—and this is a walking town if there ever was one—is to start at the highest point, the **Roman temple**, and work your way down. Afterward, if you can't face climbing back uphill to the pousada, you can grab a taxi at any of the town's many cab stands. Although nearly every cab is a Mercedes, fares are so cheap you can't help wondering how the driver makes a living (10 to 15 percent tips gratefully accepted).

Only 14 of the temple's original columns still stand, and even fewer (12) of the Corinthian capitals, which are carved from Estremoz marble. Given the temple's history—it was bricked up at one point and used as an armory, then an abattoir—you're surprised to see so much of it left. Its latest threat: Tourists scrambling up its eroded stairs for a closer look. The temple itself is now off limits, so you must be content to view it from the street. No problem; it stands in the middle of a wide, open square and you can walk all around it. The best angle for photographs is from the northwest corner looking back through the skeletal columns toward the pousada and the adjoining **chapel of the Convento dos Lóios.**

This early-15th-century chapel is private, the property of the dukes of Cadaval, but a custodian unlocks its massive wooden door each morning and afternoon. Unlike so many dour, dank, and dusty Portuguese churches, this one is bathed in light, especially in the morning, when the sun slants through high round windows, firing the gold altar to radiance and illuminating walls paved in early-18th-century blue-and-white tiles that depict the life of Saint Lawrence Justinian.

Your next stop should be the **Museu de Evora**, just around the corner from the chapel and the pousada on largo do Conde de Vila Real. It too faces the Roman temple. An archbishop's palace during the 16th and 17th centuries, the museum wraps around a central courtyard that's strewn with Roman relics and, in amongst them, a jarring collection of modern Portuguese sculpture in the creamy beige and pink marbles of Estremoz and Borba. But better to have them here than out scattered around the base of the Roman temple, as they were for years. The stone-floored arcade around the courtyard and the rooms that open off it are filled with massive marble sarcophagi, busts, and bits and pieces of sculpture from various periods back to Roman times. The two most important are probably the broken bas-relief (bottom half only) of a Roman woman in a gauzy, billowing skirt, and a rather severe Gothic Virgin at her prayers.

Up a switchback flight of stairs is a gallery, its walls hung with the work of the 15th- to 17th-century artists—Portuguese, Italian, and Flemish—who painted in Evora. Recently renovated, the rooms, with their polished floors of rare wood, white walls, and well-hung paintings, are a pleasure to stroll. In the old days a gnome of a man shuffled you through, pointing out art and air-conditioners with equal pride. Today you can move along at your own pace (do pull aside the large front gallery's curtains for a different perspective of the Roman temple).

Portuguese art takes some getting used to; you can't help wondering if these early painters all preferred dark palettes or if the canvases are just long overdue for a good cleaning. Probably a bit of both. At any rate, their mood is somber, even macabre when the subject is one of Christianity's gorier moments. Two notable exceptions: the 13 panels (late-15th-century Flemish) that chronicle the life of the Virgin (perhaps the museum's finest work), and a surprisingly graceful Nativity painted by Frei Carlos, a monk who lived at the **Convento de Nossa Senhora do Espinheiro**, 4 km (2.5 miles) north of town. Time permitting during your Evora stay, you might want to drive out to this 15th-century monastery, if only to see its Renaissance-Baroque church.

Your next stop should be the Sé (cathedral) directly behind the museum on largo do Marquês de Marialva (its mismatched conical towers soar above the museum courtyard). To reach it, leave the museum, turn left, and walk right around the museum building. En route, note (on your right) the mansion on the northwest corner of the broad leafy square in front of the Sé. This long, low, white building, with trim the color of curry powder, is where Vasco da Gama retired after his triumphant voyages to the Indies. He would scarcely recognize his old home today, so often has it been altered and enlarged. The building's other claim to fame (or rather, infamy) is that it served as Evora's court of the Inquisition.

The **cathedral** is a brooding granite pile that took 64 years to build (from 1186 to 1250). What distinguishes it, however, is the way its soaring stone columns and vaulted ceilings have been pointed with chalk-white mortar—not exactly restful or conducive to meditation. The **cloister**, which you must ask to see, is altogether peaceful, a Gothic haven. But the cathedral's high point (quite literally) is its **treasury**, cached away up a twisting stair in one of the towers. To wander from case to case marveling at the jewel-encrusted miters and reliquaries is to see at first hand what the wealthy English dilettante and frequent visitor to Portugal William Beckford had in mind in 1787 when he wrote, "Gracious goodness! The Roman Catholic religion is filled with fine stage effects!" But the glitter of the vestments, crosses, and croziers pales beside the delicacy of the 13th-century ivory Virgin, whose body opens in triptych to reveal the nine most important episodes of her life. Somewhere along the way she lost her head, and the wooden replacement doesn't begin to match the elegance of the ivory torso.

Two of Evora's best restaurants are within easy walking distance of the cathedral. The first choice, **Fialho**, at 16 travessa das Mascarenhas, is also the farthest away, but you can hoof it in ten minutes. With your back to the cathedral walk straight ahead down rua 5 de Outubro to praça do Giraldo, a distance of four blocks. Turn right and follow the arcaded sidewalk to the end of the square, then continue straight ahead along rua João de Deus seven short blocks to a small park. About halfway along the north side of the park you'll come upon a little alley that shoots off to the right. This is travessa das Mascarenhas, and to find Fialho you need only walk one block in.

By most accounts Fialho is Portugal's best provincial restaurant. Gabriel Fialho, whose father started the business nearly 50 years ago, now presides over the kitchen, while his two brothers watch the bottom line. A salty little blue-collar *tasca* (bistro) when it first opened, Fialho is decidedly white-collar today, a businessman's hangout where the portions are whopping and the prices reasonable. The place buzzes with the conversation of local scholars who've come to discuss the ways of the world and linger over such specialties as *sopa de panela* (a layered soup of sausages, chicken, bread, and fresh mint), partridges braised with cabbage, or any one of Gabriel's robust pork dishes.

If you feel like a less ambitious walk, **Cozinha de Santo Humberto**, just half a block downhill from praça do Giraldo at 39 rua da Moeda, is another excellent choice—and also a local businessman's favorite. It's a few steps down from the narrow cobbled street (this used to be Evora's Jewish quarter), and with its arches, vaulted ceilings, and terra-cotta tile floors it has the look of an old Moorish house. The chef, Joaquina Maximino, is famous for her lusty homemade soups, but most of all for her *migas*, an Alentejo classic that is nothing more than a stir-fry of pork, garlic, and crumbles of yesterday's bread. (It's a lot better than it sounds.)

If you're wondering what wines to order at either restaurant—indeed, at any Alentejo restaurant—by all means try some of the excellent local labels. The best table reds are Tapada de Chaves 1982, Borba Vinho Tinto Reserva 1976, Herdade do Esporão 1986, and Quinta do Carmo 1985. As for whites, you won't go wrong with

Reguengos de Monsaraz Regia Colheita or Vidigueira, both 1987.

After lunch return to praça do Giraldo (note the huge 16th-century marble fountain, for which a Roman arch was sacrificed), walk to the south end of the square, then follow rua da República two blocks downhill to the **church of São Francisco**. Though the church is a splendid example of Moorish-Gothic style for which the finest architects and artisans of the day pooled their talents, the main attraction here (if that's the right word) is the ghoulish **Capela dos Ossos** (Chapel of Bones). Its walls and columns supporting the frescoed barrel ceilings are entirely covered with human skulls and leg and arm bones, to induce piety, it's said.

Next, retrace your steps about 100 yards along rua da República, turn right onto rua dos Infantes for two blocks, where the road forks, then bear left on rua da Misericórdia and follow this street of splendid 16th- and 17th-century façades two long blocks to **largo das Portas de Moura**, a broad, treeless square with a spherical fountain of white marble (circa 1556) in the center. There are additional landmarks here: on the northwest corner, the early-16th-century **Soure town house** (private) topped with the curious conical dome so characteristic of Evora, and, catercorner across the square, the **Casa Cordovil** mansion (also 16th century; also private), with a delicate portico of horseshoe Mudejar arches.

Speaking of arches, on your wanderings around Evora you may have noticed snatches of a high, arched **aqueduct** around the edge of the old city walls. It looks Roman but is in fact Romanesque, a public works project put up by João III in the 16th century. It was—and is—an architectural masterpiece, an attraction so important that Camões, Portugal's beloved epic poet, mentioned it in his *Lusiads,* the story of Vasco da Gama's triumphant voyages of discovery: "Noble Evora," Camões wrote in the 16th century, "the seat once of the rebel Sertorius, famous now for the royal aqueduct with its hundreds of imposing arches...."

Where you go next depends on whether you've had your fill of architecture. If you have, retrace your steps to rua da República and the praça do Giraldo, then, on your way back up to the pousada, browse all the craft shops lined up on both sides of **rua 5 de Outubro**, Evora's "boutique row." Here you can see all of the Alentejo's famous handcrafts: rustic pottery, fancily painted wooden chests and chairs, cork ice buckets, and little copper coffeepots just like the one the waiter brings to your breakfast table each morning.

If, on the other hand, you're game for more sightseeing, leave the Portas da Moura square by way of rua Conde da Serra, and walk two long blocks east to a T intersection. Dead ahead lies the 16th-century **Jesuit University** (now a high school). The walls inside are covered with what may be Portugal's rarest collection of 16th-, 17th-, and 18th-century *azulejos,* some of them, as befits a Jesuit setting, depicting the lives of the saints. The school's classical **cloister**, with its arching double colonnade, is Evora's—indeed, one of Portugal's—most beautiful.

The fortress set high on the hill directly across largo das Colegiais from the university is the **Palace of the Counts of Basto** (you must apply for permission to enter). This Medieval castle built on Moorish foundations was the Evora residence of the kings of Portugal, and it is where Catherine of Bragança retreated after the death of her husband, Charles II of England. To return to the pousada, simply follow largo das Colegiais as it arcs uphill (the back of the pousada is directly above you; the weathered stone walls separating it from the Palace of the Counts of Basto are part Roman, part Visigothic).

It's a steep uphill hike back to the **Pousada dos Lóios**, so you'll no doubt be ravenous by dinnertime. In summer, you will dine in the glassed-in cloister (the granite doorway to the adjoining chapter room, all slender twisted columns, horseshoe arches, and delicately carved borders, is as fine an example of Luso-Moorish architecture as you're likely to see in Portugal). In cold weather, breakfast, lunch, and dinner are served in the old monks' refectory, a long, narrow room with high vaulted ceilings, velvet draperies the color of ruby Port, and floors tiled in terra-cotta.

You can't help wondering how those 15th- and 16th-century monks would view today's dining room, where crystal sparkles, silver gleams, and candles softly flicker. Or what they would think of a menu so strewn with French classics. Much as you may be tempted to order steak béarnaise, you'll fare better with such Portuguese dishes as *sopa à Alentejana* (egg-and-bread-thickened garlic-coriander soup) and *porco à Alentejana* (paprika-rouged chunks of pork braised with baby clams, still in the shell). Don't fail to try one of the superb local sheep cheeses: the little nutty ivory-hued rounds for which

Evora is famous, or better yet, the big and biting Beja, blushed with paprika. Some Portuguese actually prefer it to *queijo da serra,* Portugal's "Queen of Cheeses," which comes from the Beira Alta, farther north.

ARRAIOLOS AND ANCIENT DOLMENS

If you haven't picked up the little folder that the Evora tourist office hands out pinpointing the locations of the menhirs and dolmens in the immediate area, you should do so before setting out on this leisurely daylong outing; otherwise you'll never be able to locate them. Moreover, the leaflet describes each historic site in some detail, so you can decide which ones interest you most.

Arraiolos

You should probably begin your tour at Arraiolos, 22 km (13 miles) north of Evora via N 114-4 and N 370, 46 km (29 miles) west of Estremoz via N 4, and about 20 minutes longer from Vila Viçosa, also via N 4. The Oriental-style rugs you've been seeing all over Portugal are made in this spic-and-span white town, where almost every door and window is framed in cobalt blue "to keep the evil spirits away." (Originally, perhaps, but today these brightly painted borders are more apt to be purely for show.)

All of the important *fábricas* (rug workrooms) are lined up along the main street of this essentially one-street town (there are little alleys shooting off at odd angles but only one straight, *drivable* street stretching from one end of Arraiolos to the other). For rugs, you need only look for the *tapête* signs. The typical arrangement is a store out front and *fábrica* directly behind. **Fábrica Kalifa**, **Condestável**, and **Calântica** are just three of the shops you'll pass along this four- to five-block stretch. Many doors are left open, or at least ajar—a sign of welcome.

Most shopkeepers will gladly show you through their workrooms, especially if you've bought something—even a small pillow cover. Do ask, because you've never seen anything like these dimly lighted ateliers, piled to the rafters with rainbows of yarn. And you've never witnessed such frenzied activity. Women draw themselves into circles of six or eight to work on a single giant rug, spread from lap to lap. As they stitch in flowers, birds, geometrics, and yards and yards of background, their fingers fly over acres of stiff hemp with stunning speed, usually to the beat of rock 'n' roll twanging out of some little transistor radio tucked away in a corner. Even so, the work is so painstaking that it takes an experienced embroiderer three weeks to complete one square meter of tapestry.

If you have any intention of buying an Arraiolos rug, this is the place to do so, because you'll beat the prices of Lisbon by about 15 to 20 percent. Most of the Arraiolos shops, moreover, will pack and ship whatever you buy.

One early English fan of these intricately cross-stitched carpets, according to Dame Rose Macaulay, was that rich 18th-century aesthete William Beckford. On his way from Lisbon to Spain, she writes in *They Went to Portugal* (1946), Beckford stopped at Arraiolos "to lay in a stock of bright carpets for his journey, lest he should find himself in an uncarpeted room; in the Estremoz posada he spread them all round his bed, they made a flaming, exotic appearance and protected his feet from the damp brick floors."

How did this tiny village tucked away in the cork orchards get into the rug business? And why are the motifs so distinctly Oriental? Historians believe that Alentejo women first learned the art of rug making from the Moors, who lived in these parts for more than 400 years and whose entourages usually included plenty of talented rug weavers. But the designs so characteristic of Arraiolos rugs today were probably developed in the early 16th century, after Vasco da Gama returned from the East with piles of Persian carpets.

Before long these vividly patterned floor coverings became the rage among Portugal's rich and royal, many of whom lived nearby at Evora. This turn of events wasn't lost on savvy Arraiolos craftsmen, who decided that they could make a little money by copying them. There were plenty of sheep to provide wool. There was no shortage of plants from which bright natural dyes could be extracted, no shortage of skilled needleworkers. And, most important, no shortage of potential customers. It had to be a lucrative business. And more than 400 years later it continues to be one.

If you'd like to see some choice early Arraiolos carpets,

follow the main street to the very heart of town (no more than four or five blocks) and the little treeless square where the village elders hang out and where the Turismo (tourist office) and Câmara Municipal (town hall) stand shoulder to shoulder. There's an eye-popping tapestry exhibit on the second floor of the town hall (one flight up). The 18th- and 19th-century embroideries hung on these walls are far more finely worked than the rugs made today.

This would be an excellent day for a picnic, and at any little *tasca* or grocery along the main street you can pick up the makings: a loaf of bread, a chunk of cheese, a plastic bag of olives, a bottle of wine, and perhaps a *paio,* the plump, smoky, dry-cured sausage bound up in string for which Arraiolos is also famous. For your alfresco lunch you might simply drive uphill to the grounds of Arraiolos's 14th-century **castle**.

Alternatively, you might head for any town exit; you'll be in the countryside in minutes and will have no difficulty finding a peaceful spot in which to spread your picnic. Afterward you can spend the afternoon working your way from dolmen to menhir to cromlech to cave. Five major prehistoric sites cluster in the cork orchards to the south and west of Arraiolos and Evora, the farthest no more than 60 km (38 miles) away, and most of them much closer. These include the **Escoural Cave**, with its crude wall scribblings, the **Cromlech and Menhir of Almendres** (an entire ring of standing stones), the **Dolmen of Silval** (a national monument), the **Dolmen-Chapel of São Brissos** (a red-tile-roofed, whitewashed chapel built around a dolmen) and, finally, the **Dolmen of Comenda** (two massive upright slabs topped by a lintel of granite, a detail, it almost seems, of Stonehenge). To find any of these remote sites, however, you must consult your Turismo leaflet.

You'll be in cork country as you search for these Stone Age relics, and there's an almost biblical quality about this landscape, where trees misshapen as scarecrows dance over the horizon. Cork oaks are the Alentejo's single most important crop, providing as they do more than half the world's supply of cork. These evergreen oaks look a lot like the olive trees that often grow among them. But you *can* tell the two apart. Cork oaks have pricklier, greener leaves and their tops are flat, almost as if a crop duster had come flying low across the plains, shearing every cork in its path. It takes 40 years for an oak to produce good cork, which explains the old Alentejo saying: "If you plant for yourself, sow a vineyard; if you plant for your son, put in an olive tree; but if you are thinking of your grandson, it's a cork oak you want."

The oaks are stripped of their bark (cork) every nine years; the job is done between May and September by methods developed generations ago. Using sharp, elongated axes, men slit the bark vertically down each side of the trunk and large lower limbs. They then pry the cork away in halves or quarters, leaving a trunk so raw, so red it looks mortally wounded. But soon the rust red dulls to cinnamon brown, then chocolate, then inky black. All of this before a new layer of cork begins to grow. It's quite a show: hills and hills of cork, in different stages of development, parading across fields of wildflowers—yellow, red, purple, blue. If you squint your eyes, it's easy to imagine that someone has covered the cork orchards with Arraiolos's finest carpets.

Another interesting side trip from Evora is Evoramonte on the road (N 18) to Estremoz; see the section on Vila Viçosa and Elvas side trips that follows the Estremoz section, below.

ESTREMOZ AND THE POTTERY TOWNS

If you'd like to see the Alentejo's liveliest country market at high-octane pitch, you should begin on a Saturday morning. That's when farmers converge on Estremoz, 46 km (29 miles) northeast of Evora on N 18, from every direction. Suddenly its main downtown square becomes a two-acre cacophony of rabbits, chickens, ducks, and geese, of mopeds, pickups, and two-wheeled donkey carts. If it's cheese or sausage you seek, chewy loaves of hearth-oven bread, hand-carved wooden spoons, or even a cutaway sheepskin cloak like the ones the shepherds wear, then this is the time to come. And the earlier the better, if you want to make it to the pottery towns south of Estremoz before they close, at 1:00 P.M.

If, on the other hand, you merely want to pick up a few pieces of pottery at the Estremoz market, any day will do, because the ceramics stands stretching along the south side of the square are permanent installations. What they sell are the primitive plates and platters of Redondo, a pottery village about a half hour south of Estremoz; the somewhat more refined hand-painted earthenware of São Pedro de Corval (a half hour farther south—see below for both); stacks of the rustic terra-cotta jugs and pots made everywhere in the Alentejo; and platoons of *bonecos* (festive clay figurines), for which Estremoz is famous.

Estremoz

The market is only one of Estremoz's attractions. Facing the east side of the main downtown square, the Rossio, directly opposite the market, there's the funky little **Museu Rural** on the ground floor of the town hall, a touching, if eclectic collection gleaned, it would seem, from local outbuildings and attics. These vintage farm and kitchen implements, and the bright provincial costumes, are the essence of the Alentejo, even today.

There's an even better exhibit at the Municipal Museum, inside the 17th-century walls at the top of the old town. To reach it follow the pousada signs, which will lead you up through steep rocky streets barely wide enough to swing a Honda to the 13th-century castle (now a pousada) that presides over Estremoz. The houses squeezed in here are white, squintingly so—their snowy marble lintels and windowsills, scrubbed to high glare, will bounce your light meter's needle right off the top of the scale. There's every reason for Estremoz to call itself "The White City Where Marble Shines."

As you nose your car uphill to the castle-pousada you're likely to see women out with paint buckets and mop-handled brushes, inky figures in widow's weeds and crumpled porkpies of black felt, applying yet another coat of whitewash. These *donas de casa* no sooner finish painting a row of houses than they begin all over again. It's what psychiatrists might call obsessive-compulsive behavior. An old Alentejo joke about it may not be entirely apocryphal: It seems that a hunter once hung his gun at a café door, grabbed a bite inside, then came outside to discover that, while he'd been eating, his gun had been whitewashed along with the rest of the house.

There's plenty of space to park beside the Pousada da Rainha Santa Isabel, but be a bit wary of the children begging for escudos and cigarettes, even though their eyes are soulful enough to melt the stoniest heart—and be sure to lock car doors, windows, and trunk. If you aren't staying at this, the most palatial of Portuguese pousadas, have a quick look inside its marble halls before popping across the square to the Municipal Museum. Also ask the man at the reception desk if you can see the locked tower room where Rainha Santa Isabel is said to have died. It's a little chapel now, and the blue-and-white *azulejos* lining its walls tell the life story of this saintly 13th-century queen.

If you're staying at Estremoz in the **Pousada da Rainha Santa Isabel**, or in one of the recommended manor houses nearby (see Choosing an Alentejo Base, above), you'll certainly want to dine in the pousada's dining room. It is positively princely, two banquet-size rooms with ceilings so high they all but vault out of sight, with massive antique armoires and a menu practically identical to that of the pousada at Evora (see above). Once again, stick with the Portuguese specialties. The chef here isn't quite as good as the one at Evora, maybe because there are so many more mouths to feed here (tour-bus groups often stop to eat, if not to sleep), or maybe because the kitchen is so far removed from the dining room—down two steep marble flights at the far end of the castle. Did King Dinis and his wife, the Rainha Santa Isabel for whom the pousada is named, also have to contend sometimes with cold chops and roasts? No doubt. But things are improving today, thanks to an energetic, organized new pousada manager who has had the great good sense to let his wife, a cook of uncommon skill, prepare some of the pousada's sinfully rich *doces de ovos* (egg sweets), using old family recipes. They're trundled to your table aboard a double-decker pastry chariot, and you won't go wrong ordering the *sopa dourada* (golden soup, a cinnamon-spiked egg-yolk custard strewn with cubes of toast or cake) or *toucinho do céu* (bacon from heaven, a translucent egg-and-pumpkin tart so sweet it sets your teeth on edge).

To many visitors, it's surprising that Estremoz, a largely agricultural town, should possess a **Municipal Museum** of such cultural clout. Its street-level galleries showcase an exuberant procession of little clay *bonecos*—shepherds holding suckling lambs, peasant women balancing baskets of eggs on their heads, cavalrymen dressed up like Napoleon, and, of course, hundreds of saints, the most popular of all being Rainha Santa Isabel, who stands straight and tall with an apron full of roses. Legend has it that this queen's goodness irked King Dinis. He scolded his wife repeatedly about giving so much to the poor, but she went right ahead. Once he nearly caught her distributing bread to the homeless, but when he demanded to see what she had hidden in her apron, the loaves had turned to roses.

The Municipal Museum has an upstairs, too, full of antique weapons and agricultural and culinary implements; but most interesting of all are the model Alentejo rooms.

If you cross the Municipal Museum's rear courtyard, a clutter of broken Roman columns and capitals, you'll find sculptors at work in a little shed. They are the Ginja brothers, Arlindo and Afonso, who transform brown blobs of Alentejo clay into faithful replicas of the *bonecos* in the museum. Most of their output goes into museums and museum shops, but they do keep a few pieces on hand to sell to visitors who happen their way.

If you aren't dashing on to see the potteries at Redondo and São Pedro de Corval before they close, drive back down to the north side of the market square for lunch at the **Aguias d'Ouro** (27 rossio Marquês de Pombal). The ground-floor *tasca* will be bedlam, a high-decibel, shoulder-to-shoulder mob of townsmen and farmers in from the country. What you want is the bigger, quieter upstairs restaurant, which is subdivided into a series of cozy, informal dining rooms, most of them paneled in blond wood and floored in herringbone parquet. This is a strictly white-tablecloth operation up here, and chef João Maria Serrano Grasina, a 15-year veteran at Aguias d'Ouro, ranks as one of the Alentejo's best cooks. He concentrates on *cozinha tipo da região* (typical regional cooking), and his specialties include *arroz de faisão* (wild pheasant braised with rice—meltingly tender except for the occasional piece of buckshot), a porridgey sweet-sour game soup thickened with crumbles of bread, and a bubbling *fejão dobrada* (earthen casserole of white beans, sausages, and tripe redolent of fresh coriander).

The Pottery Towns

You'll have to leave before lunch if you want to see the pottery of **Redondo**, a distance of 25 km (16 miles) south on N 381. Although housing developments are springing up west of the town, Redondo remains a backcountry hamlet of treeless streets and one-story houses snoozing under the fierce Alentejo sun. Its raison d'être is pottery, and the buildings you see emblazoned with plates are shops, sometimes with attendant *olarias* (potteries). At any one of them you can buy classic Roman water jugs, *tachos barros* (rectangular clay casseroles), and whole sets of tableware with motifs so primitive they border on the childish. The stuff is absurdly cheap—and extremely fragile.

The more skilled potters at **São Pedro de Corval** are as likely to turn out a fancifully painted beanpot or candlestick as a plate or platter. This little town is no more than a half-hour drive from Redondo, 28 km (17.5 miles) via N 381 south to Reguengos de Monsaraz, then 8 km (5 miles) east on 214 toward Monsaraz. Most maps don't even show it, but you'll recognize it easily enough by the giant amphoras set by the side of the road (some of them even have "*olaria*" lettered on them). You don't need an appointment to visit any of the little potteries here. A cheerful *bom dia* (good morning) or *boa tarde* (good afternoon) will usually get you inside to watch potters bending over their wheels, to see kilns being loaded, and, almost needless to add, to buy. Most of these potteries have a "seconds" room, where it's often possible to unearth a treasure or two among the throwaways.

Between São Pedro de Corval and the perched walled town of Monsaraz, 8 km (5 miles) straight ahead to the east, there are two important Stone Age sites: the **Menhir of Outeiro**, an 18-foot monolith so impressive it was used to illustrate the term *menhir* in a French book on prehistoric Brittany, and the **Menhir of Bulhoa**, a simple phallic shape covered with inscriptions. (Again, you'll need the leaflet you picked up in Evora to find them in these boulder fields.)

Monsaraz

Few tourists are on to Monsaraz, a tiny Moorish town set on a jut of rock above the Guadiana river and the Spanish border. A good thing, because once tourists crowd into its sleepy streets, once they begin scrambling over the ramparts of its 13th-century **castle**, Monsaraz will slip forever out of its time warp. Halfway along stony rua Direita (the main street that extends from the town gate to the castle) you'll come upon the 16th-century village church (worth a quick look), and directly beside it an 18th-century pillory.

The local Turismo office stands at right angles to the

church, but it's rarely open. No matter. The main attraction is Monsaraz itself, the rows of 16th- and 17th-century town houses with Gothic doorways and coats of arms, the women who gather in a patch of shade to gossip and embroider, the children who play in a wedge of sunlight, and, not least, the 360-degree vistas down across the Alentejo plains from this fortified town that towers 1,060 feet above them.

One of the Alentejo's most important megalithic sites, a place where fertility rites are believed to have taken place, can be found in the valley on the back side of Monsaraz. If you're interested in tracking it down, you must wind down the mountain's southern slope on the road toward Mourão (route 214 south). Almost at the foot of the mountain, in stubby fields to the right, you'll find the **Cromlech of Xarez**, a 12-foot phallic menhir surrounded by 50 standing stones arranged in a square. It's just off the main road, and visible, too. Still, lest you miss it, it's best to consult your trusty Turismo leaflet.

If you continue several kilometers farther south along the Guadiana, route 214 will intersect N 256. A right turn onto this major highway will bring you back to Reguengos de Monsaraz in less than 20 minutes. All that remains now is to pick up the route you want to follow back to your home base in Evora, Estremoz, or Vila Viçosa (for which see the following section). None is more than an hour away.

VILA VIÇOSA AND ELVAS

This easy day trip will take you across the central Alentejo. If you're starting out from Evora, you must drive east to Estremoz (N 18, then N 4/E 4). If you leave early enough (no later than 8:30 A.M.) there will be time to snake up the mountain to **Evoramonte**, 17 km (11 miles) before Estremoz on the N 18, a Medieval castle town in the clouds that is visible from both Evora and Estremoz.

Evoramonte's **castle**, cloverleaf in design, has recently been plastered over with a hideous white preservative that gives it the appearance of a stage set. But it's real, all right, a proper 14th- to 17th-century castle built on Roman-Moorish foundations that has earned a place in Portuguese history books. Here, in 1834, Crown Prince Pedro defeated his younger brother, Miguel, ending the ten-year Miguelist

War—nothing more than fraternal squabbling over who would sit on the throne of Portugal. The brothers signed a peace treaty at the Convention House just below the castle on Evoramonte's only street. A plaque marks the spot.

Today the castle caretaker lives here, and if you knock on his door he'll unlock the castle. From its top the whole of the Alentejo spreads out below you, a rumpled counterpane of browns and greens sprinkled with paper-white villages and *montes* (country estates).

Evoramonte itself is a backward little town, a chalky row of houses with a chapel at one end and the castle at the other, all of them wrapped in massive crenellated stone ramparts, parts of which date back to the 14th century.

To reach Vila Viçosa from Evora you needn't go into the town of Estremoz. The road that N 18 runs into a bit to the northeast after Evoramonte, the N 4/E 4, sweeps around to the south of it on its way to the Spanish border. Just 15 minutes east of Estremoz there's a wide fork in the road, the right prong angling southeast to **Borba**. Take it. This wide place in the road has two claims to fame: its creamy pink marble and its robust red wine. And as some collectors have discovered, Borba is one of the best towns in Portugal for antiquing. There are shops all along your way, some marked with giant copper cauldrons, others by sidewalk clutters of bric-a-brac. You'll have no trouble spotting them. Nor should you have any difficulty finding a place to park in this one-horse town.

Vila Viçosa

Your destination, however, is Vila Viçosa, 5 km (3 miles) directly south on N 255, a much bigger town of broad streets and esplanades planted with orange and lemon trees that in spring send their tart aroma clear across town into the marble quarries beyond. (The combination of intensely perfumed air and marble dust is sometimes enough to activate the most latent allergy.)

Although a moldering 13th-century castle greets you as you enter Vila Viçosa, the real reason for visiting is the **Paço Ducal** (Ducal Palace), the country seat and summer residence of the Braganças, Portugal's last ruling dynasty. It was begun in 1501, not finished until 100 years later, and as long as the Braganças owned it was forever being changed and enlarged. Today the palace occupies more than half the town, if you include all the outbuildings, topiary gardens, and the *tapada* (walled chase), which alone measures 18 km (11 miles) around. It's quite a spread, and most visitors are duly impressed. But not Joseph Baretti, an Italian critic who toured the place in 1760. "The furniture is rather mean than old," he scoffed, "and there are a hundred houses in Genoa incomparably better."

Not likely. It's true that the palace's façade, a vast three-story sprawl of marble, has the austerity of an office building. Or maybe a barracks. But the immense macadam square (Terreiro do Paço) fronting the palace is partly to blame. It may once have been the scene of bullfights and rambunctious festivals, but today it resembles a parking lot.

What you see inside, however, is nothing if not regal, and you sense it the instant you step inside the cool, polished marble entry. You must join a guided tour, alas, to see the quarters upstairs, and even though you are hurried through these elaborately tiled, muraled, draped, and furnished rooms you'll find that an hour has elapsed by the time you are led down to the ground-floor royal kitchens (a blinding battery of copper), then out again into the sunshine.

You will leave the Paço Ducal with mixed impressions: of faded Aubusson carpets and Gobelin tapestries desperately in need of repair, of ornately inlaid marble tables, of showery crystal chandeliers, of pastel silk-lined bedrooms, of biblical wall panels worked out in tiles of Delft blue (these, it turns out, *were* designed by a Dutchman). You'll sense that ghosts wander these lonely corridors at night and that closets rattle with family skeletons (only natural, given the number of deaths and murders that took place here).

But most of all you will come away from this particular palace touched by the artistry of King Carlos's sketches and watercolors. As someone once commented, "What a pity he had to waste time on being a king!" Indeed. One wintry day in 1908, after travelling from Vila Viçosa to Lisbon, King Carlos and Crown Prince Luis Filipe were assassinated as they arrived at Lisbon's big waterfront praça do Comércio, better known as Black Horse Square.

For manor-house accommodation at Vila Viçosa, see Choosing an Alentejo Base, above.

Elvas

Once you've seen as much of Vila Viçosa as you'd like, retrace your steps through Borba to N 4, then drive 28 km (17.5 miles) east to the fortified border town of Elvas, where you can lunch at the **Pousada de Santa Luzia** (on your right as N 4 nears the main town gate). This casual little place won't win any prizes for decor (beamed ceilings that look prefab, and bare, off-white walls), but who cares? The food is first-rate and the menu usually includes a little of everything that makes Alentejo cooking the most Portuguese of the Portuguese: *sopa de grão* (thick chickpea soup greened with shreds of spinach), *ensopado de borrego* (garlicky mutton and bread stew warmed by red peppers), *pezinhos de porco de coentrada* (braised pig's trotters with fresh coriander), and *torta laranja* (rolled orange torte), to name only four of the specialties that appear on the menu with some regularity.

The pousada modestly calls its dining room "one of the best restaurants in Europe." That's stretching it, but no one can deny that it does have one of the Alentejo's—one of *Portugal's*—best country kitchens. This is the place to enjoy the plump green olives for which Elvas is famous, also the place to pick up a little wooden box of the local sugarplums. These glacéed jade-green bonbons, sold at the pousada desk, make a delightful K ration to keep in your car as you prowl the Alentejo.

After leaving the pousada, turn right onto N 4 and drive a few meters uphill to the main gate of Elvas (a left turn at a busy intersection). Elvas is one Portuguese town that's more appealing from afar than it is up close. The city center seems completely overwhelmed by the mighty 17th-century ramparts that enclose it; in fact, the sun rarely reaches the narrower alleys and back streets. Even at high noon some parts of town are so dark you feel you should wipe away the shadows. Still, it's worth your while to spend a half hour navigating Elvas's web of streets, if only to get a sense of this old Moorish bastion, one that remained in Moslem hands 100 years longer than Lisbon. You can walk the battlements, and for your trouble you'll be rewarded by wide-angle views into Spain. You can also clamber about the hulking **Moorish castle**, which continues to dominate the town.

But most people find the high-striding **Amoreira Aqueduct** directly west of town far more impressive. To reach it, return to the main city gate, drive right onto N 4 and head west toward Estremoz. No sooner have you passed the pousada and begun to arc down a long hill than you will see this architectural triumph, an ancient wall of arches four and five tiers high, dwarfing rows of eucalyptus as it marches across the plain into town. Like the aqueduct at Evora, it looks Roman—and its foundations are Roman—but the aqueduct itself was built much later, between 1498 and 1622. The citizens of Elvas paid for it themselves, and it still brings them water.

As you reach the bottom of the hill you'll see a little district road veering off to the right, toward the aqueduct. If you take it, you can drive right under those towering arches. The track turns to dirt here, but if you persist and follow it 200 or 300 yards uphill, you will get the town and aqueduct in the correct perspective—and in the proper light. The late-afternoon sun will have turned the aqueduct's old weathered stones to gold and sidelighted each white house inside the ramparts of Elvas.

From here you can make your way back to your home base, either the way you came or once again opting for any alternative route headed the right way. All secondary roads are well marked and well paved, and you're never more than a few miles from some little village.

Castelo de Vide and Marvão

Whatever your home base—Evora, Estremoz, or Vila Viçosa—you can easily tour these two Medieval walled towns in a single day, even though the jaunt will lift you out of the rolling prairieland and into the São Mamede and Marvão mountains of the northern Alentejo. From Estremoz it will take you about two hours to reach Castelo de Vide, from Vila Viçosa about 20 minutes longer, and from Evora about 40 minutes more, because in each case you must first drive to Estremoz (east on N 18 from Evora and west on N 4/E 4 from Vila Viçosa). From Estremoz it's a more-or-less straight shot 59 km (37 miles) north via N 18 to Portalegre, the first town of consequence on the road to Castelo de Vide.

This road has just been straightened and widened, and it's often heavily trafficked by trucks. The highway arcs around the west end of the not-very-attractive industrial city of Portalegre (best known for its finely woven tapestries), so you miss the inner-city gridlock. But you must watch carefully as you reach the town's northern fringes, lest you miss the right turn onto N 246 to go north the last 22 km (14 miles) to **Castelo de Vide**.

If you want a breath-catching view of this old Roman spa, a white town of red-roofed cubistic houses jumbled up the slopes of a castle hill, keep an eye out as you near Castelo de Vide for a blacktop turning off to the right. Signposted "Sa. da Penha," this narrow road climbs onto a great green shoulder of mountain directly opposite town, crests at the little **chapel of Nossa Senhora da Penha**, then winds back down to join N 246-1 directly east of town, a distance, in all, of about 6 km (4 miles). There are lumberjacks on these heights slashing their way through forests of chestnut, pine, and eucalyptus, and it's said that one of them places a candle in the chapel window each night so that it shines over Castelo de Vide, bright as an evening star. The chapel itself is about a three-minute hike up above the road via stairs and well-marked paths. But it's the *view* that's worth the climb. If you follow the forest road down the eastern flank of the mountain you'll find *miradouros* (lookouts) providing panoramas down over a town that is unquestionably one of Portugal's prettiest.

Castelo de Vide doesn't disappoint up close, either, at least once you make your way through the modern sprawl of apartment blocks up to **praça Dom Pedro V**. You can park here while you explore the rest of the town on foot. The square itself is rimmed by fine 17th- and 18th-century mansions, but the focal point is surely the towering **church of Santa Maria** (more impressive outside than in, because it's strangely barnlike). The **Judiaria** (old Jewish ghetto) ascends from the square to the castle on tilting, twisting cobbled alleys past dozens of low white houses, each of which, it seems, is entered by a Gothic doorway and festooned with pots of geraniums.

For some reason, the **castle** was built outside the original town walls. Its keep belongs to the 12th century, and the castle (finally completed in 1327, although it was begun much earlier) is now little more than a shell. It was here, in the 13th century, that arrangements were made for the marriage of King Dinis and Dona Isabel of Aragón, who, as Rainha Santa Isabel, became one of Portugal's most adored queens.

While at the castle, climb the crumbling ramparts for a kestrel's-eye view down over town. And don't fail to step inside the little **church of Nossa Senhora de Alegria**, entirely paved with 17th-century polychrome tiles, or to stroll through the old town gates into a white, flower-trimmed village that has scarcely changed since the 16th century.

Marvão, just 12 km (7.5 miles) east of Castelo de Vide via N 246-1 and practically on the Spanish border, is an even more startling walled town, gripping as it does a 2,838-foot pedestal of granite (this butte was the Herminius Minor of the Romans). As you approach from the west, Marvão looks completely impregnable, little more than an outcropping of rock. But a road twists round behind this mighty hulk, sweeps through the old 13th-century gate, and clambers uphill to the castle.

The village of **Aramenha**, where you begin your hairpin climb up to Marvão, was the ancient Roman town of Medobriga, for archaeologists a major dig. The important Roman relics unearthed here, however, have all been transferred to the National Museum of Archaeology and Ethnology at Belém just outside Lisbon.

Instead of aiming for Marvão's castle right away, head for the little **Pousada de Santa Maria** (its 14 small, rustic rooms are booked months ahead of time by honeymooners), once again following the pousada signs. The pousada's dining room, an informal, glass-walled aerie high above green patchwork plains, welcomes day-trippers. A good thing, too, because it is hands down this region's best restaurant. Home-cooked provincial food is what you'll get here—lusty soups and stews—and, if you're lucky enough to snare a window table, a view that sweeps halfway across Portugal, or so it seems.

After lunch stroll up along the cramped, rough stone streets of this essentially 16th- and 17th-century town to the 13th-century **castle**. Most of the houses along the way are fitted with lacy window grilles, and many façades are hung with canary cages and pots of red and pink geraniums. It won't take you more than ten minutes to reach the castle from the pousada. There's not much here except high, walk-around battlements from which you can see, it's said, all the way north to the Serra da Estrela, a distance of 100 km (62 miles), and as far west as the great rocky scarp of Palmela directly south of Lisbon—if, of course, the air is clear. But even in less-than-perfect weather you can gaze for miles across the Alentejo plains and over the mountains into Spain. (On damp early-spring or late-fall days, when fog wraps around this town like great billows of muslin, you'll be lucky to see as far downhill as the pousada.)

Nowhere is it written that you must return to your home base exactly the way you came. In fact, it's better to cover new ground. A quick glance at any detailed map of Portugal will show there are many alternate routes. If, for example, you're headquartered in Estremoz or Vila Viçosa, you can backtrack to Castelo de Vide and then, instead of returning to Portalegre, continue straight ahead on N 118 to the crossroads at Alpalhão, where you can turn right on N 18 to go up to Castelo Branco in the Beira Baixa (see its separate chapter) or left on N 245 for the 78-km (48-mile) drive south to Estremoz. The overall distance back south is approximately the same as the route you drove north, and the bonuses include the massive fortified monastery at **Flor da Rosa**, the old Moorish town of **Crato**, and, just a few kilometers west of Alter do Chão on N 369 (a quick side trip), a six-arched **Roman bridge** that's still in use.

If you're Evora-bound you can follow this same route as far as Alter do Chão, then angle southwest across the cork orchards via N 369 and N 370. You will cross the old Roman bridge, then zigzag along the river Seda passing the walled town of **Avis**, which clings to a crag above a mirroring lake (Henry the Navigator's father was Master of Avis before he became João I), then **Pavia** (note the tiny white chapel built into a giant Stone Age dolmen), then Arraiolos of rug fame (there won't be time to stop now), and finally Evora.

Both return trips are easy back-road runs that rarely fail to produce some unexpected bit of serendipity: a merry country wedding, for example, a Gypsy caravan, or a carnival come to town, with old-fashioned carousels being hurriedly assembled in some cornfield.

GETTING AROUND

Although there is frequent train and/or bus service to Evora and Estremoz, it makes no sense to use public transportation, because once *in* the Alentejo you'll need a car to get around. So the best plan is to rent your car in Lisbon, where all major rental firms maintain offices both in town and at the airport. What you'll need is a very compact car that can squeeze through Medieval gateways, not to mention the networks of sinewy streets inside them.

Evora couldn't be easier to reach. It's a fast two hours (144 km/90 miles) east of Lisbon if you head south to Setúbal via the *auto-estrada,* then right-angle east toward Espanha (Spain) on routes N 10, N 4/E 4, and N 14. If you're based in Estremoz, you've another half hour to drive on N 4, and, if in Vila Viçosa, still another 15 to 20 minutes.

ACCOMMODATIONS REFERENCE

▶ **Pousada dos Lóios.** Largo Conde de Vila Flor, 7000 Evora. Tel: (066) 24051 or 24052; Telex: 43288.

▶ **Castelo de Milfontes.** 7555 Vila Nova de Milfontes. Tel: (083) 96108.

▶ **Solar dos Peixinhos.** 7160 Vila Viçosa. Tel: (068) 98859.

▶ **Monte dos Pensamentos.** 7100 Estremoz. Tel: (068) 22375.

▶ **Pousada da Rainha Santa Isabel.** Largo Dom Dinis, 7100 Estremoz. Tel: (068) 22618 or 22694; Telex: 43885.

▶ **Pousada de Santa Maria.** 7330 Marvão. Tel: (045) 93201 or 93202; Telex: 42360.

▶ **Pousada de São Gens.** 7830 Serpa. Tel: (084) 90327; Telex: 43651.

Note: In the United States and Canada, all pousadas can be booked through Marketing Ahead, 433 Fifth Avenue, New York, N.Y. 10016. Tel: (212) 686-9213. British and Australian travellers can make reservations through their travel agent. For reservations at Solar dos Peixinhos or Monte dos Pensamentos, contact: P.I.T., Alto da Pampilheira, Torre D-2, 8° A., 2750 Cascais, Portugal. Tel: (01) 286-7958 or 284-4464; Telex: 43304 PITSA P.

THE ALGARVE

By Carla Hunt

Carla Hunt is a freelance writer and contributor of articles to North American and international newspapers and magazines. Her family has lived in Portugal since 1970, and she travels regularly to the Iberian Peninsula.

Prince Henry the Navigator dispatched some of Europe's most important overseas explorations from the Algarve more than 500 years ago. Twenty years ago the search for new horizons was reversed as travellers made their own discoveries and found that this southern Portugal province held vast potential as a premier vacation playground.

The Algarve region stretches below the Alentejo along the Atlantic coast from the Spanish border west to Cabo de São Vicente (Cape St. Vincent) for more than 100 miles of flowering farmlands, gardens, picturesque villages, and wooded mountainsides. Its most captivating physical assets, however, are Europe's best beaches: long, wide, white, uncrowded bands of sand, framed in the western half of the Algarve by reddish-gold cliffs eroded by the wind into fanciful shapes and indented with sheltered coves and pockets of grottoes.

The quaint little fishing towns atop these splendid cliffs and behind the beaches continue to be swallowed up by inexorable resort development, which, while not as overwhelming as that of the Costa del Sol in Spain, is nonetheless rampant. The old country coastal road is likewise now almost untraceable—lost in condo construction—

but the beaches themselves, blond sand backed by steep rust-red cliffs, have mostly held their own, and the sea is generally fresh and pure Atlantic cold.

Within this setting also lie a half-dozen championship golf courses, choice tennis facilities, horseback-riding centers, fishing and boating marinas, three gambling casinos, and scores of little restaurants where the local wines and dishes of fresh vegetables, fruits, and just-from-the-sea fish show the Algarve at its flavorful best.

The name Algarve comes from the Arabic *al-Gharb,* or the west, signifying the most westerly province of the Moorish Empire, which it once was. The economic and cultural center of the Moorish occupation was in Silves, where the invaders built both massive fortifications and graceful palaces; where they introduced new agricultural methods and products, and where they tended to the civilized arts and philosophy. At the height of its influence, which extended all along this Portuguese coast, Silves was a port on the Arade river with access to the sea. Part of its decline came with the silting up of the river, and its doom was sealed when the king of Portugal, joined by Crusaders from Germany and England, successfully laid siege to it in 1189.

The Algarve rose to new heights in the 15th century, when Prince Henry launched the Age of Discovery from his school of navigation at Sagres at the western cape. In the course of a single century Portugal explored nearly two-thirds of the inhabited world.

Before the Moors and the Discoverers, the Romans had been here as well, and the Phoenicians before them, all leaving just a scattering of archaeological remembrances of things past, although many others were probably lost during the brutal earthquake of 1755. While the region's historical and cultural features are, quite frankly, secondary, there are some sights to see as well as fine traditional crafts to admire and purchase: copperware, handknit sweaters, pottery, pewter, and straw items. Above all, this is a land where the great outdoors is indeed great.

Most visitors come from Lisbon, a 40-minute flight to the southern-coast airport at Faro. When coming from Spain in the east, passengers and cars are ferried across the frontier at the Guadiana river between the town of Ayamonte on the Spanish side and Vila Real de Santo António on the Portuguese coast.

But the best way to approach the Algarve is to drive down from Lisbon—an easy four hours on the most direct new highway or a longer, leisurely route through the heart of neighboring Alentejo province, which ends at the natural obstacle of the Caldeirão and Monchique hills on the north side of the Algarve. The mountain road then twists up through the pine and eucalyptus forests before dropping down on the far side to the Algarve plain. Along the route down to the Atlantic coast, almond trees may be blooming in January or February, and green or purple figs will be ripening in groves for picking from June to August. While water-sprinkler hoses have mostly replaced the old Arab waterwheel method of irrigation, this is still the traditional part of the Algarve, flowering and quaint, and worth exploring by taking almost any road turning inland from the main east–west highway; you might even see a wonderful old painted cart drawn by a donkey in full tassled harness pulling farmer and produce to market.

The Algarve's pleasures are informal, friendly, and very reasonably priced, with the glaring exception of gasoline to fuel that must-have rental car. Logistically, it is almost impossible to explore the area via point-to-point bus service or train; the stops and stations are far from the hotels. Local sightseeing companies, however, do have full- and half-day excursions that can be booked at the larger hotels.

The key to discovery is to base yourself somewhere along the coast and hop from beach to cove to village, between the mountains and the sea, as the spirit moves. Visitors can divide the Algarve in half: west of Faro, where major resorts dot the coast all the way to Portimão and even Lagos, and then to the more rugged terrain en route to Sagres and Cabo de São Vicente; and east of Faro, where the hotels and towns come on a smaller scale, to the Spanish border. The road running this entire length is the N 125.

MAJOR INTEREST

Beach resorts between Almansil and Lagos
Picturesque hill towns Loulé, Monchique
Historic towns (Tavira, Silves, Lagos, Sagres, Cabo de São Vicente)

Faro
Old quarter

Palácio de Visconde at Estói
Roman ruins at Milreu

East of Faro
Picturesque hamlets and fishing villages
Tavira's historic churches, Roman bridge

West of Faro
Almansil, gateway to Vale do Lobo and Quinta do Lago
Albufeira, old Moorish town, the Algarve's leading tourist center
Fishing port of Portimão, good shopping and restaurants
Lagos, 18th-century chapel of Santo António
Sagres, site of Prince Henry's navigation school
Land's end at Cabo de São Vicente

The Hill Towns
Loulé, restored Moorish castle, Saturday farmers' market
Arab castle at Silves
Caldas de Monchique spa

FARO

Since the middle of the 16th century Faro has been the provincial capital of the Algarve. Today, life here revolves around the colorful little harbor, bordered by palms and parks, and around the outdoor cafés that crowd the mosaic-paved **rua Santo António**, a pedestrian zone chockfull of small boutiques and shops selling straw and wicker baskets, cooking pots, pewter, pottery, and table linens.

Although Faro's long history predates even Moorish domination, little of the town's early architecture remains from the period prior to the earthquake of 1755. The old quarter, still surrounded in part by the ancient defensive walls, is the most peaceful and charming section of the city, one you enter through the **Arco da Vila**, an Italianate gateway whose arch is crowned by a statue of Saint Thomas Aquinas. The walls enclose narrow cobbled lanes and tree-shaded squares, as well as the austere **Sé** (cathedral), its grimness relieved by gilded chapels. The cathedral was converted from a mosque after Dom Afonso III ousted the Moors in 1249, and a statue of the Christian commander and hero of the Reconquest stands nearby. Across the cathedral square is the bishop's palace, and behind the cathedral is the 16th-century convent of Nossa Senhora da Assunção, which is home of the **Museu**

Arqueológico Lapidar do Infante Dom Henrique, with items from a Roman villa discovered at Milreu, six miles north of Faro (see below).

Just off the central square is the elegant little **Cidade Velha** restaurant, whose stone, cavelike dining room is tucked cozily into the ground floor of an old house. At lunch and dinner the chef offers up a tasty selection of house specialties such as glazed duck and roast pork with prunes, and for dessert a creamy flan or rich almond tart. The wine list features a couple of notable red Dão wines from the north, a welcome relief from the everyday whites and reds of the southern regional vineyards at Lagoa here in the Algarve.

On rua Tenente Valadem, an old street lined with yellow-tinted houses, stop at number 30, one of Faro's few buildings to have escaped earthquake damage. Its old walls house a former bishop's palace, converted by its British owner into the **Al-Faghar** restaurant. Here's a good spot for sampling the famous local *ameijoas e porco na cataplana* (clams with pork, ham, and smoked sausage). This delicious, if unlikely, mélange is steamed with garlic, white wine, onions, and tomatoes in a *cataplana*—a round, covered pressure cooker that looks like a little flying saucer—a favorite copperware buy for visitors. (The Algarve town of Loulé is the known center for handmade copperwares, but you'll find these pans in Faro as well.) Al-Faghar's house recipe for *caldeirada de peixe,* a local bouillabaisse, is also much more interesting than the thin, rather bland fish stew found in many places. The restaurant **Roque**, over the bridge on the town beach, also does a very good *cataplana*.

Algarve dishes are generally simple and hearty, and if they're not always distinguished, the fresh ingredients make them flavorful. Pork and fish (cod and sardines in particular) are mainstays, as is chicken grilled plain or with *piri-piri,* an incendiary blend of tiny Angolan red peppers with olive oil and/or vinegar. Fresh fruits and vegetables in the south are luscious, as are the fresh-baked breads. Sweets are generally *very* sweet, particularly the delicious and common egg-yolk-and-sugar concoctions flavored with almond, cinnamon, lemon, or orange—a delicious dessert legacy from the Moors.

In the north section of Faro is the Baroque **Igreja do Carmo**, with its "Chapel of Bones" faced entirely with bones and skulls, probably lifted from the neighboring former graveyard, and a little religious art museum with

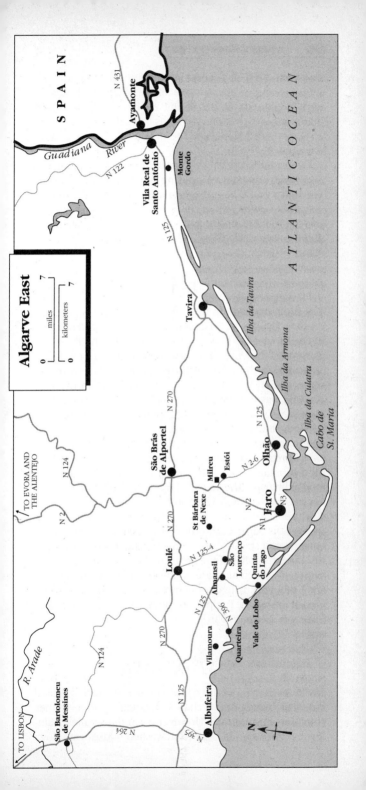

vestments, primitive Portuguese paintings, and an 18th-century statue by native-son sculptor Machado de Castro. Another church worth seeing is the 16th-century **São Francisco**, whose interior walls and chapel are richly bathed in gold work. The life of Saint Francis is told on blue-and-white tiles.

Of secular interest is the Museu Marítimo in the harbormaster's headquarters, housing numerous ship models. The **Museu de Etnografia Regional**, located in the district assembly building, illustrates traditional life in the Algarve with its reconstructions of a house with kitchen and stables, a grocer's shop and bread oven, and costumed mannequins.

Estói

The superstar sight in this part of the Algarve is the 18th-century **Palácio de Visconde de Estói**, which could be likened to a cross between Sintra's Queluz and the water gardens of the Villa d'Este near Rome—all on a miniature scale. It's in the town of Estói, inland 10 km (6 miles) north of Faro off the N 2. The palace, built in the 18th century, was until recently continuously occupied by the owners. It's not open to the public, but the splendid grounds and gardens—a fantasyland of statues (busts of famous composers and philosophers top one wall, Greek and Roman gods and goddesses another), beautifully tiled fountains, and fish-filled pools—are, and they are worth the trip. (The gates are open from 10:00 A.M. to 5:00 P.M., closed between 12:30 and 2:30 P.M.)

Close to Estói is the largest remnant of Roman occupation on the Algarve, the ruins at **Milreu**, a site thought to have been a spa of sorts for the inhabitants of Ossonoba, the Roman capital of the area, and later an early Christian center. The remains are modest: broken columns, the shell of a villa, baths, some mosaics, and a bit of an early Christian church. The portable artifacts are in the archaeological museum in Faro.

EAST OF FARO

The region east of Faro has patches of lush irrigated farms, vineyards, and orchards, standing out in the rather rough and dry terrain. However, even the smallest hamlets have their traditional whitewashed houses with flowers spilling over the window boxes and down the walls. The coast here, with less dramatic beaches than farther west, also has, as compensation, fewer, and rather ordinary, resorts. **Monte Gordo**, lying almost at the Spanish border, is about the best. (It boasts one of the Algarve's three casinos—the others are at Alvor and Vilamoura, near Almansil.)

Eight kilometers (5 miles) out of Faro is **Olhão**, a fishing village and, they say, a former smuggling port, sometimes called the Cubist Town because of its boxy, blue-trimmed white houses. The town's hardy fishermen continue the centuries-old tradition of going far out to sea for their catches. Under the covered market at the dock, great stone tables are heaped with sardines, squid, eels, snails, clams, and crabs. In August Olhão celebrates its fruits-of-the-sea bounty with a shellfish festival.

A ferry transports sunseekers from Olhão to two fine island beaches, **Armona** and **Culatra**.

Tavira

Twenty kilometers (12 miles) farther east lies Tavira, the most attractive town on this part of the coast. Tavira came through the 1755 earthquake in better shape than most Algarve towns, and its lovely white-walled buildings with brownish-pink tiled roofs—some capped with Moorish towers—its churches and ramparts, stand on two hills on either bank of a river spanned by a seven-arched Roman bridge. (Below the bridge, the silted-up waterway from the sea is called the Gilão, and above the bridge, the Séqua.)

The large number of churches here is striking. Fishing folk braving dangers of the high seas tend to be religious, and Tavira remains the most important center for tuna fishing. July and August are the months of the big catch (a single fish can weigh nearly a quarter of a ton), and the fishing itself is a fantastic melee, as fishermen jump onto the thrashing fish trapped in nets to kill them with handheld harpoons. (Visitors are able to watch this gory spectacle by going out to sea for a day on one of the boats.)

The oldest and most interesting churches are in the old town, which rises above the main square, praça da República. Passing through the wall from this main square and walking uphill, you come to the church of the Misericórdia, a good example of 16th-century Portuguese Renaissance style, and crowning the hill adjacent to the castle is the 13th-century **Santa Maria do Castelo**, built over the ruins of a former mosque. The Gothic church entrance is decorated with columns and an elaborate vegetable motif, while the major interior chapel is tiled in decorative blue-and-white 18th-century *azulejos*.

Except on Sunday, it is difficult to find any church in town open, although five seem to be actually in use. After a walking tour of the hilly old city, head back to the colonnaded square by the river for a glass of *medronho* (a local brandy made from berries of the arbutus tree) and coffee, and maybe a plate of grilled sardines. Then consider taking a picnic out to the **Ilha de Tavira**, an elongated spit of sand that cuts the town off from the sea and has two good beaches. During spring and summer months a little boat ferries passengers over and back to the island on demand.

WEST OF FARO
Almansil

As you drive west from Faro on N 125 (or from the airport, which is 8 km/5 miles west of Faro), the Atlantic lies on your left. On your right the land rolls up to hills blanketed in citrus groves and orchards of almond trees that flower at the end of January or the beginning of February, a time when the land appears to be buried in a snowfall of blossoms. An oft-told tale says that a Nordic princess was wasting away in her palace, pining for the snows of her homeland. No amount of gifts from her Moorish prince could relieve her homesickness. Then he planted a grove of almond trees, which bloomed and blanketed the land in white blossoms. The princess smiled at last in her new snow-covered home.

Along the highway (often a drag strip for Portuguese drivers, who decidedly lack the road skills of the Italians) 16 km (10 miles) out of Faro is the remarkable little **Igreja de São Lourenço**, its interior totally covered with glorious 250-year-old blue-and-white *azulejos* illustrating biblical scenes of the life of Saint Lawrence and full of appealing angels and archangels, birds and flowers.

Five farmhouses adjoining the church have been converted into the **São Lourenço Cultural Center**, boasting some fine Portuguese and English antiques as well as

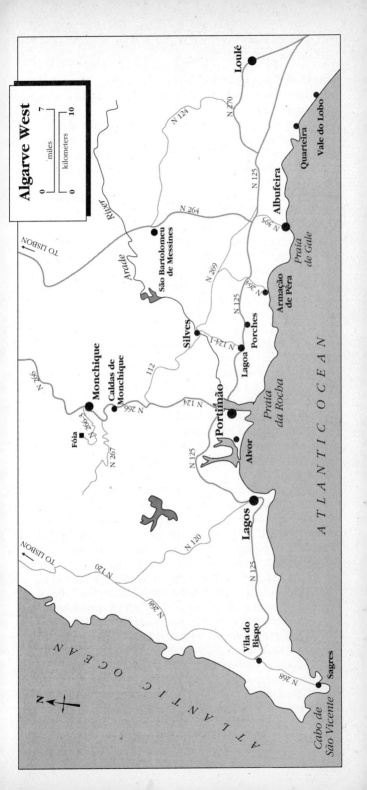

modern paintings and special art exhibitions. The center is often a setting for classical music recitals and other cultural events.

A few miles beyond São Lourenço is the turnoff to the sea at Almansil, along a rutted road that leads to two of the Algarve's nicest resort developments: **Quinta do Lago** and **Vale do Lobo**. Each has a first-class hotel, miles of connecting beaches, and excellent villas for rent for a week or more. Each resort complex has 27 holes of golf, playable in three different ways in sets of 9. The two resorts share the Roger Taylor Tennis Centre, with 12 courts (6 floodlit), a pool, a clubhouse with restaurant, and a pro shop. The Pine Trees Riding Center is in the Quinta do Lago area.

Located right on the beach at Vale do Lobo you'll find the **Dona Filipa** hotel, a member of the Trust House Forte group and for 20 years one of the nicest places to stay in the Algarve. Public rooms are elegant and airy, with terra-cotta floors, collector-quality pottery, and lots of flowers. Most of its guest rooms overlook the sea and the outdoor heated pool; there are tennis courts adjacent to the hotel, and guests have access to the Vale do Lobo golf club and the Roger Taylor Tennis Centre. There will soon be an 18-hole course just for hotel guests on the neighboring Quinta do Lago property, which covers 2,000 acres.

Quinta do Lago is the Algarve's most luxurious development. Just gazing at the futuristic sugar-white mansions, set on sprawling lawns dotted with umbrella pines and designer gardens, is a treat. Signs point to seven restaurants, two nightclubs, golf courses, a riding center, a 29-acre windsurfing lagoon, two tennis courts, a shopping center, and seven condo villages. The **Quinta do Lago** hotel, owned by young Saudi prince Kalid bin Fahd al Faisal and managed by the Orient Express Hotels, has a lovely hilltop position overlooking its own grand pool and the beach, which lies beyond an intervening part of the bird sanctuary of the ria Formosa estuary. Golf (*lots* of golf), a health club, tennis, and squash are provided for guests. Portuguese fare is the order of the day in the **Navigadores** restaurant, while the **Ca d'Oro** serves Italian dishes. Buffet lunch is served around the pool, whose bar is becoming known for a special cocktail concoction of Champagne, vodka, and blue Curaçao.

Tucked away on the country roads that connect these developments are many informal restaurants (always packed in the high season) where the fare of the day will always be good fish, shellfish, chicken, and pork dishes, plus all the fine Sagres beer and table wine you can drink. Ask the hotel concierge how to get to **Gigi's**, a thatched-roof restaurant on stilts down the beach from the Quinta do Lago Hotel, or **João Passo's**, also built out on the beach and closer to Vale do Lobo. There are also a few rather elegant eateries, such as **Shepherd's Casa Velha** at the ocean end of Quinta do Lago and the **Casa da Torre Ermitage**, off the road between Almansil and Vale do Lobo.

Loulé

Loulé, the largest of the inland villages, is 16 km (10 miles) northwest of Faro and a 10-minute drive from Almansil. Not much remains of the old town that the Christians seized from the Moors in 1249, but there is a restored Medieval **castle** right in the middle of town, and the 13th-century parish church has lovely tilework and an unusual three-nave construction. Just outside of Loulé is the chapel of Nossa Senhora da Piedade, home to the statue of Loulé's patron saint, which makes its appearance in the town's yearly mid-April processional and festival.

Long-held traditions of folklore and handicrafts make Loulé perhaps the most interesting of the *serra* (mountain) towns. She outdoes her neighbors at Carnival time with battles of flowers, floats, mask competitions, and dancing in the streets; she shines as a craft center.

In the back streets in the heart of town, craftsmen in tiny workshops can be seen fashioning copper and brassware, leather goods, wrought ironwork, wood and cane furniture, and hats and baskets from woven esparto straw. Saturday is market day, when the buying and selling of crafts and fresh food products is at its colorful best. You'll find the Algarve's finest *cataplana* pots at **Barracha's copper shop**, next to the market.

On the drive to Loulé and other inland towns, you are still likely to see decorated donkey carts along the roads, propelled sometimes by families of gypsies and other times by men and women in somber black clothes and hats, shielded from the sun by black umbrellas. One of the other things to experience when on the back roads in the Loulé environs is an haute cuisine meal at one of the Algarve's finest and most formal restaurants, **La Réserve**, in the tiny town of Santa Bárbara de Nexe. Partridge, wild boar, and hare are specialties in season, but in any season the meal will be memorable—as will the price. On the same six-acre property is the **Hotel La Réserve**, a member of the Relais & Châteaux group and a beautiful and luxurious little hideaway with grand views of the coast from almost any angle, particularly the pool. Guests are accommodated in 12 junior suites and eight duplexes, all with minibars and little kitchens.

Back on the coast and going west from Almansil, you can't miss the city-size resort development of **Vilamoura**. Its 1,000-berth marina draws yachtsmen from all over Europe and even from North America, and many of them make themselves at home in the new **Vilamoura Marinotel**, which is part of the shopping, dining, and entertainment complex. The hotel is comfortable, if unimaginatively modern, and has a pool, two restaurants, a health club, and waterskiing right outside its front door. Part of the complex includes the best movie theater on the coast, which often shows American and English films that have *not* been dubbed in Portuguese.

Very close to the hotel is the **Vilamoura Casino**, a drawing card for high rollers who come for blackjack and roulette and even those who just like to play the slot machines and bingo and watch the floor show. Dinner is served at 8:30 P.M., and entertainment begins at 10:45. Jackets and ties are required for men. (The Algarve's other casinos are in Monte Gordo and Alvor.)

Fewer people go to see the little **Museum of Roman Ruins**, right next to the mosaic floors from an ancient settlement. Between 8:30 A.M. and 5:00 P.M. you can visit this vestige of the Roman Empire, smack in the middle of ever-developing Vilamoura.

From Vilamoura, the easiest way to avoid construction en route to Albufeira, some 24 km (15 miles) west, is to return to the main highway; the road leading back down to the coast for Albufeira from N 125 is clearly marked.

Albufeira

The descent into Albufeira on the access road is steep and, because of the traffic, almost impossible to make by car during the summer season. Parking in town is no easier. Actually, the town is only tolerable out of season, and then it can be rather fun to visit, although it is stretching an association a bit to call it the "St-Tropez of the Algarve."

The town's hill-climbing streets and main square are lined with shops, restaurants, and cafés, converted from fishermen's cottages and warehouses. The main street, **rua 5 de Outubro**, leads along the cliffs to a wide terrace of parasoled tables overlooking the harbor. The street provides access to two beaches, one for folk at play and one for working fishermen. On the latter you will see colorfully painted boat prows decorated with skull and crossbones or the "evil eye," a talisman inherited either from the protective eye of the Egyptian sun god Ra or the evil eye from Moorish times, although the Portuguese say that the eye is there to look out for fish. Also of Moorish origin are the minaret-like chimneys that dot the rooftops here and throughout the Algarve. Even the name Albufeira has Arabic roots (roughly meaning "place of the small bay"). Albufeira was an important fortress town during the Christian campaign to drive the Moors from Portugal.

There are two good times of day to be in Albufeira: at the arrival of the fishing boats around 8:00 A.M., when the catch is transferred to the fish market, and again in the evening for the sunset over the Atlantic. The terrace of the cliff-top **Sol e Mar Hotel** is a good place to enjoy this golden spectacle, and even to stay for a while in the spring and fall seasons. And when the sun goes down it's time to adjourn for a fish dish—grilled sole, turbot, anchovies, sardines, or *sopa de peixe* (fish soup)—and *vinho verde* at, say, **A Ruina** (Cais Herculano), or **O Cabaz da Praia**, where regional dishes come with terrace dining and a sea view. Any time of day the thoroughly British wateringhole called **Sir Harry's Bar** is rather fun, perhaps because it has been a traditional gathering place since the Union Jack and Portuguese flag were first hung decades ago—a symbol of centuries of close relations between the two nations. The bar does a particularly brisk trade in tankards of beer, although chilled white Port is an acceptable alternative.

More elegant dining is featured 7 km (4 miles) west of Albufeira on the local coast road, in the restaurant of the cliff-top **Hotel Vila Joya** on Praia de Gale, where nouvelle cuisine specialties include breast of pigeon in juniper sauce; in the 18th-century farmhouse setting of **O Montinho** for French cuisine, with fine choices of Portuguese wines; at **La Cigale**, which is in Olhos de Agua near Albufeira; and inland and west (just off N 125 about halfway to Portimão from Albufeira) at **O Leao de Porches** in the town of **Porches** for Portuguese and English food served attractively in a converted 17th-century farmhouse.

If you're in this last neighborhood during the day, drop

by at **Olaria**, just west of the Porches turnoff, for plates, vases, candlesticks, tiles—all sorts of clay wares—and almost all of Algarve designs of blue and turquoise on a white ground. Most designs originated when the pottery center was founded on the other side of the road in 1962, and two artists, one Portuguese and the other Irish, applied regional figures to their distinctive pottery.

On the local coastal route to Porches from Albufeira is one of the Algarve's loveliest visitor retreats, **Vilalara**, an elegant two-story apartment-hotel complex that is actually in Armação de Pêra. Vilalara's charm lies in the secretive way its low-lying, Moorish-style structure matches the surrounding sun-bleached rocks, as well as its very private landscaping, including stone walkways, gardens, and little lakes. The cliffside resort is self-contained, with six tennis courts, two pools, and a secluded sandy beach to which you descend via steps cut in the cliff. The **Vilalara** restaurant is distinguished: international dishes and Portuguese standouts, including a full range of delicious codfish specialties. With these, by the way, everyone drinks red Portuguese wines, which are more abundant than and superior to the whites; all over the Algarve, red with fish is traditional. A thalassotherapy center, offering beauty treatments with seaweed and seawater, is due to be completed at the complex in 1990.

Silves

Sixteen kilometers (10 miles) or so in from the sea, roughly uphill for 15 minutes from the turnoff from N 125 at Lagoa (the wine-producing center of the Algarve), and just west of Porches on the way to Portimão, is the Algarve's oldest town, Silves, crowned by a red sandstone castle, the **Alcazaba**. Silves is thought to have been settled in the fourth century B.C., with Roman occupation coming thereafter, as evidenced by ruins of a Roman citadel unearthed beneath the walls of the castle.

But it was the Moors who brought fame and glory to Silves. They called it Chelb, and from the 8th to 12th centuries they made it a river port city more economically important than Lisbon. It was also the region's cultural center, with fountained palaces and bustling bazaars, a place where artists, writers, and philosophers thrived. Yemenite Arabs built the city walls where today visitors can walk the ramparts of the castle and peer into two huge cisterns that watered this garden spot of the Moorish Empire.

Next to the castle is a 13th-century cathedral, built over a mosque, that was partially destroyed by the 1755 quake. The ceiling, built in the shape and style of a coffin, is quite remarkable, and in the first chapel are the remains of João Gonzalvo, a navigator who travelled with the crew that discovered the Azores. Visitors can park their cars right at the base of the castle and by the church, but walking up from the lower town, along steep streets hemmed in by stone houses and too narrow for cars to pass, is a more inspiring way to conquer the summit.

At the eastern entrance to town is the **Cruz de Portugal**, carved in the 16th century from limestone, showing a finely sculpted figure of Christ on the Cross on one side and the descent from the Cross on the other.

While in town, stop at one of many shops for a treat of local almond cakes and figs stuffed with almonds. Plan a visit during the annual beer festival in early June, when everyone gathers to try the varieties of brews available in the Algarve, eat mountains of chicken grilled with *piri-piri* sauce, and watch traditional folk dancers performing. This all takes place within the walls of the castle.

Beyond Silves, higher up in the forest, is **Caldas de Monchique**, a rather cutesy but pretty little settlement nestled in a mountain ravine. The town's curative waters from mineral springs have given it spa credentials since Roman times, and nowadays there are many little hotels and restaurants and more than enough little boutiques and craft shops. A few miles higher up on the mountain road to Fóia is the town of Monchique itself, a good area for a picnic with panoramic views or for an excellent meal at the **Paraíso da Montanho**, located right on the road to Fóia—in season, try their game and casseroles of rabbit and partridge. While the area is famous for *presunto* (air-cured ham), this restaurant, and its more modest neighbors **Rampa** and **Frangos**, serve grilled chicken that is second to none.

Just across the wooded road and down a very steep entranceway is **Mon Cicus**, a gem of a mountain inn with eight very big rooms and a huge suite—all with balconies and stupendous views down to the coast. This happy hideaway has a pool, a tennis court, and inviting walking trails.

Portimão

Driving west from Porches, and past the Lagoa-Silves turn-off, you'll soon reach Portimão, one of the Algarve's largest towns, a major fishing center and a great place to watch the fleets come and go. The scene is colorful, with fishing boats tied up at the piers and fishermen selling their catches of sardines and tuna and mending their nets. Visitors can sample delicious, freshly grilled sardines (juiciest April through September), washed down with wine or beer, at open-air stalls in the adjacent park. Portimão salutes its fishing industry with a sardine festival in August, a chance to eat mounds of fish, watch freshly baked loaves of bread come out of traditional outdoor ovens, visit booths set up by local wine producers, and enjoy entertainment by top Portuguese performers.

From the port it is easy to see across the mouth of the river Arade to the fortifications that once defended this historic settlement from pirates and invaders. Beyond them to the east are the resort hotels facing out on one of the Algarve's most photographed stretches of sand, the beautiful **Praia da Rocha**. From Portimão (or Armação de Pêra, back near Albufeira), small excursion boats take visitors along the coast to see the eerie rock formations and explore the grottoes in the sandstone cliffs.

Portimão is a walker's town, with picturesque narrow streets, houses decorated with *azulejos* and iron balconies, flowering public squares, and pedestrian promenades such as the centrally located **rua do Comércio**, with craft boutiques and outdoor cafés where the locals stop for little cups of strong coffee and almond pastries.

Portimão abounds in good eating spots. The best fish, shellfish, and duck are served at **A Lanterna**, which is just over the bridge from Portimão going east. This place has been popular for years and is crowded year round. For a taste change, try fondue cooked at the table in the informal surroundings at **Mr. Bojangle's Bistro Bar** on rua da Hortinha, or shepherd's pie at the **Dennis Inn and Bar** on rua 5 de Outubro.

Portimão is also a good place to shop for handmade fishermen's sweaters, pewter, embroidery from Madeira, Portuguese Atlantis crystal (actually made north of Lisbon), Charles Jourdan shoes at Portuguese prices at the local **St. James store outlet** (one also in Albufeira), Vista Alegre porcelain, and hand-painted ceramics. **Rua de Santa Isabel** (which runs into the main praça Teixeira

Gomes) is where you will find all these specials, as well as **Vinda**, a boutique full of original clothes and gifts run by David Browne (formerly a buyer at Macy's) and his partner, Vin Gruper. They have gathered crafts from all over Portugal and design their own clothes.

Lagos

Lagos lies still farther westward along the coast, 19 km (12 miles) from Portimão. The caravels sailed by Henry the Navigator's captains were built in the town's shipyards. In the customs house on praça da República, a square ringed with historic buildings and dominated by a statue of Henry himself, captains returning from high-seas voyages held their slave auctions, the first such "markets" in Europe and a painful reminder of the worst excesses of the age of exploration. Parts of the 1,000-year-old **Moorish castle** still stand, as does the 16th-century **fortress** by the sea with its drawbridge, tunnels, towers, and a gate topped by the royal coat of arms.

A splendid survivor of the 1755 earthquake is the **chapel of Santo António**, a Baroque masterpiece in carved wood, its lower walls covered in 18th-century tiles. Next door is the **Regional Museum**, which contains a host of archaeological relics, plus examples of folk and religious arts.

The most celebrated restaurant in town (and one of the oldest, opened in the early 1970s) is **Alpendre** (rua António Barbosa Viana), which is small and cozy with an 18th-century-style decor and an extensive menu. Owner António Matos likes dishes flambéed, including his flaming steak with clams, sole, and mixed fruit. **O Castelo**, with a Medieval decor, is one of Lagos's newest dining spots, and its most elegant. Start with chilled cucumber and prawn soup, move on to poached turbot wrapped in smoked salmon with dry Martini cream sauce, and finish with strawberries (in season). Nearby at Praia da Luz, up from the beach and on the road east to town, is another good restaurant, **Darcy's**, where summer dining is on the patio and winter dining by the fire. It will be hard to decide what to order, with such items available as the house specialty of roast suckling pig, followed by myriad mouthwatering desserts and cheeses.

For the wee hours, Lagos offers an abundance of discos, boîtes, and fado clubs.

Lagos's many narrow, winding streets harbor clusters

of boutiques and art galleries. One of the best streets for shopping is **rua 25 de Abril**. All in all, Lagos is a delightful, manageable town for wandering along slanting, cobbled streets and flowered praças. Many houses—some colored ocher, others rosy tan, still others white with touches of blue—date from the late 18th century. Be sure to meander out of town to the high promontory of **Ponte da Piedade**. At sea and beach level, the reddish rocks here have eroded into strange shapes and the sea has carved out dramatic tunnels and caverns.

Sagres

Prince Henry may have built his caravel boats in Lagos, but he charted their explorations at Sagres with an enormous compass called the Rosa do Vertos (Windrose), designed with lines of stone and set in the earth inside the fort. This small fishing town, 115 km (72 miles) west of the Faro airport, is perched on a rocky escarpment that juts out into the Atlantic at Portugal's—and Europe's—southwestern corner. Unlike most of the rest of the Algarve coast, the landscape here is harsh, the cliffs are dramatic, and the views of the sea below are thrilling.

En route, take time to stop in the town of **Vila do Bispo** (16 km/10 miles north of Sagres) to see the little Baroque parish church, decorated in gilded wood carvings and tiles. Sagres itself, although not a very attractive village, boasts one of the finest seafood restaurants anywhere: **A Tasca**, down by the piers of the picturesque harbor. A Tasca is big, with seating at long tables and with an open kitchen so you can see the chef cooking freshly caught lobster (choose your own), prawns, clams, stone bass, sea bream, sea bass, and swordfish. There is also a good restaurant in the **Pousada do Infante** (which has only 23 rooms, so book ahead and ask for one with a sea-view balcony).

A short drive west of de Sagres is **Cabo de São Vicente**, the last stop westward along the coast, where the lighthouse at land's end provides guidance for ships—and a grandstand seat for spectacular sunsets. From here the world still seems to drop off into the Atlantic, just as it must have back when Prince Henry sent his sailors out into the unknown.

Today you can sit on the point (taking care to dress warmly, although vendors sell sensational hand-knit fishermen's sweaters along the road) and watch the ocean-going vessels pass by, making their way between northern Europe and the Mediterranean or Africa, or beyond.

Within hailing distance of the point of Cabo de São Vicente is a tiny stone fortress wall, enclosing a chapel, a bar, and the **Forteleza do Beliche**, a restaurant and four-room pousada where the prices are half what they are at the Pousada do Infante. It's a splendid place to have lunch or tea, perched high above the craggy coast and sea. It's equally dramatic to spend the night here, and very comfortable. A tiny chapel marks the site of Prince Henry's navigation school, where he gathered cartographers and explorers (Magellan and Vasco da Gama studied here) for what was to become—after his death—the Age of Discovery. Inside the building a rather unsophisticated film seeks to dramatize the saga, but it can hardly match the power of the real setting outside.

GETTING AROUND

Faro is the main airline gateway to the Algarve, served by TAP Air Portugal. Some of these flights are by jet aircraft and some much smaller planes, such as Dornier 228s and British-made Hawker Siddeleys. Both get you to and from the capital in 40 minutes, but be sure to reconfirm all return flights on arrival at the airport in Faro. Seats are at a premium in the summer, and getting through to TAP to reconfirm by telephone is practically impossible. Flights to the Algarve are cut back substantially in the low season, and some days there are no direct connections from overseas flights without a long wait. TAP also has small-plane service three times weekly between Lisbon and Portimão.

By car, the most direct route south from Lisbon to Faro, via Setúbal and onto the newest central highway (E 4), is a 304-km (190-mile) run. The drive from Lisbon to Lagos (N 10 to Setúbal, N 120 to Lagos) is about 265 km (160 miles), on less modern roadways, but you can take a detour to Sagres just before Lagos. And the prettiest drive of all, although longer from Lisbon, is through the Alentejo, stopping perhaps at Evora for the night (see the Alentejo chapter). Travellers arriving from Spain will take the car ferry across the Guadiana river, boarding at Ayamonte and arriving at Vila Real de Santo António in Portugal. The drive from Seville to Faro, for example, takes about three hours—if you make very good time and are lucky with ferry connections.

At both the Lisbon and Faro airports you can step off a

plane and right into a car (advance reservations are advisable). Cars can be rented in one city and returned to another with no additional charge. If you rent a car for 14 days in Lisbon or Faro and return it in Spain (or vice versa), there is a nominal additional charge. On the Iberian Peninsula, Avis seems to have the largest fleet, as well as the most fly-drive packages, which can save considerable car-rental dollars.

There is also daily train service from Lisbon to Faro. Trains for the Algarve leave from Barreiros, across the Tagus. You catch a boat at the Terreiro do Paço station (across from the praça do Comércio in the capital); its price is included in your train ticket, which you buy at the boat depot. Train travel in Portugal leaves a lot to be desired, but the Algarve run is fairly pleasant and the price is always right by rail, in contrast to the rather pricey domestic air ticket. On the Rápido (twice daily), the ride to Faro is four hours, with a stop in Albufeira en route. Some trains also stop in Portimão and Lagos en route to Faro and then continue to the Spanish border.

ACCOMMODATIONS REFERENCE

▶ **Dona Filipa.** Vale do Lobo, **Almansil**, 8100 Loulé. Tel: (089) 94141; Telex: 56848 FILIPA P; in North America, (800) 223-5672.

▶ **Forteleza do Beliche.** Estrada do Cabo de São Vicente, **Sagres**, 8650 Vila do Bispo. Tel: (082) 64124.

▶ **Pousada do Infante. Sagres**, 8650 Vila do Bispo. Tel: (082) 64222; Telex: 57491; in North America, (212) 686-0272 or (800) 223-1356.

▶ **Mon Cicus.** Estrada da Fóia, **Monchique**, 8550 Faro. Tel: (082) 92650.

▶ **Quinta do Lago. Almansil**, 8100 Loulé. Tel: (089) 96785; Telex: 58877; in North America, (212) 839-0222 or (800) 237-1236.

▶ **Hotel La Réserve. Santa Bárbara de Nexe**, 8000 Faro. Tel: (089) 90474 or 90234; Telex: 56790.

▶ **Sol e Mar Hotel.** Rua J. Bernardino de Sousa, **Albufeira**, 8200 Faro. Tel: (089) 52121.

▶ **Vilalara. Armação de Pêra**, 8655 Faro. Tel: (082) 32333.

▶ **Vilamoura Marinotel.** Vilamoura Marinha, **Vilamoura**, 8125 Faro. Tel: (089) 33332 or 33414; Telex: 58827.

Pousadas can be booked through Marketing Ahead, 433 Fifth Avenue, New York, N.Y. 10016; Tel: (212) 686-9213.

BEIRA LITORAL
WEST CENTRAL PORTUGAL

By Dwight V. Gast

Dwight V. Gast has travelled extensively in Portugal and has written about the country for Art and Auction, Travel-Holiday, *and a number of other publications. He is correspondent on Luso-American affairs for the Lisbon newsweekly* Tempo.

Whether you approach it from Lisbon to the south or Porto to the north, Beira Litoral will be your introduction to the stout and stony midsection of Portugal known collectively as the Beiras. Although they are roughly the geographic as well as the cultural center of the country, the three Beiras (the inland Beira Alta and, to the Beira Alta's south, Beira Baixa are the other two former provinces) are not as travelled as many other regions, and are a stronghold of tradition even for Portugal, which as a whole pretty much keeps to tradition.

The Beiras were the original Portugal. Afonso VI of León and Castile established the country of Portugal between the Douro and Mondego rivers at the end of the 11th century, and a century later Coimbra became the capital of the newly established kingdom of Portugal.

Coimbra is still the largest and most historically important city in Beira Litoral, but is only one reason to visit the region. The coastal (*litoral*) section is so candescent the tourist authorities call it the Costa da Prata—the Silver Coast. It is not clear if they are referring to the sheen of its waves, the shimmer of its sands, the gleam of the glassware of Marinha Grande and the porcelain of Vista Alegre, or the glint of the drying fish and the salt pans of Aveiro—all dazzling attractions along the coast tarnished only occasionally by resorts. For despite periodic editorials of protest in Coimbra's newspaper, *As Beiras,* development in Beira Litoral is hardly as extensive as in other parts of the country, and condominiums are not yet a major player in the province's centuries-old struggle with the shifting shoreline.

Nor should your visit be restricted to the coastline. If Beira Litoral was seminal in the creation of Portugal, there are many stones among the seeds. Just inland are three mountain ranges, called *serras:* the Serra da Lousã east of Pombal in the south, the foothills of the Serra da Estrela east of Coimbra, and the Serra da Gralheira north of Aveiro, below the Douro. The gray stones of their castles and hamlets and the green pines of their forests could tell tales of the bloody battles both of the Reconquest and the Peninsular War, but instead a sweeping silence rewards the visitor to these rustic refuges.

MAJOR INTEREST

Castelo de Leiria
Spectacular mountain scenery and bucolic charms of the Serra da Lousã
The romantic and historic university city of Coimbra
Roman excavations of Conimbriga
The fairy-tale forest of Buçaco
The canals and monuments of Aveiro
Natural and folkloric sights of the lagoon of Ria de Aveiro

Our route begins at the south with Leiria, your likely point of entry to the Beira Litoral. After a visit to its castle you head west for a first glimpse of the coast from which the province takes its name. The route then leads inland for a spectacular hint of the mountainous terrain in store if you later head into the eastern Beiras (for coverage see the chapter on Beira Alta and Beira Baixa, below). You continue to Coimbra, where a few days are suggested to visit the historic city and take in the numerous sights in the vicinity. Proceeding north, we propose lodging in the Aveiro area, where the Baroque fishing village, along with its lagoon and outlying villages to the north and south, should keep you pleasantly occupied for a few days.

LEIRIA

Travelling north on the main highway from Lisbon to Oporto, you will enter the west central region just above Batalha near the pines of Leiria, as the Romans did when the settlement was called Collipo, the site of their way station on the ancient road from Lisbon up to Braga. Leiria is as good a beginning as any to the rich history, flat and hilly topography, and diverse handicrafts of the Beiras.

Leiria's importance goes back to prehistory; ancient tribes probably occupied the choice site where the Lis and Lena rivers join here beneath an imposing volcanic outcropping. Traces of a Roman fortress can still be seen on the strategic rock, later contested by Christians and Moors. The present structure sprawling custodially at the summit, the **Castelo de Leiria**, is possibly the most spectacularly placed in Portugal. It dates from 1135, when as legend has it a flapping, cawing crow signaled Afonso Henriques, the first king of Portugal, to recapture the site from the Moors and build a new castle. (The town later expressed its gratitude by nesting the bird permanently on its coat of arms.) Subsequent additions were made by King Sancho II, Afonso III (who held the first *Cortes,* which the common people were allowed to attend, in the castle), and especially King Dinis, who made the castle's royal palace his principal residence with his queen, the beneficent Isabel (later Rainha Santa Isabel of Portugal).

The succeeding centuries added a literary patina to Leiria. The pastoral poet Francisco Rodrigues Lobo, known as the Portuguese Theocritus, was born there in 1580. In the 19th century, the great realist novelist José Maria de Eça de Queirós set *O Crime do Padre Amaro* (*The Sin of Father Amaro*) in Leiria. He wrote about the town's dominant feature: "The castle ruins stand out with a grand historic air, silhouetted against the sky and enveloped in the evening by the circling flight of owls."

Most of the owls have been driven away, however, for in recent years town fathers have taken to illuminating the castle at night, when it stands out golden against the black sky. Regardless of the hour, the castle is always the principal attraction of this trim, prim little district capital.

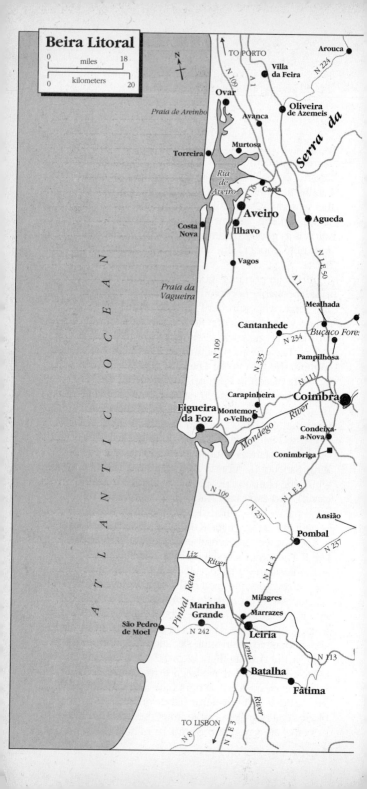

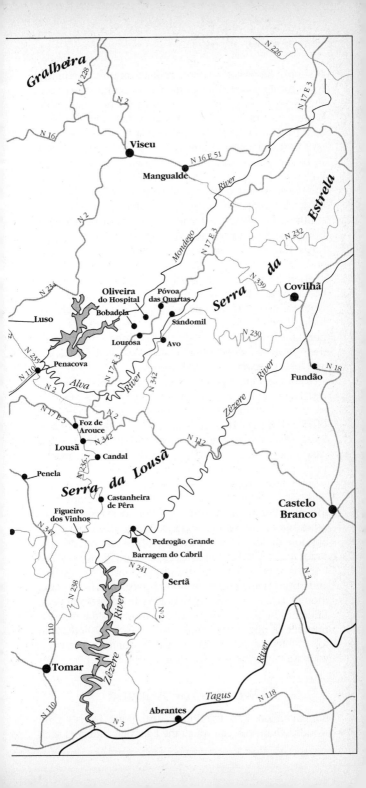

It should be visited on foot, rather than merely admired from the highway, for its other architectural merits and the views it commands of the surrounding countryside. Within its granite walls are the remains of the 15th-century **church of Nossa Senhora da Pena**, its open roof and Gothic windows framing the sky. The royal palace is in better condition, and from its loggia there are lovely views of the town. Best of all, however, is to climb up the creaky wooden stairs to the top of the keep, whence on a clear day the sweeping panorama extends as far south as the abbey of Batalha (see Day Trips from Lisbon) and west to the sea. Also westward lies the pine forest King Dinis planted in an effort to stabilize the land and furnish wood for the ships of Portugal, aptly described by 19th-century Portuguese poet Afonso Xavier Lopes Vieira as "a green and whispering cathedral, where the light plays hide-and-seek." You will likely see lucky local children doing the same—though not whispering—throughout the grounds of the castle, while their more subdued older siblings exchange whispers and kisses between the battlements.

You may want to picnic on the castle grounds, but you can enjoy almost as panoramic a view with a lunch of such regional specialties as *morcelas de arroz* (morsels of rice and pig's blood), local sausages, *brisas do Lis* (a sweet made of eggs and almonds), and *bolo do pinhão* (a cake made with pine nuts) at the **Hotel Eurosol restaurant**, rua Dom Jose Alves Correia da Silva.

After shopping for crafts (baskets, coverlets, glassware, and pottery) gathered in the district capital's shops from the surrounding area, you may want to explore Leiria's other sights—minor in comparison to the castle but pleasant nonetheless. They include a 16th-century cathedral in praça Rodriguez Lobo, a square grandiloquently presided over by a statue of the poet, and a provincial art museum and library in the former bishop's palace. Most interesting, though, is the 16th-century **Santuario de Nossa Senhora de Encarnação** on a hill opposite the castle. It is the first of a number of pilgrimage spots, each celestially sited at the top of lofty staircases, that you will encounter as you work your way northward in Portugal.

West to the Atlantic

An excursion into the **Pinha Real**, King Dinis's pine woods, where you can watch the light play hide-and-seek on the trees and the sandy soil and where you will breathe in the scent of resin, is a convenient combination with a shopping trip to **Marinha Grande**, west from Leiria on N 242. The town developed in the 18th century when the Marquês de Pombal allowed William Stephens to cut down part of the king's forest to expand a glass factory he had purchased from fellow English entrepreneur John Beare, thereby founding the Real Fábrica de Vidros (Royal Glass Factory). Stephens, and after him his brother John, also cut fine figures with the employees; they let the factory workers take music and dancing lessons and present concerts and operas in their own theater. Owned by the state since John Stephens's death, the factory still makes fine crystal by the old methods, but the ring of crystal has all but silenced the ring of the concert hall. English-speaking guides give free tours of the factory (the address, not surprisingly, is praça Stephens). You can also purchase the finished products here at less expense and in greater variety than at shops elsewhere in Portugal and, indeed, throughout the world.

Continuing west through the forest, you will sight the Atlantic at the popular beach resort of **São Pedro de Moel**. Contemplate the ocean over drinks or sample the local specialty of *sopa do vidreiro* (glassworker soup—fortunately, it is made with codfish) at the panoramic bar and restaurant of the **Hotel Mar e Sol**. Its modern but modest seaside accommodations are also among the nicest on this stretch of the Costa de Prata. For the more mountainous (and less trafficked) alternative, head northeast toward the Serra da Lousã, a preview of the spectacular pine-covered mountains characteristic of so much of the Beiras to come.

INTO THE SERRA DA LOUSA

If it's lunchtime when you start off on this leg of the journey, you might eat at the restaurant **Tromba Rija** (Tel: 044-32072; reservations necessary for dinner) in the town of Marrazes, just north of Leiria. As its name, which means "hard snout," implies, regional dishes of roast pig, cured ham, and pork sausages are its specialties. Postprandial sightseeing is just up the country road to the northeast at **Milagres**, a tiny late-Baroque church filled with marbles as well as *azulejos* lovingly depicting the *milagres* (miracles) of a local resident's recovery after being injured in a fall from his donkey cart—not an unheard of accident here even today.

Heading northeast back on the main road, N 1/E 3, through more woods, you will soon spot **Pombal**, the town from which the influential minister Sebastião de Carvalho e Melo, known to posterity primarily for rebuilding Lisbon after the 1755 earthquake, took his title of Marquês de Pombal before ending his years here in disgrace. (The town, however, is said to have taken its name from the *pombos,* or pigeons, that once flocked around its castle.) Sacked during the French retreat in 1811 and further disfigured by modern construction, Pombal has not fared much better than its marquis. Unless you are interested in surveying the foothills of the Serra da Lousã from the top of its 12th-century **castle**, Pombal can easily be bypassed.

Turning east at Pombal onto N 237 past Ansião, follow the twisting, panoramic road to the mountains. Your next stop should be the hill town of **Figueiro dos Vinhos**, which has some fine 17th-century monuments in the Igreja Matriz (parish church) and the convent of Nossa Senhora do Carmo. Farther east on a winding country road is the town of **Pedrogão Grande**, with its even older Igreja Matriz, dating from the 12th century. For sweeping views of the **Serra da Lousã**, continue on to the Barragem do Cabril, a dam in the Zêzere river valley. Proceeding north on N 236 or N 236-1 (after backtracking west to it), you will find one spectacular view after another alternating with the picturesque mountain villages of first Castanheira de Pêra and then Candal.

The road then drops sharply down to **Lousã**, a stately town set in thick woods that has long attracted artists and architects, who have embellished it with fine 18th-century houses, a Renaissance misericord, and a rambling castle made of flaking layers of the local stone. Legend has it that around 79 B.C. a certain King Arunce sequestered his lovely daughter, the Princess Peralta, and his treasure in the castle while he journeyed to Carthage to seek help against invaders. Like the castle, however, the legend is somewhat in tatters, since we do not know what became of king, princess, or treasure. We do know that thousands of treasure hunters have taken their toll on—if not treasure from—the castle, as romantic a ruin as it is amusing, for it is situated somewhat defenselessly at the bottom of the valley.

Continuing northwest you will then approach

Coimbra, passing first through the attractive town of **Foz de Arouce,** which boasts its own rows of respectable 18th-century residences.

COIMBRA

The first thing you might want to do in Coimbra is bypass it, because—perhaps out of deference to its university students—lodgings here are notoriously spartan. One noteworthy exception is **Casa dos Quintais**, a tiny manor house located on a hill overlooking the town. It has only three rooms, however, so you had probably better head for accommodations in the Buçaco Forest area a few minutes' drive north of the city (see below). Once properly lodged, you can then return with a settled mind to explore Coimbra's considerable sights. Hans Christian Andersen, who visited Portugal in 1866 and had the proper imagination to appreciate the fantastical aspects of the city, wrote: "Coimbra is a place where one should stay not just a few days, but several weeks, live with the students, fly out to the lovely open country around, give oneself up to solitude and let memory unroll pictures from legend and song, from the history of this place." Today, a few days usually have to suffice.

In many ways Coimbra represents the essence of Portugal. It is located approximately in the center of the country and was founded in prehistoric times, on the Alcáçova hill above the Mondego river. It took its present name from the nearby Roman settlement of Conimbriga (see below), though its original Roman name was Aeminium. The Mondego, unlike the Tagus and the Douro, runs its entire course in Portugal, and has been so frequent a theme in Portuguese literature it is also known as O Rio dos Poetas (the river of poets). Coimbra was the country's capital prior to Lisbon, and the birthplace of many of its early kings. Its university, founded in Lisbon in the 13th century and transferred to Coimbra, was the only one in Portugal until the beginning of this century. The purest Portuguese is still said to be spoken in Coimbra. Through the ages the city has attracted some of Portugal's most important religious, artistic, intellectual, and political figures.

Too bad that another essentially Portuguese characteristic in Coimbra is not as intangible: the horrendous traffic. Entering the city from the south, via the N 1/E 3 on the

Ponte Santa Clara, you should probably have more than sufficient time to admire the view of the whitewashed city rising on the Alcáçova hill above you as you wait to park your car on avenida Emído Navarro or in the lot at the beginning of rua do Brasil. Simply regard it as your first learning experience in this university town.

The Upper Town

For an overview of the city head for the **university**, one of the oldest in the world, situated in the Alta, or Upper, Town. By car or on foot, it is reached by negotiating the steep Medieval streets up the Alcáçova hill—the Acropolis of Lusa Atenas—to praça de Dom Dinis, where a statue of King Dinis regally welcomes you back to school. Contrary to what Camões wrote in *The Lusiads,* that "Dinis was the first to make of Coimbra a seat of learning and to induce the Muses to leave Mount Helicon for the gentle swards of the Mondego," the king actually founded the university at Lisbon in 1290. For years the two cities swapped the seat of the country's learning back and forth, until in 1537 it finally found a permanent home in Coimbra. The Marquês de Pombal reorganized its academic structure when he expelled the Jesuits in the 18th century. Two hundred years later, Salazar—an economics professor at the university before he became dictator—reorganized its physical structure with the much-criticized replacement of some of the older buildings with modern structures. Though large academic institutions exist in Lisbon and Porto and others have been established throughout the country, when the Portuguese speak of the *Lusa Atenas,* or Lusitanian Athens, they are referring to the university at Coimbra.

Student life at the university is as bohemian and steeped in tradition as is to be expected in Portugal. The students, who Andersen remarked a century ago "reminded us of Faust and Theophrastus," still wear black frock coats beneath capes ripped, they claim, with each romantic conquest. They also adorn themselves with colored ribbons called *fitas,* representing their faculties—red for law, yellow for medicine, light blue for science, dark blue for philosophy, and violet for pharmacy. Each May, near the end of the academic year, fourth-year students burn their ribbons in a ceremony called the *Queima das Fitas,* the high point of a week of student celebrations equally popular with nonacademics.

Many university students in Coimbra live in *repúblicas,* groups of a dozen or so, usually from the same part of the country, who band together to take part in the rigors and revelry of academic life. Rigor comes as much in the lecture halls as in the seniority system on which the *repúblicas* are based; revelry takes place when the students sing serenades of *fado*. *Fado de Coimbra* became distinguished from its Lisbon counterpart almost as soon as it came to Portugal from Brazil in the mid-19th century (as some musicologists believe). Its major local practitioner at the time, Augusto Hilário, established the Coimbra form by having a male voice sing the ballads—the lyrics usually mournfully romantic or intellectually witty—to the rhythms of the traditional 12-string Coimbra guitar. In the school year (other than during the Queima das Fitas), fado can be heard occasionally in the student hangouts of **Agora** (rua Simões Castro), **Santa Cruz** (praça 8 de Maio), **Diligencia** (travessa da Rua Nova), or regularly at **Trovador** (largo da Sé Velha 15), which is also a fine regional restaurant; see more on it below.

The university, then, is an appropriate place to begin your visit to Coimbra. From praça de Dom Dinis (where the statue of the king, some say justly, turns its back on the fortresslike modern faculties of arts, physics, and mathematics), proceed to the entrance to the **Velha Universidade,** or Old University Building. The 17th-century Porta Férrea (Iron Gate) opens on to the Patio do Paço das Escolas, a dusty courtyard where new students take part in ancient initiation rites. The jangly Baroque clock tower in front of you is affectionately known by the students as *a cabra* (the goat). It dates from the early 18th century and has become the symbol not only of the university but of Coimbra, appearing on everything from ceramics to sugar packets throughout Portugal. The staircase to your right leads to the via Latina, a loggia so named because Latin was once the only language spoken by its thoughtful promenaders. The arcaded walk passes the Sala dos Capelos, where degrees are conferred beneath its ornately painted ceiling and the watchful eyes of the kings of Portugal, whose portraits line the walls. It then leads to a terrace with a lovely view of the lower city and the Mondego. Upstairs are more ornate chambers—the Reitoria (Rectory) and the Sala do Exame Privado, which has a portrait gallery of stern-visaged university rectors.

Returning to the courtyard, go past the clock tower and

enter the **Capela de São Miguel**, where a Manueline portal leads to a sumptuous interior. The chapel's showpiece is a Baroque organ decorated with *talha dourada*, the gilded wood typical of the period throughout the Portuguese empire, when Brazil's mines filled the king's coffers. Of more local inspiration are the side altars, masterpieces of Coimbra Rococo.

Next to the chapel is the **Biblioteca Joanina**, built by King João V in the early 18th century, one of the most magnificent Baroque libraries in the world. Dom João's coat of arms hangs over the entrance, which leads to three huge halls embellished with chinoiserie, *talha dourada,* false perspective ceilings, *faux marbre* pilasters, and an inlaid marble floor. Though in such sumptuous company the thousands of books and manuscripts seem merely part of the decorative scheme, it is gratifying to see them actually used by students, under the glorious scrutiny of the king's portrait in a baldachin at the far end of the library.

A short walk down from the university is the **Sé Nova** (New Cathedral), which actually dates from the 16th century. It is enough to admire its ornate façade, which echoes the luxury of the former Episcopal palace across the street, and then visit the latter structure. The palace is now the **Museu Machado de Castro**, though its luxurious courtyards and loggias bespeak its former function more strongly. Named after an 18th-century Portuguese sculptor, the museum houses the country's finest collection of sculpture, an art with a long history in Coimbra. The collection begins with Medieval sculpture, the highlight of which is a mace-bearing equestrian knight who heralds the way to the loggia for another splendid view of the city and river below. The collection continues in a wing on the other side of the loggia, which displays sculpture from the 15th and 16th centuries, when Coimbra's most influential school of sculpture flourished. Artists worked the soft white limestone from nearby Ançã that has mellowed into a pleasant nougat color beneath traces of its original polychrome paint. Another chosen medium was terra-cotta. French artist Philippe Houdart's *Last Supper* is perhaps the most compelling work in that or any medium in the museum. Before a background of bas-relief Medieval architecture, saints and Saviour are portrayed with enticing individuality, down to the detail of Christ's closely cropped hair.

In addition to sculpture, the museum contains paintings, religious objects, tapestries, and coverlets—note the intricate embroidery from nearby Castelo Branco if you're planning to continue on to Beira Baixa and might like to buy a fine bedspread, a survival of the ancient craft seen here. Downstairs you can see what the structure was even before it became the bishop's palace: the dramatically lit, rough-hewn stones that are remnants of the labyrinthine foundation of Coimbra's Roman forum.

Down the street from the museum is the **Sé Velha** (Old Cathedral). One of the finest Romanesque cathedrals in Portugal, it has a rich history. Sancho I and João I were crowned here, and Saint Anthony was ordained here as well. The exterior, topped with battlements like a castle, is starkly Medieval, though somewhat warmed by the Renaissance north door by João de Rouen and the Baroque lantern turret. The austere interior contains a number of tombs and a noteworthy Flemish altarpiece. Stairs off the south aisle lead to a Gothic **cloister**, where, on a quiet day, you may hear the strains of music from students practicing in the nearby conservatory. At night the scene is enlivened by fado from **Trovador**, a restaurant serving regionally prepared trout, codfish, kidney, and other dishes in an upscale rustic setting.

From the cathedral, a cobblestone walk and steps lead down the rua Sub-Rupâs to the **Casa de Sobre Ribas**, a Renaissance palace with doors and windows carved in the Manueline style. This elaborate, exuberant decorative style, which flourished in the early 16th century under King Manuel I and is named after him, is Portugal's most original contribution to architecture. It is characterized by intricately carved knots, nets, shells, anchors, and other Portuguese nautical themes.

A legend attached to the palace is equally detailed. As told by various Portuguese writers, the story goes that the palace was the scene of the murder of Maria Teles, wife of Inês de Castro's eldest son, João. Maria's sister, the jealous Queen Leonor, convinced João that his wife was being unfaithful to him and that he should have married the queen's daughter. João promptly rushed home and stabbed Maria, prompting his disgrace and eventual exile from Portugal. The murder supposedly took place in 1379, while the palace was not built until 1547, so the tale has its detractors; but it does exemplify the kind of legend that is so much the fabric of Coimbra.

On the same street is the **Torre de Anto**, a Medieval tower where Symbolist poet António Nobre lived in the last century. These days, not words but objects are crafted here; the tower is occupied by the **Coimbra Regional Handicraft Center**, where you can purchase such specialties as hand-painted ceramics, metalwork, wools, and linens. Under the tower is the **Colegio Novo**, an attractive Renaissance cloister.

More steps lead to the Arco de Almedina, a 12th-century city gate and vestige of the Moorish presence (*medina* being Arabic for city). Through it is the Baixa, the lower, flat part of the city that stretches along the right bank of the Mondego, where the citizens of Coimbra go about their daily life.

The Lower Town

If the long walk from the university has worked up your appetite, you can easily take care of it in this part of town. *Tascas*—inexpensive restaurants much frequented by students and often indicated only by a laurel branch above the door—line rua dos Gatos and rua da Sota. One of the better ones is **Zé Manel**, beco do Forno 10, which serves an extensive Portuguese menu including *sopa da pedra* (a hearty country soup), *chouriços na brasa* (grilled sausages), *bacalhau no forno* (baked salted dry codfish), and an assortment of grilled meats in a characteristic Coimbra setting, complete with a portrait of Coimbra *fadista* Augusto Hilário.

Praça do Comércio, the square extending in front of the 12th-century church of São Tiago (closed to the public), marks the beginning of the commercial part of Coimbra. Many shops here and on the nearby rua Ferreira Borges and rua da Sofia, a few streets toward the river, sell regional crafts as well as locally produced clothing and footwear.

Just ahead is the **Mosteiro de Santa Cruz**, one of Portugal's most historic buildings. Saint Anthony studied here, and it contains the tombs of the country's first two kings, Afonso Henriques and Sancho I. Other noteworthy features of the church are the Renaissance pulpit and the carved wooden stalls in the choir, upstairs. A door in the south transept leads to the sacristy, where among other paintings you should note *The Pentecost* by Grão Vasco, an important Beira painter whose work you will be seeing more of in Viseu in Beira Alta. From there another door leads to the **Claustro do Silencio**, a Manueline cloister containing bas-reliefs of the Passion based on engravings by Dürer. In one corner is the oval Capela de São Teotónio, which houses the tomb of Saint Theotonius (prior of the monastery during the 12th century) and other relics. Upstairs are more choir stalls, decorated in *talha dourada* with scenes from the adventures of Vasco da Gama.

Farther along is rua da Sofia, the Street of Wisdom, so called because it was once lined with theological colleges. The first on your route is also the nicest: the **Igreja do Carmo**, a 16th-century church containing 18th-century paintings of clerics whose grim robes and grand headgear serve as inadvertent reminders that Coimbra, along with Lisbon and Evora in the Alentejo, was a seat of the Portuguese Inquisition. The remains of the Palácio da Inquisição, in fact, are just down the street, but they are closed.

If your interest in wisdom is piqued, continue along rua da Sofia to visit the other representative theological colleges of the Colégio da Graça, the Igreja de São Pedro, and the Igreja da Santa Justa. Otherwise, this is the part of town to appease not so much your quest for wisdom as your sweet tooth. Coimbra's traditional pastries—*arrufada* (puff pastries), *queijada* (cheese tarts), and custard tarts called *manjares brancos*—are all featured in such places as the **Santa Cruz Café**, next to the former monastery of the same name back at praça de Maio 8.

Across the Mondego

The modern bridge of Santa Clara, most conveniently crossed in a car, leads to more historic monuments of Coimbra on the western side of the river. The first, in ruin from centuries of flooding of the Mondego, is the Gothic former **convent of Santa Clara-a-Velha**, founded under the patronage of Isabel of Aragón, wife of King Dinis. She is also remembered for the Miracle of the Roses, when bread she was distributing to the poor was suddenly transformed into flowers. The miracle, along with her numerous other charitable acts of founding hospitals, orphanages, and homes for fallen women, led to her canonization as the Rainha Santa, the Queen Saint. (She is known in English as Saint Elizabeth of Portugal.)

Another evocative ruin in the vicinity is the **Quinta das Lágrimas** (Villa of Tears), a key set piece in the Portuguese national love story whose heroes are Pedro I and his Galician mistress, Inês de Castro. In the garden of the *quinta* in 1355, Inês was murdered by a contingent of courtiers who feared she would have too much influence on the Portuguese throne, and a spring gushed forth on the spot. "The nymphs of the Mondego were long to remember, with sobbing, the dark dispatch," wrote Camões in *The Lusiads,* "and their tears became a spring of pure water, that remembrance might be eternal. The fountain marks the scene of her earlier happiness, and is still known today by the name they gave it, 'Inês the Lover.' Lucky the flowers that are nurtured from such a source, its name telling of love, its water of tears." Inês de Castro was originally buried at Santa Clara-a-Velha, but her body was transferred to Alcobaça (see Day Trips from Lisbon for Alcobaça and for a variant of this tale).

Rainha Santa Isabel was also once entombed at the old convent, and her Gothic sepulcher was moved to the **convent of Santa Clara-a-Novo**, built up the hill in the 17th century, when a second tomb was added for good measure. Though now used as an army barracks, the church may be visited to see the tombs, the polychrome wood panels depicting the lives of Saint Francis and Rainha Santa Isabel, and the adjacent Renaissance cloister.

Nearby is Portugal dos Pequeninos, where Portugal's essence is delightfully distilled in a park containing child-height replicas of the most important architectural monuments in the country, plus examples of domestic architecture from throughout Portugal and the former Portuguese empire. True to its name, it is quite popular with youngsters, and it also provides a charming crash course in Portuguese architecture for grown-ups.

Other Sights in Coimbra

You should be spending a good piece of your time in central Portugal in the fresh air of the open country in the eastern Beiras. Before you leave Coimbra, though, there are a few outdoor places in the upper city that merit a visit, perhaps even a picnic. The **Jardim Botânico**, near the university, is a formal garden laid out by the Marquês de Pombal. Above it is the **Parque da Santa Cruz**, lavishly planted with flora from throughout the former empire, and above that is the **Penedo da Saudade**, a promenade offering a panorama of the city and the river below. If you would like to take in the view at table, try the nearby restaurant **Piscinas**, rua Dom Manuel, which serves traditional Portuguese cuisine.

THE COIMBRA AREA
South of Coimbra

The excavations of Conimbriga, which are well signposted, lie a few miles south of Coimbra, past **Condeixa-a-Novo**, an appealing town on the N 1/E 3 with its own little Manueline church, some nice cafés in its main square, and the **Estrela factory**, which produces and sells hand-painted ceramics.

The site of **Conimbriga**, occupied since prehistory, was of interest to a number of peoples, including the Swabian (Suevian) invaders from the north, who conquered the town in the fifth century and caused the natives to move to Coimbra. Digging began around the turn of this century; Conimbriga is now the most extensively excavated Roman site in Portugal.

A section of the same ancient road that once connected Lisbon and Braga leads visitors from the entrance past the so-called House of the Fountains, where re-created fountains plash and numerous mosaics depict simple geometric motifs or hunting and mythological characters. The road then leads to the town gate. Off to the right are the aqueduct and excavations of the forum and important public buildings; to the left is another sumptuous villa, the House of Cantaber, filled with ornamental pools in which skeletons, presumed to be from the sack, were found during excavation and remain in situ. Walk back around the wall to examine a third villa before returning to the parking lot, where there is a modern museum displaying ancient artifacts from the site.

A convenient coda to the excursion would be the town of **Penela**, a few miles farther southeast on N 347. One story relates that it was given its name during the Reconquest, when Moorish guards left their post at the town castle and the Portuguese entered, declaring, "Courage! We have a foot inside!" (*O pé nela*); others argue that the name is merely a diminutive of *penha,* the Portuguese word for rock or bluff. Whatever the origin of its name, both theories take into account the main feature of the village, its 11th-century **castle**—a well-placed structure whose views of the surrounding countryside are only enhanced by the weathering of the old structure.

West of Coimbra

Another castle lies west of Coimbra on a pleasant drive along the Mondego's north bank, on a relatively quiet road lined with rice paddies, at **Montemor-o-Velho**, on a site occupied since Roman times (though the present **castle** is predominantly a 14th-century structure built on the Mondego as part of the line of defense for Coimbra). The pale stone castle is largely in romantic ruin, and kestrels hovering above it maintain vigilance and add a Medieval air. Dining options in the area include **Ramalhão**, rua Tenente Vadim 24, Montemor-o-Velho, and **O Castel dos Caiados**, north of N 111 in Carapinheira, both excellent regional restaurants.

Continuing west along the Mondego to its mouth on the Atlantic, you will reach **Figueira da Foz**, a somewhat glitzy town for this part of Portugal that is known for its gambling casino (rua Bernardo Lopes; passport required for admission), bullfights, and expansive beach—all of which make it especially popular with Spaniards from landlocked Salamanca due east. The pleasures of Figueira da Foz are generally less cultural than those of many other towns, but it does sit on a spectacular stretch of the Costa da Prata. If the sight inspires you to want to see some real silver, that can be done at the **Museu Municipal Dr. Santos Rocha** (rua Calouste Gulbenkian), which houses an extensive archaeological collection that includes ancient silver coins. The other noteworthy institution in Figueira, the palace-museum **Casa do Paço**, is decorated with thousands of Delft tiles, a charming variation on *azulejos,* salvaged from a Dutch shipwreck.

East of Coimbra

The mountainous aspect of the Beiras can be appreciated on the relaxing and panoramic drive inland on the N 17/E 3, and lesser roads, from Coimbra toward the **Serra da Estrela**. Spectacular pine-covered mountain scenery leads to a series of picturesque villages, seemingly placed deliberately for rest stops en route. **Lourosa** is noted for its Mozarabic church, built in the 10th century. Nearby **Avo**, a hamlet on the banks of the Alva river, a tributary of the Mondego, contains the ruins of a castle built by King Dinis that towers above the town's many fine granite houses. **Bobadela**, to the north, has a Roman arch and a parish church with an inscription referring to the place as *splendissima civitas*. **Oliveira do Hospital**, a few kilometers east of Bobadela, is another town of ancient Roman origin, though as its name implies it was bestowed on the Order of the Hospitallers of Saint John in the 12th century. One such knight can be seen in the tomb of Domingos Joanes in the Capela dos Ferreiros, in the parish church. Above it is a *cavaleiro* on horseback, much like the knight in the Museu Machado de Castro in Coimbra. **São Giao**, in the foothills of the Serra da Estrela (though not on the map—watch for the sign on N 17/E 3 for the turnoff between Piaches de Alva and Sandamilo), has an elaborately decorated Baroque church known as the Cathedral of the Beiras.

Lunch of Portuguese specialties or robust regional cooking such as *truta com presunto* (trout with ham) and *ensopado de cabrito* (a casserole of kid and bread) and robust red Dão wine can be taken at the **Pousada da Santa Bárbara**, Póvoa das Quartas, a modern inn perched dramatically at the edge of a valley. If the pine-scented mountain air entices you into spending the night, or perhaps several, at the gateway to the Serra da Estrela (see the Beira Alta chapter, below), these are the most comfortable lodgings in the vicinity.

North of Coimbra

The fairy-tale setting of the **Buçaco Forest** area makes an appropriate base for your stay around Coimbra. The most enjoyable driving route there from Coimbra is east of the city on N 111, then north on N 235 at Penacova. Just before Luso, signs will direct you to turn right up a steep mountain road that leads to the gates of the forest. The **Palace Hotel do Buçaco**, a neo-Manueline extravaganza built at the turn of the century on the privileged site of the Buçaco monastery in the heart (and the height) of the forest, provides luxurious accommodations fit for a king—literally. It was constructed as a hunting lodge—not for mad King Ludwig, as it might appear—but for the Portuguese royal family. Less grandiose (and less expensive) is **Solar da Vacariça**, a refurbished 18th-century manor house just off N 336 near Pompilhosa.

The domain of monks since the sixth century, the hilly, sylvan enclave of Buçaco (sometimes spelled Bussaco) was once filled with a number of hermitages as well as the carefully cultivated indigenous and imported trees that are still going strong. In 1810 it was the scene of the Peninsular War's Battle of Buçaco, in which Wellington's troops were pitted against the French on what the duke famously referred to as the "damned long hill" of Buçaco. The French were driven downhill, whence they proceeded south to sack Coimbra, and the "valoroso e glorioso Duque de Wellington," as the Portuguese call him, emerged victorious. A few years later, when religious orders were suppressed in Portugal, the Carmelite monks were expelled from the forest (though some two dozen were later allowed to return to the monastery), which was taken over by the state and planted with even more trees. Today hundreds of species—including a stately Mexican cypress aptly named *Cypressus lusitanicus,* since it became extinct in its country of origin—flourish in the forest beside moss-covered paths and religious monuments.

Pick up a map of the forest at the Palace Hotel, where the extravagant architecture is matched by *azulejos* illustrating *The Lusiads* and the Battle of Buçaco as well as suits of armor the last Portuguese kings were unlikely to have used at the turn of the century. The map will direct you through the forest paths to the Porta de Coimbra, a gate on the outside of which are engraved papal bulls warning women not to bother the hermits and threatening excommunication to anyone who damages the trees. A more strenuous path leads past chapels containing terra-cotta sculptural representations of the Stations of the Cross to the **Cruz Alta**, where there is a museum devoted to the battle, as well as one of the most sweeping panoramas in the entire region.

The Palace Hotel can provide a regal meal of Portuguese classics with prices to match; otherwise, head north down the hill through the pleasant spa town of Luso, then west on N 234 to **Mealhada**, known throughout Portugal for its *leitão assado* (roast suckling pig), served in such regional restaurants as **Pedro dos Leitões**, on EN 1, and best accompanied by a robust Bairrada red wine, though Pocarica white and the local sparkling Mealhada white are other good choices. If you are staying in the area, you might want to vary your dining by driving a few miles west of Mealhada to the **Marquês de Marialva**, largo do Pombal 14, in the town of Catanhede. This reasonably priced restaurant offers *leitão assado,* along with more inventive creations based on traditional local ingredients.

AVEIRO

The most important city in the northern portion of Beira Litoral is the coastal city of Aveiro, the center of an area so sun-drenched that it is referred to as the Rota da Luz, the Route of Light. It is also blessed with a greater concentration of accommodations than anywhere else in the province. Choices include the **Hotel Paloma Blanca**, built as a villa in the 1930s and recently refurbished, in the heart of Aveiro; **Quinta do Paço da Ermida**, a 17th-century farmhouse overlooking the porcelain factory and museum of Vista Alegre a few miles south of town; **Albergaria de João Padeiro**, a comfortable roadside inn a few miles to the northeast in Cacia; the **Pousada da Ria**, a modern inn at the edge of a lagoon north of Aveiro in Murtosa; and the **Pousada de Santo António**, built in 1942 as one of Portugal's three original pousadas (it was remodeled in 1985) on a still-tranquil spot east of Aveiro in Serém.

The Portuguese are fond of calling Aveiro the Amsterdam or Venice of Portugal. Truth to tell, more convincing reminders of the Dutch are the Delft tiles at Figueira da Foz. The architecture, an enticing mix of Baroque excess and simpler but more colorfully painted structures, gives Aveiro its own strong character, though as Andersen justly observed, "there is nothing here except the gondola-shaped boats to remind one of the capital of the Adriatic." He was referring to the *barcos moliceiros,* wooden boats used to gather seaweed for fertilizer. Dramatically high-prowed and vividly painted with primitive motifs, the boats are so unusual that they actually bring to mind less Amsterdam or Venice than the ancient Phoenicians, said to have settled the area. *Moliceiros* are the pride of a summer regatta called the *Festa da Ria,* when the most beautifully decorated boat is given a prize.

The rest of the year, *moliceiros* and the salt-gathering *saleiros* go about their business on the canals of Aveiro, an important port until it silted over in the 16th century. The Canal Central, with its handsome mansions, and the Canal de São Roque, flanked by piles of salt drying in the sun and reached by passing through a quarter of brightly painted fishermen's houses, are reminders of Aveiro's prosperous past and continuing traditions of the present. A walk along either or both will set the mood for your visit to Aveiro.

At the height of Aveiro's affluence a local school of sculpture flourished, and the ornately carved art on display in its museum and churches is the main attraction on dry land. Before seeing the art, however, try the equally sculptural *ovos moles,* sweetened egg yolks nestled inside crisp barrel- or seashell-shaped pastries. One place to sample them is **Confeitaria Peixinho**, near the Turismo, which also stocks the local version of *arrufadas*.

You can then proceed to the visual riches of the town, beginning with the stately façades of the Câmara Municipal (town hall), across from the Turismo and, to its left, the *azulejo*-covered Igreja da Misericórdia. Nearby is the cathedral of São Domingos, which, among its splendors, houses the tomb of Catarina de Atalide, the object of much literary affection as Natércia in Camões's sonnets. Across from the cathedral is the **Museu de Aveiro**, housed in the former Convento de Jesus. In 1472 Joana, daughter of King Afonso V, left her palace for the convent, where she died. Some 200 years later she was beatified as Santa Joana Princesa, patron saint of Aveiro, and shortly afterward received her multicolored marble tomb—a confectionery showpiece of Portuguese art—in the lower chancel. Other highlights are the tomb of Dom João de Albuquerque, the *talha dourada* decorations of the chancel, the *azulejos* of the refectory, and the somber *Portrait of Santa Joana* in the painting gallery.

After taking a short walk to admire the *azulejos* and *talha dourada* of the Igreja das Carmelitas, cross the **Canal Central** for a close-up look at Aveiro's main sources of income: fishing and salt production. At the Mercado do Peixe, active in the early morning, you can watch cod, eel, and other creatures being snapped up by the local housewives who aren't married to fishermen. The little canal running off the market leads to the colorful octagonal Capela de São Gonçalinho, the scene of the annual *Festa de São Gonçalo,* during which sweet cakes are rained down on an appreciative crowd of celebrants. Beyond the chapel, along the **Canal de São Roque**, are the colorful fishermen's houses. On the other side of the canal, reached by a humpbacked bridge, are the salt pans, where piles of sodium chloride glisten in the sun.

Back past the cathedral and the museum on the other side of Canal Central is **Cozinha do Rei**, the restaurant in the Hotel Afonso V, where you can sample the fruits of Aveiro's fishermen with the local specialties of appetizers of *mexilhões* (mussels) *à moda de Aveiro,* followed by *caldeirada de enguias* (eel stew), or *bacalhau* (dried salt cod—Aveiro fishermen used to catch codfish off Newfoundland).

Ria de Aveiro

Though Aveiro may not qualify as the Venice of Portugal, the lagoon called the Ria de Aveiro, stretching north of the city, surpasses its Venetian counterpart in subtle natural beauty and intimate glimpses of an ancient livelihood. The best way of seeing it is to take the boat trip sponsored by the tourist office (Região de Turismo da Rota da Luz, praça da República; Tel: 034-23680). A small motorboat takes you past the salt pans, past the port of Gafanha, where the cod is dried, through the lagoon, past the resort and dunes of São Jacinto, to the beaches at the fishing villages of Torreira and Areinho, and lunch at the **Pousada da Ria**. Its restaurant serves the local version of *caldeirada de enguias* and other eel dishes prepared in a variety of ways, but pork and other meats are also available for ichthyophobes. Taking you drifting past sand dunes, salt marshes, pines, a wildlife refuge, islands, houses on stilts, and locals at work in their *moliceiros* and *saleiros* (as well as other characteristic boats called *bateiras, cacadeiras, erverias,* and *mercanteis*), the day-long trip is a dreamlike experience. The lagoon can also be explored by driving from Aveiro north to Murtosa, or vice versa, along the coastal route.

THE AVEIRO AREA

On the coast south of Aveiro are a number of resort towns. The most charming is **Costa Nova**, which boasts beaches on the ocean and the lagoon as well as houses boldly painted in white, blue, and green. From there you can enjoy the coastal drive down to Praia da Vagueira, from where, if you head inland and then north onto N 109 at Vagos, you will reach the famous porcelain and glass factory **Vista Alegre**. Whereas much of the art of Aveiro is folkloric, the porcelain of Vista Alegre is the last cry in sophistication. Even if shopping is not on your itinerary, the factory is worth visiting. It resembles a stage set for a Portuguese version of *Carmen,* complete with sultry workers having a smoke under the poplars in the main square. The factory can be visited by appointment;

Tel: (034) 22261. None is necessary to see the fine museum of porcelain and glass or to purchase the merchandise in the factory shop.

Farther north on N 109, at Ilhavo, is the **Museu Marítimo e Regional**. Examples of *moliceiros* and other local folkloric and sea memorabilia are displayed along with an extensive collection of shells. Should they serve to stimulate your appetite, there is a restaurant back in Costa Nova specializing in shellfish, **A Marisqueira**.

The towns north of Aveiro hold other specialized surprises. Avanca, on N 109, has a small museum dedicated to António Egas Moniz, who won a Nobel Prize for medicine in 1949. Farther north off N 109 is the *azulejo*-rich town of **Ovar**, which gave its name to Portugal's fishwives, called *varinhas,* who can still often be seen here in their country costumes, likely as not eating the eggy local version of *pão-de-ló* (sponge cake). Other ethnic garb and a large selection of Portuguese pottery are on display in the Museu Etnologico, hinting at the strong sense of tradition in Ovar evidenced during its Carnival and Easter festivals. The museum also has a section devoted to Joachim Guilherme Gomes Coelho, whose realist novels of country life in 19th-century Portugal, written under the pseudonym Julio Dinis, still delight readers of Portuguese.

Northeast of Ovar on N 113, at **Vila da Feira**, is a fanciful castle with pointed turrets. The surrounding town is lovely in its own right, with its misericord and the **Estalagem de Santa Maria**, where you may want to stay if you're headed north to Porto or the Douro valley. For more ornate art, travel farther east from Vila de Feira on N 227 and N 224 in a valley of the Serra da Gralheira to **Arouca**, where a Baroque monastery contains the mummified remains of Queen Mafalda, daughter of Sancho I, in an elaborate silver casket. The monastery also has a church filled with Baroque painting and sculpture, and a museum noted for its Portuguese primitives. If you're returning to Aveiro down N 224 from Arouca, the **Estalagem São Miguel**, at Parque de La Salette in Oliveira de Azemeis on the N 1/E 50, is a fine place to stop for a meal of shellfish and other regional specialties.

GETTING AROUND
The abundance of small communities off the main public transportation routes, especially in the mountainous inland area, makes a car the best way of getting around in

Beira Litoral. Rodoviária Nacional (RN), the national bus service, serves the larger places except Aveiro. Coimbra, Figueira da Foz, Aveiro, and Ovar have centrally located stations served by Caminhos de Ferro Portugueses (CFP), the somewhat leisurely national railway service; Leiria's station is accessible to the town only by taxi. Tourist offices in Leiria, Jardim Luiz de Camões, Tel: (044) 32748; Coimbra, largo da Portagem, Tel: (039) 25576; and Aveiro, praça da República; Tel: (034) 23680, can provide current schedules for local transportation to the smaller destinations.

In Coimbra the Queima das Fitas is celebrated each May, the Festas da Rainha Santa in July. In Aveiro the Festa da Ria takes place in July or August, and the Festa de São Gonçalo in June. Ovar's celebrations of Carnival and Easter are movable feasts.

ACCOMMODATIONS REFERENCE

- ▶ **Palace Hotel do Buçaco.** Buçaco, 3050 **Mealhada.** Tel: (031) 93101; Telex: 53049.
- ▶ **Albergaria de João Padeiro,** Cacia, 3800 Aveiro. Tel: (034) 91326.
- ▶ **Hotel Mar e Sol.** Avenida Sa Melo, **São Pedro de Moel,** 2430 Marinha Grande. Tel: (044) 59182; Telex: 15529.
- ▶ **Quinta do Paço da Ermida.** 3830 **Ilhavo.** Tel: (034) 32-24-96.
- ▶ **Hotel Paloma Blanca.** Rua Luis Gomes de Carvalho, 23, 3800 **Aveiro.** Tel: (034) 26039; Telex: 37353.
- ▶ **Casa dos Quintais.** Carvalhais de Cima-Assafarge, 3000 **Coimbra.** Tel: (039) 28821.
- ▶ **Pousada da Ria.** Bico do Muranzel, Torreira, 3870 **Murtosa.** Tel: (034) 48332; Telex: 37061.
- ▶ **Pousada de Santa Bárbara.** Póvoa das Quartas, 3400 **Oliveira do Hospital.** Tel: (038) 52252; Telex: 53794.
- ▶ **Estalagem de Santa Maria.** Rua dos Condes de Feijó, **Vila da Feira.** Tel: (056) 32411.
- ▶ **Pousada de Santo António.** 3750 **Serém.** Tel: (034) 52-12-30; Telex: 37150.
- ▶ **Solar da Vacariça.** 3050 **Mealhada.** Tel: (031) 93458.

Pousadas can be booked through Marketing Ahead, 433 Fifth Avenue, New York, N.Y. 10016; Tel: (212) 686-9213.

BEIRA ALTA AND BEIRA BAIXA
EAST CENTRAL PORTUGAL

By Dwight V. Gast

After the generally flat and open terrain of West Central Portugal, or Beira Litoral, Beira Alta and Beira Baixa (pronounced BYE-shah) unfold majestically and mysteriously. These most mountainous former provinces in Portugal are made up of several mountain ranges rippling southward from the Douro river down to the Tagus: the Serra do Montemuro just south of the Douro river, the Serra da Gralheira to their southwest, the Serra do Caramulo west of Viseu, the Serra da Estrela east of Coimbra, the Serra da Lousã southeast of Coimbra, and the Serra da Gardunha to the east of the Lousã and south of the Estrela.

Against this mountainous backdrop strewn with boulders and covered with pines (with the occasional errant palm rising defiantly), many peoples left their marks in and on the abundant local granite. Prehistoric tribes built a dolmen near Fornos de Algodres. The Romans turned a Celtic settlement at Idanha-a-Velha into a thriving town called Egitania, and constructed a mysterious structure called Centum Cellas near the present-day town of Belmonte. Inscriptions everywhere testify to the presence of Viriatus, the Lusitanian rebel who tried unsuccessfully to rout the Romans. Moors left mosques. Kings built castles. Later, a more stable population put up the white Baroque churches and residences outlined in crisp granite contours that so characterize the landscape today, only to have their efforts damaged by Spanish, French, and English troops. Those varied legacies in this spectacular mountain setting, and the traditional way of living it has spawned, are the reasons the visitor comes to the Beira Alta and Beira Baixa today.

MAJOR INTEREST

Rugged terrain of the Serra do Caramulo
Art and architecture of Viseu
Precipitous sightseeing in Lamego
Fortified castle towns near the Spanish border
Pastoral pleasures and lunar landscape of the Serra da Estrela
Jardim do Antigo Paço Episcopal (formal gardens at Castelo Branco)

Its rich history notwithstanding, a timeless pastoral quality persists in the Beira Alta and Beira Baixa. In the late 15th and early 16th centuries it inspired the fantastic backgrounds of the paintings of Viseu painter Grão Vasco, who become Portugal's most famous artist. Around the same time it provided a fitting setting for the plays of Gil Vicente, court dramatist to Manuel I and João III and the father of Portuguese drama.

Though for most outsiders the mountain area's famous passes are stunning, they do require vigilance on the driver's part. It is best to confine your consumption of the fabled Dão and lesser-known local wines to the safety of the table when the car is parked for the night, unlike the locals, who have the highest per capita wine consumption rate in Europe. The greatest seasonal road hazard is snow, which can last from December to March and render the roads impassable. The rest of the year you are likely to come upon a number of other hazards: Cows, sheep, goats, and their owners make regular roadside appearances; small barrages of orange peels suddenly shoot from a speeding vehicle; trucks and buses the size of small houses loom unexpectedly on the horizon.

Our coverage begins in the Beira Alta (meaning upper, or in this case, northern) at the Serra do Caramulo, northeast of Coimbra and east of Aveiro. After a look at the wild landscape, we continue to the burghal delights of the town of Viseu (just east of the Serra da Caramulo) then north to the town of Lamego, almost at the Douro

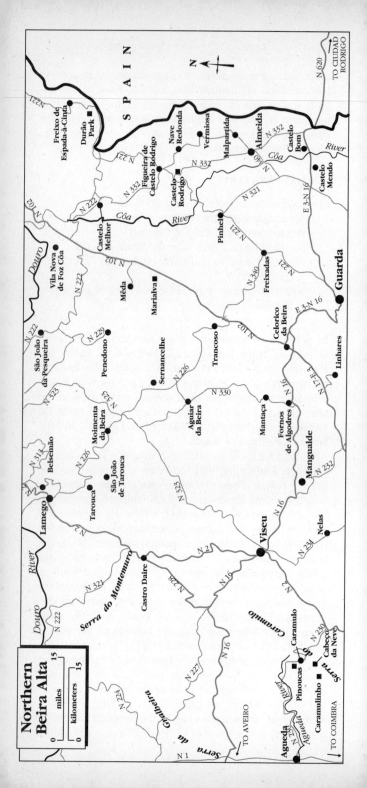

river. We then cut across to the east almost to the Spanish border to Almeida, described not long ago by two writers as a place for "only the very plucky tourist, with a very plucky car." With our recommendation of a recently opened pousada there as a base, we can now comfortably explore the fortified castle towns along the Spanish border. We then head southwest to the Serra da Estrela, the heart of the Beira mountain ranges, for a dramatic drive through the highest terrain in Portugal. We end with a dip south into the Beira Baixa (meaning lower, or, here, southern) and the town of Castelo Branco, where a garden of Baroque kings brings our route to a finish.

SERRA DO CARAMULO

Your likely point of entry to Beira Alta will be from Agueda, a Beira Litoral town 45 km (29 miles) north of Coimbra on the N 1. The N 230 east from Agueda along the Agueda river soon leaves behind the town's industrial architecture and climbs to the Serra do Caramulo, an appropriately mountainous introduction to the terrain that lies ahead. Follow the signs off N 230 to the dirt road that leads to the watchtower of **Pinoucas** for your first glimpse of the *serra*.

Back on the highway, the route continues to **Caramulo**, a spa town that displays its affluence at the **Museu do Caramulo**, housed on the main street (estrada Principal) in an institutional-looking building from the Salazar era. (The dictator was born in the Beira Alta town of Santa Comba Dão.) The museum contains an unlikely but appealingly eclectic collection strong on, of all things, vintage cars and modern art. Of the former, an 1899 Peugeot in working order is on display, along with Salazar's Mercedes, Rolls-Royces, Bugattis, and many others. The art collection consists of works by Picasso, Dalí, and other modern masters. More specifically Portuguese in subject and authorship are the 16th-century Tournai tapestries, made for Manuel I, depicting Portuguese navigational exploits, and the few examples of Viseu School paintings, which preview the pictorial glories to come.

Caramulo once had 18 sanatoriums for lung disease, and indeed, your first few breaths of fresh mountain air may well entice you to stay. The best accommodations are at the modern, Salazar-era **Pousada de São Jerónimo** just outside town, perched over the Besteiros valley. Its restaurant serves such specialties as *creme de cebola* (a creamy onion soup), *bacalhau con natas* (creamy dried salt cod), *borrego assado* (roast lamb), and *vitela estufada a camponesa* (a hearty veal stew). This could also be your introduction to the wines of the nearby Dão region. Reds such as Meia Encosta and Cardial are the most characteristic, but such whites as Serra and Coutada go well with the lighter fare.

You can also feast on the local produce. A loaf of some thick crusty bread, a bottle of Dão wine, a few thin slices of *presunto* (air-cured ham), and a *queijo da serra* (mountain ewe milk cheese) and you will soon be singing your own *serranilhas*. ("Serra," as it is known locally, is the most famous of Portuguese cheeses. In season from October to May, it has a runny, creamy quality reminiscent of Brie; in the winter and spring it also comes in a harder, riper form.) One excellent high spot for such a picnic is **Caramulinho**, a short drive southwest of the town. There, a desert landscape strewn with glistening granite boulders provides an intriguingly surreal setting. A posse or a team of spacemen could with equal plausibility come rambling out of the rocky terrain as you look over an expansive horizon that seems to extend to the limits of somebody's world. Another such high spot is the nearby **Cabeço da Neve**, where the views incorporate more recognizably earthly features such as mountain villages and the town of Viseu, your next destination.

VISEU

Driving past Caramulo to the N 2, then north, you will reach Viseu, the most important town in the Beira Alta. Because of the forests that surround it, Viseu is called "The City of Green Pines," but the sobriquet suggests nothing of the artistic treasures within the venerable gates that define the old section, in the center of town, and keep modern Viseu at bay from it. Appropriately isolated accommodations in the area (though not sparing on comfort) can be found at **Casa de Rebordinho**, a grand granite manor house some 8 km (5 miles) south of Viseu toward Nelas on N 231. In the heart of Viseu proper is the **Hotel Grão Vasco**, which provides the comparatively urban attractions of a bar, pool, and first-class restaurant on extensive grounds within walking distance of the main sights.

The hotel is named after one of Viseu's favorite sons and Portugal's most famous painter, Vasco Fernandes. Better known as Grão Vasco (Great Vasco), he was the master of a school of painting that flourished in Viseu during the 16th century. The town's remarkably well-appointed museum, the **Museu de Grão Vasco**, which features Vasco and the Viseu School, is an apt beginning to your visit to Viseu. Park your car in the square called **Adro da Sé**, in front of the cathedral. (If it's Tuesday, when a bustling farmer's market and crafts fair takes place in the square, park near the Hotel Grão Vasco or the square known as praça da República, or the Rossio, and walk through the Medieval gate called Porta do Soar to the Adro da Sé.) The museum is in the Paço dos Três Escalões, the former bishop's palace, a granite building that abuts the cathedral on the north side of the square. The top floor houses the museum's collection of religious paintings by Grão Vasco and other members of the Viseu School.

While Portuguese painting is not high on the art-history curriculum, that of this museum comes as a pleasant surprise. Its naturalism, gentle light, detailed drapery, and fantastic landscape backgrounds show the influence of Flemish painting that began with the artist Jan Van Eyck's diplomatic mission to Portugal in 1428–1429 and was nurtured by Portugal's commercial ties with northern Europe. When the Viseu School paintings were made, a century after Van Eyck's sojourn, those northern qualities had taken firm root in Portuguese soil and intermingled with indigenous motifs. Grão Vasco is best represented in the museum by *Saint Peter,* considered his masterpiece. In the painting, the saint sits on a stone throne (its ropelike arms, ending in animals bearing heraldic shields, could only have been carved by a Portuguese sculptor) placed between two squat Portuguese arches. He is dressed in elaborate robes that spread majestically on an obviously Portuguese tile floor.

Grão Vasco's *Saint Peter* is said to have been painted in reaction to a similar altarpiece his younger rival, Gaspar Vaz, made for the monastery in nearby Sao João de Tarouca. (The Vaz painting has long been removed for restoration, so you'll have to reserve your judgment of the two portrayals for when, if ever, it returns to that church.) The two artists' Christs can be compared in the museum, though, where Vasco's *Calvary* and Vaz's *Christ in the House of Martha* and *The Last Supper* are all on display. On the same subject are 14 panels depicting scenes from the life of Christ, originally part of the cathedral altarpiece, now separated and displayed individually in their own room. Though Grão Vasco's signature appears on *The Circumcision,* specialized members of his workshop did most of the work on the series. *The Adoration of the Magi* contains one of the school's most original Portuguese touches: Because of the recent discovery of Brazil, the African King Balthazar is portrayed as an exotic South American Indian, a feathered headdress replacing his crown.

Modern, some contemporary, paintings by Portuguese artists are exhibited on the floor below. Also of interest on the ground floor is the 14th- to 16th-century wood statuary and sculpture made from the soft stone quarried from the Ança region of the Beiras.

Around in the Town

Most of Viseu's considerable architectural pleasures are within the Cidade Velha (Old Town), in the immediate vicinity of the museum. The Adro da Sé square itself is bracketed by the **Igreja da Misericórdia** to the west and the Sé (cathedral) to the east. The Misericórdia is a distinctive set piece for the square as well as one of the best examples of the Baroque in all of Portugal. Its beauty lies entirely on the surface, in the white stucco façade outlined in straight and curved contours of gray granite.

The **cathedral**, on the other hand, should be explored in depth. It is dedicated to Saint Theotónio, the patron saint of Viseu, whose tomb is in Coimbra but whose statue stands above the door of the cathedral's 17th-century granite façade. Inside are a vault carved in stylized knots, an ornate altarpiece made of *talha dourada* (carved and gilded wood), *azulejos* in the north chapel, a sacristy with an intricately painted ceiling, a small museum of sacred art, and a cloister containing more *azulejos.*

Viseu's other sights are all a pleasant stroll from the Adro da Sé to nearby streets lined with stately old residences. Leading south off the square is rua da Cadeia, also called rua Dom Duarte (after the Portuguese king who was born in Viseu in 1391, traditionally in the street's Medieval **Torre de Menagem**, now adorned with the finest Manueline window in the city). Off the street runs rua Nova, known as rua Augusto Hilário after the father of

Coimbra fado singing, who was born in the small house indicated by a commemorative plaque.

Rua Nova leads to **rua Direita**, which along with its fine houses is the main venue for Viseu's many crafts shops. Black-and-red pottery, basketwork, textiles, and metalwork are all produced locally and celebrated in late summer during the Feira de São Mateus, an annual fair established by royal decree in 1510. (The Pavilhão de Artensanato da Assemblea Distrital, the district crafts office, in campo da Feira de São Mateus, has more information about the fair and Viseu's crafts.) Another regional specialty, the scrumptious *queijo da serra,* is also for sale in abundance in shops on and around the street.

If the architecture has inspired you, head over on the rua da Arvore to largo de Santa Cristina and the **Igreja do Carmo**, with its *talha dourada* and *azulejos,* then have a look at the houses south of rua Direita on rua dos Andrades. There are more on rua da Senhora da Piedade, back toward the cathedral and on the way to the Igreja de São Bento, which has the most striking *azulejos* in Viseu. If cheese interests you more than architecture, head west off rua Direita to rua Formosa, on which is the Mercado, a large covered market, where there is an abundance of cheese and other local produce.

Just ahead of the market is praça da República, or the **Rossio**, the town square around which life in Viseu revolves. It is elaborately paved, planted with lime trees, and flanked by a large *azulejo* wall. On its south side is another church decorated with *azulejos* and *talha dourada,* the Igreja dos Terceiros de São Francisco, and to the north is the **Casa Museu Almeida Moreira**, the formerly private collection of primarily decorative arts that belonged to the original director of the Museu de Grão Vasco.

The liveliness of the Rossio contrasts with Viseu's most ancient place, the **Cava de Viriato**, now a park on the north side of the Pavia river. There the Roman Decimus Junius Brutus set up a camp in 138 B.C. Despite the fact that the Lusitanian rebel Viriatus had died the year before, local legend persists that his last stand occurred in Viseu, an event commemorated by a romantic bronze-and-granite monument on the spot. Another legendary local event, the granting of Pavia water rights to the millers of the nearby town of Vil de Moinhos due to the intervention of Saint John, is still celebrated in a procession called the *Cavalhadas.* Each year the millers, mounted on horseback, lead a parade of dancers, musicians, and floats through Viseu to the saint's chapel in suburban Carreira to express their gratitude on the feast day of São João, June 24.

Year round, at the Grão Vasco hotel restaurant and the smaller **Trave Negra** restaurant (rua dos Loureiros 40), you can feast on such local specialties as *cabrito assado* (roast kid) and *trutas abafadas* (trout marinated in vinegar and oil), best accompanied by a red or white Dão wine such as the one called—what else?—Grão Vasco. Viseu also offers a rich basket of eggy desserts called *castanhas doces,* which translates as "sweet chestnuts." They have nothing to do with chestnuts, however, but consumed in excess could cause *chest knots* because of the sinful amount of sugar and egg yolks that go into them. Decorated variously with almonds or cherries or unadorned, they can be sampled in the restaurants or in such pastry shops as **Popedoce** at rua Direita, 128.

If you enjoyed the genteel architecture of Viseu, you might want to make a short detour east on the N 16 to **Mangualde** before moving on. Finest among its noble residences is the Palácio dos Anádia, on the main street. The privately owned palace can be toured if the proprietor happens to be on the premises. There is no way of knowing in advance, but it is worth trying, because the extensive *azulejo* walls and collection of decorative arts provide a rare opportunity to see how the privileged classes lived, and live. If the palace is not open, you can stroll the streets of this agreeable town and then have your own baronial dinner at the **Solar Beirão** (Hotel da Senhora do Castelo, Monte da Senhora do Castelo). A short drive east of town on N 16, this large restaurant serves regional cuisine in full view of the Serra do Caramulo and the Serra da Estrela. The Dão valley, source of some of the finer red wines of Portugal, lies northeast of Mangualde.

LAMEGO

Leaving Viseu, head north through the rocky and forested terrain on N 2. Just after Castro Daire, an unassuming little village 34 km (23 miles) from Viseu whose name bespeaks its origins as a Roman camp, the landscape opens up to a magnificent panorama of the Serra do Montemuro, rising off to the west. Admire the view of the wild country as you move on to the upland amenities of Lamego, another town of ancient origin 33 km (20 miles) farther north, and one of the loveliest towns in the region. Its Roman beginnings notwithstanding, and despite the fact that Portugal's earliest *cortes,* or national assembly, met there in 1143 to recognize Afonso Henriques as the country's first king—and despite the town's favored status by the country's next few rulers—today Lamego presents a later, largely Baroque face.

Lamego, a prosperous town in the hills above the Douro valley, makes for a pleasant stopover on a tour of the Beiras or on the way to the valley (Peso da Régua, Vila Real). **Vila Hostilina,** which offers accommodations, is a restored farmhouse above Lamego with views of the town and the surrounding countryside, including its own vineyards. Almost as scenic is the **Hotel Parque,** Lamego's oldest such establishment (it dates from the last century), now completely refurbished. It is set in gardens next to the town's famous pilgrimage church, the **Santuário de Nossa Senhora dos Remédios** on a hill up above town. Wherever you decide to stay, be sure to unpack your best walking shoes: Lamego might rightly be called "The City of Strong Legs" because of the steep climbing and long distances involved in inspecting its major monuments.

The church is a good place to begin your visit, since besides being Lamego's most important landmark it offers excellent views of the town and the outlying region as far as the Douro to the north. Its staircase, more elaborate than that at Nossa Senhora da Encarnação in Leiria but less so than Bom Jesus outside Braga, is its most prominent feature. Each September 8 thousands of the devout ascend it on their knees during the Festa de Nossa Senhora dos Remédios, a lengthy celebration that includes many other sacred and secular events, from religious processions to rock concerts. That kind of variety has its architectural correlate in the amazing array of embellishments—fountains, statues, *azulejos,* chapels— that awaits you as you make your way up the nearly 700 steps. The fantastic display of the plastic arts reaches a climax at the last landing, the largo dos Reis, where grandiose Baroque motifs and imposing authority figures appear almost folksy, owing to the naïf treatment. The church itself is anticlimactic after the staircase, but the view of the town will remedy any disappointment in Our Lady. If you would rather not make the climb on your knees or your feet, you can drive up the hill for the view (you'll have to drive up anyway if you're staying at the Hotel Parque).

Down in town is the **Sé**, the tower of which dates from Romanesque times. The rest of the cathedral is a mixture of a Gothic and Renaissance exterior (as is its lovely cloister, reached from within) and an 18th-century interior. Across from the Sé, in the 18th-century former Paço Episcopal, or bishop's palace, on largo de Camões, is the **Museu Regional de Lamego**, another surprisingly rich provincial museum, which preserves a variety of relics from Lamego's history as far back as the Romans and contains an extensive assemblage of decorative and religious art. There are many *azulejos* here from demolished structures in the vicinity, and two unusual 14th-century statues worth mentioning, both depicting the Virgin pregnant with child and given the intriguing name of Nossa Senhora do O, a popular Portuguese piety. Innocently enough, the story of this Lady of O, as Ann Bridge and Susan Lowndes recount in *The Selective Traveler in Portugal,* "comes, in part, from the seven antiphons in the Office of the days before Christmas, all of which begin with O."

Other interesting examples of the *genus loci* are ornate chapels from the monastery once attached to the town church of Chagas, as well as a number of paintings of the Viseu School, including scenes of the life of Christ by Grão Vasco and his beguiling altar panel *The Creation of the Animals.* Another highlight comes from outside the Beiras: a collection of 16th-century Flemish tapestries on classical and mythological themes. The series on the life of Oedipus merits special attention.

The bishops weren't the only ones who lived in such luxury: Have a look at the 17th- and 18th-century town houses next to the museum. There are more on rua da Pereira, which also leads to the 16th-century Igreja e Convento de Santa Cruz, as well as the 17th-century Igreja do Desterro, the interiors of both of which are filled with elaborate decoration.

A street near the Desterro chapel becomes a pleasant path along the Balsemão river to the hamlet of the same name. If your legs are still holding out, you might want to pick up some local ham, cheese, bread, and sparkling wine and follow the river about two miles downstream (northeast). Your reward, at the bottom of the valley, is the tiny **Igreja de São Pedro de Balsemão**, said to be the oldest church in Portugal. Originally built as a basilica by the Visigoths in the 7th century, it was given a facelift and a coffered ceiling in the late Renaissance. Inside is some interesting sculpture, namely the tomb of Afonso Pires, a 14th-century bishop of Porto, and another statue of Our Lady of O. (Most of this trip, too, can be made by car.)

Otherwise, you might take your picnic to Lamego's **castle**, the first of many you will come across in this part of the Beiras. To reach it, return to the museum and take the tortuous rua da Olaria, which becomes rua de Almacave and leads to the 12th-century Igreja de Almacave, the church where the Lamego *cortes* met. The street continues past shops selling the local craft items of baskets, wool blankets, and stockings to praça do Comércio, bordered by the walls and grounds of the castle. The keep dates from the 12th century, and along with the rest of the compound is well kept by the local Boy Scouts (which accounts for the exhibits of trustworthy scouting skills on display).

The restaurant in the Hotel Parque, **Nossa Senhora dos Remédios**, serves the regional specialties of the Beiras and nearby Trás-os-Montes and Douro Alto as well as more local delicacies, such as the famous Lamego mahogany-hued *presunto,* made (as it is throughout Portugal) from hogs fed on chestnuts and/or cooked potatoes. It is eaten with melon and figs during the warmer months and appears year round baked in a pastry crust as *bolo de presunto.* Other regional pies are *bolo de bacalhau,* made with dried salt cod, and *bolo de sardinhas,* made with sardines. The Lamego sparkling wine, Portugal's Champagne, comes in rosé and white—the *seco* is clear, dry, and prickly. If you'd like to taste it even closer to its source, the Turismo office, avenida Visconde Guedes Teixeira, Tel: (054) 62005, can arrange visits to vineyards. Caves da Raposeira is the closest and the best known.

Southeast toward Almeida

A panorama of Portugal's history from the ancient Romans to the Peninsular Wars unfolds in front of you in the varied series of towns along the 127 km (80 miles) between Lamego and Almeida. Unfortunately, there's no such excitement in the restaurants en route, so be sure to stock up on provisions in Lamego before setting out. The first stop, on a side road off N 226 (itself not a major road), is **São João de Tarouca** (*not* the *town* of Tarouca), the site of Portugal's first **Cistercian monastery**, begun in the 12th century. Though the monastery no longer houses Gaspar Vaz's painting *Saint Peter,* it does contain the remains of Dom Pedro, the bastard son of King Dinis, who became count of Barcelos and author of *O Livro de Linhagens,* a Medieval blue book. The fairy-tale subject matter and the fact that the monastery is now in ruins make for some romantic ruminations.

Farther ahead on N 226 is **Moimenta da Beira**, an agreeable town with some pleasing *azulejos* in the Mosteiro de Nossa Sehnora da Purificação convent church. Stop for a snack of the local *pão de ló* (sponge cake), accompanied by coffee or a glass of Terras do Demo, the local white wine. Or you may want to wait until you get to the next town, **Sernancelhe**, reached from an uphill side road east of the highway and situated beneath a ruined castle built by the Knights of Malta. Its monuments include a Romanesque church, a slender *pelhourinho* (a column erected in many Portuguese villages since Roman times to denote municipal power), several elegant residences—and its own dessert, *cavacas de Frexinho,* a sugary white pastry shaped like a clamshell.

A turnoff to the west back on the highway takes you to **Aguiar da Beira**, an ancient town with its own castle, Medieval clock tower, Manueline *pelhourinho,* and a Romanesque church, the Capela da Nossa Senhora do Castelo. The N 226 then leads to **Trancoso**, the first (and busiest) of many walled towns in this part of Portugal built up to protect the country from Spain. Such friction was witnessed by the battle between the Portuguese and the Spaniards that took place in Trancoso in 1385, if not by the marriage between King Dinis and Isabel of Aragón there a century earlier. The worst skirmish you risk here today is with the town's inordinately heavy traffic, since Trancoso lies uncomfortably near a main highway. Battle your way through the modern town to the old city. Park at the gate and walk through the cobblestone streets to the castle, heavily fortified, as were so many castles in the region, by Dom Dinis, for the victory of a spectacular survey of the silent landscape surrounding the town.

The N 226 continues scenically southeast to the hamlet of Freixadas, where you turn left (north) onto N 221 for the castle town of **Pinhel**. Its **Museu Municipal** (praça de Sacadura Cabral) contains a few archaeological and religious relics that hint at the town's former importance as a Roman outpost and an Episcopal seat. The faded grace of its churches and residences underscores the point that you have entered one of the least populated parts of

Portugal. That fact becomes even more evident as you take N 321 (to the southeast) and N 340 (to the east and northeast) through the parched terrain to Almeida, so before leaving Pinhel, buy a bottle of mineral water or the local wine (you'll see white igloo-shaped vats of it around town) for the trip.

Almeida

Almeida is a flat fortress town protected by ramparts in the shape of a six-pointed star. Though captured by the Spanish in 1762 and held by the French during the Peninsular Wars, the town offers little activity today besides tawny dogs running along the walls and cows and horses grazing outside the gates. Inside is the **Pousada Senhora das Neves** (opened in April 1987), elegantly rustic with a polished wood and stucco interior. Because the pousada offers the only accommodations for miles around, it is best to book well in advance for the two or more nights' stay you'll need to explore the outlying region.

Begin your tour with a walk around Almeida itself, along the ramparts said to have been completed by the French military engineer Sébastien Le Prestre de Vauban in the early 18th century. Despite the new pousada, the town still has an appealingly run-down appearance. Its dilapidated military barracks, churches, and residences are of little importance individually, but taken together are a pleasure to discover as you wander aimlessly around at sunset, when local children play games in the streets and their parents sit gossiping. Then return to the pousada restaurant to choose your dinner from among its Beira Alta specialties. *Bacalhau con queijo da serra* (dried salt cod with mountain cheese), *lingua de vitela* (veal tongue), *bifes de presunto* (air-cured ham and steak), and *carneiro à moda de fornos de Algodres* (mutton stewed in local red wine) are served with a fine selection of wines from the Dão and Douro valleys. After a hearty meal to the sounds of the youngsters' laughter and singing outside, you should begin to be captivated by this magic land of castles.

CASTLES NEAR SPAIN

"Thou shalt make castels thanne in Spayne, / And dreme of joye, all but in vayne." The pertinent part of Chaucer's translation of Jean de Meun is neither the country (though it is near enough) nor the futility, but the *joy* of castle dreaming. This part of Portugal, with its remote location, barren terrain, sparse population—not to mention the castles themselves—is highly conducive to such fantasies. Rather than being surrounded by sprawling new towns and souvenir stands, most of the castles you will encounter on the loop north of Almeida, as well as farther south, stand in solitary, dreamlike ruin.

Head northeast on the country road to Malpartida, where the invading French troops fought a battle at the beginning of the last century. (Today's invaders are a rather more tame contingent of storks that roost on the region's roofs and in the fruit and vegetable plots.) The road then leads through the village of Vermiosa and past the man-made lake and dam of Santa Maria. Just beyond Nave Redonda, have a look at the **Antigo Convento de Santa Maria de Aguiar**, a former Cistercian monastery with a noteworthy Gothic church. Farther on is Figueira de Castelo Rodrigo, where you can stop at the Baroque Igreja Matriz to admire the gilded interior and the unusual upper-choir arch built of granite stones cut in interlocking S shapes. **Castelo Rodrigo** is a short drive south on N 221. Its castle suffered much from border skirmishes and is now in a state of exquisite ruin worthy of Chaucerian dreams. Crumbling Gothic arches give way to ivy-covered towers, and ancient windows frame fantastic views of the surrounding countryside. The site itself sits prettily when viewed from the nearby Via Crucis, a short drive up the hill so indicated on road signs.

Take N 221 back north via Figueira de Castelo Rodrigo (if you are getting hungry, stop into a bakery for a treat of *orelhas de dom abade*—"abbot's ears" cookies) on through the orchards of olive and almond trees and across the Douro river for a brief expedition into the Alto Douro. The highway leads to the fortified town of **Freixo de Espada-à-Cinta**, the birthplace of the 16th-century navigator Jorge Alvares and the 19th-century poet Abilio Manuel Guerra Junqueiro. Under the watchful seven-sided tower built by Dom Dinis, the **castle** stands guard over the town. Step into the Igreja Matriz, a Gothic church remodeled with Manueline details, to see a series of panel paintings attributed to Grão Vasco. Returning south on the N 221, make a right just a couple of kilometers out of town on the winding road that leads to the summit of the **Durão peak** for more spectacular views.

Retrace your route back across the Douro river to Figueira de Castelo Rodrigo. There you can pick up provisions for a picnic en route northwest along N 332 and 222 to **Castelo Melhor**, a village wrapped around a conical hill topped with a Medieval wall and ruined castle, a vision out of a Grão Vasco painting (if not a science-fiction book jacket). Proceed beyond Castelo Melhor to **Vila Nova de Foz Côa** for a look at its Manueline church and a snack of its bountiful dried figs and almonds, then farther west along N 222 to the handsome town of **São João da Pesqueira** for a stop in its main square, praça da República, and perhaps a glass of the local Port. Back from there, N 222 and country roads lead south to **Penedono**, where the tiny golden castle is as elaborately crowned as the pillory at its entrance. Inside, note its interesting triangular plan and the extensive views from the top. More country roads take you east via Mêda to the main highway, N 102, where you travel south to the turnoff to the right to **Marialva**, one of the most dramatically deserted of all the castle towns.

The N 102 leads farther south to the intersection with N 226 near Trancoso, where you turn left (east) for the zigzag route past Freixedas and Pinhel back to Almeida.

THE SERRA DA ESTRELA

If Almeida's proximity to Spain tempts you to cross the frontier, a fast dash of Spanish culture is ready to hand in **Ciudad Rodrigo**, a fairly sizable town with an authentically Spanish castle and cathedral. (Don't go on a Saturday, when a huge market of everything from potted chickens to pocket calculators in the Portuguese border town of Vilar Formoso creates considerable delays—a phenomenon not mitigated by the hour's time difference between the two countries.)

In keeping with the spirit of place, you will more likely want to continue your drive through the Beiras. Due south of Almeida are **Castelo Bom** and **Castelo Mendo**, two virtually interchangeable towns where cabbage patches and free-range chickens invade the castle ruins. The superhighway E 3/N 16 leads west to the fortified town of **Guarda**, the highest city in Portugal and known as "The City of the Four Fs." *Fria, farta, forte,* and *feia* are Portuguese for "cold," "full," "strong," and "ugly." Tradition thus excuses not lingering in the busy town, though a quick stop at

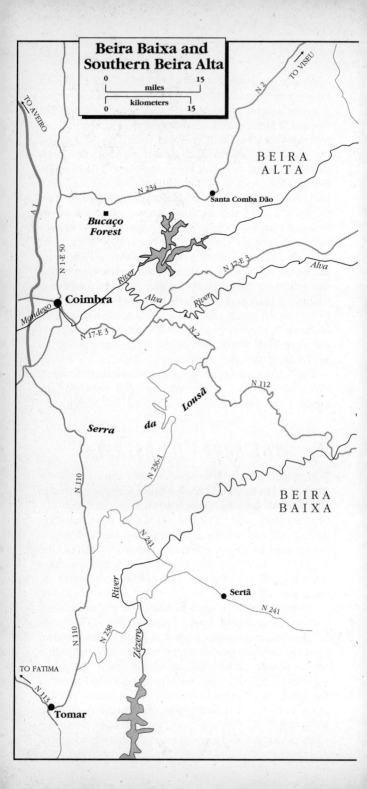

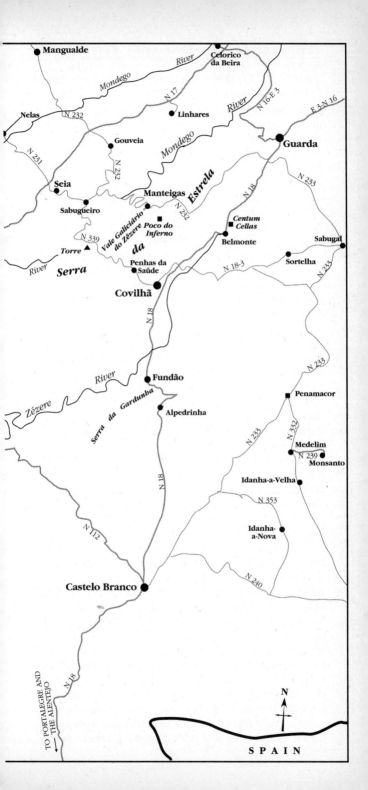

the **Sé** will dispel the last attribution. Like the French Gothic it was modeled on, via Batalha, the cathedral has flying buttresses and gargoyles, grim-looking in the local granite. Inside is a retable by Jean de Rouen, who did the monumental door to the Coimbra cathedral. Any lingering implications of *feia* will be chased away next door at the **Museu da Guarda** (Antigo Seminário Episcopal), housing an exhaustive survey of local archaeological artifacts and religious art. If your timing is right, a meal at **O Telheiro** (5 km/3 miles east on EN 16), a restaurant that specializes in regional dishes and that has a panoramic view, will provide respite from the bustle of Guarda.

Otherwise, relax by driving west and northwest on N 16 to the smaller crossroads town of **Celorico da Beira**. Visit its lumbering castle, perhaps of Roman origin and certainly refurbished by King Dinis. (For a look at some even older stones, follow N 16 west to Fornos de Algodres, whence the country road north to Mantaça passes a dolmen.) Another castle, also strengthened by Dom Dinis, stands in the more isolated town of **Linhares**, south of Celorico on the N 17/E 3. From there, country roads lead west to **Gouveia**, where you will really begin to feel surrounded by the beauty of the Serra da Estrela, officially designated a *parque natural*. A small town where the distinguished architecture includes a gentleman's residence called Casa da Torre, Gouveia is also known for the Serra da Estrela sheepdog. In the city, the Montes Herminios, estrada da Serra, Algueiro, is worth a visit, as is another kennel, Caverna de Viriato, near the Pousada de São Lourenço, for which see below. The dogs are on show during the Festas do Senhor do Calvário in Gouveia in August.

From Gouveia, the drive south on N 232 toward Manteigas is filled with adventure. It passes granite boulders and strange rock formations such as the one dubbed *cabeça do velho* (old man's head) and the source of the beloved Mondego river on the way to the **Pousada de São Lourenço**, on the main road before Manteigas. The pousada, which looks like a combination ski lodge and fortress, was built in the 1940s out of the local granite to protect guests from the harsh winters and sweltering summers of the Serra da Estrela. Alternative lodgings for the couple of nights you will want to stay in the *serra* are available by following the country road to nearby Sabugueiro. There you will find the **Casa do Cruzeiro**, a granite manor house complete with a working cheese factory, smokehouse, and bread oven. Dine at the Pousada de São Lourenço restaurant, which serves the local specialties of *bacalhau* (dried salt cod), *truta* (trout), *cabrito à Serrana* (kid stew), and *queijo da serra*. Fish dishes go well with Castelo Rodrigo white wines, meat with Covilhã Reserva reds. After dinner, try the warming local brandy, Zimbro.

The Heart of the Serra da Estrela

From the pousada (if you are staying in Sabuqueiro, rejoin the route by driving back east on the country road), N 232 descends in switchbacks to **Manteigas**, an Alpine-looking town (its older houses have wooden balconies) with crafts to match. Its textiles and leatherwork are on display at the Centro Civico, in the heart of town. Pick up some local *queijo da serra* and other provisions for a picnic at Poço do Inferno, a small waterfall up a winding gravel road south and then southeast of town. Doubling back to the road south from town, make the turn left for the glacial valley called the **Vale Glaciário do Zêzere** for another out-of-this-world experience. The first part—a straight road that seems to lead right off the edge of the earth—is enough to explain how the Portuguese navigators could fearlessly hold steady for the horizon. The route then twists and turns in a landscape thick as *cabrito à Serrana* with granite boulders west to **Torre**, which is not a tower but the highest peak in Portugal, at 6,537 feet. Park your car at the sort of space-age traffic circle with cement-block buildings and geodesic domes, pick up some ham and cheese at any of the numerous stands, and drive on to digest the sweeping views.

As the scenic drive continues back east through the ski resort of Penhas da Saúde down to Covilhã southwest of Guarda near the N 18, you get your first glimpse of the Beira Baixa. **Covilhã** has a past that rather outshines its present. Legendarily founded in the 7th century by the Visigoth Julião, it was populated by Sancho I in the 12th century, saw the birth of explorer Pero de Covilhã in the 15th century and that of the mystic Hector Pinto in the 16th, and became a cloth-producing town in the 17th. Its tradition as an industrial center continues today, but its blandness is somewhat compensated for by a large number of rugged culinary specialties. If time allows, stop at the restaurant at **Hotel Solneve**, rua Visconde da Curiscada, 126, for your choice of *feijoada* (a white-bean version of the famed Brazilian stew made with pork and sausages), *panela do forno* (the same cuts of meat mixed with rice), *trutas de escabeche* (a trout casserole), and *batatas bebedas* (drunken potatoes), made with red wine. Try Covilhã and Fundão red and white wines with your meal. The restaurant also makes a full array of dessert cookies.

Northwest from Torre to Seia, instead of east to Covilhã, takes you on a panoramic drive across the entire breadth of the Serra da Estrela. Seia's pleasant houses and churches are memorable in their own right, but the nicest souvenir of the Serra da Estrela, available here, might be *cabeça da velha*. Named after a local rock formation that resembles the head of an old woman (a short drive away up a country road), it is considered the best variety of *queijo da serra*.

From Seia, you return to accommodations at Sabugueiro by heading east on N 339; from there a country road connects to N 232 to reach the Pousada de São Lourenço.

THE BEIRA BAIXA

Taking N 232 east of Manteigas, you will make your final crossing of the Serra da Estrela into the Beira Baixa. **Centum Cellas**, on the other side of N 18 where N 232 ends, will give you a solid idea of just how ancient this part of Portugal is. The original function of the ruin remains a mystery; one theory is that it was a Roman inn. If so, it was at least as well constructed as any modern pousada, as its three stories of pink granite still stand.

A series of more enchanting castle towns follows. Just down N 18 from Centum Cellas is **Belmonte**, where there is a panoramic view of the area from the top of the castle wall built by Dom Dinis. Country roads lead east to **Sortelha**, a deserted-looking village whose castle rises steeply on a rocky outcropping. Many of its granite houses, however, are inhabited, and some signs of gentrification are beginning to be seen here and there. The nicest for the visitor is **Restaurante Alboroque**, an authentically rustic eatery in an ancient granite house. Its regional trout, rabbit, and kid dishes, with the wines of Figueira, Covilhã, and Fundão, are hearty fare fit for King Dinis.

Down the country road to the east of Sortelha is **Sabugal**, which shows few signs of rehabilitation except for the swallows that have converted loft space in the castle's unusual pentagonal keep into a choice nesting spot. The exceptional expansiveness of the castle walls is perhaps due to the special attention King Dinis lavished on its rebuilding, for the formerly Spanish town only became Portuguese when he married Isabel of Aragón. The N 233 leads south from Sabugal to the castle of **Penamacor**, whose keep is surrounded by less-well-preserved fortifications. Within its walls, Catherine the Great's personal physician, António Nuñes Ribeiro Sanches, was born to one of the Jewish families who once inhabited much of the region.

Such families flourished at **Monsanto**, south of Penamacor off N 239 east of Medelim. Today the town, which the Portuguese like to refer to as *a aldeia mais portuguese* (the most Portuguese village), flourishes as a popular place for second homes. The Lisbon gentry are justly attracted to the quaint granite houses in the ancient village built among the boulders perilously perched on its steep hill. The only thing that regularly comes tumbling down, however, occurs each May during the Festa das Cruzes, when local beauties reenact the town victory over besiegers whom it frightened away by tossing a calf over the walls (the modern version is made of flowers). Sturdy legs are required for the hike to the ruins of the castle, but the payoff is a vast panorama up to the Serra da Estrela and down to the town of Castelo Branco.

Castelo Branco will be the last town on your sightseeing itinerary in the Beiras, but before visiting it stop off at **Idanha-a-Velha** on country roads south of Monsanto. An ancient Celtic village, it was turned by the Romans into the thriving town of Egitania, and became the supposed birthplace of Wamba, king of the Goths. Roman ruins and a Paleo-Christian church remain.

Castelo Branco

Travel south and then southwest on the N 353, a country road that goes through the village of Idanha-a-Nova, where the inhabitants of Idanha-a-Velha moved after a plague of ants that lasted 100 years. Then turn right on N 354 and drive 13 km (8 miles) to N 240; turn right again and head west to Castelo Branco, the most important center in the Beira Baixa. Castelo Branco's busy history of occupations and sackings has left little of interest for the visitor. What does remain can be surveyed from the Miradouro de São Gens, a belvedere above the east side of town. Throughout its disturbances, Castelo Branco remained famous for its *colchas,* elaborately embroidered (and expensive) bedspreads that are on display (and for sale) at the **Museu Francisco Tavares Proença Júnior**, a regional museum housed in the Paço Episcopal (bishop's palace). Other noteworthy holdings of the museum include 16th-century Flemish tapestries and Portuguese primitive paintings.

Their sculptural counterparts are around the corner from the museum at the **Jardim do Antigo Paço Episcopal**, terraced gardens laid out in the 18th century. Its trees, hedges, shrubs, and flower beds are groomed with provincial formality. The real delights of the garden, though, are its statues. Pockmarked, moss-covered stone animals, apostles, fathers of the church, and kings of Portugal greet you at every step with an innocence and sagacity at once cartoonlike and sophisticated—note that the Spanish kings who ruled Portugal during the Hapsburg domination are depicted half the size of the rest.

The best accommodations in the area are at **Casa do Barreiro**, a manor house in the pleasant hill town of Alpedrinha about 40 km (25 miles) north of Castelo Branco on the N 18. Whether or not you have bought some Castelo Branco olive oil or cheese—its *cabreiro* is made from goats' milk, and the cheese known as Castelo Branco is a kissing cousin of *queijo da serra*—try **Casa do Bico**, the restaurant in the Estalagem da Neve, in the nearby village of Fundão (Quinta de São Sebastião, Fundão). It serves regional specialties as well as the local dish of *lampreia* (lamprey eel) and plenty of Fundão wine.

GETTING AROUND

The interesting small communities off the main public transportation routes here make a car the best way of getting around in Beira Alta and Beira Baixa. Rodoviária Nacional (RN), the national bus service, serves Viseu, Lamego, Guarda, Covilhã, and Castelo Branco. Viseu, Lamego, Covilhã, and Castelo Branco have centrally located stations served by Caminhos de Ferro Portugueses (CFP), the somewhat leisurely national railway service; Guarda's station is accessible to the town by bus and taxi. Viseu and Covilhã have small airports, if you'd prefer to fly and rent a car in one of those towns.

Turismo offices in Viseu (avenida Gulbenkian; Tel: 032-22294), Lamego (avenida Visconde Guedes Teixeira; Tel: 054-62005), Covilhã (praça do Município; Tel: 075-22170), and Castelo Branco (Alameda da Liberdade; Tel: 072-

21002) can provide current schedules for local transportation to the smaller destinations.

In Viseu, the Cavalhadas de Vil de Moinhos is celebrated on June 24 and the Feira de São Mateus is held from August to September. In Lamego, the Festas da Nossa Senhora dos Remédios takes place in August and September. In Gouveia, the Festa do Senhor do Calvário is from August 6 to 10. In Monsanto, the Festa das Cruzes is held the first Sunday after May 3.

ACCOMMODATIONS REFERENCE
▶ **Casa do Barreiro.** 6230 **Alpedrinha.** Tel: (075) 57120.
▶ **Casa do Cruzeiro.** 6270 **Sabugueiro.** Tel: (038) 22825.
▶ **Hotel Grão Vasco.** Rua Gaspar Barreiros, 3500 **Viseu.** Tel: (032) 23511.
▶ **Vila Hostilina.** 5100 **Lamego.** Tel: (054) 62394.
▶ **Hotel Parque.** Santuário de Nossa Senhora dos Remédios, 5100 **Lamego.** Tel: (054) 62105.
▶ **Casa de Rebordinho.** 3500 **Rebordinho.** Tel: (032) 21258.
▶ **Pousada de São Jerónimo.** 3475 **Caramulo.** Tel: (032) 86291.
▶ **Pousada de São Lourenço.** 6260 **Manteigas.** Tel: (075) 47150.
▶ **Pousada Senhora das Neves.** 6350 **Almeida.** Tel: (071) 54283 or 54290.

Pousadas can be booked through Marketing Ahead, 433 Fifth Avenue, New York, N.Y. 10016; Tel: (212) 686-9213.

PORTO AND THE DOURO VALLEY

By Thomas de la Cal

In less than an hour's drive east of Porto the terrain of this northern region, which stretches from the Atlantic Ocean to Spain, changes quickly from the humid, flat, populous industrial belt around the city of Porto, the Douro Litoral (Lower Douro), to the dry, mountainous, and thinly populated interior of the Alto Douro (Upper Douro). Tucked away in the heart of this region lies the rugged and secluded Vale do Douro (Douro river valley). Its soil and microclimate are ideal not only for the grapes that produce Port wine but also for travellers in search of scenic and vintage Portugal.

Despite their physical and climatic differences, the two Douros are joined historically and economically by the river, from whose golden complexion (*douro* means "gold" in Portuguese) they derive their name. The river's strategic importance—it links Portugal to Zamora and Valladolid in Spain and delineates Portugal's north—and the region's rich natural resources have over the centuries attracted traders, settlers, and armies who in turn have left their mark on its population, its food, and the land itself. Its people inherited the Celtic love of lore, the Phoenician savvy for commerce and maritime exploration, the Roman affinity for large urban projects, the Visigoth individuality and work ethic, the Swabian predilection for sausages, and the Moorish sweet tooth and terrace-farming techniques. And they have learned to live with the British, who have played an important role in the region's economy through the Port-wine trade for more than 250 years.

Our route starts with Porto, as the gateway to the region, and moves counterclockwise, like a Port decanter around the dinner table, through the heart of the Douro. It begins by running east along the steep, wooded slopes on the right (north) bank of the Douro, crosses over to the left (south) bank at Entre-os-Rios, and makes its way eastward on the N 222 along the high slopes that line the southern flank of the river, past the trellised table-wine vineyards surrounding the town of Cinfães.

At Barrô, some 100 km (62 miles) east of Porto, we leave the Douro Litoral behind and enter into the domain of the Port-wine region, Alto Douro, with its whitewashed towns, stately quintas (farm estates), and steep, terraced slopes densely planted with vines. Following the loop through the heart of the Douro region we cover the popular resort town of Amarante on the banks of the bucolic Tâmega river. After viewing its surrounding woods, archaeological remains, Romanesque churches, and whitewashed manor houses, we return to Porto via the N 15, stopping off at the tiny parish church at Travanca for a last peaceful moment before returning to the big city.

MAJOR INTEREST

Porto
Sé (Gothic cloister and crypt of the bishops of Porto)
Medieval quarter of the Barredo
Museu de Arte Sacra (religious treasures)
Museu Guerra Junqueiro (Hispano-Arabic pottery and Flemish tapestries)
Eating and drinking in the waterfront quarter of Ribeira
Igreja de São Francisco (gilt)
Palácio da Bolsa (stock exchange)
Baixa shopping district
Sweeping views of the city and environs from the Clérigos tower
Museu Soares dos Reis (Portuguese art masters)
Museu Romântico (and its Port-wine lodge Solar do Vinho do Porto)
Jardim Botânico
Port-wine lodges in Vila Nova de Gaia

View of Porto from the convent of Nossa Senhora do Pilar

Foz
Castelo de São João da Foz
Castelo do Queijo

Matosinhos
Waterfront restaurants
Igreja do Bom Jesus de Matosinhos

The Douro Valley
Santa Maria de Cárquere priory at Montemuro
Sweeping views of Port country at Barrô
Peso da Régua Port-wine center
Pinhão's annual grape harvest
Alijó's Celtic ruins and manor houses
Mesão Frio view of the valley
Train tours of the Douro, Trás-os-Montes, Minho

Amarante
Houses hanging over the Tâmega
Church of São Gonçalo
Arraial de São Gonçalo folk festival

The Food and Wine of the Douro

Fish is the staple of the coastal areas, while meat and sausages are favored by the people of the interior. Codfish, which Douro fishermen have been catching off Newfoundland since the 15th century, is particularly dear to the Litoral diet in its dried salt form, *bacalhau*. The Portuguese not only taught the world how to preserve the fish by salting, but have also devised more than 365 ways of preparing it. *Bacalhau à Gomes de Sá,* named after a Porto restaurant owner, is a delectable baked cod, potato, and onion casserole garnished with eggs and olives. *Tripas à moda do Porto,* a spicy combination of beans, sausages, and tripe, is the city's historic dish, invented in the 15th century by ingenious Porto housewives after Prince Henry the Navigator requisitioned their meat to provision one of his armadas and left them to make do with the offal. Porto's citizens were eventually rewarded for their sacrifice when Henry's efforts to discover a sea route to the spice trade succeeded, some years after his death, in bringing to the city's larders a host of exotic spices and ingredients.

In the mountain and pastoral areas of the Alto Douro,

cordeiro (lamb) and *cabrito* (baby goat) are popular items, particularly braised lamb served with baked rice. Dark blood sausages, *morcelas,* are used widely in stews, while the more common garlicky pork *chouriços* are incorporated in soups and grilled as appetizers. River trout stuffed with golden brown *presunto* (air-cured ham) from Lamego or Chaves is an Alto Douro delicacy.

The people of the Douro share Portugal's affinity for egg-based and caramelized sweets—and have a sense of humor. Where else can you taste sweets with names like *barrigas de freira* (nun's tummies) and *testiculos de São Gonçalo?* The figs, oranges, and other fresh fruits of the Vale do Douro area are lower-calorie alternatives.

The Douro is one huge wine cellar. Apart from the famous fortified Ports, of which there are more than 350 varieties, there are also young, tart *vinhos verdes,* Douro reds and whites, *vinhos espumantes* (sparkling wines), and after-dinner spirits such as *bagaço,* Portugal's equivalent of grappa, and Cognac-styled *aguardente,*

Port is a fortified wine produced solely in the Douro river valley and its tributaries from a variety of grapes. The secret lies in its fortification process. When high-proof *bagaço* is added to young wines at the proper time, fermentation (sugar being converted to alcohol) is stopped to help maintain the fruity flavor of the grapes. The process results in a unique wine with a rich color, a natural sweetness, and extraordinary longevity.

Port is named after the city of Porto, where it is aged, bottled, and shipped. Before obtaining its present name, however, it was known variously as *vinho de embarque* (embarcation wine), on account of the way it was shipped by boat, and priest Port, because most of it came from monasteries.

There are several versions on how the making of Port came about. The most accepted theory is espoused by Nicolau d'Almeida, master blender of the venerated Ferreira Port house, who believes that Port was produced by accident in 1820 when a change in weather yielded higher-than-normal sugar content in the grapes and stopped the fermentation process. The Anglo community in Porto, however, claim that it was a British subject by the name of Peter Bearsley who invented Port by chance one day at an inn when he added elderberry juice to his wine and found that it improved the wine's color and taste.

Purists maintained that this barbarous practice adulterated an otherwise fine wine, but waged a losing battle against the proponents of fortification. Their protests were not entirely in vain. The making of Port has improved since the early 19th century: Elderberry juice has been replaced by the more refined and effective *bagaço* (distilled from the hulls of crushed grapes), and the production and aging of the wine is carefully supervised by the government-run Port Wine Institute.

The making of Port wine starts at the grape harvest each fall in the Douro wine region (the first demarcated in the world, in 1756—a century before the French came up with the Appellation Contrôlée), which begins roughly 60 miles east of Porto and stretches along the river and its tributaries to the Spanish border. The grapes are crushed and stored in warehouses upriver at Peso da Régua and its environs for the winter, when the cool weather helps the lees settle. When fermentation reaches a desired point, brandy is added (roughly one-fifth of the wine volume), stopping fermentation within roughly 48 hours.

In the spring the new wine is transported to the shippers' lodges in Vila Nova de Gaia across the river from Porto, where it is allowed to mature. The wine is first kept in large wooden barrels called *pipas* for two to three years, while the lees continue to be drawn out. At the end of this period it is tasted and categorized. Some Ports continue to be aged in wooden barrels, others in bottles. The more common Ports, aged in barrels, generally are blended with other years' wines, which helps maintain the quality and standard of a particular brand, while the early bottled Ports normally come from a single harvest.

There are Ports for every occasion and taste. White Ports, which are the product of several types of white grapes and are blended, are aged in casks and come in sweet, dry, or extra-dry varieties. The latter are light bodied and make an excellent aperitif. Ruby Ports are also blended, but are more full bodied, younger and sweeter, and serve as ideal dessert wines and mixers. Tawny Ports have been called the "Port man's Port" because of their mellow taste, which makes them suitable for all occasions. Some inexpensive tawnies are blended from ruby and white Ports, but the better-quality ones are often allowed to acquire their amber color and smooth flavor through aging in wooden barrels for 7 to more than 40 years. It is expensive to maintain wines in a cask for a long time, so some older tawny Port can be dearer than a bottle of vintage Port.

Vintage Port, however, is the queen of Ports. It is the

product of an exceptional harvest. The unblended wine is normally bottled two years after the vintage, and matured for no less than ten years. It is rich in color and full bodied. It is stored lying down to prevent the cork from drying out, and throws a heavy sediment, which explains why it is decanted. The next best thing to the vintage is the late-bottled vintage, or L.B.V., also the product of a fine vintage, which is allowed to mature longer in the cask before being bottled sometime from the fourth to sixth years of its age. The difference between the vintage and the L.B.V., however, is that the latter can be sold right after it is corked and does not need decanting. Another important vintage is *colheita* (also sometimes called "Port of the Vintage"), which requires at least seven years in cask before bottling. Vintage, L.B.V., and *colheita* Ports are normally served as after-dinner drinks.

The British, who made Ports fashionable throughout the world, have recently been surpassed by the French as the largest importers of Port wines, but have increased their consumption of the finer vintage Ports. You can taste or acquire Port wine at the plush Solar do Vinho do Porto on the grounds of the Museu Romântico in Porto or at the wine lodges that line the dock at Vila Nova de Gaia across from the city.

The same grapes of the Upper Douro are used to produce unfortified table wines of note, such as Ferreira's superb red Barca Velha and Constantino's white Monopólio, and some of Portugal's best *vinhos espumantes,* such as the brut and meio-seco Raposeira bubblies. The latter are aged and fermented in cool, dank caves carved out of a mountain above the town of Lamego. Except during the month of August, the caves are open to visitors.

PORTO

Porto (Oporto in English) does not inspire love at first sight. Its sprawling industrial suburbs and the stern gray architecture of its financial district (granite being the region's most abundant stone) do not conjure up visions of a romantic holiday. Probe deeper, however, and you will find a more aesthetically pleasing and colorful Porto, a city of both Gothic elegance and Baroque flair. Like the tiny, picturesque houses on its steep slopes, time appears to be suspended here. This is vintage Porto, an ancient and proud city that gave the nation both its name and its language, helped liberate Lisbon from the Moors, and produced Henry the Navigator, the father of Portuguese maritime exploration. Its important contributions to the Portuguese nation, and the working-class values and independent streak of its citizens, make it the quintessentially Portuguese city. And though Porto, Portugal's second largest city, may have lost some of its temporal power to its flashier rival, Lisbon, in the eyes of most of the nation it is still the hereditary guardian of all things Portuguese.

Porto is somewhat reluctant, unlike Lisbon, to flaunt its wealth in public. Its treasures lie hidden behind the ancient doors of granite palaces and museums, which house the art and antiques collections of the city's wealthiest merchants, and in the wines maturing in the cool cellars of its wine lodges at Vila Nova de Gaia. The narrow, cobbled alleyways and old houses of the working-class neighborhoods, and the stalls of flower vendors and fishmongers along the river, display the city's colorful side. Allow time to get to know Porto. Savor it slowly, like a fine Port.

Early Porto

The Porto area has been inhabited for more than 4,000 years, but wars, earthquakes, and new construction have erased most of the signs of this early habitation. Some vestiges of pre-Celtic and Celtic civilization have been unearthed on Pena Ventosa hill, where the cathedral stands today, and can be seen in the city museum. Lusitanos (Lusitanians) lived in fortified hill towns and carried out trading with Phoenician merchants attracted to the area's metal deposits. The hamlets ranged from the smaller *castros* (fortified villages) containing individual clans to *citânias* (towns) of up to 200 households. When the Romans finally conquered the area in the third century B.C., after a long, arduous struggle, they fortified the existing *cividade* (city) on the right bank and renamed it Portus. Across from it, on the left bank, they built a new metropolis, which they called Cale. The twin cities came to be known as Portucale, and their dialect and name later served as the models for the language and the name of the new nation, Portugal. The Romans were replaced by the Swabians and Visigoths in the fifth and sixth centuries A.D. (parts of the former Swabian wall can be seen near the cathedral); they, in turn, were vanquished by Moorish armies, which leveled the cities.

Porto has always been in the forefront of Portuguese history. It was one of the first cities on the peninsula to shake off Moorish domination, in the 11th century. A Porto bishop, Dom Pedro Pitões, persuaded English Crusaders on their way to the Holy Land to help liberate Lisbon. Porto's merchants, equally resourceful and independent, were pioneers in championing civilian rule in the 14th century. By supporting the Crown against powerful nobles, they obtained a royal decree barring the nobility from residing in their district. Their money and shipyards were used in Portugal's 15th- and 16th-century maritime exploration, and their fortunes, and those of the city, became tied to the new territories. In the 16th century, for example, the city was hard hit by its loss of the spice monopoly, but in the 18th century it became very prosperous through the gold and diamond mines in Brazil.

Napoleonic troops took Porto twice, in 1808 and 1809, but were expelled by troops led by Sir Arthur Wellesley, the future Duke of Wellington. The French invasions, however, sowed the seed of republicanism. In 1820, Porto masons formed a liberal movement that spread to Lisbon and ended in a constitution limiting the power of the Crown and terminating the Inquisition. This was followed by a civil war, won by the liberals. To pay off the huge war debt, the new government abolished the monasteries and sold off their property—which is why so many of these institutions in Porto are owned today by private persons or the civil authorities.

The enterprising spirit of Porto's merchants ran free during the late 19th century. Gustave Eiffel built a steel railway bridge linking the right bank with Vila Nova de Gaia (formerly Cale) and the rest of Portugal to the south. This was followed by an impressive two-tier metal road bridge, the Ponte Dom Luis I, designed by Eiffel's disciple, Seyrig, which joins the upper and lower levels of Porto and Vila Nova de Gaia.

The beginning of the 20th century brought a new era of economic development and public works. The age-old problem of flash floods, which for centuries had devastated the lower part of the city and the Port-storage facilities at Vila Nova de Gaia, was finally solved with the damming of the Douro. A third bridge, the Ponte de Arrábida near the mouth of the river, completed in 1963, spans its 890-foot width in one single reinforced concrete block and now carries the A 1 highway. The A 1 and connecting main routes on the north side of the river, however, constitute by far the worst bottleneck in the entire country of Portugal.

Today, the economic emphasis has shifted away from the river to the seafront north of the river mouth, where such industries as fish canning, textile manufacture, furniture making, and ceramics are thriving. The old city and its Port wine have been left to age in peace.

The British and Porto

The British have traded with Porto since the 14th century, and have been a permanent fixture in the city since the 18th. At first they came to the river's mouth and traded cloth and codfish for Portuguese wine, honey, and fruit. Many of them eventually settled here and continued a brisk trade that was made official by the signing of the Methuen trade treaty between England and Porto in 1703. The Douro replaced the Minho as England's main wine supplier, and the Port wine industry developed. The British wine exporters grew rich carrying out their business in the rua dos Ingleses in Porto, and built their own Factory House (named after factors, or wine-buying agents, of the 16th century), where they held lavish parties. But life in Porto was not without its problems. The English Port merchants had to deal with the Inquisition (which among other things barred them from burying their dead in Portuguese soil), various attempts to break up their monopoly, Napoleonic invasion, a blight that nearly wiped out the vineyards, then fascism and revolution. Through their pluck and courage, and with occasional help from British forces, they have managed to endure.

The history of the Anglo community in Porto teems with colorful and resourceful characters. There was Scotsman George Sandeman, who arrived in Porto in 1790 with 300 pounds to his name and built it into a fortune and one of the largest of the Port houses. The future doyenne of the Delaforce Port house arrived in Portugal clinging to an empty barrel after a shipwreck. And there was the liberty-loving Richard Noble, who, whenever he saw a crowd fighting the police, would pick up his cane and lead the mob. There were also Renaissance men such as Joseph James Forrester, whose talents as an artist, surveyor, and cartographer were used to chart the Douro wine region and river, for which he was awarded a barony by the king of Portugal in 1848. He was also a Port purist who fought a bitter but losing battle with the British wine trade in Porto and London on the subject of adulteration. He drowned in his beloved Douro river in 1861, when his boat capsized in the dangerous Valeira gorge. His two female companions, members of the Portuguese Ferreira Port dynasty, floated to safety, buoyed by their voluminous petticoats.

The descendants of those first Port merchants continue to thrive in Porto today. They remain English: They play cricket on Saturdays at their Lawn Tennis Club, swim at the Praia dos Ingleses near Foz, send their children to the Porto British school, attend services at their Protestant church, and celebrate the queen's birthday. And every Wednesday, as they have for more than 200 years, the male members of the British Association, some of whom trace their ancestry to the founding Port houses, meet at the Factory House to discuss business over lunch and Port. (They started meeting on Wednesdays because that was the day there was no delivery of mail from Britain, and they could therefore take their time over Port and cigars.) On the weekends they retire upriver to their quintas (farm estates) on the hills overlooking the Douro to oversee the maturing of the grapes.

Porto is a city of hills on the right (north) bank of the Douro. Its oldest and most photogenic quarters are situated three miles upriver from the estuary, in the southeastern corner of the sprawling city. The colorful waterside *bairro* (quarter) of the Ribeira is known for its street vendors and tiny bistros; the Medieval Barredo quarter climbs the steep Pena Ventosa above it. At the summit, commanding a view of the city and its environs, is Porto's cathedral. The town of Vila Nova de Gaia, home of the Port wine lodges, lies directly across on the left bank. Porto and Vila Nova de Gaia are linked here by the two-tier Ponte Dom Luis I, a 19th century metal bridge. The center of Porto is a five-minute walk north from the cathedral via the avenida Afonso Henriques, past the São Bento train station. At its center is the busy praça da Liberdade, which once served as the main northern entrance to the former walled Medieval city; the 14th-century wall was torn down in the 18th century as the city grew northward. Remnants of the former two-mile wall can be seen in the Ribeira and Freixo to the east. The area around the square is called the Baixa and serves as Porto's shopping and commercial district. Running north from it is the wide, elegant avenida

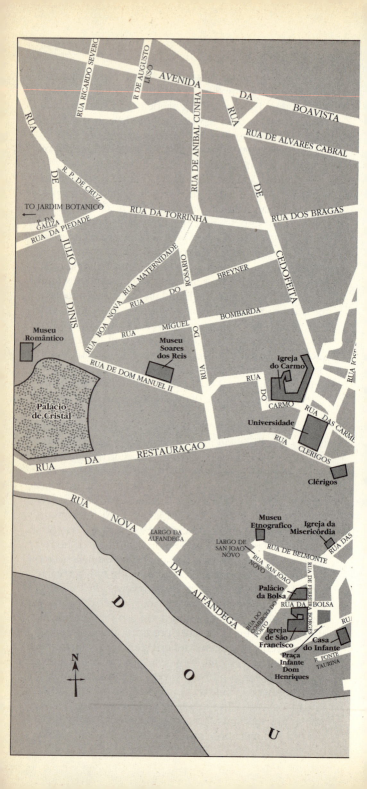

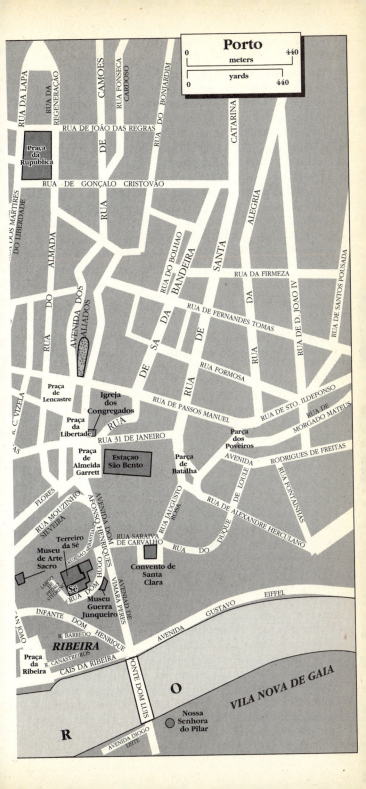

dos Aliados, planted with flower beds and populated with outdoor cafés, restaurants, and banks and other businesses. Some of Porto's older hotels and pensions lie on the tiny streets and squares off it. At the top of the avenue is the imposing 20th-century city hall, flanked by the tourist and the main post offices. The city's modern hotels are located a ten-minute drive west of the Aliados on the avenida da Boavista, a modern thoroughfare that connects the city to the airport and Porto's beach suburbs of Foz and Matosinhos.

Porto is a walking, bus, and cab city. Most of its sights are contained in the one main hub. Cars are best left at the hotels or in one of the main parking areas. Parking on the main thoroughfare, the avenida dos Aliados, is by meter.

Give yourself two full days to get to know the city. Make sure you wear comfortable walking shoes with rubber soles capable of handling the steep slopes and slippery cobbled streets. Most institutions are open from 10:00 A.M. to noon and 2:00 to 5:00 P.M. Tuesdays to Sundays (shops also open Saturday mornings), except for the Museu Romântico, Museu de Arte Sacro, and the Museu Guerra Junqueiro, which close on Sundays. The wine lodges can be visited Mondays through Fridays during the winter, and add Saturdays to their roster from June through August. The Sandeman and Real Vinícola lodges are open on Saturdays throughout the year.

The Cathedral

On the southwest side of avenida Dom Afonso Henriques, at the top of the steep, wind-swept Pena Ventosa, stands Porto's cathedral, or Sé, where the parents of Prince Henry the Navigator, Philippa of Lancaster and João I of Portugal, were married in 1387, and where Henry was later christened. The Sé's foundations were laid in the 12th century, but many additions have been made over the ages to the original fortresslike Romanesque structure. Of note on the exterior are its elaborate Baroque doorway and elegant 13th-century rose window. The interior is rich in gold and silver. The 17th-century silver altar in the main chapel was painted over during the French invasions to conceal its splendor from marauding troops. Other items of note are a bronze relief of the baptism of Christ in the baptistry to the left as you enter the church; the crypt of the bishops of Porto, with a 17th-century gold-carved retable; and the 14th-century Gothic **cloister**, decorated with tiles depicting scenes from the life of the Virgin and from Ovid's *Metamorphoses*.

The tiny square in front of the Sé contains the statue of Vimara Peres, who liberated the city from the Moors. On Saturdays the square turns into the Vandoma flea market, where antique curios and knickknacks can be picked up at bargain rates. The Terreiro da Sé holds the former Baroque palace of the archbishops of Porto, which now serves as a municipal office. It is an ideal spot from which to admire the picturesque Barredo and Ribeira quarters tumbling down to the river.

The Barredo

The tiny houses of this ancient *bairro* cling precariously to the steep slopes of Pena Ventosa. It is a miracle that so many of these homes have withstood earthquakes throughout the centuries. Segments of a sixth-century Swabian wall stand directly below the northwestern corner of the Terreiro da Sé. (The Swabians overran Portugal when the Roman Empire began to wane.) A few steps south of the wall, at largo de Pedro Vitorino, is the **Museu de Arte Sacra**, which contains what religious treasures (plate, liturgical books, and vestments) the citizens of Porto were able to hide from Napoleon's troops, a valuable coin collection, and liturgical instruments (organs and stringed instruments such as lutes and guitars) from the 15th to the 19th centuries collected by Porto's wealthy bishops. The former residence of the satirical poet Guerra Junqueiro (1850 to 1923), southeast of the museum at rua de Dom Hugo, 32, is now the **Museu Guerra Junqueiro**, a lavish dwelling offering a glimpse of patrician life in Victorian Portugal. It contains some of Junqueiro's work as well as Hispano-Arabic pottery, Flemish tapestries, and Portuguese furniture from the 16th century collected by the wealthy artist.

A maze of stone stairs, one of which is the Escada do Barredo, runs down from rua de Dom Hugo to the rua do Barredo, past homes festooned with colorful wash billowing against the wind like spinnakers.

The Ribeira

The quaint but crumbling waterfront quarter of Ribeira lies directly south of the rua do Barredo, and west of the Ponte Dom Luis I. It is crossed west to east by the cobbled cais (quay) da Ribeira, which contains the remains of the 14th-century Fernandina wall. Parts of the quay's thick wall have been converted into taverns and bistros from which you can gaze at the river, where wooden *rabelos* (square-riggers), loaded with wine kegs, are docked. These long, handsome vessels once carried the precious wine cargoes down the fast waters of the Douro to Porto. The **Taverna Bébodos** is a typical Ribeira tavern, where such simple regional fare as *sardinhas grelhadas* (grilled sardines) or a *caldeirada* (multi-fish stew) can be washed down with glasses of *vinho verde* drawn from a cask. Closed Sundays; no credit cards accepted.

Chez Lapin, a few steps west at rua dos Canastreiros, 40, lodged in an arcade, is a tiny family-run *tasca* with a view of the river. The establishment, which has an open kitchen, is decorated with hunting paraphernalia and specializes, of course, in *coelho* (rabbit), cooked in white wine sauce. Expect the place to be crowded during the summer months. No credit cards accepted. The same family has now opened the more upscale **Downing Street** restaurant, on the praça da Ribeira at the western end of the quay. Housed in a former warehouse, Downing Street has a third-floor dining room decorated with vintage photos of Porto and looks out onto the ancient cobbled square with its colorful renovated Ribeira houses. A house specialty is *arroz de tamboril* (monkfish and rice stew).

The Ribeira is the setting for the city's most popular *festa,* the feast days of São João on June 23 and 24. The event is a pagan summer-solstice ritual, adopted by the Church, in which the population of Porto spends two nights of revelry consuming rivers of *vinho verde* and eating roast kid. Huge bonfires are lit and young couples jump over them.

The Financial District

Porto's financial district lies a few steps northwest of the Ribeira square. At the juncture of the rua Infante Dom Henriques (formerly rua dos Ingleses) and rua de São João, above the square, you will encounter the three-story Georgian **Factory House**, which was built in the 18th century by British consul Whitehead. The area in which it stands was once an elegant commercial center; now it is run down and somewhat shabby. Behind the austere colonnaded façade of gray granite, however, is a richly decorated club where the young Wellington and his officers danced the night away in the early 19th century. Its well-stocked library is cared for by the wine families' historian. Entrance is barred to the general public, but you may catch a glimpse of the interior through one of its windows.

The rua Infante Dom Henriques runs west into the Infante Dom Henriques square, dominated by a statue of the city's most famous son, Henry the Navigator. South of the square, on rua da Alfândega, is the **Casa do Infante**, popularly (but not academically) believed to be the birthplace of Henry. The 14th-century structure, which served as a customs house until the last century, has now been restored and converted into the city's historical museum. The southwestern corner of the palm-lined square houses the Gothic-style **Igreja de São Francisco**. The fact that it is next door to the stock exchange may explain why it has one of the richest and busiest interiors in Porto. Its walls, vaulting, pillars, and altar are covered with carved and gilded wood representations of animals, plants, and angels. The visitor's eyes are soon drawn to the 13th-century altar, where the simple granite statue of Saint Francis provides a respite from the dizzying display.

Porto's temple to business and financial enterprise, the **Palácio da Bolsa** (stock exchange) takes up most of the northwestern corner of the square. The exterior is solid and conservative, while its interior sanctum is more ostentatiously bold, rich in marble, stucco, and wood. The 19th-century Salão Arabe, with its arabesques and stained-glass windows, was inspired by the Moorish splendor of the palace at Granada. Built at the height of the Romantic movement, which captured the Portuguese imagination, it belongs more in a scene out of *A Thousand and One Nights* than in a stock exchange.

Guided tours of the Bolsa are available. The headquarters of the Association of Wine Exporters is also housed in the building.

For a more down-to-earth experience, visit the **Museu Etnografico** directly west of the Bolsa, at largo de São João Novo, a small but fine showcase of the traditional life of the Douro peasantry. An ancient wine press, peasant costumes and implements, and a weaver's workshop are on display, and regional handicrafts can be purchased. The museum is located in a former Jewish quarter, where some of Spain's most important Jewish families took refuge in the 15th century after being expelled from Spain. Some of Porto's best jewelry shops are found nearby, to the northeast toward praça da Liberdade, on rua das Flores. The **Igreja da Misericórdia**, an 18th-century Baroque structure designed by the Italian architect Nicolau Nasoni in collaboration with the Portuguese engineer Manuel Alvares, is also in the same street. A beautifully executed 16th-century painting is housed in the adjoining **Casa da Misericórdia** hospice owned by the same order that runs the church. The canvas, attributed to Colijn de Coter, has the Portuguese royal family present at the Crucifixion.

The Baixa

The Baixa, around the praça da Liberdade, is the city's main shopping district. (Store hours in Porto run from 9:00 A.M. to noon and 2:30 to 7:00 P.M. during the week, and from 9:00 A.M. to 1:00 P.M. on Saturdays.) Porto is not only Portugal's textile and leather center, but is also esteemed for its intricate gold and silver filigree work, introduced by the Moors and perfected in the 17th and 18th centuries, when gold and silver began to pour in from the Portuguese colonies. **José Rosas & Cie**, at rua das Flores, 245, deals in antique and secondhand jewelry; **Rosier**, in the neighboring rua da Cunha, at number 38, manufactures reasonably priced classical and modern jewelry.

There are no bargains in the antiques world of Porto, but interesting pieces such as Indo-Portuguese ivory-inlaid furniture do crop up at auctions at the **Galerias de Vandoma**, at rua Mouzinho Silveira, 181, which parallels rua das Flores. East of praça da Liberdade is the rua de Santa Catarina, a pedestrian street known for its gift shops and fashionable clothing stores. The side streets that run into it also have their specialty shops. Leather and glassware can be purchased on rua 31 de Janeiro, while hand embroidery and linen are a century-old tradition at the **Casa dos Linhos**, at rua Fernandes Tomás, 660. Clothes bargains and inexpensive regional handicrafts, such as wicker and pottery, are sold all day Mondays to Fridays and Saturday mornings at the colorful local market of **Bolhão** (rua Sá da Bandeira), west of Santa Catarina. The larger **Bom Sucesso** market is a short cab ride northeast, at its namesake square.

The **Grande Hotel do Porto**, also on Santa Catarina, provides an opportunity for shoppers to be in the thick of things. The former grande dame of Porto's hotels is in need of a facelift to restore her past glory, but the prices, attentive service, parking facilities, and Belle Epoque restaurant and look help make up for her genteel shabbiness. Situated near the Grande is the **Majestic Café** (number 112), one of the oldest coffeehouses and landmarks of the city. Its sculptured cherubs atop pilasters, jasper pillars, and the finely carved wood here would make William Morris proud. Coffee is served with reverence in copper holders.

The area around praça da Liberdade and the wide avenida dos Aliados is also dotted with sidewalk cafés, pastry shops, and teahouses. **Arcadia**, at praça da Liberdade, 63, is one of the oldest pastry shops in Porto. Its Old World decor and Baroque-style pastries make it a temple of confectionery frequented by the affluent tea set and the intelligentsia.

Southeast of Liberdade

The tiled exterior of the **Igreja dos Congregados** brightens the Almeida Garrett square (named after Porto's romantic writer) southeast of Liberdade. The interior of the **São Bento** train station next door has an interesting collection of *azulejos* by the 20th-century master Jorge Colaco, combining Portuguese history and the evolution of the train. The capture of Ceuta (in North Africa) by João I in the 15th century is the centerpiece. Southeast of the square, off the avenida Dom Afonso Henriques at rua Saraiva de Carvalho, is the former **Convento de Santa Clara**. The cross-fertilization of styles, from the Gothic, Manueline, and Renaissance stonework of its doorway to the Mudejar (Moorish-style) ceiling of its interior, will tax the keenest student of architecture. The panel of the Immaculate Conception by Joaquim Raphael is also worth noting in this small church, whose opulent touches echo the rich past of the religious orders in Portugal.

West of Liberdade

The **Clérigos tower**, a Baroque structure built by Italian architect Nicolau Nasoni, dominates the skyline of its namesake street on a hill west of Liberdade. If you climb its 200-plus steps you will be rewarded with a sweeping view of the sea to the west, Vila Nova de Gaia to the south, and the mountains to the east. Northwest of the Clérigos, past the book and pottery shops of the rua das Carmelitas, is the lovely palm-lined praça dos Léos (Square of the Lions), flanked on the south by Porto's university and the tiled exterior of the 18th-century **Igreja do Carmo** to the west. The eastern exterior of the church is decorated with 20th-century *azulejos,* designed by Silvestro Silvestri, depicting important events of the discoveries. The adjoining Igreja das Carmelitas and its monastic quarters have been turned into the barracks of the National Republican Guard.

The **Museu Soares dos Reis**, named after Portugal's most famous sculptor, is housed in the Carrancas palace (former residence of the counts of Terreira José) behind the neighboring Santo António hospital, on rua de Dom Manuel II. Apart from exhibiting works by the sculptor, who is known for his evocation of *saudade* (nostalgia), the museum houses one of the nation's most complete collections of paintings by 15th- to 20th-century Portuguese masters. The top floor contains valuable Limoges enamels and a sword belonging to the first king of Portugal, Afonso Henriques.

Porto's other great museum, the **Museu Romântico**, lies off the western end of rua de Dom Manuel II at rua de Entre Quintas, 220, in the 19th-century former Maceirinha estate, where King Carlos Alberto of Sardinia spent his last days in exile. The building draws attention not only for its valuable collection of 19th-century European art and furniture but also for its basement **Solar do Vinho do Porto**, which offers more than 350 varieties of Port and a view of the river below. The bar is closed on Sundays.

Porto's Gardens

The Portuguese green thumb can be admired at several locations on the west side of the city. The gardens and manmade pond of the **Palácio de Cristal** exhibition center, at rua de Dom Manuel II, are the closest to the center and offer a cool haven in the summer. The **Jardim Botânico**, at rua do Campo Alegre, grows rare plants and trees from all corners of the former Portuguese Empire. (The garden is open weekdays from 2:00 P.M. till dusk; use bus line 35 or 37.) The other green space in Porto, the **Casa dos Serralvas**, lies farther west. The sprawling estate, which belonged originally to the counts of Vizela, passed through several hands in the 19th and 20th centuries before being acquired by the state. The estate, at rua de Serralvas, 977, is open Tuesdays through Sundays from 2:00 P.M. till dusk, and is a ten-minute bus ride (line 35) from the city center.

Vila Nova de Gaia

Vila Nova de Gaia, across the Douro south of Porto, sits on top of a pre-Roman fortified *castro* (hamlet) and the former Roman settlement of Cale. It was made officially into a town in the Middle Ages by burghers and nobles to counteract the power of the bishops of Porto. It also suffered greatly over the ages from flash floods and is somewhat shabby and run down. The town still serves as the vault for millions of bottles of Port maturing in the damp and cool cellars of some 60 wine lodges facing the river. Vila Nova de Gaia was picked over Porto proper for practical reasons: Its north-facing location favors higher humidity and cooler air, which cut down the rate of evaporation of the wine in the cellars.

Cross the lower level of the Ponte Dom Luis I, by car or on foot, and turn right onto avenida Diogo Leite, which runs along the quay where the elegant rabelos are docked, to visit the wine lodges. Some of the best known are Sandeman, Croft, Ferreira, Cintra, Taylor, Cálem, Cockburn, Barros, Fonseca, and Real Vinícola. The lodges offer guided tours in English, during which you can see the aging and blending process, sample their wines free of charge, and purchase bottles. All lodges can be visited weekdays except at lunchtime; the Sandeman and Real Vinícola lodges are open on Saturdays, and Real Vinícola on Sunday mornings.

Sandeman, at largo Miguel Bombarda, 2, is housed in a former 16th-century Jesuit convent beside the river. The 200-year-old company, whose symbol is a cloaked student from Coimbra university, has been acquired by Seagrams of Canada, but the Sandeman family continues to supervise the wine production. The lodge has a small museum with tools and implements used in wine making dating back to the 18th century. The oldest section of the lodge has soft wooden stilts placed upright on the floor as a cushion to prevent damage to the oak barrels as they are rolled over them. The wood's texture is close to that of velour.

The Real Companhia Vinícola do Norte de Portugal, founded by royal decree in 1756, is housed in a large estate at the eastern and upper end of Vila Nova de Gaia, at rua Azevedo Magalhães, 314. It produces both Port and *espumante*. To get to this lodge, cross on the upper tier of the Ponte Dom Luis I and turn left at the second crossing, off avenida da República.

Several outdoor cafés on the esplanade by the river offer fine views of old Porto. The best picture-postcard view, though, is available at the former **convent of Nossa Senhora do Pilar**, which sits on a high promontory on the eastern corner of Vila Nova de Gaia overlooking the river. From the esplanade in front you can gaze down at the bridge, the old town, crowned by the Sé, and the remains of the 14th-century Fernandina wall to the east. The former convent has a Renaissance cloister and an unusual 17th-century barrel-vaulted roof. Its strategic importance has always attracted military attention. Wellington set up camp here in his campaigns to oust the French from Porto, and liberal forces made it their headquarters during the civil war. The hill continues to be occupied by army barracks, but the former convent can be visited.

Vila Nova comes alive every year on the second Sunday of January during the Festas de São Gonçalo e São Cristóvão, which are more like a pagan fertility rite than a Catholic celebration. An image of São Gonçalo, known as the saint who helps women find husbands, discovered centuries ago in the river, is paraded through the streets by local boatmen accompanied by a phalanx of drummers. São Cristóvão and São Roque are also honored, and gallons of Port wine are drunk, accompanied by phallus-shaped cakes.

The Foz and Matosinhos

The Atlantic coastal area west and northwest of Porto, from the Douro estuary to Matosinhos, is the city's mini-Riviera. Leave Porto by the river road (rua do Ouro) and follow it (5 km/3 miles) to the *foz* (mouth), where the **Castelo de São João da Foz** guards the entrance to the river. The 16th-century fortress was built on the site of a 13th-century Benedictine monastery despite protestations from the order. To placate the monks, the chancel of the former monastery was spared as part of the garrison's chapel, and can be visited. Our route then turns right (north) onto the avenida do Brazil, which parallels a palm-lined esplanade past the Praia dos Inglezes. The tiny, homey **Hotel Boa Vista** sits on a small promontory overlooking the fort and the Foz. Its pub, rooftop restaurant, and small indoor pool and gym make it an attractive place to stay for travellers in search of a relaxed environment. The hotel is near some of the better Porto restaurants and fashionable discos.

The avenida do Brazil turns into the avenida de Montevideu, which is flanked to the east by seaside villas. One of these, now the **Dom Manuel** restaurant, at number 384, is among the area's best eating facilities, with an impressive fish menu. The restaurant is closed on Sundays. Tel: (02) 67-23-04.

The **Castelo do Queijo** or **São Francisco Javier Fortress** is right on the coast, one kilometer down the road beside the praça de Gonçalves Zarco. Zarco, discoverer of Madeira, came from neighboring Matosinhos. The foundation of the 17th-century garrison contains an ancient sacrificial boulder used by Celtic Druids in the sixth century B.C.

Continue northwest to **Matosinhos** via the esplanada do Rio de Janeiro and the N 208. The former fishing village has grown tremendously in recent years following the construction of an artificial port and lost some of its charm to industry, but its waterfront restaurants continue to serve some of the best fish and shellfish in the region. The **Esplanada Marisqueira**, at rua Roberto Ivens, 628–638, has its own private vivarium. Here you can try mouth-watering *arroz de marisco, caldeirada de peixe* (fish stew), and *açorda de marisco* (coriander-spiked, bread-thickened shellfish stew into which raw eggs are dropped just before serving). *Broinhas de Leixoes* are a typical local honeycake dessert.

Past the busy port of Leixoes and over a viaduct, you will encounter the **Igreja do Bom Jesus de Matosinhos**, a 16th-century shrine containing a wooden statue of Christ on the cross that washed up on the beach several hundred years ago. Legend has it that it is one of four carved by the disciple Nicodemus, destined for the four corners of the earth. The statue had lost an arm on its voyage. Fifty years after the statue's discovery, an old woman combing the beach for firewood found a wooden arm. When the arm would not ignite, she took it to the shrine, where it miraculously attached itself to the Nicodemus statue.

The Senhor de Matosinhos pilgrimage, in the first two weeks of June, is one of the liveliest and most colorful of its kind in the region, with singing, dancing, fireworks, and outdoor eating. The Baroque façade of the shrine is by the prolific Nicolau Nasoni. The ceilings of the nave and the chancel are covered by a sumptuous recessed panel depicting scenes from the Passion.

The return trip to Porto can be shortened by turning left at praça de Gonçalves Zarco by the Queijo fortress onto the avenida da Boavista. Avoid driving in the late afternoon on weekends during the summer months, however, or you may be stuck in bumper-to-bumper traffic with locals returning from a day at the beach.

Staying in Porto

"Oporto has nothing to boast with respect to its hotels. Indeed I know of no city in Europe of this size and consideration that possesses so few," wrote a disappointed William Kingston in 1845. The situation was finally resolved a century later with the construction of the luxury **Hotel de Infante Sagres**, at number 62 praça de Lencastre, just west of the avenida dos Aliados and several blocks northwest of praça da Liberdade. This elegant hotel has the look and feel of a stately town house with all the genteel touches and service of the Belle Epoque. Several members of the British royal family have stayed here. The impressive wood-carved fireplace at the entrance was the work of a former night porter. The restaurant in the hotel is the most luxurious in the city, with a well-stocked cellar.

Modern luxury chain hotels, with all the recreational amenities that go with them, have also made their appearance in Porto during the last few years. The 232-room **Hotel Méridien** has a fine French restaurant and a popular discotheque. The hotel's conference facilities draw executives. The Méridien is situated in a modern neighborhood in the northwestern side of the city, ten minutes from the center by cab or bus, at avenida da Boavista, 1466.

The **Hotel Sheraton Porto**, nearby at avenida da Boavista, 1269, offers a heated, indoor pool and a squash and health club.

We discuss the dowager Grand Hotel do Porto above, in the Baixa section.

Dining in Porto

When it comes to food, Portuenses can be reactionary in the extreme. Any variation on their centuries-old cuisine is viewed with suspicion, which explains why the menus in the restaurants and *tascas* here tend to be of a sameness. But the food is flavorful and betrays some of its North African, Eastern, and New World influences.

The food and varied menu of **Portucale**, its penthouse view of the city, the sea, and the surrounding countryside, and its attentive service make it the most complete dining experience in Porto and a local favorite. Its somewhat brash modern decor is compensated for by its mouth-watering dishes, which include lobster with rice stew, pheasant stuffed with almonds, wild boar, and a rich version of Porto's traditional tripe dish. This moderate-to-expensive restaurant, which occupies the 14th floor of an *albergaria* (modern inn) at rua da Alegria, 598, is a short cab ride northeast from the city center. Tel: (02) 57-07-17.

The **Infante de Sagres**, lodged in the hotel of the same name (praça de Lencastre, 62), is Porto's most elegant restaurant, frequented by the city's old guard. Its opulence—crystal chandeliers, wood-paneled mirrors, tapestries, and thick carpeting—is matched by its equally sumptuous food and vintage wine list, served by a phalanx of discreetly efficient black-tied waiters. The soufflés and flambées, with Port, are the trademark of the maître d', while the chef's artistry in the dessert area can be viewed on the pastry cart. Fresh flowers, candles, and fine Portuguese silver and china decorate the restaurant's 15 or so tables. Tel: (02) 28176.

The **Grande Hotel do Porto** restaurant, with its stucco ceiling, topaz walls, velour curtains, and glass chandeliers, offers a less expensive fin-de-siècle alternative to the Infante de Sagres. Guests have a choice of à la carte or prix fixe dining. Rua de Santa Catarina, 197; Tel: (02) 28176.

The **Escondidinho**, a popular, down-to-earth establishment near the town center at rua dos Passos Manuel, 144, serves some of the city's best food of the Douro region. The atmosphere of this modestly priced, family-run establishment, which is a replica of a typical Douro country house, is relaxed and homey. Closed Sundays. Tel: (02) 21079.

Nightlife in Porto

A good way to start the evening in Porto is by paying a visit to the Solar do Vinho do Porto wine bar (see above, West of Liberdade). The **Mal Cozinhado** restaurant, at rua do Outeirinho, 13, on the western tip of the Ribeira dock, features regional folk dancing and music during the summer, though the **Casa das Mariquinhas** fado house, at rua São Sebastião, 25, near the cathedral, provides a mellower alternative with its checkered cloth tables and dim lights. Open from 9:00 P.M. every night; Tel: (02) 31-60-83.

The Ribeira area offers a more animated choice of music. **Postigo do Carvão**, a lively restaurant and piano bar at rua Fonte Taurina, 26–34, is housed in a former warehouse. **Aniki-Bobo**, next door, caters to jazz and folk lovers; no credit cards accepted.

Porto's chic crowd tends to head out toward the pubs and discos west of the city. **Swing**, at rua Júlio Diniz, 766, near the Palácio de Cristal, is frequented by Porto's young swinging set, who like its combination of upstairs pub and downstairs disco. Sophisticated and well-heeled Portuenses frequent establishments in the affluent suburb of Foz do Douro, a ten-minute ride from the center, where pub-disco-restaurant combinations at Twins and Greens are the latest craze. **Twins**, at rua do Passeio Alegre, 1000, is supposed to be a members-only club, but the rule is generally waived. The decor and menu are old-guard Continental. Meals are served Mondays to Saturdays. **Greens**, at rua Padre Luis Cabral, 1086, is less clubby and the cuisine more nouvelle. The restaurant is closed Saturday nights and Sundays.

THE DOURO VALLEY

Think of the Douro valley as a fortress hemmed in by high walls—in this case by mountains soaring at times up to 3,000 feet—guarded by a powerful coalition of wine barons, defending their bucolic fiefdom against the onslaught of industry. Within this domain lies a spectacular and rugged valley where tiny villages, stately quintas, and vineyards compete for space on steep slopes of pink granite and schist, intricately striated with terraces, as if some giant had raked a comb across the hills. The terraces look over the Douro, which twists and turns like a serpent through the valley. The Douro's legendary fury— for centuries flash floods inundated the low-lying towns on its banks—has now been contained by eight dams, and the wooden *rabelos* that until recently carried the wine to Porto have been replaced by tour boats. Bed-and-breakfast establishments and inns have begun to sprout on the slopes and along the river's tributaries, and tours of the vineyards are becoming popular. Like a good vintage coming to maturity, the Douro valley is being uncorked for an appreciative public.

The grapes that produce Port wine are grown in the Alto Douro's demarcated wine zone, which begins 62

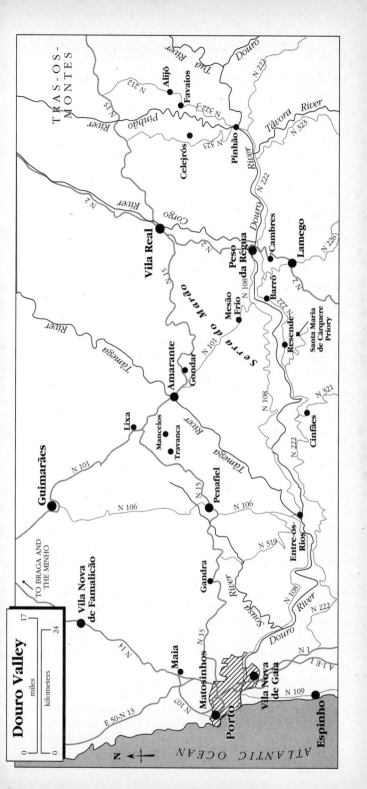

miles upstream from Porto and stretches some 3 miles south and 16 miles north along the river, all the way to the Spanish border. The El Dorado for Port-wine vineyards, however, is a 13-mile strip at its center between Peso da Régua and Pinhão, where the soil and climatic conditions are just right for the grapes. After Pinhão the landscape gradually becomes wilder and more primitive as the river moves east toward Spain (see the Trás-os-Montes chapter for more details). There are few towns beyond Pinhão, and some of the barren hillside vineyards still show the scars of a 19th-century phylloxera plague that devastated the region's vines. American vines, nicknamed *americanos,* saved the day when their root stocks, immune to phylloxera, were grafted with the endangered domestic varieties.

But the region east of Porto is not only the domain of Port. The grapes of the region also produce some fine unfortified wines, such as the red Barca Velha and white Monopólio. And although the heart of *vinho verde* production is the Minho province to the north, some of the estates and former monasteries of the Douro Litoral produce some refreshing *verdes*.

Our route concentrates on the wine areas along the Douro as far as Pinhão and its environs. It begins some 40 km (25 miles) east of Porto, by crossing from the northern to the southern bank of the river at Entre-os-Rios (a town at the confluence of the Douro and Tâmega rivers, known for its river lamprey and the neighboring Convento de Alpendurada *vinho verde*). It follows the left, or southern, bank (N 222) east on a roller-coaster run high above the river, past trellised vineyards, handkerchief-size cornfields, and an occasional row or grove of olive trees. Every so often there is a fine vista of the wooded right bank and its mountains. An opening in the dense foliage may reveal a tiny village clinging to a slope above the river or women washing laundry on the banks of the Douro, as they have done for centuries. The road visits the *vinho verde* town of Cinfães and its neighboring historic monastery of Santa Maria de Cárquere, meanders on to Resende, known for its egg-and-sugar sweets and bed-and-breakfasts.

After Barrô, where silver-gray ground-baked pottery is sold beside the road, the clay soil and trellised landscape of the Douro Litoral are left behind and replaced by the schist and ground-hugging vines of the Alto Douro Port-wine region. The steep mountains surrounding the valley protect it from moist Atlantic winds, producing warm winters with light rainfall and scorching hot summers. The best grapes grow near the river, where they obtain moisture and are protected from the wind. Schist is the other element behind their success. It gathers heat during the day and releases it during the night, thereby providing an even temperature for the grapes to mature. The vertical grain and porous nature of the granite and schist allow water to soak in and remain as reserves for the roots to tap into during the scorching summers with temperatures up to 40 degrees Celsius (106 degrees Fahrenheit).

Outside Barrô you have a choice of continuing on the N 222 as it twists down toward Peso da Régua (which is on the right bank of the river), the administrative center of the Port-wine business in the Alto Douro, or taking a longer, more scenic route (N 226) there via the historic city of Lamego (for which see the Beira Alta chapter). From Peso da Régua the N 222 continues on the south bank along the demarcated region's most coveted vine slopes and handsome quintas. It crosses to the right bank at Pinhão, the geographic center of the Port-wine region, climbs (N 322-3) a ravine to Alijó, known for its pousada's fine Douro cooking, and loops back to Pinhão on the N 323-1 and N 323 past granite Medieval villages with views over vineyards spread out like a giant corduroy quilt.

After crossing back to the left bank at Pinhão, the N 222 backtracks, returns to the right over a bridge to Peso da Régua, and climbs west to Mesão Frio on the Serra do Marão, where you can continue toward Porto on the windy but scenic northern slopes of the Douro or veer right onto the N 101 and visit the enchanting resort town of Amarante, on the banks of the Tâmega. The wooded area around Amarante is littered with archaeological remains, Romanesque churches, and manor houses and offers swimming, fishing, and hiking opportunities. The town's Victorian tea houses, lodged on balconies over the river, and weekly outdoor *arraiais* (carnivalesque barn-style parties that go on to the wee hours) are other attractions. The tour ends on the N 15 back to Porto after stops at the tiny parish church of Travanca, and the Aveleda estate at Penafiel, where a walk in the semitropical gardens and a taste of its fine *vinho verde* provide a suitable finale to the Douro.

Give yourself three to four days for a leisurely visit to the valley. The limited number of accommodations here makes it essential that you reserve your stay in advance. The best time to visit is during the *vindima* (grape harvest) in late September and early October, when the grape leaves turn as bright as maples and the valley comes alive with activity and echoes with the songs of the grape pickers. Women and children pick the grapes, and the men carry baskets of grapes weighing over 100 pounds up and down dizzying slopes. Traditionally, the grapes were trodden in *lagares* (concrete vats) by barefoot men to the beat of a drum or the wheeze of a concertina or an accordion. Although human labor has been replaced mostly by mechanical crushers (which purists say rob the wine of some of its taste), some of the large estates still crush a small amount of their crop the old way for the benefit of tradition and tourists. Merry postharvest parties are held at the quintas, and wine is consumed liberally by all. Visits to the *vindima* can be arranged by travel agents and the Turismo offices in Porto and Peso da Régua. It is possible to visit the valley by boat or train or a combination of the two (see the Getting Around section at the end of the chapter).

Along the Douro River

Cinfães, 35 km (22 miles) east of Entre-os-Rios, surrounded by cornfields, olive groves, and trellised vines, is the area's commercial center for *vinho verde,* and a good spot to taste it. The light estate wine Quinta do Crasto is one of the area's finer "green" wines. Dom Afonso Henriques, the first king of Portugal, spent his early years in the town under the care of his godfather. The town's handsome 12th-century church of Santa Maria de Tarouquela belonged to a former Augustine monastery.

The **Santa Maria de Cárquere priory**, off the N 222 east of Cinfães (some 9 km/5 miles southeast of Anreade), is a historic landmark for Portugal. In 1114, on the summit of Montemuro, surrounded by rocky crests, the young Afonso Henriques was miraculously cured of a crippling disease. His godfather, Egaz Moniz, was led to the site by the Virgin Mary in a dream. A Romanesque church and priory were constructed in honor of the event. The priory has since disappeared, but the church, which has been remodeled several times over the centuries, and the chapel crypt of the region's once-powerful lords of Resende provide a glimpse of the priory's former glory: a crenellated tower, a Gothic chapter house, an ornate Manueline façade, a colonnaded Romanesque doorway, an unusual Romanesque window supported by capitals of sculptured pelicans, and four sarcophagi with Medieval inscriptions.

Resende is a tiny town some 19 km (12 miles) east of Cinfães, known for its sweet sugar-and-egg *cavacas* ("straw hats") and its semisweet Casa de Rendufe *vinho verde*. Several antique-filled *casas* (country homes) owned by members of the local aristocracy have opened their doors to bed-and-breakfast guests here. The **Casa de Resende** is a pleasant town house near the town center, with one double bedroom and one single, while the **Casa de São Gens** and the **Casa do Mato** offer more secluded alternatives on the outskirts of the village, with gardens and two antique-filled double bedrooms apiece. Their owners are country gentry with the famous explorer's name of Magalhães (Magellan). Continental breakfast is served, but more substantial meals have to be obtained outside in towns such as Cinfães or in the village bistros at Resende.

The name of the 12th-century fortress church of **São Martinho de Moros** alludes to the brief Moorish tenure in the area. Stories abound of Moorish treasures buried under rocks, fountains, and ruins in the surrounding countryside. The rural church, commanding a desolate hill pass, has an intricately carved stone tympanum. Its cool and airy interior contains the remains of primitive wall paintings depicting scenes of Saint Martin's life. The church lies less than one kilometer off the N 222, some 6 km (4 miles) east of Resende.

Barrô, some 12.5 km (8 miles) northeast of Resende, clings to a high, wooded promontory with a sweeping view of the Douro valley and the Marão mountains to the north. The area around Barrô is known for its silver-gray *olaria* (ground-baked pottery). Basket-shaped pots used to bake rice and round jugs are among the common household items fashioned by the area's craftsmen, who use holes in the ground filled with smoldering wood ashes as their kilns. The ashes, together with the gray, schist soil of the region, give the pottery its distinctive color.

Barrô is both the geological and official border between the Douro Litoral (Coastal Douro) and the Alto (Upper) Douro. From here on to the east the soil becomes drier and clay gives way to schist. Trellised vineyards begin to disappear, replaced by ground-hugging vines. From Barrô on lies the first demarcated wine zone in the world, stretching some 2 miles south and about 15 miles north along the river all the way to the Spanish border. In 1756 a company formed by Prime Minister Pombal to oversee production and fix prices in an effort to eliminate the British monopoly placed 325 granite posts as markers along the valley's borders. The company failed to break the British hold on the export industry but did succeed in setting standards and regulations. Today, some of the original markers still guard the hillsides, others have been requisitioned by farmers for doorposts.

Six kilometers (4 miles) east of Barrô you have a choice of routes to reach the Port country. You can either continue on the N 222 to Peso da Régua (22 km/14 miles) in the heart of Port country or turn right onto the N 226 for a slightly longer (13 km/8 miles) but more scenic journey via the bucolic and historic town of Lamego (see the Beira Alta chapter). If you decide on the former, you should first make a short 3-km (2-mile) detour on the N 226 to the **Miradouro da Boa Vista**, a belvedere commanding some of the most sweeping views of the Douro valley, the town of Peso da Régua across the river, and the Marão mountains to the north.

Peso da Régua, the administrative center of Port wine of the Douro valley, lies 28 km (18 miles) east of Barrô on the right bank of the Douro. It is also the starting point for several scenic train routes (see Getting Around, below), and one of the stops on the national railroad's Linha do Douro. The latter follows the Douro to Barca de Alva, 5 km (3 miles) west of the Spanish border, where the railroad company runs a small inn and restaurant.

Although Peso da Régua lacks the architectural beauty and monuments of, say, Amarante to the northwest, this is partly compensated for by the stark beauty of the river and surrounding countryside. It was from Peso da Régua, before the advent of the railway and the taming of the river, that the square-rigged *rabelos,* laden with wine barrels, set off on their perilous journey down the river to Porto. The boatmen eased the hazardous trip sometimes by dipping into the wine barrels and later topping them off with river water, much to the annoyance of the shippers. Today you can still catch a glimpse of these retired wooden ships soaking in the sun on the banks of the river.

Peso da Régua is the headquarters for the winegrowers' association. Their offices in the Casa do Douro contain a register of some 85,000 vineyards of the Alto Douro region, and the casa's entrance is lit up by a set of stained-glass windows depicting the production and history of

Port. The Turismo office beside the station, at largo da Estação (Tel: 054-22846), will provide maps and other information on the region and help make arrangements for accommodations or arrange a visit to a vineyard.

The **Casa dos Varais** is a bed-and-breakfast housed in an elegant 18th-century home just outside the town of Cambres, 5 km (3 miles) south of Peso da Régua on the high ground above the left bank of the Douro. The house, which has a lovely tropical garden and looks out onto terraced vineyards and the river, is an ideal spot from which to enjoy the scenic flavor of the Port-wine valley. There are two double bedrooms and a private living room, decorated with antiques, open to guests. To get here from Peso da Régua, cross the bridge and take the N 2 toward Cambres. There are no outstanding restaurants in the immediate vicinity, but the bistros in Peso da Régua provide fairly good regional food, such as *cabrito assado* (roast kid) accompanied by *arroz de forno* (baked riče), and trout stuffed with ham.

The best Port-wine vineyards start at Peso da Régua and stretch east along the sides of the Douro and its tributaries. The N 222 follows the left bank of the river east. The steep slopes on both sides of the river, which sometimes reach inclines of close to 90 degrees, have been intricately terraced by hand, stone by stone, with a skill and precision that would win the respect of Aztec stonemasons. Even the thin layer of dirt on which the vines grow had to be carried up, bucketful by bucketful. The endless rows of steps sometimes lead to a whitewashed quinta of one of the wine barons, crowning the slopes above the river. The trails on either side of the river and its slopes were made by boatmen to pull their boats upriver on their return trips from Porto.

Pinhão, on the confluence of the Douro and Pinhão rivers, 22 km (14 miles) upriver from Peso da Régua, is the epicenter of the Port-wine vineyards. It occupies a small strip of flat land on the right bank of the Douro. Behind it, the terraced mountains rise perpendicularly. Some of the major Port houses maintain storage houses beside the pretty train station, which is tiled with blue, white, and yellow panels depicting the Port-wine story. It is a sleepy town for most of the year, but, come the fall grape harvest, its population swells as grape pickers from the surrounding countryside congregate here. The intoxicating smell of wine fills the streets, and the canyon above the town echoes with the sounds of the *vindima,* which usually runs from the last week in September to the middle of October (but can be delayed or advanced depending on the weather conditions in a given year).

The **Pousada do Barão de Forrester** at Alijó, a rustic town set on a high plateau 18 km (11 miles) north of Pinhão, offers comfortable accommodations and good food. The road from Pinhão (N 322-3) to Alijó twists and climbs the terraced eastern side of the canyon above the Pinhão river. During the *vindima* you can stop your car and watch the picking from the road, and may be invited to share a glass of wine with the pickers. The pousada, which is named after the Britisher who mapped, and drowned in, his beloved Douro, is in a large house in the town's center. Remodeled several years ago, it has 11 comfortable rooms done up in bright fabrics and furnished with reproductions of antiques, a well-stocked Port bar, and a fine country restaurant with a mural of grape trellises serving some of the region's specialties, which include skillet-fried trout wrapped in tissue-thin slices of *presunto,* the Portuguese equivalent of prosciutto, *cabrito assado com arroz de forno* (kid baked en casserole with rice), *cozido a Portuguesa* (meat, chicken, and vegetable stew), *pudim de amêndoa* (almond pudding), and sugar-and-egg *cavacas de Santa Eugenia.* The local wines are Alijó, Favaios, Sanfins do Douro, and Pegarinhos. If you are not satisfied with them, go on to the Douro-denominated reds and whites. The pousada can also arrange visits to the vineyards.

Alijó, which is known for its oranges, received its royal charter in 1226. Its origins are much older, as can be witnessed in the ruins of Celtic *castros* (fortified Iron Age hill towns with ramparts and moats, which were common in Portugal between 800 B.C. and A.D. 200) that lie in the vicinity and in the Roman names of some of the neighboring towns such as Favaios (a bastardization of the Roman *Flavius*). The *castros* provide ideal spots for picnics and walks. There are several private *solares* (manor houses) of note in Alijó's town square and its adjoining streets, which sport the coats of arms of several of the region's patrician families. Alijó's most striking feature is a large tree planted in 1856 that broods over the main square, provides shade during the blistering summers, and is an idyllic spot throughout the year to trade news and gossip. Alijó is the perfect place to get away from it all, eat good country cooking, sample the Douro's huge selection of wines, breathe fresh mountain air, and take endless walks. Twice a year, during the annual fair (August 14) and the feast of São Martinho (November 11), the quiet and peace are shattered by the sounds and merriment of a fairground, and the sky is lit up by fireworks.

You can return to Pinhão the way you came or loop around some 30 km (19 miles) and visit the western side of the plateau, which offers more breath-catching views over the vineyards and a glimpse of primitive Medieval villages where *carro duriense,* burro-drawn wooden carts that look like Roman chariots, are still used.

For the loop, leave Alijó the way you came and drive 5 km (3 miles) to **Favaios**, a granite village that retains its Medieval flavor and has a communal fountain from which villagers still draw their water. The town cooperative sells Favaios's sweet muscatel wine. From here, take the N 323-1 north past evergreens and small granite huts to Sanfins do Douro, given by King Dinis to his bastard son in 1258. Southwest of Sanfins, at Sabrosa, which claims the birth of the famous Portuguese explorer Ferdinand Magellan (scholars, however, place it in the Minho), take the N 323 south and drive through vineyards scattered thick over the plateau. The descent to Pinhão is like a corkscrew plunging into a bottle, and should be attempted during daylight hours.

At Pinhão cross the Douro again to the left bank, follow the N 222 to the Peso da Régua bridge, recross the river to the right bank, and follow N 108 west.

Mesão Frio sits high above the Douro, 12 km (7.5 miles) northwest (on N 101) of Peso da Régua in the Marão mountains on the way to Amarante. These mountains allow the Douro valley to enjoy a semi-Mediterranean climate by acting as a buffer against the cold Atlantic winds. The town's main street is lined with orange trees and 18th-century *solares.* Its Gothic parish church and the former Franciscan monastery of Santa Cristina, now converted into a hospital, adorn this street. A Baroque gate crowned by animals, the façade, and the iron-adorned fountain embellish the stately **Casa da Rede**, situated above the main road on the western outskirts of the town above the river. You can admire this private home, one of the region's finest, from the road.

At Mesão Frio you can either continue back to Porto on the N 108, which has stunning views of the river and the left bank, or turn north onto the N 101 toward Amarante, one of northern Portugal's most picturesque towns.

Amarante

A picture-postcard town with a dreamy enchantment to it, Amarante lies 25 km (16 miles) northwest of Mesão Frio on the wooded banks of the Tâmega on the border of Trás-os-Montes, the Minho, and the Douro Litoral. The wooden balconies and covered porches of its riverside homes and Victorian-style teahouses are reflected in the clear waters of the Tâmega and afford views of the town's monuments. The verandahs of the teahouses are ideal for watching youngsters and old men fish while you sample the town's famous pastries.

The people of Amarante are known for their happy dispositions. *Amar* (love), the first part of the town's name, tells it all. Their patron saint is São Gonçalo, who finds husbands for unmarried women. The Romaria de São Gonçalo is a popular pilgrimage held on the first weekend of June, when single women visit the **church of São Gonçalo** to pray for husbands. The exterior loggia of the handsome 16th-century church is flanked by statues of four Portuguese kings who reigned while it was being built, while its interior contains the remains of the saint and an elegant 17th-century organ supported by Tritons. The church faces an 18th-century double-arched granite bridge, flanked by long obelisks and graced with semicircular platforms where pedestrians pause to gaze at the river and courting couples court. In 1809 the town put up stiff resistance against Napoleonic forces on this bridge.

Other interesting sights include the church of São Pedro with its lively Baroque façade and nave decorated with early-17th-century *azulejos*. The Câmara (town hall) museum houses the town's two *dêmonios* (a she-devil and a he-devil), believed to be a holdover from ancient devil worship. A 19th-century bishop of Braga decided to dispose of the devils and sold them to an English buyer, but this caused such a local furor that they had to be returned.

The *arraial de São Gonçalo* is held Thursdays and Saturdays at the municipal gardens. For a small fee you can eat, drink, dance, watch folk dancing, and participate in a *marcha popular* led by *gigantes* (giants) of the forest, played by young men sporting huge heads made of glazed paper. The origin of the *gigantes* is lost in time, but they are believed to have some ties to northern European lore. The festivities are illuminated by lavish fireworks displays, the loud noise supposedly keeping away the devil.

The wooded area around Amarante has been likened to Germany's Black Forest. This similarity may have attracted Germanic tribes such as the Swabians to it, and may explain why there are many remnants of pagan worship still in existence here. Stone Age dolmens, early Iron Age *castros,* and unusual formations called *pedras baloiçantes* (balancing rocks) can be seen in the vicinity. The *castro* ruins of the Carneiro (16 km/10 miles southeast on N 101) and Candemil (14 km/9 miles southeast on N 15) are two of the largest in the area. The country around Amarante is also graced with Romanesque churches: Freixo de Baixo (5 km/3 miles northwest on N 101) contains a 12th-century parish church with primitive frescoes; Mancelos (14 km/9 miles west, off the N 211-1), has interesting carved tombs; Lufrei (3 km/2 miles east, off the N 312) has a highly carved doorway; Gondar (6 km/4 miles southeast, on the N 15) has both a parish church and ruins of a former monastery.

A one-day excursion on the single-track **Linha do Tâmega** (you can pick it up in Amarante; 31 miles each way) up the Tâmega into the *bastos* (pasturelands) of Trás-os-Montes will treat you to some of the most unspoiled bucolic countryside in the north of Portugal. The tiny toy of a train climbs past forests of pine and oak, vineyards and whitewashed manor houses, and fields of heather and rosemary before ending its journey at Arco de Baulhe, with its quaint railway museum. Tickets for this train ride, which takes two hours each way, can be purchased at any of the railway stations on the line.

There is trout fishing (permits can be obtained in Lisbon from the Direção-Geral dos Serviços Florestais e Agrícolas, at avenida João Crisótomo, 2628), swimming, and rowboats for hire (the latter are inexpensive and can be booked by the hour or day by your hotel) on the Tâmega, and hiking on trails around Amarante. There is also a superb camping area with a rustic restaurant beside the river on the outskirts of the town, at **Quinta dos Frades** (Tel: 055-42-21-33). More information and maps on the region, its sights, and activities can be obtained at Amarante's local tourism office, located near the bridge on rua Cândido dos Reis (Tel: 055-42-29-80).

Amarante has a nice selection of accommodations. The modern **Hotel Navarras**, at rua António Carneiro, has air-conditioned rooms, a heated indoor swimming pool, and outdoor dining facilities. The **Hotel Amarante**, at rua Madalena, is a more modest alternative, with a panoramic view of the town. The drawback is the noise of its public bar. The **Casa Zé da Calçada** at rua de Janeiro, 31, is a large, comfortable town house with three double bedrooms decorated with regional artifacts. It belongs to the **Zé da Calçada** riverside restaurant across the street, which is known throughout the Douro for its namesake, a baked dish of dried salt cod and potatoes, and for regional specialties such as baked kid and sugar, egg, and almond sweets like caramelized, peaked *foguetes* (rockets) and smooth, light *brisas do Tâmega* (Tâmega breezes). The wine list includes the local Quinta da Livração estate wine and the popular light Adega Cooperativa de Gatão. Amarante's most colorful *tasca* (tavern), the **Adega Regional**, is housed in a man-made cave on the tiny rua António Carneiro, near the river and town center. It's easy to find and a perfect spot for a predinner appetizer of *presunto* and *salpicão* (wine-cured and smoked sausages). Senhor Cardoso, the owner, is a colorful and hospitable character who will make sure your glass remains topped up.

Having completed the northwestern and final leg of the tour of the Douro, take the N 15 back from Amarante. Drive 10 km (6 miles) northwest to Lixa and turn left. (The N 15 going northwest out of Amarante is also the N 101. If you stay straight on 101 at Lixa instead of turning off on the N 15 to the left, you'll come to Guimarães and then Braga in the Minho.) Before returning to Porto, get a final taste of vintage Portugal by visiting the Romanesque parish church at **Travanca** off the N 15, with its splendid capital inscribed with dragons. Then continue southwest on the N 15 to the leafy hilltop town of **Penafiel** and stop to stroll in the lush subtropical garden and taste the fine *vinho verde* wines of the **Quinta de Aveleda** estate.

GETTING AROUND

Porto's international airport, Pedras Rubras, is located at Maia, 15 km (9 miles) northwest of the city. A taxi ride with tip should run to 2,000 escudos (make sure you agree on the fare with the driver before you get in). The number 56 bus connects the airport with the city center and the Campanhã railway station, at rua da Estação. The station, which is at the eastern end of the city, connects Porto internationally as well as with the Douro and the south of the country. The Trindade train station, at the end of rua

António Saldanha, handles the northern routes. The São Bento commuter station, at praça Almeida Garrett, has a shuttle service to Campanhã.

The Rodoviária Nacional, or national bus company, at praça de Lencastre, sells tourist passes for the city bus and tram system. The passes, good for four to seven days of unlimited travel, are only worth buying if you intend to use buses fairly often. Tel: (02) 22-69-54. Taxis are fairly ubiquitous; they can be caught at a cab stand at the southern end of the avenida dos Aliados or summoned by phone; Tel: (02) 38-80-61.

Double-decker Cityrama buses (rua Entre Paredes; Tel: 02-31-71-55), with English-speaking hostesses, tour the city and visit the Port-wine lodges. Ferry boats also tour the river, leaving on the hour from the quay at Vila Nova de Gaia. The 45-minute boat ride provides vistas of Porto and includes a visit to the Foz. The boat runs from 10:00 A.M. to 6:00 P.M. between May and October, except Saturdays.

Give yourself two full days to get to know Porto—and wear comfortable walking shoes. Also, pay a visit to the main Turismo office at rua Clube Fernianos, 25 (open Mondays through Fridays from 9:00 A.M. to 7:00 P.M.; Saturdays 9:00 A.M. to 4:00 P.M.; Sundays 10:00 A.M. to 1:00 P.M.), to pick up its handy red pamphlet on the city, a map of Porto and its bus routes, and a miniguide with a short history of Port wine.

Several scenic train routes range along the Douro; tickets can be purchased at the stations or through travel agents, as can tourist passes with discounts of 25 percent for one to three weeks' duration. (We recommend travelling first class, as second class can be pretty grungy.) Children under 4 travel free as long as they don't occupy a seat; otherwise they are charged a second-class fare. Children between 4 and 12 pay half the adult rate. Soft drinks and beer can be purchased on these lines, but not meals.

The **Linha do Douro** begins at the São Bento station in Porto and follows the Douro through the heart of Port-wine country to Barca de Alva in the southeast, near the Spanish border. Three trains make the seven-hour trip every day. The journey can be broken up by stopping at important wine centers such as Peso da Régua or Pinhão. After Pinhão the terrain becomes wilder, and the river narrows. *Mortorios* (vine cemeteries) ravaged by the phylloxera plague of 1868 begin to appear, surrounded by abandoned stone villages. At Pocinho, before Barca de

Alva, you can take the **Linha do Sabor** east for three hours to **Miranda do Douro**, a historic town with its own dialect and dances and a fairly good pousada. At **Barca de Alva** the railroad company runs a small restaurant and a boardinghouse with five bedrooms (see the Trás-os-Montes chapter).

The single-track **Linha do Tâmega** follows the river northeast past pines, vineyards, and manor houses and stops at picturesque plateau towns such as Celorico and Mondim do Basto, where heraldic manor homes offer bed and breakfast (see the Trás-os-Montes chapter). The line ends at Arco de Baulhe, where you can visit a railway museum with vintage trains and rail paraphernalia. It takes nearly two hours to do the 31-mile trip. The **Linha do Corgo** line runs north from Peso da Régua along the deep gorge of the river Corgo past Vila Real (see the Trás-os-Montes chapter), known for its Mateus rosé. It climbs through the rugged Padrão and Padrela mountains on its three-hour journey to the spa town of Chaves, near the Spanish border. The **Linha da Tua** runs from Tua, northeast of Pinhão, to Bragança in the northeastern corner of Portugal. The primitive coal-fired train, with wooden carriages and seats, crosses two mountain ranges at a leisurely pace on its four-hour journey through Portugal's outback.

A car is the best way to visit the interior, however, where many of the scenic and monumental attractions are off the main road and train lines. Cars can be rented at the airport or in Porto. The main-artery traffic around Porto, however, is horrendous and even dangerous. Expect long delays around here. Avoid night driving on the winding and poorly marked Douro roads.

There are one- and two-day package tours of the Portwine region via boat and train. The best include wine tasting and lunch at a wine lodge at Pinhão. Trips can be booked through travel agents or Endouro, praça da Ribeira, 20D, 4000 Porto; Tel: (02) 32436; Telex: 27347. There are several tour options. The one-day Douro Maravilhoso tour begins on the double-decker, 100-seat *Ribadouro* sightseeing boat (bar service on board), which cruises from Porto to Peso da Régua. Several dams en route are negotiated by locks. There is a one-hour stopover at Peso da Régua, where lunch can be procured before the return to Porto. The two-day program begins with a train ride to Peso da Régua on a special first-class coach with bar service and guide. Lunch at Peso da Régua is followed by a tour via bus of the neighboring town of Lamego. After an overnight stay at Peso da Régua you return to Porto by boat, stopping for lunch at the former convent of Alpendurada.

The Cruzeiros da Rota do Vinho do Porto tours offer a pair of two-day cruises. Program A starts with the boat ride to Peso da Régua, followed by dinner and overnight accommodations in a simple inn. On the second day the cruise continues upriver to Pinhão and Vilarinho de Cotas in the heart of the vineyards, stops for lunch in the gardens of the Taylor, Fladgate & Yeatman lodge, and returns to Porto via a special coach. Program B begins with the train ride to Pinhão, lunch at the lodge, a boat trip up to Vilarinho de Cotas and down to Peso da Régua, and an overnight stay there before resuming the cruise to Porto.

ACCOMMODATIONS REFERENCE

▶ **Hotel Amarante.** Rua Madalena, **Amarante**, 4600 Porto. Tel: (055) 42-21-06.

▶ **Pousada do Barão de Forrester.** Rua José Rufino, **Alijó**, 5070 Vila Real. Tel: (059) 95467; Telex: 26364.

▶ **Hotel Boa Vista.** Esplanada do Castelo, 58, **Foz do Douro**, 4100 Porto. Tel: (02) 67-05-88; Telex: 25574.

▶ **Grande Hotel do Porto.** Rua Santa Catarina, 197, 4000 **Porto**. Tel: (02) 28176; Telex: 22553.

▶ **Hotel de Infante Sagres.** Praça de Lencastre, 62, 4000 **Porto**. Tel: (02) 28101; Telex: 22378.

▶ **Casa do Mato.** 4660 **Resende**; contact Maria Lucinda Magalhães. Tel: (054) 97307.

▶ **Hotel Méridien.** Avenida da Boavista, 1466, 4000 **Porto**. Tel: (02) 66-88-63; Telex: 27301.

▶ **Hotel Navarras.** Rua António Carneiro, **Amarante**, 4600 Porto. Tel: (055) 42-40-35.

▶ **Casa de Resende.** Rua Conego Correia Pinto, 14, 4660 **Resende**; contact Maria Isabel de Sousa Moreira. Tel: (054) 97104.

▶ **Casa de São Gens.** 4660 **Resende**; contact Maria Susana Magalhães. Tel: (054) 97307.

▶ **Hotel Sheraton Porto.** Avenida da Boavista, 1269, 4000 **Porto**. Tel: (02) 66-88-22.

▶ **Casa dos Varais. Cambres**, Peso da Régua, 5050 Vila Real; contact Lucia de Castro Girão. Tel: (054) 23251 or (02) 66-74-42.

▶ **Casa Zé da Calçada.** Rua de Janeiro, 31, **Amarante**, 4600 Porto. Tel: (02) 42-20-23.

Pousadas can be booked through Marketing Ahead, 433 Fifth Avenue, New York, N.Y. 10016; Tel: (212) 686-9213.

THE MINHO

By Thomas de la Cal

The Minho, tucked away in the northwest corner of the country, between the Minho river and Spain to the north and Porto and the Douro river to the south, with the remote province of Trás-os-Montes to the east, is Portugal's Garden of Eden. Its rich soil and an ample supply of water from rainfall and thermal springs keep it eternally verdant. Mists shroud its interior in mystery and give the land an aura of sublime peace. Blessed with such beauty, its inhabitants, a happy and hospitable lot, fittingly chose the heart as their crest.

Physically, the Minho has been likened to a huge amphitheater. The serras of Peneda, Gerês, and Padrela in the east form a semicircle facing west onto a stage comprising the bucolic Lima, Cávado, and Tâmega valleys. Some of Portugal's most dramatic historical events—including the very birth of the nation—have been staged here by a mixed cast of Celtic, Germanic, Slavic, Spanish, and other Mediterranean peoples. The performances took place amid a vast array of natural settings—a luxuriant Atlantic coastline, rolling hills, pristine lakes, and majestic peaks—and an equally impressive number of man-made props: from Iron Age *castros* (fortified hilltop stone villages) and granite Medieval hamlets to elegant Renaissance *solares* (manor houses) and elaborate Baroque churches.

The Minhotos' personality is as mixed and their imagination as fertile as their region's landscape. They inherited their affection and their perpetual nostalgia from the Celts, who settled the area around 3000 B.C., some of their poetic and artistic inspiration from Greek visitors of the Bronze and Iron ages, and their spirit of adventure from the Phoenicians (the Minho claims several renowned explorers). The Romans built roads, started the wine business, and passed on many of their superstitions, while the Swabians (Suevi), a Germanic tribe, introduced the notion of hard work and small, independent landholdings. The next influx, the Visigoths, populated the Minho's mountainous interior and gave the Portuguese language its Baltic sounds, while the Moors left behind their taste for sweets and spices and for enchanted castles and princesses. The Minhotos' independent streak—the Moors and Romans were never able to subjugate them totally—led to a secession from the domain of León and Castile in the 12th century, and the establishment of the Portuguese kingdom by Afonso Henriques of Guimarães.

The Minhotos' most impressive quality, however, is their ability to blend the northern work ethic with the southern *joie de vivre* without letting one succumb to the other. Hard work has made their region one of the country's principal cattle-growing (mostly oxen), wine-producing, and textile-manufacturing centers. But the Minhotos can also play with equal vigor. Their all-night *arraiais* (barn parties) and their spirited folk dances, the *viras* and the *malhão,* are a match for the most intense party animal.

They are also extremely religious, but here too they have blended their Christian faith with their pagan past. Their *festas* (feast days) and *romarias* (pilgrimages) are an amalgamation of what some might call the sacred and the profane. Somber church ritual is accompanied by carnival-like rites of spring celebrating the Minhoto love of nature. The ancient Mother Goddess religion, with its ties to fertility and the earth, has merged in the Minho with the cult of the Virgin. In some villages Mother Nature, the Minho's unofficial patron goddess, is worshipped with splendid flower pageants and parades.

Women also play an important role in the region's economy. They can often be seen in the fields tending the family plot while the men work outside the country. Behind this practice are the traditional inheritance customs of the Minho: Small family plots are divided equally among all descendants, making the fragmented land too small to support families. Minho women have also played a role in politics. The region's history is filled with heroines such as Deu-la-Deu Martins, who outsmarted Spanish besiegers in the 14th century, and Maria da Fonte, who led a revolt against state authority in the early 19th century. The Minhota beauty, also legendary in Portugal, is displayed at its best during feast days, when the Minho women don their traditional costumes and intricate gold filigreed jewelry.

While the past is still alive in the Minho, progress, with all its aesthetic drawbacks, is slowly altering the face of its Atlantic coastal areas, where tacky resorts spoil some of Portugal's most splendid beachfront property. Ancient historic towns such as Guimarães and Braga are beginning to be smothered by small factories, and the countryside invaded by foreign architecture, as men return from their work stints abroad and build cheap, gaudy copies of North and South American and northern European homes.

Minho hospitality, however, continues to endure both here and in the rural areas, again doing justice to the heart as the symbol of this region, and there are still large stretches of the rural interior where the natural beauty of this province has yet to be tampered with.

MAJOR INTEREST

Guimarães
Romanesque Igreja de São Miguel, ducal palace, and castle
Nossa Senhora da Oliveira convent and museum
Martins Sarmento museum (Celtic artifacts and stone sculptures)
Iron Age Citânia de Briteiros
Ancient Castro de Sabroso

Braga
Rua do Souto shopping and cafés
Cathedral chapels and treasury
Former archbishops' palace and square
Palácio dos Biscainhos city museum
Jardim de Santa Bárbara
Torre de Menagem (keep)
Baroque façade of the Palácio Raio
Holy Week festivities and annual wine fair
Shopping for crafts, religious art, and leather goods

The Braga Area
Baroque staircase at sanctuary of Bom Jesus do Monte
Santuário de Monte Sameiro's view of the Minho
Baroque church of Santa Maria Madalena
Neo-Byzantine chapel of São Frutuoso
Póvoa de Lanhoso (castle and filigree)

Parque Nacional de Peneda-Gerês (hiking, swimming, Roman remains, spa, wild horses)

Alto Minho
Idyllic rural scenery
Staying in manor houses
Ponte de Lima's crafts and agriculture market
Serras do Soajo and da Peneda
Medieval fortress at Lindoso

Minho River Valley
Palácio de Brejoeira wine estate at Monção
Valença do Minho's views of the Minho river and Spain's Galician mountains
Caminha's handsome town square and Renaissance parish church

Viana do Castelo
Picture-postcard main square
Municipal museum (tiles and earthenware, Indo-Portuguese furniture)
Baroque chapel of Nossa Senhora da Agonia
Shops selling peasant scarves, regional costumes, *palmitos,* and other folk items of the Minho
Festivals and flower pageants
Restaurants with Minho folk music and dancing

Barcelos
Pottery, carved cattle yokes, and antiques
Weekly country market
Palácio Ducal (open-air archaeological museum)
Romanesque doorway of parish church

The Atlantic Beaches
Hotels, casino, and beaches
Marina and deep-sea fishing
Fish and shellfish dining
Póvoa de Varzim's picturesque fishermen's *bairro,* woollen sweaters, and gold- and silversmiths
Vila do Conde's lace-making school and annual crafts fair

Food and Wine of the Minho

Minho dishes have a straight-from-the-farm-to-the-pot flavor and a diversity commensurate with the region's topography. The substantial culinary repertoire ranges from kid

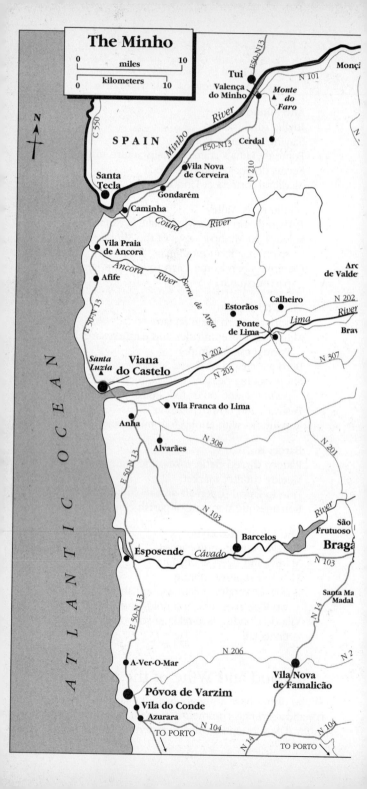

and lamb dishes in the mountainous midriff to fresh river trout and lamprey eel in the river valleys, from fish stews, cod, shellfish, and sardines in the coastal areas to pork, cured hams, sausages, and veal steaks in the valleys. The region's *caldo verde,* a thick potato-and-cabbage soup with a dash of olive oil and slices of sausage, is aptly named after the verdant countryside. (The cabbage is the emerald green, nonheading Galician cabbage, or collard.) *Sopa seca* (dry soup), an odds-and-ends dish invented by frugal housewives in mountain areas to recycle meats, vegetables, and bread, is a meal in itself: Leftovers are resuscitated with hot broth, seasoned with mint, layered into a terra-cotta casserole, and baked.

Other indigenous Minho delectables include the heavy, vinegary *rojões e sarrabulho à moda do Minho* (pork stew with maize dumplings) and the dark-meated *lampreia* (river eel), marinated in its own blood with wine, then cooked in it. Some lamprey dishes are also curried. The latter spice, together with saffron, became popular in the 16th century after Vasco da Gama returned with his ships laden with spices from India. Minhotos love lamprey so much that they make effigies of it, using an intensely sweet egg-yolk custard that is poached in an eel-shaped mold with eyes, mouth, and teeth sculpted with icing.

Pork is a major and tasty staple of the Minho diet. Nutritious meals of cooked potatoes, corn, chestnuts, and wheat are lavished on pigs throughout the year, in order to guarantee their delectable flavor. Pork curing and sausage making are cottage industries. Every fall the pigs are butchered, hams are laid out to cure, and yards of casing are stuffed with blends of pork and spices to produce such popular sausages as *salpicão,* a pork tenderloin cured in dry wine, salt, and garlic, then smoked, or the dry, long, thin *linguiça,* consisting of chopped pork shoulder, garlic, and paprika. Sausages and hams make great appetizers and add consistency to stews like the hearty *cozido à Portuguesa,* a mélange of meats and vegetables.

Meals are accompanied by rich and crunchy *pão de milho* (corn bread), or the more traditional *broa,* a dense and chewy yeast-raised corn bread, and washed down with the region's *vinho verde,* named not for its color but for its relative youth and the green countryside. *Vinhos verdes,* reds and whites, young and fizzy, should be drunk during their first two years. The British call them "eager" wines on account of their effervescence. The best *vinhos verdes* are the estate whites such as Palácio da Brejoeira, Solar de Bouças, and Quinta da Aveleda. The vines grow and cling to trellises, telephone poles, and any other object they find, reaching heights of up to 150 feet. The trellising practice, which was introduced by the Romans, frees the precious ground soil for a second crop and prevents the grapes from overripening, so that they yield a medium-dry, crisp, low-alcohol beverage. A word of caution, though, about *vinho verde:* Because of its relatively high acid content, too much of it before going to bed may cause indigestion and/or wild dreams.

Give yourself a minimum of a week to explore the Minho. Our essentially circular coverage begins at the royal town of Guimarães, where it all started, moves next door to Braga, the religious capital of Portugal and a major center of Baroque art, and then moves northeast into the Peneda-Gerês national park. It veers west into the bucolic Lima river valley, studded with patrician estates, goes up through the Alto Minho, meanders along the fortress-lined Minho river valley, which borders Spain and which gave the region its name and some of its most famous heroines and wines, and starts south along the Atlantic coast to Viana, the capital of folklore of the Minho. A short detour from Viana east to Barcelos, the ceramic center of the north, is discussed before we return to the Minho's Atlantic coastline.

GUIMARAES

Guimarães, the cradle of the Portuguese nation, lies in a tree-studded valley surrounded by mountains 51 km (32 miles) northeast of Porto via the N 105-2 and N 105 or the N 14 and N 206. It was founded by the Visigoth countess Mumadona in the tenth century under the name of Vimaranes and grew around her fortress tower and monastery. In 1118 it soared into prominence by being in the vanguard of the revolt that shook off the yoke of Spanish domination. The liberator was the young Count Afonso, son of Henry of Burgundy and Princess Teresa (Tareja in Visigoth), bastard daughter of the king of León and Castile, who had inherited the region as part of her dowry in 1095. When Henry died Teresa became acting regent on behalf of her young son, but alienated her subjects by taking a Galician count as her lover and siding with the Spanish against her subjects' aspirations for autonomy.

When Afonso came of age he led the Portuguese barons and religious leaders against the combined forces of his mother and her lover, defeating them in a bloody battle on the outskirts of the city in 1128. The victorious Afonso, a giant of a man and a military genius as well, went on to liberate large tracts of Portugal from the Moors and was proclaimed king by his troops. Papal recognition, however, did not come until 1179, after a hefty financial contribution was made to the Vatican.

Medieval Guimarães is re-created yearly on the first Sunday of August during the Festas Gualterianas, during which the residents don period costumes and perform Medieval plays.

The Town

Guimarães is composed of two cities. By far the more charming is old Guimarães, with its numerous churches, tiny cobbled streets, and Medieval town houses and arches, which runs roughly from the largo da Oliveira at its center, northward up to the Colina Sagrada, the sacred hill where stand some of the monuments tied to Portugal's beginnings as a nation. You can walk from the Oliveria square to the Colina in 15 minutes. Then there is modern, dynamic Guimarães, which lies south of the square and is composed mostly of small business establishments, medium-sized shoe and textile factories, and uninspired apartment blocks.

The Porto road (N 105) enters Guimarães through this part of town, and turns into the avenida Dom Afonso Henriques, which runs south to north. Monumental Guimarães starts at the end of this avenue, on the flower-lined alameda da Resistência ão Fascismo (the local Turismo office is at the junction of the two avenues). Oliveira square is a block north of the fountain on the eastern side of this street.

The Sacred Hill

The **Colina Sagrada** is dear to the Portuguese heart. It was in the **castelo** at the top of this hill that Afonso Henriques is believed to have been born. The castle's heavily restored 10th-century **Torre de Menagem** (Keep) and its eight surrounding towers were the inspiration behind the Portuguese coat of arms. On the green beside the castle's western ramparts is the tiny 12th-century Romanesque **Igreja de São Miguel do Castelo**, where Afonso is said to have been baptized. The floor of the chapel is covered with gravestones of Portuguese nobles, and reads like a Who's Who of Portuguese Medieval nobility. The hollow stone basin to the right as you enter the chapel was used for offerings of grain before coins became commonplace.

São Miguel is dwarfed by the giant building next door, the 15th-century **Paço Ducal** (Ducal Palace) of Dom Afonso, Count of Barcelos and first duke of Bragança. This Afonso, the bastard son of King João I, travelled extensively throughout Europe on diplomatic missions for his father and apparently acquired a taste for things northern, which explains the Burgundian "maison" architecture of the building. The second duke, Fernando II, was beheaded by King João II, and the building was abandoned. The Braganças, a resilient and politically astute family, survived and returned to power in 1640, ruling Portugal until they were ousted by the First Republic in 1910. In 1933 António Salazar had the old palace restored and converted into a presidential residence and **city museum**. The roof of the palace is lined with tall brick chimneys that look like the lances of knights marching to battle. The inside courtyard bears the coat of arms of the Bragança family; the coat of arms is tilted to the left to indicate the family's bastard status.

The palace contains something for everyone: an armory, Indo-Portuguese furniture, copies of French and Flemish tapestries of the 16th to 18th centuries, paintings by Portuguese, Italian, and Dutch masters, and a valuable collection of Persian rugs from the 15th to 17th centuries. There are several canvases attributed to the 17th-century painter Josefa de Ayala (better known in painting circles as Josefa de Obidos, after the town in the south where she painted and died). The chestnut ceilings of its banquet and dining halls are shaped like the inside ribbing of a Portuguese *caravel,* in tribute to Portugal's maritime exploits.

To reach the hill by car, drive northeast up avenida Alberto Sampaio (starts at the eastern end of the alameda da Resistência ao Fascismo), veer left at the end of this street onto rua Serpa Pinto, and take the first right onto largo do Carmo.

Largo da Oliveira

Directly south of the Colina Sagrada, via the Carmo square and the tiny cobbled rua Santa Maria, lies the largo da Oliveira, a typical Medieval square lined with Gothic stone arches and somewhat shabby but distinguished 15th-century town houses with elaborate wrought-iron grilles. The iron bells of the tower of the **Igreja de Nossa Senhora da Oliveira** (Our Lady of the Olive Tree) on the southeastern corner of the square still toll as they have for centuries. Children play here unimpeded by cars, watched by their mothers from the square's outdoor café. Legend has it that the Visigoth warrior Wamba was asked by his people to be their king. Seeking a divine signal, Wamba drove a staff into the ground and declared that he would become king only if it put forth leaves. Leaves did sprout and Wamba bowed to the inevitable—and centuries later Nossa Senhora da Oliveira was built on the site of the miracle.

The **Museu de Alberto Sampaio** is housed on the grounds of the former convent building next door. The only vestige of the original monastery is the door on the eastern corner of the cloister. The museum contains priceless art and other objects collected from convents and churches in the area. Curios include the buffcoat worn by Dom João I, father of Prince Henry the Navigator and founder of the royal house of Avis, in his victory over a much larger Spanish army at Aljubarrota in 1385. The second floor of the museum holds a glittering display of ecclesiastical plate, including a portable silver triptych popularly believed to have been captured from the Spanish in the battle, but apparently of Portuguese origin. Other highlights are a 35-pound silver cross carved with scenes from the Passion of Christ; a stunning 15th-century silver chalice inlaid with Limoges enamel; and a Manueline monstrance attributed to Gil Vicente, who, apart from being the father of Portuguese theater, was one of the most talented goldsmiths of his era. This 16th-century personage entertained the court with his tragicomedies and farces and inspired church audiences with his moralistic *autos-da-fé* during Portugal's Age of Discovery.

The museum was the scene of a spectacular heist in 1975. Among the goods stolen were gem-studded crowns and a gold chain dating from the reign of João I that was made to stretch from the entrance of the town to the church. The thieves have apparently been identified, but the treasures have yet to be be returned.

Other highlights in the square include the handsome 14th-century **Padrão da Batalha do Salado** (a porch lined with saints carved by French masons in limestone) and the **Antigos Paços do Conselho** (old town hall), an elegant crenellated structure built over Gothic arches that now serves as the municipal library. The square, now a pedestrian island, is the ideal spot to escape from the noise and fast pace of modern Guimarães, where new textile, tanning, and kitchen-appliance industries are replacing traditional crafts such as silver- and goldsmithing, hand embroidering, and linen weaving.

Some of the spacious guest rooms and the elegant dining room of the **Pousada da Nossa Senhora da Oliveira** front the northeastern corner of the square. Several aristocratic town houses from the 15th to the 17th centuries were remodeled and joined together, decorated with fine reproductions of antique furnishings, and staffed with hospitable Minhotos to re-create a Medieval-style inn. The establishment is run by the efficient and attentive Dinorah Costa, who will make your stay comfortable. If you are a light sleeper, however, be prepared to be kept up at night by the banter of the teenagers who congregate under the arches of the old town hall.

In keeping with its Medieval flavor, the inn's fine restaurant is housed in the kitchen of the former baronial residence and is furnished in heavy wood and wrought iron. What makes the restaurant especially pleasant and exciting is its massive gray stone fireplace that is open front and back and can be enjoyed by diners sitting on either side of it. The kitchen serves regional specialties and is known for its richly flavored *rojões a Minhota* (pork stew), made with pickled cauliflower and carrots. The pork is so tender that it falls from the bones.

For a more intimate and romantic bistro ambience, try the cozy **El Rei** restaurant behind the pousada, at largo de São Tiago. The most popular lunch spot in town is the family-run **Jordão** restaurant, near the city center at avenida Dom Afonso Henriques, 55, with regional decor and food.

The Sarmento Museum

The **Museu Martins Sarmento** lies west of the largo da Oliveira on rua Paio Galvão. Lodged partly in a Gothic cloister, the museum contains the findings of the 19th-century archaeologist Francisco Martins Sarmento, Portugal's Schliemann, who spent his life and fortune excavating the Iron Age cities of Briteiros and Sabroso, north of Guimarães. The collection includes coins, jewelry, and artifacts dating back to the Celts. Its two most interesting pieces are the Pedra Formosa, one of two large granite slabs from Briteiros, inscribed with human forms, which scholars believe could have been from entrances to Celtic crematoriums, and the four-foot-high colossus of Pedralva. This latter freestanding statue, which was found in a field near Briteiros in 1930, is so large that it took 24 oxen to move it. Some scholars believe it was carved in the pre-Roman era. Others, arguing that it is too advanced for that period, insist that it may have been executed in modern times.

Outside Guimarães

The luxury **Pousada de Santa Marinha da Costa**, which lies 2 km (1.3 miles) east of the city center on the N 101-2, halfway up the Serra da Catarina overlooking Guimarães and on the way to Penha (see below), is the ultimate in getting away from it all. The gardens of the former Augustinian monastery, which meander up the mountain behind the pousada, are irrigated by its freshwater springs. Guests can sleep in former monks' cells, in large suites decorated with antiques from the royal palace of Ajuda in Lisbon, or in a modern annex. The marble pillars and arches of the old monastery kitchen provide a dignified backdrop for sumptuous dining. The property was donated to the monks by Mafalda, wife of Afonso Henriques, in the 12th century and is named after Santa Marinha, the patron saint of mothers. Recent restoration work, however, has uncovered signs of earlier habitation, including a Mozarabic arch. The sprawling monastery, whose east wing was practically consumed by fire in 1951, was recently remodeled by the state. It has more than 50 double rooms and can accommodate large tour groups.

A breathtaking view of the region can be had from the top of the mountain (follow the signs indicating **Penha**) above the pousada. At the summit is a monument to Gago

Coutinho, the first person to cross the southern Atlantic (1922) to Brazil in an airplane, and the 20th-century Santuário de Nossa Senhora da Penha, the patron saint of travellers. Small curio shops, cafés, and restaurants on the summit are popular with pilgrims visiting on weekends.

Travellers in search of the leisurely life of the region's country squires can find it in the **Paço de São Cipriano**, a baronial manor house with an imposing crenellated tower, sprawling gardens, and a pool surrounded by trimmed box hedges. This lovely home, with five double bedrooms to let, is 5 km (3 miles) south of Guimarães (signposted). Take the N 105 toward Porto. Turn left at the sign to Tabuadelo, less than 4 km (2.5 miles) out of town, and drive for another 2 km (1.25 miles). The sprawling estate is beside the parish church on the southern outskirts of this tiny village. The **Casa do Ribeiro**, 5 km (3 miles) west of Guimarães at Selho, is a perfect example of an 18th-century manor house. It is solidly built in granite, contains its own chapel, and has the crest of the Ferras Pinto family carved in stone over an imposing gate. The two double rooms and one single bedroom, furnished with antiques, look out onto forested hills.

North of Guimarães

The Iron Age **Citânia de Briteiros** lies 15 km (6 miles) north of Guimarães on a hill overlooking the pristine waters of the Ave river. The 19th-century Portuguese archaeologist Martins Sarmento spent his adult life uncovering the secrets of this citânia, which is the largest of its kind in Portugal. The site, walled at one time, whose layout is reminiscent of ancient Mycenae, contains the remains of some 200 round, rectangular, and elliptical houses (some of which have been reconstructed, to the disdain of purists) and a large cistern. In the southwestern corner of the citânia lies an interesting granite slab that scholars believe may have had a part in a Celtic reincarnation ritual: The cremated person was symbolically returned to the womb when he or she was introduced through a hole in the slab to the cremation chamber behind it. Carved on the slab above the hole is the figure of a person with legs spread. The Romans are believed to have converted the crematorium into hot baths. The artifacts discovered on the site are displayed at the Martins Sarmento musuem in Guimarães.

To get to Briteiros head north out of Guimarães on the N 101, turn right onto the N 310 at Taipas (known for its ancient Roman baths), and left at Santo Estêvão. (Beyond the citânia, north and west on the same road, N 309, are Monte Sameiro and Bom Jesus do Monte; see The Braga Area, below.)

The **Castro de Sabroso**, also excavated by Sarmento, can be seen from Briteiros on a hill to the northwest. It is smaller than Briteiros (only some 35 dwellings), and is believed to be the older of the two sites. Its walls are thicker and better joined than those at Briteiros. Sabroso stands on a hill above the tiny town of Cancela, and can be reached from Taipas by heading north on the N 309 toward Cristina de Longos. About 4 km (2.5 miles) from Taipas, turn right and climb past Cancela to the top of the hill.

BRAGA

Braga, 22 km (14 miles) northwest of Guimarães on the N 101 and just 7.5 km (5 miles) north of Sabroso on the N 309, is Portugal's Eternal City, with perhaps more churches and more saints per capita than Rome. At the height of Church power, the nuns and priests of Braga outnumbered laymen nearly two to one. For more than 600 years its archbishops were the lords of Braga, answerable only to Rome. The nobility was barred from owning land inside the city's walls, where all business was centered around the needs of the church. With the growth of secular power in the late 18th century, things changed: The Medieval walls came down, the bourgeoisie moved in and diversified the economy, and the archbishops were forced to relinquish their administrative grip on the city.

Today, industrial parks and shopping arcades have replaced churches and palaces on the builders' agenda, and new industries such as auto-accessory manufacturing thrive alongside the older candle making and religious-artifacts crafts. For the first time since the Inquisition the Church is having to compete for parishioners with other religious sects, including Mormons and Jehovah's Witnesses, and its Catholic schools and university with state educational institutions.

The archbishop here continues to wield tremendous power as the religious and spiritual leader of Portugal. During Holy Week (the week before Easter), the most important religious event in Portugal, Braga's churches and street chapels are kept constantly lit by votive candles, and its religious shops are filled with a constant stream of pilgrims. It appears that the adage "Porto earns, Lisbon spends, Coimbra studies, and Braga prays" still holds true for Braga today.

Braga got its name from *Bracari,* the name given by the Romans to the Gadhelic Celts who settled it around 300 B.C. It eventually received the seed of Christianity from the late Romans, who had conquered it in 250 B.C. and made it the hub of a network of five roads. When the empire crumbled, the area's fertile prospect was too tempting a catch for the northern hordes to pass up. The Swabians swooped down in 409 and ruled it till 585, when they were in turn vanquished by the Visigoths. The next threat came from the south, when in 711 a Moorish army leveled the city. But Braga had too important a location—in a large valley at the foot of three major mountain ranges—to be left in enemy hands, and for the next 300 years Christians fought Moors for this strategic enclave. When it finally reverted to Christian hands, it landed in the lap of Henry of Burgundy through his marriage to Princess Teresa of León and Castile (discussed in the Guimarães section). Braga was elevated from a bishopric to an archbishopric, and a French prelate was installed in the post; he was the future Saint Gerard.

In 1112 Henry handed over the city to Archbishop Dom Mauricio, making him lord of Braga. With their deed of ownership secured, the new ecclesiastical masters of Braga begin to expand their power, throwing their spiritual weight behind Dom Afonso Henriques in his successful bid to establish an independent kingdom. Next, they waged a diplomatic and spiritual war with Santiago de Compostela and Toledo for the religious leadership of the peninsula. Failing in that attempt, they turned their attention south to the reconquest of Portugal from the Moors and, later, to carrying the message of God to the new continents opened up by the Portuguese explorers in the late 15th century.

Large building projects were undertaken with the profits from the spice trade in the 16th century, under the auspices of the flamboyant archbishop Dom Diogo Sousa, who imported artisans from Spain to work on the cathedral and added a Renaissance wing to the archbishops' palace. He also dazzled Europe with a sumptuous and spectacular embassy to Rome on behalf of the Portuguese Crown, which flaunted Portugal's new-found wealth. Gold from Brazil and the religious zeal fostered by the Counter-Reformation helped turn Braga into the center of Baroque art in Portugal during the 18th century. (The art style itself took its name from the Portuguese word *barroco,* rough pearl.) The bishops and their retinues dressed in satin and jewels and even had their own private orchestras. The prelates were at the zenith of their power—but trouble lay around the corner.

The city was caught up in the social upheavals of the late 18th century, and in 1792 the bishops were forced to give up their feudal title of lords of Braga to civilian authorities. In 1808 the city was overrun by Napoleonic troops, and the churches sacked. The final blow came in 1910, when Church properties were confiscated by the First Republic. Although some of these were later returned, the bishops of Braga never recovered their former power.

The Old City

Some of Braga's religious spirit has given way recently to a commercial fervor. The favorable business climate has spawned its own building boom that has forced the city to spill out of its old boundaries and spread across the valley, with all the modern drawbacks like traffic congestion and uninspired if utilitarian buildings. The city's main artery, the avenida da Liberdade, which runs from the praça da República in the north to the river Este, is lined with banks and concrete office blocks and smothered in a permanent shroud of diesel fumes from a constant stream of cars.

Parts of old Braga have been spared this modern jungle, however, and offer an oasis more in tune with the clerical tradition of this ancient city. This sector, which comprises most of the former domains of the bishops of Braga, lies directly west of Liberdade and is fairly concentrated. The pedestrians-only **rua do Souto** is the conduit into this haven. It begins in the tiny Barão São Martinho square, directly west of the praça da República, and runs east to west past some of the city's oldest and poshest shops, selling antiques, designer clothes, and jewelry, and trendy outdoor coffeehouses crowded with shoppers and university students. It ends at the picture-postcard largo do Paço, which is the nerve center of the old city. The square is graced by a Flamboyant fountain and flanked by the former archbishops' palace to the north and the cathedral to the south. Most of Braga's other interesting sights are located to the north and south of this square and require no more than a ten-minute walk. The rua Dom Diogo de Sousa picks up the westerly trajectory of the rua do Souto and ends at the 16th-century Porta Nova arch, which is the former western perimeter of the city. Restaurant row is located directly outside the Porta Nova, in the tree-lined campo de Hortas. Inexpensive municipal parking can be had at the Conde de Agrolongo square, two blocks directly north of the largo do Paço.

The Cathedral

The Sé (cathedral), off the rua Dom Diogo de Sousa, is Braga's centerpiece. Construction was begun in the 12th century under the patronage of Henry of Burgundy on the site of the 6th-century church of Santa Maria, which had been destroyed by the Moors in 711, and of an even earlier (A.D. 43) temple to the Egyptian goddess Isis. (A Latin inscription on a stone outside the chapel of Saint Gerard states that the priestess Lucrecia Fida, from the convent of Braga, erected a temple to Isis on this spot.) The original plan was to build a five-nave church to compete with Santiago de Compostela, but financial restraints pared the builder's plan to two.

Over the centuries various archbishops left their mark on the Sé's architecture. The result is an interesting mélange of styles that taxes the visitor's architectural knowledge. The first Cluniac archbishops, imported by Henry of Burgundy from France, were responsible for the elegant Romanesque arching over the main entrance, depicting scenes from 13th-century allegorical French tales in the *Roman de Renart,* about the fox created by Eve after she and Adam were expelled from the Garden of Eden. The ostentatious archbishop Dom Diogo de Sousa imported Bizcayan artists, who tampered with the Romanesque, incorporating Gothic arches into the portico and giving a Flamboyant look to the apse. The busy Baroque façade and imposing bell towers were built in the 18th century.

The courtyard of the Sé complex is lined with chapels. The Gothic **Capela dos Reis** on the south end contains the tombs of the founders of the cathedral, Henry and Teresa. Teresa's remains were returned to Braga upon her death and buried beside those of her husband, despite her having taken up with a Galician count. In an apparent attempt to reconcile the two, Dom Diogo de Sousa had Teresa's bones interred with her husband's in 1513; this shocked a more conservative colleague, who later had the bones separated. The embalmed remains of Lourenço Vicente, the "warrior" archbishop, are also displayed, in a glass casing in the chapel. The prelate gained his fighting spurs at the 14th-century battle of Aljubarrota, where the Portuguese, with the help of British archers, defeated a much larger Spanish army. Vicente's body was discovered intact during restoration work years after his death, which prompted many to call him a saint.

The Capela de São Geraldo, at the eastern end of the courtyard, is lined with 18th-century *azulejos* depicting the life of Braga's first archbishop, Saint Gerard. Every December 5, believers bring gifts of fruit to the chapel in commemoration of Saint Gerard's first miracle, in which he saved a sick child by conjuring up fresh fruit in the middle of the winter. The Capela da Glória, next door, contains the beautifully carved tomb of Archbishop Gonçalo, the uncle of Nuno Alvares Pereira, the military genius behind the battle of Aljubarrota. The tomb is guarded by six lions and lined by images of deacons said to be chanting the litany of the dead. The walls of the room reveal vestiges of Mudejar and Renaissance frescoes.

The courtyard and adjacent cloisters house several shrines to Nossa Senhora do Leite (Our Lady of the Milk), nursing the infant Jesus. The chapels are surrounded by wax and plastic breasts left by women asking the Virgin to bless them with ample milk. Scholars believe the practice may have a pre-Christian origin. Perhaps the finest artistic tribute to the Virgin in Braga is the Renaissance statue of the Virgin suckling the Holy Child, which stands under a lovely baldachin at the back of the Sé at rua do Leite, and is attributed to the 16th-century French sculptor Nicolas Chanterene.

The interior of the cathedral, though heavy and dark, contains several items of artistic merit. The 16th-century bronze tomb of the Infante Dom Afonso, one of Henry the Navigator's brothers, in the southwest wing exhibits its Flemish creator's flair for the ornate. The choir walls teem with representations of animals and plants from the New World, intertwined with the brass pipes of two 18th-century organs and rising from them like musical notes. Organ recitals are given here on Saturday mornings and on feast days.

The religious treasures of the cathedral, which date back to the tenth century, are stored in the **Museu de Arte Sacra** in the northwest wing. Many were hidden from marauding Napoleonic troops in the early 19th century. Of all the gold and silver exhibited, the silver monstrance of 18th-century Archbishop Gaspar de Bragança, son of King João V, will hold you the most. It weighs nearly 19 pounds and is encrusted with 450 precious stones. Of more historical value is a tiny iron cross carried by the priest who accompanied the Portuguese explorer Pedro Alvares Cabral when he discovered Brazil in 1500. The same cross travelled back to Brazil in 1960 for the blessing of the new Brazilian capital, Brasília. An amusing item in the collection is the pair of platform shoes worn by the diminutive Archbishop Rodrigo de Moura Teles, who needed them to reach the altar.

There are guided tours of the treasury and the chapels (afternoons only in the winter).

Largo do Paço

The **Chafariz do largo do Paço**, or bishop's fountain, as it is popularly called, stands directly opposite the Sé in a peaceful cobbled square lined with arches. The fountain was built by Archbishop Rodrigo de Moura Teles to glorify his family; its basin, embellished with miniature models of the six towers that once defended the city, is supported by a troop of angels, while a seventh tower, displaying the coat of arms of the archbishop's family, serves as a base for the Madonna. The picturesque square (depicted on Portugal's 500-escudo note) is a favorite meeting place for students from the neighboring university.

The **Antigo Paço Episcopal**, or former archbishop's palace, on the north side of the largo do Paço, is composed of 14th-, 17th-, and 18th-century wings. The palace was confiscated in the 19th century by the state and its goods sold at auction. The 18th-century wing burned soon after, leading some to suspect arson. The palace now serves as the city library and as the rectory of the university of the Minho. The library, which can be visited, houses more than 300,000 volumes, some dating from the 9th century. Its rarest documents are contained in the magnificent ivory-and-wood **Sala do Arcaz**. Library documents include detailed family genealogies of persons who applied to join the Church during the Inquisition. Special permission is required to visit the Sala do Arcaz, but documents can be requested and read in the wood-lined reading room. Also of interest is the entrance to the university rectory, whose walls display some fine examples of 17th- and 18th-century *azulejos* recovered from homes and churches.

Around the Cathedral

The **Arco da Porta Nova**, west of the Sé at the end of the rua Dom Diogo de Sousa, exemplifies the battle waged by the archbishops of Braga to retain control of their city. In 1778 the 16th-century main gate of the city was torn down and replaced with a wider one. The city prelates might have welcomed the new door had it not been for the fact that King José I surmounted it with an arch bearing his family's coat of arms. Furious, the reigning archbishop appealed to the municipality, which solved the controversy by tactfully adding an episcopal hat to the top of the royal coat of arms and encircling it with an ecclesiastical cape and tassels.

In keeping with tradition, the noble family that built the 17th-century **Palácio dos Biscainhos** had it erected outside the walls of the city of the archbishops, northwest of the Arco da Porta Nova on the street bearing its name. The two-story nobleman's palace, remodeled in the 18th century and now the city museum, shows something of the sumptuous lifestyle of the old Portuguese nobility. The walls of its grand salon are lined with 18th-century *azulejos* depicting the leisurely activities; its wooden ceiling re-creates in oil the burning of a family member, Miguel de Carvalho, in Japan in 1624. The rooms, arranged and decorated by period, contain elegant furniture from the 17th to 19th centuries. The *casas de fresco* (cool houses), huge umbrellalike trees with niches trimmed out of the vegetation, offer the visitor a cool haven from the hot sun in the terraced garden.

East of the palace, in front of the 18th-century wing of the former archbishops' palace, is the **Câmara Municipal** (town hall), built in the late 18th century by André Soares, the most renowned Baroque architect of his time. Facing east toward the former archbishops' palace, the well-balanced building marks the turning point of political power in Braga. Its grand stairway is lined with *azulejos* showing the arrival in Braga of Archbishop José de Bragança (bastard brother of King João V) to assume his new post, but it is evident that the reins of the city are now in civilian hands and that the post does not carry any temporal power. The council room contains exquisite crystal chandeliers and portraits of important figures in Braga's history. Guided tours are given on weekdays.

The **Jardim de Santa Bárbara**, farther east, behind the former archbishops' palace, is an oasis of tranquillity and beauty. The tiny garden is a sea of color, with more than 50 varieties of flowers. The flower beds, arranged in elaborate designs, do justice to the Minho's reputation as the garden of Portugal. The crenellations of the Medieval wing of the former archbishops' palace and the sharp geometry of several arches recovered from a fire that gutted the Baroque wing provide a fitting backdrop for young lovers and landscape photographers alike.

The all-purpose eatery **Lusitana**, situated at the southeast corner of the garden, is the ideal spot for a light lunch or tea. Patrons can sit outside on a small esplanade and admire the sweet-smelling garden or eat in a tiny room lined with counters exhibiting a cornucopia of such delicacies as shrimp and cod croquettes (ideal for picnics), and with shelves brimming with drinks, jars of candy, and boxes of chocolates. They can also nibble on *combinados* (combination platters) such as cold cuts, tender lamb stew, Braga's hearty *frigideiras* (meat pies), and almond-, egg-, and sugar-based delicacies such as *fatias de Braga* (poached loaves of egg yolks and sugar, sliced and submerged in cinnamon syrup). The sweets are manufactured in the Lusitana's own nearby pastry shop.

If you want to burn off calories and get a bird's-eye view of the city, climb the steps of the 18th-century **Torre de Menagem** (keep), on largo de São Francisco. This imposing crenellated structure is the last of six towers that once guarded the city; the others were torn down as Braga expanded. Nearby, the Moorish-style filigreed wooden screens of the 17th-century **Casa dos Crivos**, at rua de São Marcos, are also the last of their kind in Braga. The first screens were built in the 16th century to allow cloistered nuns a view of the world outside while protecting them from inquisitive eyes. The doors of this building are now open to the public for art and other cultural exhibitions put on by the city. Between the Casa dos Crivos and the keep, the coffeehouse tradition is alive and well at the 19th-century **Café Brazileira**. Its strategic position at the entrance to the fashionable rua do Souto makes it a favorite among the city's artists and intellectuals. Marble, copper, and glass fittings and ancient waiters in white livery provide a refined, Old World elegance and suitable ambience for lingering discourses. Both indoor and outdoor seating allow you to indulge in Europe's favorite sport of people watching.

The handsome iron- and stonework of the **Capela de Nossa Senhora de Conceição** (Our Lady of Conception chapel) and the lacy Manueline work of the windows of the adjoining **Casa dos Coimbras**, in São João de Souto square, one block south of the rua do Souto by way of rua Francisco Sanches, were built in the 17th century for Dom João de Coimbra, the financial administrator of the flamboyant archbishop Diogo de Sousa, who apparently spared no expense to feed his ego and glorify his family name. The two are still privately owned, but can be admired from the street. The exterior of the **Hospital São Marcos**, in the square to the south, has an amusing façade designed by the 18th-century architect Carlos Amarante, who had a flair for theatrics: He lined the ledge of the roof with granite statues of the Apostles gesticulating madly.

The front of the 18th-century **Palácio Raio**, one block to the south in the street sporting its name, is considered one of the most beautiful and original examples of civil Baroque architecture in the country. In this palace André Soares, the designer of the town hall, brought together Portugal's tile, wood, and stone crafts in an elegant yet voluptuous composition that avoids gaudiness. The locals call it the Casa do Mexicano, because peasants in the area mistook an exotic Turkish wooden figure in the entrance vestibule for a Mexican.

Most of ancient Braga lies under the modern city, waiting to be unearthed. A few archaeological treasures have been discovered quite by accident. One of these, the **Fonte do Idolo** (Fountain of the Idol), at rua do Raio, 309, was uncovered by workers installing a sewage pipe. Behind an inconspicuous green gate and at the foot of some steps lies part of a collapsed altar believed to have been used in immersion rituals in a temple to the Lusitanian idol Tongenabiago. Latin inscriptions indicate that the Romans later adapted it for their own purposes. Gardeners planting orange trees in the patio of the **Museu Pio XII**, at campos de São Tiago to the west of the fountain, recently discovered a Roman pool, inlaid with a beautifully preserved mosaic of fish and squid, that formed part of a Roman patrician's home. The museum building, which also houses a seminary, contains antiquities dating back to the Neolithic period. The fairly large collection has been put together in a haphazard way and will test the knowledge of archaeology buffs.

Holy Week in Braga

Braga's religious passion reaches its height during Semana Santa (Holy Week), when the city is transformed into one huge temple of worship, as church icons and other treasures are paraded in streets lined with banners of ancient families whose ancestors fought to liberate Portugal from the Moors. The nights are spectacularly lit by thousands of candles carried by the penitent. Hooded men with torches provide a dark side to the daily processions; at one time in history such men would single out the houses of suspected sinners.

On a lighter note are the Festas de São João, from June 23 to 25. Although they are under the banner of the Church, these events actually date back to pre-Christian times and the observance of the summer solstice. All-night parties are held in streets illuminated by raging bonfires, *vinho verde* flows freely, and the odors of roast pork and grilled sardines compete with the fragrance of burning wax and incense.

The third big event of the year here is the *vinho verde* fair at the end of September, a week-long event held in the **Palácio Municipal de Exposições**, or industrial fairground, located in a large park at the southern end of avenida da Liberdade. The region's main wine producers and smaller estate bottlers exhibit their wares and provide tastings.

Staying in Braga

For a city with a constant flow of pilgrims, Braga's accommodations leave much to be desired; finding a room in the city is *never* easy. When the summer tourist season is over conventioners pour in for Braga's many agriculture, wine, and industrial shows. Holy Week and other religious holidays keep the hotels filled in the spring. Make your reservations months ahead of time.

Some of the best hotels in the region are in the cool and luxurious surroundings of the Bom Jesus sanctuary in the hills above Braga (see the Braga Area section, below, for details). Cheaper and less luxurious accommodations can be had in Braga's *residencias* (boarding houses). **Inácio Filho**, one of the better ones, has a cozy little sitting room, furnished in the style of a Minho country house, and is ideally located in the old quarter. The **Casa da Pedra Cavalgada**, a 19th-century villa at Palmeira on the northeastern outskirts of Braga, via N 101, offers a more traditional Victorian Portuguese ambience and decor. Two large double bedrooms and a large living room are available to guests, as are its small, well-kept grounds. No credit cards.

Dining in Braga

The monastic heritage of Braga may be the reason why there are relatively few restaurants in the city. **Inácio**, across from the Arco da Porta Nova, is Braga's most popular and endearing restaurant. The family-run establishment is strictly a regional affair, with wooden beams and whitewashed walls covered with regional artifacts, providing a rustic backdrop to such Minho delectables as wood-fired *cabrito no forno* (roast kid), *rojões a Minhota,* and the house specialty, *lampreia com arroz.* (Call ahead of time if you want to taste this last mouth-watering dish.) Owner Claudionor Sobral, an attentive host, keeps a well-stocked cellar with the best Alvarinho green wines. He also carries Solar das Bouças, a semisweet green wine bottled in neighboring Amares by the Count Albano de Castro. Closed Mondays; campo das Hortas, 4; Tel: (053) 22335.

The **Conde Dom Henrique**, a tiny bistro behind the Sé, specializes in fish and is frequented by city officials and intellectuals. Its decorative theme, like its name, is old Portugal: Pictures of popular figures from Portugal's past line its walls. No credit cards accepted in this moderately priced establishment at rua do Forno, 17. Closed Mondays. For a more elegant dinner, you need to head for the neighboring hills of Bom Jesus (5 km/3 miles away) to the restaurant of the **Hotel do Elevador** (see below in the Braga Area section). Its Old World decor, its deferential service, and its view of manicured gardens, Braga, and the surrounding valley attract the elite of Portuguese society. Both the set and à la carte menus include regional and Continental dishes that are good value for the money. In Braga tradition, sweets are a heavy favorite here, particularly the chef's *bolo de amêndoa* (almond cake). To get here follow the avenida da Liberdade south, turn left onto the avenida João XXI (you will see the Hotel Turismo on the north side of the street), and head east (the avenue changes its name to avenida João Paulo II), following the signs to Bom Jesus. The Elevador is to your left as you arrive at the sanctuary.

Tiny eateries along the rua do Souto offer snacks throughout the day, and more than 20 pastry shops cater to sweet tooths. The city is known for its rich desserts. The *pudim à abade de Priscos* (abbot of Priscos pudding), named after a plump priest with an insatiable appetite, requires 15 egg yolks and a generous topping of caramel.

Shopping in Braga

Lace and embroidery, damask bedspreads, earthenware goods such as chestnut roasters, wicker and straw baskets, and religious art make up much of the cottage-industry produce of Braga and its environs. Bargains can be obtained at the weekly Tuesday fair (ask for directions at the local Turismo office, avenida da Liberdade, 1, on the town's main park). The Turismo also carries many of these same goods at only slightly higher prices. The rua do Souto west of the Turismo is Braga's fashionable shopping street, with boutiques and antiques shops and coffee and pastry shops. The sedate, elegant **Chapelaria de Abreu Araújo**, at number 124, is the last of the great hat shops, selling handmade Portuguese and foreign creations. The religious artifacts industry is alive and thriving. The **Casa Fânzeres**, at number 132–134, the oldest and most picturesque, specializes in the sale and repair of religious antiques. Braga's trendy **Rosal Boutique**, at number 36, features women's ready-to-wear labels by foreign and Portuguese designers.

Braga is also one of the country's main centers of leather goods. The **Sapatária Teresinha**, at number 84, specializes in handmade shoes; **Herdeiros de Francisco José Ferreira**, at number 124, sells handbags, briefcases, and suitcases. The *viola Braguesa* or the *cavaquinho* guitar, which served as models for the ukulele, can be bought or admired at the top of rua do Souto at **Vadeca** (largo Barão São Martinho, 14). **Casa Eden**, across from the Santa Bárbara garden, at Justino Cruz, 28, sells damask bedspreads and hand-embroidered linens.

THE BRAGA AREA

The hills around to the south of Braga are covered with religious sanctuaries. The most spectacular is **Bom Jesus do Monte**, which sits high up in a lovely wooded area surrounded by grottoes and streams 5 km (3 miles) east of the city via the avenidas João XXI and João Paulo II. The 19th-century travel writer William Kingston called the site "a lovely prospect to excite the poet's muse, or the warmest adoration of the true worshipper of nature and of nature's God." Legend has it that the area became sacred after the discovery of a beautifully carved cross on the site of the church centuries ago.

The sanctuary's most striking feature is a monumental Baroque staircase, sculpted in stone and adorned with fountains and other waterworks. The structure, which rises 940 feet to the shrine of Saint Clement, is one huge allegory, divided into three parts. At the bottom is the Sacred Way, with scenes from the Passion, making use of terra-cotta figures. The second section, a stone face, pays tribute to the five senses: water gushing from the eyes to illustrate sight, from the nose for smell, etc. The final section is called the Stairway of the Three Virtues. In front of the shrine, which was designed by Carlos Amarante, are life-size statues of the men who persecuted Jesus: Annas, Caiaphas, Herod, and Pilate. The altar of the Neo-Classical shrine itself, the church of Bom Jesus, completes the allegorical scheme of the stairs with larger-than-life figures.

You can drive up to the shrine, then walk down the stairs and return to your car at the top via a water-powered funicular that runs every 15 minutes; or you can leave your car at the bottom, climb the stairs, and take the funicular down. Either way, gaze up from the bottom to see how the granite sculptures form a giant chalice.

An outdoor café, a teahouse, and gift shops are at the site, as well as some of the most welcoming accommodations in the region. Most guests prefer to stay up here while visiting Braga because it offers a cool sanctuary from the heat and pollution that often engulf the plain of Braga below. The most exclusive and genteel hotel is the **Elevador**, on the northwestern side of the square facing the sanctuary. Plush furnishings, attentive staff, an elegant restaurant, and large rooms with sweeping views of its gardens and the Braga valley make it a memorable place at which to stay. The recently refurbished **Parque Hotel**, on a slope above the church, has been tastefully renovated without losing its turn-of-the-century flavor. The hotel has a paneled bar, a breakfast room, and club-styled salon, but no restaurant. (Lunch and dinner can be had a few steps away at the Elevador, which is owned by the same company.) If you are looking for a change of pace from the hotel circuit, try **Casa dos Lagos**, at the entrance of Bom Jesus. The Barbosa family rents out part of their terraced country house, which they have converted into a self-sufficient apartment with two bedrooms, a bathroom, and a kitchen, with access to a small cobbled garden lined with palm trees.

The turn-of-the-century **Santuário de Monte Sameiro**, 4 km (2.5 miles) east of Bom Jesus on the N 103-3, is known more for its breathtaking views of the Minho and its huge dimensions than for its architecture. Masses are held in a football-field-size courtyard below the church. A larger-than-life statue of Pope Pius XII at the entrance of the staircase leading to the courtyard commemorates his visit to the site in 1954. The woods and paths around the shrine are popular with picnickers.

The shrine also attracts another breed of pilgrim, seeking a more earthly delight: the **Sameiro** restaurant, beside the church. The cook and owner of the restaurant, Maria da Conceição, is a short, portly, middle-aged woman who has won several awards for her cooking at regional and national competitions. House specialties, all cooked on wood-fired stoves, include baked lamprey and codfish in cream sauce. During the summer river trout and kid from the surrounding area go well with the house's tart *vinho verde*. Maria will not divulge the secret behind her famous *tarta de chila* (spaghetti-squash tart), but Port and honey seem to be among its ingredients; the squash is candied to give it texture. The restaurant's simple wood panels and white linen provide an austere environment in keeping with the shrine next door. Closed Mondays.

Eight kilometers (5 miles) southwest of Sameiro, on the thickly wooded slopes of Mount Falperra, is the **Igreja de Santa Maria Madalena**, one of the finest examples of rocaille architecture in Portugal. The handsome building was designed by André Soares, whose clever use of swirls and lines brings the façade to life. The woods around the sanctuary once harbored a local Robin Hood by the name of Ze Telhado, who may have been attracted to the area because it is named after Santa Marta da Falperra, the patron saint of thieves. You can also reach Falperra from Braga using the N 309 (5.5 km/3.5 miles).

The tiny 7th-century **Capela da São Frutuoso**, 3.5 km (2.2 miles) north of Braga off the N 201 on the way to Ponte de Lima, at Real, is one of the few remaining examples of Suevic Neo-Byzantine architecture left in Portugal. The ancient chapel, partially destroyed by the Moors in 711, was rebuilt in the 11th century. The simple beauty of its design clashes with the ornateness of the Igreja de São Francisco next door. To go inside São Frutuoso, apply for the key from the chaplain at São Francisco.

The 12th-century crenellated castle at **Póvoa de Lanhoso**, 19 km (12 miles) east of Braga (take the N 103 16 km/10 miles to Pinheiro, then turn left onto the N 205 here at the signpost to Póvoa), is endowed with tragic stories. According to legend, Afonso Henriques had his mother locked up here after defeating her in the battle of São Mamede in 1128. Others say it was her sister, Urraca, who had her placed there for refusing to become her vassal when she was widowed by the king of León. These legends pale, however, beside the story that the lord of the castle, returning from a trip to find his wife and her father confessor in flagrant adultery, had them and all the people in the castle burned alive. His reason for burning the other occupants of the castle was that they too were guilty, for not warning him. On a more uplifting note, Póvoa is also known as the birthplace of filigree work in Portugal.

PENEDA-GERES PARK

The spectacular alpine **Parque Nacional de Peneda-Gerês**, northeast of Braga, which stretches between Spain to the north and the river Cávado to the south, is a balm to nature enthusiasts, who are drawn to its 178,000 acres of forests, man-made lakes, rivers, waterfalls, and rocky ridges rising up to 5,075 feet. It is divided into several valleys by the serras of Soajo, Peneda, Amarela, and Gerês and by the Lima, Homen, and Cávado rivers. Annual precipitation in the region is considerable, and the bare granite summits of the horseshoe-shaped park are covered in snow during the winter. Slopes cascade down to the lush, deep-cut valleys abloom with Gerês iris and other colorful indigenous plants. The more remote areas house a varied wildlife, including roe deer, wolves, and wild Luso-Galician horses. Fishermen are attracted to the park's trout-brimming rivers; boat enthusiasts and windsurfers have several artificial lakes to pick from; hikers and mountaineers can spend days on man-made trails.

Vestiges of human habitation have been found in the area dating back 5,000 years, and the ancient artifacts can be reviewed in the ethnography museum outside the tiny village of São João do Campo on the northern border of the park below the Vilarinho das Furnas dam. The southern side of this reservoir is lined with Latin-inscribed milestones belonging to the Roman road built by Emperor Vespasian.

Organized tours of the park by bus, on horseback, or on foot can be booked through travel agencies or through T. G. Trote, Cabril, 5495 Borralha; Tel: (053) 59292. Maps and itineraries are available at the rangers' lodge at the main entrance of the park just past Caniçada or at the Turismo office in the spa town of Gerês (on avenida Manuel Francisco da Costa). The park is a one-hour drive northeast of Braga. Take the N 103 east to just past Cerdeirinhas, then turn left onto the N 304. After crossing the Cávado river past Caniçada, follow the N 308-1 off to the right and drive north 12.5 km (7.8 miles) to Gerês.

The most scenic and luxurious accommodations in the area are back at the junction of the N 103 and N 304 on the hills directly south of the entrance to the park. The **Pousada de São Bento**, on the N 304, 1.5 km (0.9 miles) north of the junction, was named after a sixth-century saint who is reputed to have lived in a cave near the entrance to the park. It has the look and the modern comforts of a Swiss chalet and the relaxed atmosphere of a Portuguese home. Its glass-enclosed restaurant and outdoor verandah afford sweeping views of the magnificent Cávado river. The 18-room inn also has a small pool. Reservations should be made in advance in summer.

The **Aldeamento da Pedra Verde**, which sits in solitary splendor at the top of another hill (on the N 103, half a kilometer east of the 103/304 junction toward Chaves), is a bargain. The solidly built stone cabins of this mountain retreat command views of the surrounding mountains and are fitted with fireplaces and supplied with wood. The decor of the spacious two-bedroom apartments is rustic and warm, adding to the romantic atmosphere. Guests have access to a pool and gardens as well as a small pub. Meals are not served on the grounds, but can be taken at the nearby pousada.

Casa da Santa Lucia, half a mile down the road east of the aldeamento on the N 103 on a hill overlooking Gerês park, is a Swiss-style mountain house with a definite homey flavor and cooking provided by the attentive owner, Rosa de Araújo, at hotel prices. Its four bedrooms are furnished with Portuguese antiques. Dinners are supervised by Senhora de Araújo, who is proud of her chicken in Champagne sauce and rich custard pies. She will also pack you a picnic lunch with local fruits and wine, give guidance on park tours, or steer you to the weekly open-air market at **Vieira do Minho** if you happen to be her guest on a Monday. To get to the market take the N 103 west for 1.9 km (1.2 miles), turn left and drive another 5 km (3 miles) south on the N 304. The market, where merchants share the field with farmers selling the region's beautiful, long-horned *barroso* oxen, is a good place to buy shag and wool rugs, linen, country bread and cheese, and beautifully carved *cangas* (ox yokes) with Celtic inscriptions (which make handsome headboards).

Gerês, which sits on the eastern edge of a gorge at the base of the Gerês mountain range, has been a spa since Roman times. This one-street town became a fashionable watering hole in the 18th century and now serves as the excursion and provision center for the park. Its drinking waters, rich in fluorine, were used to treat intestinal disorders.

A popular one-day drive in the Peneda-Gerês park begins by climbing the wooded slopes directly north of Gerês along the left bank of the Gerês river gorge for about 10 km (6.2 miles) on N 308, past waterfalls and picnic areas. Turn left at the *albergaria* (hostelry) onto a dirt road and drive for 5 km (3 miles) through woods lined with Roman milestones (Emperor Vespasian's road) and moss-covered rocks. The Vilarinho das Furnas reservoir suddenly appears to your right. Underneath the placid man-made lake lies the town of Outeiro da Cadeia, whose bell is said to toll when the water level drops. The reservoir is flanked on the north by the jagged, bald peaks of the Serra da Amarela. If you are lucky you might catch a glimpse of the park's wild horses drinking in the lake at dawn or sunset.

Turn left at the first T junction and drive 2 km (1.25 miles) on a paved road past the tiny village of **São João do Campo** to the ethnography museum, with its traditional iron kitchen, looms, spinning wheels, Celtic yokes, and farm implements, and a regional crafts store selling wool sweaters and colorful shag rugs. On the side of the road beside the museum is a Roman milestone surmounted by a stone crucifix. Turn left onto another dirt road and drive several kilometers to the **Junceda Belvedere**, a rocky lookout point with a prehistoric feel and a spectacular view of the Gerês valley. To complete the semicircular tour backtrack several kilometers and take another dirt road southeast toward the Casa Abrigo da Bela Vista. The road meets the N 308-1 just above Gerês. East of Gerês, at Ponte do Arado, you can take a refreshing dip at the foot of waterfalls.

ALTO MINHO

The heart of the Minho, the Alto Minho (Upper Minho) begins north of Braga in the hills surrounding the bucolic banks of the river Lima and stretches north to the Minho river. The Atlantic Ocean forms its western boundary and is the backdrop for Viana do Castelo, its administrative capital; the wild Soajo mountains, sandwiched between the Peneda mountains to the north and the Amarela mountains to the south, form the eastern border with Trás-os-Montes. The interior is dotted with elegant manor houses and granite *cruzetas* (crosses) threaded with grapevines and with tiny farms and wood and granite *espigueiros* (corn cribs) that resemble miniature temples on stilts. The *espigueiros* have openings like venetian blinds that allow the air to circulate freely so the corn can stay dry; they stand on stilts to keep the rats away.

There is a peaceful, idyllic look to this lush and soothing landscape that belies its turbulent past. The area surrounding the Lima river became the bulwark of Christian defenses against the Moors and produced many of the knights who fought under Afonso Henriques to liberate the region from Spanish rule. The descendants of many of these families still live in their ancestral homes beside the river Lima, and some rent out rooms to visitors. There are close to 30 manor houses in the Alto Minho that take in guests.

Ponte de Lima

This small town on the banks of the Lima, 33 km (20 miles) north of Braga on the N 201, has always beguiled visitors. The invading Roman legions were so enchanted by the river's beauty that they believed it to be the Lethe, the legendary river of forgetfulness, and refused to cross it until their general, Junio Bruto, swam across. In time they built a bridge, of which the last four arches on the right bank still stand, and named the town on the left bank Forum Lincurium.

During the early Middle Ages Ponte de Lima played a pivotal role in the border defenses of the Minho against the Moors. Today only vestiges remain of the defensive walls that once encircled the town. The 15th-century **fortress-palace** of the Marquês de Ponte de Lima has been converted into the town hall, and the Medieval **prison tower** has been turned into the town archives, with a tiny workshop to restore the city manuscripts, which date back to 1322. In the courtyard of the 18th-century church of São Francisco (west of the square facing the river), which houses the town's religious-art museum, there is a stone with scratch marks supposedly left by the devil.

The café-lined main square, cooled by a large Baroque fountain, provides an ideal spot from which to admire the multiarched bridge mirrored in the lazy waters of the river, guarded by the white onion-domed bell tower of the **Igreja de Santo António da Torre Velha** on the right bank and framed by rumpled blue-black mountains to the north. You can watch women kneeling on the sandy broad banks of the river doing their washing, which billows colorfully in the afternoon breeze.

The best time to visit the town is during the feast of São João in June or on September 17 to 19, when you will be treated to folk dancing and singing along the river or invited to an all-night *arraial* (corn-husking) party at a manor house. Ponte de Lima is also known for its colorful open-air market. Every second Monday of the month since the Middle Ages the wide, sandy left bank of the river by the bridge has been transformed into a huge tent bazaar for all kinds of farm products, horses and oxen included, plus locally produced crafts such as hand-carved wooden furniture, tin lamps, linen, woollen blankets, glazed pottery, and wicker. Sardines are roasted on charcoal stoves and eaten with rich moist *pão de milho* (corn bread), accompanied by the fine local *vinho verde*.

The *Alvarinho* grape, the most coveted of the green-wine stocks for its low acid content and high alcohol level, is said to have been grafted nearby in the tiny town of Sá. (Most common *vinhos verdes* are varietals, grafted from several stocks.)

Dining in Ponte de Lima used to be limited to fairly simple meals at a few establishments on the riverfront. Now the **Churrasqueiria Tulha**, in rua Formosa east of the main square, has helped fill the gap. Pine and oak furniture and an indoor grill provide a warm and welcoming atmosphere to this rotisserie, which is lodged in a converted grain-storage barn. The family-run establishment specializes in grilled meat and fish cooked over a wood fire and carries Paço de Cardido, a white estate-bottled *vinho verde,* as well as fine Ponte de Lima cooperative *verdes.* Closed Tuesdays.

For more ambitious fare, drive up the hill on N 307 6 km (3.75 miles) directly south of Ponte de Lima to the secluded **Monte de Madalena** restaurant. You will be rewarded not only with glorious views of the town and the Lima valley, but also with gracious service and creative, well-presented regional cooking. The classically decorated establishment, with formally attired waiters and heavy Portuguese furniture, is a favorite of the local aristocracy and officialdom. House specialties include small game and river trout from the region. Closed Mondays.

Manor Houses

Ponte de Lima and its environs, Minho's manor row, make the ideal base from which to explore the region. A group of manor-house owners have formed an association, Turihab, to handle reservations for the Minho. Turihab shares its offices with the national Turismo office. The address is praça da República, Ponte de Lima, 4970 Viana do Castelo; Tel: (058) 94-23-35; Telex: 32618. Turihab will make reservations and mail you a brochure with details and pictures of the homes as well as prices for bed-and-breakfasts. The English-speaking personnel at this office will also help steer you to the manor houses, some of which are off the beaten track. If you write to the national Turismo office at the same address, they will mail brochures and maps with walking tours of the region.

There are more than 20 manor houses in the borough of Ponte de Lima, most on the right bank, that offer rooms to guests. The 17th-century **Casa de Pomarchão** lies directly east of Outeiro, 2 km (1.25 miles) north of Ponte de Lima off the N 202 toward Arcos de Valdevez. It is an impressive manor with a monumental entrance, surrounded by vineyards and orchards. Guests stay in a modern two-story house decorated with rustic touches and equipped with a kitchen, English-language books, and a fireplace—ideal for families or couples who want a change from hotels and guest houses.

An even more secluded and romantic experience can be had at the **Moinho de Estorãos**, a converted watermill on the banks of the tiny Estorãos river. The mill, beside an old Roman bridge 6 km (4 miles) west of Ponte de Lima off the N 202 on the way to the Atlantic coast and Viana do Castelo, is equipped with all the amenities, including a large fireplace for intimate evenings. While you are out in this neck of the woods, take a peek at the magnificent Solar de Bertiandos on the N 202 south of Estorãos, composed of two adjoining 18th-century buildings and an older crenellated tower from the 15th century. The large baronial home (which does not take in guests) is one of the most impressive of Portugal's manor houses. It was built with two wings because of a feud between two factions of the Pereira family; when the dispute was finally settled, through marriages, the walls separating the two wings came down.

The view of the valley and Ponte de Lima from the terraced gardens and main house of the **Paço de Calheiros** (6 km/4 miles northeast of Ponte de Lima) is one of the enticing features of this 18th-century manor. The home has been restored by the young, dynamic count of Calheiros. Available for rent are four double bedrooms with private baths in the main house, all facing a garden, and six more modern apartments with kitchenettes by the magnolia-lined courtyard. Guests have access to two large salons decorated with Portuguese antiques and a large baronial fireplace. The hospitable count, who traces his ancestry back to before the birth of the nation, may invite you to dinner or to visit his textile factory at Barcelos.

The **Solar de Cortegaça**, at Subportela on the left bank of the Lima river toward Viana do Castelo, is another heraldic manor house, filled with heirlooms of the Abreu family. Of the three double bedrooms with bath, the tower suite is the most coveted, with windows on two sides and an elegant bath brightened with *azulejos*. The family cook will prepare special Minho dishes for guests.

East Along the Lima

The drive from Ponte de Lima east on the N 203 along the left bank of the river Lima is dotted with Minho estates, ancient watermills, granite homes with wooden balconies streaked with the colors of farm goods drying, and monasteries. The most striking structure is the early Romanesque **Igreja de São Salvador** at Bravães, 14.5 km (9 miles) east of Ponte de Lima, whose arresting doorways are carved with animal and geometric designs, vestiges of the magical and astral side of Christianity in the early Middle Ages. The interior contains the remains of Renaissance frescoes discovered during restoration work in the 1940s.

The view across the river from the right bank of the Lima 18 km (11 miles) east of Ponte de Lima of the town of **Ponte da Barca** and its solid 18th-century bridge is one of the most pleasant in the Minho. (Baptisms of unborn babies were at one time performed at midnight under the bridge, with the first man to pass by designated as the godfather.)

The baronial splendor and lineage of the **Paço Vedro de Magalhães**, southeast of Ponte da Barca, off the N 101 toward Braga, is equally impressive. The magnificent 18th-century estate belongs to the Corte Real and Lima family, which is blessed with a long line of explorers and statesmen; two Corte Real brothers explored part of the North American coast during the 16th century under a British flag. The property sits in secluded woods surrounded by mountains. Its imposing portico is itself dwarfed by the family's baronial hall, its walls covered with paintings of the family's famous ancestors and sporting a standard of the lieutenant-general of the Order of Malta. The main hall is so large that at one time equestrian events were staged inside it. Three double bedrooms have been set aside for guests and are decorated with genteel elegance. The 18th-century **Casa da Agrela**, farther south on the N 101, at São Pedro do Vale (6 km/ 3.75 miles from Ponte da Barca), is a smaller, pleasant alternative. Three rooms with views of the colorful garden and the surrounding valley are available.

There are unfortunately no restaurants in the area to match the patrician splendor of its manor houses; dining out here is simple and rustic. The **Adega Regional** restaurant in a converted farmhouse on the banks of the Vez river in **Arcos de Valdevez**, 5 km (3 miles) north of Ponte da Barca on the N 101, takes special pride in its trout and steaks. Guests have a choice of dining alfresco in a vine-covered courtyard or indoors surrounded by antique farm implements. Again, the local cooperative's *vinhos verdes* should fit your needs.

Ponte da Barca and Arcos de Valdevez both provide an entrance to the Peneda section of the Peneda-Gerês park, which is cut off from the Gerês area by the Serra da Amarela. The tourist information booth by the Ponte da Barca provides hiking maps of the park and information on where to rent rowboats to explore the river.

An enjoyable one-day drive (80 km/50 miles) through this part of the park includes both banks of the Lima river. The N 203/304-1 follows the left bank of the river all the way east to the 13th-century **fortress of Lindoso**, which was built by King Dinis to guard the pass where the Lima enters from Spain. From the battlements to the south you can admire a cluster of stone *espigueiros* where the farmers still store their corn. Before Lindoso the road passes a turnoff to the right to **Ermida**, about 10 km (6 miles) from Ponte da Barca, the site of several prehistoric dolmens. The majestic stones stand in a circular field on the summit, surrounded by trees and frequently mists.

Backtrack 11 km (7 miles) to the Ponte de Paradamonte, cross the river, and head for the mountain village of **Soajo** on the N 304 (3 km/2 miles), where the *monteiros,* as the mountain people are called, are known for their independent streak. For centuries they made a living hunting. Under an arrangement with King Dinis in the 13th century they were allowed autonomy so long as they kept his court stocked with game and came to his aid during invasions. To cement the partnership, King Dinis also prohibited the nobility from taking residence in Soajo: They could spend no more time in the village, he ruled, than it took a piece of bread toasted at the end of a spear to cool down. This edict is said to be the origin of the unusual pillory in the main square: a triangular shape with a mischievous face carved in it held up by a long granite pole. The cluster of *espigueiros* mounted on a huge boulder here overlooking the barren peaks of Peneda are a symbol of the community, which owns them in partnership. Lively corn-husking parties with singing and dancing are held here during the fall harvest.

Although its rates take advantage of its being the only lodging in the area, the **Casa do Adro** here is a clean and functional inn in a typical 18th-century town house near the main square. It has singles, doubles, and suites, furnished in ordinary modern taste. The Casa do Adro's main attraction is the kitchen, where guests are served breakfast facing a large granite chimney where game was once roasted. The two cafés near the square provide simple meals (rabbit and lamb, specialties of the area) and local color. From Soajo you can visit the dolmens at **Mezio**, 19 km (12 miles) west on the N 202 toward Arcos de Valdevez, which have shapes similar to those at Stonehenge.

To return to Ponte da Barca on the right bank of the Lima, follow the signs out of Soajo toward **Ermelo**. Before reaching this charming village you will cross a pass dotted with primitive round *brandos,* rock shelters used by shepherds in the summer. To visit Ermelo, with its pretty Romanesque chapel and ornate Manueline pillory, you must leave your car and walk down a stone path worn by hundreds of years of use. Farther down the road you will pass *canastros,* round wicker containers with thatched roofs used to store grain.

The N 101 north of Ponte da Barca climbs to the spectacular Serra da Bualhosa gorge, where whitewashed villages, onion-domed churches, and terraced farms cling tenuously to the steep slopes. On the other side of the pass lies the Minho river valley.

MINHO RIVER VALLEY

The Minho river and its narrow valley run west to east for about 60 miles from Melgaço in the northeast to Caminha at the mouth. They are flanked south and north by mountains: on the left bank (the southern, Portuguese side) by the high peaks of the Serra da Peneda and several other smaller ranges; and on the right bank by the equally impressive mountains of the Cordillera Cantabrica, in the Galician province of Spain. A series of forts, some still standing, guarded Portugal's northern frontier against invasion for centuries. Some of the forts have been converted into pousadas and tourist attractions. The Minho river continues to be a major source of food, providing lamprey in the spring and succulent *meixao* (mussels). The valley's eastern plateau still yields some of the most precious Minho wines, extracted from the Alvarinho grape.

The area around **Monção**, 39 km (24 miles) north of Ponte da Barca on the N 101, particularly the district around Pinheiros to the south, is considered the Mecca of *vinho verde*. The huge 19th-century **Palácio de Brejoeira**, 5 km (3 miles) south of Monção on the N 101, is reputed to produce the most outstanding—and most expensive—of the estate white *vinhos verdes* and *aguardentes* (brandies), with vines grafted exclusively from the Alvarinho stock. Part of its success can be attributed to its dowager owner and administrator, Herminia Silva D'Oliveira Pais, who personally oversees her wine production from vine to bottle. The sprawling mansion, modeled after the royal palace of Ajuda outside Lisbon, can be admired from the iron gates (and on the label of its bottles). The last king of Portugal slept in the palace on his way to exile, and António Salazar received his Spanish counterpart, Francisco Franco, here in 1950. England's Prince Andrew was a recent guest.

The former fortress town of Monção, on the banks of the Minho river in the middle of the stretch facing Spain across the water, is known for its courageous women. The first was Deu-la-Deu Martins, who saved it in 1369 from Spanish besiegers. After months of siege, she flung the last of the town's bread over the wall, defiantly informing the Spanish that there was plenty more where that came from. The Spanish, believing the Portuguese had enough supplies to hold out indefinitely, lifted their siege. Her statue now stands in the main square. Ines Negra, another heroine, fought to retake Monção from the Spanish in the 14th century. King João I and his ally John of Gaunt, the Duke of Lancaster (John's daughter married João and was the mother of Henry the Navigator), had been laying siege to the town for 50 days. Inês Negra challenged and defeated in combat a woman from the fortress, to settle the siege. The remains of the town's fortifications line the river facing Spain, a stone's throw away.

The **Casa de Rodas**, on the southeastern outskirts of Monção, is a beautiful example of 18th-century manorial Portugal, surrounded by pines and vineyards. Four bedrooms are open to guests, who also have access to most of the elegant house, which is furnished in fin-de-siècle style.

The 19-km (12-mile) ride west to Valença do Minho on the N 101 is very picturesque. The hills above the tiny Medieval town of **Lapella** provide a magnificent vista of its crenellated keep, the river, and the majestic mountains of

Galicia to the northwest. For an even more impressive view, drive to the summit of **Monte do Faro**, 7 km (4.5 miles) southeast of Valença do Minho. To get to this lookout point, turn left onto the N 101-7 toward Cerdal just before Valença. From the chapel of Santa Ana there you can admire the Soajo and Peneda mountain ranges to the east, Galicia to the north, and the Minho river mouth to the southwest. The **Pensão Monte do Faro**, at the summit, decorated with a heavy Victorian hand, has as well as accommodations a fine restaurant serving regional specialties such as lamprey with rice—and panoramic views.

Valença do Minho

The double fortress town of Valença do Minho, overlooking Tui in Spain, epitomizes the once violent nature of Luso-Spanish relations. It rests on a hill above the Minho, guarding Portugal's northern border. Its 18th-century Vaubanesque defenses divide the old quarter into two crown-shaped towns. Each fortress is surrounded by a moat and guarded by six bastions with parapets and watchtowers. The main entrance to the town is through the Porta da Coroada, a monumental doorway emblazoned with the coats of arms of the kingdom, and then through a covered passage. Despite its seemingly impregnable façade, Napoleonic troops were able to capture the town in 1807 before being repelled by a combined force of British and Portuguese regulars. During the second Napoleonic invasion in 1809 the French bombed the town from the Spanish town of Tui across the river, but that time the defenders held out.

Today the garrison town has been largely transformed into a bazaar, and the French and Spanish alike may invade as long as they leave their francs or pesetas behind. Many of the houses have been turned into shops selling such Portuguese handicrafts as linen, pottery, wicker, leatherware, tin and copper goods, peasant dresses, and colorful Portuguese scarves. The crafts shop connected to the Pousada de São Teotónio also provides a large selection of Minho folk art.

Apart from the shops, the two quarters provide quaintly cobbled streets, fountain-cooled squares, cafés, tiny whitewashed churches, and handsome town houses with ornate Manueline windows and crenellations.

The **Pousada de São Teotónio** is lodged on top of the

bastion overlooking the river and the iron bridge that spans it, built by Charles Eiffel in the early 1900s. The architect of the "California Modern" pousada made good use of the river view, incorporating it into most of the 16 bedrooms and the bar, terrace, garden, and restaurant. The restaurant serves quality regional food such as spicy saffron rice, lamprey, kid, and Valença's very own *angulas com toucinho* (eels with bacon). Try its hearty country vegetable soup, which carries the full variety of the Minho's produce, precooked a day in advance to allow the ingredients to blend.

Other dining spots in Valença include the **Parque**, a typical Portuguese bistro with colorful regional decorations, a warm and friendly staff, and a reputable grill. It is tucked away in the rua da Oliveira facing the western battlements of the southern polygon. **Muralhas**, a lively bistro specializing in fish, is lodged literally inside the walls of the fortress at the main entrance of the town (hence its name, which means "walls"). You can dine either in the coolness of the former guardhouse or outside in a small esplanade looking onto a small square. If you choose the latter, be advised of potentially bothersome fumes from traffic, particularly on weekends.

If you like vintage trains, head east for the railway station, outside the fortress perimeter, to visit the train museum, housed across the tracks from the stationmaster's office, east of the N 13 as you enter town. It contains a steam engine built in Manchester in 1875 by Beyer Peacock and an elegant salon car constructed in France for the Portuguese royal family.

Southwest to Viana do Castelo

The 27 km (17 miles) ride from Valença on the N 13 southwest to Caminha is one of the most enchanting in the Minho. The rocky terrain, patched by pine forests and vineyards, gives way to a more mellow landscape tempered by the pastels of orchards and grain fields. The river widens and the tiny islands of Boega and Amores appear. The elegant **Pousada de Dom Dinis** in Vila Nova de Cerveira was built inside the ruins of a 14th-century walled town overlooking the Minho. Segments of the old castle and some outbuildings inside the ramparts have been converted into 26 rooms and three suites with terraces, furnished with replicas of old Minho wooden furniture; two bars; a small disco; and a glass-enclosed restaurant where you can sample the area's tender *arroz de savel* (stewed rice and shad), curried or baked lamprey (in spring), and *biscoitos de milho doce* (sweet corn wafers). The compound is peaceful and palatial: all stone, stucco, and oleander, surrounded by crenellated ramparts that are penetrated by a massive arched gate. The square glass box of a building that houses the restaurant detracts somewhat from the otherwise charming pousada.

Caminha sits at the mouth of the Minho and Coura rivers, facing the Portuguese fortress island of Insua in the estuary and the Spanish town of Santa Tecla on the right bank. Over the centuries it has undergone countless vicissitudes on account of its strategic position, guarding the mainland from invaders—including the Vikings. Today it is largely a fishing and coppersmithing center. Its quaint, spotless main square is a mosaic of architectural periods, from the Medieval crenellated **Torre do Relójio** (clock tower) to the elegant **Palácio dos Pitas**, with its ornate Manueline windows, to the 17th-century **Paços do Conselho** (town hall). Nearby, the lovely panels of the wood-carved ceiling of the 15th-century **Igreja Matriz** (parish church) were apparently the work of a Mudejar artist. Outside on the northern wall there is an amusing gargoyle of a man relieving himself, his derrière pointing at Spain.

South of the Caminha main square is the **Adega Machado**, a small, intimate bistro tucked away on the quiet Visconde Sousa Rego street, tastefully decorated with tile, wood, and regional furniture. Its proximity to the sea and two rivers is evident on its menu, which includes shellfish, pickled shad, fleshy trout from the Coura river accompanied by a green parsley sauce and cured ham, and the house special, *tainha assada no forno* (baked mullet). Meat lovers can select the tender *cabrito assado* (roast kid) from the neighboring Serra D'Arga. Another restaurant, the **Remo**, sits on stilts on the riverside wharf of the tiny sailing club of Caminha as you enter the town from Valença on the N 13. The large, glass-enclosed establishment diplomatically serves both Portuguese and Spanish dishes, but specializes in *arroz de mariscos,* a mouth-watering shellfish and rice stew that bears little relationship to Spanish paella.

After Caminha the N 13 turns south and travels along the Atlantic **Costa Verde**, with its wide, sandy beaches, passing tourist resorts of varying quality (some extremely tacky) and fishing villages with interesting histories. **Vila**

Praia de Ancora and its namesake river along here got their name from a tragic story in which a comely wife who had run off with a Moorish emir was captured and returned to her husband, who had her strapped to an *âncora* (anchor) and thrown into the river to drown. The neighboring town of Afife is also proud of its reputation for beautiful women, although it has the curious custom of burning old women in effigy during Lent.

VIANA DO CASTELO

This prosperous, busy city sits on a plain on the right bank of the Lima river estuary west of Ponte de Lima. Behind it, to the north, the Santuária de Santa Luzia stands guard on a steep wooded hill. Viana is a popular tourist center, known for its colorful folk festivals, fireworks, and deep-sea fishing.

Viana has a long history. Vestiges of human habitation dating back as far as the Stone Age have been uncovered on both the shore and the mountain. The Greeks and the Phoenicians both visited it in the Iron Age and left their mark on the art and adventurous spirit of the people. Viana's name, some say, is actually a bastardization of Diana, the Greek goddess of the hunt.

In the 16th century the sailors of Viana put their town on the world map: Gonçalo Velho colonized the Azores; João Velho charted the mouth of the Congo river; and João Alvares Fernandes mapped the banks of Newfoundland for Portuguese cod fishermen. The handsome Renaissance and Manueline buildings that grace the old quarter were constructed during this period. Viana merchants—many of them Jews forced to convert to Christianity who gravitated to Viana because it was not as hard on them as other cities—also began to trade with the Hanseatic League and Great Britain, exchanging wine, fruit, cork, honey, and other produce for cloth and other finished goods. It was out of Viana do Castelo that the first Port wine was shipped to England. The wine trade and gold from Brazil helped fuel a Baroque building boom in the 18th century. Today, Viana continues to have an important fishing community as well as boat building, pottery, and crafts industries.

Boat tours explore the shore and river on Tuesdays and Saturdays; book them at the Avic travel agency in the avenida dos Combatentes da Grande Guerra (Tel: 058-24081). Walking tours depart from the Turismo office, lodged in a handsome 15th-century palace on the rua do Hospital Velho, near the praça da República. The palace also houses tourist shops selling blue-and-white Viana ceramics, linen, copperware, gold and silver filigree, colorful regional costumes, now worn mostly on feast days (green or red for feast days, blue for mourning, black for brides to set off their gold filigree), multicolored peasant scarves, *palmitos* (sprays of artificial flowers), and handkerchiefs with hearts sewn on them, traditionally given by young maidens to their swains.

The area in and around the delightful **praça da República**, north of the Turismo office, contains the city's most impressive buildings and its best outdoor cafés, shops, and restaurants. At its center is the ornate 16th-century fountain designed by the master stonemason João Lopes the Elder, who crowned it with an armillary sphere representing the world to remind all proudly that it was a Minhoto, Fernando de Magalhães (Ferdinand Magellan), who proved that the world was round. Facing the fountain are several architectural jewels. On the east is the 16th-century crenellated and arcaded **Antigo Paços do Conselho** (former town hall), now an exhibition and cultural center. The Renaissance façade of the **Misericórdia Hospice**, designed by João Lopes the Younger, is an ode to Greece, held up by Athenian atlantes and caryatids. (The adjoining church contains important 18th-century *azulejos* by António Oliveira Bernardes and his son, Policarpo.) The Gothic portal of the **Igreja Matriz** (parish church), south of the square, pays homage to the merchants of Viana, who are shown being carried on the shoulders of the Apostles.

West of the town center, toward the mouth of the river, on rua Manuel Espregueira, is the **Museu Municipal**, housed in the 18th-century former Maceias Barbosa family palace. The building has wonderful *azulejos* also painted by Policarpo, who, together with his father, António, led the Portuguese tile revolution to combat the Dutch influence in Portugal. The ground floor has coffered ceilings and exquisite Indo-Portuguese furniture; the second floor holds a rare collection of 18th-century Coimbra glazed pottery. Other items include a granite statue of an ancient Lusitanian warrior, whose uniform is strikingly similar to those worn by Iron Age Greeks, and Roman coins.

The **castle of São Tiago da Barra** lies several blocks southwest of the museum near the mouth of river. The fortress, which has undergone several adaptations over the centuries, has a quaint little chapel inside it dedicated to Saint James and can be visited.

Northwest of the castle, off rua de Monserrate, is the tiny Baroque **Capela de Nossa Senhora da Agonia**, which despite its name is the center of one of the most spectacular and lively feasts in Portugal. For three days, at the end of the third week in August, Viana becomes one huge festival, doing justice to its reputation as the country's folk-culture capital. The streets glitter with thousands of colorful lights and are spanned by hundreds of wooden arches decorated with colorful paper and ornamental flowers and ribbons. The squares are filled with choral folk groups, who perform the fast-paced traditional *viras* and *cana verde* dances. Towering *gigantones,* played by young men standing on stilts and wearing large cardboard heads, enliven the crowds and inspire the awe of the children. The city is redolent with the tantalizing odors of sausages, pork, and sardines being grilled over coals in outdoor stalls. Young women parade in colorful, embroidered regional costumes with complicated human, animal, and flower designs, weighed down by a fortune in gold filigree necklaces, passed down from generation to generation, mother to daughter. The avenues are crowded with long linedances in which everyone participates, accompanied by marching brass bands or more traditional bagpipe, drum, and cymbal ensembles.

After the statue of Nossa Senhora da Agonia is paraded through the streets paved with millions of flower petals and floated out to sea to bless the fishing fleet, the festival ends in a blaze of fireworks at the harbor.

The towns around Viana are also known for lavish spring flower pageants, bearing out the Minho's reputation as the garden of Portugal. The Festas da Senhora das Rosas are held in the neighboring town of Vila Franca do Lima (May 7 and 8). The women of the village weave intricate rose tapestries, which they carry on their heads. At the Festas dos Andores Floridos (May 24 and 25) in Alvares, floats covered entirely with roses are drawn through streets carpeted with intricate flower designs.

Staying in Viana do Castelo

Viana has a fairly large and varied selection of accommodations. The most scenic is the **Hotel de Santa Luzia**, at the top of Mount Santa Luzia. Its suites and 44 rooms, recently refurbished in Art Deco style, echo a more relaxed and opulent era. Many of them command a grand view of Viana, its river, and the ocean. The outdoor swimming pool is discreetly surrounded by hedges. The food in the glass-lined dining room is mostly Continental. The hotel is owned by the government and is used to provide on-the-job experience for future pousada employees and hoteliers, so the staff is young and eager.

The **Paço D'Anha**, across the river, is the most luxurious of the area's manor houses and one of the grandest in the region. It was here that the prior of Crato was informed in 1580 that he had been proclaimed king of Portugal after the death of his uncle and regent, the former cardinal of Evora. The rule of Dom António, however, was one of the shortest in Portuguese history: the Spanish invaded soon after he was invested and forced him to flee the country.

The sprawling property, at Anha, 5 km (3 miles) to the southeast of Viana, produces, bottles, and sells an esteemed white *vinho verde* named after it. Guests stay in converted grain houses equipped with all the amenities, including kitchens. Meals and horseback riding are also provided at the estate, which is owned by the Alpouim family.

Dining in Viana do Castelo

The **Cozinha das Malheiras**, on rua Gago Coutinho, is a posh new restaurant directly south of the paços do Conselho frequented by city businessmen. The decor is pure white, with modern Portuguese art on the walls. The kitchen offers a varied assortment of international, traditional Minho, and nouvelle Portuguese cuisine. Less sedate and more typical Minho fare, entertainment, and decor are available at **Os Três Potes**, housed inside a former bakery in a cul-de-sac on the rua dos Fornos, a two-minute walk southwest of the main square. Waitresses in Minho dress serve prix fixe or à la carte meals. The English-owned establishment provides a sampling of Minho appetizers, including cured ham and other meats such as roast kid and *rojões*. Reservations are required in the summer, particularly on the weekends, when Minho folk dancing and singing shows are put on for the public; Tel: (058) 23432.

The **Casa D'Armas** is a new waterfront restaurant lodged in a former armory, which may have something to do with its stiff Medieval decor but does not detract from its tasty, well-presented food. Its extensive wine list includes white *vinho verde* from the neighboring Paço D'Anha estate. House delicacies include river salmon, veal with mushrooms in a white wine sauce, and *torta de amêndoa* (almond torte).

The vine-covered outdoor dining room and a solid reputation for Minho fare make **O Espigueiro**, 5 km (3 miles) south of Viana on the main (N 13) road to Porto, popular with families on the weekends. It is about 300 yards off the road to your right and is signposted. The **Quinta do Santoinho** next door is the ultimate dining and party experience in the area, where all-night *arraiais* are held for the benefit of tourists. For a prix fixe, guests eat and drink to their hearts' content and dance the night away. There are even fireworks and *gigantones* to animate the party. Those who survive till the end are served a *champorreão,* a powerful punch of Champagne, *vinho verde,* beer, lemon, sugar, and ice. The parties are held Tuesdays, Thursdays, and Saturdays during August; Thursdays and Saturdays during June, July, and September; and Saturdays in May and October. Reservations for the event, which begins at 8:00 P.M., can be made in Viana at avenida dos Combatentes, 206; Tel: (058) 24081.

Before leaving town, drive 4 km (2.5 miles) north or take a seven-minute funicular ride (leaves on the hour in the morning and every half hour after 2:00 P.M.) from rua 25 de Abril to the summit of the wooded Mount Santa Luzia, which served for centuries as the refuge for the people of Viana in times of plague or invasions. From the tower of the Neo-Byzantine basilica of Santa Luzia, a copy of Sacré-Coeur in Paris, you have a panoramic view of the Lima estuary and the southern Minho. Behind the Hotel Santa Luzia above the basilica are the ruins of an Iron Age city, which was later populated by Romans and Swabians and then encircled by a wall in the Middle Ages.

BARCELOS

The center of pottery making in the north—and home of the Portuguese good-luck symbol, the rooster—is Barcelos, on the right bank of the Cávado river 30 km (19 miles) southeast of Viana do Castelo via the N 103 on the way to Braga. The cock became equated with good luck and justice, according to the legend, when a man on a pilgrimage to Santiago de Compostelo was accused of stealing silver and was sentenced to death by hanging. As his last wish he requested an audience with the magistrate who had condemned him and was received as his judge was sitting down to a dinner of roast cockerel. Pointing to the dinner plate, the accused declared that the cockerel would proclaim his innocence. The judge laughed and had him led away, but did not eat his meal. Just as the unfortunate man was being hanged, the cock stood up, crowed, and fell dead again. The judge rushed to the gallows and found the prisoner still breathing because the noose had failed to tighten around his neck. The **Cruzeiro do Senhor do Galo**, a 15th-century cross commemorating the event, stands on the esplanade beside the ruins of the palace of the Count of Barcelos and first duke of Bragança, the **Palácio Ducal**, now an open-air museum. The esplanade looks down at a Gothic bridge that spans the steep ravine of the Cávado river.

Across from the palace, on the northwestern corner of the square, is the elegant 15th-century **Solar dos Pinheiros**, nicknamed Casa do Barbadão (the bearded one) after one of its former occupants. The southern tower has a relief of this Barbadão, a Jew, pulling at his beard, which he vowed never to cut after his daughter fell in love and bore a son to a gentile out of wedlock. The gentile happened to be King João I, who made his bastard son the first duke of Bragança. East of the house, on the largo do Município, is the 13th-century Romano-Gothic **Igreja Matriz** (parish church), rich in gilt and carved capitals. Near the town center, to the northeast, is the octagonal Baroque **Igreja de Senhor da Cruz**, built on the site where João Pires, a peasant who insisted on working on the day of the Holy Cross, saw a black Cross on the ground in front of him. He immediately stopped working and repented. The church is decorated with flowers and lights during the first week of May for the feast of the Cross. Farther north, on the avenida dos Combatentes da Grande Guerra, is the former church of the Benedictine **monastery of Nossa Senhora de Terço**, filled with 18th-century *azulejos* depicting the life of Saint Benedict.

Barcelos's main attraction, however, is its pottery. A huge country **market** is held every Thursday in the campo da República, a large esplanade in the center of the town. At the fair, one of the most colorful in the country, you can pick up multicolored rag rugs, bags, fruit trays, wine holders and baskets made of rushes, lacework, linen, and *cangas* (hand-carved yokes), in addition to pottery, at bargain prices. The multicolored and varied pottery—figurative, decorative, and kitchen oriented—is produced in the surrounding countryside in small and medium-sized workshops. There are popular figurines such as the large-headed *gigantones,* devils, ox carts, multipiece municipal bands, roosters, and altar pieces done in a rough primitivism that would enchant students of anthropology. Some of the more amusing pieces are anthropomorphic, echoing the region's pagan past. The foremost proponent of this art was Rosa Ramalho, whose pregnant goats are said to have inspired Picasso. Her granddaughter, Julia, has carried on the family trade. Her work, as well as other goods produced in the region, can be purchased in the Medieval crenellated keep on the largo da Porta Nova, which has been converted into the local Turismo office and regional crafts center. Barcelos is also known as an antiques center. The **Casa das Antiguidades** on the pedestrian rua Duques de Bragança, a block west of the largo da Porta Nova, is the most prestigious of these establishments. Here you will find carved oak furniture, china, silver, and Indo-Portuguese teak furniture inlaid with ivory.

The best restaurants in Barcelos are near the Turismo office. The **Casa dos Arcos** is a tiny, comfortable establishment on the rua Duques de Bragança, with stone walls, thick wooden beams, and low lighting. The Medieval-style restaurant, which is popular with the city's intelligentsia, offers a fine selection of regional dishes such as *rojões* and *cabrito* and Barcelos' estate-bottled white Quinta do Tamariz, and the tarty Quinta da Portela. A few steps east of the Turismo office is the simple and rustic **Muralha**, which serves good wholesome food. More upscale, the **Bagoeira**, several blocks to the east, caters to the old guard, with traditional dishes and Victorian decor. This restaurant, on avenida Dr. Sidónio Pais, is a good place to try the region's *laranjas doces* (oranges stuffed with sweet pumpkin sauce) or *quei jadinhas* (egg-and-almond sweets).

The accommodations of merit in the Barcelos area are in the town's suburbs. The British owners of the **Quinta do Convento Franqueira**, a former Franciscan monastery surrounded by 35 acres of pine woods and vineyards, have set aside two elegantly furnished rooms in the main house for guests. The rooms look out onto manicured gardens and over the pristine waters of a rustic swimming pool. Meals, available upon request, are served with the estate's own *vinho verde*. The property is located 4 km (2.5 miles) south of Barcelos off the N 205 toward Póvoa de Varzim. About one kilometer (half a mile) out of Barcelos, turn right at the filling station and drive 3 km (1.9 miles).

The **Casa do Monte**, 6 km (4 miles) north of Barcelos (signposted) off the N 103, is a two-story farm-type house with ivy-covered walls and neatly trimmed lawns. Its four rooms, furnished in a refined country style, overlook the gardens and a pine-studded valley. The atmosphere is relaxed and rural.

THE ATLANTIC BEACHES

The best-known beach resorts of the Minho can be found south of Viana do Castelo on the way to Porto along the N 13, where the flat, gently curving coastline is graced with golden beaches, sand dunes speckled with shrubs, and an occasional river mouth. While most of the coast south of Viana is developed, you can still find a few secluded stretches. Among the developed centers is **Póvoa de Varzim**, where such traditional industries as fishing and silversmithing exist next to the thriving tourist businesses, dividing Póvoa into two towns. The tourist area is on the north end of the town and encompasses four miles of sandy beaches, lined with hotels, water slides, tennis and golf facilities, discotheques, and all the other recreations that adorn mass-market summer playgrounds. Sloops are docked at the man-made marina beside the elegant Casino Monumental. The 208-room **Vermar Dom Pedro** is the most exclusive beachfront hotel in town, with all the modern trimmings, including tennis courts, sauna, grill, and restaurant with views of the beach, piano bar, discotheque, and two heated pools. More secluded and rustic is the **Estalagem Santo André**, on the beach at A-Ver-o-Mar, 6 km (4 miles) north of the town, with a pool and a restaurant facing the beach. The huts of seaweed harvesters (the weed is dried and used as fertilizer) line the beach nearby.

As would be expected, fish and shellfish are the dishes of preference in Póvoa de Varzim. The **Casino Monumental** on the southern end of the beachfront avenida dos Banhos offers the most sybaritic table and decor, as well as views of the marina. Its *lagosta suada* (steamed lobster) is a house special—order it if money is of no consequence. You can burn the calories off at the cabaret next door, but bring your passport if you want to try to win back the money you spent for your repast. The **Enseada**, a more modest beachfront property across the street from the casino, has a large menu and a tank for fresh fish. It serves *caldeirada dos poveiros,* a mixed fish stew or chowder developed by the town's fishing community that varies according to the catch.

The fishing port south of the marina faces the picturesque fishermen's *bairro*. The women continue to mend the nets by hand and sell fish as they have done for generations, while the men tend to the boats and the fishing. For centuries the fishing community practiced endogamy. The practice is dying off, but other customs remain alive, such as passing down the inheritance to the youngest son so that he can take care of his aging parents. Families continue to have their individual signs on their equipment and boats, a practice some scholars believe they may have inherited from Scandinavian and other northern European fishermen, who populated the flat coast over the centuries and formed close-knit clans to safeguard their traditions and property.

The fishing community comes alive on August 14 and 15 during the feast of Nossa Senhora da Assunção, when the life-size statue of the patron saint is carried down to the beach to bless the fleet. The event is followed by a beachside *arraial* and fireworks.

Of interest to shoppers here are the heavy wool fishermen's sweaters and the silver and gold creations fashioned and sold at the famous **Gomes** shop on rua da Junqueira. You can watch the silversmiths working the metal behind a glass partition, creating elaborate platters, soup vessels, candelabra, and other dining and household goods. There's also a liquor store, outside town on the N 13 toward Porto, where Alberto Montenegro has collected more than 150,000 bottles to satisfy all tastes and pocketbooks.

Vila do Conde, a quaint maritime town with an old fishing quarter, sits on the right bank of the Ave river estuary, 3 km (2 miles) south of Póvoa de Varzim. It became an important shipbuilding center during the Age of Discovery, and continues to fashion wooden ships for the Portuguese cod fleet. In 1987 its yards completed a replica of the caravel that transported Bartolomeu Dias around the tip of South Africa and opened the way for

Vasco da Gama's historic trip to India. The ship is now docked off Cape Town, South Africa.

Lacemaking has also been a business here since the 17th century. This labor-intensive craft is taught at the **Escola de Bilros** (Lace School) in the largo do Carmo, where *rendas de bilros* (bobbin lace) can be purchased. In 1719, following the tradition of Minhota heroines, a Vila do Conde lacemaker by the name of Joana Maria de Jesus saved her industry from extinction by persuading the court in Lisbon to modify a royal decree ordering Portuguese householders to use only Flemish lace.

Portugal's largest **crafts fair** is held here during the last week of July and the first week of August. All of the country's regions are represented by artisans demonstrating their skills to the public. The feast of São João (June 23 and 24) is also a popular event, during which the town is spectacularly lit with bonfires, thousands of lights, and fireworks. The two days of partying end with a candlelit procession to the beach led by lacemakers and other town women dressed in typical Minho dress.

There are several buildings of note in Vila do Conde. The most impressive monument is the **convent of Santa Clara** complex beside the bridge. The chapel of its handsome 14th-century Gothic church contains the intricately carved Renaissance tombs of its founders: Don Afonso Sanches, the bastard son of King Dinis, his wife, Dona Teresa Martins, and their two sons. The 18th-century fountain in the center of the close was fed by an aqueduct from the same period (parts of which are still standing) that ran from Póvoa de Varzim and that was built with 999 arches (because the builders thought that 1,000 would have been too presumptuous and might have offended God). The convent is now a rehabilitation center, but there are guided tours of the church. The view of Vila do Conde, lapped by the Atlantic to the west and the Ave river to the east, is one of the finest in the area. The ornate Plateresque doorway of the crenellated **Igreja Matriz** (parish church), north of the Turismo office (avenida 25 de Abril), was fashioned by Bizcayan stonemasons in the 16th century.

The **Estalagem do Brasão**, near the Vila do Conde town center, is a comfortable modern inn with 26 rooms, a bar, and a fairly good restaurant where egg-and-sugar convent desserts, such as the soft, caramelized *pastéis de Santa Clara,* fill the dessert cart. All the modern comforts, including a sauna and heated indoor pool, can be had at the modern **Motel de Sant'Ana**, on a small hill at Azurara across the river from Vila do Conde. Guests have a choice of an outdoor grill and terrace or dining in a softly lit indoor restaurant, where a pianist plays romantic music. Before leaving Azurara, stop off at its pretty 16th-century Manueline parish church, the patron saint of which is Santa Maria-a-Nova, who is supposed to bring happiness to wedded couples.

South of Azurara the main road tends a bit inland on the way down to Porto.

GETTING AROUND

The Minho is fairly well linked by train from Porto, which has an international airport. The Linha do Minho runs from Porto's Trindade station, up the coast past Vila do Conde, Póvoa de Varzim, Barcelos, Viana do Castelo, and Caminha, where it turns east and follows the Minho river along the border with Spain all the way up to Monção. You can also catch commuter trains to Guimarães and Braga from this station.

Bus service between the towns is fairly good but, as you might expect, slow. The best way by far to see the Minho is by car. Traffic congestion around the main towns is common, particularly during rush hour. At the height of the summer season the N 13 from Valença to Porto is taxed with both tourists and returning Portuguese guest workers from the north. Otherwise, the roads are fairly well marked and reasonably well paved.

Most of the sights and towns of merit in the Minho can be visited following a circular route. As laid out in our narrative, a tour by car might begin at Guimarães, continue to Braga, up to the Peneda-Gerês park, across to Ponte de Lima and Ponte da Barca, up to Monção, west to Valença, and down the coast past Viana do Castelo, Barcelos, Póvoa de Varzim, Vila do Conde, and Azurara. From Azurara you could cut back east to Guimarães or go south to Porto and its airport. Give yourself at least a week to digest all the region's natural, architectural, and gastronomic delights—ten days would be better.

Braga

Braga suffers from the same traffic problems as other major cities, but its historic quarter is fairly small and best done on foot. Park at the guarded municipal parking lot directly north of the cathedral, on the praça Conde de

Agrolongo, and proceed south to the cathedral on foot. Avoid driving on the main street, the avenida da Liberdade, during rush hours. Taxis can be obtained in front of the Turismo office at the western edge of the central park, or summoned by phone; Tel: (053) 28019. The train station is a short ride north of the center, at praça da Estação Rodoviária. The bus station is next door at travessa da praça do Comércio.

ACCOMMODATIONS REFERENCE

▶ **Casa do Adro.** Soajo, 4970 Arcos de Valdevez. Tel: (058) 47327.

▶ **Casa da Agrela.** São Pedro do Vale, 4980 Ponte da Barca. Tel: (058) 42642.

▶ **Paço D'Anha. Anha,** 4900 Viana do Castelo. Tel: (058) 28459.

▶ **Estalagem do Brasão.** Avenida Coronel Alberto Graça, 4480 **Vila do Conde.** Tel: (052) 62-40-16.

▶ **Paço de Calheiros. Calheiros,** 4990 Ponte de Lima. Tel: (058) 94-71-64 or 94-13-64.

▶ **Quinta do Convento Franqueira.** 4750 **Barcelos.** Tel: (053) 81-16-06.

▶ **Solar de Cortegaça.** Subportela, 4900 Viana do Castelo. Tel: (058) 97-16-39.

▶ **Pousada de Dom Dinis.** 4920 **Vila Nova de Cerveira.** Tel: (051) 95601; Telex: 32821.

▶ **Hotel do Elevador. Bom Jesus do Monte,** 4700 Braga. Tel: (053) 25011; Telex: 33401.

▶ **Inácio Filho.** Rua Francisco Sanches, 42, 4700 **Braga.** Tel: (053) 23849.

▶ **Casa dos Lagos.** Bom Jesus do Monte, 4700 Braga. Tel: (053) 24563.

▶ **Moinho de Estorãos. Estorãos,** 4990 Ponte de Lima. Tel: (01) 921-3733 or (058) 94-23-72.

▶ **Casa do Monte.** Abade de Neiva, 4750 Barcelos. Tel: (053) 82519.

▶ **Pensão Monte do Faro. Monte do Faro,** Ganfei, 4930 Valença do Minho. Tel: (051) 22411.

▶ **Pousada da Nossa Senhora da Oliveira.** Rua de Santa Maria, 4800 **Guimarães.** Tel: (053) 41-21-57.

▶ **Parque Hotel.** Bom Jesus do Monte, 4700 Braga. Tel: (053) 22048; Telex: 26179.

▶ **Casa da Pedra Cavalgada.** Lugar do Assente-Palmeira, 4700 **Braga.** Tel: (053) 24596.

- **Aldeamento da Pedra Verde.** Cerdeirinhas, 4850 Vieira do Minho. Tel: (053) 57444.
- **Casa de Pomarchão.** Arcozelo, 4990 Ponte de Lima. Tel: (058) 94-11-39.
- **Casa do Ribeiro.** São Cristovão de Selho, 4800 **Guimarães.** Tel: (053) 41-08-81.
- **Casa de Rodas.** 4950 **Monção.** Tel: (051) 52105 or 52355.
- **Casa da Santa Lucia.** Cerdeirinhas, 4850 Vieira do Minho. Tel: (053) 57452.
- **Hotel de Santa Luzia.** Monte de Santa Luzia, 4900 **Viana do Castelo.** Tel: (058) 22192; Telex: 32420.
- **Pousada de Santa Marinha da Costa.** 4800 **Guimarães.** Tel: (053) 41-84-53.
- **Motel de Sant'Ana.** Azurara, 4480 Vila do Conde. Tel: (052) 62-16-94; Telex: 27695.
- **Estalagem Santo André.** A-Ver-o-Mar, 4490 Póvoa de Varzim. Tel: (052) 68-18-81.
- **Pousada de São Bento.** Caniçada, 4850 Vieira do Minho. Tel: (053) 57190; Telex: 32339.
- **Paço de São Cipriano.** Tabuadelo, 4800 Guimarães. Tel: (053) 48-13-37.
- **Pousada de São Teotónio.** 4930 **Valença do Minho.** Tel: (051) 23374.
- **Paço Vedro de Magalhães.** 4980 **Ponte da Barca.** Tel: (058) 42117.
- **Vermar Dom Pedro.** Avenida dos Banhos, 4490 **Póvoa de Varzim.** Tel: (052) 68-34-01; Telex: 25261.

The Minho manor-house association handles reservations and information from its headquarters here. Write or call Turihab, praça da República, Ponte de Lima, 4970 Viana do Castelo; Tel: (058) 94-23-35, Telex: 32618.

Pousadas can be booked through Marketing Ahead, 433 Fifth Avenue, New York, N.Y. 10016; Tel: (212) 686-9213.

TRÁS-OS-MONTES

By Thomas de la Cal

The region of Trás-os-Montes (Behind the Mountains) is as remote as its name implies. Cut off from the rest of Portugal by the Marão and Gerês mountains to the west and the Douro river to the south, and bordered on the north and east by Spain, the province is the country's outback. Adding to its isolation are four mountain ranges—Alvão, Padrela, Nogueira, and Mogadouro—which run roughly north to south, dividing the province into high plateaus and deep-cut valleys. Trás-os-Montes was considered so remote in the 14th century that King Dinis, who wanted to secure his borders, had to give away land in order to get people to settle there. A string of fortresses was built along the frontier. The region became a hardship post for civil servants and army officers out of Lisbon and Porto and a haven for criminals and for political and religious exiles. Spanish and Portuguese Jews fled here from the Inquisition during the 16th century. Many of them were *Marranos,* or "New Christians," who ostensibly had converted to Christianity but continued to practice their Jewish faith in secret.

Trás-os-Montes is a backward region of extremes: Winters are harsh and summers are blistering hot; its plateaus are covered with stunted vegetation, which supports the region's sheep, and crowned by massive rocky crests, while its valleys, gentler and more lush, support a mixed agricultural economy of corn, grapes, olives, figs, oranges, apples, and almonds. Commerce and agriculture are the staples of this thinly populated region, and industry is virtually nonexistent. The past is very much alive in unspoiled, self-sufficient communal villages of granite and schist, such as Rio de Onor at its northeastern border, where belief in *bruxas* (witches) and *currandeiros* (medicine men) is still a way of life. Some of these villages are so ancient that you will feel as though you are entering the Europe of the Middle Ages, possibly earlier. Here you will see women in black carrying large loads on their heads and men-and-ox teams tilling fields as they have done for centuries and smell the sweet, yeasty aroma of bread baking in communal ovens.

Trás-os-Montes is ideal for those who want to get away from it *all* and enjoy simple, vanishing pleasures such as fresh, clean air and water, wide-open spaces, and unadulterated food. You can see Paleolithic art engraved on the walls of the Douro canyon, explore Celtic *castros* (fortified villages) more than 3,000 years old, and climb the battlements of the fortress towns lining the Spanish border. You can taste the waters of spas used since Roman times, hunt partridge and rabbit on the plateaus, watch rare birds in rocky crests, fish in pristine rivers and mountain streams, and shop for handmade copper, tin, leather, linen, and woollen goods.

The best time to visit Trás-os-Montes is during the mild seasons: spring, when the almond and chestnut trees bloom in the valleys, and early fall, during the grape harvest.

MAJOR INTEREST

Vila Real's Palácio Mateus
Environs of Vila Real (mountain villages of Serra do Alvão and Terra do Basto and manor house accommodations)
Romeu (granite village)
Miranda do Douro (museum, cathedral, and folk dances)
Bragança (museum, citadel, and Romanesque civic building)
Environs of Bragança
Parque Natural de Montesinhos
Chaves (museum, keep, spa, Vaubanesque fortresses, colorful verandahs)

Trás-os-Montes has been inhabited for thousands of years. Stone Age markings adorn the Douro river canyon at

Mazouco, on its southeastern border with Spain. Celtic vestiges dot the landscape in the ruins of fortified hamlets and rock carvings that were used by Druids and now live on in the customs, religion, and folkways of the area, where ancient rites still celebrate birth, puberty, marriage, and death. In some villages epic stories passed down from generation to generation provide an oral record of peoples and events. The Romans mined the region's gold quarries and tapped its warm-water springs in the northwest near Chaves; the Swabians, a people from southern Germany, settled the Trás-os-Montes valleys; the Visigoths, another Germanic tribe, from the Baltic area, gravitated toward its upper plateaus.

Trás-os-Montes is slowly entering the 20th century. A major highway will traverse the region by 1990, passing through Vila Real, Mirandela, and Bragança, to link Portugal to Zamora, in Spain. Plans are afoot to start mining the large iron and coal deposits along the Douro river and on the northeastern interior near Bragança. Signs of modernity are also cropping up in remote villages as new wings and television antennas burgeon on ancestral homes.

The Food and Wine of Trás-os-Montes

The food of Trás-os-Montes is as simple, unpretentious, and hearty as its people. The quality of its produce guarantees its taste: The region is known for its potatoes and cabbages, river trout, veal, lamb, kid, ham, and sausages. Garlic, paprika, and mint are its basic herbs and spices. *Sopa seca* (dry soup) contains most of these ingredients, plus bread. The various meats and vegetables that go into it are precooked, then doused with scalding stock, sprinkled with mint, and baked before serving. Sausages are popular in stews. *Azedo,* made of beef, pork parts, paprika, and hot peppers, has been called the "king of sausages." *Alheira* (spiced sausage) was invented during the Inquisition by Marranos to fool the Catholic population into believing they were eating pork. Instead, this sausage was made with chicken, rabbit, partridge, and bread, cleverly camouflaged by garlic, hot peppers, and paprika. (Pork was eventually added as the sausage made its way into the general population.) Mahogany-colored *presunto* (Portuguese prosciutto), from Chaves and Valpaços, another of the region's delicacies, can be served as an appetizer (with or without melon), stuffed in trout, or wrapped around the latter, then quickly sautéed.

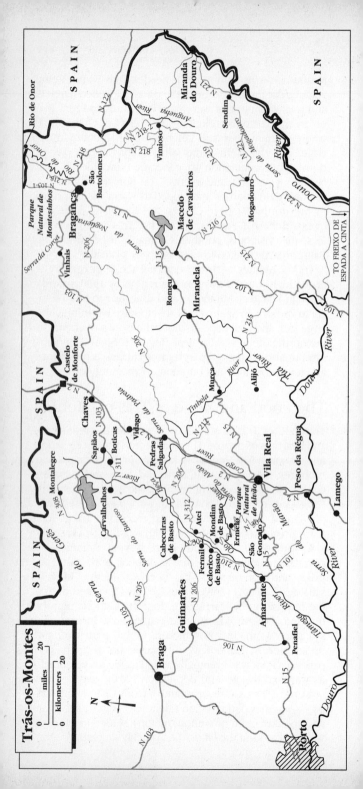

Almonds and eggs are a major ingredient in Trás-os-Montes desserts. They, together with pumpkin, make up Murça's rich *toucinho do ceu* (bacon from heaven) flan, said to have been invented by nuns, who named it after its heavenly flavor. (Lard or bacon fat may have also been used in the original recipe.)

Pão (bread) is the staple of Trás-os-Montes, and one of its finest treats. It is normally baked at high temperatures in brick or stone ovens, which accounts for its thick crust and moist, chewy interior. The best-flavored breads are baked in wood-burning ovens, together with aromatic wild flowers that add to the odor and taste. In some remote areas the bread is formed into symbolic shapes: Stars represent the sun, which provides light and warmth, and human figures refer to fertilization of the soil. During winter feast days bread pyramids, or *charolos,* are built to signify harvest plenty. The bread, blessed by the village priest, is supposed to ward off sickness and evil spirits. Scholars believe the bread cult may be a holdover from fertility rites tied to an ancient religion.

The route outlined below starts at Vila Real, near the eastern end of the Douro. It tours highlights of the scenic Serra do Alvão to its north and the Terra do Basto plateau to the northwest, before heading northeast on the N 15 toward Bragança. A southeasterly detour through almond and olive country also offers a view of the impressive Douro river ravine before it plunges into Spain, and of tiny border towns like Miranda do Douro, renowned for its veal steaks, its ancient dances, and its unique Mirandes dialect. The Parque Natural de Montesinho and its communal villages can be explored from the walled city of Bragança in the far northeast before heading west (N 103) to the spa town of Chaves, famous for its Roman bridge, its picturesque verandahs, and its *presunto,* air-cured ham, which many connoisseurs rate higher than Italian prosciutto.

VILA REAL

Vila Real, the administrative and commercial center of southern Trás-os-Montes, is the birthplace of Diogo Cão, the explorer of the Congo basin. It sits at an altitude of 4,750 feet at the edge of a gorge at the juncture of the Marão, Alvão, and Padrela mountains and the Cabril and

Corgo rivers, 57 km (36 miles) east of the eastern Douro town of Amarante, on the N 15. It is also a thriving agricultural center surrounded by apple, plum, and fig orchards, known primarily for its rosé, its Borges & Irmão Port, its earth-baked, silver-gray *olaria* (pottery), and its hand-loomed *linho* (linen) from Argarez, all of which can be purchased at the Turismo office, at avenida Carvalho Araújo, 94, or at the annual feast of Saint Peter (June 27 to 29).

The *olaria* comes primarily from the neighboring town of Bisalhães, where holes in the ground serve as kilns. The kitchen and decorative pottery (pots, jugs, platters, etc.) is placed over coals, the hole is covered so that air cannot get in, and the ashes and smoke transform the clay into an ashen-gray color. The pottery is embellished with hand-carved flower patterns and geometric designs passed down from generation to generation.

Vila Real was named after the ancient sanctuary of Panóias (5 km/3 miles northeast of the city), where the Romans used to sacrifice animals to their gods. In 1895 it became the first town to be electrified in Portugal. Today it continues to grow and modernize, but its center maintains its old charm.

The main sights are contained on and along the cobbled **avenida Carvalho Araújo**. The Sé, a former Dominican monastery with Romanesque and Gothic touches, has an unusual statue of the Virgin standing on top of a dragon. The Renaissance façade at number 19 is what remains of what is believed to have been the house of Diogo Cão, the 15th-century navigator. Farther west the impressive, monumental double staircase of the 19th-century Câmara Municipal (town hall) welcomes visitors with Baroque flair. The view of the Corgo ravine from the esplanade behind the Câmara is impressive.

The **Palácio Mateus**, 3 km (2 miles) south of Vila Real, is one of the area's showpieces and its principal claim to fame. The Baroque façade, designed by Italian architect Nicolau Nasoni, is featured on the label of the rosé and other Mateus wines. Although the building is still a residence, parts of it can be visited. Its tiny, quaint museum contains, among other things, a collection of letters from 19th-century personalities such as Wellington, Talleyrand, and Metternich. The Fundação da Casa Mateus sponsors classical music concerts and organizes guitar and music courses on the premises in August and September.

The palace can be visited daily, but is closed at

lunchtime. Unfortunately, wine tasting is not conducted on the grounds but in a modern bottling plant nearby (open 9:00 A.M. to 12:00 P.M. and 2:00 P.M. to 5:00 P.M.; closed Saturdays and Sundays).

Vila Real proper is devoid of interesting restaurants and memorable accommodations, but its environs offer idyllic alternatives. The **Casa das Quartas**, a 16th-century manor house surrounded by orchards and vineyards, sits perched on a wooded hill 4 km (2.5 miles) southeast of Vila Real (off the N 15 to Murça). The country house has three guest rooms with private baths. Guests can stroll in several levels of gardens of rose bushes, box-trimmed hedges, and fruit trees, play cards or watch television in comfortable sitting rooms elegantly furnished with patrician country antiques, or visit the private family chapel. Continental breakfast is served in your room or in the garden. Rates are reasonable, below those charged by state-run inns and some three-star hotels.

The **Pousada de São Gonçalo** lies in the serene solitude of the Marão mountains, 22 km (14 miles) west of Vila Real on the N 15. Its 15 rooms with private bath are somewhat small and uninspiring, but its views are breathtakingly rugged and its restaurant offers the best of regional cooking.

The **Pousada do Barão de Forrester**, at Alijó, 27 km (17 miles) east of Vila Real on a bucolic, vine-covered plateau, also has good food and a full selection of wines. Its rooms are done up in bright fabrics and reproductions of antiques, and its dining room is decorated with murals of grape trellises. The friendly, English-speaking staff can arrange for visits to the neighboring vineyards, where grapes are grown for some of Portugal's most famous Port wine.

Excursions from Vila Real

Retreats of great beauty and tranquillity near Vila Real are the **Parque Nacional de Alvão** and the **Terra do Basto** plateau north and northwest of Vila Real. In the spring, the rolling countryside is awash in color from thousands of wildflowers. During the winter, when its peaks are snowcapped, its valleys are dotted with *medas de palha,* corn stalks woven and centered around a pole. The *medas* are shaped like upside-down cones, in order to force rainwater to run off quickly. The stalks are used as bedding for farm animals. Crystal-clear streams run through the area's pine-studded valleys, where thatched houses are occasionally still seen. In the high passes the wind soughs over rocky crests, interrupted by the occasional shrill whistle of a shepherd calling his dogs or the tinkle of a goat's bell. A panoramic sweep of this rugged, rumpled region can be enjoyed from the heights of the **Alto do Velão**, 20 km (12.5 miles) northwest of Vila Real, on the N 304. You may spot eagles nesting above the waterfall at **Figas do Ermelo**, located farther up the road on the Olo river.

The sister towns of Mondim de Basto, Celorico de Basto, and Cabeceiras de Basto, all part of a powerful Medieval earldom, obtained their names from a famous Lusitanian warrior. **Mondim de Basto**, past Ermelo (N 304), 44 km (28 miles) northwest of Vila Real, is a charming venue on the banks of the Tâmega river, with ancient cobbled streets and Romanesque and Gothic churches. **Celorico de Basto** (N 210), a bit farther downstream on the right bank toward Amarante, is lined with manor houses and guarded by an 18th-century castle. Northwest of Mondim, on the N 304, the imposing three-story **Casa do Barão de Fermil** lords it over the family's namesake ancestral town. The yellow villa has the lines of a French château and colonial trimmings, such as raised tiles on the edges of the roof, Chinese style. It is now a bed-and-breakfast operation with all the luxuries and trappings of a Portuguese country estate. Four bedrooms (two doubles and two singles) have been set aside for guests, who can also enjoy the comforts of a spacious sitting room furnished with antiques, a large garden, and a small swimming pool. Continental breakfast is provided, and Dona Maria Fernanda Mourão, the hostess, will steer you to the best bistros in the area for hearty mountain food.

The **Casa da Granja**, an 18th-century granite manor house surrounded by box-trimmed hedges and forest, also takes in guests. It is situated in Vila Nune, 8 km (5 miles) north of Fermil on N 210. Its three double bedrooms, furnished with antiques, have views of the surrounding wooded countryside and share a cozy common room with a large fireplace. The hostess, Dona Maria da Conceição Teles de Vasconcelos, can direct you to the nearest dining spot.

In the hamlet of Cabeceiras de Basto (N 205), 11 km (7 miles) to the north, the former **Convento de Refojos**, now a church, contains a statue of the Lusitanian warrior Basto, ancient ritualistic masks, and a gilded organ supported by fauns. The Basto statue was headless until the 17th century, when it received a new one, complete with moustache and military headdress. **Atei**, across the Tâmega from Vila Nune (north on the N 312 from Mondim), has Roman ruins and a subterranean passage from the town to the banks of the river, believed to have been used as an escape route during sieges. The Basto area is known for its trout, its *cabrito assado no forno com arroz* (roast kid and rice), and its leather (belts), tin (lamps), and baskets, all of which can be bought at the local Turismo office at Mondim de Basto, on rua Comendador Alfredo Alves de Carvalho (Tel: 059-38479), or at the fair held at Mondim on the second and twenty-second of every month.

CENTRAL TRAS-OS-MONTES

The road northeast from Vila Real to Bragança (N 15) begins as a tapestry of pine trees, vineyards, olive groves, and fields of grain, and gradually gives way to an impressive lunar landscape. **Murça**, 32 km (20 miles) east of Vila Real, lies on a promontory above the Tinhela river ravine. Its famous *porca*, an Iron Age granite boar, stands in a bed of petunias in the main square. This curious animal is believed to have played a role in some prehistoric cult: Some scholars believe it may have been placed in fields to protect crops from evil spirits. During the political struggles of the 19th century the *porca* was painted blue when the conservatives won an election and red if the progressives were victorious. Murça is also known for its *toucinho do ceu* flan and for its honey, sausages, and goat cheese.

Mirandela, 31 km (19 miles) east on the sandy banks of the river Tua, has a 16th-century bridge with 20 arches. It is also celebrated for its tin and wrought-iron work, such as pots and pans, stoves, and elaborate window grilles, which can be bought in shops lining the main street in front of the river. Mirandela has a lively annual crafts fair from the last week in July to the end of the first week in August. The rolling hills around Jerusalém do Romeu (11 km/7 miles to the east) are covered with olive and cork.

After Jerusalém do Romeu turn right for a short (2.5-km/ 1.5-mile) detour to the restored granite-and-shale village of **Romeu**, home of the region's most famous eating establishment. The **Maria Rita** restaurant, on the village's sole street, is styled after a typical Trás-os-Montes patrician town house, with large dining rooms, stone fireplaces, and rustic furniture. The regional menu includes *sopa de alheiras,* a thick and spicy garlic soup loaded with *alheira* sausages, wild game, and asparagus. Whole turkeys, baby pigs, and lambs are cooked to order for parties who call in advance; Tel: (078) 93134. House wines include homemade Romeu (red), Julieta (rosé), and Romeu (Port). Don't miss the **Museu de Curiosidades** next door, which contains 19th-century fire trucks, four Model-Ts, and antique sewing machines and musical and photographic equipment. The village, its restaurant, and the museum are owned by the patrician family of Clemente Meneses, as is most of the outlying land.

After Jerusalém do Romeu, as you continue northeast on N 15 toward Bragança, 66 km (41 miles) away, the trees begin to disappear and a barren landscape takes over, as you traverse some of the most thinly populated countryside in southern Europe. If you have enough time and prefer more architecture and human contact, veer right 9 km (5.5 miles) east of Jerusalém do Romeu onto N 216, toward Macedo de Cavaleiros, for a longer route (181 km/113 miles) to Bragança via southeastern Trás-os-Montes.

SOUTHEASTERN TRAS-OS-MONTES

Almost every town in southeastern Trás-os-Montes, no matter how humble, boasts a Romanesque, a Gothic, and a Baroque church or a blend of the three, and often a castle, or at least the remains of one. The castles were mostly built in the 14th century by Dom Dinis, Portugal's builder king, to protect the country's eastern border.

Macedo de Cavaleiros

Macedo de Cavaleiros, about 6.5 km (4 miles) after the turnoff from N 15, is said to have obtained its name from two Medieval knights adept at fighting Moors with *macedos* (clubs). With the Moors now gone the sport has turned to game, and the weapons are rifles. The town continues to be a favorite of aristocrats from the north of Portugal, who maintain manor houses and hunting lodges within its limits. It is also known for its wicker baskets and crocheted bedspreads and activities including swimming at the Azibe dam and visits to the sanctuaries of Santo Ambrósio and

Nossa Senhora de Balsamão. The **Estalagem do Caçador**, lodged in the former town hall, is one of the region's finer privately owned inns. Its 25 bedrooms are all furnished with Portuguese antiques and handmade bedspreads and linen. The lodge's large salon contains a huge marble fireplace, leather chairs, elaborate gros-point rugs from Arraiolos, and hunting curios. Its dining room is traditionally Portuguese, with carved leather-backed chairs, hand-crocheted tablecloths, and elaborate silverware and china. Game dishes, prepared during the hunting season (September through February), include Port-marinated partridge and fricasseed hare; veal steaks stuffed with *presunto* are a year-round specialty. The cellar stocks the family estate-bottled Valperdinhas red wine. A rose garden and a marble-lined swimming pool are other attractive features. This moderately priced establishment, owned by a Porto publishing magnate, tends to fill up in hunting season, so if you plan to visit during the fall, you had better book well in advance.

The ruins of a 12th-century fortress overlook the town of **Mogadouro**, 50 km (31 miles) southeast of Macedo on N 216, which is known for its wood crafts (chairs, religious objects, and kitchenware), and its woollen (blankets and clothes) and leather goods (harnesses). In the early spring the neighboring Serra da Castanheira is clothed in a white mantle of blooming chestnut trees.

Guarded by an imposing tower, **Freixo de Espada à Cinta** sits surrounded by millions of almond trees on a fertile plain in the southeastern corner of Trás-os-Montes, 45 km (28 miles) south of Mogadouro on N 221. There are several versions as to how the town obtained its unusual name of "Ash Tree with a Sword around It": from a Visigoth nobleman named Espadacinta; from Dom Dinis, who hung his sword on an ash tree here and rested in its shade. Another tale says the town was named after a valiant nobleman from León, whose coat of arms bore an ash and a sword, who defended Freixo against the Moors.

To encourage the settlement of this remote town 4 km/ 2.5 miles from the Spanish border, Portuguese kings made Freixo a sanctuary for fugitives, giving selected condemned prisoners their freedom in exchange for living here. King Afonso Henriques gave the town its charter in the 12th century, and King Dinis built its main fortifications in the late 13th century. It subsequently became a prosperous silk center.

The seven-sided **Torre do Galo** (Cock's Tower), which offers a fine view of the almond-tree-studded valley, is the last of four similar structures built by King Dinis. It stands beside the lovely parish church, construction of which was begun in the 14th century and completed 400 years later. The famous Spanish Plateresque, or Neo-Manueline, architect João de Castilho, who was married to a woman from Freixo, added the Renaissance touches to the elegant Gothic doorway. The interior is rich and impressive, adorned with an elaborate wrought-iron pulpit, a wood-carved chancel, and painted wall panels attributed to the 16th-century master Vasco Fernandes (Grão Vasco), for whom see the Beira Alta chapter.

Freixo produced some of Portugal's greatest missionaries, including Jorge Alvares, the first monk to preach in Japan. It is also the birthplace of the satirical poet Guerra Junqueiro (1850 to 1923).

The best time to visit the town is in the early spring, when the millions of flowering almond trees transform the valley into a white bower. The **Quinta da Boa Vista**, a small tourist development on the town's outskirts, consists of four independent houses, with three airy bedrooms furnished with modern touches. There is a fairly good restaurant, a bar, a swimming pool, and tennis courts.

Take N 221 toward Mogadouro for 10 km (6 miles), and turn right at the sign for **Mazouco**, where donkeys continue to be a major means of transport and some villagers still make their own sausages and cheeses. Leave your car in the square and ask any of the locals to guide you to **O Carneiro** (the sheep), a Paleolithic rock carving engraved on the steep canyon wall that drops precipitously down to the Douro river southeast of the village.

Golden eagles, black storks, and Egyptian vultures still nest on the ledges and crannies of the tall cliffs of this gorge, which runs north to south for 70 miles from Miranda do Douro to Barca de Alva.

Despite its small size, **Sendim**, on N 221 near the border (27 km/17 miles east of Mogadouro), boasts one of Portugal's most famous restaurants, **Gabriela**. Alice, the cook and second-generation owner of the 70-year-old restaurant, has beguiled Portuguese presidents with her food and catered banquets. Her culinary awards include a Coq d'Or. Guests of this rustic no-frills establishment, located in the town square, can watch Alice preside over a wood fire in her large kitchen. Her mouth-watering *posta*

Mirandesa à Gabriela is a large veal steak cooked over an open fire fueled by grape and olive vines. She guards the recipes of her sauces as closely as the local *curandeiros* do their cures.

Miranda do Douro

Miranda do Douro, perched above the Douro river and its ravine across from Spain, 22 km (14 miles) northeast of Sendim on N 221, was for centuries the linchpin in the string of fortified towns defending the northeastern border and the seat of an important bishopric. It grew prosperous from its trade with Spain under the rule of the powerful Tâvora grandees, and was the center of culture and religion of Trás-os-Montes during the Renaissance. During the 18th century, however, the persecution of the Tâvoras by the autocratic prime minister Marquês de Pombal, who grew wary of their growing power, a series of invasions, and the loss of the bishop's seat to Bragança plunged Miranda do Douro into a decline from which it is only now starting to emerge. A new border post, new road links to Spain, and the recent construction of a dam are all behind its reemergence.

Miranda's 16th-century cathedral, rich in gold, houses the curious statue of the Meníno Jesus da Cartolina, a baby Jesus sporting a top hat. It is said to represent a boy who miraculously appeared during a siege of the town by the Spanish in 1711 and led the Portuguese to victory. Little remains of Miranda's castle, which was destroyed during another Spanish siege in 1762, but its crenellated **Torre de Menagem** (keep), the temporary headquarters of Wellington during the Peninsular Wars, still stands.

Miranda's culture and folklore are still thriving. It has its own dialect, Mirandes, a blend of low Latin, archaic Portuguese, Galician (northwestern Spanish), and Hebrew, which is still spoken and taught locally. The **Museu da Terra de Miranda** contains furniture and costumes of the region and archaeological artifacts, such as pre-Roman double-edged axes and spears, Celtic jewelry, Roman lapidaries, scales, and pottery, Moorish daggers, and carved stones from an old synagogue. During the Festas da Santa Bárbara (third Sunday in August) and the Romaria de Nossa Senhora de Nazaré (early September) you can admire the town's ancient and colorful folk dances: the *pingacho* (rough ballet), the *Geribalda* (a round dance), and the *Mira-me Miguel* (a square dance);

and watch its *pauliteiros* (stick dancers), men clad in white flannel shirts, aprons, and flower-covered hats who perform ritualized sword fights to the accompaniment of bagpipes, cymbals, and drums. The *pauliteiro* troop is run by the energetic former priest of neighboring Duas Igrejas, the director of Miranda's museum, who is the self-appointed champion of Mirandes culture.

Miranda is known for its hooded, hand-embroidered brown woollen capes and waistcoats, worn by the town's important men during ceremonies and feast days; its *facas de palacoulo* (knives with forks attached to them, used by the shepherds of the region); and its braised *posta à Mirandesa* (veal steaks), which can be tasted at the **Mirandes**, a rustic family-run restaurant. The **Pousada Santa Catarina**, a simple 12-room inn 3 km (2 miles) northeast of Miranda do Douro (N 122), overlooking the dam, is spartanly decorated but has nice views of the calm waters of the dam and across the plain of Zamora. The restaurant serves small game such as stewed partridge and rabbit during the winter hunting season, and Douro river trout wrapped in *presunto* and sautéed in butter. The area's garlicky *fumeiro* (smoked mixed sausage) is a savory appetizer.

NORTHEASTERN TRAS-OS-MONTES

The tiny **Castelo de Algoso**, which sits on the rocky Cabeço da Penedia promontory above the river Angueira about halfway between Miranda and the northeastern town of Bragança, has a fine vista of the surrounding countryside, dotted with olive groves, and the Maças river below. To get to the castle, which at one time belonged to the Knights of Malta, drive 29 km (18 miles) northwest from Miranda do Douro on N 218 toward Bragança and turn right onto N 219 near Vimioso. The castle, commanded by a large tower, is 2 km (1.2 miles) past Vimioso. Leave the car by the river and walk up a steep hill to the rocky crest.

Bragança

For a remote outpost in the northeastern corner of Portugal, the walled town of Bragança (known as Brigantia by the Celts and Juliobriga by the Romans) has left a decided mark on Portuguese history. The house of Bragança, founded by the bastard son of King João I in 1442, ruled Portugal from 1640 until 1910, when it was ousted by the Republic.

The town commands a high promontory on the barren slopes of the Serra da Nogueira 2,165 feet above sea level. Its Medieval walls and citadel are among the best preserved in Portugal. It was a major rope-making and silk center in the 15th and 16th centuries, with an important community of Jewish merchants. Although the Inquisition forced many Jews to convert, some families chose to go underground and continue to practice their faith in secret. Copper (kitchenware), leather goods (jackets, belts, bags), wool blankets, and basket weaving have replaced silk in the shops in the praça da Sé, the town's main square.

The citadel's **Torre de Menagem** (keep) houses the town's military museum and memorabilia from the Spanish and Napoleonic wars, during which Bragança was occupied. The **Torre da Princesa**, beside it, is haunted by tragic ghosts. The comely wife of the fourth duke of Bragança, Dona Leonor, was locked up here by her husband, who could not bear that any other man should lay eyes on her. When he moved his court south he had her murdered. The shaft of a Medieval pillory in front of the castle is driven through a granite statue of a boar, believed to have formed part of an Iron Age cult. Some scholars believe that the boar, like Murça's *porca,* served as a large amulet against evil spirits. The **Domus Municipalis**, a rare and beautiful example of an Iberian Romanesque civic building, lies on the southern end of the citadel beside the 16th-century **church of Santa Maria**. The pentagonal 12th-century building has an elegant frieze of carved medallions lining its walls and a cistern in the middle. The building served as the meeting place of the *homens bons* (good men), or city officials, and now offers a cool haven from the scorching summer heat.

Outside the citadel walls, at rua Conselheiro Abílio Beça, in the 18th-century palace of the bishops, is the **Museu Regional Abade de Baçal** (Abbot of Baçal). Its garden contains archaeological remains dating back to the Iron Age, and its two floors exhibit Trás-os-Montes furniture, tools, ancient coins, church plate and vestments, Indo-Portuguese furniture, and paintings. The abbot of Baçal (1865 to 1945) was a diminutive and energetic scholar who recorded the history and customs of the region, including those of its Jews, who played a major role in the silk trade. The museum is closed at lunchtime and on Mondays.

Bragança gained prominence in 1780, when the bishop moved there from Miranda do Douro. His seat was installed in a heavy 16th-century Jesuit building in the praça da Sé. On the north side of the square lies the **Solar Bragançano**, an intimate restaurant housed in a former town house. Wooden ceilings, chandeliers, and Arraiolos rugs provide an Old World touch, but don't affect the reasonable prices of this establishment frequented by Bragança's elite. House specialties are *cabrito branco a Montesinho* (white Montesinho kid), baked cod with boiled potatoes, and veal steak *solar* style, with egg and orange rinds. The region's semisweet *favalos* (muscatel) can be enjoyed with hors d'oeuvres of *alheiras* (spiced sausages) or Portugal's "queen of cheeses," *queijo de serra* (sheep cheese from the Beira Alta). **La em Casa**, on rua Marquês de Pombal, is an earthier alternative, with rustic regional touches in its pottery, copper, and ironware (closed Mondays).

A splendid view of the walls and citadel of Bragança and the surrounding mountains can be had from the balconies of the 16 rooms and from the restaurant of the **Pousada de São Bartolomeu**, which sits on a hill about a mile west of town. The inn also has a comfortable salon, with a huge stone fireplace and wood-paneled bar. Its posh restaurant serves both regional and international cuisine, and wild boar, partridge, and hare during the hunting season. The cook is also known for his *cozido à transmontana,* a hearty stew containing several meats and vegetables, and *feijoada à transmontana,* a good winter white-bean casserole containing pork and sausage (be warned, however, that the dish contains pig's ears). The pousada is popular with travelling businessmen throughout the year and tends to fill up, so we suggest booking several months in advance.

The former monastery of **Castro de Avelas**, 5 km (3 miles) north of Bragança off the N 103 to Chaves, is a handsome, unusual structure composed of three curious cylindrical towers. This former Benedictine center of worship has Moorish and Romanesque touches and is believed to have been built in the 12th century. It was abandoned in the 19th century when the religious orders were banned and is now inhabited by doves. Try chanting inside, and its walls will reward your efforts.

Parque Natural de Montesinhos

Wolves, foxes, and wild boars inhabit the 185,000-acre Parque Natural de Montesinhos, between Bragança and the northern border with Spain, which contains some of the wildest bush country in Portugal. The park also comprises self-sufficient villages like Rio de Onor, where communal life and pre-Christian pagan rituals are still practiced. The inhabitants still believe in the evil eye and *bruxas* (witches). This is one of the areas in which bread plays a major role in religious events: Between Christmas and Epiphany, the unmarried men in some villages, such as Sacoias and Varge (north on 218-1), don hideous devil masks and "frighten" the women of the village into donating food and wine to the church. Villagers construct tall pyramids of bread, eggs, and sausages, called *charolos,* and take them to the church to be blessed and auctioned off, then ceremoniously eaten. The blessed bread is supposed to ward off sickness and evil spirits. It is also said to represent fecundity.

The village of **Rio de Onor** straddles the border with Spain in a fertile valley 24 km (15 miles) northeast of Bragança on N 218-1. Its citizens still own certain pastures in common, rotate chores, and have a democratic (albeit all-male) governing body. Two *mordomos* (majordomos) are elected yearly to conduct town business. Not long ago the village owned a communal pair of shoes that men wore on their visits to the "big city" of Bragança. The rest of the year they went barefoot or wore wooden clogs. The village is a diplomatic anomaly: Half of it lies in Portugal and the other in Spain. Its inhabitants cross freely from one side to the other, share the same grocery store on the Spanish side, and have intermarried for centuries. To reach Rio de Onor from Bragança (24 km/ 15 miles) take the N 218 east out of town, veer left onto N 218-1, turn right 2 km (1.25 miles) past the airport, and follow the signs to Rio de Onor.

West of Bragança

The N 103 west to Chaves (96 km/60 miles) from Bragança is a scenic route winding through oak and chestnut woods surmounted by the bare peaks of the *serras* (mountain ranges) of Montesinho and Coroa. Round, whitewashed *pombais* (pigeon houses), where pigeons are raised for eating, alternate with trout farms and cattle grazing on steep slopes.

Vinhais and the remains of its 14th-century castle crown a high mountain pass overlooking a fertile valley planted with apple orchards 34 km (21 miles) west of Bragança. An important and wealthy monastic enclave up to the 19th century, when the religious orders were banished, Vinhais has lost some of its prosperity and glitter. Villagers have built homes inside the castle grounds and chickens and goats run free in its former courtyard. The **Igreja de São Francisco**, which perches atop a flight of steps off the main rua dos Frades, is a faded beauty today. Gone are its rich ceiling paintings, but the elaborate gilded altar and polychrome statues of saints survive. The church was originally part of a larger convent, which was divided during the religious turmoil of the 19th century in order to keep it from falling into private hands. Seminarians have since returned to the convent next door, renamed Encarnação. To visit the church, get the keys from the nuns, who live in a yellow house on the western corner of the courtyard. The pretty Visigothic **Igreja de São Facundo** sits on the grounds of the cemetery in the valley below the town. It has a fine exterior decorated with carved heads.

More contemporary wood carving, such as yokes for ox carts, wooden furniture, walking sticks, and kitchen utensils, can be obtained at the town's colorful biweekly market held on the ninth and twenty-third of each month at the soccer field, on the western corner of the town past the convent. Other items include the area's Pinheiro cream cheeses, woollen blankets, mountain boots, donkey and mule saddles, and other farming paraphernalia, sold by black-garbed Gypsies and other itinerant merchants. Peasants from the surrounding countryside park their donkeys and carts on the main street to visit the market.

THE ALTO TAMEGA

The wide, fertile valley of the upper Tâmega river, surrounding the town of Chaves, has always attracted settlers and invaders alike: the former for its rich soil, the latter because it represented a breach in the otherwise impregnable wall of mountains protecting the north from Spain. It is strewn with Celtic and Roman remains, with thermal springs and spas. Luiz de Camões, Portugal's 16th-century poet laureate, was a native of the region.

Chaves

Chaves ("keys") lies at the center of the Alto Tâmega valley. It received its name from the keys given to Nuno Alvares Pereira by João I, father of Prince Henry the Navigator, for his valiant service at the battle of Aljubarrota in 1385, in which the Portuguese vanquished a much larger Spanish force.

Chaves is known for its *presunto* and for its thermal springs. The Romans named it Aqua Flaviae and mined the gold and iron of the area. The Ponte Trajano, built in A.D. 104, turned the town into an important junction on the Roman road linking Braga to the south with the northern town of Astorga in Galicia, Spain. The bridge is still in use, but the rest of the Roman town lies under modern Chaves, waiting to be excavated.

Most of the historic sites are in and around the Medieval **praça de Camões**. The **Museu da Região Flaviense**, with objects depicting the life of the people in the region, is housed in a former 15th-century palace of the dukes of Bragança. It also contains an important collection of Roman coins from the first to the fourth centuries A.D., along with minting instruments. The adjoining **Museu Militar** is lodged in the town's 12th-century keep. The manicured gardens of the keep display archaeological remains dating back to the Iron Age, and its ramparts provide a sweeping view of the Tâmega and the surrounding countryside. You can gaze at the garden from **Dionisyos**, a bistro-style restaurant with both indoor and outdoor dining, located in the adjacent praça do Município.

The praça de Camões also contains an ornate Manueline **Pelourinho** (pillory), which was a symbolic column bestowed on towns by kings giving the municipality the right to dispense justice. (Earlier versions also served as a gallows.) The lovely Romanesque doorway of the parish church beside it was uncovered during recent restorative work. The interior of the Baroque **Igreja da Misericórdia** next door is embellished with 18th-century *azulejos* depicting the life of Christ.

Chaves is called the *"cidade das varandas"* because of the colorfully painted wooden verandahs on the eastern side of the square and the neighboring rua Direita.

On the eastern side of town are the two 17th-century

Vaubanesque fortresses of São Francisco and São Neutal (neither open to the public). The curative waters at the health spa beside the river, at 73 degrees Celsius (160 degrees Fahrenheit), are said to be Europe's warmest. For something more filling, cross the Ponte Trajano to the left bank, turn left, and head down to the largo de São Roque. The tiny **Restaurante Campismo**, named after the camping area in front of it, a rustic family-run establishment, offers gracious service and fine cooking. Trout stuffed with the town's renowned *presunto* and *cabrito no churrasco* (spit-roasted kid) are specialties. The tart, somewhat cloudy house white wine goes well with fish. A more robust, dry red from neighboring Valpaços is also recommended. No credit cards accepted. Closed Thursdays.

O Pote, a lively restaurant about a kilometer from the center of town on the main road to Spain (N 103-5), is a good place to try *bolas de carne* (minced beef balls in tomato sauce). Another treat is *pão de presunto,* a hearty bread baked with slices of the area's rich ham.

Chaves may boast about its food, but its accommodations are another matter. The **Hotel Trajano**, a comfortable though colorless hotel with a wood-and-tile decor, is your best bet. The rooms are clean and furnished with pine furniture and linen bedspreads. Its dining room is somewhat dark but does serve fairly good food. The hotel stands on the quiet and cobbled travessa Cândido dos Reis, east of the praça de Camões. Roman baths, discovered during the hotel's construction, were unfortunately covered up again.

Faustino and Filhos, one of the country's largest *tascas* (taverns), housed in a warehouse nearby at travessa do Olival, 12, is a good place to mingle with farmers and other local folk and taste regional wines, drawn from huge vats.

Chaves is at the end of the national railway's scenic **Linha do Corgo**, which links it to Peso da Régua 90 km (56 miles) to the south on the Douro river (see Getting Around, below). A railway museum is lodged in a hangar beside the main train station.

The imposing **Castelo de Monforte** lies off N 103 14 km (9 miles) northeast of Chaves on a wind-swept promontory. The 14th-century structure was built by King Dinis around the remains of a Romanized Lusitanian *castro* to protect the Tâmega valley. It was used at different times as a prison and as a refuge for fugitives. From its ramparts you have a clear view of Spain and the mountains to the north and can gain a sense of the isolation and hard life of the frontier people. To reach the *castelo* you must brave a bumpy, but short (1 km), dirt road. Visits are conducted from 3:00 P.M. to 6:00 P.M. daily.

Vidago

The spa town of Vidago, 17 km (10 miles) southwest of Chaves on the N 2, holds the key to accommodations in the area. The royal family frequented this spa and made it popular at the end of the 19th century. The **Vidago Palace Hotel** was inaugurated in 1910 by Manuel II, the last king of Portugal. The Belle Epoque hotel sits in a lush park west of the train station, surrounded by gardens, ponds, and fountains. The old girl has lost some of her luster over the years, but you can still detect her earlier original glory in the majestic entrance and the large, imposing dining room lined with wrought-iron Doric columns, where waiters in white livery serve a choice of set meals consisting of international hotel food and some regional dishes. The charming, moderately priced hotel does have a modern annex behind it, with state-of-the-art rooms, an outdoor swimming pool, a disco, and several tennis courts. Romantic afternoons can be spent rowing in the hotel's man-made pond, which is populated by swans.

Outeiro Machado

Of all the archaeological remains that abound in the area around Chaves, the rock carvings outside Outeiro Machado may be the most interesting. The 165-foot-long granite boulder, carved by Neolithic artists with ladders, axes, and other symbols, is believed to have been used by Celtic Druids for sacrifices. Part of the stone was damaged when villagers, inspired by rumors of hidden gold, used dynamite to try to dislodge it.

To reach the stone head west out of Chaves on the Vale de Anta and Soutelo road, turn right at a yellow sign advertising "Arte Rupestre" about 3 km (2 miles) out of Chaves, and follow the dirt road and signs for about 1 km to an open field. The boulder is easy to spot, right in the middle of the field.

The Serra do Barroso

The Serra do Barroso, centered some 50 km (31 miles) west-southwest of Chaves, is famous for its beautiful longhorned Barroso oxen and for its drinking waters. The people of Boticas, at the entrance of the *serra* (turn left [south] at Sapiãos onto N 312 from N 103, west out of Chaves) are known for their curious practice of burying their wine in the ground for a year. The custom began in the early 19th century, during the Napoleonic invasions, when the townsfolk decided to hide their wine rather than let the French soldiers consume it. When the French left and they unearthed the wine, they discovered that it had improved. They began calling the buried wine bottles *mortos* (dead), and the unearthing process *levantar um morto* (raising the dead). You can taste the wine at the vine-covered **Santa Cruz** restaurant, poised on a hill overlooking the Beça river. Large, succulent portions of braised beef, hare, and trout, plus moist country bread, are prepared in an open kitchen by village women. The look is pure country. Homemade sausages and ham are also served. No credit cards accepted.

For entertainment, and to improve their cattle stock, villages in the vicinity compete during the summer in *chegas de toros,* pitting their champion bulls against each other. The bulls are treated like sports heroes, paraded with bands and given food by the patrons, who cheer them on and goad them to battle. The fight ends when one bull gores the other to death or one turns and runs away. At the end of the season the champion is rewarded by being put to pasture with the local cows.

The **Estalagem de Carvalhelhos** is a simple country inn set in the midst of woods, springs, and gardens in Carvalhelhos, 8 km (5 miles) west of Boticas on N 311. Its drinking water is among the best in the north, its restaurant's service is attentive, and the cooking is homey and country style. The moderately priced establishment, with 20 spacious double bedrooms with bath, is open only from June to October.

The neighboring Iron Age *castro,* with its moat, double-walled perimeter, and circular homes, is one of the best-preserved in the country. It sits at the end of a dirt road on the hill above the estalagem. Don't be surprised to see an occasional blond shepherd in the region; he is probably the descendant of the Swabians, a Germanic pastoral people who populated the area in the fifth century A.D.

For maps and further information on the region, contact the Turismo office in Chaves at terreiro da Cacalaria; Tel: (076) 21029. Its staff speaks English and is very helpful.

Montalegre sits 3,000 feet above sea level on a rocky promontory facing the Larouco mountains and Spain to the north, in the northwestern corner of the province, 43 km (27 miles) west of Chaves. The town, known for its tasty potatoes, is dominated by an imposing, heavyset castle, built by King Dinis in the 14th century over the ruins of a 13th-century fortress. The castle, which is composed of two towers and a keep and surrounded by a semicircular wall and battlements, has been extensively restored. Roman stones with Latin inscriptions, found in the surrounding area, are also exhibited in the courtyard. From the battlements you see a small stream spanned by an ancient stone bridge; women often do laundry on its banks.

The tiny **church of Misericórdia**, which stands in the main village square, has an elaborate three-layered gilt reredos, its columns adorned with carvings of acanthus leaves.

Montalegre is slowly emerging from the Middle Ages, with government money coming in to fund an agricultural research facility and to support a new army barracks. Right now, however, donkey carts with round wooden frames continue to be the main form of transport to border villages inside the rugged *serra* to the north.

GETTING AROUND

Major places in the Trás-os-Montes are fairly well connected by road, train, and plane. The best way to see the region, however, is by car, which has to be picked up in Porto or Lisbon, as there are no agency rentals in the region. The Linhas Aereas Regionais (LAR) flies to Vila Real and Bragança from Lisbon and Porto. LAR reservations can be made domestically at Porto's airport (Tel: 02-24656; Telex: 20406) and the Lisbon airport (Tel: 01-88-71-62; Telex: 63505), or through the national airline offices.

Three scenic train lines connect the region with the Douro valley and Porto. The **Linha do Corgo** runs from Peso da Régua on the Douro north through Port-wine country to Vila Real, then on to the upper Tâmega valley. Before reaching Chaves on its five-hour journey, the train climbs the spectacular Alvão mountains and stops at the wooded spa towns of Pedras Salgadas and Vidago.

The **Linha da Tua**, which has vintage wooden cars and seats and is pulled by a coal-fired engine, is the most scenic and rustic in all of Portugal. Its four-hour journey starts at Tua, east of Pinhão in the eastern Douro, and runs northeast toward Bragança past two mountain ranges.

The single-track **Linha do Tâmega** line links the tiny town of Arco de Baulhe in the high western Terra do Basto plateau to the western Douro. Its most interesting stretch is a 50-km (31-mile) run between Arco de Baulhe and Amarante, at the junction of Trás-os-Montes, the Douro, and the Minho. The train begins its run through a green countryside streaked with stone fences. It stops at picturesque country towns like Celorico and Mondim de Basto, whose stations are decorated with tiled panels and flowers, and follows the river through forests and vineyards and past country estates to Amarante. The trip takes about two hours, in either direction. There is a train museum at Arco de Baulhe housing vintage engines and train paraphernalia. You can take a bus to this tiny station from Chaves or drive (76 km/48 miles) by taking the N 2 south toward Vila Real and turning west onto N 226 at Vila Pouça de Aguiar.

Tickets for all three trains can be bought at the railway stations or through travel agencies. Tourist passes are available with discounts of 25 percent for one to three weeks' duration. Rail travel in Portugal is inexpensive, and first class is definitely worth the small extra cost. Children under 4 travel free on laps, and youngsters between 4 and 12 pay half fare. Soft drinks can be purchased, and passengers bring snacks—or sometimes whole meals, complete with wine, which they are known to share. Advance booking is normally not necessary. Information on schedules and tickets can be obtained at the Turismo offices and at the main train station of Campanhã in Porto; Tel: (02) 56-41-41.

ACCOMMODATIONS REFERENCE

▶ **Casa do Barão de Fermil**. 4890 **Fermil** (Veade). Tel: (055) 36211.

▶ **Pousada do Barão de Forrester**. Rua José Rufino, **Alijó**, 5070 Vila Real. Tel: (059) 95467; Telex: 26364.

▶ **Quinta da Boa Vista**. 5180 **Freixo de Espada à Cinta**. Tel: (078) 62145.

▶ **Estalagem do Caçador**. Largo Manuel Pinto Azevedo, **Macedo de Cavaleiros**, 5340 Bragança. Tel: (078) 42354.

▶ **Estalagem de Carvalhelhos**. Carvalhelhos, 5460 Boticas. Tel: (076) 42116.

- **Casa da Granja. Vila Nune,** 4860 Cabeceiras de Basto. Tel: (053) 52195.
- **Casa das Quartas. Alambres,** 5000 Vila Real. Tel: (059) 22976.
- **Pousada Santa Catarina.** Estrada da Barragem, **Miranda do Douro,** 5210 Bragança. Tel: (073) 42255.
- **Pousada de São Bartolomeu.** Estrada de Turismo, 5300 **Bragança.** Tel: (073) 22493; Telex: 22613.
- **Pousada de São Gonçalo.** Serra do Marão, **Amarante,** 4600 Porto. Tel: (055) 46-11-13; Telex: 26321.
- **Hotel Trajano.** Travessa Cândido dos Reis, **Chaves,** 5400 Vila Real. Tel: (076) 22415.
- **Vidago Palace Hotel.** 5425 **Vidago.** Tel: (076) 97356.

Pousadas can be booked through Marketing Ahead, 433 Fifth Avenue, New York, N.Y. 10016; Tel: (212) 686-9213.

MADEIRA

By Jean Anderson

And now our course took us into regions and past islands already discovered by the great Prince Henrique. First came Madeira, so called from its many forests. This was the earliest of the islands to be settled by Portugal and the best known to fame. Although set on the very edge of the known world, none of those beloved by Venus can outshine it, had it too been hers she would quickly have forgotten Cyprus, Gnido, Paphos, and Cythera. (Camões, The Lusiads, 1572)

Could Portugal's epic poet have oversold the island of Madeira? Not at all. Its effect, even in today's age of tourism, is magical.

Some say that Madeira is a vestige of Atlantis, that legendary—or maybe not so legendary—continent that vanished beneath the sea sometime before the dawn of history. Certainly there's the look of legend everywhere about Madeira, the otherworldliness of Shangri-La.

For João Gonçalves Zarco and Tristão Vaz Teixeira, two of Prince Henry's able Portuguese navigators who sailed here in 1420, this green, rumpled island was paradise found—particularly after puny, barren Porto Santo just 25 miles northeast, where they'd been blown ashore a year earlier with fellow navigator Bartolomeu Perestrelo. Stranded on Porto Santo for weeks while they readied their storm-battered ships for their return to Portugal, the explorers surveyed the southern horizon and the cloudbank that always seemed to hover there. Did the Ocean of Darkness lie just beyond? The end of the world? This was the early 15th century, a time when the Atlantic was still known as "The Green Sea of

Gloom," when sailors, more superstitious than scientific, believed in a flat earth, mermaids, and monsters of the deep.

The following year, on orders from their prince, who reasoned that land lay behind the shroud of fog, the navigators returned to Porto Santo to investigate. Cautiously they pushed south and slipped into the curtain of cloud. What they beheld, rising thousands of feet above them, was an island so majestic, so lushly forested that they promptly named it Madeira (which means "wood").

With the voyages of discovery just beginning, Madeira's sheltered harbor, at what is now Funchal, offered Prince Henry's navigators a strategic way station as they explored the west coast of Africa. And its forests provided valuable timber for the caravels that would conquer the seas during the rest of the 15th century.

What those early explorers soon learned—and most travellers today fail to realize—is that Madeira is not a single island but an entire Atlantic archipelago, located some 360 miles off the west coast of Morocco and 557 miles southwest of Lisbon.

There are eight Madeira islands in all: the three Desertas, clearly visible on the eastern horizon from Funchal, the three barren Selvagens, more than 190 miles farther south near the Canary islands (which belong to Spain), and the two inhabited islands that concern us here—Madeira and Porto Santo. All of the islands are volcanic, and their tumultuous topography suggests the violence with which they were heaved during the Tertiary Era from an ocean floor more than four miles down. These island peaks today, especially those of Madeira, seem so savage, so razor sharp, it's difficult to believe that the primeval holocaust that shaped them took place more than 30 million years ago.

As islands go, the Madeiras are small, mere volcanic chips that seem to float upon the sea. Porto Santo, which has little to brag about other than 6 miles of sandy beach, measures a meager 9 by 3 miles, and Madeira (Prince Henry's "bigger, better island") just 36 by 14 miles. But consider this: Madeira's mountainous backbone, which runs from east to west, rises to heights of more than 6,000 feet, which means that in 11 short km (7 miles) you can drive from sea level to crags above the clouds, passing through at least five distinct botanical zones. Along the coast there are banana and sugar-cane plantations; as you move upward these give way to vineyards, then scraps of garden planted with cabbages and potatoes, then misty forests of mimosa and *vinháticos* (Madeira mahogany), and finally to heathery moors reminiscent of Scotland.

Madeira itself offers just about anything else a body could want: plenty of posh resort hotels with pools as big as soccer fields (to compensate for the lack of sandy beaches)... remote country inns... major wine, wicker, and embroidery industries... a sophisticated capital (Funchal) with a casino and loads of good restaurants... storybook towns shelved high in the hills... a terrain so green, so creased by terraces it looks as if someone had draped the island with emerald corduroy... and, not least, balmy daytime temperatures that seem permanently stuck around 70 degrees Fahrenheit—at least along the south shore. In the mountains and on the north shore temperatures are always cooler, sometimes significantly so, and there's always more rain there, too, so it's best to carry a sweater and raincoat as you travel about the island.

MAJOR INTEREST

The capital city of Funchal
Madeira wine
Embroidery and other handicrafts
Mercado dos Lavradores (market)
The great gardens
The volcano village of Curral das Freiras
The wicker village of Camacha
Pico do Arieiro and Pico Ruivo, Madeira's highest peaks
The thatched village of Santana
The south shore, especially clifftop views from Câmara de Lobos and Cabo Girão
The rugged north shore
The drive around the western tip of Madeira
The high plateau of Paúl da Serra
The island of Porto Santo (for those who demand nothing more than a sandy beach to snooze upon)

Given the big-city gridlock of contemporary Funchal, not to mention the extraordinary complexity of the postage-stamp farms, vineyards, and irrigation ditches (*levadas*) hacked into Madeira's near-vertical slopes, it seems impossible that this island was uninhabited when Prince

Henry's navigators discovered it in the 15th century. But the colonists sent to settle it and Porto Santo began with a blank canvas.

Prince Henry wasted no time developing the islands, especially water- and soil-rich Madeira. It's said that in their haste to clear the land the colonists set fire to the forests, which then smoldered for seven years. It may be so. At any rate, a rich ash was laid down in which cuttings of the Malvasia grape, imported from Crete, and shoots of Sicilian sugar cane quickly took root.

Within decades, Madeira sugar and wine were both turning a profit. Just 30 years after Madeira was discovered, the Venetian explorer Cadamosto remarked on the quality of the island wine. And not so very much later Shakespeare mentioned it in *Henry IV:* "Jack," Poins asks Falstaff in act I, scene two, "how agrees the devil and thee about thy soul that thou soldest to him on Good Friday last for a cup of Madeira and a cold capon's leg?"

Both industries thrive today, but tourism is the big money machine. This isn't, as you might think, a jet-age phenomenon. Quite the contrary. Island tourism began more than 200 years ago, when fragile British ladies were sent down to winter in Madeira's sunny climes. At about the same time the British navy discovered that this palmy Atlantic island was a perfect spot for R & R and routinely put its sailors ashore there after months at sea.

In addition, Britons homeward bound from Africa or India believed that nothing could reacclimatize them to the cold, raw winters of home, even prevent consumption, like a few weeks on Madeira, so they began to break their journeys there. Some of them never left, which explains why you see so many blond, blue-eyed Madeirans.

A number of Scots and Englishmen, deciding that there were fortunes to be made in Madeira, relocated there, and to this day their descendants control much of the local hotel, shipping, bunkering, wine, and embroidery businesses. A little-known fact: Portugal very nearly handed Madeira over to England in 1661 as part of the marriage agreement between Catherine of Bragança and Charles II, but decided to hold back and play its trump card only if England demanded more in the way of a dowry from the Portuguese princess. England didn't, and so the Madeira islands remain Portuguese to this day, an autonomous entity with representation in the national parliament.

Even 200 years ago it didn't take long for word of Madeira's healthful climate to spread, and soon many of

Europe's noble families, its princes of finance, even a few of its crowned heads, began building expensive quintas (estates) in and around Funchal. For a while during the 19th and early 20th centuries, Madeira was a watering hole every bit as fashionable as Baden-Baden and the French Riviera.

The island's place in the sun lasted longer than that of most stylish resorts, mostly because it was too difficult—and expensive—for Everyman to reach. But by the 1960s, when engineers finally managed to hack a landing strip into the side of a mountain on the eastern end of Madeira, the gilded set had already defected to exotic new dots on the map.

As might be expected, the winter-weary of Europe now whizzing down to Madeira aboard 727s from Lisbon—and charters from elsewhere—are more hip and less stuffy than their predecessors. But it's the island's 12-months-of-June climate that they seek, just as their forerunners did. They find it, as visitors always have, at Funchal, on the sheltered south shore, which is spared most of the "weather" blustering in from the north.

How much time should you allow Madeira? It all depends on your interests and, to some degree, your budget, because Madeira costs more than the rest of Portugal (except maybe for the resort complexes in the Algarve). In the old days visitors settled in for the winter. Even today winter remains the high season, from a social standpoint at least. You'll find it difficult to obtain rooms in Funchal during the Christmas/New Year's and Easter holidays, because the "regulars" book months ahead of time, often reserving the same quarters year after year. But the weather changes little, so it really doesn't matter what time of year you come, although it's apt to rain around the spring and fall equinoxes.

Most travellers today spend about a week on Madeira, or maybe split a week between Madeira and Porto Santo. There's no question that a week will give you plenty of time to sunbathe, to "do" Funchal, and to see most of the rest of the island as well. However, although you may think that you can just whiz around an island that measures only 36 miles long and 14 miles wide, it's not so. On these narrow, twisting blacktops you can scarcely average 20 miles an hour. Nor would you want to drive any faster, because children and animals are forever popping onto the highway unannounced.

If you have nerves of steel and no trace of vertigo, the

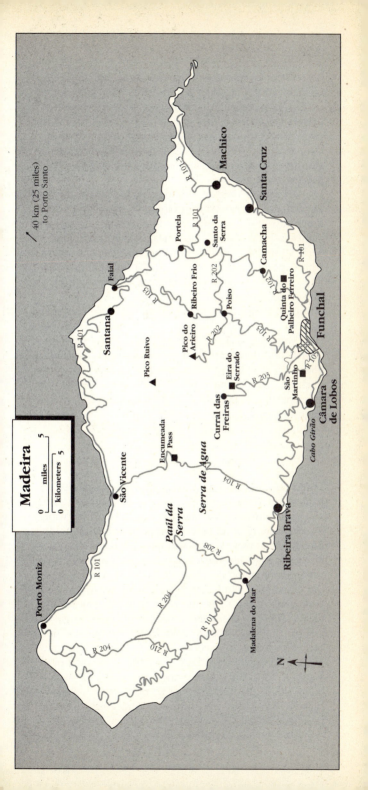

best way to see Madeira is by rental car. But if you're faint of heart you'll be better off in a car with driver (every hotel concierge is plugged into the network of local cab drivers who hire out for the day) or aboard one of the many island tour buses. These behemoths slam around the mountains with terrifying speed, ricocheting passengers from side to side, so be sure to keep Dramamine handy.

Every tour of Madeira should begin in the capital city of Funchal, which resembles nothing so much as a scaled-down Rio. It too sprawls around a crescent harbor and climbs a great green amphitheater of mountains at its back. Mini-Rio or no, Funchal is nonetheless a proper city with a population of about 100,000. Its sidewalks, like those of Rio, are worked out in intricate mosaics of black and white.

Your first Funchal stop should be the Turismo office at avenida Arriaga, 18, the jacaranda-canopied main street. Here you can pick up free city and island maps, brochures, and details about all island excursions, including hikes along Madeira's mountaintop *levadas* (irrigation ditches). This Turismo office, by the way, may be the most efficient and helpful in all of Portugal. Its staff is large, English speaking, and knows Madeira and Porto Santo in detail.

Madeira Wines

Then step directly next door to the **Madeira Wine Company** (avenida Arriaga, 28), housed—or at least partly so—in a 16th-century Franciscan monastery. Many wineries today are all steel pipes, tanks, and ducts, but not this one. It's what you expect a winery to be: massive wooden beams strung with cobwebs, cool stone floors, and oaken vats of wine aging in a sort of perpetual twilight. In the old days you could just wander about the São Francisco wine lodges, but today the operation is far more organized. There is a regular schedule of well-thought-out tours with English-speaking guides; to join one you need only show up at the reception area.

The São Francisco lodges aren't where the bulk of the Madeira Wine Company's wines are produced. Most of them, and this includes such well-known labels as Blandy's, Cossarts, Miles, Leacock's, and Welsh, are made in modern plants elsewhere around town. The São Francisco lodges are mostly for show, a place to introduce visitors to the four basic types of Madeira wine: pale dry Sercial; nutty, semidry Verdelho; sweet and mellow Bual; and the dessert-rich Malmsey (an Anglicization of Malvasia)—in a butt of which George, Duke of Clarence (the brother of Edward IV and Richard III), was drowned in 1478 in the Tower of London. Or so the popular English schoolboy tale goes.

The Madeira wine industry, as we've already said, began shortly after Prince Henry the Navigator's colonists arrived on the island. But the wines didn't develop their complexity, their depth of character, their finesse until a couple of centuries later, and even then quite by accident. It seems that British schooners bound for the New World routinely called at Madeira to provision, and while there took aboard casks of island wine (fortified with brandy to stop fermentation). The ships then proceeded to America, following the favorable trade winds through the South Atlantic and Caribbean, where the sun was so hot it melted the pitch in the ship's planking and, quite literally, cooked the wines. But instead of being ruined, the wines actually improved. They emerged from their steamy voyage smoother, richer, nobler than identical wines that had never left the island. And they aged better, too.

For a time, island wines were sent as ballast aboard ships to India just so that they would develop the longevity and slightly "burnt" taste that connoisseurs had come to expect of fine Madeiras. Today the tropical journeys are all simulated at the wineries: The wines are gradually heated in a process known as *estufagem* to temperatures as high as 120 degrees Fahrenheit. But the result is the same. This complicated process is explained as you tour the São Francisco lodges, as is the *solera* system, the topping off of older wines with carefully chosen newer vintages, which not only improves the quality of the wines but also ensures uniformity. Like most winery tours, this one ends in the tasting room, where you can sample—and buy—a variety of Madeiras.

Few places are easier to tour than Madeira, first, because Funchal is so compact, and second, because you can make easy day trips out of town, looping in a different direction each day. Although there are some points of historical interest, what makes Madeira special are its emerald-in-the-rough beauty, its Equator-to-England botanical diversity, and its wine, wicker, and embroidery industries. It's a rich menu and you can pick and choose at leisure, alternating days in town with days in the country.

At the outset, you should spend a few days in Funchal relaxing, orienting yourself, and poking around in the city center. On another day you might head for the hills directly above Funchal to see the Jardim Botânico (Botanical Garden) and the oddity of Curral das Freiras, a hamlet built inside a volcano. You might spend part of another day on top of the island at Pico do Arieiro, catching en route the exotic gardens at Quinta do Palheiro Ferreiro and the wicker town of Camacha, then pressing on to Pico Ruivo, to the thatched village of Santana, or to the wide bay at Machico, where Prince Henry's navigators stepped ashore in 1420. The cliff-hanger, however, is the day-long drive around the western land's end at Porto Moniz. Along the way you can visit the fishing village of Câmara de Lobos, the lofty headland of Cabo Girão, the tumultuous north shore, and the brooding moonscape of Paúl de Serra (a high plateau on the western half of the island). Porto Santo, Madeira's satellite island, deserves another day or two—*if* you seek nothing more than sun, sea, and sand.

Staying on Madeira

Because Madeira is so small, there's no need to plan a complicated itinerary with shifting accommodations. All you need is a comfortable spot where you can lounge in the sun, a home base from which to make leisurely day trips about the island. Not surprisingly, Funchal offers the best choice of hotels, most of which line up on cliffs on the western edge of town. There's the huge, futuristic **Casino Park Hotel**, with floor shows and the on-grounds **Casino da Madeira** for those who like to live it up after dark (it was designed by Oscar Niemeyer, whose signature work is the Brazilian capital, Brasília); the smaller, posher **Savoy** (an architectural extravaganza that's part ancient Greece, part ancient Rome, and mostly 20th-century Las Vegas); a high-rising **Madeira-Sheraton**, which, to its credit, has tried to capture the "feel" of Madeira by installing beams in its ceilings, covering its floors with terra-cotta, and hanging its roughly plastered white walls with island folk art.

And then there is **Reid's Hotel**, a turn-of-the-century grande dame that reminds you of nothing so much as one of those elegant old Cunarders, somehow run aground—in Eden. Reid's perches atop its open promontory and is very nearly swallowed up by ten acres of tropical gardens. There are secluded walks and lookouts hidden in this jungle of bougainvillaea, oleander, and hibiscus. Given Reid's elegance, its idyllic setting, and the guarantee of privacy, it's scarcely surprising that its guest list reads like a Who's Who. Winston Churchill came here to paint, George Bernard Shaw learned to dance here, the king and queen of Sweden visited recently, and down the years Reid's has welcomed too many kings and queens of the silver screen to count.

If you prefer something cozier you couldn't do better than the 39-room **Quinta da Penha de França**, an old garden-engulfed house located midway between the Casino Park and Savoy hotels (the rooms in the new wing are the choicest).

If you crave something outside the city and utterly away from it all, there are two little pousadas in the clouds. The newer, and nicer, one is the brand-new 22-room **Pousada Pico do Arieiro**, at the very top of Arieiro, Madeira's second highest mountain (5,939 feet), about a half-hour drive straight up the mountain above Funchal. The more rustic 12-room **Pousada dos Vinháticos** perches halfway up Serra de Agua in the middle of the island; the views from it are absolutely mesmerizing. The bad news is that you are a long way from Funchal—a good hour's drive over hair-raising roads guaranteed to try both your nerves and your skill at the wheel. Under no circumstances should you drive them after dark.

FUNCHAL

You will find Funchal perfect for walking as long as you parallel the sea. Most of the main streets do. But the cross streets climb or drop at alarming angles, and unless you're fit, you'll soon be huffing and puffing.

In addition to Madeira wine, what interests most island visitors are the handicrafts. The best way to get a fix on them is to cross avenida Arriaga from the São Francisco wine lodges and stroll a block south to Perestrello's photo shop. A right here onto rua do Conselheiro José Silvestre Ribeiro and one short downhill block will bring you to the **Casa do Turista** (number 2). Don't be misled by the shop's name; its inventory is strictly top of the line. Inside this old admiral's house you will see two full floors of the most intricately worked Madeira linens, the most handsome wicker baskets, and the finest tapestries, together with delicate china and crystal from the Portuguese mainland. There's quite a bit of folk art, too (costume dolls, handknit woolen helmets like those island farmers wear, fishermen's sweaters). Best of all, the shop will pack and ship anything you buy (not true of many island shops).

You have several options for lunch. You can pause at any of the little sidewalk cafés along the town's main street, avenida Arriaga (most are located a couple of blocks east, nearer the cathedral); you could buy some cherimoyas (a green, alligator-skinned tropical fruit the size of an apple with perfumey white flesh), bananas, and passion fruit in front of the big public garden directly across avenida Arriaga from Perestrello's photo shop, then find a shady bench and picnic inside this block-square garden where black swans preen, water gardens trickle, and poinsettias as big as oaks bloom right around the calendar with no special consideration for Christmas.

Or you could walk west past the park toward the rotunda at the west end of avenida Arriaga, where a brooding bronze Prince Henry the Navigator sits above the clamor of traffic. Just one block beyond the public garden (and one block before the rotunda), rua dos Aranhas angles right and uphill. And about half a block along it on the right, at number 22, you'll come upon what many consider to be Funchal's best restaurant: **Celeiro**—definitely the sort of place local businessmen like to keep to themselves; Tel: (091) 33322.

You may have to wait to get in even if you've called ahead for a table because there are only two rooms, and an antique gristmill appropriates about half of one of them (the restaurant building was originally a granary). But you will be rewarded with first-rate island cooking: a tomatoey *sopa de peixe* (fish soup) made with *espada,* the delicious though undeniably ugly black scabbard fish that swims in island waters, or maybe a skewer of prawns, mushrooms, and sweet red peppers brought sizzling to table. You can order a *garafa* of the local *tinto* or *branco* (white), but these are usually unpleasantly tannic, and you'll probably be happier with one of the fine table wines from the Portuguese mainland. Every good Madeira restaurant stocks them in abundance.

After lunch, stroll back east along avenida Arriaga past the wine lodges and tourist office to the **Sé** looming above you. The cathedral was built at the end of the 15th century, and though it's said to be early Gothic with flourishes of the Manueline (an exuberant architectural style introduced by Manuel I that incorporates ropes, knots, spheres, and other nautical motifs to commemorate Portugal's great discoveries), it seems altogether tame compared to the tower of Belém and the Jerónimos monastery near Lisbon. In fact its façade—white stucco edged in black basalt—is downright dour. But the interior is magnificent, especially the coffered cedar ceiling inlaid with ivory and the rows of lacily carved and gilded 17th-century choir stalls. It's an impressive setting for Mass and for the concerts that are played here every June during the Madeira Music Festival.

From the cathedral it's three short blocks uphill along rua João Tavira to rua do Bispo. Turn right, mosey half a block along this shady street, and you'll find, at number 21 just across the street, the **Museu de Arte Sacra**. Like so many Madeira museums, this one occupies an old palace, in this case the bishopric, which dates back to 1600. The collection of religious artifacts within positively glitters. Although some were rescued from village churches threatened by neglect or ruin, the more opulent, and certainly many of the paintings, are 15th- and 16th-century Flemish. There's good reason for this: In the early days, Madeira's most valuable export was sugar, a costly commodity often bartered for works of art. The Flemish were the master artists of the day, and, not so coincidentally, some of the people Prince Henry sent down to help colonize Madeira were Flemish (his sister had married the king of Flanders).

Once you leave the museum, step next door into the broad, sunstruck **praça do Município** (Municipal Square), a sea of ocean-wave mosaics worked out in marble chips of black and white. It's dizzying to cross, but you should make your way to the west side of the square, if only to slip inside the **Colégio church** (begun in 1569 by the Jesuits but now home to the island's embryo university). This is an ornate church with a richly gilded retable (circa 1660) behind the high altar. That it has survived is a miracle, given the fact that this house of worship became a barracks after the Marquês de Pombal banished the Jesuits in 1759 (see the Chronology at the end of the book).

From the Colégio it's a short uphill block or so along rua dos Ferreiros to the venerable **D'Oliveiras wine lodge**. Compared to the Madeira Wine Company this is a small family operation, but D'Oliveiras sells some singularly fine old Madeiras, such as an 1850 Verdelho. This is the place to buy a Madeira bottled in the year of your birth, or perhaps of your marriage, a wine to save and savor during a special celebration.

You might spend what's left of the afternoon walking through the oldest part of town—easy enough to reach from D'Oliveiras. Simply return to the Colégio, walk one block east (left) along rua M. Funchal to rua 5 de Outubro, then saunter five blocks downhill to rua da Alfandega. A right onto this narrow cobbled street will plunge you into Funchal of old. There are tinsmiths here, recycling oil drums into washbasins and water sprinklers. There are shops and *tascas* (bistros) galore, women pausing to chat with friends, men hanging out in little coffeehouses. It's all very "slice of life."

After six short blocks rua da Alfandega dead-ends into the imposing 16th-century **Palácio de São Lourenço**, a fortress-castle that served as the home of Madeira's military governors. Turn right here onto avenida Zarco and walk past the fort (not open to the public) two steep—but mercifully short—uphill blocks to Funchal's main drag, avenida Arriaga.

Turn left and make your way two blocks west past the rotunda to the swatch of greenery on avenida do Infante directly above the harbor. This is the **Parque de Santa Catarina**, where you'll find the pristine little **Capela de Santa Catarina**. Built by Zarco in 1425, it is the island's oldest church, but it has been partially rebuilt at least twice, in the late 15th century and again in the 17th, each time so skillfully that it's impossible to tell what's original.

You might end the afternoon in high style by taking a proper English tea on the terrace at **Reid's Hotel**, at estrada Monumental, 139, on the west end of town, from which there's a dynamite view across Funchal harbor. You don't have to be a hotel guest in order to pause here for tea; don't miss the *bolo de mel* (honey cake) if it's on the tea trolley. Or you could take tea instead at **Quinta Magnólia** across estrada Monumental from Reid's, then 100 yards uphill on rua do Dr. Pita. With its stately trees and tidy lawns, the quinta resembles nothing so much as a British country club, which in fact it was until the old British "regulars" either died off or stopped wintering in Madeira. Today the quinta is home both to an art gallery and to Madeira's hotel school, whose students are carrying on the English tradition of afternoon tea. They also serve lunch (but no dinner), and the menu changes daily to feature whatever was studied that morning. Quinta Magnólia's dining room is small, so if you'd like to lunch there you'll have to reserve a place; Tel: (091) 64614.

Around the Mercado dos Lavradores

Begin another day in Funchal at the **Mercado dos Lavradores** (Workers' Market), near the foot of rua Brigadeiro Oudinot at the eastern end of Funchal. It's open every day except Sunday, but Friday morning is when it's at its busiest and best, so you may want to juggle your schedule in order to visit the market at prime time. With its flower sellers in red capes and full skirts striped in hot colors surrounded by acres of orchids and birds of paradise, with its pyramids of home-grown cabbages, tomatoes, bananas, and custard apples, with its baskets of *espada* and sardines, still streaming seawater, it is a photographic golden opportunity.

Be sure to climb up one flight to the second-floor balcony, where small vendors in from the country sell braids of garlic, strings of *piri-piri* (the incendiary little red peppers slipped into so many island recipes), and huge orange wedges of winter squash. If you can weave your way through the booths to the railing, you'll be rewarded with a straight-down view of the market melee just below. It's a terrific angle for a photograph.

After leaving the market, climb two blocks up rua Brigadeiro Oudinot and cross the bridge over a bougainvillaea-shrouded ravine to the **Instituto do Bordado Tapeçarias e Artesanato** (Embroidery and Tapestry Institute), at rua do Visconde de Anadia, 44. One flight up there's a charming little museum full of frothy eyelet-trimmed pinafores and petticoats, silken linens embroidered in stunning detail, and petit-point portraits of Prince Henry the Navigator, Pope Paul, and, of all people, Jacqueline Kennedy Onassis. The stitches are so fine, the shadings so delicate, you'd swear the portraits were done in pastels.

The Madeira embroidery industry was begun some 150 years ago by a young Englishwoman named Elizabeth Phelps, the daughter of Funchal wine shipper Joseph Phelps. She had long admired the needlework of Madeira country women, and in the 1850s, when the dreaded *oidium* blight that had already wiped out many of the vines in Europe began decimating island vineyards and impoverishing hundreds of small farmers, inspiration struck. If Madeira women could be taught to embroider fine linens with the designs beloved by the English, Miss Phelps reasoned, they could surely make enough money to help support their families in this time of crisis.

Working at first with a small group of women, Elizabeth Phelps taught them new stitches, and soon had them embroidering top-quality Irish and Belgian linens. On her next trip to London she showed samples of the Madeira embroidery to British friends, who snapped them up and begged for more. Soon Miss Phelps found a London agent for the Madeira embroideries, and the rest is history.

Even today, although the Instituto do Bordado Tapeçarias e Artesanato exercises strict quality controls, Madeira embroidery remains very much a cottage industry. As you drive around the island you'll see groups of women and girls gossiping and embroidering—on mountainsides, in doorways, under grape arbors. Usually each works on a single item—a napkin, a tea towel, or a handkerchief—but sometimes a particularly skilled group will combine talents on a large tablecloth.

A block downhill from the Instituto do Bordado Tapeçarias e Artesanato at **Patrício & Gouveia** (rua do Visconde de Anadia, 24) you can, if you ask, watch linens being stamped with the designs that will be sent out into the countryside to be embroidered, or finished linens being laundered, pressed, and packaged for sale in the company showrooms.

Funchal is chockablock with embroidery shops, but some of them are choicer than others. Patrício & Gouveia has a broad inventory of delicate table linens, many with intricate open work. If needlework is of particular interest, however, you should also visit two other top shops, each about a five-minute walk from Patrício & Gouveia. For tablecloths, placemats, tea towels, and handkerchiefs embroidered and appliquéd in bright colors, stroll over to **Imperial Linens** at rua de São Pedro, 26, near the Colégio. And for daintily embroidered pastel blouses and lingerie, simply walk downhill to the Sé and to **Teixeiras**, located directly across the street from it at rua do Aljube, 13–15.

The Quinta das Cruzes Area

Afterward, grab a bite at a sidewalk café (there's no shortage of them around the cathedral), then taxi up to

Quinta das Cruzes, at calçada do Pico, 1, about a kilometer straight up from the public garden on avenida Arriaga. (You can walk, but it's a tortuous climb.) Most guidebooks tell you that this old villa, now a museum, was the home of Madeira's discoverer, João Gonçalves Zarco, and that it was built in the 15th century. Well, most guidebooks are wrong. Zarco did build a home here, but the house you see today is 18th century. No matter: The reason you come to this quinta is not so much the house as the orchid greenhouses out back, the archaeological shards strewn about the grounds, which come down to us from the island's earliest settlers, and most of all the exhibits of 17th- to 19th-century Euro-Asian porcelains, paintings, and furnishings inside. It's an impressive collection, all gathered from island homes and churches, and it proves how sophisticated life was in this Portuguese colony two and even three centuries ago.

Zarco lies buried in the little tiled chapel of the 17th-century **Convento de Santa Clara**, directly next door to the Quinta das Cruzes. Like so many island churches today, it's kept locked, so you'll have to ring the bell to get in. For a small contribution one of the nuns will put down her embroidery and show you through.

Just a block below the convent you'll find Madeira's newest museum, **Casa Museu Frederico de Freitas**. Opened only in 1987, the museum is housed in an 18th-century mansion that was the home of the prominent Funchal barrister for whom it is named. In fact, it is still under construction, and the patio where Dr. de Freitas's rare early *azulejos* will be displayed has yet to open. But there's plenty to see already: a new, double-height front gallery devoted to rotating exhibits (island watercolors and etchings made up one recent show), then, in the house itself, 12 showplace rooms of furniture, paintings, and artifacts, left exactly the way Dr. de Freitas arranged them.

From the museum you can stroll down to the public garden on avenida Arriaga, about five blocks below, then make your way back to your hotel, either on foot or by taxi (there's a cab stand in front of the garden).

Dining in Funchal

For dinner, there is no shortage of choices in Funchal. You might, for example, doll up and go to **Reid's Grill**, a rooftop restaurant in the hotel, with wraparound windows, fabulous views of Funchal harbor, and classic French cuisine; Tel: (091) 23001. Or you might head for **Casa dos Reis** at rua da Penha de França, 6, just two blocks from the Casino Park Hotel and almost directly across the street from the Quinta da Penha de França. The cozy upstairs-downstairs restaurant, all snowy linens and gleaming crystal, serves a mix of French, East Indian, and Portuguese specialties: lobster crêpes, shrimp curry, or a real Madeira fish muddle made with plenty of garlic, tomatoes, and whatever the fishermen's nets have fetched up. Tel: (091) 25182.

The **Casino da Madeira**, a futuristic round building on the grounds of the Casino Park Hotel, is less than a five-minute walk from Casa dos Reis, so this might be the night to try your luck at roulette or blackjack.

One of Funchal's finest restaurants, **Solar do F**, at avenida Luiz de Camões, 19, is only a five-minute walk from Reid's, the Madeira-Sheraton and Casino Park hotels, and the Quinta da Penha de França, so it makes a convenient choice for dinner. Because this old quinta is an indoor-outdoor restaurant, at least in warm weather, it's possible to dine here either under the stars or in one of its elegant but understated rooms. Seafood's the main thing here, as befits an island restaurant, and much of it is grilled over open coals and brought sizzling to table. A house specialty to look for is the skewer of giant prawns and the ubiquitous *espada*, green pepper, and tomato, a supremely succulent marine shish kebab. Tel: (091) 20212.

You might do as the locals do and go down to **Caravela**, a casual harbor-view restaurant atop an office building at avenida do Mar, 15–17, that is famous for its ocean-fresh seafood. Or you might head for the old fishermen's quarter at the eastern end of the harbor to dine at **Romana**, an atmospheric spot at largo Corpo Santo, 15, with dark beamed ceilings and rough plaster walls hung with hand-painted plates. There are two menus at Romana, one French and one Portuguese; the Portuguese is the one to insist upon, because it offers such Madeira specialties as *carne de vinho e alhos* (braised chunks of pork marinated with crisp white wine and garlic). Avoid the house dessert, a perfumy, stiffly set passion-fruit pudding, which one wit has dubbed "The Portuguese Jell-O." Tel: (091) 28956.

Another dinner might be at a *restaurante típico* (folk restaurant) in the hills above town. **A Seta**, at estrada do

Livramento, 80, is the best choice. It's too far to walk and too confusing a route to drive, so you should hire a taxi for the evening (not expensive). Then settle in for a hearty dinner of *espetada* (charcoal-grilled skewers of beef redolent of garlic and bay leaves) and *bolo de caco* (chewy rounds of yeast bread baked on top of the stove on lava stones) accompanied by island-grown potatoes, yams, beans, and carrots fatter and sweeter than those produced anywhere else. But food is only one of A Seta's attractions. You'll be serenaded as you dine by *fado,* mournful ballads belted out here by a young *fadista* enveloped, like every proper female fado singer, in a voluminous black shawl. And when she takes her break, you'll be entertained by folk dancers in bright regional costume. It's all a bit touristy, true, but lots of fun. Tel: (091) 47673.

If you're feeling ambitious, you might even drive 9 km (6 miles) west of Funchal to the town of Câmara de Lobos to watch the sun set behind Cabo Girão from the second-floor dining terrace of **Coral,** a lively bar-restaurant located on a little waterfront square called largo da República. Its chef can prepare *espada* at least half a dozen different ways, all of them delicious. (Black of skin, snakelike of body, and fearsome of tooth, *espada* is blessed with surprisingly delicate lean white flesh.) The special dessert here is a fresh banana pudding, but it isn't much better than Romana's passion-fruit number. Besides, it languishes all day on the unrefrigerated pastry wagon. Tel: (091) 94-24-69.

The Hills above Funchal

Madeira's luxuriant **Jardim Botânico** in the hills above Funchal is no more than a 15-minute drive from the city center up to the **Quinta do Bom Sucesso,** until 1936 the home of the Reid family (of Reid's Hotel). The grounds were later turned into a botanical garden and horticultural laboratory and opened to the public in 1960. With its flower beds and hothouses stair-stepping 450 feet up the side of a mountain and its near-aerial views of Funchal, Bom Sucesso is breathtaking. There are great blocks of color everywhere, so the effect is of an outsized, living Mondrian: hot red squares of salvia, bright yellow rectangles of ginger lily, intense blue ribbons of hydrangea. There are magnolias, too, and fern trees, even umbrella pines under which you can enjoy a simple lunch.

If you don't dawdle at the garden you'll have time to return to Funchal, head west out of town along avenida do Infante (route 101), then, just as you approach Reid's Hotel, turn right onto rua do Dr. Pita (route 105) and climb a couple of kilometers uphill past Quinta Magnólia to the stark black-and-white **Igreja de São Martinho**, which crowns a lonely pinnacle and is visible for miles.

Your destination is one of Madeira's curiosities, the village of **Curral das Freiras**, built inside the crater of an extinct volcano. The round trip will take you two hours, and for once it's less than a daredevil drive. Once you reach São Martinho, edge right along route 105, and twist 7 km (4 miles) through the upper fringes of Funchal to **Pico dos Barcelos** (pause here long enough to enjoy the gull's-eye view of town).

Less than 2 km (1 mile) ahead, the road forks; bear left and switch back 16 km (10 miles) to **Eira do Serrado**, the lookout at the top of the crater. Soon houses and vineyards give way to cool glades of eucalyptus, then clouds of hydrangeas, then deep pine woods.

You should reach the crater, 3,318 feet up, just as shafts of late-afternoon sun spill over its rim and down onto the houses sprinkled up and down near-perpendicular slopes like white flower petals. According to the story all Madeira schoolchildren learn, the nuns from the Santa Clara convent in Funchal fled to this secret valley in the 16th century to escape the pirates pillaging the city (*curral das freiras* means "corral of the nuns"). In time a tiny settlement developed here but it was completely cut off. Not until 1959 was a road built down into the crater linking this little community with the outside world. Before then, the only way in and out was by foot along a tortuous route. Although less than 20 km (12 miles) from Funchal, Curral das Freiras is still more isolated than many towns on Madeira's remote western tip. It didn't get television until the mid-1980s.

When you're ready to return to Funchal, simply go back the way you came.

TO THE TOP OF THE ISLAND

A leisurely day's tour in the heights above Funchal might include a visit to Quinta do Palheiro Ferreiro, one of the island's dreamy gardens, a pause at the wicker town of Camacha, and lunch 5,939 feet up at the very top of Pico do Arieiro, Madeira's second-highest mountain. (At 6,048 feet, Pico Ruivo is the loftiest, and it's clearly visible to the north from Pico do Arieiro.)

The route out of town is altogether confusing, because street names and highway numbers change often. The best plan is to ask your hotel concierge to mark your map, routing you through town the easiest way, then up into the hills to **Quinta do Palheiro Ferreiro**. It's only 8 km (5 miles) northeast of Funchal, but given city traffic it may take you half an hour to reach. These gardens belong to the Blandy family, who also own, among other things, Reid's Hotel and one of the major wine houses.

The house at this estate is surprisingly modest, but the gardens are ravishing. They showcase hundreds of botanical exotics from around the world that coexist happily with Madeira's own spiky dragon trees and stately mahoganies. As you stroll the formal and informal gardens, passing arbors, reflecting pools, and pavilions, you'll see South African proteas, Japanese loquats, Mexican blood lilies, and New Zealand fern trees. The gardens were laid out by a French landscape architect in the 18th century for the first Conde de Carvalhal. The Blandys bought the estate in 1884, and it was Mildred Blandy, the mother of today's owner, who began importing flowering trees, shrubs, and plants. Something blooms here nearly every day of the year. You're free to roam the gardens at your leisure; the house, however, is off limits.

Camacha

On leaving the quinta, go right onto route 102 for an 8-km (5-mile) run through misty woodlands to Camacha, headquarters of Madeira's wicker industry. This business was also introduced by the English, in this case by William Hinton and James Taylor. In Victorian times many wealthy British families built summer houses in the cool mountain village of Camacha and filled them with Italian wicker. Seeing all the willow and cane growing in the area, Hinton and Taylor decided to teach villagers to make the wicker furniture so popular in other parts of Europe. They could undercut the Italian prices and make a bundle. Quite so, and the business continues to boom today.

Most of the wickerwork is done behind closed doors in and around Camacha, but if you visit in late spring you'll encounter whole families out on the slopes peeling willow shoots, which have been boiled in a tar bath to loosen the bark. You will also see osiers and young stalks of cane leaning against fences everywhere, drying in the open air, masses of straw spread on rooftops under the downpouring sun, and men loading bundles of each onto flatbed trucks for distribution to the weavers, most of whom free-lance out of their own homes just as the embroiderers do. By fall everything will have been woven into chairs and baskets, which will be stacked up along miles of highway, awaiting pickup.

The best place at Camacha to see men weave osiers into baskets and cane into tables and chairs is in the basement of **Café Relógio**, a great barn of a shop facing the broad town square. Its inventory simply staggers: baskets and hampers of every conceivable size and shape, dog and cat beds, trunks and foot lockers, whole sets of porch furniture, all piled to the rafters.

Although Café Relógio is, as its name suggests, a restaurant as well as a shop, you'll fare much better if you push on to the new Pousada Pico do Arieiro, less than half an hour away. To reach it, follow route 102 north out of Camacha, lined now by banks of hydrangeas and thickets of watercress. After a squiggly 8 km (5 miles), make a sharp left onto route 202, the road to Poiso and Pico do Arieiro, 13 km (8 miles) straight ahead (as straight, that is, as any Madeira road is likely to be).

The road climbs quickly, leaving behind foggy groves of pine and eucalyptus and soaring into the clouds. Soon you're on top of a great fleecy field pierced here and there by savage crags. You might be in an airplane. Animals range free on these hardscrabble heights, so you must watch for the occasional sheep and hog. There are even wild ponies scavenging about up here, although few people are lucky enough to glimpse them.

You couldn't pick a more panoramic spot for lunch than the **Pousada Pico do Arieiro**. Or a better country restaurant. You can feast here on such Madeira specialties as fresh watercress soup, pork loin stuffed with garlicky sausage, even roast suckling pig. The pousada's architect has given the place the rustic look of a hunting lodge, then wrapped the lounge–bar–dining room—one vast sweep of space—with glass so that you won't miss any of the ever-changing roof-of-the-world drama just outside.

After lunch, how you spend the rest of the day will depend upon your particular interests. First and foremost, however, you must climb 150 feet or so up to the lookout at the very peak of **Pico do Arieiro**. On a clear, cloudless day you can see Pico Ruivo, the granddaddy of them all, in full splendor to the north, Funchal far below, even the island of Porto Santo some 25 miles northeast. There's a well-marked trail leading from Pico do Arieiro to **Pico Ruivo** that crests Madeira's mountainous spine most of the way. It's three miles each way, not overly arduous; if you don't tarry, the round trip will take you about four hours—time enough to make it back to town before nightfall if you set out by 1:30 or 2:00 P.M. The hike is option number one, because it will lead you deep into Madeira's unspoiled interior as no highway can.

Santana

Option number two is to roller-coaster by car over to the thatched village of Santana on the precipitous north shore. You've only to retrace your steps from Pico do Arieiro to Poiso, then turn left onto route 103 and snake past Ribeiro Frio (there's a government trout hatchery in this valley) and São Roque do Faial to Degolada, where 103 dead-ends into route 101. A left turn onto this two-lane blacktop will send you careening along the cliffs to the village of Faial, then Santana. This sounds like a long drive, but in fact it shouldn't take even an hour. The total distance from Pico do Arieiro to Santana is barely 40 km (25 miles).

What's unusual about Santana are its brightly painted, thatched A-frames. "Munchkin houses," someone once called them, and there's no denying that they'd be quite at home in *The Wizard of Oz*. Giant nonheading cabbages grow in the yards of these fairy-tale houses, framed with sunny spills of nasturtium. Children, puppies, and kittens all tumble about the flower beds, and women sit in doorways embroidering linens that will one day cover dining tables thousands of miles away.

These cheerful thatched houses are unique to Santana, but no one can say when—or why—they were first built. Probably some clever Santanan figured that if the thatched triangular huts used to shelter livestock worked so well, then a larger version would do nicely for his family. It would be sturdy and furnish good protection from the wind and rain that blew down from the North Atlantic as well as provide a snug haven from the fog that so often hovered over Santana.

As for the houses' gaily striped façades, who knows? Madeirans do love color, as a glance at any home garden quickly proves. So very likely some inventive woman (it is the wife and mother who keeps the house freshly painted) decided to brighten the front of her house (and perhaps the sometimes gloomy north-shore days) with the primary colors she loved. Then friends and neighbors followed suit.

Santana is just the place to poke around, trying first one side road, then another. You never know what lies around the next bend, but you can be certain it will be something trapped in an earlier time warp. Some of Santana's prettiest A-frames line the road that aims toward Pico Ruivo—a sharp left in the center of town.

To return to Funchal, you have only to double back to Poiso, then proceed straight ahead via route 103, winding down into town. The total distance is about 40 km (25 miles), and the return trip shouldn't take you more than an hour.

Machico

Option number three would be to drive from Pico do Arieiro past Poiso to the intersection of 102 (the route up to the pousada), then, instead of turning south toward Camacha, bearing north (left) and zigzagging past Santo da Serra to Portela. A right turn here onto route 101 will bring you twisting and turning down the island's steep eastern flank to the little seaside village of Machico. This is not a lengthy drive—about 30 km (19 miles) in all—but you'd better allow at least three-quarters of an hour to negotiate all the hairpin turns.

Machico is where Prince Henry's navigators first came ashore in 1420, and where, legend has it, they found evidence of an earlier visitor. When Zarco and Teixeira beached their boat on Machico's gray gravel strand, the story goes, they found a crude wooden cross with a Latin inscription, which one of them translated: "Here came Machim, an Englishman, driven by the tempest, and here lies buried Anna d'Arfet, a woman who was with him."

The navigators had heard the story of Robert Machim, as had most of 15th-century Europe. But the tale of the star-crossed lovers had been just that—a tale. It seems that Machim, rather than marry the woman of high birth chosen for him, eloped aboard a ship bound for Spain with his true love, Anna D'Arfet. The ship was caught in a ferocious storm and blown far off course, and when land was at long last sighted the lovers begged to be put ashore. They were, at what is now Machico. Anna died a few days later, and, although ill and weak, Machim managed to give her a proper burial. He himself died shortly thereafter. This all happened about 75 years before the arrival of the Portuguese navigators. Or so it's said.

Today tourism is overtaking the little town of Machico. Pleasure boats mingle in the bay with fishing smacks, and tennis courts are encroaching on the shore. It's a pretty enough town, with broad streets and squares shaded by plane trees, and it boasts two churches worth a peek. First there's the **Capela dos Milagres** (Chapel of the Miracles) on the east bank of the river that bisects the village. Tristão Vaz Teixeira, whom Prince Henry had appointed governor of the Machico region (Zarco got Funchal), had the little church built early in the 15th century. It was destroyed by a flood in the early 19th century and had to be rebuilt. The second church, the 15th-century **Nossa Senhora da Conceição**, stands in the middle of town on a little square shaded by sycamores. Its distinguishing feature is the fancy portal donated by Manuel I, for whom Manueline architecture is named.

The return to Funchal is easy—you just follow the coast road (route 101) south past the airport at **Santa Cruz**, then continue on into town via the airport road. The drive will take you less than an hour, because this is Madeira's best highway. Time permitting, pause at Santa Cruz to see the mostly Gothic 16th-century church, one of the biggest and most architecturally impressive outside of Funchal—odd for a town that is no more than a dot on the map, and no one can explain just why it is here.

AROUND THE WESTERN TIP OF MADEIRA

Save this trip for a day when the sun is shining on the north side of the island—and check the weather report to make sure. You can't judge what's happening on the other side of Madeira by local weather, because in Funchal's microclimate the sun is almost always visible. On this day-long excursion you will hurdle Madeira's mountainous spine to explore the little-developed north shore, the steep slopes of which plummet into pounding surf and to beaches so small they look like fingernail parings, then you will move west along this inhospitable coast to land's end at Porto Moniz. The total distance is less than 160 km (100 miles), so depending upon how often you stop to "ooh" and "ahh," you will be back in plenty of time for dinner. But you must set out by 8:00 A.M.

Leave Funchal via route 101 (avenida do Infante), passing hotel and condo row on its way west and continuing some 9 km (6 miles) through banana plantations and vineyards en route to the aquatint fishing village of **Câmara de Lobos** (home of the restaurant Coral; see Dining in Funchal). Winston Churchill used to set up his easel on a little knoll above the horseshoe of black lava that cups the town. It was a good vantage point from which he could look down upon dozens of red, blue, and yellow boats careened on the shingle beach, brown fishing nets strung up like butterfly wings to dry, and squat, square white houses roofed in red tile that cling to the cliffs of Câmara de Lobos as if magnetized.

Things haven't changed much since Churchill's day. Toddlers still go skinny-dipping in the surf, older youths continue to dig for clams beneath boulders veloured with algae. And fishermen bring in boatloads of *espada,* the local catch that dominates island menus everywhere. There are even racks of cod drying in the sun and well on their way to becoming *bacalhau,* the dried salt cod beloved by every true Portuguese.

The only recent development at Câmara de Lobos is the gaggle of children begging for escudos. They are hard to resist, especially when you look beyond the picture-postcard façade of this little town and see the primitive conditions in which many of them live. A policy that usually works is to hand the oldest child a 50-escudo coin, indicating that he is to share it with all of his friends. This generally sends the children scurrying off to make change. You can also refuse them with a stern "No," or, better yet, an emphatic German *"Nein,"* but you may feel like Scrooge for the rest of the day.

When you've seen as much of Câmara de Lobos as you like, continue west to Cabo Girão, which looms some 9 km (6 miles) straight ahead. The scraggly vineyards you pass are said to be Madeira's best, and it seems miraculous that their grapes are juicy and sugary enough to produce any wine, let alone the noble Madeiras. You will see scraps of vineyard all along the south shore, demonstrating what a cottage industry winemaking is on this island.

Cabo Girão, Europe's second-highest sea cape (after Norway's North Cape), rises 1,933 feet straight out of a roiling sea. As you stand at the little stone-walled belvedere at its brink you'll be astounded to see, far below, postage-stamp gardens wrested from this almost perpendicular headland. You can't help wondering how on earth they are tended and watered. Punishing work, to say the least.

The view from the cape simply dazzles. To the left you can see Funchal, sparkling in the sun, and beyond it all the way to the eastern end of the island. Ahead to the south there's nothing but open ocean, and to the right more precipitous cliffs, matted with prickly pear and stalks of aloe. Never mind the little lizards darting here and there—they are completely harmless—but if you leave your purse or camera bag open, don't be surprised to discover that one of them has crawled inside.

Your climb toward the north shore begins at Ribeira Brava, some 13 km (8 miles) farther along, although it may well take you half an hour to reach it, because the highway switches back down the western flank of Cabo Girão at a pitch so steep you'll have to shift into second gear, maybe even first, to spare your brakes. You'll soon find yourself driving the Madeira way, honking just before each new curve to alert anyone just around it that a car is coming—a good policy.

Once in Ribeira Brava, cross the gravelly riverbed that cleaves this little town and turn right onto route 104. From here to São Vicente on the north shore it's 26 km (16 miles) and flat, at first, as the blacktop parallels the river. But soon you wind up, up, up into the puffy clouds that always seem to obscure Encumeada pass, then unwind on the downhill run to the north shore, plunging from misty groves of mahogany and mimosa to green slopes so tightly terraced that cows must be confined in *palheiros* (thatched huts) lest they gobble up precious crops or, worse, fall off the mountain.

The next 18 km (11 miles) are guaranteed to test both your driving ability and your cool, for the highway (route 101) is nothing more than a shelf hacked into bedrock. It lurches along high above the surf on its way to **Porto Moniz**, splashing through waterfalls and swooshing in and out of tunnels. Much of the way the road is scarcely one lane wide, so if a tour bus should come barreling around a bend toward you, either you or it will have to back up to the nearest lay-by to let the other pass. This is not a drive for the meek or the acrophobic.

By the time you reach Porto Moniz it will be noon, maybe even later. At any rate, it will be time to break for lunch, and you have two respectable, if not outstanding, restaurants from which to choose. They roost almost side by side on low lava cliffs overlooking this hamlet's main attraction: natural saltwater swimming pools. In reality, these are nothing more than giant cauldrons in a black lava flow solidified eons ago during Madeira's formative stages.

Both restaurants, **Cachalote** and **Orca**, cater to tour-bus groups, so the best plan is to pick whichever one looks emptier. Nondescript, modern eateries with glass windows gazing seaward, both are clean and efficient, and you won't go wrong at either ordering anything that swims.

The next leg of the tour will bring you across a high, barren moor of brutal beauty called **Paúl da Serra**. To reach it, take route 101 west out of Porto Moniz, although, in truth, the road hairpins skyward. After about 8 km (5 miles) a blacktop angles off to the left (route 204), and that's the road you want. The highway, at long last straight, runs for 16 km (10 miles) along Madeira's spine, where half-wild sheep graze amid bits of stubble. The elemental bleakness of the terrain is pure moonscape.

Before long, however, tufts of green begin to push up through the pebbles, and blushes of heather appear; the road veers sharply right, then tightens into a corkscrew and plunges through 11 km (7 miles) of pines, eucalyptus, and vineyards to rejoin route 101 on the south coast a few miles east of Madalena do Mar. You have only 14.5 km (9 miles) to drive farther east to reach Ribeira Brava, where you took the Encumeada pass road earlier in the day. Then it's back to Funchal the way you came. You should make it home well before dark.

THE ISLAND OF PORTO SANTO

This low-slung, semiarid island located just 25 miles to the northeast of Madeira isn't for everyone. It's tiny—only 9 miles long and 3 miles wide—so unless you crave a lazy day or two on the beach you'll probably find little reason to make the 15-minute flight over from Madeira.

The island capital of Vila Baleira isn't much, either: a cluster of red-roofed white houses, a church, a few shops set about a square pebbled in black and white.

The island's main claim to fame (other than its 6 miles of sugary beach) is the house where Christopher Columbus is said to have lived shortly after his marriage to the daughter of Bartolomeu Perestrelo, one of Prince Henry's navigators and the island's first governor. It's just off the main square, a rough stone building two stories tall with a walled garden where fuchsia-colored bougainvillaea seems to have run amok. For years the town fathers have been saying that the house will "open soon" as a museum, but don't hold your breath.

A jumbo airstrip (used by NATO as well as TAP Air Portugal jets on the South America–Lisbon run) stretches across the middle of Porto Santo, dividing the flat agricultural western half from the hillier east. The island's highest point, Pico do Facho, stands a mere 1,521 feet above sea level. There are some craggy cliffs along the northeast shore, but the island is for the most part a rolling checkerboard of wheat fields, vineyards, and small gardens where tomatoes, melons, and figs grow. Water is desperately short on the island, and cloth-sailed windmills help pump what little of it is available.

Although few non-Portuguese come to Porto Santo, Madeirans flock over in August to windsurf, sail, and sack out on the sand. Autumn belongs to the wealthy hunters who fly in to shoot rabbits and partridges, both of which outnumber people hereabouts.

Rabbits very nearly decimated this island once, all because Bartolomeu Perestrelo had smuggled a pregnant doe rabbit aboard ship in Lisbon and released her in the Porto Santo wilds. By the time the colonists were ready to reap their first Porto Santo harvest, that one doe rabbit (and her first litter) had multiplied and remultiplied many times. In a matter of months rabbits had overrun the island, devouring everything in sight, including, alas, the colonists' carefully tended crops. His shortsightedness cost Perestrelo the governorship of Madeira; he got Porto Santo instead, rabbits and all.

There's a first-rate hotel on Porto Santo, cleverly named the **Porto Santo**, on the beach just below Vila Baleira. Its 100 rooms are snapped up early, so if you have any intention of overnighting here you'd better reserve your rooms well in advance.

When it comes to food, Porto Santo can't compete with Madeira. You may get fresher fish at one of the little fishermen's stands along the beach than at any fine Madeira restaurant, however, because your dinner here is not only cooked but *caught* to order. Fresher, too, than that served at the Porto Santo hotel dining room, which is hands down Porto Santo's best restaurant. The cook's rib-sticking home-style soups are simply marvelous, and so are his stews. Almost needless to add, he also has a way with fish, and serves plenty of it.

Life barely creaks along on Porto Santo; in fact, it moves so slowly that not much seems to have happened since Columbus left more than 500 years ago. Bring a good book.

GETTING AROUND

The only way to reach Funchal is from Lisbon or Porto via TAP Air Portugal. From Lisbon, Boeing 727s whiz back and forth to Madeira with near commuter frequency; there are also several nonstop flights each week from Porto. The island of Porto Santo fares less well, with only one weekly Lisbon–Porto Santo flight, on a Sunday. The flying time to either island from Lisbon is one and a half hours, from Porto to Madeira it's about two.

Madeira's airport has always had a reputation for being a "white knuckler," not only because its runway is so short but also because it is hacked into the side of a mountain far above the sea. Things have improved recently, thanks to the engineers who added several hundred extra yards of runway on a trestle high above the ground that strides eastward almost to the village of Machico. Although landings and takeoffs are no piece of cake, at least they don't seem as death defying as they once did. Even with the longer runway, the only large jets with engines and brakes powerful enough to make it are Boeing 727s and 737s. Madeira's dream of a jumbo jetport may never come to pass—and that could very well be its salvation. For if jumbos ever began disgorging tourists by the thousands, Madeira would surely lose the remoteness and otherworldliness that have made it special all of these centuries.

TAP 18-passenger Hawker-Siddeley prop planes make four Madeira–Porto Santo round trips each day between early April and late October; off season, service is less frequent. Either direction, it's a 15-minute hop. For flight information and reservations while you are in Madeira, contact TAP Air Portugal at avenida Dr. António José de Almeida, 17-4°, in downtown Funchal; Tel: (091) 30151 or 26077. Because these planes are so small, it's best to reserve a seat well in advance.

You can also sail between Madeira and Porto Santo. Ask about schedules from the Turismo, at avenida Arriaga, 18, in Funchal. The crossing is usually so rough that even old salts would rather fly. By catamaran, the trip takes one and a half hours under ideal conditions, longer in heavy seas; by conventional interisland boat it's three to four hours, again depending on the weather.

Many different companies offer a broad assortment of excursions around Madeira. Two major firms in Funchal are Savoy Travel, located at the Savoy hotel, on avenida do Infante (Tel: 091-22030), and Windsor, at estrada Monumental, 252 (Tel: 091-31056). You can also pick up excursion brochures by the handful at the Turismo office and in the lobbies of all major hotels.

If you prefer to see Madeira at your own pace, you'll find that many major automobile rental companies maintain offices in town and/or at the airport. The car you want is a powerful little mountain goat that can climb Madeira's narrow serpentine roads without complaint. A big, bulky model simply won't do. And be sure to fill your car's gas tank before you set out on an excursion—you'll use a lot more gas than you'd think on the hills, and there are virtually no filling stations outside the major towns.

To hire a car with an English-speaking driver you have only to speak to your hotel concierge.

On Porto Santo the best way to get about is probably by taxi. Fares are cheap, the drivers know just where to take you, and there's little point in renting a car when you can see everything in a morning or an afternoon.

ACCOMMODATIONS REFERENCE

▶ **Casino Park Hotel.** Avenida do Infante, P-9000 **Funchal**, Madeira. Tel: (091) 33111; Telex: 72118 ITI P.

▶ **Madeira-Sheraton Hotel.** Largo Antonio Nobre, P-9007 **Funchal**, Madeira. Tel: (091) 31031; Telex: 72122 SHERFU P; in North America, (800) 325-3535.

▶ **Quinta da Penha de França.** Rua da Penha de França, P-9000 **Funchal**, Madeira. Tel: (091) 29080.

▶ **Pousada Pico do Arieiro. Monte,** P-9000 Funchal, Madeira. Tel: (091) 48188; Telex: 72622.

▶ **Hotel Porto Santo**. P-9400 **Ilha do Porto Santo**. Tel: (091) 98-23-81; Telex: 72210 P.

▶ **Reid's Hotel**. Estrada Monumental, 139, P-9000 **Funchal**, Madeira. Tel: (091) 23001; Telex: 72139 REIDS P; in North America, (800) 223-6800; in New York, (212) 838-3110.

▶ **Hotel Savoy**. Avenida do Infante, P-9000 **Funchal**, Madeira. Tel: (091) 22031. Telex: 72153 SAVOY P.

▶ **Pousada dos Vinháticos**. Encumeada, Serra de Agua, P-9350 **Ribeira Brava**, Madeira. Tel: (091) 95-23-44.

Pousadas can be booked through Marketing Ahead, 433 Fifth Avenue, New York, N.Y. 10016; Tel: (212) 686-9213.

THE AZORES

By Dwight V. Gast

Two-thirds of the way across the Atlantic between New York and Lisbon lie the Azores (Açores in Portuguese, pronounced ah-ZOH-resh). On the map the archipelago looks like a Calder mobile dangling from the 40th parallel. In reality, though, these nine islands, firmly fixed in the ocean, are as stable as their volcanic origins allow. "Great green ships / themselves, they ride / at anchor forever; / beneath the tide," wrote John Updike in his poem "Azores."

Their greenness is due in large part to a certain atmospheric stability: A high-pressure area known to meteorologists as the "Azores High" often builds up over the islands, heralding good weather for continental Portugal and the rest of Europe, and sustaining (with the warmth of the Gulf Stream and an ample amount of precipitation) a variety of vegetation. Most of the flora was imported from the far reaches of the Portuguese empire over the centuries and painstakingly cultivated into patchwork quilts of fields that are stitched together with lava fences, often covered with hydrangeas. Don't go to the Azores expecting Tahiti, however, or even Madeira. Hard cinders rather than soft sands—there are few sand beaches—make up most of the island's shoreline. Though the climate is technically subtropical, you will enjoy the Azores most if you regard them as a rather weather-beaten greenhouse. Damp gusts more than occasionally come along, so travel with adequate rain gear year-round.

This metaphorical greenhouse is of the somewhat fussy Victorian variety. Politically conservative and proudly Roman Catholic, the Azoreans are as staunchly rooted in tradition as their islands are in the sea. The family unit remains strong; old-fashioned courtship rituals persist among the young; and *festas,* or religious ceremonies, take place year-round throughout the archipelago, as evidenced by the gaily decorated Pentecostal chapels called *teatros* or *impérios.*

Other features of the Azorean landscape are more earthly in nature, though they may not look it. Seismic activity has given rise to *caldeiras,* or craters, *furnas,* or caverns, and lava wastelands philosophically named *mistérios,* or mysteries. These phenomena are as characteristic of the terrain as the brightly painted chapels and the Baroque churches chiseled out of black basalt, which provide an ornate backdrop for the folkloric events that reach their peak on the Day of Pentecost. In addition to religious festivals, different traditions of singing and dancing are followed concurrently on each island then, so if local color is your interest, Pentecost is the time to go.

If the constraints of tradition and the harshness of the land were responsible in varying degrees for massive waves of Azorean emigration (first to Brazil and later to the United States and Canada), those very factors now attract people to the archipelago. The vast majority of visitors are emigrants returning to their homeland, but others have come to appreciate the colorful and luxuriant folklore and flora. One such recent visitor was the conservative American author and critic William F. Buckley, Jr., who with uncharacteristic verbal leanness in his book *Atlantic High* called the Azores "quite simply . . . the most beautiful group of islands in the world."

MAJOR INTEREST

Volcanic crater lakes and hot springs of São Miguel
Architecturally and historically important town of Angra do Heroismo on Terceira
View of surrounding islands from São Jorge
Yacht port of Horta and volcanic landscape of Capelinhos on Faial
View of perfect volcanic crater of Pico from Faial
Magnificent flora and waterfalls of Graciosa and Flores
Religious and folkloric festivals of Espírito Santo (Pentecost) in all the islands

Over the years the Azores have been associated with the lost continent of Atlantis, the ancient Phoenicians, and with certain islands appearing in Genoese maps as early as 1351. The Azores are thought to have been discovered, though, or at least rediscovered, by Diogo de Silves some time around 1430. The earliest extant document about the archipelago is a royal decree dated 1439 ordering that the easternmost group of islands—São Miguel and Santa Maria—be populated; the settlers came primarily from Estremadura, the Alentejo, and the Algarve. Population of the central group—Terceira, Graciosa, São Jorge, Faial, and Pico—was due in large part to Prince Henry the Navigator's sister Isabel, who in 1430 married Philip the Good, Duke of Burgundy, and soon provided a Flemish connection for peopling those islands, especially Terceira, São Jorge, and Faial. The islands, in turn, supplied Flanders with raw plant materials to dye its famous textiles. The westernmost group—Flores and Corvo—were discovered in 1452 and remained unsettled until the following century.

During the expansion of the empire the Azores served as a stopping-off place for Portuguese navigators, who brought the wealth of the Americas and the India trade to the islands, especially Terceira. Like the rest of Portugal, the archipelago came under the domination of Spain during the so-called Babylonian captivity, when Philip II invaded Portugal and proclaimed himself King Felipe I. The Portuguese revolt against the Spanish, however, began in the town of Angra on Terceira in 1640. In the 1820s, during the struggle for the throne between King Pedro and his brother Miguel, Pedro set up court in Angra and for a few months considered the city the capital of the Portuguese empire. Then he moved to Brazil.

Coincidentally, other emigration soon followed, much of it in connection with the whaling industry. Melville wrote in *Moby-Dick* how "no small number of these whaling seamen belong to the Azores, where the outward bound Nantucket seamen frequently touch to augment their crews from the hearty peasants of these rocky shores.... How it is, there is no telling, but Islanders seem to make the best whalemen." These emigrants eventually settled as far afield as New England, Canada, California, and Hawaii, where communities of Azorean descendants continue such customs as the feast of Pentecost.

The 19th century saw expanded commercial contact between the Azores and the outside world. In addition to supplying whalers, the islands exported wheat, flax, dye plants, wine, and oranges. Migration worked both

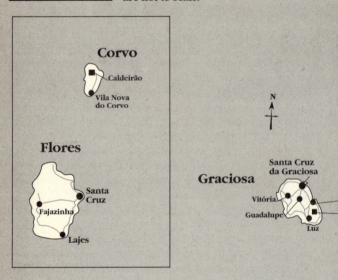

ways. Early in the century, two enterprising Boston families, the Hicklings and the Dabneys, moved to São Miguel and Faial respectively to manage much of the export business (their descendants have since left the islands). Early in this century, the strategic importance of the archipelago made it a vital link in cable transmission, as well as a stopover for ships and, finally, aircraft.

Throughout, however, Azoreans remained conscious of their distinct identity, which goes beyond general insularity (*insularidade* in Portuguese) to specific Azoreanness (*açorianidade*), a term coined by Azorean writer Vitorino Nemésio to refer to the island's *Weltanschauung*. The islands' isolation has shaped the sensibilities of some of Portugal's greatest modern writers. The Azores have produced a large number of journalists, too. As Azorean scholar Onésimo T. Almeida has pointed out, "for the outsider it is astonishing to hear that the islands have had more than six hundred different newspapers throughout their history and today still publish seven dailies, one of which, *O Açoriano Oriental,* is the third oldest newspaper in Europe, seven weeklies, and four journals dedicated to works on literature, history, art, folklore and culture."

The political manifestation of Azoreanness is the fact that the islands became an autonomous region in 1979. Today the archipelago prints its own stamps and proudly flies its flag of the goshawk and nine stars throughout the islands alongside the Portuguese banner. (The goshawk, *açore* in Portuguese, from which the islands take their name, is a romantic misidentification of a less majestic bird, with the less majestic name of *milhafre,* indigenous to the islands.)

Added to the idiosyncrasy of the Azores is the fact that each island has its own sense of identity, not to mention superiority. Of most interest to the visitor are the islands of São Miguel, Terceira, and Faial. A couple of days' stay in each will allow you to see the most important sights in the Azores. If you have more time at your disposal, however, do discover the charms of the other islands. For the sake of the intrepid our coverage describes all of them, roughly paralleling the Portuguese discovery of the archipelago. It begins with the eastern group of São Miguel and Santa Maria; moves on to the central islands of Terceira, Graciosa, São Jorge, Faial, and Pico; and ends with the western group of Flores and Corvo.

SAO MIGUEL

The largest and easternmost island in the Azores (it measures 38.5 by 10 miles), crescent-shaped São Miguel has been inhabited since 1444. Today it has half of the archipelago's total population of about 250,000—and the best tourist facilities. The nicest accommodations for the couple of nights required for exploring the western portion of the island are at the **Hotel São Pedro** in the sizable city of Ponta Delgada (with a population of about 100,000 it is the largest in the archipelago). Built in the 19th century as the Hickling family town house, the hotel has a harbor view and preserves a Georgian air in its antiques-appointed rooms.

Ponta Delgada

The salt air will soon put you in the mood for a stroll, and despite some unsightly modern construction, Ponta Delgada still has enough of its history to make for a pleasant promenade. Pick up a map at the tourist office on avenida Dom Henrique near the stage-flat arches of the 18th-century town gates. Proceed across the pavements decorated in black and white stones, reminiscent of Rio de Janeiro, to the waterfront. Walk along to **Forte de São Bras**, a fortress begun in the 16th century to defend the city against corsairs, then head away from the harbor and have a look at the religious buildings, the **Igreja de São José** with its dark stone framing white surfaces, and the lavish interior of the **Convento de Nossa Senhora da Esperança**. You'll pass two palaces, the 17th-century Conceição and the 19th-century Fonte Bela, and the 17th-century mermaid-covered town house, Casa de Carlos Bicudo, as you make your way back past the town gates and the Igreja Matriz de São Sebastão, the parish church, with its ornate Baroque and Manueline portals.

If you'd like a preview of the pottery you'll be seeing *in situ* in the villages of Lagoa and Vila Franca do Campo, stop into the **Casa Regional da Ilha Verde** (largo da Matriz, 25), a shop where local crafts are sold. From there, rua dos Manaias leads past the Igreja de Santa Bárbara and the Baroque Paço do Concelho, the town hall. On the following street, rua João Moreira, is the **Museu Carlos Machado**, housed in the former convent of Santo André and containing sections on Azorean natural history and folklore. One of the most unusual artifacts of island life on display is the *capote-à-capelo,* an extravagantly hooded cape worn by island women until just a few decades ago.

If the museum has piqued your interest in island culture, proceed to the **Livraria Nove Estrelas** at rua do Mercado, 35, where prints and English-language books about the Azores are on sale. Also on Mercado are the town theater and open-air market next to it. A cross street, ladeira da Mãe de Deus, leads to an overview of Ponta Delgada at the **Refúgio da Mãe de Deus**, an old fortification where in 1944 an antiaircraft battery mistakenly fired on the plane carrying General Dwight D. Eisenhower home to the United States from North Africa. Back down on the waterfront below it is the Baroque Igreja de São Pedro, which houses the 18th-century *Nossa Senhora das Dores* (Our Lady of Sorrows), one of the finest sculptures in the Azores.

Follow your stroll around Ponta Delgada with a meal at the **Hotel São Pedro** restaurant, largo Almirante Dunn. It serves all the Azorean specialties, including *caldo azedo* (bean and potato soup), *couves solteiras* and *couves fervedouros* (cabbage soups), *polvo guisado em vinho de cheiro* (octopus stewed in local wine), *caldeiradas de peixe* (fish stews), *arroz de lapas* (limpets with rice), and *lapas de molho Afonso* (limpets in a spicy sauce). São Miguel is also famous for its beer, and if you're lucky, the hotel will have a supply of the local *vinho de cheiro,* a strong red table wine. Besides the ubiquitous island sweets, one of the nicest desserts is a slice of the locally cultivated pineapple.

The other sites on the west end of São Miguel require a car, and the tourist office will be able to provide you with information about where to rent one. One popular diversion is a visit to a pineapple hothouse, the most extensive being **Estufas Agosto Arruda** just north of town. There you can see the plants in various stages of cultivation, sample the fruit and a liqueur made from the juice, and stroll around the carefully tended grounds with nice views of Ponta Delgada and the harbor.

From there the drive inland to the northwest leads to the panoramic mountain, Pico do Carvão, and **Caldeira das Sete Cidades**, a volcanic crater that according to legend contains the remains of seven cities founded by Spanish bishops who fled to the Azores to escape the Moors. Today it is the site of a small village and two lakes, one green and one blue, separated by a narrow strip of land. Next to the blue lake, Lago Azul, are extensive gardens planted with flowering trees and shrubs, which will begin to give you an idea why São Miguel is known as the Ilha Verde, Green Island. **Hotel Monte Palace**, just built above the lakes, is overpoweringly modern, but it does have a regional restaurant with nice views of the lakes.

From here the scenic route continues northeast to the rocky terrain at Mosteiros and along the coast past a promontory called Ponta da Bretanha, a reminder of the Breton settlers who along with the Flemish are said to be responsible for the French pronunciation of "u" in São Miguel speech. From there, continue to the cliffside village of **Capelas**, the center of São Miguel's tobacco plantations. There, the hill called Morro das Capelas affords more sweeping views of the coast.

The next stop is the handsome town of **Ribeira Grande**, the center of tea plantations. It has a number of noteworthy monuments in its churches (the 16th-century Nossa Senhora da Estrela, the 17th-century São Francisco and Espírito Santo, and the 18th-century Nossa Senhora da Concepção) and a 16th-century town hall. Its regional restaurant is **O Fervedouro** (rua do Passal); you might also want to make a detour to the village of Santa Bárbara for a regional meal at **Cavalo Branco**, rua do Melo Moio, 23.

Heading toward the eastern end of the island on the southern coast road, you'll pass a number of sand beaches before going through the fishing port of **Lagoa**, which has a few shops selling glazed blue-and-white pottery made from volcanic clay, and the villages of Agua de Pau and Caloura. **Vila Franco do Campo** is worth a stop to see its churches. The 15th-century **Igreja de São Miguel** has a marvelous interior containing Gothic arches carved with vegetable motifs and a relief of *Souls in Purgatory*. The 18th-century **church of São Pedro** contains a statue of Saint Peter carved out of the creamy Ança stone from the Beiras in mainland Portugal. The **church of Santo André** has a lavish interior with *azulejos* and a paneled ceiling.

You may then want to shop for more pottery before heading inland past the crater lake of Lagoa das Furnas to the town of **Furnas**. The most relaxing accommodations on the island are here at the **Hotel Terra Nostra**, where another couple of nights' stay will give you a pleasant sense of this part of the island. The oldest part of the complex is none other than Yankee Hall, the summer home built by the Hickling family around a thermal spring in the 19th century. Later additions, including an Art Deco hotel with an excellent regional restaurant and a recently opened new wing, make it the closest thing the Azores has to a fashionable resort. Whether or not you stay here, be sure to visit the hotel's lush botanical garden, planted with vegetation imported to the Green Island from around the world, and ask to have a dip in its outdoor pool, which is filled with heated mineral waters the color of orange juice.

Furnas gets its name from the *furnas,* or caverns, that were created by a volcanic eruption in the 17th century. Today the hot ground is also used to cook *cozido de Lagoa das Furnas,* a regional dish of meats and vegetables steamed in a cloth bag buried in the earth. The **Terra Nostra** hotel restaurant serves it in style, as does the **Casa de Chá Terra Nostra** (Lagoa das Furnas), with its great views of the crater lake.

From Furnas, the coastal drive will take you to the principal sights on this side of São Miguel, for which you might want to pack a picnic of *cabreiro* (goat's milk cheese) or some *queijo da ilha,* a local cheese made from cow's milk. Your first stop is **Povoação**, a fishing village that grew up around the Capela de Santa Bárbara, a chapel considered the first place of worship built on the island. Farther east, at Tronqueira, is **Pico de Vara**, the highest point on the island, with excellent views. Nordeste, at the northeast extreme of the island, has an interesting church, **Igreja de São Jorge**, with basalt pillars amid the wood carvings and statuary inside, and **Achadinha** also merits a stop to see the lavish interior of its church, **Igreja de Nossa Senhora do Rosário**. The final point of interest on this part of the island is **Porto Formoso**, where if you're in the mood for a swim you might want to try **Praia dos Moinhos**, one of the nicest little beaches on the island. From there, an inland road leads back to Furnas.

SANTA MARIA

Santa Maria, the roughly rectangular (10.5 by 6 miles), southernmost island in the Azores, is easily seen in a day's drive through quiet fields dotted with windmills and whitewashed low, cubic houses with red tile roofs. The first island in the archipelago to be discovered, Santa Maria owes its distinctive architecture to the fact that its original settlers came from the Algarve. Columbus was allegedly another early visitor, said to have sent his men to give thanks in the **Igreja de Nossa Senhora dos Anjos** in the fishing village of **Anjos** for deliverance from a shipwreck in 1493. Though the church is a reconstruction, it is still interesting from a historical point of view; and the village, a short drive north of the airport, makes a convenient first stop on your way around the island.

The next two places en route are the interior villages of **São Pedro** and **Santa Bárbara**, each with simple and ancient churches. The landscape is best appreciated at a lookout called **Miradouro do Espigão**, overlooking vineyards and the **bay of São Lourenço**. From here you can head inland to **Santo Espírito**, where the sights include whitewashed houses, windmills, and the **Museu de Etnografia**, a small ethnographic museum. West of it is the pleasant village of Almagreira, and beneath it the fishing port of Praia, which gets its name from the long beach. (Santa Maria, the only island in the Azores that is not volcanic in origin, is also the only one with golden sandy beaches.)

Farther west is the island's main town, **Vila do Porto**. Among its many monuments is the Manueline church, the **Igreja de Nossa Senhora da Assunção**. **Café Restaurante Atlantida** (rua Teófilo de Braga) is the place for a regional meal of *caldo de Nobos* (a turnip soup), *sopa do Império* (meat stew), or just the local pastry, a sugar-coated cookie called *cavaca,* accompanied by a glass of the local *vinho de cheiro* or dessert wines called *vinho abafado* and *vinho bastardinho.*

The only accommodations on the island are here in Vila do Porto at the **Hotel do Aeroporto**, originally built as part of a U.S. Air Force base during World War II.

TERCEIRA

The third (*terceira*) island in the Azores to be discovered, egg-shaped Terceira (18 by 11 miles) is also the third largest. But culturally it is of primary importance, and its main town, Angra do Heroismo, is on UNESCO's World Heritage List because of its architectural and historical significance. For that reason, you may want to stay in Angra for the couple of days you'll need to see the town and drive around the island.

Settlement of Terceira began in about 1450, with immigrants primarily from the Algarve and the Alentejo. Initially agricultural, Terceira soon became an important stop for galleons from India and the Americas, attracting French, English, and Flemish corsairs, whose constant presence brought about the construction of the fortifications that are still an important part of the landscape in Angra do Heroismo. In 1474 the settlement of Angra became the seat of the military government and remained an administrative center of the Azores for over three centuries. In 1534 it was given the status of a city—the first in the Azores—and the seat of a bishopric. When Philip II of Spain became king of Portugal in 1580, the Portuguese pretender Dom António took refuge on Terceira.

The Spanish, whose forces included the writers Cervantes and Lope de Vega, invaded the island the following year, initially with little success. The locals won the battle of Salga ingeniously by driving away the Spanish with wild cattle. Following more bloody fighting, however, the Spanish finally gained control in 1583. In 1589 Sir Francis Drake unsuccessfully attacked the town of Angra, as did the Earl of Essex in 1597. After the restoration of the Portuguese throne in 1640, the Spanish presence came to a violent end. Further struggles took place in the 19th century, when Angra became the seat of the liberal regency of Pedro IV. Because of its citizens' bravery at that time, Pedro's daughter, Maria II, extended the city's name to Angra do Heroismo (Bay of Heroism) at the suggestion of Almeida Garrett, the romantic poet and dramatist who spent his youth on Terceira.

Angra do Heroismo

Though much surviving from its past was damaged in an earthquake in 1980, Angra do Heroismo remains a pleasant town for a walk along orderly cobblestone streets lined with whitewashed stone buildings with terra-cotta tile roofs. Though the islanders are familiar with outsiders from the American military base at Lajes, accommodations are surprisingly spartan. One choice is the **Hotel Beira Mar**, a clean and modest establishment with some rooms right on the bay. It also has one of the nicest regional restaurants in town. From the hotel, begin on the parallel street, rua Direita, where you can visit the 18th-century **Igreja da Misericórdia** to see the paintings and sculptures dating from the same century. From there, rua do Conselheiro Jacinto Cândido leads to the **Palácio Bettencourt**, an extravagant private residence from the Baroque era, open to the public as the town library. Across from it is the **Sé**, or cathedral, recently restored to a pristine condition that practically obscures its 16th-century origins. Rua do Marquês then leads past the richly planted Jardim Municipal, or city park, to the **Igreja do Colégio**, a Jesuit church decorated with *azulejos* and Brazilian jacaranda wood, and the Palácio dos Capitães-Generais, the former palace of the military governors, now occupied by the regional government.

If you return to the park, you will pass the Paço do Concelho, or city hall, and the Igreja da Nossa Senhora da Guia on the rua João de Deus. The **Museu da Angra** is just around the corner on the rua Chagas, in a former convent. It houses an unusual collection of weapons and, more fittingly, religious paintings and sculpture. Note especially the Flemish works, a reminder that Henry the Navigator originally granted the governorship of Angra to Jacome de Bruges. A more extensive collection is housed privately at the **Casa Museu Francisco Ernesto de Oliveira Martins**, for which an appointment through the tourist office on rua Rio de Janeiro (Tel: 095-23393) is necessary. For a final overview of the city, take rua do Pisão to the **Alto da Memória**, an obelisk erected to the memory of Pedro IV on the site of Angra's first castle.

The **Beira Mar** hotel restaurant (rua de São João, 1–5) serves local specialties such as *alcatra* (a beef stew especially popular during the Holy Ghost feasts), *alcatra de cherne* (made with grouper), *polvo guisado* (octopus stewed in wine), and *morcela* (a type of sausage). The island produces its own *verdelho* white wine as well as *queijo da ilha* cheese. Another regional restaurant is **Adega Lusitania**, rua de São Pedro, 63–65.

Pick up a car and picnic provisions to see the rest of the island with its Algarve- and Alentejo-type houses, some with peaked chimneys and flanked by wooden structures for drying corn. In season the roads are lined with hydrangeas and roses, and the herds of cattle that are so important to the island's economy feed indolently in the green fields. (Terceira has its own peculiar form of bullfighting, in which the beast is led about by ropes; called *tourada à corda,* it takes place during the Festa de São João around June 24.)

But begin your island tour with a view of Angra and the bay from Monte Brazil on the outskirts of town. Head inland from there for more views of Terra Chá, then over to Ponto das Contendas on the southeast corner of the island. Driving to the north coast, stop at **Ponta do Mistério** for a look at an otherworldly landscape, then across to **Ponta do Queimado** for a stroll to its lighthouse. This quiet spot, and the forest called Mata da Serreta across the road, are nice spots for a picnic. Head inland again to the natural beauties of the grottoes of **Algar do Carvão**, then stop at the **Caldeira de Guilherme Moniz**, the largest volcanic crater in the Azores.

GRACIOSA

With more gentle slopes than the other islands, pear-shaped Graciosa (8 by 5 miles) lives up to its name, which means gracious. Its open terrain is dotted with windmills, a tradition that may or may not derive from the island's original Flemish settlers, who were perhaps joined by people from the Beiras and Minho of mainland Portugal. Other traditions, such as widespread use of donkeys and the cultivation of wine, make Graciosa one of the most relaxing of the Azores for the visitor. The French author and statesman Chateaubriand, who stopped on the island on his way to the United States during the French Revolution, mentioned Graciosa fondly in his writings.

Santa Cruz da Graciosa is the town nearest to the airport, and should be seen for its **Museu de Etnografia**, as well as for its handsome black stone churches. Inland are the villages of **Vitória** (which houses some lovely Portuguese primitive painting in the **Capela de Nossa Senhora da Vitória**), **Guadalupe**, and **Luz**, and the coast has another picturesque village, Praia. One of the most fascinating aspects of the island, however, is the volcanic crater called **Caldeira do Enxofre**, with a cavern where there are several still-active fumaroles. At its rim there are views of the four other islands of the central group.

Graciosa's only lodgings are in the simple **Residencial Santa Cruz**, with 20 modest rooms and home-cooked meals of seafood specialties. The local wines are the dry white *vinho de cheiro* and the sweeter *angélica*.

SAO JORGE

Updike must have had São Jorge (35 by 5 miles) in mind when he wrote about the "great green ships" of the Azores, for it sits staunchly in the middle of the central group like a vigilant surfaced submarine. Despite its location, its early settlement was spotty due to its lack of good harbors. Nevertheless, the island attracted corsairs from around the world, who must have mistakenly thought it held riches like those on Terceira.

Though São Jorge has some pretty villages—notably Velas, Urzelina, Manadas, Calheta, Ribera Seca, and Topo (the last is where the local women make brightly colored *colchas,* or coverlets)—the island's real riches are primarily natural. One of its most unusual features are the **fajas,** flat parcels of farmland extending from the base of cliffs like scatter rugs over the sea. The nicest fajas extend along the north coast from the Faja do Ouvidor to the Faja da Caldeira de Santo Cristo, and a walk along that part of the island, with wonderful views of Graciosa and Terceira in the distance, is highly refreshing—especially when fueled by some bread, wine, and the local *queijo da ilha,* the most highly prized cheese in the Azores, exported to Portuguese communities throughout the world. **Pico de Esperança,** a mountain peak at the center of the island, offers excellent views of the whole central group.

Accommodations are provided by the **Estalagem das Velas,** which makes up for its stark modern style not only with great views of the islands of Faial and Pico but also with a good regional restaurant that serves all the specialties of the islands.

FAIAL

Faial fans out irregularly from five sides of the **caldeira,** the volcanic cone in the center of the island (13 by 9 miles). Faial takes its name from its beech shrubs (*faias* in Portuguese), even though the island's most prominent plants are the ubiquitous hydrangeas that prompted the writer Raul Brandão to christen Faial the Ilha Azul, or Blue Island.

Originally settled by the Portuguese, the island was later populated by the Flemish, who went there in search of fortune with their countryman Josse van Huerter, whose name was eventually corrupted into **Horta,** the name of the island's principal city and the only natural port in the Azores. Another prominent foreigner was John Dabney, who became the American consul to the Azores in 1808 and whose family soon controlled the local whaling industry as well as the export of wine and oranges from the neighboring island of Pico. Further development came with Horta's role as a cable center linking Europe with North and South America, which brought foreign companies, such as Deutsch-Atlantische Telegraphengesellschaft and Western Union, to the island at the beginning of this century. The old Western Union compound is now the **Hotel Faial**, the social hub of the upscale locals. Quieter accommodations are at the **Estalagem de Santa Cruz**, located in a restored 16th-century fort on the harbor across from the peak of Pico island. Perhaps it was the fortress's defensive aspect that appealed to actor Raymond Burr—known for his portrayal of defense attorney Perry Mason—who ran the place a few years back before purchasing other property on the island.

Horta wasn't always so accommodating to travellers. Mark Twain, describing his 1867 stopover there in *Innocents Abroad,* wrote that the "community is eminently Portuguese, that is to say, it is slow, poor, shiftless, sleepy, and lazy.... The people lie, and cheat the stranger, and they are desperately ignorant, and have hardly any reverence for their dead." Times have changed. Today the outsiders who call at Horta are mainly yachtsmen. In season, you can find them at **Pete's Café Sport** at rua Tenente Valadim, 9, a scene straight out of the Spouter-Inn in *Moby-Dick*—and a lively introduction to Faial. Above it, Pete (whose real name is José Azevedo) recently opened a private museum to house his collection of scrimshaw, the traditional old whalers' craft of carving whales' teeth and bone.

Throughout the year you can see a modern artistic tradition at Horta's marina, where yachtsmen have applied their painting skills with varying degrees of success to cover the concrete walls with bright naif paintings that are supposed to ensure safe passage. The marina is also the setting for Horta's annual **Semana do Mar**, or Week of the Sea, a festival that features sporting events, crafts, music, and food.

Horta's other cultural riches are more historical. In addition to the **Museu de Arte Sacra**, or sacred art museum, there is the **Museu de Horta**, which has an exhibit of scenes of Azorean life painstakingly executed in the unusual medium of fig-tree wood. The mostly Baroque churches Igreja Matriz de São Salvador, Igreja de São Francisco, Igreja de Nossa Senhora do Carmo, and Igreja de Nossa Senhora das Angústias, as well as the panoramic chapel called the Ermida de Nossa Senhora do Pilar, complete the city's sights.

The relaxed atmosphere of Horta may make you want to stay in the town, but do venture out to have a look at Faial's volcanic legacy. Besides the caldeira, the volcanic cone at the center of the island, there is **Capelinhos**, the site of the volcanic eruption that occurred at the western end of the island in 1957–1958. There, a lighthouse stands half-buried by lava in an angry landscape, and a little museum displays documentation of the event.

Restaurants include the **Estalagem de Santa Cruz** (rua Vasco da Gama), **Cosme** (rua nova Angústias), and **Club Naval** (rua Vasco da Gama); all are in Horta and serve Azorean food as well as local specialties made with rabbit.

PICO

"The isle of Pico has its name from the peak or high mountain upon it, which is frequently capt with clouds, and serves the inhabitants of Fayal nearly the same purpose as a barometer." So wrote George Forster in *A Voyage Round the World* in 1777, and it still holds true.

The peak, the highest in Portugal at 7,710 feet, is so gracefully shaped it seems like Mount Fuji lost at sea. It has long been the principal reason for visiting the island (26 by 9 miles), especially since blight killed off most of the vines that once produced a wine served as far away as the tables of the tsars. For information about climbing the mountain, contact the tourist office in Horta on Faial at rua Vasco da Gama; Tel: (092) 22237.

If you're not a climber but would just like a pleasant day trip from Faial, cross the channel from Horta (Vitorino Nemésio's novel *Bad Weather in the Channel* immortalized the crossing in literature) for a closer look at Pico or a drive along its perimeter through the towns and villages interspersed with stark lava *mistérios*. Heading south from Madalena, you'll pass the **Mistério de São João** on the way to **Lajes do Pico**, where a modern whaling museum, the **Museu da Baleia**, is all that remains of this industry once so much a part of life on Pico and Faial.

(Whaling, long on the decline, ended with Portugal's entry into the European Community in 1986, but sportfishing is popular in this part of the Azores. The tourist office in Horta on Faial can provide further information.)

From Lajes, take the inland road through the little lake district to see the **Mistério da Prainha**, then head across the base of the peak to **Mistério de Santa Luzia** before returning to Madalena for the boat back to Horta, which has the best accommodations in Faial (see above).

FLORES AND CORVO

"At Flores in the Azores Sir Richard Grenville lay," begins Tennyson's famous poem about the English privateer's fateful encounter with the Spanish fleet off the island in 1591. Such stories of violence (there is another one about the Confederate *Alabama,* which wreaked havoc among Union ships off Flores during the American Civil War) are hard to believe about Flores. The flowers that gave Flores its name flourish on the island, which is blessed with twice as much rain as São Miguel. For many, the flora makes the island, the westernmost of the Azores, the most beautiful, too. Even the fussy Twain was eventually pleased: "It seemed only a mountain of mud standing up out of the dull mists of the sea," he wrote. "But as we bore down on it the sun came out and made it a beautiful picture—a mass of green farms and meadows that welled up to a height of fifteen hundred feet, and mingled its upper outlines with the clouds.... It was the aurora borealis of the frozen pole exiled to a summer land!"

There are other sights on this pineapple-shaped island (10.5 by 8 miles). **Santa Cruz**, the main town, has its small **Museu Etnográfico**, as well as several Baroque churches. Other places to see are the village of **Fajazinha**, picturesquely located near the waterfall of Ribeira Grande, and the numerous chapels and waterfalls scattered around the island. Also of interest are the island's rock formations, especially the Exareus grotto. **Pensão Lajes das Flores** in Lajes provides modest lodgings and serves simple Azorean specialties.

In Flores you may be able to persuade a local boatman to make the crossing to **Corvo**, the northernmost, smallest (4 by 2.5 miles), and last of the Azores, inhabited by only a few hundred people who speak an archaic form of Portuguese. If so, you may also be able to talk him into sailing around the tiny island. In any case, visit the village of **Vila Nova do Corvo**, which prides itself on being the smallest town in Portugal (population 300), and hitch a ride on a tractor to **Caldeirão**, Corvo's extinct volcano. Inside is a crater lake with nine tiny islands, a microcosm of the Azores themselves.

GETTING AROUND

TAP Air Portugal, the Portuguese national airline, flies from Lisbon directly to São Miguel, Terceira, and Faial; from Boston directly to São Miguel; and from Los Angeles directly to Terceira. Direct charter flights are often available from such travel agencies as Azores Express (199 South Main Street, Fall River, MA 02721; Tel: 800-762-9995 or 508-677-0555), Map Tours (6 Highland Cross, Rutherford, NJ 07070; Tel: 201-438-8002), Suntrips (2350 Paragon Drive, San Jose, CA 95131; Tel: 800-444-7866 or 408-432-1101), and Lawson Tours (2 Carlton Street, Toronto M5B 1J2, Canada; Tel: 416-977-3000).

Within the archipelago SATA Air Açores (main office: avenida Dom Henrique, 55; 9500 Ponta Delgada, São Miguel; Tel: 096-27221) flies on a whimsical schedule among all the islands except Corvo, using a fleet of British Aerospace turboprops. The islands are spread out: It takes about 40 minutes to fly from São Miguel to Terceira; another 40 minutes from Terceira to Faial; and about 25 minutes from Faial to Graciosa. Space is limited and overbookings are not infrequent, so be sure to confirm your reservations and arrive at the airport at least an hour before departure time.

Passenger boats and smaller craft sail to all the islands. Current schedules are available from the Ornelas Travel Agency (avenida Infante Dom Henrique, 9500 Ponta Delgada, São Miguel; Tel: 096-25379) and government tourist offices (avenida Infante Dom Henrique, 9500 Ponta Delgada, São Miguel; Tel: 096-25743; Airport, Santa Maria; Tel: 096-82155; rua Rio de Janeiro, 9700 Angra do Heroismo, Terceira; Tel: 095-23393; rua Vasco da Gama, 9900 Horta, Faial; Tel: 092-22237).

On individual islands, the most flexible means of transportation is a car. Tourist offices have information about renting them as well as motorcycles and bicycles.

In addition to the Easter cycle—religious feasts that take place between Lent and the feast of the Sacred Heart—a number of other celebrations occur regularly. On São Miguel the Procissão do Senhor dos Enfermos takes place the first Sunday after Easter in Vale das Furnas; the Procissão do Trabalho May 9 to 11 in Vila Franca do Campo, and the Festa do Senhor Bom Jesus da Pedra the last weekend in August in Vila Franca do Campo; there are special ceremonies throughout the island called Véspera de Reis on January 6 and Cantorias das Estrelas on February 2. On Santa Maria, the Festa de Santo Amaro takes place January 15 in Almagreria and the Festas da Vila August 15 in Vila do Porto. On Terceira, the *tourada à corda* bullfighting takes place in the period around June 24 alternately in Angra do Heroismo and Praia da Vitoria. On São Jorge, a procession takes place the first Sunday in September in Faja do Santo Cristo. On Faial the Festa de São João takes place June 24 in Horta; the Semana do Mar from the first to the second Sunday in August. On Pico, the Festa de Bom Jesus takes place in São Mateus on August 6. On Corvo, the Festa do Fio takes place in May and September.

ACCOMMODATIONS REFERENCE

▶ **Hotel do Aeroporto. Vila do Porto,** 9580 Santa Maria. Tel: (096) 82211.

▶ **Hotel Beira Mar.** Rua de São João, 1–5, **Angra do Heroismo,** 9700 Terceira. Tel: (095) 25188.

▶ **Hotel Faial.** Rua Consul Dabney, **Horta,** 9900 Faial. Tel: (092) 22181.

▶ **Pensão Lajes das Flores.** Lajes das Flores, 66, **Lajes das Flores,** 9960 Flores. Tel: (092) 52496.

▶ **Estalagem de Santa Cruz.** Rua Vasco da Gama, **Horta,** 9900 Faial. Tel: (092) 23021.

▶ **Residencial Santa Cruz. Santa Cruz da Graciosa,** 9880 Graciosa. Tel: (095) 72345.

▶ **Hotel São Pedro.** Largo Almirante Dunn, **Ponta Delgada,** 9500 São Miguel. Tel: (096) 22223.

▶ **Hotel Terra Nostra.** Rua Padre José Francisco Botelho, **Furnas,** 9675 São Miguel. Tel: (096) 54304.

▶ **Estalagem das Velas. Velas,** 9800 São Jorge. Tel: (095) 42632.

CHRONOLOGY OF THE HISTORY OF PORTUGAL

Prehistory

Portugal's long and rambunctious history began in Paleolithic times, perhaps half a million years ago. Chellean and Acheulian hand axes have been unearthed near Lisbon, together with tools and weapons shaped of flint and bone (some of these are on display in the ethnological museum next door to Jerónimos monastery in the Lisbon suburb of Belém). According to *Past Worlds: The Times Atlas of Archaeology* there have been significant finds up and down the west coast of Portugal between the Algarve-Alentejo border and in Coimbra in the Beira Litoral, some 185 miles to the north. But the most exciting discovery is the most recent: In the early 1960s a small painted cave was found in the Alentejo, 80 miles southeast of Lisbon.

- **18,000–13,000 B.C.:** The bull, horse, and hybrid figures crudely drawn on the walls of the Escoural Cave (9 miles south of Montemor-o-Novo and 38 miles west of Evora) may not be as extensive as those at Lascaux in France or Altamira in Spain, but they may be even older and they certainly give some notion as to the manner of man that roamed these red-brown plains before the dawn of recorded history.
- **4000–1500 B.C.:** Megalithic culture flowers in Portugal, particularly around present-day Evora in the Alentejo. This cult of standing stones, of stone gods, then spread north to France and Britain—or so archaeologists now suspect. Clusters of dolmens, menhirs, and chromlechs (areas marked off by stones) still exist throughout the Alentejo. Elsewhere in Portugal the major megalithic sites are

the splendidly preserved Dolmen de Barrosa near the Minho seaside resort of Ancora, and, in Trás-os-Montes just northwest of Chaves, the great rock at Outeiro Machado, upon which early Neolithic artists have left more than 350 carvings—axes, ladders, even human faces.

Migrations and Invasions

- **1100–600 B.C.:** Phoenicians trade along the south and west coasts of Portugal, establishing the post of Alisubbo (now Lisbon), then moving as far north as Nazaré and Aveiro. The people of these two fishing towns claim to be descended from the Phoenicians, and certainly the design of their boats—flat bottoms and high, turned-up prows—is pure Phoenician. Next came the Carthaginians (Phoenicians who had settled in North Africa near Tunis in the ninth century B.C.) and then the Greeks, each sailing out of the Mediterranean through the Straits of Gibraltar, then moving west along the Algarve coast before rounding the land's-end promontory of Cabo de São Vicente and following the rugged shore north to Lisbon.
- **600–300 B.C.:** Invasion and occupation by the Celts, who build fortified towns on hilltops throughout the northern half of Portugal. The major remaining sites (Portugal's oldest settlements) are Citânia de Briteiros and Castro de Sabroso, southeast of Braga in the Minho province. At the larger, more impressive Briteiros, two houses (circular structures of stone) have been reconstructed, the better to show what life was like in this Celtic town. There was a public water system here, a well-laid-out street plan, even an escape tunnel leading down to the river Ave hundreds of yards below. Celtic ornaments, implements, and painted pottery recovered at the site can be seen in Guimarães at the **Martins Sarmento museum** (named for the 19th-century archaeologist who excavated these sites). While Celts were taking over the north of Portugal, the Iberians, possibly from North Africa, occupied the south but unfortunately left few traces.

Roman Portugal

Romans arrive on the Iberian Peninsula in 218 B.C. after the second Punic War, but don't reach the westernmost part of it (what is now Portugal) until some decades later. During their 600-year occupation, the Romans build extensively throughout Portugal: temples, roads, aqueducts, and cities, the wealthiest city being Conimbriga (second century B.C.–A.D. 468), not far south of today's Coimbra. Now being excavated, Conimbriga sprawls across a field. There are colonnaded streets, reflecting pools, fountains, and intricate mosaics worked out in chips of red, white, and black marble.

Iberia's best preserved Roman temple stands in Portugal, too: the little Corinthian temple of Diana at Evora (second century A.D.).

- **197–179 B.C.:** The Lusitanian War rages between the Romans and the Lusitanians, the warlike Celtic tribes and other peoples already occupying what is now Portugal, and at the end of it Lusitania becomes a part of the Roman province of Hispania Ulterior.
- **147–139 B.C.:** Lusitanian resisters try to oust the Romans. Their leader, a valiant warrior named Viriathe ("The Man with the Bracelets"), is today a Portuguese national hero of epic proportion.
- **138 B.C.:** Romans kill Viriathe at Viseu, smash the resistance, and begin colonizing Portugal in earnest. Local resistance continues for more than 100 years.
- **61–45 B.C.:** Julius Caesar manages to subdue the restive population of Hispania Ulterior. In 60 B.C. he establishes a provincial capital at the Roman seaport of Olisippo (Lisbon) and begins building towns at Santarém, Evora, Elvas, and Beja. Caesar also turns the Alentejo into "the granary of Rome" (it remains Portugal's breadbasket today).
- **27–15 B.C.:** Under Augustus (and the *Pax Romana*) Iberia is almost wholly Romanized. The old Hispania Ulterior is split into two provinces: Baetica (now Andalusia) and Lusitania (the lower three-fourths of Portugal plus the modern-day Spanish provinces of Extremadura and Salamanca). That part of Portugal north of the Douro river becomes part of the Roman province of Gallaecia.

- **A.D. 200 onward**: The Christianization of Portugal begins, and bishoprics are established at Braga, Lisbon, Evora, and Faro.

Visigothic Portugal

The fifth century sees the decline of the Roman Empire in Iberia as the Germanic Suevi, Vandals, Alans, and Visigoths sweep in from the north and east. At first the Visigoths respect the Roman Order, but by the end of the sixth century they rule Iberia themselves from their powerful seat at Toledo.

- **409**: The first wave of barbarians—Vandals, Alans, Suevi, and Visigoths—cross the Pyrenees into Spain, then, in time, move westward to Portugal. Only the Germanic Suevi, sometimes called Swabians, who settled between the Roman city of Portus (Porto) on the Douro and the Minho river farther north, and the Visigoths, who ultimately ruled Portugal, left their mark. Although Visigothic ruins are scattered over much of Portugal, the only Suevic relic of significance is the seventh-century Byzantine church of São Frutuoso at Braga in the Minho.
- **414–418**: Visigoths overcome the Alans and Vandals, who retreat into Spain.
- **585**: Led by King Leovigild, the Visigoths suppress the Suevi and annex Seuvic territory to their kingdom of Toledo.
- **589 onward**: Now ruled by King Reccared, the Visigoths become Roman Catholics and begin persecuting Spanish and Portuguese Jews.

Moorish Portugal

When they first call on North African Moslems to help them defeat the Visigoths, few of the native peoples living on the Iberian Peninsula dream that the Moors would overrun them, then rule for more than 500 years. Or that they would change the very look of their land and leave imprints—architectural, agricultural, and otherwise—that are still clearly visible. The *azulejos* (decorative glazed tiles) that face so many Portuguese buildings today were introduced by the Moors, for example, as were the tall filigreed chimney pots and giant water wheels still in use in the Algarve (*itself* an Arabic word meaning "the west"), the arcaded streets, the fountain-splashed courtyards, and the water gardens so characteristic of Portugal.

- **711**: Iberian dissidents appeal to North Africa for help in defeating the imperious, intolerant Visigoths. The Moors cross the Straits of Gibraltar into Spain and begin their conquest of Iberia.
- **716**: Braga, the former Suevic capital, falls to the Moors.
- **717**: All of Iberia is in Moorish hands except for the mountainous north. The Visigoths, still in control of Asturias in north-central Spain, begin the Christian Reconquest of Arab-held peninsular lands.
- **722 onward**: The north of Portugal is reclaimed from the Moors as far south as Porto.
- **945**: The Countess Mumadona founds the Monastery of Vimarenes, the origin of the important Minho town of Guimarães.
- **961–1015**: Viking and Arab raids prompt Mumadona to build a strong defense tower at Vimarenes. It becomes the castle of Guimarães, which in turn becomes "The Cradle of Portugal."

The Dawn of Portuguese Nationhood

- **1095**: Alfonso VI, king of León and Castile, marries his daughter Teresa to the French knight, Henry of Burgundy, who had fought so valiantly against the Moors. He dubs Henry Earl of Portucale.
- **1109**: The Spanish kingdom of León and Castile makes Portucale an independent county within its realm.
- **1111**: Birth of the Earl of Portucale's first son at the castle of Guimarães. Named Afonso Henriques, he will become the first king of Portugal.
- **1128**: The Earl of Portucale dies; at the urging of local barons, young Afonso Henriques revolts against his mother, defeats her forces at the battle of São Mamede at Guimarães, and seizes control: the first decisive step toward the formation of the Kingdom of Portugal.
- **1139**: Afonso Henriques declares Portucale independent of the Spanish kingdom of León and Castile and proclaims himself King Afonso I.
- **1147**: Afonso marches south from Porto and, with the help of Crusaders, drives the Moors from Lisbon.

- **1179**: After half a century of squabbling between León and Castile and Portugal, Rome recognizes Afonso as king of the "sovereign and independent state of Portugal."
- **1185–1223**: Afonso's successors in the Burgundian dynasty, Sancho I and Afonso II, work to consolidate and unify Portugal south along the coast. During this period Portugal's mighty military orders are founded, among them the Hospitalers and the Templars (whose cathedral at Tomar is a major landmark).
- **1249**: Afonso III recaptures Faro in the Algarve, and the last of the Moorish forces leave Portugal.
- **1256**: Lisbon is named capital of Portugal.
- **1279–1325**: The reign of Dinis I. This forward-thinking king unifies Portugal, institutes programs of economic and agricultural reform, and builds 50 fortresses along the Spanish border (among them the hilltop castles at Estremoz, Marvão, and Monsaraz). He also negotiates the Treaty of Alcañices (1297), forcing Castile to honor Portugal's boundaries, and founds a university at Lisbon (1290). Later moved to Coimbra, it is Continental Europe's second-oldest university (after Bologna).

The Age of Discovery

Troubles with Castile (now separate from León) continue. When Fernando I, the last of the Burgundian-dynasty kings, dies, power passes to his widow, who marries their only child, a daughter, to Juan I of Castile, with the condition that the Portuguese throne passes to her unborn grandson. But the people rise up and name as "regent and defender of the realm" João, Grand Master of Avis (a bastard son of Pedro I, known both as "the Cruel" and "the Just").

- **1385**: On August 15 João defeats the Castilians at the battle of Aljubarrota and ascends the throne as João I, the founder of the Avis dynasty.
- **1386**: João I signs the Treaty of Windsor with England, which ensures "an inviolable, eternal, strong, perpetual and true league of friendship, alliance and union."

- **1387**: João I marries Philippa of Lancaster, daughter of John of Gaunt, further cementing Portugal's ties with England.
- **1394**: Dom Infante Henrique (Prince Henry the Navigator), the third son of João I and Queen Philippa, is born in Porto.
- **1419**: Prince Henry goes to Sagres and Cabo de São Vicente in the Algarve to found his school of navigation, remains of which can still be seen.
- **1419–1425**: Portugal discovers and colonizes the Madeira islands.
- **1431–1432**: Portugal discovers and claims the Azores.
- **1433**: João I dies, and Prince Henry's older brother, Dom Duarte, ascends the throne.
- **1434–1435**: Portuguese navigators round Cape Bojador on the west coast of Africa.
- **1436–1437**: Prince Henry leads an attack against Tangier but is defeated.
- **1438**: Prince Henry returns to Sagres and the voyages of discovery.
- **1444**: Portuguese navigators reach Cape Verde; slave trade begins at Lagos in the Algarve.
- **1445–1457**: Portuguese forces push farther down Africa's west coast, reaching Senegal, Gambia, and the Cape Verde Islands.
- **1458**: The king of Portugal commissions Venetian cartographer Fra Mauro to draft a new map of the world incorporating all of Prince Henry's discoveries.
- **1460**: Prince Henry dies at Sagres at the age of 66.
- **1469**: Vasco da Gama is born.
- **1482**: Portuguese navigators reach the mouth of the Congo river.
- **1485**: King João II refuses to finance the voyages of a Genoese explorer who had served Prince Henry and married the daughter of one of his navigators. His name: Christopher Columbus. (A controversial new theory holds that Columbus was not Italian but Portuguese.)
- **1487**: Portuguese explorer Bartolomeu Dias rounds Africa's Cape of Good Hope.
- **1492**: Columbus, sailing under the Spanish flag, discovers the West Indies.
- **1494**: Portugal and Castile sign the Treaty of

Tordesillas, which grants to Castile all discoveries west of a mid-Atlantic meridian (370 sea leagues west of the Cape Verde Islands) and to Portugal all discoveries east of it, which includes Brazil (historians believe the Portuguese already had some inkling of its existence at the time of the treaty).

- **1495–1521**: Reign of Manuel I (Prince Henry's great-great nephew) and the flowering of the exuberant architectural style named for him. The best examples of Manueline architecture are the tower of Belém and Jerónimos monastery near Lisbon, the famous "rope" window at the convent of Christ at Tomar, and the cloister and "unfinished chapels" at the great cathedral at Batalha, which Prince Henry's father began building to commemorate Portugal's victory over Castile at Aljubarrota. Prince Henry lies buried here together with members of his immediate family.
- **1497–1498**: Vasco da Gama leaves Lisbon for the East Indies, rounds the Cape of Good Hope, arrives at Mozambique, then sails on to India.
- **1500**: Pedro Alvares Cabral discovers Brazil (but see 1494, above).
- **1510**: The Portuguese annex Goa on the southwest coast of India.
- **1515**: The Portuguese control the Indian Ocean.
- **1519–1521**: Magellan sails east from Lisbon to circle the globe. He is killed in the Philippines, but one of his captains completes the round-the-world voyage in 1522.
- **1521–1557**: Portugal, now heavily in debt because of its voyages of discovery, suffers a decline.
- **1524**: Luiz Vaz de Camões, Portugal's great epic poet, is born in Lisbon. Vasco da Gama dies.
- **1536–1558**: The Portuguese Inquisition.
- **1557**: The Portuguese open a trading post at Macão in China.
- **1572**: *The Lusiads,* Camões's epic poem immortalizing Portugal's voyages of discovery, is published in Lisbon.
- **1579**: Camões dies in Lisbon.
- **1638**: C. M. Kopke, a German living in Porto, founds the first Port wine company. It still bears his name and is the most distinguished house in the Barrios Almeida group.

The Spanish Domination

In 1580, with Portugal impoverished, Philip II of Spain pounces, annexing not only mainland Portugal but also such colonies as Madeira. When he denies Dutch ships entry to Lisbon to load spices from the Portuguese islands in the East, they sail on to the Indies and soon not only shut the Portuguese out of the spice trade but also seize such valuable possessions as the Moluccas, São Tomé (in the Gulf of Guinea off the west coast of Africa), Angola, and Brazil. Under the three Philips, II, III, and IV, Spain dominates Portugal for 60 years. At the end of Spanish rule in 1640, Portugal is little more than a backward province.

The Rise of the House of Bragança

Outraged by the crushing taxes levied to finance Spanish wars, the nobles of Lisbon rebel. Led by the Duke of Bragança and aided by their old enemy, the Dutch, the Portuguese regain their independence.

- **1640–1656**: João, Duke of Bragança, rules newly liberated Portugal as João IV. During his reign Portugal regains Brazil, Angola, and São Tomé (since 1975 the independent Republic of São Tomé and Principe).
- **1661**: Catherine of Bragança, sister of Afonso VI, marries Charles II of England (it is for her that New York City's borough of Queens is named).
- **1668**: The Treaty of Lisbon is signed, and Spain at last recognizes Portugal's independence.
- **1703**: The Treaty of Methuen is signed with Britain, allowing Portuguese wines to be sold in Britain and British woolens in Portugal, whereupon the Portuguese textile industry collapses.
- **1706–1750**: The reign of João V. Portugal once again grows rich and powerful thanks to the discovery of gold and diamonds in Brazil. Many of the country's most resplendent buildings are built, including the palace at Mafra, the summer palace at Queluz just outside Lisbon, and the Baroque library at Coimbra (by most accounts, the world's most beautiful library because of its painted ceilings and rare gilded and inlaid woods).
- **1755**: The great earthquake and fire destroys most

of Lisbon and kills more than 30,000 people. With the blessing of José I, the Marquês de Pombal redesigns the city and Lisbon becomes a town of leafy squares and broad boulevards lined with buildings four and five stories tall.
- **1755–1777**: José I all but hands the throne to the rigid and tyrannical Marquês de Pombal, who tries, among other things, to throw off the English yoke and make Portugal economically independent. He also expels the Jesuits because they had become too powerful.
- **1756**: Port-wine-growing region demarcated (100 years before France's *appellation contrôlée*).
- **1777–1792**: José I dies, Maria I (The Mad) ascends the throne, and the Marquês de Pombal falls from grace. Most of Pombal's reforms are rescinded; the Jesuits return to Portugal.
- **1792**: With Maria I now deranged, João VI becomes regent.

The Peninsular War

Because of its great alliance with Britain, Portugal is drawn more or less unwillingly into the Napoleonic Wars, and, as a result, battles are fought on her soil.

- **1793**: Portugal joins Britain in its struggle against Napoleon.
- **1807**: Junot's French troops invade Portugal. The Portuguese royal family flees to Brazil.
- **1808**: Wellington arrives with detachments of British soldiers to fight the French.
- **1810**: Wellington scores the decisive victory against the French by winning the battle of Buçaco just north of Coimbra.

The Decline and Fall of the Monarchy

- **1811**: The French are driven out of Portugal into Spain. With the Portuguese royal family still in exile in Brazil, British General William Carr Beresford governs newly liberated Portugal.
- **1817–1820**: Weary of British rule, Portuguese liberals rise up repeatedly, only to be quelled by British soldiers.

- **1821:** A new liberal Portuguese constitution is drafted and approved by the Cortes (the legislative body), which confirms João VI king of Portugal. He returns from Brazil with Queen Carlota and their younger son, Miguel. Crown Prince Pedro remains in Brazil. The king agrees to the terms of the new constitution; Queen Carlota and Prince Miguel do not.
- **1822:** Brazil declares its independence.
- **1825–1834:** João VI dies and Crown Prince Pedro, now emperor of Brazil, is proclaimed king. Pedro refuses to return to Portugal and vows, instead, to pass the crown to his baby daughter, Maria da Glória, and to let his younger brother, Miguel, serve as regent until she comes of age. Prince Miguel agrees, but soon after assuming power he reneges, abolishes the new constitution, and returns to the absolutist ways. Crown Prince Pedro, deposed as emperor of Brazil, returns to Portugal to find that his brother has seized the throne. The Miguelist Wars follow, until Pedro defeats Miguel once and for all at Evoramonte. Pedro IV no sooner gains power than he dies. His daughter succeeds him as Maria II.
- **1836:** Maria II marries Duke Ferdinand of Saxe-Coburg-Koháry, a cousin of Queen Victoria's consort, Prince Albert.
- **1837–1907:** Unrest continues with repeated power plays among the liberals and conservatives. An anticlerical movement leaves many great monasteries derelict.
- **1908:** King Carlos I is assassinated in Lisbon along with Crown Prince Luis Filipe. Carlos's second son ascends the throne as Manuel II.
- **1910:** To save Portugal from civil war, King Manuel abdicates, retreats to England, and remains there in exile until his death in 1932. The Republic is born on October 5.

The Republic of Portugal

The young republic struggles to restore order and a sound economy, but with little success.

- **1916**: Portugal joins the Allies and declares war on Germany.
- **1920**: The war leaves Portugal financially depleted and minus much of its manpower.
- **1926**: A military coup overthrows the government and General António Carmona soon emerges as Portugal's new president; he remains in office until his death in 1951.
- **1928**: Dr. António de Oliveira Salazar, an economics professor from the university at Coimbra, is named finance minister; he quickly balances Portugal's budget and helps restore political order.
- **1932 onward**: Salazar becomes prime minister and within a year masterminds the organization of the New State, which gives him the powers of a dictator.
- **1939–1945**: Portugal remains neutral during World War II but allows Great Britain and the United States to build air bases in the Azores.
- **1961**: Portugal loses its colony of Goa to India.
- **1968**: A freak accident incapacitates Salazar (his deck chair collapses and he suffers irreversible brain damage). His successor, Marcelo Caetano, continues the rigid Salazar policies, including an unpopular war with the African colonies.
- **1970**: Salazar dies.
- **1970s**: Africans from the Cape Verde Islands are brought to Lisbon to do general construction work. Many stay, but there is little work available for them, and some become peddlers and, alas, thieves.
- **1974**: On April 25 the military seizes power in a virtually bloodless coup now known as the "Flower Revolution" (soldiers marched through Lisbon with red carnations stuck into the barrels of their guns). Portugal veers sharply toward the left as Communists and Socialists gain strength at the polls. Communism is especially popular among the farmers of the Alentejo, who work the vast estates of absentee owners for very little pay.
- **1974–1975**: Portugal's African colonies of Angola and Mozambique gain independence, and 750,000 refugees flood into Lisbon. Because of a housing shortage, the leftist government domiciles them in worker-run tourist hotels (even the Ritz is commandeered).
- **1976 onward**: A new constitution is adopted. Politi-

cal power struggles continue among rightists, centrists, and leftists, but gradually a more stable coalition government is stitched together. General António Eanes is elected president.
- **1986**: Dr. Mário Soares, a Socialist, is elected president. Portugal joins the European Community.

—Jean Anderson

INDEX

Abrantes, 145
Achadinha, 410
Adega Lusitania, 413
Adega Machado: Caminha, 331; Lisbon, 72
Adega Regional: Amarante, 286; Arcos de Valdevez, 325
Adega Regional de Colares, 95
Adega Saloio, 90
Ad Lib, 73
Adro da Sé, 231
Agora, 211
Aguiar da Beira, 238
Aguias d'Ouro, 169
Albergaria de João Padeiro, 221, 225
Albergaria Senhora do Monte, 67
Albufeira, 192
Alcântara Mar, 73
Alcazaba, 194
Alcobaça, 104
Aldeamento da Pedra Verde, 319, 344
Aldeamento Turístico Marinha Village, 87, 116
Alentejo, 10, 13, 14, 16, 19, 151
Al-Faghar, 184
Alfama, 6, 45
Algamar, 111
Algar do Carvão, 414
Algarve, 8, 180
Alhandra, 126
Alijó, 282
Almansil, 188
Almeida, 239
Almeirim, 146
Alpendre, 197
Alpiarça, 146
Alto Douro, 250
Alto da Memória, 413
Alto Minho, 321
Alto Tamega, 362
Alto do Velão, 352
Amarante, 284
Amoreira Aqueduct, 174
Ana Salazar, 73
Angra do Heroismo, 412
Aniki-Bobo, 274
Anjos, 411
Antigo Convento de Santa Maria de Aguiar, 240
Antigo Paço Episcopal, 309
Antigo Paços do Conselho, 333
Antigos Paços do Conselho, 301
Aparthotel Magnoliamar, 114, 116

Aparthotel de Tróia, 114, 116
Apeadeiro Restaurante, 86
Aqueduto das Aguas Livres, 60
Aramenha, 177
Arcadia, 267
Arco da Porta Nova, 310
Arcos de Valdevez, 326
Arco da Vila, 183
Armona, 187
Arouca, 224
Arrábida Peninsula, 15, 17, 110
Arraiolos, 163
Atei, 353
Atelier Fotográfico de Carlos Relvas, 134
Atlantis: Cascais, 85; Lisbon, 74
Aveiro, 221
Avenida Palace, 66
Avis, 178
Avis Restaurant, 56
Aviz, 69
Avo, 218
Azambuja, 126
Azeitão, 112
Azenhas do Mar, 96
Azores, 18, 401

Bacchus, 56
Bagoeira, 338
Bairro Alto, 55, 73
Baixa: Lisbon, 42, 73; Porto, 266
Banana Power, 72
Barca de Alva, 288
Barcelos, 336
Barracha's Copper Shop, 191
Barredo, 263
Barreto and Gonçalves, 74
Barrô, 279
Batalha, 105
O Batel, 86
Bay of São Lourenço, 411
Bazar do Parque, 84
Beco do Carneiro, 50
Beco do Chão Salgado, 63
Beira Alta, 18, 226
Beira Baixa, 226, 246
Beira Litoral, 10, 14, 16, 201
Beira Mar, 413
Belém, 9, 12, 61, 81
Belmonte, 246
Benfica, 16
Berlengas, 100
Berta Marinho, 74
Bertrand's, 54
Biblioteca Joanina, 212
Bobadela, 218
Bôca do Inferno, 87

Bolhão, 266
Bom Jesus do Monte, 12, 316
Bom Sucesso, 266
Borba, 172
Bordalo Pinheiro Factory Museum, 102
Braga, 304
Bragança, 358
Brazileira, 54
Buçaco National Park, 17, 18, 219

O Cabaz da Praia, 193
Cabeço da Neve, 230
Cabo Espichel, 111
Cabo Girão, 395
Cabo da Roca, 88
Cabo São Vicente, 198
Cachalote, 396
Cacilhas, 108
Café Brazileira, 311
Café Relógio, 390
Café Restaurante Atlantida, 411
Calântica, 163
Caldas de Monchique, 195
Caldas da Rainha, 102
Caldeira do Enxofre, 414
Caldeira de Guilherme Moniz, 414
Caldeirão, 419
Caldeira das Sete Cidades, 408
Camacha, 389
Câmara de Lobos, 394
Câmara Municipal, 310
Caminha, 331
Campo da Feira, 131
Canal Central, 222
Canal de São Roque, 222
Ca d'Oro, 190
Caparica, 108
Capela do Fundador, 106
Capela dos Milagres, 393
Capela de Nossa Senhora da Agonia, 334
Capela de Nossa Senhora de Conceição, 312
Capela de Nossa Senhora da Piedade, 140
Capela de Nossa Senhora da Vitória, 414
Capela dos Ossos, 161
Capela dos Reis, 307
Capelas, 409
Capela de Santa Catarina, 382
Capela de Santo António, 51
Capela da São Frutuoso, 318
Capela de São Miguel, 212
Capela do Senhor dos Passos, 127

434

INDEX 435

Capelinhos, 417
Capuchos, 93
Caramulinho, 230
Caramulo, 229
Caravela, 386
Carcavelos, 81
O Carneiro, 356
Cartaxo, 126
La em Casa, 360
Casa do Adro, 326, 343
Casa da Agrela, 325, 343
Casa das Antiguidades, 338
Casa dos Arcos, 338
Casa D'Armas, 335
Casa d'Avo, 129
Casa do Barão de Fermil, 352, 368
Casa do Barreiro, 248, 249
Casa do Bico, 248
Casa dos Bicos, 53
Casa Canada, 73
Casa dos Cedros, 133, 149
Casa de Chá Terra Nostra, 410
Casa dos Coimbras, 312
Casa da Comida, 70
Casa Cordovil, 161
Casa dos Crivos, 311
Casa do Cruzeiro, 244, 249
Casa Eden, 315
Casa Fânzeres, 315
Casa da Granja, 352, 369
Casa do Infante, 265
Casa dos Lagos, 317, 343
Casa do Leão, 46, 69
Casa Leonel, 74
Casa dos Linhos, 266
Casal da Torre, 134, 149
Casa das Mariquinhas, 273
Casa do Mato, 279, 289
Casa da Misericórdia, 266
Casa do Monte, 339, 343
Casa Museu Almeida Moreira, 233
Casa Museu Francisco Ernesto de Oliveira Martins, 413
Casa Museu Frederico de Freitas, 385
Casa Museu dos Patudos, 146
Casa do Paço, 218
Casa da Pedra Cavalgada, 314, 343
Casa de Pomarchão, 323, 344
Casa da Ponte, 95
Casa das Quartas, 351, 369
Casa dos Quintais, 209, 225
Casa Quintão, 75
Casa de Rebordinho, 230, 249
Casa da Rede, 283
Casa Regional da Ilha Verde: Lisbon, 74; Ponta Delgada, 407
Casa dos Reis, 386
Casa de Resende, 279, 289
Casa do Ribeiro, 303, 344
Casa de Rodas, 328, 344
Casa da Santa Lucia, 320, 344

Casa de São Gens, 279, 289
Casa dos Serralvas, 268
Casa de Sobre Ribas, 213
Casa da Torre Ermitage, 191
Casa do Turista, 379
Casa dos Varais, 281, 289
Casa Zé da Calçada, 286, 289
Cascais, 15, 85
Casino da Madeira, 378, 386
Casino Monumental, 339
Casino Park Hotel, 378, 399
O Castel dos Caiados, 218
O Castelo, 197
Castelo de Algoso, 358
Castelo de Bode, 141
Castelo Bom, 241
Castelo Branco, 247
Castelo de Leiria, 203
Castelo Melhor, 241
Castelo Mendo, 241
Castelo de Milfontes, 155, 179
Castelo de Monforte, 364
Castelo dos Mouros, 93
Castelo da Pena, 93
Castelo do Queijo, 271
Castelo Rodrigo, 240
Castelo de São João da Foz, 270
Castelo de São Jorge, 46
Castelo de Vide, 175
Castle of Almourol, 143
Castle of São Tiago da Barra, 333
Castro de Avelas, 360
Castro de Sabroso, 304
Cava de Viriato, 233
Cavalo Branco, 409
Celeiro, 380
Celorico de Basto, 352
Celorico da Beira, 244
Centum Cellas, 246
Cerâmica de Bicesse, 84
Ceramicarte, 86
Cêrca Moura, 47
Cervejaria Trindade, 56
Chafariz do largo do Paço, 309
Chapelaria de Abreu Araújo, 315
Chapel of the Convento dos Lóios, 158
Chapel of Nossa Senhora da Penha, 176
Chapel of Nossa Senhora dos Remédios, 100
Chapel of Santo António, 197
Chaves, 363
Chez Lapin, 264
Chiado, 54, 73
Chico Elias, 140
A Choupana, 84
Church of Misericórdia, 367

Church of Nossa Senhora de Alegria, 176
Church of Nossa Senhora da Assunção, 135
Church of Nossa Senhora de Assunção, 85
Church of Nossa Senhora de Nazaré, 104
Church of Nossa Senhora da Pena, 206
Church of Santa Maria, 101, 176, 359
Church of Santo André, 409
Church of São Francisco, 161
Church of São Gonçalo, 284
Church of São Mamede, 96
Church of São Pedro, 99, 100, 109, 409
Churrasqueiria Tulha, 323
Cidade Velha, 184
La Cigale, 193
Cinfães, 278
Citânia de Briteiros, 303
Ciudad Rodrigo, Spain, 241
Clara, 70
Claustro Real, 106
Claustro do Silencio, 214
Clavi di Nos, 72
Clérigos Tower, 267
Cloister of Silence, 104
Club Naval, 417
Coconut's, 86
Coimbra, 209
Coimbra Regional Handicraft Center, 214
Colares, 95
Colégio Church, 381
Colegio Novo, 214
Colina Sagrada, 298
Comida de Santo, 71
Conde de Castro Guimarães Museum, 85
Conde Dom Henrique, 314
Condeixa-a-Novo, 217
Condestável, 163
Confeitaria Peixinho, 222
Conimbriga, 217
Constância, 144
Convent of Nossa Senhora do Pilar, 270
Convento de Cristo, 137
Convento de Nossa Senhora da Esperança, 407
Convento de Nossa Senhora do Espinheiro, 159
Convento de Refojos, 352
Convento de Santa Clara: Funchal, 385; Porto, 267
Convento da Santa Iria, 139
Convent of Santa Clara, 341
Convent of Santa Clara-a-Novo, 216
Convent of Santa Clara-a-Velha, 215
Conventual, 70
Copodetres, 72
Coral, 387
Corvo, 418
Cosme, 417
Costa Nova, 223
Costa do Sol, 80

INDEX

Costa Verde, 331
Covilhã, 245
Cozinha das Malheiras, 335
Cozinha do Rei, 222
Cozinha de Santo Humberto, 160
Cozinha Velha, 90
Crato, 178
Cristo Rei, 108
Cromlech and Menhir of Almendres, 165
Cromlech of Xarez, 171
Cruz Alta: Coimbra, 217; Sintra, 93
Cruzeiro do Senhor do Galo, 337
Cruz de Portugal, 195
Cucos, 99
Culatra, 187
Curral das Freiras, 388

Darcy's, 197
Dennis Inn and Bar, 196
Diligencia, 211
Dionisyos, 363
D'Oliveiras Wine Lodge, 381
Dolmen-Chapel of São Brissos, 165
Dolmen of Comenda, 165
Dolmen of Silval, 165
Dom Manuel, 271
Domus Municipalis, 359
Dona Filipa, 190, 200
Dornes, 142
Douro Litoral, 15, 17, 250
Douro Valley, 15, 250, 274
Downing Street, 264
Durão Peak, 240

Eduardo Azenha, 96
Eira do Serrado, 388
Elevador, 316
Elevador da Gloria Cable Car, 57
Eloy de Jesus, 74
Elvas, 174
English Bar, 84
Enseada, 340
Ericeira, 96
Ermelo, 327
Ermida, 326
Escola de Bilros, 341
Escondidinho, 273
Escoural Cave, 165
O Espigueiro, 336
Esplanada Marisqueira, 271
Estação Zootécnica Nacional, 126, 134
Estalagem do Brasão, 341, 343
Estalagem do Caçador, 355, 368
Estalagem de Carvalhelhos, 366, 368
Estalagem Ilha do Lombo, 141, 149
Estalagem Muchaxo, 88, 116
Estalagem Nossa Senhora da Guia, 87, 116
Estalagem de Santa Cruz, 416, 417, 420

Estalagem Santa Iria, 139, 149
Estalagem de Santa Maria, 224, 225
Estalagem Santo André, 339, 344
Estalagem São Miguel, 224
Estalagem Vale da Ursa, 141, 150
Estalagem das Velas, 415, 420
Estói, 186
Estoril, 8, 82
Estoril-Cascais-Guincho Coast, 8
Estoril Casino, 83
Estrela Factory, 217
Estremadura, 9, 76
Estremoz, 166
Estufa Fria, 59
Estufa Quente, 59
Estufas Agosto Arruda, 408
Evora, 156
Evoramonte, 171

Fábrica Kalifa, 163
Fabrica da Sant'Anna, 74
Factory House, 264
Faial, 415
Faianças Artisticas Bordalo Pinheiro, 102
Fajazinha, 418
Falcão Restaurant, 144
Faro, 183
Fátima, 11, 142
Faustino and Filhos, 364
Favaios, 283
Feira da Ladra, 52, 75
Feira Nacional do Cavalo, 134
Ferrari, 75
O Fervedouro, 409
Festas dos Santos Populares, 51
Fialho, 16, 160
Figas de Ermelo, 352
Figueira da Foz, 218
Figueiro dos Vinhos, 208
Flores, 418
Flor da Rosa, 178
Fonte do Idolo, 312
Fortaleza, 100
Forte Dom Rodrigo, 86
Forteleza do Beliche, 199, 200
Forte de São Bras, 407
Fortress of Lindoso, 326
Fortress of São João Baptista, 101
Foz de Arouce, 209
Foz Palace Motel, 103, 115
Francisco Ramos, 75
Frangos, 195
Freixo de Espada-à-Cinta: Beira Alta, 240; Tras-os-Montes, 355
Funchal, 379
Fundação Calouste Gulbenkian, 59
Furnas, 409
Furnas Lagosteira, 87

Gabriela, 356
Gafieira, 72
Galeao, 73
Galerias de Vandoma, 266
Gambrinus, 44, 70
Gerês, 320
Gigi's, 191
Golegã, 134
Gomes, 340
Gouveia, 244
Graciosa, 414
Grande Hotel do Porto, 266, 273, 289
Greens, 274
Guadalupe, 414
Guarda, 241
Guimarães, 11, 297
Guincho, 15, 88
Gulbenkian Foundation, 59

Helio, 73
Herdeiros de Francisco José Ferreira, 315
Horta, 415
Hospital São Marcos, 312
Hot Clube de Portugal, 72
Hotel Abides, 133, 149
Hotel do Aeroporto, 411, 420
Hotel Albatroz, 87, 115
Hotel Amarante, 285, 289
Hotel Atlántico, 84, 115
Hotel Baia, 86, 115
Hotel Beira Mar, 412, 420
Hotel Boa Vista, 270, 289
Hotel Central, 91
Hotel Dom José, 142, 149
Hotel do Elevador, 314, 343
Hotel Estoril-Sol, 84, 115
Hotel Eurosol, 206
Hotel Faial, 416, 420
Hotel Grão Vasco, 230, 249
Hotel do Guincho, 88, 116
Hotel de Infante Sagres, 272, 273, 289
Hotel do Mar, 111, 116
Hotel Mar e Sol, 207, 225
Hotel Méridien, 272, 289
Hotel Monte Palace, 409
Hotel Navarras, 285, 289
Hotel Palácio, 83, 116
Hotel Palácio dos Seteais, 94, 116
Hotel Paloma Blanca, 221, 225
Hotel Parque, 235, 249
Hotel Porto Santo, 397, 400
Hotel La Réserve, 192, 200
Hotel Rex, 67
Hotel de Santa Luzia, 334, 344
Hotel São Pedro, 407, 408, 420
Hotel Savoy, 378, 400
Hotel Sheraton Porto, 272, 289
Hotel Solneve, 245
Hotel dos Templários, 140, 150
Hotel Terra Nostra, 409, 420
Hotel Tivoli, 91, 116
Hotel Trajano, 364, 369

INDEX 437

Hotel de Turismo, 145
Hotel Vila Joya, 193

Idanha-a-Velha, 247
Igreja do Bom Jesus de Matosinhos, 271
Igreja do Carmo: Coimbra, 215; Faro, 184; Lisbon, 55; Porto, 268; Viseu, 233
Igreja do Colégio, 413
Igreja dos Congregados, 267
Igreja da Graça, 130
Igreja dos Grilos, 109
Igreja de Jesús, 109
Igreja da Madre de Deus, 53
Igreja de Marvila, 129
Igreja Matriz: Barcelos, 337; Caminha, 331; Golega, 134; Sesimbra, 111; Viana do Castelo, 333; Vila do Conde, 341
Igreja da Misericórdia: Angra do Heroismo, 412; Chaves, 363; Porto, 266; Viseu, 232
Igreja de Nossa Senhora dos Anjos, 411
Igreja de Nossa Senhora da Assunção, 411
Igreja de Nossa Senhora da Oliveira, 300
Igreja de Nossa Senhora do Rosário, 410
Igreja de Santa Clara, 132
Igreja de Santa Iria, 133
Igreja de Santa Maria da Alcáçova, 130
Igreja de Santa Maria do Castelo, 145
Igreja de Santa Maria Madalena, 317
Igreja de Santiago e São Mateus, 146
Igreja do Santíssimo Milagre, 131
Igreja de Santo António da Torre Velha, 322
Igreja de São Facundo, 362
Igreja de São Francisco: Porto, 265; Vinhais, 362
Igreja de São João Baptista, 138
Igreja de São Jorge, 410
Igreja de São José, 407
Igreja de São Lourenço, 188
Igreja de São Martinho, 388
Igreja de São Miguel, 409
Igreja de São Miguel do Castelo, 299
Igreja de São Pedro de Balsemão, 236
Igreja de São Roque, 57
Igreja do São Salvador, 325
Igreja do Seminário, 129
Igreja de Senhor da Cruz, 337
Ilha de Tavira, 188
Imperial Linens, 384
Inácio Filho, 314, 343
Instituto do Bordado Tapeçarias e Artesanato, 383
Isto e Aquilo, 86

Jardim do Antigo Paço Episcopal, 248
Jardim Botânico: Coimbra, 216; Funchal, 387; Lisbon, 57; Porto, 268
Jardim de Santa Bárbara, 311
Jardim Zoológico, 60
Jesuit University, 162
João Padeira, 86
João Passo's, 191
Jordão, 301
José Rosas & Cie, 266
Judiaria, 176
Junceda Belvedere, 321

Lagoa, 409
Lagos, 197
Lajes do Pico, 417
Lamego, 203
A Lanterna, 196
Lapella, 328
Largo da Oliveira, 300
Largo do Paço, 309
Largo das Portas de Moura, 161
Largo das Portas do Sol, 47
Laurentina, 71
Lavores, 74
O Leao de Porches, 193
Leiria, 203
Linha do Corgo, 288, 364, 367
Linha do Douro, 287
Linhares, 244
Linha do Sabor, 287
Linha do Tâmega, 285, 288, 368
Linha da Tua, 288, 367
Lisboa A Noite, 71
Lisboa Sheraton, 66
Lisbon, 6, 9, 14, 15, 16, 35
Livraria Nove Estrelas, 408
Lontra, 72
Loulé, 191
Lourinhã, 99
Lourosa, 218
Lousã, 208
Lusitana, 311
Luz, 414

Macedo de Cavaleiros, 354
Machico, 392
Madeira, 9, 14, 18, 370
Madeira House, 73
Madeira-Sheraton Hotel, 378, 399
Madeira Wine Company, 376
Mafra, 96
Majestic Café, 267
Mal Cozinhado, 273
O Mal Cozinhado, 132
Mangualde, 234
Manteigas, 245
Mare Viva, 64
Marialva, 241
Maria Rita, 353
Marinha Grande, 207
A Marisqueira, 224
Marquês de Marialva, 220
Martins and Costa, 75

Martins Sarmento Museum, 422
Marvão, 19, 177
Matosinhos, 270
Mazouco, 356
Mealhada, 16, 220
Menhir of Bulhoa, 170
Menhir of Outeiro, 170
Mercado dos Lavradores, 383
Mercado da Ribeira, 39
Méridien, 66
Mesão Frio, 283
Mezio, 327
Michel, 69
Milagres, 207
Milreu, 186
Minho, 10, 11, 13, 19, 290
Miradouro da Boa Vista, 280
Miradouro de Santa Luzia, 280
Miradouro do Espigão, 411
Miranda do Douro, 288, 357
Mirandela, 353
Mirandes, 358
Miscricórdia Hospice, 333
Mr. Bojangle's Bistro Bar, 196
Mistério da Prainha, 418
Mistério de Santa Luzia, 418
Mistério de São João, 417
Mogadouro, 355
Moimenta da Beira, 238
Moinho de Estorãos, 324, 343
Moita do Ribatejo, 148
Monastery of Batalha, 105
Monastery of Jerónimos, 81
Monastery of Nossa Senhora de Terço, 337
Monção, 328
Mon Cicus, 195, 200
Mondim de Basto, 352
Monsanto, 247
Monsaraz, 170
Monserrate, 17, 95
Montalegre, 367
Monte Cara, 70
Monte do Faro, 329
Monte Gordo, 187
Monte de Madalena, 323
Montemor-o-Velho, 218
Monte dos Pensamentos, 154, 179
O Montinho, 193
Mosteiro dos Jerónimos, 62
Mosteiro de Santa Cruz, 214
Mosteiro de São Francisco, 133
Motel de Sant'Ana, 342, 344
Municipal Gallery of Visual Arts, 109
Municipal Museum: Estremoz, 168; Obidos, 101
Muralha, 338
Muralhas, 330
Murça, 353
Museu de Alberto Sampaio, 300
Museu da Angra, 413
Museu Arqueológico Lapidar do Infante Dom Henrique, 183

INDEX

Museu Arqueológico de São João de Alporão, 129
Museu de Arte Popular, 12, 62
Museu de Arte Sacra: Braga, 308; Funchal, 381; Horta, 416; Porto, 263
Museu de Aveiro, 222
Museu da Baleia, 417
Museu do Caramulo, 229
Museu Carlos Machado, 407
Museu de Cera de Fátima, 142
Museu de Coches, 63
Museu de Curiosidades, 354
Museu Escola de Artes Decorativas, 47
Museu de Etnografia, 411, 414
Museu de Etnografia Regional, 186
Museu Etnográfico, 147, 265, 418
Museu de Evora, 158
Museu Francisco Tavares Proença Júnior, 248
Museu de Grão Vasco, 231
Museu da Guarda, 244
Museu Guerra Junqueiro, 263
Museu de Horta, 416
Museu de José Malhõa, 102
Museu Luso-Hebraico, 139
Museu Machado de Castro, 212
Museu de Marinha, 63
Museu Marítimo e Regional, 224
Museu Martins Sarmento, 302
Museu Militar, 52, 363
Museum of Roman Ruins, 192
Museu Municipal, 238, 333
Museu Municipal Dr. Santos Rocha, 218
Museu Nacional de Arqueologia e Etnologia, 63
Museu Nacional de Arte Antiga, 44
Museu Nacional de Arte Contemporânea, 55
Museu Nacional do Azulejo, 53
Museu Pio XII, 312
Museu da Região Flaviense, 363
Museu Regional Abade de Baçal, 359
Museu Regional de Lamego, 236
Museu Romântico, 268
Museu Rural, 167
Museu Rural e do Vinho, 127
Museu Soares dos Reis, 268
Museu da Terra de Miranda, 357

Navigadores, 190
Nazaré, 103
Nicola, 42
Nossa Senhora da Conceição, 393
Nossa Senhora da Memória, 103
Nossa Senhora do Pópulo, 102
Nossa Senhora dos Remédios, 12, 237

Obidos, 101
Odrinhas, 96
Oeiras, 81
Olaria, 194
Olhão, 187
Oliveira do Hospital, 219
Orca, 396
Outeiro Machado, 365
Ovar, 224

Paço D'Anha, 335, 343
Paço de Calheiros, 324, 343
Paço Ducal, 172, 299
Paço de São Cipriano, 303, 344
Paços do Conselho, 331
Paço Vedro de Magalhães, 325, 344
Padrão da Batalha do Salado, 301
Padrão dos Descobrimentos, 62
O Pagem, 70
Palace of the Counts of Basto, 162
Palace Hotel do Buçaco, 219, 225
Palace of Monserrate, 95
Palácio da Alorna, 147
Palácio Bettencourt, 413
Palácio dos Biscainhos, 310
Palácio da Bolsa, 265
Palácio de Brejoeira, 328
Palácio de Constância, 144, 149
Palácio de Cristal, 268
Palácio Ducal, 337
Palácio Mateus, 350
Palácio Municipal de Exposições, 313
Palácio Nacional, 92
Palácio Nacional da Ajuda, 64
Palácio Nacional de Mafra, 97
Palácio Nacional de Queluz, 89
Palácio dos Pitas, 331
Palácio Raio, 312
Palácio de São Lourenço, 382
Palácio de Visconde de Estói, 186
Palm Beach, 86
Palmela, 108
Pão de Açucar, 85
Pap'Açorda, 70
Paraíso da Montanho, 195
Parque Eduardo VII, 58
Parque Hotel, 317, 343
Parque de Marinha, 87
Parque Mouchão, 139
Parque Nacional de Alvão, 351
Parque Nacional de Peneda-Gerês, 18, 318
Parque Natural de Montesinhos, 361
Parque Restaurant, 330
Parque de Santa Catarina, 382
Parque da Santa Cruz, 216
Pastelaria Suissa, 43
Patrício & Gouveia, 384
Paúl da Serra, 396
Pavia, 178
Pavilhão Chines, 72
Pedrogão Grande, 208
Pedro dos Leitões, 220
Pelourinho, 363
Pena, 93
Penafiel, 286
Penamacor, 247
Peneda-Gerês National Park, 18, 318
Penedono, 241
Penedo da Saudade, 216
Penela, 217
Penha, 302
Peniche, 100
Peninha, 93
Pensão Lajes das Flores, 418, 420
Pensão Monte do Faro, 329, 343
Pensão Residencia Santa Maria da Arrábida, 110
Pensão Ribamar, 103, 116
O Pescador, 86
Peso da Régua, 280
Pete's Café Sport, 416
Picnic, 43
Pico, 417
Pico do Arieiro, 391
Pico dos Barcelos, 388
Pico de Esperança, 415
Pico Ruivo, 391
Pico de Vara, 410
Pinhão, 15, 281
Pinha Real, 206
Pinhel, 238
Pinoucas, 229
Piscinas, 217
Pombal, 208
Ponta Delgada, 407
Ponta do Mistério, 414
Ponta do Queimado, 414
Ponte da Barca, 325
Ponte de Lima, 322
Ponte da Piedade, 198
Popedoce, 234
Porches, 193
Portas do Sol, 130
Portimão, 196
Portinho da Arrábida, 110
Porto, 15, 250
Porto Covo, 155
Porto Formoso, 410
Porto Moniz, 395
Porto de Santa Maria, 88
Porto Santo, 396
Portucale, 272
Postigo do Carvão, 274
O Pote, 364

INDEX 439

Pousada do Barão de Forrester, 15, 282, 289, 351, 368
Pousada do Castelo, 101, 115
Pousada do Castelo de Palmela, 109, 115
Pousada de Dom Dinis, 330, 343
Pousada do Infante, 198, 200
Pousada dos Lóios, 154, 157, 162, 179
Pousada do Mestre Afonso Domingues, 106, 116
Pousada da Nossa Senhora da Oliveira, 301, 343
Pousada Pico do Arieiro, 379, 390, 399
Pousada da Rainha Santa Isabel, 154, 168, 179
Pousada da Ria, 221, 223, 225
Pousada de Santa Bárbara, 19, 219, 225
Pousada Santa Catarina, 358, 369
Pousada de Santa Luzia, 174
Pousada de Santa Maria, 19, 154, 177, 179
Pousada de Santa Marinha da Costa, 302, 344
Pousada de Santo António, 221, 225
Pousada de São Bartolomeu, 360, 369
Pousada de São Bento, 319, 344
Pousada de São Filipe, 110, 116
Pousada de São Gens, 154, 179
Pousada de São Gonçalo, 351, 369
Pousada de São Jerónimo, 229, 249
Pousada de São Lourenço, 244, 249
Pousada de São Pedro, 141, 149
Pousada de São Teotónio, 329, 344
Pousada Senhora das Neves, 239, 249
Pousada dos Vinháticos, 379, 400
Povoação, 410
Póvoa de Lanhoso, 318
Póvoa de Varzim, 339
Praça de Camões, 363
Praça do Comércio, 39
Praça Dom Pedro V, 176
Praça Dom Pedro IV, 42
Praça Marquês de Pombal, 58
Praça do Município, 381
Praça da República: Tomar, 138; Viana, 333
Praça dos Restauradores, 44
Praia das Maças, 96
Praia dos Moinhos, 410
Praia da Rocha, 196
Príncipe Real, 67
Procopio, 72

Queluz, 17, 89
Quinta de Aveleda, 286
Quinta da Bacalhoa, 113, 115
Quinta da Boa Vista, 356, 368
Quinta do Bom Sucesso, 387
Quinta da Capela, 95, 115
Quinta da Cardiga, 135
Quinta do Convento Franqueira, 338, 343
Quinta das Cruzes, 384
Quinta dos Frades, 285
Quinta do Lago, 190, 200
Quinta das Lágrimas, 215
Quinta Magnólia, 382
Quinta dos Marqueses de Fronteira, 60
Quinta do Paço da Ermida, 221, 225
Quinta do Palheiro Ferreiro, 389
Quinta da Penha de França, 379, 399
Quinta do Santoinho, 336
Quinta de São José, 99, 116
Quinta de São Thiago, 94, 116
Quinta da Sobreira, 133, 150
Quinta das Torres, 113, 116
Quinta Vale de Lobos, 150
Quinta do Vinagre, 95

Ramalhão, 218
Rampa, 195
Ranniro Lea, 74
Redondo, 169
Refúgio da Mãe de Deus, 408
Refúgio da Roca, 88
Regional Archaeological and Ethnographic Museum, 109
Regionalia, 84
Regional Museum, 197
El Rei, 301
Remo, 331
Resende, 279
La Réserve, 191
Residencia Inglêsa, 67
Residencial Santa Cruz, 414, 420
Restaurante Alboroque, 246
Restaurante Campismo, 364
Restaurante Castizo, 132
Restaurante Mar Bravo, 103
Ria de Aveiro, 223
Ribatejo, 10, 11, 16, 117
Ribeira, 263
Ribeira Grande, 409
Rio de Onor, 361
Ritz Grill, 70
Ritz Inter-Continental Hotel, 59, 65
Romana, 386
Romeu, 353
Roque, 184
Rosal Boutique, 315
Rosier, 266
Rossio: Lisbon, 42, 73; Viseu, 233
Rota Do Vinho, 126
A Ruina, 193

Sabugal, 246
Sado Estuary Natural Reserve, 114
Sagres, 198
St. James Store Outlet, 196
Saisa, 82
Sala do Arcaz, 309
Sameiro, 317
Santa Bárbara, 411
Santa Cruz: Flores, 418; Madeira, 393
Santa Cruz Café, 211, 215
Santa Cruz da Graciosa, 414
Santa Cruz Restaurant, 366
Santa Engracia, 52
Santa Justa Elevador, 55
Santa Luzia, 47
Santa Margarida Beach, 110
Santa Maria, 410
Santa Maria de Cárquere Priory, 278
Santa Maria do Castelo, 188
Santa Maria Monastery, 104
Santana, 391
Sant'Anna, 74
Santarém, 127
Santo Espírito, 411
Santuário de Monte Sameiro, 317
Santuário de Nossa Senhora de Encarnação, 206
Santuário de Nossa Senhora dos Remédios, 235
São Bento, 267
São Francisco, 186
São Francisco Javier Fortress, 271
São Gião, 219
São João do Campo, 321
São João da Pesqueira, 241
São João de Tarouca, 237
Sao Jorge, 415
São Julião da Barra, 81
São Lourenço Cultural Center, 188
São Luis da Francesca, 43
São Martinho de Moros, 279
Sao Miguel, 407
São Pedro, 411
São Pedro do Corval, 170
São Pedro de Moel, 207
São Pedro de Sintra, 90
São Rafael Pequeno Museum, 102
São Vicente de Fora, 52
Sapa, 90
Sapatária Teresinha, 315
Sardoal, 145
Sarmento, 74
Sarmento Museum, 302
Sé: Angra do Heroismo, 413; Faro, 183; Funchal, 380; Guarda, 244; Lamego, 236; Lisbon, 51; Vila Real, 350
Semana do Mar, 416

Sendim, 356
Senhor Vinho, 71
Sé Nova, 212
Sernancelhe, 238
Serra da Arrábida, 107
Serra do Barroso, 366
Serra do Caramulo, 229
Serra da Estrela, 19, 218, 241
Serra da Lousã, 208
Sesimbra, 111
Sesimbra Castle, 111
A Seta, 386
Seteais, 94
Setúbal, 109
Sé Velha, 213
A Severa, 71
Shepherd's Casa Velha, 191
Shrine of Nossa Senhora do Cabo, 112
Silves, 194
Sintra, 17, 88
Sir Harry's Bar, 193
Soajo, 326
Solar, 75
Solar Beirão, 234
Solar Bragançano, 360
Solar dos Chavões, 127
Solar de Cortegaça at Subportela, 324, 343
Solar do F, 386
Solar dos Peixinhos, 155, 179
Solar dos Pinheiros, 337
Solar de São Pedro, 90
Solar da Vacariça, 219, 225
Solar de Vinho do Porto, 57
Solar do Vinho do Porto, 268
Sol e Mar Hotel, 193, 200
Sortelha, 246
Stones, 73
Stringfellows, 73
Sua Excelência, 70
Swing, 274

Tabuleiros Festival, 138
Tágide, 69
A Tasca, 198
Tavares, 56, 69
Taverna Bébodos, 264
Tavira, 187
Teatro de São Carlos, 55
Teatro Nacional, 43
Teixeiras, 384
O Telheiro, 244
Terceira, 411
Terra do Basto, 351
Terra Nostra, 410
Tivoli, 66
Tivoli Jardim, 66
Toca do Caboz, 96
Tomar, 135
Torre, 245
Torre de Anto, 213
Torre de Belém, 62
Torre das Cabaças, 130
Torre do Galo, 356
Torre de Menagem: Braga, 311; Bragança, 359; Guimares, 298; Miranda do Douro, 357; Viseu, 232
Torre da Princesa, 359
Torre do Relójio, 331
Torres Vedras, 99
O Toucinho, 147
Tower of Belém, 81
Trancoso, 238
Trás-os-Montes, 10, 16, 17, 345
Travanca, 286
Trave Negra, 234
Os Três Potes, 335
Tróia, 113
Tromba Rija, 207
Trovador, 211, 213
Tun Fon, 71
Twins, 274

Vadeca, 315
Vale Glaciário do Zêzere, 245
Vale do Lobo, 190
Vale de Lobos, 133
Valença do Minho, 329
Varanda, 65

Varanda do Oceano, 108
Vasco da Gama Aquarium, 81
Velha Goa, 71
Velha Universidade, 211
Vermar Dom Pedro, 339, 344
Vestal Faianças de Alcobaça, 105
Viana Do Castelo, 332
Vidago, 365
Vidago Palace Hotel, 365, 369
Vieira do Minho, 320
Vila do Bispo, 198
Vila do Conde, 340
Vila da Feira, 224
Vila Franca De Xira, 123
Vila Franco do Campo, 409
Vila Hostilina, 235, 249
Vilalara, 194, 200
Vilamoura, 192
Vilamoura Casino, 192
Vilamoura Marinotel, 192, 200
Vila Nogueira de Azeitão, 112
Vila Nova de Foz Côa, 241
Vila Nova de Gaia, 269
Vila Nova de Ourém, 142
Vila do Porto, 411
Vila Praia de Ancora, 331
Vila Real, 349
Vila Viçosa, 171
Vimeiro, 99
Vinda, 197
Vinhais, 362
Viseu, 230
Vista Alegre: Aveiro, 223; Lisbon, 74
Vitória, 414
Viuva Lamego, 74

York House, 45, 66

Zé da Calçada, 286
Zé Manel, 214